D0429341

THE
EMPEROR
OF OCEAN
PARK

THE
EMPEROR
OF OCEAN
PARK

STEPHEN L.
CARTER

JONATHAN CAPE
LONDON

Published by Jonathan Cape 2002

2 4 6 8 10 9 7 5 3 1

First published in Great Britain in 2002 by
Jonathan Cape
Random House, 20 Vauxhall Bridge Road, London sw1v 2sa

Random House Australia (Pty) Limited
20 Alfred Street, Milsons Point, Sydney,
New South Wales 2061, Australia

Random House New Zealand Limited
18 Poland Road, Glenfield,
Auckland 10, New Zealand

Random House South Africa (Pty) Limited
Endulini, 5A Jubilee Road, Parktown 2193, South Africa

The Random House Group Limited Reg. No. 954009
www.randomhouse.co.uk

A CIP catalogue record for this book is available from the British Library

ISBN 0-224-06284-0

Papers used by The Random House Group are natural,
recyclable products made from wood grown in sustainable forests;
the manufacturing processes conform to the environmental
regulations of the country of origin

Printed and bound in Great Britain by
Clays Ltd, St Ives plc

For Mom, who loved a mystery,
and for Dad, who is not in this one:
I love you both, always

Deux fous gagnent toujours, mais trois fous, non!
(Loosely: Two fools always win, but three fools, never!)

—Siegbert Tarrasch

(Note: The chess piece Americans call the bishop,
the French call *le fou*.)

THE
EMPEROR
OF OCEAN
PARK

THE VINEYARD HOUSE

WHEN MY FATHER finally died, he left the Redskins tickets to my brother, the house on Shepard Street to my sister, and the house on the Vineyard to me. The football tickets, of course, were the most valuable item in the estate, but then Addison was always the biggest favorite and the biggest fan, the only one of the children who came close to sharing my father's obsession, as well as the only one of us actually on speaking terms with my father the last time he drew his will. Addison is a gem, if you don't mind the religious nonsense, but Mariah and I have not been close in the years since I joined the enemy, as she puts it, which is why my father bequeathed us houses four hundred miles apart.

I was glad to have the Vineyard house, a tidy little Victorian on Ocean Park in the town of Oak Bluffs, with lots of frilly carpenter's Gothic along the sagging porch and a lovely morning view of the white band shell set amidst a vast sea of smooth green grass and outlined against a vaster sea of bright blue water. My parents liked to tell how they bought the house for a song back in the sixties, when Martha's Vineyard, and the black middle-class colony that summers there, were still smart and secret. Lately, in my father's oft-repeated view, the Vineyard had tumbled downhill, for it was crowded and noisy and, besides, they let everyone in now, by which he meant black people less well off than we. There were too many new houses going up, he would moan, many of them despoiling the roads and woods near the best beaches. There were even condominiums, of all things, especially near Edgartown, which he could not understand, because the southern part of the island is what he always called Kennedy country, the land where rich white vacationers and their bratty children congregate, and a part-angry, part-jealous article of my father's faith held that white people allow the members of what he liked to call the darker nation to swarm and crowd while keeping the open spaces for themselves.

And yet, amidst all the clamor, the Vineyard house is a small marvel. I loved it as a child and love it more now. Every room, every dark wooden stair, every window whispers its secret share of memories. As a child, I broke an ankle and a wrist in a fall from the gabled roof outside the master bedroom; now, more than thirty years after, I no longer recall why I thought it would be fun to climb there. Two summers later, as I wandered the house in post-midnight darkness, searching for a drink of water, an odd mewling sound dropped me into a crouch on the landing, whence, a week or so shy of my tenth birthday, I peered through the balustrade and thus caught my first stimulating glimpse of the primal mystery of the adult world. I saw my brother, Addison, four years older than I, tussling with our cousin Sally, a dark beauty of fifteen, on the threadbare burgundy sofa opposite the television down in the shadowy nook of the stairwell, neither of them quite fully dressed, although I was somehow unable to figure out precisely what articles of clothing were missing. My instinct was to flee. Instead, seized by a weirdly thrilling lethargy, I watched them roll about, their arms and legs intertwined in seemingly random postures—making out, we called it in those simpler days, a phrase pregnant with purposeful ambiguity, perhaps as a protection against the burden of specificity.

My own teen years, like my adulthood dreary and overlong, brought no similar adventures, least of all on the Vineyard; the highlight, I suppose, came near the end of our last summer sojourn as a full family, when I was about thirteen, and Mariah, a rather pudgy fifteen and angry at me for some smart-mouthed crack about her weight, borrowed a box of kitchen matches, then stole a Topps Willie Mays baseball card that I treasured and climbed the dangerous pull-down ladder to the attic, eight rickety wooden slats, most of them loose. When I caught up with her, my sister burned the card before my eyes as I wept helplessly, falling to my knees in the wretched afternoon heat of the dusty, low-ceilinged loft—the two of us already set in our lifelong pattern of animosity. That same summer, my sister Abigail, in those days still known as the baby, even though just a bit more than a year younger than I, made the local paper, the *Vineyard Gazette*, when she won something like eight different prizes at the county fair on a muggy August night by throwing darts at balloons and baseballs at milk bottles, and so solidified her position as the family's only potential athlete—none of the rest of us dared try, for our parents always preached brains over brawn.

Four Augusts later, Abby's boyish laughter was no longer heard along Ocean Park, or anywhere else, her joy in life, and ours in her, having vanished in a confused instant of rain-slicked asphalt and an inexperienced teenager's fruitless effort to evade an out-of-control sports car, something fancy, seen by several witnesses but never accurately described and therefore never found; for the driver who killed my baby sister a few blocks north of the Washington Cathedral in that first spring of Jimmy Carter's presidency left the scene long before the police arrived. That Abby had only a learner's permit, not a license, never became a matter of public knowledge; and the marijuana that was found in her borrowed car was never again mentioned, least of all by the police or even the press, because my father was who he was and had the connections that he did, and, besides, in those days it was not yet our national sport to ravage the reputations of the great. Abby was therefore able to die as innocently as we pretended that she had lived. Addison by that time was on the verge of finishing college and Mariah was about to begin her sophomore year, leaving me in the nervous role of what my mother kept calling her only child. And all that Oak Bluffs summer, as my father, tight-lipped, commuted to the federal court-house in Washington and my mother shuffled aimlessly from one downstairs room to the next, I made it my task to hunt through the house for memories of Abby—at the bottom of a stack of books on the black metal cart underneath the television, her favorite game of Life; in the back of the glass-fronted cabinet over the sink, a white ceramic mug emblazoned with the legend BLACK IS BEAUTIFUL, purchased to annoy my father; and, hiding in a corner of the airless attic, a stuffed panda named George, after the martyred black militant George Jackson, won at the fair and now leaking from its joints some hideous pink substance—memories, I must confess in my perilous middle age, that have grown ever fainter with the passage of time.

Ah, the Vineyard house! Addison was married in it, twice, once more or less successfully, and I smashed the leaded glass in the double front door, also twice, once more or less intentionally. Every summer of my youth we went there to live, because that is what one does with a summer home. Every winter my father griped about the upkeep and threatened to sell it, because that is what one does when happiness is a questionable investment. And when the cancer that pursued her for six years finally won, my mother died in it, in the smallest bedroom, with the nicest view of Nantucket Sound, because that is what one does if one can choose one's end.

My father died at his desk. And, at first, only my sister and a few stoned callers to late-night radio shows believed he had been murdered.

PART I

NOWOTNY INTERFERENCE

Nowotny interference—In the composition of chess problems, a theme in which two Black pieces obstruct one another's ability to protect vital squares.

CHAPTER I

THE LATEST NEWS BY PHONE

(1)

"THIS IS the happiest day of my life," burbles my wife of nearly nine years on what will shortly become one of the saddest days of mine.

"I see," I answer, my tone conveying my hurt.

"Oh, Misha, grow up. I'm not comparing it with marrying you." A pause. "Or with having a baby," she adds as a footnote.

"I know, I understand."

Another pause. I hate pauses on the telephone, but, then, I hate the telephone itself, and much else besides. In the background, I hear a laughing male voice. Although it is almost eleven in the morning in the East, it is just nearing eight in San Francisco. But there is no need to be suspicious: she could be calling from a restaurant, a shopping mall, or a conference room.

Or not.

"I thought you would be happy for me," Kimmer says at last.

"I am happy for you," I assure her, far too late. "It's just—"

"Oh, Misha, come on." She is impatient now. "I'm not your father, okay? I know what I'm getting into. What happened to him is not going to happen to me. What happened to you is not going to happen to our son. Okay? Honey?"

Nothing happened to me, I almost lie, but I refrain, in part because I like the rare and scrumptious taste of *Honey*. With Kimmer for once so happy, I do not want to cause trouble. I certainly do not want to tell her that the joy I feel at her accomplishment is diminished by my concern over how my father will react. I say softly, "I just worry about you, that's all."

"I can take care of myself," Kimmer assures me, a proposition so utterly true that it is frightening. I marvel at my wife's capacity to hide good news, at least from her husband. She learned some time yesterday that her years of subtle lobbying and careful political contributions have at last paid off, that she is among the finalists for a vacancy on the federal court of appeals. I try not to wonder how many people she shared her joy with before she got around to calling home.

"I miss you," I say.

"Well, that's sweet, but, unfortunately, it's starting to look like I gotta stay out here till tomorrow."

"I thought you were coming home tonight."

"I was, but—well, I just can't."

"I see."

"Oh, Misha, I'm not staying away on purpose. It's my job. There's nothing I can do about it." A few seconds while we think this through together. "I'll be home as soon as I can, you know that."

"I know, darling, I know." I am standing behind my desk and looking down into the courtyard at the students lying on the grass, noses in their casebooks, or playing volleyball, trying to stretch the New England summer as they leap about in the dying October sun. My office is spacious and bright but a bit disorderly, which is also generally the state of my life. "I know," I say a third time, for we are at that stage in our marriage when we seem to be running out of conversation.

After a suitable period of silence, Kimmer returns to practicalities. "Guess what? The FBI will be starting to talk to my friends soon. My husband too. When Ruthie said that, I'm like, 'I hope he won't tell them *all* my sins.'" A small laugh, wary and confident at the same time. My wife knows she can count on me. And, so knowing, she turns suddenly humble. "I realize they're thinking about other people," she continues, "and some of them have awfully good résumés. But Ruthie says I have a really good shot." *Ruthie* being Ruth Silverman, our law school classmate, Kimmer's sometime friend, and now deputy White House counsel.

"You do if they go on merit," I say loyally.

"You don't sound like you think I'm gonna get it."

"I think you *should* get it." And this is true. My wife is the second-smartest lawyer I know. She is a partner in the biggest law firm in Elm Harbor, which Kimmer considers a small town and I consider a fair-sized city. Only two other women have risen so high, and nobody else who isn't white.

"I guess the fix could be in," she concedes.

"I hope it isn't. I want you to get what you want. And deserve." I hesitate, then plunge. "I love you, Kimmer. I always will."

My wife, reluctant to return this sentiment, strikes out in another direction. "There are maybe four or five finalists. Ruthie says some of them are law professors. She says two or three of them are your colleagues." This makes me smile, but not with pleasure. Ruthie is far too cagey to have mentioned any names, but Kimmer and I both know perfectly well that *two or three colleagues* boils down to Marc Hadley, considered by some the most brilliant member of the faculty, even though he has published exactly one book in a quarter-century of law teaching, and that came almost twenty years ago. Marc and I used to be fairly close, and I am not close to many people, especially at the university; but the unexpected death of Judge Julius Krantz four months ago ruined what slight friendship we had, sparking the behind-the-scenes competition that has led us to this moment.

"It's hard to believe the President would pick another law professor," I offer, just for something to say. Marc has been lobbying for a judgeship longer than my wife, and helped Ruthie, once a favored student, land her current position.

"The best judges are people who have practiced real law for a while." My wife speaks as though quoting an official contest rule.

"I tend to agree."

"Let's hope the President agrees."

"Right." I stretch a creaky arm. My body is aching in just the right places to make it impossible to sit still. After breakfast this morning, I dropped Bentley at his overpriced preschool, then met Rob Saltpeter, another colleague, although not quite a friend, for our occasional game of basketball, not at the university gym, where we might embarrass ourselves in front of the students, but at the YMCA, where everybody else was at least as middle-aged as we.

"Ruthie says they'll be deciding in the next six to eight weeks," my wife adds, reinforcing my secret suspicion that she is celebrating far too soon. Kimmer pronounces Ruthie's name with remarkable affection, given that, just two weeks ago, she derided her old friend to my private ear as *Little Miss Judge-Picker.* "Just in time for Christmas."

"Well, I think it's great news, darling. Maybe when you come home we can—"

"Oh, Misha, honey, I have to go. Jerry's calling me. Sorry. I'll talk to you later."

"Okay. I love you," I offer again. But I am declaring my affection to empty air.

(11)

Jerry's calling me. To a meeting? To the telephone? Back to bed? I torture myself with risqué speculations until it is time for my eleven o'clock class, then gather my books together and rush off to teach. I am, as you may have gathered, a professor of law. I am in the vicinity of forty years of age and was once, in the mists of history, a practicing lawyer. Nowadays, I earn my bread by writing learned articles too arcane to have any influence and, several mornings a week, trying to stuff some torts (fall term) or administrative law (spring term) into the heads of students too intelligent to content themselves with B's but too self-absorbed to waste their precious energy on the tedious details one must master to earn A's. Most of our students crave only the credential we award, not the knowledge we offer; and as generation after generation, each more than the last, views us as a merely vocational school, the connection between the desire for the degree and the desire to understand the law grows more and more attenuated. These are not, perhaps, the happiest thoughts a law professor might endure, but most of us think them at some time or other, and today seems to be my day.

I hurry through my torts class—what new is there to say, really, on the subject of no-fault insurance?—and I get off several nice lines, none of them original, that keep my fifty-three students laughing for much of the hour. At half past twelve, I trudge off to lunch with two of my colleagues, Ethan Brinkley, who is young enough still to be excited about being a tenured professor, and Theo Mountain, who taught constitutional law to my father as well as to me and who, thanks to the Age Discrimination in Employment Act and an indefatigable physical constitution, may well teach my grandchildren. Sitting with them in a disintegrating booth at Post (only the uninitiated call it Post's), a grim deli two blocks from the law school, I listen as Ethan tells a story about something hilarious that Tish Kirschbaum said at a party last weekend at Peter Van Dyke's house, and I am struck, as so often, by the sense that there is a white law school social circle that whirls around me so fast that I discern it only in tiny glimpses: until Ethan mentioned it,

I had no idea that there *was* a party last weekend at Peter Van Dyke's house, and I certainly was offered no opportunity to decline to attend. Peter lives two blocks away from me, but stands miles above me in the law school's hierarchy. Ethan, in theory, stands miles below. But skin color, even on the most liberal of campuses, contrives a hierarchy of its own.

Ethan keeps talking. Theo, his bushy white beard spotted with mustard, laughs in delight; as I try my best to join in, I wonder whether to tell them about Kimmer, just to see the pomposity drain for a splendid moment from their satisfied Caucasian faces. I want to tell *somebody*. Then it occurs to me that if I spread the news around and Marc subsequently beats out Kimmer for the nomination—as I suspect he will, albeit undeservingly—all the arrogance will come flooding back, only worse.

Besides, Marc probably knows anyway. Ruthie would not tell Kimmer Marc's name, but I bet she has told Marc Kimmer's. Or so I assure myself as I walk, alone, back along Town Street to the law school. Lunch is over. Theo, old enough to have a granddaughter at the college when most of us still have children in grade school, is off to a meeting; Ethan, an expert on both terrorism and the law of war, is off to the gym, for he keeps himself athletically taut in case MSNBC or CNN should call. I, with nothing in particular to do, return to the office. Students flurry past, all colors, all styles of dress, and all shambling along in that oddly insolent gait that today's young people affect, heads down, shoulders hunched, elbows in at the sides, feet hardly leaving the ground, yet managing all the same to convey a sense of energy ready to be unleashed. Marc probably knows anyway. I cannot escape the thought. I pass the granite glory of the Science Quad, into which the university seems to pour all its spare cash nowadays. I pass a gaggle of beggars, all members of the darker nation, to each of whom I give a dollar—*paying guilt money*, Kimmer calls this habit of mine. I wonder, briefly, how many of them are hustlers, but this is what my father used to call an "unworthy thought": *You are better than such ideas*, he would preach to his children, with rare anger, commanding us to patrol our minds.

Marc probably knows, I tell myself once more as I trip up the wide stairs at the main entrance to the law buildings. Ruthie Silverman, I am willing to bet, has told him everything. Theo taught Ruthie, too, and my wife and I were her classmates; but it is Marc Hadley upon whom she, like so many of our students, lavishes her most lasting devotion.

"That's the problem with students," I murmur just under my breath as I cross the threshold, for talking to myself, which my wife assures me is a sign of insanity, has been my lifelong habit. "They never stop being grateful."

Nevertheless, prudence prevails. I decide to keep Kimmer's news to myself. I keep most things to myself. My world, although occasionally painful, is usually quiet, which is how I like it. That it might suddenly be overtaken by violence and terror is, on this sunny autumn afternoon, quite beyond my imagining.

(III)

IN THE HIGH-CEILINGED LOBBY, I run into one of my favorite students, Crysta Smallwood, who has a tremendous crush on data. Crysta is a dark, chunky woman of not inconsiderable intellectual gifts who, before law school, majored in French at Pomona and was never called upon to manipulate numbers. Since her arrival in Elm Harbor, the discovery of statistics has made her delightfully crazy. She was in my torts class last fall and has spent most of her time since on her twin loves: our legal-aid clinic, where she helps welfare mothers avoid eviction, and her collection of statistics, by which she hopes to show that the white race is headed for self-destruction, a prospect that gladdens her.

"Hey, Professor Garland?" she calls in her best West Coast slur.

"Good afternoon, Ms. Smallwood," I answer formally, because I have learned through hard experience not to be too familiar with students. I walk toward the stairs.

"Guess what?" she enthuses, cutting off my escape, heedless of the possibility that I might be headed someplace. Her hair is a very short Afro, one of the last in the school. I am old enough to remember when few black women of her age wore their hair any other way, but nationalism turned out to be less an ideology than a fad. Her eyes are a little too far apart, giving her a mildly unsettling walleyed look when she meets your gaze. She moves very fast for a woman of her bulk, and is consequently not so easy to avoid. "I've been looking at those numbers again. On white women?"

"I see." Trapped, I gaze up at the ceiling, decorated with ornate plaster sculptures: religious symbols, garlands of yew leaves, hints of justice, all repainted so often that they are losing their sharp definition.

"Yeah, and, so, guess what? Their fertility rate—white women?—is so low now that there won't *be* any white babies by about 2050."

"Ah—are you sure about those figures?" Because Crysta, although brilliant, is also completely nuts. As her teacher, I have discovered that her enthusiasm makes her careless, for she often cites data, with great confidence, before taking the time to understand them.

"Maybe 2075?" she proposes, her friendly tone implying that we can negotiate.

"Sounds a little shaky, Ms. Smallwood."

"It's because of abortion." I am on the move again, but Crysta easily keeps stride. "Because they're killing their babies? That's the main reason."

"I really think you should consider another topic for your paper," I answer, feinting around her to reach the sweeping marble staircase to the faculty offices.

"It's not just abortion"—her voice carries up the stairwell after me, causing one of my colleagues, nervous little Joe Janowsky, to peer over the marble railing in his thick glasses to see who is shouting—"it's also interracial marriages, because white women—"

Then I am through the double doors to the corridor and Crysta's speculations are mercifully inaudible.

I was like her once, I remind myself as I slip into my office. Every bit as certain I was right on subjects I knew nothing about. Which is probably how I got hired in the first place, for I was intellectually bolder when I was intellectually younger.

That, plus the happenstance of being my father's son, for his influence around the campus faded only slightly after the trauma of his confirmation hearings. Even today, well over a decade after the Judge's fall, I am buttonholed by students who want to hear from my own mouth that my father is indeed who they have heard he is, and by colleagues who want me to explain to them how it *felt* to sit there day after miserable day, listening stoically as the Senate methodically destroyed him.

"Like watching somebody in *zugzwang*," I always say, but they are not serious chess players, so they never get it. Although, being professors, they pretend to.

Searching for a distraction, I leaf through my IN box. A memorandum from the provost's office about parking rates. An invitation to a conference on tort reform in California three months from now, but only if I pay my own way. A postcard from some fellow out in Idaho, my opponent in a postal chess tournament, who has found the one move I hoped he would miss. A reminder from Ben Montoya, the deputy dean, about some big lawyer who is speaking tonight. A moderately threatening letter from the university library about some book I have evidently lost. From the middle of the stack, I pull out the new *Harvard Law Review*, skim the table of contents, then drop it, fast, after coming across yet another scholarly article explaining why my infamous father is a traitor to his race, for that is the level to which the darker nation has been reduced: being unable to influence the course of a single event in white America, we waste our precious time and intellectual energy maligning each other, as though we best serve the cause of racial progress by kicking other black folks around.

All right, I have done my work for the day.

The telephone rings.

I stare at the instrument, thinking—not for the first time—what a nasty, intrusive, uncivil thing the telephone really is, demanding, irritating, interrupting, invading the mind's space. I wonder why Alexander Graham Bell is such a hero. His invention destroyed the private realm. The device has no conscience. It rings when we are sleeping, showering, praying, arguing, reading, making love. Or when we just want desperately to be left alone. I think about not answering. I have suffered enough. And not only because my mercurial wife hung up so abruptly. This has been one of those peculiar Thursdays on which the telephone refuses to stop its angry clamor for attention: a frustrated law-review editor demanding that I dispatch an overdue draft of an article, an unhappy student seeking an appointment, American Express looking for last month's payment, all have had their innings. The dean of the law school, Lynda Wyatt—or Dean Lynda, as she likes to be addressed by everybody, students, faculty, and alumni alike—called just before lunch to assign me to yet another of the *ad hoc* committees she is always creating. "I only ask because I love you," she crooned in her motherly way, which is what she says to everybody she dislikes.

The phone keeps ringing. I wait for the voice mail to answer, but the voice mail, like most of the university's cut-rate technology, operates best when not needed. I decide to ignore it, but then I remember that my conversation with Kimmer ended badly, so perhaps she is calling to make up.

Or to argue some more.

Bracing myself for either alternative, I snatch up the handset, hoping for the voice of my possibly repentant wife, but it is only the great Mallory Corcoran, my father's law partner and last remaining friend, as well as a Washington fixer of some repute, calling to tell me that the Judge is gone.

A VISIT TO THE COAST

(1)

I ARRIVE in Washington on Friday afternoon, the day after my father's death, leave my bags at the home of Miles and Vera Madison, my wife's diffident and proper parents, then go over to the Shepard Street house, only to find that Mariah, in her orderly way, has done most of what needs doing. (By unspoken agreement, we both know the family cannot rely on flighty Addison, who has yet to relay any travel plans.) Long ago, Mariah was a plump, disorderly child, with a terrible inferiority complex about her younger, fair-skinned sister, for an obsession with pigmentation is even now the curse of our race, especially in families like mine. As she grew older, Mariah became a stately, almost regal, beauty, somehow ignored nevertheless by the men of the Gold Coast (as we style our narrow, upper-middle-class strip of the darker nation), perhaps running now to fleshiness, but that is to be expected after bearing five children, according to sour Kimmer, professional lawyer and amateur fitness guru. (Kimmer has borne exactly one, a half-planned accident we named Bentley after his maternal grandmother's maiden name.) The adult Mariah is also fabulously well organized, the only one of the children who takes after the Judge in that respect, and she does not believe in rest. But moments after I walk through the door of the rambling and ugly Shepard Street house where we both spent our teen years, Mariah dumps the rest of the work on me. She does this, I think, not out of grief or malice or even exhaustion, but out of the same trait that led her to quit journalism for a career of raising her children, a peculiar willed deference to men, inherited from our mother, who required of her two daughters less that they play a role than that they display an attitude: there were tasks unfit for their gender. Kimmer hates this in my sister, and has accused her, once to her face, of wasting the brain that earned her Phi Beta Kappa in her junior year at Stanford. Kimmer tossed out this line at a Christmas party in this very house that we foolishly attended two years ago. Mariah, smiling, responded calmly that her children deserve the best years of her life. Kimmer, who scarcely broke her professional stride when Bentley was born, took this as a personal attack and said so, which gave my sister and me another reason, if one was needed, not to speak to each other.

You should understand that in many ways I love and respect my sister. When we were younger, Mariah was, by common agreement, the most intellectually able of my parents' four children, and the one most earnestly and touchingly devoted to the impossible work of gaining their approval. Her successes in high school and college warmed my father's heart. To warm my mother's, Mariah married once and happily, an earlier fiancé who would have been a disaster having conveniently absconded with her best friend, and she produced grandchildren with a regularity and an enthusiasm that delighted my parents. Her husband is white and boring, an investment banker ten years her senior whom she met, she told the family, on a blind date, although sweet Kimmer always insists that it could only have been the personals. And, if I admit the truth, Mariah has always preferred white men, all the way back to her high-school years at Sidwell Friends, when, under the hawklike scrutiny of our brooding father, she began to date.

At Shepard Street, Mariah is greeting callers in the foyer, formal and sober in a midnight blue dress and a single strand of pearls, very much the lady of the house, as my mother might have said. From somewhere in the house wafts my father's terrible taste in classical music: Puccini with an English-language libretto. The foyer is small and murky and crowded with mismatched pieces of heavy wooden furniture. It opens on the left to the living room, on the right to the dining room, and in the back to a hallway leading to family room and kitchen. A broad but undistinguished staircase strides upward next to the dining-room door, and along the upstairs hall is a gallery where I used to crouch in order to spy on my parents' dinner parties and poker games, and where Addison once made me hide in a successful effort to prove to me that there is no Santa Claus. Beyond the gallery is the cavernous study where my father died. To my surprise, I see two or three people up there now, leaning on the banister as though it belongs to them. In fact, there are more people in the house than I expect. The entire first floor seems filled with somber suits, a larger slice of financially comfortable African America than most white Americans probably think exists outside the sports and entertainment worlds, and I wonder how many of the guests are happier about my father's death than their faces attest.

When I step through the front door, my sister offers me not a hug but a distant kiss, one cheek, other cheek, and murmurs, "I'm so glad you're here," the way she might say it to one of my father's law partners or poker buddies. Then, holding my shoulders in something still short of a hug, she looks past me down the walk, eyes tired but bright and mischievous: "Where's Kimberly?" (Mariah refuses to say *Kimmer*, which reeks, she once told me, of faux preppiness, although my wife attended Miss Porter's School and is thus fully qualified as a preppie.)

"On her way back from San Francisco," I say. "She's been out there for a few days on business." Bentley, I add, much too fast, is with our neighbors: I picked him up early from his preschool yesterday and then left him again this morning to make this trip, assuming I would be too busy today to spend much time with him. Kimmer will retrieve him tonight, and they will be down tomorrow on the train. Explaining all these logistical details, knowing already that I am talking too much, I experience a yawning emptiness that I hope my face does not show, for I am missing my wife in ways I am not yet prepared to review for the family.

But I need not have bothered to mask my emotions, for Mariah has plenty of her own to cope with, and makes no effort to hide her pain or her confusion. She has already forgotten asking for my wife. "I don't understand it," she says softly, shaking her head, her fingers digging into my upper arms. Actually, I am sure Mariah understands perfectly. Just last year the Judge was in the hospital to repair the imprecise results of his bypass operation of two years before, a fact my sister knows as well as I do; our father's death, if not precisely awaited, was hardly unexpected.

"It could have happened anytime," I murmur.

"I wish it hadn't happened *now*."

To that there is little to say, other than to mention God's will, which, in our family, nobody ever does. I nod and pat her hand, which seems to offend her, so I stop. She closes her tired eyes, gathering her control, then opens them and is all Garland again. She sighs and tosses her head back, as though she still has the long hair she struggled to care for as a teenager, then says unapologetically: "I'm sorry there's no room for you guys in the house, but I've got the kids down in the basement and half the cousins up in the attic." Mariah shrugs as though to say she has no choice, but I sense her true intention in making these dispositions: she is quietly asserting her dominion and daring me to challenge her.

I do not.

"Fine," I say, never losing the smile that always seems to confound her.

But, to my surprise, my sister's face bears no look of triumph. She seems, with this victory, more miserable than ever, for once not sure what to say. I cannot recall when I have seen Mariah less confident; but, then, she loved the Judge best, even though there were times when she couldn't stand him.

"Hey, kid," I say softly, *kid* being what we used to call each other when we were teens and experimented with liking each other. "Hey, come on, it's going to be okay."

Mariah nods uncertainly, not reassured by a single word from my mouth. But, since she distrusts me, this is scarcely surprising. She nibbles her lower lip, an act she would never perform in front of one of her children. Then she gets up on her toes and speaks in a high-pitched whisper, her breath tickling my ear: "I need to talk to you about something, Tal. It's important. Something . . . something's not right." As I incline my puzzled head, Mariah glances from one side of the shadowy foyer to the other, as though afraid of being overheard. I follow her gaze, my eyes, like hers, running over obscure distant relatives and fair-weather friends, including some the family has not seen since my father's mortifying confirmation fight, and at last settling on the hovering figure of her husband, Howard Denton, looking prosperous and fit and somehow perfectly in place in spite of his whiteness. Howard worships at the shrine of bodybuilding; even in his fifties, his broad shoulders seem to float above his tapered waist. He adores Mariah. He also adores money. Although he sneaks the occasional reverential look in my sister's direction, Howard is mainly carrying on an animated conversation with a clutch of young men and women I do not quite recognize. From their trim energy and Brooks Brothers attire, and from the fact that one of them is pressing a card into his hand, I suppose business is being done, even here, even now.

The same thing used to happen to my father, even after his fall: he would walk into a room, and suddenly everybody would want something from him. He projected that aura, sending a subliminal message that he was a person around whom and through whom *things happened*—a person it would benefit you to know. And here is lean Howard, of all people, he of the thinning brown hair and hand-tailored suits and seven-figure income, or maybe it is eight now, able to exercise the same power. So now it is my turn to be offended, less on behalf of the family than on behalf of the race: my vision is suddenly overlaid with bright splotches of red, a thing that happens from time to time when my connection to the darker nation and its oppression is most powerfully stimulated. The room fades around me. Through the red curtain, I still see, albeit dimly, these ambitious black kids in their ambitious little suits, young people not much older than my students, vying for the favor of my brother-in-law because he is a managing director at Goldman Sachs, and I suddenly understand the passion of the many black nationalists of the sixties who opposed affirmative action, warning that it would strip the community of the best among its potential leaders, sending them off to the most prestigious colleges, and turning them into . . . well, into young corporate apparatchiks in Brooks Brothers suits, desperate for the favor of powerful white capitalists. Our leaders, they argued, would be tricked into supporting a new goal. Fancy college degrees and fancier money for the few would supplant justice for the many. And the nationalists were right. I am the few. My wife is the few. My sister is the few. My students are the few. These kids pressing business cards on my brother-in-law are the few. And the world is such a bright, angry red. My legs are stone. My face is stone. I stand very still, letting the redness wash over me, wallowing in it the way a man who has nearly died of thirst might wallow in the shower, absorbing it through every pore, feeling the very cells of my body swell with it, and sensing a near-electric charge in the air, a portent, a symbol of a coming storm, and reliving and reviling in this frozen, furious instant every apple I have ever polished for everybody white who could help me get ahead—

"Leave it alone, kid," says my conscience, except that it is really Mariah, her voice surprisingly patient, her hand on my arm. "It's just the way he is." I look down and see that my fingers have curled into a fist. I know that almost no time has passed—a second, perhaps two. No time ever passes when the red curtain falls across my vision, and I often have the sense that I can reach out my will and freeze those moments for eternity, remain locked forever between this second and the next, living in a world of glorious red fury. I have that sense now. Then I look up and see, through the redness, the pain—no, the *neediness*—in my sister's dark brown eyes. What is it that she needs and Howard is not providing? Not for the first time, I wonder what (other than money) she sees in him. It is my wife's notion that Mariah was running away from something when she chose her mate, but all of my parents' children were running away, as hard and fast as possible, running from the very same something, or someone, and neither Addison nor I ever married anyone as insipid as Howard.

On the other hand, my sister's marriage is happy.

Mariah murmurs my name and touches my face and is, for an instant, my sister and not my adversary. The red is gone, the room is back. I almost hug her, which I do not think I have done in ten years, and I even believe that she would let me; but the moment passes. "We can talk later," she says, and pushes me gently but definitely away. "Go say hello to Sally," she adds as she turns to greet her next guest. "She's crying in the kitchen."

I nod dumbly, still not sure why these moods come over me, trying to remember when last this malady struck. As I turn into the dreary hallway, Mariah is already telling somebody else how good it was of him to come and bestowing a kiss on each cheek. I greet Howard as I pass, but he is too busy collecting business cards to do more than grimace and wave. A quick shimmer of red dances around his head and is gone. I turn away. The numberless cousins, as my father used to call them, seem to pack every square foot of the first floor: numberless simply because the Judge never really bothered to get them straight. Presiding over the cousins, as always, is the ageless Alma, or Aunt Alma, as our parents insisted we call her, although Alma herself, in secret, embracing us in great clouds of sachet, commanded us all to call her "just Alma," which we often took literally, although not to her face: *Mariah, is Just Alma here yet?* Or even: *Mommy! Daddy! Just Alma is on the phone!* Just Alma, who is my father's second cousin or great-aunt or something, admits to some eighty-one years and has probably lived longer, skinny as a tree branch and loud and fun and raunchy, never quite still, gracefully deporting herself in the jazzy rhythms that have sustained the darker nation ever since its coerced beginnings. As a child, I sought her out at every family gathering, because she was always pulling nickels and dimes out of unexpected pockets and forcing them upon us; I seek her out now because she has been, since our mother died, the family's gravitational force, drawing us toward her as though she can curve space.

"Tal*cott!*" Alma cries when she sees me, leaning on her intricately carved cane, smiling her flirtatious grin. "Getcha self on over here!"

I kiss Alma gently, and she awards me a quick squeeze. I can feel her fragile bones move, and I marvel that the winds of age have not managed to blow Alma away. Her breath smells of cigarettes: Kools, which she has been smoking since some legendary act of protest when she was a high-schooler in Philadelphia almost seven decades ago. She was married for more than half a century to a preacher who was a power in Pennsylvania politics, and who was eulogized by the Vice-President of the United States.

"It's good to see you, Alma."

"That's the problem! All good-lookin men ever wanna do with me is *see!*" She cackles and slaps my shoulder, fairly hard. Alma, despite her tiny frame, bore six children, all of whom are still living, five of whom are college graduates, four of whom are still in first marriages, three of whom work for the city of Philadelphia, two of whom are doctors, one of whom is gay: there is some sort of numerical principle at work. Together Alma's children, along with her grands and great-grands, account for the largest subset of the numberless cousins. She lives in a cramped apartment in one of the less desirable neighborhoods of Philadelphia but spends so much time visiting her descendants that she is away more than she is home.

"You'd probably be too much for me, Alma."

I give her another quick squeeze and prepare to move on. Alma grips my biceps, holding me in place. Her eyes are half covered with thick yellow cataracts, but her gaze is sharp and alive. "You know your daddy loved you very much, don't you, Talcott?"

"Yes," I say, although with the Judge love was less knowledge than guess.

"He had plans for you, Talcott."

"Plans?"

"For the sake of the family. You're the head of the family now, Talcott."

"I would think that would be Addison." Stiffly. I am offended and not sure why.

She shakes her little head. "No, no, no. Not Addison. You. That's the way your daddy wanted it."

I purse my lips, trying to figure out if she is serious. I am flattered and worried at the same time. The idea of being the head of the Garland family, whatever it might mean, has an odd appeal, no doubt the expression of some ancient male gene for dominance.

"Okay, Alma."

She hugs me a little tighter, refusing to be mollified. "Talcott, he had plans for you. He wanted you to be the one who . . ." Alma blinks and leans away again. "Well, never mind, never mind. He'll let you know."

"Who'll let me know, Alma?"

She chooses to answer a different question. "You have the chance to make everything right, Talcott. You can fix it."

"Fix what?"

"The family."

I shake my head. "Alma, I don't know what you're talking about."

"You know what I mean, Talcott. Remember the good times we used to have in Oak Bluffs? You kids, your daddy and mommy, me, Uncle Derek—back when Abigail was still with us," Alma concludes suddenly, surprising me with a small sob.

I take her hand. "I don't think human beings can fix things like that."

"Right. But your daddy will let you know what to do when the time comes."

"My daddy? You mean the Judge?"

"You got some other daddy?"

This is the other thing everybody says about Alma: she is no longer quite all there.

Extricating myself at last, I remember that I am supposed to be looking for Sally. All the crazy Garland women, I am thinking: is it we Garland men who give them their neuroses, or is it just coincidence? I struggle through the throng. I wonder why all these people are here now, why they couldn't wait for the wake. Maybe Mariah isn't planning one. A couple of strangers thrust their hands at me. Somebody whispers that the Judge didn't suffer and we should count our blessings, and I want to spin around and ask, *Were you there? . . .* but instead I nod and walk on, as my father would have. Somebody else, another white face, mumbles that the torch has been passed and it is all up to the children now, but neglects to define *it.* Just outside the kitchen, I frown at the hearty handshake of an elderly Baptist minister, high in the councils of one of the older civil rights organizations, a man who, I am pretty sure, actually testified against my father's confirmation to the Supreme

Court. And now has the temerity to pretend to mourn with us. The handshake seems interminable, his ancient fingertips keep moving on my flesh, and I finally realize that he is trying to impart the secret hailing sign of some fraternity, not knowing, perhaps, that rejecting the overtures of such groups was one of my very few acts of rebellion against my parents' way of life—the life, I often think, from which Kimmer, my fellow rebel, rescued me. Nor is it my pleasure to enlighten him. I simply want to escape his insincere unctuousness, and I can feel the veil of red about to return. He refuses to let go. He is talking about how close he and my father were in the past. How sorry he is about the way things turned out. I am about to respond with something rather un-Christian, when all at once a whirlwind of small bodies hurricanes past, nearly knocking us both to the floor; the five Denton children, ages four through twelve, are rushing in their leaderless headlong way to trash some other area of the house. They number Malcolm, Marshall, the twins Martin and Martina, and the baby, Marcus. Mariah, I know, is even now hunting desperately for a name for the very obvious sixth little Denton, due in late February or early March, but is at a loss to find a way to honor both our history and her pattern. This latest pregnancy is in any case a scandal, at least within the four walls of my house. A year ago, when she was forty-two, Mariah confided to my astonished wife that she wanted to bear one more child, which Kimmer denounced, to my private ear, as an irresponsible waste and self-indulgence: for Kimmer, like my father, values most those who differ from her least.

(11)

OURS IS an old family, which, among people of our color, is a reference less to social than to legal status. Ancestors of ours were free and earning a living when most members of the darker nation were in chains. Not all of our ancestors were free, of course, but some, and the family does not dwell on the others: we have buried that bit of historical memory as effectively as the rest of America has buried the larger crime. And, like good Americans, we not only forgive the crime of chattel slavery but celebrate the criminals. My older brother is named for a particular forebear, Waldo Addison, often viewed as our patriarch, a freed slave who, in freedom, owned slaves of his own until forced to flee northward in the 1830s, after Nat Turner's rebellion led the Commonwealth of Virginia to rethink the status of the free negroes—small "n"—as they were then called. He stopped briefly in Washington, D.C., where he lived in the mosquito-infested slum known as George Town, more briefly still in Pennsylvania, and at last wound up in Buffalo, where he made the transition from farmer to barge worker. What became of Waldo's six slaves family history does not reveal. We do, however, know something of the man himself. Grandfather Waldo, as my father liked to call him, became involved in the abolitionist movement. Grandfather Waldo knew Frederick Douglass, my father always said, although it is difficult to imagine that they were friends, or, indeed, that they had much in common, aside from the fact that both had been enslaved. My father liked to speculate about Grandfather Waldo's possible involvement in the underground railroad—his work on the lakes and canals made it logical, my father would say, bright-eyed with hope. As my father aged, the speculation hardened into fact, and we would sit out on the wraparound porch of the Vineyard house in the evening cool, sipping pink lemonade and swatting away mosquitoes, while he described Waldo's unlikely exploits as though he had seen them himself: the risks he ran, the schemes he hatched, the credit he deserved. But there was never any evidence. What few facts we have suggest that Grandfather Waldo was a drunken, thieving, self-interested scoundrel. Waldo's four sons, as far as we know, were all scoundrels too, and his lovely daughter Abigail married another, but it was her no-good husband, a textile worker in Connecticut, who gave us the family name. Abigail's only son was a preacher, and his eldest son a college professor, and *his* second son was my father, who has been many things, including, at his highest, a federal judge, the close confidant of two Presidents, and, almost, a Justice of the Supreme Court; and, at his lowest, the unindicted but publicly humiliated target (Mariah, who inclines toward melodrama, says *victim*) of investigations by every newspaper and television network in the country, to say nothing of two grand juries and three congressional committees.

And now he is dead. Death is an important test for families as old and, I might say, as haughty as ours: repressing our anguish is as natural as driving German cars, participating in the Boule, vacationing in Oak Bluffs, and making money. My father would not have wanted tears. He always preached leaving the past in the past—*drawing a line*, he called it. *You draw a line and you put yourself on one side of the line and the past on the other.* My father had many of these little epigrams; in the proper mood, he would recite them in his ponderous way as though expecting us to take notes. My siblings and I eventually learned not to go to him with our problems, for all we would ever receive in return were his stern face and heavy voice as he lectured us on life, or law, or love . . . especially love, for he and our mother had one of the great marriages, and he imagined himself, in consequence, one of the great experts. *Nobody can resist temptation all the time,* the Judge warned me once, when he thought, wrongly, that I was contemplating an affair with my future wife's sister. *The trick, Talcott, is to avoid it.* Not a particularly profound or original insight, of course, but my father, with his heavy judicial mien, could make the most mundane and obvious points sound like the wisdom of the ages.

Talcott, I should explain, is my given name—not Misha. My parents selected it to honor my mother's father, whom they expected to leave us money in consequence, which he dutifully did; but I have hated it ever since I was old enough to be teased by schoolmates, a very long time. Although my parents forbade the use of diminutives, friends and siblings mercifully shortened my name to Tal. But my closest comrades call me Misha, which, you will correctly have guessed, is the Anglicized version of a Russian name, the diminutive for Mikhail, which has been, from time to time, one of my other sobriquets. I am not Russian. I speak no Russian. And my parents did not give me a Russian name, for, other than a few dedicated Communists in the thirties and forties, what black parents ever did? But I have my reasons for preferring Misha, even though my father hated it.

Or perhaps *because* he did.

For my father, like most fathers, had that effect on us too: my siblings and I have all been defined in part by our rebellion against his autocratic rule. And, like most rebels, we often fail to see how much we have come to resemble the very thing we pretend to loathe.

(I I I)

I NEED A BREAK.

To please Mariah, I spend a few minutes in the kitchen with the tearful Sally, who was raised by my father's only brother, my late Uncle Derek, whom the Judge abhorred for his politics. She is a cousin by marriage, not blood: she was the daughter of Derek's second wife, Thera, and her first husband, but Sally refers to Derek as her father. Sally has become a pudgy, lonely woman, with unhappy doe eyes and wildly styled hair; comforting her now, I see nothing of the daring, aggressive teenager who was, long ago, Addison's secret lover. These days, Sally works on Capitol Hill for some unknown subcommittee, a job she secured through my father's waning influence when she could hold no other. Sally, who has had her troubles, focuses every conversation, within seconds of its beginning, on how badly she has been treated by every person she has ever known. She wears dresses in alarming floral patterns, always too tight, and, although she no longer drinks the way she used to, Kimmer reports seeing her slip pills by the handful from the canvas tote bag she carries everywhere. She has the bag with her now. Patting Sally's broad back, I try to measure her intake of whatever she is hiding by the slurring of her voice. I remind myself that she was once warm and vivacious and funny. I accept a slurpy kiss a little too close to my lips, and at last escape to the foyer. I hear Alma's wheezy cackle but do not turn. I notice Howard again, still doing business, the red nimbus still flashing from his neck. I need to escape, but Mariah will be furious if I leave the house, and I have never been very good at bearing the fury of women. I yearn for the simple rejuvenating pleasure of chess, perhaps played online, using the laptop I left back at the Madisons'.

But, for now, simple privacy will have to do.

I slip into the small room that was once my father's study, since converted to a small library, with low cherrywood bookshelves along two walls and, beneath the window, a tiny antique desk with a two-line telephone. The paneling is cherry too, decorated not with self-congratulatory photographs (those are upstairs) but with a handful of small tasteful drawings by unknown artists, along with an original Larry Johnson watercolor—not his best—and a tiny but very nice Miró sketch, a recent gift to the Judge from some conservative millionaire. I wonder, for a greedy moment, which of the children gets the Miró, but I suppose it stays with the house.

"As the rich get richer," I whisper uncharitably.

I close the door and sit at the desk. On the bookshelves behind the red leather swivel chair are dozens of scrapbooks, some fancy, some cheap, all bulging with photographs, for my mother was a meticulous chronicler of the family's life. I pull one out at random and discover a spread of Addison's baby pictures. A second is of Abby. The page to which it falls open displays her around age ten in Little League uniform, the cap tipped back jauntily on her head, a bat on her shoulder: my parents had to threaten to sue, I remember, before she was allowed to play. The old days. My father, no matter what he was doing, never missed a game. The Judge used to talk about those old days, fondly: *the way it was before*, he would call it, in odd nostalgic moments, meaning, before Abby died. Nevertheless, he drew his line, put the past in the past, and moved on.

I keep leafing through the albums. A third is full of graduation pictures—mine, Mariah's, Addison's, from all levels of our education—along with shots of Mariah and Addison receiving various awards. Especially Addison. None of me, but I have never won anything. Forcing a smile, I keep flipping pages. Most of the book is empty. Space for shots of the grandchildren, perhaps. I put the album away. The next one has the most attractive binder, soft old leather stained a dark blue, and is full of newspaper clippings, all of which seem to be about—

Oh, no.

I close the book quickly and close my eyes slowly and see my father rushing out of the house late on a spring evening, commanding my mother to *stay put, Claire, just stay put, we have three other children to worry about, I'll call you from the hospital!* And, later still, my mother answering the phone on the kitchen wall, her hand trembling, then moaning in maternal horror and sagging against the counter, before turning businesslike and distant, which both my parents could do at a snap. I was the lone witness to this display. Mariah and Addison were away at college and Abby was out somewhere; at fifteen, Abby seemed always to be out somewhere, quarreling constantly with our parents. My mother made me dress and hurried me over to a neighbor's house, even though, at close to seventeen years of age, I was more than capable of staying home unguarded. She left me with quick, desperate kisses, vanishing in the other car on unexplained but obviously tragic business. It was after midnight when my father came to pick me up and sat me down in the living room at Shepard Street and told me in a quivering voice, quite far from his usual radio-announcer tone, that Abby was dead.

From the day of her funeral until the day he died, my father hardly mentioned Abby's name.

But he kept a scrapbook. A decidedly weird scrapbook.

I open my eyes once more and leaf through the pages.

And notice at once that something is wrong.

Only the first four clippings have anything to do with Abby. The news story of her death. The formal obituary. A follow-up a week later informing readers that the police had no leads. Another article two months further on reporting the same joyless tidings.

My father was angry in those days, I remember. He was angry all the time. And he began to drink. Alone, the way prominent alcoholics do, locked in this very room. Perhaps poring over this very scrapbook.

I turn the page. The next clipping, dated a few months later, records the death of a small child in a hit-and-run accident in Maryland. I shudder. The following page carries another clipping: a young seminary student, also a hit-and-run victim. I turn and turn. The contents chill me. Page after page of newspaper stories about innocent people killed by hit-and-run drivers, all over the United States. Two, almost three years of them. An elderly woman leaving a supermarket in a small town. A police officer directing traffic in a big city. A rich, politically connected college student, her convertible crushed by a tractor-trailer. A news reporter smashed by a station wagon while changing a flat on a busy highway. A high-school football coach, mangled by a taxi. An impoverished mother of six, a famous writer, a bank clerk, a heart surgeon, a wanted burglar, a teenager on her way to a babysitting job, the son of a prominent politician, a potpourri of American tragedy. Some of the stories bear the inky stamps of the various clipping services that used to send you articles from around the country on a subject of your choice, back before online research; many are no more than tiny one-paragraph items from the *Post* and the old *Star*; and a few, very few, are marked with faded blue asterisks and, scribbled in the margins, dates, usually much later than the publication dates of the stories themselves. By working backward from other stories in the album, I soon figure out that the asterisks mark the hit-and-runs in which the driver who did the hitting and running was eventually caught. And a few of the articles about arrests are further annotated with brief, angry notes in my father's crabbed handwriting: *I hope they fry the bastard*, or *You'd better have a good lawyer, my friend*, or *At least somebody's parents got justice*.

I flip quickly to the back of the book. The collection ends in the very late seventies, about the time the Judge's drinking stopped. Makes sense. But nothing else does.

This is not the nostalgic scrapbook of a parent who misses a child;

this is the product of a mind obsessed. It strikes me as diabolical in the traditional Christian sense, a thing of the devil. The air around the book seems thick with an aura of mental corruption, as though haunted by the spirit of the madman who assembled it . . . or the spirit that possessed him to do so. I quickly slide the binder back into its place, fearing that somehow it might infect me with its gleeful lunacy. Odd that it should be sitting here this way, mixed in with the happier memories. Insanity of this sort, even if temporary, is precisely what few children want to know about their parents . . . and what few parents want their children to know about. The Garlands have many little secrets, and this is among them: when Abby died, my father went a little nuts, and then he got better.

I close my eyes again and sink into the chair. He got better. That is the important thing. He got better. The man we are burying next week is not the man who sat here in this ugly little room, drinking himself insensible night after night, flipping through the pages of this sick scrapbook, terrorizing the family not with anger or violence but with the awful silence of emotional destitution.

He got better.

And yet my fanatically private father preserved this album, the record of his short-lived insanity, where any visitor to the house might blunder across it. I can readily believe that the Judge would have created the scrapbook during his madness, but it seems reckless, out of character, to have held on to it in the years since. All other evidence was discarded years ago. There are, for example, no liquor bottles in the house. The book, however, survives, right on the shelf. Fortunately for my father's reputation, nobody happened upon the book at the time that the Senate Judiciary Committee was holding its hearings on his—

The door to the little room snaps open. Sally is standing there in her unreasonably tight gray dress, her substantial chest heaving, a rapturous yet somehow helpless smile shining through the tears. She looks slightly confused, as though surprised to find me the first place she looks. Addison has called, she finally announces. Her eyes are alight, ecstatic, sharing her joy. He is on his way, Sally adds happily, oblivious to the possibility that others might not be as thrilled as she. He will be here no later than tomorrow. I blink my eyes, struggling for focus. She sounds like a character out of Beckett. I am on my feet, nodding, blocking the bookcase with my body, absurdly worried that she might get a look at the Judge's mad scrapbook. Addison is coming, she repeats.

Transformed by this news, she has achieved a sudden allure. He will be here soon, Sally assures me. Very soon.

From her deliriously fawning tone, she might be announcing the pending arrival of the Messiah. Although, if you ask most of my brother's many women, they would probably describe him as very much the other thing.

CHAPTER 3

THE WHITE KITCHEN

(I)

THE NEWS of the Judge's death reached us several times in the years before the event actually occurred. It is not that he was ill; he was, as a rule, so vigorous that one tended to forget his wavering health, which is why the heart attack that at last cut him down was, at first, so difficult to credit. It is simply that he led the sort of life that generated rumor. People disliked my father, intensely, and he returned the favor. They spread stories of his death because they prayed the stories were true. To his enemies—they were legion, a fact in which he gloried—my father was a plague, and rumors of a cure always raise hopes in those who suffer, or love those who do. And, in this case, some of those my father plagued were not people but causes, which, in America, can always count their lovers in the millions, unlike individual people, who die unloved every day. Not one of his enemies but hated my father, and not one but spread the stories. Self-styled friends would call. They were always whispering how sorry they were. They had heard, they would say, about my father's heart attack while promoting his latest book up in Boston. Or his stroke while taping a television interview out in Cincinnati. Except that there would not have been one: he would be alive and well in San Antonio, speaking to the convention of some conservative political action committee—the Rightpacs, Kimmer calls them. But, oh, the gleeful rumors of his demise! My mother hated the rumors, not for the heartache, she said, but for the humiliation—there were standards, after all. But not in the rumor mill. Waiting in the checkout line at the supermarket, just before my son Bentley was born, I was astonished to read on the cover of one of the more imaginative tabloids, just beneath the weekly Whitney Houston story (TALKS CANDIDLY ABOUT HER HEARTBREAK) and just above the latest way to lose as much weight as you want without diet or exercise (A MIRACLE DOCTORS WON'T TELL YOU), the gladsome tidings that the Mafia had put out a contract on my father, because of his cooperation with federal prosecutors—although, when Kimmer made me go back to the store and buy it and I read the whole thing, all one hundred fifty words, I noticed a pointed lack of detail as to what my father could possibly have to cooperate with prosecutors about, or what he might know about the Mafia that would be so dangerous. I called Mrs. Rose, the Judge's long-suffering assistant, and finally caught up with him on the road in Seattle. He took the opportunity to warn me yet again on the insidiousness of his enemies.

"They will do anything, Talcott, *anything* to destroy me," he announced in the oracular tone he tended to adopt when discussing those who disliked him. He repeated the word a third time, in case my hearing was off: "Anything."

Including, I noted while leafing through the pessimistic pages of *The Nation* a few years back, accuse him of paranoia. Or was it megalomania? Anyway, my father was sure they were out to get him, and my sister was sure they were right. When the Judge skipped Bentley's christening three years ago, worried the press might be there, Mariah defended him, pointing out that he had missed half the baptisms of her children—no difficult feat, given the numbers—but by then she and I were barely speaking anyway.

Once a false story of my father's demise made the real papers—not the supermarket tabloids, but the *Washington Post*, which killed him on a wintry morning in a commuter plane crash in Virginia, one among a dozen victims, his apparent presence on board noted poignantly, but also coyly: CONTROVERSIAL FORMER JUDGE FEARED DEAD IN CRASH is what the headline said. The irony was plain to the most casual follower of current events, because what people feared was not my father dead but my father alive; and because of the unhappy turning his career took, which was also, my father liked to say, the fault of the *Post* and "its ilk." Left-wing muckrakers, my father called them in his well-remunerated speeches to the Rightpacs, who were pleased to hear this angry, articulate black lawyer blaming the media for his resignation from the federal bench not long after the collapse of his anticipated elevation to the Supreme Court, where, his conservative fans loved to remind his liberal critics, he had argued and won two key desegregation cases in the sixties. Oh, but he could be confounding! Which is why Mariah was certain that there were smiles of relief all along the Cambridge–Washington axis (where she picked up that hackneyed phrase I will never know, but I suspect it was from Addison, who could always stand her) when the early editions of the *Post* carried the crash story and a couple of the more careless news-radio stations repeated it. The plague, it seemed for a glorious instant, was at an end. But my wily father was not on board. Although his name was on the manifest and he had checked in, he had prudently chosen that occasion to argue via long distance with my mother, then busily dying at the Vineyard house, over the cost of some repairs to the gutters, and the discussion grew sufficiently extended that he missed the flight. The airline got its passenger list wrong, this being back in the days when it was still possible to do such a thing. "That's how much she loved me," the Judge told us in a drunken ramble the night of Claire Garland's funeral. He cried, too, which none of us had seen before—only Addison even claimed to have seen him take a drink since the bad period just after Abby died—and Mariah slapped my face when, the very next day, I pointed out to her that, in the six years of my mother's illness, my father spent as much time on the road as he did at her bedside. "So what?" my sister demanded as I groped for a suitable riposte to a palm across the cheek—a question, once I thought about it, that I was ill-prepared to answer.

And perhaps I deserved the rebuke, for the Judge, despite his coldness toward most of the world, including, usually, his children, was never anything but tender and affectionate with our mother. Even when my father was a practicing lawyer, before the move to government service, he was constantly leaving meetings with clients to take calls from his Claire. Later, on the Securities and Exchange Commission and then on the bench, he would sometimes leave litigants waiting while he chatted with his wife, who seemed to take such treatment as her due. He smiled for her in a natural delight that told the world how grateful he was for the day Claire Morrow said yes; at least until Abby died, after which he did not do much smiling for a while. Once a semblance of family stability was re-established, my parents used to take evening walks along Shepard Street, holding hands.

Of course, my father was on the road constantly. At the time of his death, he liked to call himself just another Washington lawyer, which meant that when he wanted to reach me he would have Mrs. Rose place the call, his own time being too precious, and, when I came on the line, he would invariably put me on the speakerphone, perhaps to leave his hands free for other work. Mrs. Rose told me once that I should not be upset: he put everybody on the speakerphone, treating it as though it had just been invented. Indeed, everything that he was doing was new to him. He was, formally, of counsel to the law firm of Corcoran & Klein—*of counsel* being a term of art covering a multitude of awkward relationships, from the retired partner who no longer does any lawyering to the out-of-work bureaucrat trying to bring in enough business to earn a full partnership to the go-go consultant looking for a respectable place to hang a shingle. In my father's case, the firm offered a veneer of gentility and a place to take his messages, but little more. He saw few clients. He practiced no law. He wrote books, went on nationwide speaking tours, and, when he needed a rest, showed up on *Nightline* and *Crossfire* and *Imus* to beguile the evil armies of the left. Indeed, he was the perfect talk-show guest: he was willing to say nearly anything about nearly anybody, and he would call anyone who argued with him the most erudite and puzzling names. (The censors would have a terrible time when he used words like *wittol* and *pettifoggery*, and he was once bleeped out on one of the radio talk shows for describing a particular candidate's shift to the right during the Republican presidential primaries as an act of *ecdysis*.) Oh, yes, people hated him, and he reveled in their enmity.

Mariah, naturally, made more of all this than I did. I have always thought that the far left and far right need each other, desperately, for if either one were to vanish the other would lose its reason to exist, a conviction that has freshened in me from year to year, as each grows ever more vehement in its search for somebody to hate. Now and then, I even wondered aloud to Kimmer—I would say it to no one else—whether my father manufactured half his political views in order to keep his face on television, his enemies at his heels, and his speaking fees in the range of half a million dollars a year. But Mariah, having been in her time both philosophy major and investigative journalist, sees oppositions as real; the Judge and his enemies, she would say, were playing out the great ideological debates of the era. It was the culture war, she would insist, that brought him down. I thought this proposition quite silly, and came to think, after years of reading about it, that the scandal-mongers who drove him from the bench might have had a point; and I made the mistake of saying this, too, on the telephone to

Mariah, not long after Bob Woodward published his best-selling book about the case. The book, I told her, was pretty convincing: the Judge was not a victim but a perjurer.

Aghast at this unexpected break in the family ranks, even in private, Mariah swore in my presence for what I am fairly certain was the first time in our mutual lives. I asked her whether she had actually read the book, and she responded that she had no time for such trash, although *trash* was not the word she actually selected. She had called, you should understand, because she wanted the entire family—that is, the three children—to write a joint letter to the *Times* as a protest against its favorable review of the Woodward book. She still had friends there who would see that it was published, she said. I declined and told her why. She told me that I had to do it, that it was my duty. I mumbled something about letting sleeping dogs lie. She told me that I never did anything she wanted me to do, dredging up a story I myself had forgotten about some lonely friend of hers she begged me to ask out when I was in college. Mariah said I should, just once, stand up for her. She said she had never done anything to deserve being treated the way I treated her. I thought about my Willie Mays baseball card, but decided not to mention it. Instead, a bit irritated, I am afraid I called her immature—no, tell the truth, the term I used was *spoiled brat*—and Mariah, after a heavy pause, answered with what I considered an unprovoked assault on my wife, which began, "Speaking of lying down with bratty dogs, how's your bitch?" My sister can play the dozens with anybody, and certainly with me, having honed her skills during her long and passionate membership in a rather exclusive and notoriously catty black sorority. When I suggested huffily that it was inappropriate for her to talk about Kimmer in those terms—very well, I put it a bit more strongly than that—Mariah asked angrily whether I ever raised the same objection to the things she knew my wife said about her. As I floundered in search of an answer, she added that blood was thicker than water, that this was something I owed to the family. And when I tried to climb up on my pedagogical high horse, proposing that my higher duty was to truth, she asked me why in that case I didn't just take out a full-page ad in the paper: MY FATHER IS GUILTY AND MY WIFE IS UNFAITHFUL. But that is how badly we always get along. So, when Mariah pulls me aside in the grim family-filled foyer at Shepard Street and whispers that she has to talk to me later on in private, I assume she wants to discuss the remaining details of the funeral, for what else have we two lifelong enemies left to talk about? But I am wrong: what my sister wants to tell me is the name of the man who murdered our father.

(11)

I LAUGH when Mariah tells me. I confess it freely, if guiltily. It is terrible of me, but I do it anyway. Perhaps it is a matter of exhaustion. We have no time together until after midnight, when we at last sit down at the kitchen table drinking hot cocoa, me still in my tie, my sister, fresh from the shower, in a fluffy blue robe. Howard and the children and some subset of the numberless cousins are asleep, crammed into various corners of the grand old house. The kitchen, which my father recently had redone, is sparkling white; the counters, the appliances, the walls, the curtains, the table, everything the same sheeny white. At night, with all the lights on, the reflections hurt my eyes, lending an air of insanity to what is already surreal.

"What exactly are you laughing at?" Mariah demands, rearing back from the table. "What's the matter with you?"

"You think *Jack Ziegler* killed Dad?" I splutter, still not quite able to get my mind around it. "Uncle Jack? What for?"

"You know what for! And don't call him Uncle Jack!"

I shake my head, trying to be gentle, wishing Addison would arrive after all, because he is far more patient with Mariah than I will ever be. A moment ago, before uttering the name, my sister was nervous, maybe even frightened. Now she is furious. So I guess you could say I have at least improved her mood.

"No, I don't. I don't know. I don't even know what makes you think somebody killed him. He had a heart attack, remember?"

"Why would he suddenly have a heart attack now?"

"That's how they are. They're sudden." My impatience is making me cruel, and I try to force myself to slow down. My sister is no fool, often discerning things that others miss. Mariah was the subject of a small piece in *Ebony* magazine back in the mid-1980s, when, as a twenty-six-year-old reporter at the *New York Times*, she achieved a Pulitzer nomination for a series of stories about the diverse lives of children who eat in soup kitchens. But she suddenly quit her job not long after, when the paper began investigating my father in earnest. Although Mariah called it a protest, the truth is that she left the workforce entirely and, together with her very new husband, moved to a lovely old colonial in Darien—the first of three, each larger than the last—promising to devote all her time to her children, and in this way endeared herself to our mother, who believed to the day she died that women belong in the home. Darien is not that far from Elm Harbor, but these days Mariah and I see each other twice a year, if unlucky. It is not so much that we do not love each other, I think, as that we do not quite like each other. I resolve, for perhaps the hundredth time, to do better by my sister. "Besides," I add, softly, "he wasn't exactly young."

"Seventy isn't old. Not any more."

"Still, he did have a heart attack. The hospital said so."

"Oh, Tal," she sighs, flapping a hand at me and feigning world-weariness, "there are so many drugs that can cause heart attacks. I used to work the police beat, remember? This is my area. And it's really hard to catch this stuff in the autopsy. I mean, you are really so innocent."

I decide to give that one a miss, especially since Kimmer is constantly saying the same thing about me, for different reasons. I offer an olive branch: "Okay, okay. So why would Uncle Jack want to kill him?"

"To shut him up," she says heavily, then stops and draws in her breath so suddenly that I cast a quick look over my shoulder, to see whether Jack Ziegler, the family bogeyman, might be peering in the window. I see only my mother's collection of crystal paperweights, gathered from countries all over the world, lined up on the sill like shiny eggs with transparent shells, and, in the glass of the window, my own reflection mocking me: an exhausted, sagging Talcott Garland, looking less like a law professor in his unfashionable horn-rimmed glasses and close-cropped hair and crooked tie than like a child wishing it would all be over. I turn back to look at my sister. Like Mallory Corcoran, our "Uncle Mal," the man we call Uncle Jack is not related to us by blood or marriage. The family bestowed upon these white friends of my father honorary titles when they became godparents—Uncle Mal to Mariah, Uncle Jack to Abby—but, unlike Uncle Mal, Jack Ziegler had far more to do with my father's destruction than with his redemption.

"Shut him up about what?" I ask softly, because it has always been Mariah's position that my father knew nothing about Uncle Jack's more questionable activities, that the suggestion of any business connection between the two of them was no more than a white-liberal plot against a brilliant and therefore dangerous black conservative. Maybe that is why Mariah stops: she sees the trap into which her own reasoning leads.

"I don't know," she mutters, looking down and clutching her mug with a mother's fierce protectiveness.

This might be a good moment to let my sister's fantasy drop, but, having listened this far, I decide that it is my duty to help her see how nutty an idea it is. "Then what makes you think Uncle Jack had anything to do with it?"

"Ever since the hearings, he's been waiting for the right moment. You know he has, Tal. Don't tell me you haven't felt it!"

I ask a lawyer's question. "What would make this the right moment?"

"I don't know, Tal. But I know I'm right."

Again: "Do we have any actual evidence?"

She shakes her head. "Not yet. But you could help me, Tal. You're a lawyer, I'm . . . I used to be a journalist. We could, you know, investigate it together. Look for proof."

I frown slightly. Mariah has always been both spontaneous and obsessive, and talking her out of her latest impulse will not be easy. "Well, we would need a reason first."

"Jack Ziegler is a murderer. How's that for a reason?"

"Even assuming that's true . . ."

"It's not an *assumption*." Her eyes flash with fresh fury. "How can you defend a man like that?"

"I'm not defending anyone." I do not want to pick a fight, so I answer her challenge with another: "So, do you have a plan in mind? Do you want to call Uncle Mal?"

Mariah is trapped and she knows it. She does not really want an investigation, and knows as well as I do that nothing would change, that the heart attack would still be a heart attack, that she would be made to look a fool. She cannot call Mallory Corcoran, one of the most powerful lawyers in the city, and demand, on nothing but hope, that he shake up the world for her. Mariah refuses to look at me, scowling instead in the direction of the gleaming white SubZero refrigerator, already decorated, through some domestic alchemy, with the inevitable pictures of dogs and trees and ships, crudely drawn in crayon by her younger children—the sort of sentimental bric-a-brac that the Judge would never have tolerated.

"I don't know," Mariah mumbles, the lines of exhaustion plain on her stubborn face.

"Well, if—"

"I don't know what to do." She shakes her head slowly, her gaze on the white table between us. And this tiny chink in Mariah's emotional armor offers me a bright, sad insight into the life she leads all day as Howard rides off to far provinces to slay financial dragons for the clients, and the profits, of Goldman Sachs. The pictures on the refrigerator are the fruits of my sister's frantic efforts yesterday to keep her children busy as she went about the debilitating business of planning, virtually alone, a funeral service for the father she spent four decades trying unsuccessfully to please.

"I'm so tired," Mariah declares, a rare admission of weakness. I look away for a moment, not wanting her to see how these three simple words have touched me, not even wanting to acknowledge the commonality. The truth is that Mariah and Addison and I always seem to be exhausted. The scandal that destroyed our father's career somehow energized him for a new one but left his family debilitated. We children have never quite recovered.

"You've been working hard."

"Don't patronize me, Tal." Her tone is matter-of-fact, but her eyes flash again, and I know she has been offended by a nuance that was not even there. "You're not taking me seriously."

"I am, but . . ."

"Take me seriously!"

My sister is practicing her best glare. The weariness is gone. The confusion is gone. I remember reading in college that social psychologists believe anger is functional, that it builds self-confidence and even creativity. Well, I don't know about the creative part, but Mariah, angry at me as usual, is suddenly as confident as ever.

"Okay," I offer, "okay, I'm sorry." My sister waits, giving nothing. She wants me to make the move, saying something to show that I am taking her crazy idea seriously. So I formulate a serious question:

"What can I do to help?" Leaving open the matter of what exactly I am offering to help with.

Mariah shakes her head, starts to speak, then shrugs. To my surprise, tears begin a slow course down her cheeks.

"Hey," I say. I almost reach out to brush them away, then remember the foyer and decide to sit still. "Hey, kid, it's okay. It is."

"No, it isn't okay," Mariah sobs, making a fist with her dainty hand and striking the table with considerable force. "I don't think . . . I don't think it will ever be okay."

"I miss him too," I say, which is quite possibly a lie, but is also, I hope, the right thing to say.

Crying openly now, Mariah buries her face in her hands, still shaking her head. And still I dare not touch her.

"It's okay," I say again.

My sister lifts her head. In her grief and despair, she has attained a truly haunting beauty, as though pain has freed her from mere mortal concerns.

"Jack Ziegler is a monster," she says shortly. Well, that at least is true, even if only a fraction of the wicked things the papers say about him ever happened. But it is also true that he has been tried and acquitted at least three times, including once for murder, and, as far as I know, continues to live up in Aspen, Colorado, fabulously wealthy and as safe from the world's law-enforcement authorities as the Constitution of the United States can make him.

"Mariah," I say, still softly, "I don't think anybody in the family has seen Uncle Jack in more than ten years. Not since . . . well, you know."

"That's not true," she says tonelessly. "Daddy saw him last week. They had dinner."

For a moment, I can think of nothing to say. I find myself wondering how she can know who the Judge saw and when. I almost embarrass myself by raising this question, but Mariah saves me:

"Daddy told me. I talked to him. To Daddy. He called me two days . . . two days, uh, before . . ."

She trails off and turns away, because it is not the habit of our family to share our deepest pains, even to each other. She covers her eyes. I consider walking around the table, crouching next to my sister, slipping my arms around her, offering what physical comfort I can, maybe even telling her that the Judge telephoned me, too, although, in good Garland fashion, I was too busy to call him back. I envision the scene, her response, her joy, her fresh tears: *Tal, Tal, oh, it's so good to be friends again!* But that is not who I am, still less who Mariah is, so, instead, I sit still, preserving my poker face, wondering whether any reporters have gotten hold of the story, which would only be a fresh disaster. I can see the headlines now: DISGRACED JUDGE MET WITH ACCUSED MURDERER DAYS BEFORE HIS DEATH. I nearly shudder. The conspiracy theorists, for whom no famous death ever flows from natural causes, have already started to work, granted time on the wilder radio talk shows ("Rats," Kimmer calls them, who has a way with acronyms) to explain why the heart attack that felled my father is necessarily a lie. I have scarcely noticed their antics, but now, imagining what some of the callers might say if they heard about the Judge's meeting with Uncle Jack, I begin to understand the strange turnings of my sister's paranoia. Then Mariah makes it worse.

"That isn't all," she goes on in the same flat voice, her eyes on something beyond the room. "I talked to him last night. To Uncle Jack."

"Last night? He called? Here?" I should be proud of myself, managing to ask three stupid questions where most people could squeeze in only one.

"Yes. And he gave me the creeps."

Now it is my turn to be set back. Far back. Again, I search for something to say, settling at last on the obvious.

"Okay, so what did he want?"

"He offered his condolences. But mostly he wanted to talk about you."

"About me? What about me?"

Mariah pauses, and she seems to wrestle with her own instincts. "He said you were the only one Daddy would trust," she explains at last. "The only one who would know about the arrangements Daddy had made for his death. That was what he kept saying. That he needed to know the arrangements." The tears are flowing again. "I told him that the funeral was Tuesday, I told him where, but he—he said those weren't the arrangements he meant. He said he needed to know about the *other* arrangements. And he said you would probably know. He kept on saying it. Tal, what was he talking about?"

"I don't have any idea," I admit. "If he wanted to talk to me, why didn't he call me?"

"I don't know."

"This is too weird." I remember Just Alma. *He had plans for you, Talcott. That's the way your daddy wanted it.* Is this what Alma was talking about? "Just too weird."

Something in my tone gets a rise out of my sister, as something in my tone often does. "Are you sure you don't have any idea, Tal? About what Jack Ziegler might have wanted?"

"How would I know?"

"I don't know how you'd know. That's what I'm wondering." As Mariah glares her distrust, I feel, rising between us, the shade of our lifelong argument, Mariah's sense that I am never there for her, and mine that she is far too demanding. But surely she does not believe that I would somehow be involved with . . . with somebody like Jack Ziegler. . . .

"Mariah, I'm telling you, I don't have the slightest idea what this is all about. I don't even know the last time I heard from . . . from Jack Ziegler."

She flips a hand, brushing this away, but makes no verbal response. She is not saying she trusts me; she is signaling a willingness to call a truce.

"So, all he asked about was . . . arrangements?"

"Pretty much. Oh, and he also said he would probably see us at the funeral."

"Oh, boy," I mutter, in an awful stab at sarcasm, wondering if there is some way to keep him out. "We can all look forward to that."

"He scares me," says Mariah, her earlier speculations about Uncle Jack evidently off the table for now, although certainly not forgotten. Then she squeezes my fingers. I look down in surprise: we have linked hands, but I cannot remember just when.

"He scares me, too," I say. Which is, I am pretty sure, the most honest sentence I have uttered all day.

CHAPTER 4

THE CHARMER

(1)

IT WAS the Judge's occasional hope to die before Richard Nixon, who would then be obliged—so my father reasoned—to attend his funeral, and perhaps even to say a few words. President Nixon, you might say, helped to create my father, discovering him as an unknown trial judge with a moderately conservative bent, inviting him to the White House often, and, at last, appointing him to the United States Court of Appeals, where, a bit over a decade later, Ronald Reagan discovered him all over again, and nearly managed what the newspapers of the moment called a "diversity double" at the Supreme Court: Reagan, struggling against his hard-won image as the savior of the nation's white males, would appoint the Judge and, at a stroke, double the number of black Justices and, at the same time, become the first President to appoint two Justices who were not white males. Reagan's grab at history failed, and my father, who like many successful people never quite untangled ambition from principle, refused to forgive him for the sin of giving up on the nomination.

But my father's attitude toward Nixon was otherwise. The Judge returned Nixon's favor, still insisting a quarter-century after the only presidential resignation in our history that it was a cabal of vengeful liberals, not Nixon's own venality, that drove the man from office. The Judge saw in Nixon's fall remarkable parallels to his own, and loved to point them out to his eager lecture audiences: two enlightened, thoughtful conservatives, one white, one black, each of whom, on the verge of making history, had his career destroyed by the ruthless forces of the left. Or something like that: I heard that particular stump speech only twice, and it turned my stomach both times—not for ideological reasons or because of its patent distortion of history but because of its gruesome, un-Garland-like bath of self-pity.

Alas, my father did not achieve his dream. It was he who attended Nixon's funeral, not the other way around. The Judge flew off to California, hoping, on what evidence I can scarcely imagine, for an invitation to eulogize his mentor. If you watched the service on television, you know it did not happen. My father's face was never even visible. He was squeezed into about the fifteenth row, lost among a smattering of former deputy assistant secretaries of no-longer-extant Cabinet departments, some of them convicted felons. Chafing from yet another disappointment, my father hastened home, wondering, no doubt, who of any note would attend his funeral.

Who, indeed? I ponder my father's morbid question as, tightly clutching the hand of my beautiful wife, I follow the casket down the nave aisle of the Church of Trinity and St. Michael, a drafty granite monstrosity just below Chevy Chase Circle where, nine years ago this December, to the general astonishment of our families and friends, Kimmer and I were married. Most, I might add, are even more astonished that we are married still, for our tumultuous mutuality has been marked by many false beginnings.

Who, indeed? We children are following the casket. Addison, whose creaky eulogy a few minutes ago displayed all the same saccharine religiosity of his radio call-in show, is flanked, in defiance of etiquette, by his girlfriend of the moment. Mariah is ahead of me, her husband, Howard, adoring at her side, some subset of her children trailing in her wake, the rest of them either back at Shepard Street with the au pair or perhaps wandering the church, climbing somewhere they shouldn't. Then, remembering that Mariah and her offspring are family, I command my musings away from their unexpectedly spiteful path, for, as I believe I have mentioned, the Judge always counseled his children to avoid unworthy thoughts.

Who, indeed? I wonder, stifling a cough from the choking cloud of incense that is still part of the ritual of traditional Episcopal churches, even if most have forgotten why. Who, indeed? The answer, I suspect, would have been a fresh disappointment to my name-conscious father. Because nobody is here—nobody who would have mattered to the Judge. None of the big liberals who loved him when he was young. None of the big conservatives who loved him when he was old. Just bits and pieces of the family, some longtime friends, a few of his law partners, and a handful of nervous journalists, most of them far too young to know why my father's name was so notorious, but a few who remember and have come to see for themselves that the monster is really gone.

Mallory Corcoran is here, of course, leading a small phalanx of lawyers from the firm, and the Judge's quiet assistant, Mrs. Rose, who has been with him since he was on the bench, has also come. The Gold Coast has naturally sent a contingent, mostly yellow-skinned men of my father's generation, expensively dressed, all anxiously checking their Rolexes, probably to be sure the funeral ends before their tee times. A handful of judges who served with my father are present, including, to my astonishment, one who went on to the Supreme Court, although he is seated near the back, as though worried about being seen. A dozen or so of my father's old law clerks are scattered about the church, most of them looking more embarrassed than unhappy; but I am grateful nevertheless for their loyalty. I spot my friends Dana Worth and Eddie Dozier, who used to be married to each other, back when Dana thought she might be interested in men, primly seated three rows apart, as befits the angrily divorced. Eddie's face is set in hard, defiant lines, but the usually tough Dana seems a little weepy. We have fallen away from each other, the three of us, since their marriage collapsed. They met while serving together as law clerks for my father in the early 1980s, and they were the first—and will, I suspect, be the last—married couple ever hired to teach at the law school. Dana, tiny and white, and Eddie, broad and black, were an odd couple to begin with, unfashionably defiant in their right politics, and neither of them ever quite mastered the fine academic art of telling people to their faces something other than what you really think.

Off alone in the far rear corner, I note with surprise, sits the one law clerk I was sure would be among the missing: Greg Haramoto, the earnest yet shy young man whose openly reluctant testimony a decade ago did as much as any interest group to sink my father's nomination to the Supreme Court. Greg was a surprise witness—a surprise to the Judge, at least—and he repeatedly insisted during his riveting four hours before the television cameras that he did not want to be there at all. But he nailed my father to the wall. Sitting in the hearing room in obvious discomfort, blinking too often behind his thick glasses, Greg told the Senators that Jack Ziegler called my father's chambers after hours so often that he came to recognize his distinctive voice. He said Jack Ziegler and my father met for lunch. He said Jack Ziegler even stopped by the courthouse at least once, late at night. He said the Judge swore him to silence. He said lots of things, and my father unconvincingly denied some and unwillingly recalled others. The security logs for the federal courthouse, in which the guards record everybody who enters and leaves, did much to refresh the Judge's recollection.

After the hearings, Greg became a wandering nomad of the legal profession. He quit his post with the general counsel of the Federal Communications Commission, and, despite his excellent academic record at Berkeley, no law firm wanted him, because they all worried about whether a man who was willing to crucify his own boss on national television would keep the confidences of unsavory clients; no corporation would hire him, because most of their CEOs were on my father's side; and no law school could keep him, because he was too shattered to commit serious scholarship. He tried working as a public defender, to bury his own pain beneath the far more significant pains of those from whom life on the bottom has squeezed any vestige of morality, but his soul was never in it, his clients suffered, and his employer invited him to try something else. Greg Haramoto, who once imagined life at the top of the profession, suddenly had trouble landing a job. The last I heard, he was working in his family's export-import firm in Los Angeles—a comedown, according to Mariah, that serves him right. Yet here is Greg, his earnest eyes shiny with tears, mourning along with the rest of us, saying goodbye to the man he helped to ruin. In his testimony, he insisted over and over that his admiration for my father had never flagged. But, then, it is often surprisingly easy to destroy the things we love.

My eyes continue to roam. I spot another colleague from the law school, the fastidious Lemaster Carlyle, born in Barbados, who has been on the faculty just two years longer than I but stands many tiers higher in reputation. Lem is a tough little spark-plug of a man, whose beautifully tailored suits hide a well-muscled form, and whose flowery and idiomatic language hides a well-muscled mind. He and I are hardly close friends, and he did not know the Judge at all, so I suppose he came out of solidarity, for he believes in race as an utterly mystical yet deeply personal connective tissue. During the battle over my father's nomination, Lem, despite his assiduously liberal politics, took the Judge's side quite publicly: "Two blacks on the Supreme Court are better than one," was his dubious slogan. Although Lem is not a likable man, I loved him for this conviction long before I met him.

Dana, Lemaster, and I are the only representatives of the law school my father so loved. (Eddie decamped for Texas following the divorce.) Dean Lynda was thoughtful enough to send an enormous wreath, and even the students, to my amazement, sent flowers, two neatly segregated arrangements, one from the black students, one from the white. But flowers are not people, and, even adding in poker buddies, journalists, simple sensation-seekers, bits and pieces of Kimmer's family, and those who remain from the numberless cousins (age and geography have somewhat thinned their ranks, but they are there, gossiping together in the back of the church), I do not think there are two hundred people present in a church built to hold more than thrice that number. And Jack Ziegler, whatever he was really asking about "arrangements," is not among them.

(11)

IN THE FAMILY, we do not like to talk about Jack Ziegler. Not any more. He was my father's college roommate as well as Abby's godfather, but during the last decade of his life, the Judge could not bear the mention of his old friend's name. Indeed, it has become an article of conservative faith that my father ultimately lost his bid for the Supreme Court because he chose to honor their lifelong acquaintance; or, more precisely, because he had lunch with Jack Ziegler. Twice. That was the sum total of Greg Haramoto's testimony, that my father and an old friend met for lunch, and that, later on, the old friend got a tour of the courthouse. So they talked on the phone a few times: nothing sinister about that! Certainly that is the way the case is put by the Judge's partisans, Mariah ever in the lead, for his nomination to the Supreme Court was sailing along back in 1986, the Senate's liberal Democrats far too intimidated by his skin color and his qualifications to raise any serious fuss, until the story of the lunches came out. And the background of his luncheon partner. The press immediately swirled into one of its ecstasies of condemnation. Jack Ziegler, a disgraced former employee of the Central Intelligence Agency, had somehow managed to become a footnote to half the political scandals in the second half of the twentieth century—or so it often seemed. He testified on some peripheral but quite embarrassing matter before Sam Ervin's Watergate Committee, his name turned up unflatteringly in an appendix to the Church report on wrongdoing by the CIA, and a book or two have hinted at his distant involvement with the Iran-Contra mess, although he was, by that time, long out of the Agency; even the Warren Commission supposedly took his statement, behind closed doors, for he had, in his days in the field, filed a report from Mexico City on the peculiar activities of one Lee Harvey Oswald. But Jack Ziegler stayed mostly in the shadows, until the disaster of my father's nomination to the Supreme Court made him famous. Still, if the carrion-eating journalists who looked into his relationship with the Judge managed to find a sinister *allegation* or two, nothing was ever *proved* except the lunches, at least against my father: thus ran my sister's position. And the position of the Rightpacs and the editorial page of the *Wall Street Journal*. And, for a while, mine as well. (Addison, unable to see a way to squeeze any money from the contretemps, kept his cards tightly to his chest.)

But the daily stream of fresh allegations proved too weighty. Within days of Greg Haramoto's appearance, the security logs turned up, and my father's most fervent supporters in the Senate were diving for cover. A few friends urged him to fight, but the Judge, a team player to the end, gamely asked the White House to withdraw his nomination. To his dismay, President Reagan made no effort to dissuade him. And so the seat on the Court for which my father had spent half a lifetime jockeying went instead to a little-known federal judge and former law professor named Antonin Scalia, who was, in the general relief, confirmed unanimously. "And Nino Scalia is doing a hell of a job," the Judge would sing gleefully in his lectures to the Rightpacs, a remark which, like many of my father's, always made me wince, especially because whenever he said it—and he said it often—I would be forced to endure the barbs of my liberal colleagues, Theo Mountain very much to the fore, who, unable to hurt my father, decided to prick the son instead.

That, of course, came later. At the time, my father's fall seemed impossible, so high had he been raised by the brilliance of his mind and the utility of his politics. "He didn't do anything!" Mariah would cry during the nightly telephone conversations that marked, in that instant of crisis, a brief truce in our running war.

"It's not about what he did," I would answer patiently, trying to explain for her lay and partisan ear a judge's duty to avoid even the appearance of impropriety, only half believing it myself, given some of the characters who have managed to hang on to their seats on the federal bench, including the Supreme Court. "It's about hiding what he did."

"That's ridiculous!" she would shoot back, unable in those days to wrap her voice around the rougher forms of dismissal so characteristic of our country's increasingly vulgar discourse. "They were out to get him all along, and *you know it.*" As though having real enemies was a defense against any charge of wrongdoing. Or as though the fact that Jack Ziegler was about to stand trial for a bewildering variety of offenses at the time of what the press called the secret lunches was a triviality; or as though the fact that my father and Uncle Jack were apparently still in touch when his old roommate was a fugitive from justice was beside the point. After all, Uncle Jack was ultimately acquitted of nearly all the charges, and, if he was truly a fugitive, he was a fugitive only from the justice of liberals who hated him for his perhaps over-enthusiastic prosecution of the Cold War: so quoth the editorial page of the *Journal.*

And if whispers along the legal grapevine spoke of jury tampering, of bribed or intimidated witnesses, of the felicitous disappearance of crucial pieces of evidence, well, there are always whispers.

(I I I)

KIMMER, EXHAUSTED after taking the red-eye from San Francisco and then collecting our son and training down here, dozes on my shoulder in the limousine as we head for the cemetery out in Northeast Washington, a few blocks north of Catholic University. Bentley snuggles nervously against her other side, his gray suit hanging loosely on his tiny frame, because frugal Kimmer believes in buying children's clothes two or three sizes ahead. I gaze at my wife's profile. In her simple black dress, unadorned except by subtle gold earrings and a single strand of pearls, she is arresting. My wife is tall and quite intensely handsome, with a long, thoughtful face, a bold, aggressive chin, engaging brown eyes, a broadly prominent and very kissable nose, and soft, encompassing lips that I adore. Even her steel-rimmed glasses seem sexy: she is constantly slipping them on and off, nibbling on the ends, twirling them as she talks on the phone, all of which I find enthralling. I have loved looking at her since the day we met. She is, by her own description, big-boned, with wide shoulders and broad hips that have finally, after years of sometimes wild fluctuations, settled into a roundness she finds comfortable. Her skin is a shade or so lighter than mine, reflecting her upper-class Jamaican heritage. She wears her dark brown hair in a defiant short Afro, as if to contradict the stern expectations of her clan (where hair is always permed and often colored), and her slow smile and quick temper hint at a passionate core. There is a lushness to Kimmer, but a stolidity as well. She carries herself with a sensual dignity that simultaneously draws you in and sets firm limits. She keeps the world off balance, and is burdened by a raging desire for fairness. Her intellect is quick and wide-ranging. Given the opportunity, Kimmer would be an excellent judge. Nobody really wants to mess with her: not the opposing lawyers she encounters in her work, not the friends she collects with such disturbing ease, and certainly not I.

For example, I have not lately challenged my wife about her frequent trips to San Francisco, where she is ostensibly doing what lawyers call "due diligence," reviewing the financial records of a software company that her firm's most important client—a local leveraged-buyout group called EHP, formerly Elm Harbor Partners—plans to acquire. She would shoot me down if I mentioned it: Kimmer goes where EHP sends her, and if EHP wants her in California, well, California, here she comes. It is the strength of her relationship with EHP that earned her the quick partnership she pretends to disdain, for EHP asked for her by name at Newhall & Vann almost from the day she walked in the door. And EHP is, formally, the client of Gerald Nathanson, one of her firm's most influential partners, a very married man with whom my very married wife is, or is not, having an affair.

Maybe the furtive telephone calls and the long, unexplained disappearances from her office are mere coincidences. And maybe my father is about to leap from his casket and do the funky chicken.

Now, as my jealousy flames afresh, Kimmer unexpectedly intertwines her fingers with mine, where they lately have spent little time. I look over at her in surprise and notice the start of a smile on her face, but she never looks in my direction. Bentley is now fast asleep, and Kimmer's free hand is absently stroking his curly black hair. Bentley sighs. They have something special, these two, some genetically mysterious mother-son connection that excludes me, and always will. In this strange, broken world, men often love their wives as much, or as little, as they do their children, but, for women, biology seems to trump personal choice: they may love their husbands, but their children come first. Were the balance otherwise, I doubt that the human race would have survived. Indeed, I suspect that one reason I have remained true to Kimmer, whatever she has done, is that I know that if we ever parted she would take Bentley with her. Even though I spend far more time with our son than she does, she could not bear to let him go. I steal another glance at Kimmer, then look up at Addison, cuddling shamelessly with his white girlfriend in the opposite seat, wondering, as I have so often, if the mutual passions in their very different natures have ever led to mutual sparks.

Addison is perhaps an inch shorter than I am, and broader through the shoulders, but it is muscle, not fat; although not really an athlete, he has always kept himself in good shape. His face is both friendlier and more handsome than mine, his brows less intrusive, his eyes more evenly set, his demeanor more calm and open. Addison has wit and style and grace, none of which I possess. When we were children, Addison was charming and fun and I was merely a grind, and I always had the sense, at parties, on vacations, in church, that my parents were more excited about introducing my brother to their friends than introducing me. In our school days, I would arrive in each classroom four years after Addison left, and I would achieve better grades, but the teachers would always be persuaded that he possessed the better brain. If I brought home an A, my father would nod, but if Addison brought home a B, he gained a slap on the back for his effort. As a child, I read over and over the story of the prodigal son, and was invariably incensed by it. I argued about it with Sunday-school teachers galore. When we read the parable of the lost sheep, I told my teachers I thought most people would keep the ninety-nine sheep rather than go searching for the missing one. The answer would be an angry glower. Adulthood changed nothing. That I would remain married to the same difficult woman my father accepted as a matter of course, but each time Addison introduced a new and ever-more-compliant one, the Judge would smile and put an arm around his shoulders: "So, son, ready to settle down at last?" Any answer my brother offered seemed to satisfy. And my father always seemed a good deal less impressed by my tenure at one of the nation's best law schools than by Addison's eerie ability to strike gold wherever he digs.

Nowadays, my older brother has become a type common to the darker nation: smart, ambitious, well educated, utterly dedicated to the romanticism of the long-shattered civil rights movement, living on the fringes of what remains. Racial unity has long ago disappeared, as has the larger nation's commitment, if it existed, to the basic principles of the movement. Dozens of organizations claim the mantle of Wilkins and King and Hamer, along with an army of academics, a brace of television commentators, and every group of newly anointed victims of oppression, not one of which can resist pointing out the astonishing similarities between its own endeavor and the black freedom struggle.

As for Addison, he has played the circuit like the tennis pro my father once hoped he would be: after the University of Pennsylvania, a post at a community-development corporation in Philadelphia, followed by a mid-level staff position for one of the state's congressmen, a few years in Baltimore at the national office of the NAACP, a high position in the Democratic National Committee, a desk at the Ford Foundation, key advisory spots in three national political campaigns, a semester as a visiting scholar at Amherst, a stint at the ACLU, a couple of years at the Education Department under Clinton, that Ford Foundation desk again, a semester at Berkeley, a year in Italy, six months in South Africa, a year in Atlanta, all three funded by a Guggenheim as he works on his yet unfinished great book on the movement. In unguarded moments, my brother whispers hopefully of the MacArthur award that will certainly never come, and so, forced to earn a living, Addison has transformed himself into a man of the new century, hosting a radio call-in show five nights a week in Chicago, joyfully intimidating guests as he proclaims to the world—or at least to his audience—his own orthodox liberal views on everything from the death penalty to gays in the military, insisting at least twice each night, even now, that George W. Bush was never really elected President, peppering his commentary with mountains of Biblical quotations, some of them accurate, along with alleged gleanings from Mahavira, Chuangtzu, and other sages with whom his listeners are unlikely to be familiar. I suppose one would call the slant of his religiosity New Age, for he mixes in what he finds useful and discards what he dislikes. He lives in a small and aging but nevertheless elegant townhouse in Lincoln Park, sometimes alone, sometimes with any of his several girlfriends, most of them white, waiting for the next big thing to come along to add to his résumé. Pressed, he will admit that he was married once or twice, but he invariably adds that he has come to harbor doubts about the institution, and is therefore glad that his didn't last.

Ah, sweet marriage! My parents always described it as the fundamental institution on which civilization rests. My sister and I, whatever our weaknesses, have tried to behave as though we believe it. But Addison, for all his outward signs of religious fervor, behaves otherwise. His first wife was a schoolteacher in the Philadelphia public schools, a sweet, quiet woman of the darker nation, whose name was Patsy. Patsy and my brother immediately fell to fighting over when they would be able to begin a family. My brother, like many a man not ready to commit himself to the marriage to which he is already committed, had a single, consistent answer: *Later.* Patsy left him in the third year. Disaster followed. For a while, there was, it seemed, a woman a week, including one horrible Thanksgiving two years after my father's disgrace when he arrived at Shepard Street with a garishly made-up child who looked about fifteen and dressed like a hooker. (She was, we quickly learned to our relief through smooth questions from my mother, twenty-two and some sort of minor star on the soaps; Sally, late as usual, recognized her at once and went into paroxysms of jealous awe.) Addison and Cali—for that was the unlikely name of his date—stayed at dinner just long enough to be rude, then hurried off, explaining that they had a long drive back to New York, but really, so he told me out in the driveway, to visit other friends in Maryland, two male screenwriters who had built a gorgeous house on the water near Queenstown. That was Addison, at least until recently. He liked to be seen with actresses, models, singers, little mindless wisps of sexuality—but not always. For a while, he set up housekeeping in Brooklyn with a half-mad convicted bomber named Selina Sandoval, who never met a protest she didn't like, unless it was against abortion. Selina kept guns all over the apartment and saw Addison as fascist but educable, which is roughly the way that Addison sees me. As for Addison, he described his interest in Selina as "research for a novel"—which, like so many of his ideas, has yet to be started. When Selina finally got too crazy and landed back in jail, she was followed by a flight attendant, then a commodities broker, then a moderately famous tennis player, then a waitress at his favorite deli, then one of the stars of the Dance Theater of Harlem, then a police detective, which was my brother's idea of a joke. Eventually, Addison settled on a second wife, Virginia Shelby, a graduate student at the University of Chicago, an anthropologist, a woman of friendly smile and intimidating intellect, someone at last my father and mother thought good enough, a union that we thought would calm him down. Everybody loved Ginnie, everybody but Addison, who swiftly tired of her nagging him about— what else?—starting a family. He left her a year and a half ago for a twenty-four-year-old production assistant on his radio show. Although it is styled as a trial separation, nobody seriously expects Addison and Ginnie to resume their conjugality, which is why nobody is surprised when he shows up at the funeral with a perfect stranger, a skinny, shamelessly clinging white woman named Beth Olin, who is some sort of minor poet, or maybe a playwright—there isn't time to find out the details during this brief visit, and we never see her again.

CHAPTER 5

A GRAVESIDE ENCOUNTER

(1)

KIMMER KEEPS firm hold of my hand as we stand beside the grave, shivering in the chill as Father Bishop pronounces the words of committal. Freeman Bishop, who has been rector of Trinity and St. Michael, it sometimes seems, since before the Deluge, is in the Episcopal tradition of scholarly priests, possessing the deep knowledge of theology and church history that was once the common expectation for clergy of the Anglican communion. My father, however, always spoke ill of the man. The reason was politics. The Episcopal Church has lately been battered by stormy conflicts on everything from the ordination of gays and lesbians to the authority of the Bible. Father Bishop, in the Judge's view, was on the wrong side of every fight. *They don't understand,* my father would moan, referring to those with whom he disagreed, *that the church is steward and custodian of moral knowledge, not its originator! They think they're free to change whatever they want to fit the fashion of the moment!* Right or wrong, the Judge was always strident; and, always, he seemed more comfortable mourning the world that had passed away than planning for the one rushing toward him.

As for Freeman Bishop, whatever his complicated politics, he is a man of enormous faith, and a considerable gift for preaching. He puts on a fine show, the Judge used to say, and this is true: with his pleasantly bald brown pate, his thick spectacles (as he likes to call them), and a heavy, rolling voice that seems to roar up like a hurricane from somewhere well down the Atlantic coast—he is actually from Englewood, New Jersey—Father Bishop could easily pass for one of the great preachers of the African American tradition . . . as long as one does not listen too closely to the content. And, for all the Judge's disdain for the man, they were, if not exactly friends, at least on relatively warm terms. Recently, my father's ever-smaller circle of intimates along the Gold Coast even admitted Freeman Bishop to their own most sacred institution, the Friday-night poker game. So, although a couple of well-known conservative preachers called to volunteer their services, there was never really any question about who would officiate at the funeral.

I have always loved cemeteries, especially old ones: their satisfied sense of the past and its connection to the present, their almost supernatural quietude, their stark reassurance that the wheel of history turns indeed. For most of us, cemeteries exude a mystical power, which explains both the hold the vampire myths have on our imagination and the fact that the desecration of gravestones, whenever it happens, will always be the lead story on the local evening news. But I love cemeteries most as places of discovery. Sometimes, visiting a strange city for the first time, I will find the oldest burial ground and walk there, learning the local history by studying family relationships. Sometimes I will stroll for hours to find the grave of a great figure from the past. A year or so before Bentley was born, Kimmer and I both had to be in Europe on business—I was in The Hague for a conference on how the tort law of the European Community should compensate for pain-and-suffering damages, she was in London doing goodness-knows-what for EHP—and we stole a day and a half for a visit to Paris, where neither of us had ever been. Kimmer wanted to see the Louvre and the Left Bank and the Cathedral of Notre Dame, but I had other plans, insisting that we take a taxi all the way out to the grim Montparnasse Cemetery in a furious thunderstorm to look at the grave of Alexander Alekhine, the raving anti-Semite and alcoholic who was chess champion of the world back in the 1930s and possibly the most brilliant player the game has ever known.

More evidence, if my wife needed any, that I am moderately raving myself.

And now another cemetery. The brief graveside ceremony passes in a blur. I find myself unable to concentrate, looking around for the bulldozer that will cover the casket after the last mourner has drifted away, but it is too well hidden. I gaze briefly at the polished marble headstone, where my mother's name is already carved, and the small marker, off to the side, for Abby. The family plot my father purchased years ago tops a little rise; he always said he bought it for the view. From up here, we can see most of the grounds. The cemetery is wooded and vast, headstones marching away in implausibly straight rows over sloping hills. Even in the sharp autumn sun, there are shadows everywhere. In the middle distance, some of the shadows seem to move—reporters, perhaps. A trick of the light? My fervid imagination? If I am not careful I will catch my sister's paranoia. I focus on the graveside once more. This is my third burial on the quiet little hill, and the family is smaller each time. First we buried Abby here, then my mother. Now the Judge.

Murdered, I remind myself, glancing over at my sister, who wept throughout the service. A chilly breeze carries a few fresh leaves to the earth: every year, the trees seem to shed them a little bit sooner, but I am watching with the eyes of age. Mariah says the Judge was murdered. We are burying our father next to Abby, and Mariah thinks Abby's god-father killed him.

Possible. Not possible. True. False.

Insufficient data, I decide, fidgeting with worry.

Kimmer squeezes my hand. Mariah is still sniffling; Howard, straight and strong, cradles his wife as though worried she might float away. They seem to have brought only part of their brood, but I lack the energy to get the count straight. Standing just beyond the Denton children, Addison seems bored, or perhaps he wishes he could say a few words here, too. His girlfriend, or whatever she is this week, has wandered irreverently away, evidently engrossed in a study of the other headstones. Next to Addison, Mallory Corcoran, pale and wide, glances at his watch, making no effort to hide his impatience. But Father Bishop is finished anyway. His bald brown head reflecting the sun, he adjusts his glasses and utters the final words of the final prayer: "O Lord Jesus Christ, Son of the living God, we pray thee to set thy passion, cross, and death, between thy judgment and our souls, now and in the hour of our death. Give mercy and grace to the living, pardon and rest to the dead, to thy holy Church peace and concord, and to us sinners everlasting life and glory; who with the Father and the Holy Spirit livest and reignest, one God, now and for ever."

We all recite the *Amen*. The service is over. The mourners stir, but I stand for a moment, awed by the frightening power of this prayer: *between thy judgment and our souls*. My father, if all I have tried to believe is true, now knows God's judgment on his soul. I wonder what that judgment is, what it might be like to leave mortal existence behind and know there are no more second chances, or, perhaps, to find forgiveness after all. To the atheist, the cemetery is a place of the dead, vulgar and absurd, ultimately pointless; to the believer, a place of scary questions and terrifying answers. I gaze at the casket, poised on its runners, surrounded by plastic grass, ready to slide into the ground as soon as we have dispersed.

Give pardon and rest to the dead.

Kimmer squeezes my fingers to snap me back into the secular world of post-funeral handshakes. The leave-taking begins. Friends and cousins and law partners gather round again. A black man who looks to be about a hundred years old throws skinny arms around me, whispering that he is the uncle of somebody else whose name means nothing to me. A tall, striking woman in a veil, another member of the darker nation, replaces him, explaining that she is the sister of some aunt of whom I have never heard. I wish I knew my extended family, but I never will. Still embracing unknown relations, I spot Dana Worth, who waves sadly and then disappears. I suffer a bear hug from a teary Eddie Dozier, Dana's ex, who then turns to hug Kimmer, who cringes but allows it. I say goodbye and thanks to Uncle Mal and his wife, Edie; to the Madisons, who, as usual, say all the right things; to Cousin Sally and her longtime boyfriend Bud, a onetime boxer of no distinction whose jealous fists sometimes mistake anybody who looks at her too long for one of his opponents. I lose track of the people whose hands I am shaking and begin to get their names wrong, an error my father would never have committed. *Head of the family*, I remember.

Kimmer slips an unexpected arm around my waist and squeezes, even offering a smile to jolly me from my reverie. She is trying, I realize, to comfort me—not out of a wifely instinct, I know, but out of deliberation. Her other hand clutches Bentley's tiny one. Our son looks tiny and lost in his long black coat, purchased just yesterday at Nordstrom's. He is also beginning to yawn.

"Time to go, baby," says Kimmer, but not to me.

We stroll back toward the cars, bunches of people no longer united in the commemoration of a life; we are individuals again, with jobs and families and joys and pains of our own, and my father, for most of the mourners, is already in the past. Mariah continues to whimper, but seems alone in this activity. A cell phone burrs somewhere, and a dozen hands, including my wife's, dig into pockets and purses to check. The lucky winner is Howard, who listens briefly, then launches into a quiet dispute over the proper valuation of convertible debentures, and is still blabbering happily as he squeezes into the limousine.

A few more handshakes and hugs and kisses, and then we are alone again. Addison, I notice, is still up at the grave. He is hunched over, hands thrust into his coat despite the warmth of the afternoon, gazing forlornly into the shadows. What is he thinking about? Beth? Ginnie? The unwritten book on the movement? Next week's lineup of guests? I tell Kimmer I will be right back, release her hand reluctantly, and head back toward my brother. I would like to say that the sight of Addison in his loneliness has touched some wellspring of empathy or even love, but that would be a lie; more likely, I am worried that my brother is experiencing an epiphany, communing with great forces, learning some mystical truth that I am missing. Like when he knew, and I did not, that Santa was a fraud. Tawdry though it may seem, it is the old jealousy, the *Why Addison?*, that drives me back to his side.

"Hey, Misha," he murmurs as I reach the top of the hill, as insistent on using my nickname as Mariah is on avoiding it. He does not turn his head but manages nevertheless to reach out and lay his hand on my shoulder. It occurs to me that I have interrupted him at prayer. And that, in his eulogy, he did not mention God once.

"You okay?" I ask, trying to figure out what he is looking at. All I see are trees and headstones.

"I think so. I don't know. I was just thinking."

"About what?"

"Oh, you know. What Guru Arjan said about the tortures of death."

Well, of course. That was my next guess.

A moment passes. I have long admired and envied my big brother, and we have had a lot of fun over the years, but, just now, we have little to say to each other.

"It's beautiful up here," says Addison. "I guess I'll be up here one day. You, too."

It takes a few seconds for me to understand that he is talking about death. No, not talking about it: worrying about it. My big brother, who was never afraid of anything, and whose charm and grace have carried him effortlessly through his life, is suddenly worried about dying. Did he really rely on my father that heavily? I wonder. Or maybe I am the abnormal one, to watch my father's casket lowered into the ground and feel no twinge of concern over my own mortality. In either case, my brother wants comfort. Plainly, Beth Olin is not the comforting type. But neither am I.

"Come on," I whisper, taking his elbow. "We should go."

He shakes off my arm and points. "You know, Misha, every time I look at Abby's grave, I still hope we'll find them."

"Find who?"

"The folks in the car that killed her." In my older brother's voice I hear all my father's bitter fury. I stare at him for a moment, puzzled.

"Addison—"

"Right," he says. "You go on, I'll be down in a minute. Go on."

I wait a few more seconds, but Addison does not budge, so I turn at last and head back down the path toward the cars. Drawing near, I notice that Kimmer is now on her cell phone, her strong back to me, awkwardly taking notes on a piece of paper she has flattened on top of the limousine. Howard and Mariah are already gone, but a few family loyalists still wait, including Uncle Mal, who should have been back at the office a long time ago. I flush with warmth at his affection for us, until I realize that he, too, is on the phone. I shake my head at the ways of the corporate world. Maybe he and Kimmer are talking to each other.

"Talcott!"

I spin around at the sound of my name, first thinking it is Addison, but he is now on the path, moving in this direction, and he, too, has heard the call and is craning his neck toward a nearby hill.

"Talcott! Talcott, wait!" But faintly, more an echo than a voice.

I turn toward the back of the cemetery, where bare trees cast lengthening shadows in the late-afternoon sunlight. A low mist is gathering, so the vista has lost a bit of its crisp brightness. At first, I see only shadows and more shadows in the direction of the voice. Then two of the shadows detach themselves and turn, wraithlike, into people, two men, both white, striding in my direction.

I recognize one of them, and the autumn sky goes gray.

"Hello, Talcott," says Jack Ziegler. "Thank you for waiting for me."

(11)

THE FIRST THING I notice about Uncle Jack is that he is ill. Jack Ziegler was never a very large man, but he always seemed a menacing one. I do not know how many people he has killed, although I often fear that it is more than the numbers hinted at in the press. I have not seen him in well over a decade and have not missed him. But the changes in the man! Now he is frail, the suit of fine gray wool and the dark blue scarf hanging loosely on his emaciated frame. The square, strong face I remember from my boyhood, when he would visit us on the Vineyard, armed with expensive gifts, wonderful brainteasers, and terrible jokes, is falling in on itself; the silver hair, still reasonably thick, lies matted on his head; and his pale pink lips tremble when he is not speaking, and sometimes when he is. He approaches in the company of a taller and broader and much younger man, who silently steadies him when he stumbles. A friend, I think, except that the Jack Zieglers of the world have no friends. A bodyguard, then. Or, given Uncle Jack's physical condition, perhaps a nurse.

"Well, look who's here," Addison seethes.

"Let me handle this," I insist with my usual stupidity. I discipline myself not to speculate about what Mariah suggested as we sat in the kitchen Friday night.

"All yours."

Before Jack Ziegler quite reaches us, I warn Kimmer to stay down by the car with Bentley, and, for once, she does as I ask without an argument, for no potential judge can be seen even chatting with such a man. Uncle Mal steps forward as though to run the same interference for me that he does for his clients as they leave the grand jury, but I motion him back and tell him I will be fine. Then I turn and hurry up the hill. Mariah, of course, is already gone, which is just as well, for this apparition might push her over the edge. Only Addison remains nearby, just far enough away to be polite, but close enough to be of help if . . . if what?

"Hello, Uncle Jack," I say as Abby's godfather and I arrive, simultaneously, at the grave. Then I wait. He does not extend his hand and I do not offer mine. His bodyguard or whatever stands off to the side and a little bit behind, eyeing my brother uneasily. (I myself am evidently too unthreatening to excite his vigilance.)

"I bring you my condolences, Talcott," Jack Ziegler murmurs in his peculiar accent, vaguely East European, vaguely Brooklyn, vaguely Harvard, which my father always insisted was manufactured, as phony as Eddie Dozier's East Texas drawl. As Uncle Jack speaks, his eyes are cast downward, toward the grave. "I am so sorry about the death of your father."

"Thank you. I'm afraid we missed you at the church—"

"I despise funerals." Spoken matter-of-factly, like a discussion of weather, or sports, or interstate flight to avoid prosecution. "I have no interest in the celebration of death. I have seen too many good men die."

Some by your own hand, I am thinking, and I wonder if the other, rarely mentioned rumors are true, if I am talking to a man who murdered his own wife. Again Mariah's fears assail me. My sister's chronology possesses a certain mad logic—emphasis on the adjective: my father saw Jack Ziegler, my father called Mariah, my father died a few days later, then Jack Ziegler called Mariah, and now Jack Ziegler is here. I finally shared Mariah's notion with Kimmer as we lay in bed last night. My wife, head on my shoulder, giggled and said that it sounds to her more like two old friends who see each other all the time. Having no basis, yet, to decide, I say only: "Thank you for coming. Now, if you will excuse me—"

"Wait," says Jack Ziegler, and, for the first time, he turns his eyes up to meet mine. I take half a step back, for his face, close up, is a horror. His pale, papery skin is ravaged by nameless diseases that seem to me— whatever they are—an appropriate punishment for the life he has chosen to live. But it is his eyes that draw my attention. They are twin coals, hot and alive, burning with a dark, happy madness that should be visited on all murderers at some time before they die.

"Uncle Jack, I'm s-sorry," I manage. *Did I actually stammer?* "I have—I have to get going—"

"Talcott, I have traveled thousands of miles to see you. Surely you can spare me five of your valuable minutes." His voice has a terrible wheeze in it, and it occurs to me that I might be breathing whatever has made him this way. But I stand my ground.

"I understand you've been looking for me," I say at last.

"Yes." He seems childishly eager now, and he almost smiles, but thinks better of it. "Yes, that is so, I have been looking for you."

"You knew where to find me." I was raised to be polite, but seeing Uncle Jack like this, after all these years, brings out in me an irresistible urge to be rude. "You could have called me at home."

"That would not be—it was not possible. They know, you see, they would consider that, and I thought—I thought perhaps . . ." He trails off, the dark eyes all at once confused, and I realize that Uncle Jack is frightened of something. I hope it is the specter of prison or of his obviously approaching death that is scaring him, because anything else bad enough to scare Jack Ziegler is . . . well, something I do not want to meet.

"Okay, okay. You found me." Perhaps this is forward, but I am not so frightened of him now; on the other hand, I am not very happy about spending time in his company either. I want to flee this sickly scarecrow and retreat to the warmth, such as it is, of my family.

"Your father was a very fine man," says Uncle Jack, "and a very good friend. We did much together. Not much business, mostly pleasure."

"I see."

"The newspapers, you know, they wrote of our *business dealings*. There were no *business dealings*. It was nonsense. Trumped-up nonsense."

"I know," I lie, for Uncle Jack's benefit, but he is not interested in my opinions.

"That law clerk of his, perjuring himself that way." He makes a spitting noise but does not actually spit. "Scum." He shakes his head in feigned disbelief. "The papers, of course, they loved it. Left-wing bastards. Because they hated your father."

Not having exchanged a word with Jack Ziegler since well before my father's hearings, I have never heard his opinions about what happened. Given the tenor of his comments, I doubt he would be interested in mine. I remain silent.

"I hear the fool has never been able to get a job," says Uncle Jack, without a trace of humor, and I know who has been pulling at least a few of the strings. "I am not surprised."

"He was doing what he thought was right."

"He was lying in an effort to destroy a great man, and he is deserving of his fate."

I cannot take much more of this. As Jack Ziegler continues to rant, Mariah's nutty speculations of Friday seem . . . not so nutty. "Uncle Jack . . ."

"He *was* a great man, your father," Jack Ziegler interrupts. "A very great man, a very good friend. But now that he is dead, well . . ." He trails off and raises his hand, palm upmost, and tilts it one way, then the other. "Now I would very much like to be of assistance to *you*."

"To me?"

"Correct, Talcott. And to your family, naturally," he adds softly, rubbing his temples. The skin is so loose it seems to move under his fingers. I imagine it tearing away to leave only an unhappy skull.

I glance over at the cars. Kimmer is impatient. So is Uncle Mal. I look down at my baby sister's godfather once more. His help is the very last thing I want.

"Well, thank you, but I think we have everything under control."

"But you will call? If you need anything, you will call? Especially if . . . an emergency should arise?"

I shrug. "Okay."

"With your wife, for instance," he continues. "I understand that she is going to become a judge. I think that is wonderful. I understand that she has always wanted this."

"It isn't certain yet," I answer automatically, surprised that the secret has spread up into the Rocky Mountains, and also not wanting Jack Ziegler anywhere near her nomination. He has already spoiled one judicial career too many. "She isn't the only candidate."

"I know this." The burning eyes are gleeful again. "I understand that a colleague of yours believes the job to be his for the taking. Some would call him the front-runner."

I am thrown, once more, by the breadth of his knowledge; I choose not to wonder how he knows what he knows. I am glad that Kimmer is not within earshot.

"I suppose so. But, look, I have to—"

"Listen, Talcott. Are you listening?" He has drawn close to me again. "I do not think he has the staying power, this colleague of yours. It is my understanding that a fairly large skeleton is rattling around in his closet. And we all know what that means, eh?" He coughs violently. "Sooner or later, it is bound to tumble out."

"What kind of skeleton?" I ask, sudden eagerness overwhelming my caution.

"I would not concern myself with such things if I were you. I would not share them with your lovely wife. I would wait patiently for the wheel to turn."

I am mystified, but not precisely unhappy. If there is information that would kill off Marc Hadley's chances, I can hardly wait for it to— what did he say?—tumble out. Even though Marc and I were once friends, I cannot resist a rising excitement. Perhaps America's obsession with the use of scandal to disqualify nominees for the bench is absurd, but this is my wife we are talking about.

Still, what can Jack Ziegler possibly know about Marc Hadley that nobody else does?

"Thank you, Uncle Jack," I say uncertainly.

"I am always happy to be of assistance to any of Oliver's children." His voice has assumed a curiously formal tone. I am chilled once more. Is the skeleton something that he has somehow created? Is a criminal maneuvering to help my wife attain her longed-for seat on the bench? I have to say something, and it is not easy to decide what.

"Uh, Uncle Jack, I . . . I'm grateful that you would think to help, but . . ."

His disintegrating eyebrows slowly rise. Otherwise his expression does not change. He knows what I am trying to say but has no intention of making it easy.

"Well, it's just that I think Kimmer . . . Kimberly . . . wants to have the selection go forward so that, um, the better candidate wins. On the merits. She wouldn't want anybody to . . . interfere." And I am suddenly sure, as I say the difficult words, that what I am telling him is true. My smart, ambitious wife never wants to be beholden to anybody, for anything. When we were students, she made a name for herself around the building with her outspoken opposition to affirmative action, which she saw as just another way for white liberals to place black people in their debt.

Maybe she was right.

Uncle Jack, meanwhile, has his answer ready: "Oh, Talcott, Talcott, please have no fear on that account. I am not proposing to . . . interfere." He chuckles lightly, then coughs. "I am only predicting what is to occur. I have information. I am not going to use it. Nor do you need to do so. Your colleague, your wife's rival, has many, many enemies. One of them is certain to unlock the door and allow the skeleton to tumble out. The service I am doing for you is simply to let you know. Nothing more."

I nod. Standing up to Jack Ziegler has drained me.

"And now it is your turn," he continues. "I think perhaps you, Talcott, might be of assistance to me."

I close my eyes briefly. What did I expect? He did not travel all this way to tell me that Marc Hadley's candidacy is going to collapse, or to pay his last respects to my father. He came because he wants something.

"Talcott, you must listen to me. Listen with care. I must ask you one question."

"Go ahead." I want suddenly to be free of him. I want to share his odd news with Kimmer, even though he told me not to. I want her to kiss me happily, overjoyed that she seems to be on the verge of getting what she wants.

"Others will ask this of you, some with good motives, some with ill," he explains unhelpfully in his mysterious accent. "Not all of them will be who they say they are, and not all of them will mean you well."

I forgot Uncle Jack's eerie, unfathomable certainty that all the world is conspiring, but he evidently has changed little from the days when he used to drop by the Vineyard house with gifts from foreign ports and complaints about the machinations of the Kennedys, whose irresolution, he used to say, cost us Cuba. None of the children knew what he was talking about, but we loved the passion of his stories.

"Okay," I say.

"And so I must ask what they will ask," he continues, the mad eyes sparkling.

"Well, fire away," I sigh. Over by the limousine, Kimmer is glancing at her watch and raising her hand, beckoning, to urge me to hurry. Maybe she has another telephone meeting coming up. Maybe she, too, is scared of Jack Ziegler, whom she has never quite met. Maybe I need to get this over with. "But I really only have a few minutes to . . ."

"The arrangements, Talcott," he interrupts in that wheezy whisper. "I must know everything about the arrangements."

"The arrangements," I repeat stupidly, aware that my sister is not as crazy as I have been hoping, and that my brother, sensing that something is going on but not sure what, has moved half a step closer to us, in the manner of a protector or a wary parent—very often the same thing.

"Yes, the arrangements." The hot, joyful lunacy on his face sears my own. "What arrangements did your father make in the event of his death?"

"I'm not sure what you—"

"I believe you know precisely what I mean." A hint of steel: here, for the first time, is the Jack Ziegler about whom everybody was reporting back in 1986.

"No, I don't. Mariah told me you called and asked her the same thing. And I have to tell you what I told her. I don't have the slightest idea what you're talking about."

Uncle Jack shakes his sickly head impatiently. "Come, Talcott, we are not children, you and I. I have known you since you were born. I am your sister's godfather, may she rest in peace." A gesture toward the plot. "I was your father's friend. You know what I am asking, I think, you know what it means, and you know why I inquire. I must know the arrangements."

"I'm still not quite sure what you mean. I'm sorry."

"Your father's arrangements, Talcott." He is exasperated. "Come. The arrangements he worked out with you in the event of his, ah, unexpected demise."

I do not make Mariah's mistake: I am sure he does not mean *funeral arrangements*, not least because the funeral just ended. And then I see what I did not when Mariah grabbed me on Friday night. He is thinking about the will. The disposition of my father's estate. Which is odd, because, although my father was hardly poor, Jack Ziegler is quite rich; or so say the newspapers.

"You mean the financial arrangements," I say softly, with the confidence of a lawyer who has worked it all out. "Well, we haven't had the official reading of the—"

"That is not what I mean at all and you know it," he hisses, spraying me with his old man's spittle. "Do not fox with me."

"I'm not *foxing*." Allowing him to see my irritation.

"I understand that your father swore you to secrecy. That was sensible of him. But you surely must see that your vow does not include me."

I spread my arms wide. "Uncle Jack, look. I'm sorry. I don't think I can help you. There just aren't any arrangements that—"

In a movement almost faster than I can follow, his skeletal hand snakes out and grabs my wrist. I shut up. I can feel the heat of his illness, whatever it is, coursing beneath the papery skin, but his strength is amazing. His nails furrow my arm.

"What arrangements?" he demands.

As I stand, mouth open, my wrist still trapped in Uncle Jack's thin fingers, Addison moves a worried step closer, so does the bodyguard, and I sense more than see the two of them sizing one another up; something primal and male is suddenly in the air, a mutual scenting, as though they are beasts preparing for battle, and I see the first faint tinges of red beginning to blot out the trampled green grass.

"Please take your hand off me," I say calmly, but the hand is already off, and Uncle Jack is looking down at it as though it betrayed him.

"I am sorry, Talcott," he murmurs, speaking, it seems, more to the hand than to me, and somehow sounding not so much contrite as cautionary. "I ask what I ask because I must. I do so for your sake. Please understand that. I have nothing to gain, except to protect you, all of you, as I always promised your father I would. He asked me to look after his children if anything happened to him. I agreed to do so. And"—this almost sadly—"I am a man of my word." He shoves the offending hand into his pocket. The lunatic, gleeful eyes lift slowly to meet mine. Off to the side, Addison relaxes. The wary bodyguard does not.

"Uncle Jack, I . . . I appreciate that, but, uh, we're grown-ups now. . . ."

"Even adults may require looking after." He coughs softly, covering his mouth with his fist. "Talcott, there is not much time. I love you and your brother and your sister as though you were my own. I ask you now for help. So, please, Talcott, for the good of the family we both love, tell me of the arrangements."

I take a moment to think. I know I must get this precisely right.

"Uncle Jack, look. I appreciate you being here. I'm sure the whole family does. And I know it would mean a lot to my father. Please believe me, I would help you if I could. But I—I just don't know what you are talking about." I can feel myself botching it. "If you would just tell me what arrangements you mean."

"You know what arrangements I mean." This in a hard tone, with a touch of the fire I saw a minute ago, just enough to remind me that I am dealing with a dangerous man. The day is growing darker and my head is beginning to pound. "You appreciate that I am here? Excellent. Now I would appreciate the information."

"I don't have any information!" Finally losing my temper, for nothing causes quite so sharp a red aura as condescension. "I told you, I don't know what in the world you're talking about!" I am so loud that heads turn among the mourners who have not yet departed, and the bodyguard looks ready to grab Uncle Jack and make a run for it. Out of the corner of my eye, I notice that long-suffering Kimmer is striding heavily toward us. It occurs to me that it would be best to finish this conversation before she arrives. "I'm sorry I raised my voice," I tell him. "But there is nothing I can do to help you."

A long silence as the eerily dancing eyes search mine. Then Jack Ziegler shakes his head and purses his thin lips. "I have asked my question," he whispers, perhaps to himself. "I have delivered my warning. I have done what I came to do."

"Uncle Jack—"

"Talcott, I must go." His hot glare fixes briefly on Addison, standing ten paces away, who frowns and turns toward us as though aware of scrutiny. Jack Ziegler crowds closer to me, perhaps afraid of being overheard. Then the skinny hand snakes out again, once more amazing me with its speed, and I take another step back. But he is holding only a small white card. "Beware of the others I have told you about. And when you decide that you would like to talk about . . . about the *arrangements* . . . you must call me. I will come to any place you name, at any time you name. And I will help you in any way that I can." A pause as he waits, frowning. "I do not usually make such promises, Talcott."

Now I get it. He expects me to thank him. I hate that.

"I understand," is all I can bring myself to say. I pluck the card from his fingers.

"I hope so," he says sadly, "for I would not want to see you harmed." All at once he smiles, inclining his head toward my advancing wife. "You or your family."

I cannot believe what I have just heard, and the red is suddenly very sharp and bright. My voice is more gasp than objection: "Are you . . . Is that a threat?"

"Of course not, Talcott, of course not." He is still smiling, except that it is more an ugly rictus than a sign of happiness. "I am warning you of the thoughts of others. For me, a promise is a promise. I promised to protect you, and so I shall."

"Uncle Jack, I don't really know what—"

"Enough," he says sharply. "You must do what you must do. Allow no one to dissuade you." For a long moment, the dark, demented eyes bore into mine, making me lightheaded, as though part of his insanity is crossing the two feet between us, burrowing down my optic nerve into my brain. And then, very suddenly, Jack Ziegler gives me his back. "Mr. Henderson, we are going," he snaps at the bodyguard, who favors us with a final suspicious glance before also turning away. Mr. Henderson steadies his master. They walk off along the shadowy path through the marching headstones, turn a corner, and soon are lost in the deeper shadows, as though they are ghosts whose time in the world of the living is done and who therefore must return to the earth.

Still stunned, I feel Addison's steadying hand on my shoulder. "You did great," he murmurs, knowing, perhaps, that I doubt it. "He's a fruitcake."

"True." I tap the card against my teeth. "True."

"You okay?"

"Sure."

My brother gives me a look, then shrugs. "See you at the house," he promises, and heads off to look for his weird little poet or whatever she is. I take a step nearer the grave, unable somehow to believe that my father, casket or not, was able to lie quietly through the entire exchange with Uncle Jack. His silence, perhaps, is the best evidence that he is actually dead.

"What was that all about?" asks Kimmer, now at my side.

"I wish I knew," I say. I consider telling her what Jack Ziegler said about Marc Hadley, but decide to wait; better she be pleasantly surprised than cruelly disappointed.

Kimmer frowns, then kisses me on the cheek, takes my hand again, and leads me down the hill. But as I ride back to Shepard Street in the limousine, clutching my wife's cold hand, Jack Ziegler's words run like a mantra through my troubled mind: *The others. Beware of the others. . . . I am warning you of the thoughts of others. For me, a promise is a promise.*

And the rest of it: *I would not want to see you harmed. You or your family.*

CHAPTER 6

THE PROBLEMIST

(1)

ALTHOUGH IT IS no longer our home, Washington is very much Kimmer's city. With the Congress, the White House, a gaggle of federal regulatory agencies, countless judges, and more lawyers per capita than any locale on the face of the earth, it is a place for those who like to make deals, and making deals is what my wife does best. My wife's first task when she arrived in the city was to build a base camp, complete with laptop and portable fax machine, in the guest room of her parents' home, on Sixteenth Street up near the Carter Barron Theatre, a half-mile or so north of Shepard Street. She spent Monday, the day before the funeral, lining up appointments for Wednesday, the day after, one meeting over at the Federal Trade Commission on behalf of a client, the rest in furtherance of her candidacy for the court of appeals. And so this morning she leaves her parents' house early, for breakfast with another old friend—"the new girls' network," she gushes, although some are men. This particular friend is a political reporter at the *Post*, a woman appropriately named Battle, a buddy from Mount Holyoke, who is said to be connected.

Kimmer has always cultivated the press and is frequently quoted in the pages of our local newspaper, the *Clarion*, and, now and then, in the *Times*. I have a different attitude toward journalists, one I have exercised frequently over the past few days. When reporters call me, I have no comment, no matter what the subject. If they persist, I simply hang up. I never talk to reporters, not since the press savaged my father during his hearings. Never. I have a student named Lionel Eldridge, a one-time professional basketball star who, having ruined his knee, now hopes to be a lawyer. Kimmer and I know him and his wife a little bit, because he worked at her firm last summer, a job I helped him to obtain at a time when other firms, vexed by his grades and trying to prove they were not awed by his celebrity, turned him down. Lots of journalists still do stories about "young Mr. Eldridge," as Theo Mountain likes to call him—I think in jest, for Lionel may be half a century younger than Theo, but he is almost a decade older than the rest of the second-year students. In any event, the media still adore young Mr. Eldridge, and love to chronicle his doings. Once a reporter was foolish enough to call me. She was writing a profile of Sweet Nellie, as he was called in his playing days, and wanted, she said, to capture his eagerness to master this new challenge. She had spoken to Lionel, who had identified me as his favorite professor. I was flattered, I suppose, although I am not in this business to be liked. But still I had no comment. She asked why, and, as she caught me at a weak moment, I told her. "But this is a *nice* piece I'm writing," she wailed. "I write *sports*, for goodness' sake, not politics." As though the distinction would reassure me. "I hate sports," I told her, which was a lie, "and I'm not a nice man," which is the truth.

Even though my wife keeps telling me otherwise.

But Kimmer thinks her newspaper friend can help her, and perhaps she is right, for my wife has a nose for knowing who might be able to boost her closer to her goal. Later, she will meet with the Democratic Senator from our state, a graduate of the law school, to try to cajole him out of Marc Hadley's corner and, at minimum, onto the sidelines: a meeting I went hat in hand to Theo Mountain, the Senator's favorite teacher, to arrange. She is lunching with Ruthie Silverman, who warned her that everything about the process is confidential but at last agreed to see her anyway, for everybody who knows Kimmer develops the habit of doing what she wants. After lunch, my wife will visit the chief lobbyist for the NAACP, an appointment arranged by her father, the Colonel, who is also connected. Then, in the late afternoon, Kimmer and I will join forces, because the great Mallory Corcoran himself has squeezed the two of us into his calendar at four; Kimmer and I will see Uncle Mal together, in the hope that he will agree to put a portion of his considerable influence her way.

Washington, as I said, is Kimmer's city. It is not, however, mine, and it never will be; it is far too easy to close my eyes and remember all the long, bleak hours of hearings as my father sat before the Senate Judiciary Committee, first confident, next disbelieving, then angry, and finally sullen and defeated. I remember the days when my mother sat behind him, the days when I did. How Mariah was too upset to attend after the scandal broke, and how Addison, often summoned, never showed, to my father's distress. How the Judge's distress irritated me when I was so loyal and so ignored and Addison, as usual, so flighty and so loved: the prodigal son indeed. I remember the television lights, after the hearing was moved down the hall to a larger room, and everybody sweating. I had no idea that television lights were so hot. Senate staffers dabbed the members' foreheads; my father dabbed his own. I remember his grim refusal to accept any coaching from Uncle Mal, from the White House, from anybody who might help. I remember looking up at the Senators and thinking how distant and high and powerful they seemed, but also noticing how they read most of their long, pompous questions from cue cards, and how some of them grew confused if the conversation wandered too far from their briefings. I recall the baize on the tables: until I had the chance to touch it, I never realized it was simply stapled in place, a kind of special effect for the cameras. In reality, the tables were plain wood. I remember the crowds of reporters in the hallways and the entrances, shouting for attention like preschoolers. But most of all, like everybody else, I remember the dreary and repetitive and ultimately necessary questions: *When did you last see Jack Ziegler? Did you meet with Jack Ziegler in March of last year? What was the subject matter of the discussion? Were you aware of the pending indictment at that time?* On and on and on. And my father's dreary, monotonous answers, which sounded less and less convincing with every repetition: *I don't know, Senator. No, I did not, Senator. I do not recall, Senator. No, I had no idea, Senator.* And, finally, the beginning of the end, which always starts with friends running for cover and with the same signal to the now disgraced nominee, usually spoken by the chairman: *Now, Judge, I know you to be a decent man, and I have a great deal of respect for your accomplishments, and I would really like to believe that you are being candid with this committee, but, frankly . . .*

Nomination withdrawn at nominee's request.

Nominee and family humiliated.

Grand jury convenes.

Fade to black.

Or, as I might have said back in college, during my more overtly nationalist days, to white.

Even now I shudder at the memory. But there is no escaping it, at least not here in Washington. Last night, Kimmer and I sat up with her parents, watching the eleven o'clock news. When the anchorwoman reached the funeral of Oliver Garland, about the third story in, there, suddenly, were scenes not of today's events but of the humiliation of many years ago, my father seated before the Judiciary Committee, his mouth moving soundlessly as the reporter continued to talk. Cut to footage of Jack Ziegler in handcuffs following one of his many arrests: a nice, if biased, touch. Cut to the Judge giving a fiery speech before one of the Rightpacs as the reporter chattered about his later career. Cut to the rueful face of Greg Haramoto, interviewed outside the church just after the funeral, expressing his sorrow at the passing of "a great man" and extending his condolences to the family—although he made no effort to condole us in person, or by telephone, or even by note. Greg turns out to be the only attendee whose post-funeral comments made the news; but perhaps he was the only one the journalists found worth interviewing. Just as he was, before the Judiciary Committee in 1986, the only witness who mattered.

Even after all these years, knowing that the committee might have been right does nothing to assuage the pain of my father's disgrace. Strangers accost me at conferences: *Aren't you Oliver Garland's son?* I mutter banalities through thick curtains of red and flee as quickly as I can. So it is just as well that I do not accompany Kimmer on her Washington rounds; my pain would hinder her and, in the end, might injure her. Besides, Bentley and I have made other plans for the day. In a little while, we will head over to Shepard Street and then off with Mariah and her crew for a morning of in-line skating at some suburban roller-drome. Miles Madison, whose professional life now consists of occasional conversations with the managers of his various properties, has left for the golf course, despite the rainy weather. "If they can't play golf," sighs Vera Madison, "they'll just play cards and drink all day." My mother-in-law, who always asks me to address her by her first name, has all of Kimmer's handsomeness and height but is a good deal thinner; my wife's breadth comes from the Colonel, who has grown buttery since his retirement, and who, on his good days, allows me to call him Mr. Madison. Vera has offered to watch Bentley if I need to talk to my sister. I decline. I am keeping my son very close to me until I figure out what Uncle Jack was talking about. Probably nothing, but still. I have not yet told Kimmer, unsure how she will react, but when I asked her before she left this morning to please be careful, she looked at me hard—Kimmer misses little—and then kissed me lightly on the lips and said, "Oh, I will, Misha, I will." I was smiling at Kimmer when she walked out into the cold morning drizzle. She was smiling too, probably in anticipation of her day.

Kimmer headed into town in her mother's midnight-blue Cadillac, so Bentley and I take the rental car—a prosaic white Taurus—for the five-minute drive down Sixteenth Street to Shepard. Our journey takes us through the heart of the Gold Coast, a lovely corner of Northwest Washington where, over the middle decades of the twentieth century, hundreds of lawyers and physicians and businessmen and professors of the darker nation created an idyllic and sheltered community for their families in the midst of racial segregation. The lots tend to be large, the lawns manicured to perfection, and the houses spacious and beautifully furnished; in the white suburbs, they would sell for double or triple their value in the city. On the other hand, the ritzy black enclave of the Gold Coast might be integrating: Jay Rockefeller, for example, now lives on a vast estate that sprawls from just beyond Shepard Street down to Rock Creek Park. Perhaps for aesthetic balance, many rising black professionals who would once have purchased homes here are now busily integrating the suburbs.

Stopping briefly for a red light, I peek at my son in the rearview mirror. Bentley is a good-looking boy. He has my thick black hair, pointy chin, and deep chocolate skin, along with his mother's huge brown eyes, striking eyebrows, and full lips. He is also a quiet and very serious child, given to shyness around others and introspection when alone. Our son talked late: so late that we consulted pediatricians and even a pediatric neurologist—some friend of some cousin of Kimmer's—all of whom assured us that, although most children have spoken a few words midway through their second year, and some much earlier, it is neither unusual nor a sign of an impending mental deficiency for a child to start talking later. Just wait it out, everybody told us. And Bentley made us wait. Now, half a year past his third birthday, he has begun to babble in that peculiar mixture of proper English and mysterious prelinguistic code that so many toddlers discover shortly after turning one. He is talking it now, sternly lecturing his new dog, fiery orange and filled with stuffing, a gift from Addison, who never misses a chance to create a fan: "And no and doggie no said no cause Mama red you uh-oh doggie bad okay go home now go no no dare doggie Mama no no said dare okay no no okay dare doggie bad dare you . . ."

I interrupt this string of gorgeous gibberish:

"You okay, buddy?"

My son shuts up and eyes me warily, his pudgy hands clutching the yet unnamed dog as though he fears it might disappear.

"Dare doggie," he whispers.

"Right."

"Dare *you!*" he bursts out happily, for he adds new words and phrases just about daily. I wonder which television show he picked this line up from. "Dare *don't!*"

"Okay, buddy. I love you."

"Wuv you. Dare you."

"Dare you, too," I answer, but this only puzzles him, and his laughter subsides into uneasy silence.

I shake my head. Sometimes Bentley makes us uneasy, too—Kimmer especially. She spoils him hopelessly, unable to bear his unhappiness for an instant, because she has always blamed herself for whatever is wrong with our son, if, indeed, anything is. His first morning outside the womb swung rapidly from exhilarating to terrifying. Laboring in one of the brightly colored birthing rooms at the university hospital's sparkling maternity wing, pressing down when ordered, holding back on request, working on her breathing, doing all of it exactly right in typically splendid Kimmer fashion, my wife suddenly started to bleed very heavily, even though the baby's head had hardly crowned. I watched in amazement as the white sheets and green hospital gown turned bright, viscous red. The jolly, encouraging midwife who had been supervising the event all at once lost her jolliness and stopped encouraging. From my coaching perch on a wooden stool, I asked if everything was all right. The midwife hesitated, then offered me a wobbly smile and said that pregnant women can easily afford to lose a lot of blood, because their blood supply doubles. But she also whispered to a second nurse, who hurried from the room. The bleeding continued, a coppery red sea, as the midwife tried to deliver the baby's head. Her gloved hands slipped and she cursed. Kimmer felt things going awry, then looked down and saw all the blood and screamed in terror, which I had never heard before and have never heard since. I had never seen so much blood either. Our baby's little head was awash in it. The fetal monitor began braying a series of desperate objections. A doctor I had never seen before materialized to replace the midwife. She took a quick look and barked a series of swift orders; without further conversation, I was pressed physically from the room by two nurses as a phalanx of blue gowns converged on the bed, leaving me all alone in the modern, soulless waiting area to contemplate the possibility that I would lose both wife and son on what should have been the happiest day of my life.

Kimmer, it later turned out, was suffering from abruptio placentae, a premature separation of the uterine lining, similar to a menstrual period, but often deadly when one is carrying a late-term child; more specifically, as we were later told, Kimmer suffered a rupture of the myometrium, which might easily have been fatal, for she could have bled to death and our baby could have asphyxiated. To this day, my wife believes the condition was brought on by her continuing to drink during pregnancy, for she scoffed at claims that her personal habits could possibly do the baby (or fetus, as she called our child growing inside her) any harm. If her fears are true, then I must share the blame, not because I am a drinker—I am not—but because I have never been strong where Kimmer is concerned. After she thrice angrily ignored my nervous entreaties, I gave up trying to stop her. The first few hours of our son's life were harrowing: there was a chance, the doctors told us, stone-faced, that we might lose him. And Kimmer herself needed treatment for the blood she'd lost. A day or so later, when everybody turned out alive after all, my wife and I knelt in prayer, the last time we have done so outside of a church, thanking a God we have usually ignored.

Bentley, I believe, was God's answer.

Yet our son's birth also marks the point from which our marriage began its downhill slide. Today, my wife and I live together on uneasy terms. There are things she does not want to know and things she wants me not to know. If she is out of town, for instance, she calls me, not the other way around. Only in emergencies do I dare break the rules. When Mallory Corcoran called on Thursday afternoon to tell me my father had died, I checked our home answering machine by remote to see whether my wife had called. She had not. I immediately tried her at her hotel in San Francisco. She was out. I called her cell phone. It was turned off. I picked up Bentley from day care, explained to him solemnly what had happened to his grandfather, then returned to our house and tried again. She was still out. I called for hours, until midnight in the West—3 a.m. in Elm Harbor—and Kimmer was always out. Finally, in a burst of dreadful inspiration, I called the hotel again and asked for Gerald Nathanson. Jerry was in his room. He was nervous. The work was still going on, he told me. He did not know where my wife was, but he was sure she was safe. He promised to have her call if he ran into her. She called me ten minutes later. I never asked from where.

AT SHEPARD STREET, the door is opened by Cousin Sally, who is skipping work this morning in order to sit in my father's kitchen torturing my sister with dubious stories from our shared childhoods. Sally smothers me in those powerful arms, which is the way she greets just about everybody, but Addison in particular. Inside the house, smooth jazz is playing: Grover Washington, I think.

Bentley shrieks at his first sight of little Martin and Martina, who are, as usual, hand in hand. Within minutes, my son has joined the younger members of my sister's posse in some complicated game that has them trooping through the house in a dignified line, led by Marcus, the youngest, touching one and exactly one piece of furniture in each room before proceeding to the next, then reversing course and doing the same backward. I find Mariah and Just Alma in the twin wicker rocking chairs on the back porch. Alma, a Kool protruding jauntily from her mouth, grins in what could be delight, and Mariah allows me to kiss her cheek. Alma seems to be at the tail end of one of her raunchy stories, as well as her energy: she has to be going, she says, explaining for my benefit that one of her granddaughters will be along any minute to drive her back to Philadelphia. As she stands up, Alma pulls one of her famous tricks, squeezing the tip of the cigarette to put it out, then slipping it into the pocket of her cardigan.

I nod at the empty rocker, and Sally, reading my signal, takes Just Alma's seat. I then walk with Alma into the house. In the foyer, while she hunts for her coat, I ask her casually what she meant when she said the other day that *they* would let me know about the plans my father had made for me.

Alma's wise old eyes move in her dark face, but she does not quite look at me. "It ain't nothin to do with me," she murmurs after a moment.

I haven't a clue what she is talking about, and I say so.

"Ain't no *they*," she explains as I help her into her coat. "Just you and your family."

"Alma . . ."

"Your job is to take care of the family."

The honking of a horn announces the arrival of her granddaughter, who is, like quite a few of the numberless cousins, too young to consider the possibility that one should try to be polite, even the day after a funeral.

"Gotta go," Alma informs me.

"Alma, wait a second. Wait."

She is walking away from me, but her voice floats over her shoulder. "If your daddy has plans, he'll tell you soon enough."

"How can he possibly . . ."

We are standing at the open front door. Alma's huge suitcase is sitting on the floor of the foyer. A brown Dodge Durango is in the driveway, her rude granddaughter a blur behind the windshield. Alma takes my hand, and this time she does look at me.

"Your daddy was smarter than all of them, Talcott. That's why they were afraid of him." This is another precious bit of family mythology: that the Judge was denied his seat on the Supreme Court by lesser intellects who were jealous and racist at the same time. "You just wait and see."

"See what?"

"See how afraid of your father they were. When they come. But don't let it worry you none."

"When who comes?"

"They might not come, though. Your father thought they would. But they might be afraid."

"I'm not following. . . ."

"Like Jack. Jack Ziegler. He was afraid of your father, too."

It takes me a moment to process this. Somewhere deep in the house, I hear the shrieks of joyful children.

"Alma, I . . ."

"Gotta go, Talcott." She has rescued her Kool from her pocket and seems to want to light it. "I just emptied my bladder and I wanna get back to Philly before I gotta do it again."

"Alma, wait. Please. Wait a second."

"What *is* it, Talcott?" The peeved tone of an exhausted but indulgent parent.

"Jack Ziegler—what were you saying about him?"

"He's just an old man, Talcott, Jack Ziegler is. Don't let him scare you. He didn't scare your father none, and he shouldn't scare you none either."

(I I I)

I suggest we go for a walk, but my sister declines. Mariah is lonely, tired, and irritable—not hard to understand, perhaps, when her only grown-up company so far this morning has consisted of the self-centered, confusing Alma and the intermittently reliable Sally. I persuade my sister to come in from the porch. We sit down together in the kitchen. Mariah's makeup lacks its usual precision, her hair is in curlers, and the house she will formally inherit as soon as the will is admitted to probate is already the worse for wear, with evidence of young inhabitants—everything from tiny shoes to Playmobil sailors—scattered everywhere. Howard is gone, having returned to New York on the first shuttle to repair some collapsing deal, and leaving Sally and me to sit in that remarkably white kitchen listening to Mariah rail against Addison for his insufficiently vigorous defense of the Judge when he spoke at the funeral. And, indeed, I found my brother's brief reference to the hearings confusing, perhaps because he was trying to please too many constituencies: *Some of the attacks on my father were unfair. Some were pretty nasty. But some were thoughtful. Some were respectful. There were issues about which reasonable people could differ. We must never, in our love for Dad, forget that. And, certainly, the Christian in me will not allow me to condemn those who took the other side, because they, too, were doing what they thought was right.*

"He can be a real bastard," my sister informs us, her finger stabbing the air. "All Addison ever thinks about is Addison." Her tone suggesting that this is news. Sally's pug mouth twists in a half-grin, half-grimace: she adores my big brother, but also knows him to be a selfish . . . what-Mariah-said. Sally's mother, Thera, avoids my father's side of the family, even skipping the funeral, and I suppose what happened between Addison and her daughter is one of the reasons. Addison himself, along with Beth Olin, the great white poet, left town shortly after the funeral, heading on to Fort Lauderdale, where my brother had a speaking engagement. "Love amongst the Rats," sniffed Kimmer, when she learned that Beth was going along. "Good riddance," sniffs Mariah now, who is more like my wife than she will ever admit.

Yet Addison also has another side, the side for which I admire him. At Shepard Street yesterday afternoon, before he left with Beth, my brother took me aside, into the library, the same room where I found the diabolical scrapbook. Some relative murmured condescendingly that the brothers were going off to plan the future of the family. With the door closed behind us, I once more managed to place my body in front of the bookshelf, not wanting Addison to see the worrisome volume. But he wasn't looking. He surprised me with an earnest bear hug, then let me loose and offered his handsome smile. He told me he had caught snatches of the conversation with Jack Ziegler, and that I had acquitted myself admirably—one of the Judge's favorite phrases. We both laughed. He asked me what I planned to do about whatever Uncle Jack was looking for, and added, before I could speak, that he would help in any way he could. I had only to call. My heart hammered with sibling love. For so much of my youth, and even my early adulthood, Addison was protector, helper, role model. He cheered when I succeeded and consoled me when I failed. Strong Addison, wise Addison, popular Addison, whose advice at critical turnings of my life was far more helpful than the Judge's. He was there for the trivial—like when I was trounced in the election for editor in chief of the law review—and for the profound—like when my work kept me from making a planned trip to see my ailing mother, and she died while I was busily writing an article on mass tort litigation. And he urged me, against the wishes of the family, to go ahead and marry Kimmer—a decision, despite its occasional difficulties, that I believe I will never regret.

Looking into his somber, caring eyes yesterday, however, I could think of nothing with which I needed help. I told him the truth: that I had no idea what Uncle Jack was asking about, and therefore had no plans to do anything about it. Addison shifted tracks swiftly, as a good politician should, and said that might be best: Jack Ziegler is crazy as a loon.

(I V)

MARIAH, after three cups of coffee, finally announces that it is time to depart. But the intention, as so often, is easier than the act. Last night, my sister's king-sized family was augmented by the au pair of the moment, a matronly and delightful woman from the Balkans whose name I never do get straight. Even with the au pair's assistance and Sally's, it takes an astonishingly long time to get five children dressed to go off to the rink. And Mariah herself must prepare for the day. Waiting, I wander the house with Bentley, who stares around my father's long study with wide-eyed wonder. It occurs to me that my son has not been in this room in a year. My father loved his privacy, and this was his most private room. I lift Bentley in my arms and point to the signed photographs of my father with the great that line the wall opposite the windows, pronouncing the names carefully for my son, even though he will never remember them: John Kennedy, Lyndon Johnson,

Roy Wilkins, Martin Luther King, A. Philip Randolph, then the doorway to the hall and, at the far side, a sharp shift in political emphasis to Richard Nixon, Ronald Reagan, George Bush *père et fils*, Dan Quayle, Bob Dole, John McCain, Pat Robertson. Bentley giggles and frowns and giggles again, pointing at some of the pictures and ignoring others, but I can find no ideological pattern to his responses.

At the time of his death, my father had at his disposal a formal and suitably impressive corner office right down the hall from Uncle Mal's, on the tenth floor of a glass-walled building at Seventeenth and Eye, a short walk from the White House, where, despite all that happened, he was still an occasional guest, at least during Republican administrations. In Washington, downtown office buildings are much shorter than in other large cities. The tenth floor is considered fairly posh, and posh was very much my father's style in the last, tortured years of his life. He seemed determined to earn, all at once, the money denied him during his two decades on the bench. Although he lived so frugally that what he spent it on is anybody's guess.

The Judge rarely used his corner office downtown. He preferred to work at home, sitting alone in this cavernous study, which he constructed after my mother's death. To build it, my father simply knocked down the walls that separated the three family bedrooms ranged along the gallery at the top of the curved stair that swept upward from the foyer. This meant that, whenever any of his children visited overnight, we slept on a fold-out sofa down in the musty basement playroom, or in the dilapidated and probably illegal maid's quarters some earlier owner had shoehorned into one end of the attic. Which is how Kimmer and Bentley and I got into the habit of staying at her parents' home whenever we were in Washington. The Judge seemed not to mind. He was not the sort of grandfather who doted on his children's children. He hated to give up, even temporarily, his access to any corner of his house. He would chafe and fume if we came down late any morning from the maid's room, then run up the stairs for an inspection. He would shush Bentley if his laughter grew too loud. How he put up with Mariah and her enormous brood, I have no idea, for after the death of our mother, he came to like the security of chosen silence. Put simply, my father preferred his privacy. Unlike most of us, my father probably would not much have minded dying alone, which, it seems, is exactly what he did.

I glance down the long room to my father's large but shabby desk—an antique, he likely would have called it—an old partners desk, with kneeholes on both sides, each surrounded by a surfeit of drawers for all occasions. The wood is dark and pitted and desperately in need of a polishing, but I suppose my fanatically private father never brought anybody up here, so there was nobody to polish it for. Besides, the desktop itself is in perfect order, the pens and blotter and telephone and photographs—only of Claire, not of the children—all arranged with a realistic precision signaling that the office is used, yes, but by an individual of extraordinary self-discipline, which is how my father thought of himself. And, as with all the elements of good character, acting as though you are disciplined is not much different from actually being disciplined.

This is where my father died, sprawling across the desk, found by the housekeeper an hour or so later (a woman we will wind up paying a goodly sum to keep her away from the eager tabloids, Mallory Corcoran's minions drafting the ironclad contract for her signature, Howard Denton providing the cash). No note clasped in my father's hand, no finger pointing to a clue, and no evidence of foul play. I wonder what crossed his mind at the end, what fear of judgment or oblivion, what anger at a life's work left unfinished. Mariah imagines a killer standing over him, hypodermic in hand, but the police found no sign of a struggle, and her determination to show that the Judge was murdered seems to me, at this moment, no more than a mechanism for staving off anguish she would rather not experience. Or am I failing to penetrate to a deeper reality that only my sister so far perceives? I gaze at the desk and see my father, a bulky man, grabbing at his chest, eyes sick with disbelief, an angry old man with a bad heart, dying with none of his family nearby or even forewarned. The housekeeper called 911 and then called the firm, as the Judge had instructed her to do should something like this happen, and, although Mariah has had the carpet shampooed, I still discern faint outlines here and there where the paramedics left dirty footprints.

Across the room from the desk, positioned before one of the three windows looking out on the yard, is the low wooden table, manufactured by Drueke, on which my father used to compose his chess problems. Atop the table is a marble chessboard, the alternating gray and black squares each almost three inches on a side. Wandering over to the windows, I caress the ornately carved Indian box that holds the Judge's treasured chess set, the lid neatly shut, conveying a sense of abandonment, perhaps even bereavement. Call it anthropomorphism, call it romanticism: I envision the pieces mourning their master, the touch of whose fingers they will never feel again. I was, once upon a time, a serious chess player, having learned the moves from my father, who loved the game but rarely played against an actual opponent, for he was of a different, more exclusive fraternity, the chess problemist. Problemists try to find new and unusual ways to use the fewest possible pieces as they challenge solvers to figure out how white can play and checkmate black in two moves, and so on. Problems were never to my taste; I always preferred to play an actual game, against a flesh-and-blood opponent; but the Judge insisted that the only true chess artist was the composer. A few of his problems were even published in minor magazines here and there, and once, back in the early Reagan years, in what was then known as *Chess Life and Review*, the leading chess publication in the country, a page that hangs framed, even now, in the upstairs hallway of the Oak Bluffs house.

I open the box and admire the three-inch-high chess pieces stuffed into their two felted compartments, each beautifully stained piece carved of ebony or boxwood, traditional in design but with enough added fillips and whorls to make the set distinctive. I smile a bit, remembering the way we used to come into the study when it was downstairs—before the Judge knocked down the walls to make this one—and find him hunched over the table, a notebook at his side, working out his compositions. It relaxed him, he said; although at times it resembled an obsession, it was better than his drinking.

Then I frown. I sense something peculiar about the set, even as it lies in the box, but I cannot quite work it out.

I glance around at Bentley, who has plucked a volume of C. S. Lewis from my father's shelf and seated himself in my father's recliner. The Judge used to quote Lewis by the yard. His grandson has selected a page at random and is running his stubby fingers along the lines of type, his mouth moving as though he can read the words. Well, maybe he can a little, maybe he will surprise us all, as he so often has.

I close the box and put it back on the table. I cross to the desk and settle myself in the executive swivel chair, the oxblood leather old and cracked. I am not sure what I am doing, why I am even in this room, much less why I am sitting at the Judge's desk. On the credenza behind the desk stands a computer, complete with a printer–scanner–fax machine, nothing but the best, meaning the most expensive, for the Honorable Oliver C. Garland, as much of his mail was still addressed when he died. As usual, the computer is enveloped in a form-fitting green plastic dust cover—a dust cover!—because, although Addison, who loves computers, insisted that the Judge ought to have the latest technology and often went out and purchased it for him, my father hardly ever used it, preferring to compose his speeches and essays and angry letters to the editor, even his books, on yellow legal pads, which Mrs. Rose, his assistant, would later transcribe. Two pads sit on his desk, one of them missing the top few pages, both of them entirely blank.

No clue there, either.

I slide open a file drawer at random and find a few drafts of this and that, along with a scattering of financial records. Leafing through the next drawer, which seems to contain letters, I am startled briefly by a rapping sound behind me. Bentley has crawled into the kneehole on the far side of the desk and is knocking on the wood and giggling. I realize that I am supposed to answer, like at a door.

"Who's there?" I say, very loud, holding in my hand some mutually flattering correspondence between the Judge and a syndicated columnist sufficiently far to the right that the Heritage Foundation probably would not have him in.

"Knock-knock," my son says with a laugh, getting the joke backward.

"Who's there?" I repeat.

"Bemmy. Bemmy dere." He comes flying out, uncoiling at that remarkable speed that three-year-olds of both sexes seem able to summon at an instant, sprawling cross-legged on the vast Oriental carpet, then rolling to his feet like a paratrooper who has made a perfect landing. "Bemmy dere! Dare you!"

I step deftly around the desk to hug my son, but he shoves happily free of me and tears off toward a little sitting area my father arranged under the largest of the three windows on the long side of the room. From his parents, or at least his father, Bentley has inherited a certain reckless clumsiness. So I am not entirely surprised when, looking back to see whether I am playing, my son smashes into the Judge's chess table. The marble board lifts, then crashes back onto the glass-topped table. Nothing breaks, but the elegant box tumbles onto its side and the hand-turned pieces patter like rain against window and walls, then drop to the floor. Bentley tumbles backward, landing on his well-padded rump with a surprised grunt.

"Bemmy hurt," my son announces in wonderment. He sheds no tears, perhaps because he possesses, already at age three, the Garland frugality with displays of emotion. "Bemmy ouch."

"You're okay," I assure him, crouching for a hug he does not seem to want. "You're just fine, sweetheart."

"Bemmy ouch," he reminds me. "Bemmy fine. Bemmy okay."

"That's right, you're okay."

Bentley climbs to his feet and toddles off in the direction of my father's desk. I stoop to pick up the scattered chess pieces, setting them not in the box but in the positions from which they would begin a game. I note with irritation that two pawns are missing, one white and one black. I glance around the carpet again but see nothing. Pieces of this size are not easy to miss. I peek under the wooden chairs on either side of the chess table: still nothing.

From out in the hallway, I hear the mischievous chatter of two or three of my sister's children, fresh from the shower, and, as Bentley rushes out to join them, my mind sparks with unreasoning anger. Why do the pawns number only fourteen instead of sixteen? The answer is infuriatingly obvious. The missing chess pieces are evidence that Mariah's children have been frolicking in here. My sister, as usual, sets no limits on the freedom of her spoiled little brood. True, the house will soon be hers, but she might wait more than a week before letting her kids turn the room where the Judge died into a playpen—or a pig-pen.

Still, having a rambunctious child of my own, I can see why the cavernous room might qualify as an attractive nuisance. Unfortunately, a collectible chess set, like the one my father used to compose his problems, is worth a good deal less with pieces missing. I assume that the missing pieces will turn up, and I catch myself wondering whether Mariah, about to inherit the house and all its contents, might be persuaded to let me have the chess set. I could even return it to the Vineyard, where my father used to work on his compositions in the good old days, sitting alone on the porch in the evening, sipping lemonade, hunched over the board—

Downstairs, the doorbell rings, and I shiver, suddenly certain that somebody has come to the house to deliver more bad news. I am already halfway out the door when Sally's substantial voice comes blasting up from the foyer:

"Tal, there's some men here to see you." A pause. "They're from the FBI."

CHAPTER 7

THE ROLLER WOMAN

(I)

"YOU PEOPLE WORK FAST," I tell the two agents as we settle in the living room. I have offered them something to drink, which they have declined. I am more nervous than I want to be, but that is because I am not quite ready to talk to them; I am not quite sure how to handle some of the questions they are sure to ask about my wife. Mariah, in dark slacks and bright red socks, stands in the arched entry to the foyer, watching us carefully. Sally, wearing one of her endless supply of too-tight dresses, peeks around the corner with wide, agitated eyes.

"Just doing our job," says the tall one, a black man named Foreman. I wonder if he is deliberately misunderstanding me.

"What I mean is, we buried my father yesterday," I explain. "My wife told me you would be coming by soon, but I would think that this could wait."

The two men exchange a look. The shorter man, McDermott, has an angry white face, sandy hair, and a large, unsightly birthmark on the back of his hand. He seems old for this work, sixtyish, but I am wary of stereotypes. The taller one is calm and wears glasses. His hands are in constant motion, the hands of a magician. The two agents are seated awkwardly on the cream-colored sofa, as though worried about marring it. Both wear suits far cheaper than anything the mourners who crowded into the foyer last Friday would buy. I am across from them in a creaky rocker. Somewhere in the house, I hear shrieks of joy, and I know that five Dentons, plus one Garland, are off on another destructive rampage.

"We don't think it can," McDermott reports, staring me down.

"Well, I think this is inappropriate. I mean, naturally, I'll be happy to help in any way I can. But surely it doesn't have to be done today."

There is an odd moment of silence. I have the slightly scary sense that they know secrets they are contemplating whether to reveal. I remind myself that this is America.

"What did your wife tell you, exactly?" asks McDermott at last.

"Nothing confidential," I assure them. "She told me that you would be coming by to interview me in connection with . . . well, her possible nomination."

"That *we* would be coming by?" Foreman sounds amused.

"Well, that somebody from the FBI would—"

"What about her nomination?" McDermott interrupts, rudely.

Before I can answer the agent's question, Sally surprises us all by stepping forward and putting one of her own:

"Have we met before, Agent McDermott?"

He is silent for a beat, as though sorting through the visual memories of a long and distinguished career of performing background checks.

"Not that I recall, Mrs. Stillman," he says at last. With a twinge of dismay, I note his precision: he knows who in the family has taken whose last name, and who has not. If even a timeserver like McDermott is being this thorough, Kimmer is unlikely to succeed in hiding what she most wishes to. My wife must be longing for the old days, when Washington did not care about adultery.

Once upon a time.

I make myself relax. At least we have never hired an illegal alien, my wife has never committed sexual harassment, and we have had no more trouble with our taxes than any other two-earner professional family.

"Are you sure?" Sally persists.

"Yes, ma'am," he says shortly, and cuts his eyes toward Foreman, who nods and stands up and walks over to Sally. An appalled Mariah is already pulling at her arm. The three of them have a whispered conversation, but it is obvious that Foreman is indicating, as gently as he can, that the agents would like to talk to me alone.

"Thank you," Foreman calls after her as Sally stomps across the foyer, half led by Mariah and half leading her. There is no response.

"Now, then," says McDermott, looking down at his little notebook. He has already dismissed my cousin from his thoughts. I wonder, briefly, why she decided to challenge him.

"Right," I say, for no reason. I sit back, bewildered. There is something nudging the edge of my consciousness, something to do with Sally's reaction, but I cannot quite get it. "Right," I repeat, losing my place.

"You were talking about your wife's nomination," Foreman prompts, glancing at his puzzled partner as he speaks.

"Oh, oh, right." I gather myself. "I know she hasn't been formally nominated. But the background check comes first, right?"

"Background check?" asks McDermott.

"Concerning her nomination," I explain, glancing quickly toward the foyer, and also wondering whether I am idiotic or they are. "Uh, her possible nomination."

They look at each other again. It is Foreman's turn.

"Mr. Garland, we are not here about your wife."

"I beg your pardon."

"We should have made things clear." He crosses his long legs. "We know about what is going on with your wife, of course, but I'm afraid that's not the reason for this visit. Believe me, we would not interrupt your bereavement for a background check."

"Okay. Okay, then, why are you here?" But, even as I speak, I know what is coming, and my heart seems to slow down.

McDermott again: "Yesterday afternoon, in the cemetery, you spoke with one Jack Ziegler. True?"

I like that: *One Jack Ziegler.* Conveying suspicion, but not actually saying much.

"Well, yes . . ."

"We need to know what you talked about. That's why we're here." Just like that. He has made his demands and he is finished.

"Why?"

"We can't tell you that," says McDermott quickly, as well as rudely.

"We would if we could," adds Foreman, just as fast, which earns him a dirty look from his partner. "I can say that this is in reference to an ongoing criminal investigation, and please let me assure you that neither you nor any member of your family is in any way a subject of that investigation."

Because I am my father's son, I am tempted, for a silly moment, to correct his use of the alleged verb *ongo.* In the next instant, I am tempted to tell him precisely what Uncle Jack said to me. But discipline holds in the end; one of the terrible things about being a lawyer is that cautious precision is second nature.

Besides, I already mistrust them.

I say: "How do you happen to know that I spoke with Jack Ziegler yesterday?"

"We can't tell you that," says McDermott, the broken record, again too fast.

"I would like to think that my government does not spy on funerals."

"We do what we have to do," McDermott chirps.

"We don't spy at all." Foreman cuts in like a bully at a high-school dance. "In a criminal investigation, as you know, being a lawyer yourself, there are certain exigencies. The methodology is often complex, but, I assure you, we always proceed in accord with pertinent regulations." He is saying precisely the same thing as McDermott, just using a lot more words to do it. He is probably a lawyer too.

I am running out of ideas. I ask: "Is Jack Ziegler the subject of the investigation? No, never mind," I add, before McDermott can repeat his line.

"We need your help," says Foreman. "We need it badly."

I use one of my father's most effective tools when he used to lecture: I make them wait. I think about my encounter with Uncle Jack, and try to understand what it is that I am guarding. I think that perhaps I should relate, word for word, what happened. I nearly do. And then, in his impatience, McDermott ruins it.

"We can make you tell us, you know."

Foreman nearly groans. My head snaps around. I have been angry, on and off, for the last several days, and yesterday I was frightened. I have had enough.

"I beg your pardon."

"You *have* to tell us what you know. It's your legal obligation."

"Don't be ridiculous," I snap, my eyes blazing through suddenly red air into Agent McDermott's unanticipated umbrage. "That isn't the law, as I'm sure you know. You can't coerce somebody into cooperating with your investigation. You can, *maybe*, punish me if I tell you something that isn't true, but you can't make me tell you what you want to know, no matter how badly you need to know it, not unless you convene a grand jury and issue a subpoena. Now, is that what you want to do?"

"We could do that," says McDermott. I do not understand his fury or, for that matter, his tactics. "We don't want to, but we could."

I am not finished. "Federal prosecutors convene grand juries, not FBI agents. And, as I recall, there is a very specific regulation prohibiting you from making threats."

"We're not making threats," Foreman tries, but McDermott will not stop.

"We don't have time to play games," McDermott snarls. His voice has taken on a faint accent, probably Southern. "Jack Ziegler is scum. He's a murderer. He sells arms. He sells drugs. I don't know what else he sells. I do know nobody's been able to nail him. Well, this time we're going to do it. We're this close, Professor." He holds up thumb and forefinger a centimeter or so apart. Then he leans toward me. "Now, your wife is up for a judgeship. Great, I hope she gets it. But it's not going to look very good, is it, when it turns out that her husband refused to cooperate in a criminal investigation of a scumbag like good old Uncle Jack Ziegler. So—are you going to help us or not?"

I glance over at Foreman in disbelief, but his face is professionally blank. Full of fiery indignation, I am about to snap out an answer—goodness knows what I plan to say—when Sally's stout voice drifts into the room from the foyer:

"I'm leaving, Tal. Gotta go to work. I guess I'll have to talk to you later." Judging from her tone, she is still offended at being excluded. But she also wants to talk to me *now*.

I jump to my feet and excuse myself for a moment, buying time to think. And, if I can, to calm down. I walk Sally to the door. On the front step, she pauses, turns to face me, and asks if I happened to get Agent McDermott's first name. I confess that he does not seem to have mentioned it, then ask her why she wants to know.

"I just have the feeling I've seen him before," Cousin Sally says, her bold brown eyes holding mine. Except on the subject of Addison, Sally lacks an outlandish imagination, so, if she says she has met him, I am required to take her seriously.

"Where?"

"I don't know, Tal, but—did you see his hand?"

"The birthmark? Yes."

"Yeah, and his lip." I think about it for a few seconds, then nod. There is a small, pale spot on McDermott's upper lip, a kind of scar, far more prominent when he is angry. "I've seen that mark before," says my cousin, who, thanks to a bad marriage in her past, has a few scars of her own.

"Where?"

"I . . . I'm not sure."

"On the Hill? In connection with your work?"

Sally shakes her head. "A long time ago."

Before I can respond to this, Sally shrugs and smiles and says never mind, more than likely she is mistaken.

I wait a beat, then ask her if she is all right. "I'm fine," she says, a sad, thoughtful look coming into her eyes. Sally squeezes my hand, and, when she lets go, my anger goes too, just like that, as though she has drawn it out of me.

"Thanks for your help," I smile.

She smiles back, then turns and heads for her car, carrying one of the oversized totes that always remind Kimmer of a bag lady.

I return to the living room, far calmer than I was a few minutes ago. McDermott and Foreman are both on their feet, alert and impatient, but confident too. Well, why shouldn't they be confident? They have played the good-cop, bad-cop routine perfectly, and they both know I am beaten. I know it too. I have no idea whether Sally really has seen McDermott before, but I have learned a lot over the years about cutting your losses; one of the things the Judge drummed into our heads was the old rhyme about living to fight another day. I look at the agents steadily and say: "I'm sorry if I seemed uncooperative. That wasn't my intention. Now, what exactly do you want to know?"

(11)

MY SISTER AND I get moving later than we planned, but eventually we arrive at the crowded skating rink, which is across the highway from one of Washington's countless suburban shopping malls. Marcus has a cold and stays at Shepard Street with the au pair, so we are seven altogether, and can all squeeze into Mariah's just-acquired Lincoln Navigator, that luxurious monster masquerading as a sports-utility vehicle. Everybody skates but me. Mariah's children, who apparently do this all the time, are quite good, and Bentley, who has never done it before, is eager to try, for his introspective streak does nothing to reduce his childlike bravado. Mariah takes personal charge of him and promises not to leave his side. Mariah takes promises more seriously than anybody I have ever known, so I have no doubts about his safety. Bentley, however, must have a few; just before stepping onto the rink itself, he turns to me, so festooned with pads and helmet that he can scarcely be seen, and whispers, "Dare *you?*" Smiling, I shake my head and assure my son that Aunt Mariah will take good care of him. Bentley smiles tentatively back at me, then steps out into the rink, holding on to my sister with both hands. The Denton children have long since whirled away, to the beat of a song by Celine Dion or Mariah Carey or some other PG-motion-picture-soundtrack diva.

I lean on the heavy wooden boards that form the sides of the rink, and watch. I am not skating because I do not want to embarrass myself, but also because I want to think. I want to think because I want to make sure that I am not in trouble. I want to make sure that I am not in trouble because I did not tell Foreman and McDermott everything that happened. I did not lie to them, exactly, but I did not reveal the entire conversation with Uncle Jack. I told them about the condolences he offered. I told them he seemed sick. I told them about his repeated demands to know about *the arrangements.* I told them about his concern that others, who would mean us ill, would ask the same questions. But I did not tell them about his promise to protect me and my family, for fear that it might be misconstrued. I did not tell them what he said about Marc Hadley.

The odd part was that, after I finished my recitation (which they interrupted only now and then, for minor clarifications), the FBI men had just one question, asked with polite emphasis by Agent Foreman: "So, Mr. Garland, what arrangements *did* your father make?" When I repeated what I had earlier told Uncle Jack, that I did not have the slightest idea what arrangements he was talking about, Foreman walked me, with lawyerlike precision, through a series of possibilities: Were there any special financial arrangements? Burial arrangements? Had my father left any special instructions about what should be done upon his death? Special instructions to open a safe-deposit box, for example? Or an envelope to be sealed until after he died? Did I recall any conversations or communications over the past year in which my father used the word *arrangements?* (That last question would have left me laughing had their faces, and McDermott's silky threat about Kimmer, not been so serious.)

I responded to every question with some version of the same hackneyed Washington phrase: *I don't know, Not to my knowledge, I don't recall,* sounding much like my father before the Judiciary Committee, and reminding me yet again just how much I hate the city. Once it became clear that this was the only answer I was prepared to offer, McDermott seemed ready to lose his temper again. But, for once, Foreman got there first. He told me how helpful I had been. He told me how they knew it was a difficult time and they were grateful for my cooperation. He told me that he would personally see to it that none of this created the slightest adverse reflection on my wife's chances for nomination—another nicely meaningless lawyerly turn of a phrase. And he told me they would see themselves out, which I allowed them to do.

A few minutes after the agents left, I found myself regretting that I had not told them all I knew—and only then did I realize that they had not left me business cards telling me how to get in touch with them if I remembered anything else. This struck me as odd, because the many FBI agents I regularly encounter when my former students go through security checks for government jobs always leave their cards. I worried over this omission, wondering why they were so confident that they had all they needed to know, wondering whether I had, without realizing it, given them the decisive link in their investigation. Then I forgot all about the question, because an impatient Mariah, tapping her foot in the foyer, pointed out that we had to leave, lest we not have time to skate and still get back for my appointment with Mallory Corcoran. On the way to the skating rink, she sat in silence for a while, then asked whether I thought Sally really knew McDermott. I said something inconsequential about how I had no way to tell. Mariah said she did not think Sally was the sort to make stuff up. As it happens, I agree, but I only nodded, humoring my worried sister. Next, I figured, she would be telling me that the FBI killed the Judge. Or a cabal of liberals with strawberry birthmarks on their hands. Or a conspiracy of men with scars on their lips. But she said nothing, just brooded all the rest of the way to the rink, and I apologized telepathically for my unworthy thoughts.

Now, watching my son grow gradually less tentative under my sister's tutelage, I am impressed by her patience, her maternal thoroughness. She has coaxed him to the point where he is willing to let go of her hand. I smile. Mariah knows how to mother, puts lots of time and thought into it. I wish I knew as much about how to father. Feeling a sudden surge of love for my sister, I try to put her wild theories out of my mind, pondering instead a far more pressing question: how to catch up with the work I am paid for. I must schedule makeup classes for torts and for my seminar, which I am missing for this entire week, and still find time to finish the overdue revised draft of my article on mass tort litigation for the law review, which I originally planned to pursue this past weekend. Maybe if I—

Suddenly, an astonishingly well muscled woman of our nation thwacks against the boards below me, grabs the top of the wall with two gloved hands, and favors me with a sunny smile. She is clad in black spandex and red skates, and she moves with the easy grace of the natural athlete. "Hey, handsome, how come you're not skating?" she calls, as though we have known each other for years. Her skin is gorgeously brown, her face plain yet roundly pleasant, her mouth full of huge teeth, her head unfortunately topped by a shock of hideously pressed flat curls. Two gold loops, one large, one small, hang from each pierced ear. She is close to six feet tall, and older than I first thought: perhaps in her mid-thirties. "Are you there?" she asks, still smiling, when at first I say nothing. "Hello?" She is, I realize in surprise, flirting with me, not an activity with which I have much recent experience. Her eyes sparkle with secret mischief, and her toothy grin is contagious.

I find myself smiling back, but my throat is dry, and it is an effort for me to say, "I'm afraid I'm not much of a skater."

"So what?" she laughs, shuffling her feet in place, a fist on each strong hip. "I'll teach you if you want." She reaches a hand toward me, palm upward, fingers splayed, and tilts her head to one side as if to stretch her neck. "Come on, handsome, you need to have some fun, I can tell."

Unexpectedly stirred by her aggressiveness, and, I confess, already having fun, I am about to reply with a remark every bit as flirtatious as hers, when she casts a practiced eye down at my hand, observes my wedding band, loses her smile, says, "Oops, oh, hey, sorry," spreads her long arms, and skates off, backward. With a last saucy wave, she swirls away and is lost in the crowded rink. To my surprise, I am pierced with a sense of loss so strong that for an instant I forget to watch out for Bentley, who naturally chooses that moment to collide with another skater. He leaves the rink wailing, his lip split bloodily. Mariah, full of apologies, is in tears herself. A couple of her spoiled children laugh at Bentley's clumsiness, the others sob at all the blood. I hug my son and apply an ice pack helpfully supplied by the management, but he is shaking his head and crying for his mother. I was nowhere near him when the accident happened and could have done nothing to prevent it, but Bentley seems to think I am guilty nevertheless.

Most likely, he is right, for the roller woman cavorts through my dreams for weeks to come.

CHAPTER 8

MORE NEWS BY PHONE

(1)

AT TWENTY MINUTES OF FOUR, I step out of a taxi in front of the building in which, just a week ago, my father had his office. I have traded in my blue jeans for the same charcoal suit I wore to the funeral, the only suit I happen to have brought with me to Washington, and one of only two I happen to own. I am early, so I window-shop. There is a jeweler in the lobby and a dealer in rare books on the corner, and I visit both, happy to be in a city so comfortable with its black middle class that I am not an object of suspicion in either establishment. In the jewelry store, I fight the temptation to buy Kimmer a small but budget-busting present—she has a weakness for diamonds, and I see a pair of earrings I know she would love. On the corner, I talk with the proprietor of the bookshop about a scarce pamphlet for which I have been searching, Bobby Fischer's self-published account of his mistaken arrest for bank robbery, melodramatically entitled *I Was Tortured in the Pasadena Jailhouse!* I leave the owner my card; he promises to see what he can do. When I return to the lobby, Kimmer is already there, pointing at her watch and glaring at me. It is still three minutes of four, but one does not take the slightest chance of keeping Mallory Corcoran waiting. The great Mallory Corcoran does not wait.

Except that he does wait for Kimmer and me. Not only waits, but receives us with all the considerable charm he can muster. He comes out to the reception area himself, wearing no jacket, but, with crisp blue shirt and yellow club tie and yellow braces stretched over his substantial belly, kisses Kimmer's cheek, shakes my hand formally, and leads us back to the enormous corner office, which, like most offices in the city, has views mainly of buildings across the street, but with a peek at the

Washington Monument if you look at just the right angle. His desk is piled high with briefs and memoranda. It is one of the few desks in any law firm in the city with no computer in evidence. He leads us to a leather sofa, faced by two original Eames chairs, one of which he selects for himself. I marvel that it can hold him, but Mallory Corcoran, like many successful litigators, seems to have the trick of adjusting his weight to fit the situation. One of his three secretaries takes drink orders: tea for Uncle Mal and Kimmer, ginger ale for me. A tray of finger sandwiches materializes. We chat about the funeral and the weather and the press and the latest scandal on Capitol Hill. He tells us that a team of paralegals has packed all my father's personal things and the firm will ship them wherever we specify; he asks if I want to take a last look at Oliver's office, and I decline, not least because my wife is about to jump out of her skin.

Then we get down to business.

Uncle Mal begins by inviting a senior associate, a nervous woman he introduces as Cassie Meadows, to sit in and take notes. Kimmer is uneasy talking in the presence of a stranger, but Uncle Mal tells us to treat Meadows (as he calls her) like furniture. Not a very nice thing to say, and Meadows, a rail-thin denizen of the paler nation, blushes furiously, but I see his point: with so many people indicted for so many things in Washington these days, and so many indictments resting on vague contradictions in hazily remembered conversations, the great Mallory Corcoran wants a friendly witness in the room.

"Meadows is a hell of a litigator," he tells us, as though we are about to go into court, "and she knows everybody worth knowing on the Hill."

"I used to work for Senator Hatch," she explains.

"And she was a Supreme Court law clerk and the top of her class at Columbia," he enthuses, playing the usual Washington game of using résumé power to bat away questions of trust. If she is this smart, he is saying, you have no business asking why she is sitting in. Then he adds the real point: "And, Kimberly, she'll be working with me very closely on this matter. Everything I know, she'll know." Meaning that Mallory Corcoran, beyond this one meeting with us, will likely be too busy to help my wife out, so that she will be foisted off henceforth on an associate.

Kimmer stops resisting.

Uncle Mal is not the kind of man who is easily pinned down; nevertheless, the meeting goes well. He understands why we are here and he does almost all the talking. He asks Kimmer how her other meetings went, but barely listens to her answers. Kimmer has not had time to tell me much, but I gather she has not, so far, heard the answers she wants. The Senator, who gave her only fifteen minutes (with two aides in the room to prompt him), is firmly in Marc Hadley's camp and kept telling her there will be other chances down the road; Ruthie Silverman was smooth and evasive; the civil rights lobbyist promised to try, but warned that the administration was unlikely to listen. Mallory Corcoran waves all of this away. What matters is who knows whom. He has his ear firmly to the ground, he says, for he loves clichés, rolling them grandly off his tongue so that his listeners will know he knows they know it is all an act. I wonder whether he will tell us about the skeleton that a cackling Jack Ziegler promised. Instead, Uncle Mal says that Marc Hadley is calling in all his markers, putting on a full-court press, pulling out all the stops—the metaphors go bumping into each other in fine Washington sound-bite fashion—and lots of my colleagues at the law school are helping him. "Probably to get rid of him," Kimmer mutters, which I think might actually be true, but it is plain that she is upset.

Uncle Mal sees it too. He smiles broadly and shakes his head. Kimmer is not to worry, he says. Meadows can talk to people on the Hill, he explains, and his anorexic associate nods her head to show that she knows this is a command. The rest of it, says Uncle Mal, he will handle himself. Marc and his friends know some people, true, but—he thumps his chest—"Mallory Corcoran probably knows a few more people than Marc Hadley does," which is exactly what Kimmer wants to hear. He will make a few calls, Uncle Mal assures us, which means he will talk to the President and, more important, the White House Counsel, Ruthie's boss, who will make the final recommendation, and happens to be a former partner in the firm. Uncle Mal does not promise to lobby for Kimmer's candidacy, but he does say he will nose around and find out what is going on, which often amounts to the same thing; for, in the mirror maze of the federal appointments process, sometimes what matters most is having the right person ask the right questions. All of this, he says, should be considered his gift to us, because of the respect in which he held my father—which means, of course, that he will expect us to pay him back without hesitation should he ever ask.

Kimmer by this time is beaming—she is no poker player, my brilliant wife—but I know Uncle Mal is not that easy. When he has us sufficiently awed by his munificence, he adjusts his cuffs and then, somehow contriving to look us both in the eye at the same time, folds his hands and asks what is, in contemporary Washington, the one question that really matters: "Is there anything in your background, Kimberly, anything at all, or yours, Talcott, that, were it to become public knowledge, would embarrass the President, or you?" *Or me?* is the unspoken but clearly implied third term in the series: *Embarrass me and you will never, ever be able to count on the firm again.*

"Nothing," says Kimmer, so quickly that we both look at her in astonishment.

"You're absolutely sure?" asks the great Mallory Corcoran.

"Absolutely."

She slips off her glasses and offers her most dazzling smile, which turns most men into fawning sycophants, and invariably devastates me, on the rare occasions that she bothers to try. It is wasted. Uncle Mal has weathered smiles from the world's leading experts. He raises an eyebrow at my wife and then turns to me. Kimmer grabs my hand and shoots me a glance. This seems unwise: does she think he will overlook it?

"Talcott?" he inquires.

"Well," I begin. Kimmer squeezes desperately. Surely I would not mention, in front of Uncle Mal and this total stranger . . . surely . . .

"Misha," she murmurs, casting her eyes toward Meadows, who, obviously bored, is staring into space. She has written perhaps two sentences on her pad.

But my wife has no need to worry, for her infidelities are not on my mind. "Well, there is one thing bothering me," I admit. Then I tell them about this morning's visit from the FBI. As I lay out the details, I can feel Kimmer growing distant and annoyed . . . and worried. She returns my hand.

Uncle Mal interrupts.

"Did they really say that if you didn't talk to them about Jack Ziegler it could hurt your wife's chances?"

"Yes."

"Those bastards," he says, but softly, leaning back and shaking his head. Then he picks up one of the four telephones scattered around the room and stabs a button with a sausagey finger. "Grace, get me the Attorney General. If he's not available, the deputy. It's urgent." He hangs up. "We'll get to the bottom of this, oh, yes." He turns to Meadows. "Get me a copy of the regs governing FBI interviews with witnesses."

"You mean now?" she asks, startled out of some private reverie.

"No, next week. Of course now. Go."

She scurries from the room, still clutching her notepad. I see at once—and I assume Meadows does too—that Uncle Mal does not want her to be around for what is coming next. What I do not see is why. Nor is Mallory Corcoran about to enlighten us. Instead, he takes us on a side trip: "Oh, Tal, by the way, I turned on the television the other night, and who do you think I saw? Your brother." And he is off, describing Addison's appearance on *The News Hour*, during which he railed against some recent Republican legislative initiative. Kimmer cringes, worrying now that my brother's politics will hurt her chances, and Uncle Mal, noticing her discomfort, veers off into a story about my father's days on the bench, a very funny one about a befuddled litigant, to which I hardly pay any attention, not only because I have heard it many times before, but because I am remembering the business card the FBI agents never gave me. I suddenly know why Uncle Mal sent Meadows away. He has figured out that whatever the Justice Department is about to tell him is going to be awful, and nothing to do with Kimmer and her judicial ambitions. After Mariah's dispiriting speculations, it scares me in advance.

The phone buzzes. Uncle Mal stops in mid-sentence and picks it up. "Yes? Who? Okay." He puts his hand over the receiver. "It's the AG's deputy." Then he is lost to us again: "Mort, how the hell are you? . . . I hear that Frank is going to Harvard next year. That's great. . . . When are you going to start making an honest living? . . . Well, you know there's always a place for you here. . . . What? Los *Angeles?* Oh, come on, our smog is much better than theirs. . . . Uh-huh . . . Oh, I know, I know. . . . Well, listen, let me tell you why I called. I am sitting here in my office with a couple of very irate citizens of this fine republic, one of whom rejoices in the name of Talcott Garland, and the other of whom is known as Kimberly Madison. . . . Yes, that Kimberly Madison . . . No, I know you have nothing to do with picking judges, but that's not what I'm calling about. . . . Uh-huh." He puts his hand over the receiver and says to us: "Aren't there any secrets in this town?" Back to the phone: "Well, listen. It seems that a couple of not very polite FBI guys visited Mr. Garland this morning. . . . No, nothing about that. A criminal investigation. The subject appears to be a certain Jack Ziegler, whose name I assume you have heard. . . . What? . . . No, no, I'm not representing Mr. Ziegler any longer, you know Brendan Sullivan over at Williams & Connolly does that these days. . . . No, Morton, no, not that either . . . No, my guy is Talcott Garland. . . . Uh-huh . . . Morton, listen. Here's the thing. In the first place, as I suspect you know, my client just buried his father yesterday. So I'd say the timing is a little bit lousy. Second, one of these FBI guys threatened Mr. Garland." I am shaking my head emphatically, but Uncle Mal, once he gets going, is relentless. "Yes, that's right. . . . No, not with bodily harm. He said that if Mr. Garland did not tell him exactly what he wanted to know, right then and there, it would hurt Ms. Madison's chances for the nomination. . . . Yes, I know they're not supposed to, that's why I'm calling. . . . Yes . . . No, I haven't. . . . Yes, I do, and an apology from your boss would be even better. . . . Yes . . . Yes, I will. . . . Exactly one hour, though . . . Okay."

He hangs up without saying goodbye, which has become a status symbol in our uncivil times: the less you have to worry about offending people, the more powerful you must be.

"Uncle Mal," I begin, but he rides right over me.

"Right. So this is the thing. These FBI guys seem to have broken lots of rules. So Morton Pearlman is going to talk to his boss, and then we'll see."

"You didn't have to do that," says Kimmer, nervously.

"Kimberly, Kimberly, dear, don't worry." He actually pats her hand. "This will not snap back on you, I promise. This is just how the game is played in this town. Take the word of an old hand. You have to let them know they can't fu—, uh, can't mess with you, and you have to let them know early. So, this is what I suggest." He is on his feet now, so we are, too. Outside, it is silvery twilight. "Why don't you two lovebirds get a bite to eat? Call me right here in, say, an hour. I'll tell Grace to put you through. I'll have an answer by then, or I'll be down at DOJ eating somebody's lunch."

During this splendid little speech, he has somehow moved us to the door. I notice Meadows approaching down the hall, a colorful volume of the *Code of Federal Regulations* in her hand.

"Thank you, Mr. Corcoran," says Kimmer.

"'Mal' is fine," he says, for about the tenth time.

"Thank you, Uncle Mal," I add.

This time I get the hug. And a furtive whisper in my ear: "This smells, Tal. It stinks to high Heaven." I turn in surprise, thinking, for some reason, that he is talking about me, not to me. But I see in his wise, experienced insider's eyes only warning. "Be very, very careful," he says. "Something isn't right."

MY SISTER and the terrifying au pair are watching Bentley. Mariah said he can stay with her as late as we need to be out, so worried Kimmer and I, lovebirds or not, walk up to K Street to one of the city's many steak houses. Our nation's capital is not noted for the quality of its restaurants, but its chefs do seem to know steak. It is just past five, so we are able to get a quiet corner table without waiting. Kimmer, who has been silent for most of the four blocks we have walked, throws herself into her chair, orders a brandy Alexander before the waiter can get a word out, and favors me with a disapproving glance. I reach for her hand, but she snatches it away.

"What is it?" I ask in frustration.

"Nothing," she snaps. She looks across the room, then looks back. "I thought you were on my side. I thought you loved me. Then all this bullshit about the FBI. I mean, why the hell did you bring that up?"

Kimmer knows that vulgarity bothers me, which is why she uses it when she is angry; I do not believe she speaks this way to anybody else.

"I thought Uncle Mal could help," I tell her. "And he is helping."

"Helping! He picks up the phone and yells at some idiot who works for the Attorney General, and then says I told him to do it, and that's supposed to *help?*" She slumps in her chair, yanks off her glasses, closes her eyes for a moment. I glance around nervously, but none of the other diners seem to have noticed her outburst. Kimmer perks up again. "I mean, I thought he was supposed to be some kind of major player. Doesn't he have more sense than that?"

Now, the truth is that Uncle Mal's reaction bothered me too. So did his decision to send Meadows out of the room. But I am not sure how to make either of these points to my wife. Goodness knows, nobody in my family ever says anything directly.

"Kimmer, don't you think the best thing is to get this out in the open—"

"Get *what* out in the open?"

"Whatever's going on."

"Nothing's *going on.*"

"How can you say that after Jack Ziegler—"

"Your damn father just won't leave us alone, will he?"

"What are you talking about?"

She seems almost ready to cry. "Your parents never wanted you to marry me in the first place! You *told* me that."

I am stunned. My wife has not mentioned this story in years but, obviously, has not forgotten it. Well, that your in-laws opposed your marriage cannot be easy to forget. "Oh, darling, that was years ago, and they weren't *against* it exactly. . . ."

"They said it would be scandalous. You told me."

And they were right. It was. But this is hardly the time to remind my wife how the two of us gleefully shocked black Washington. "Well, sure, but you have to understand the way they meant it. . . ."

"Your father's in the grave, and he's still making trouble."

"Kimmer!"

She sighs, then puts up her hands in a gesture of truce. "Okay, okay, I'm sorry. I didn't mean that. That wasn't fair." She leans forward and sips her drink, closes her eyes for an instant, then takes my hand. Despite my own growing anger, I let her do it. Being touched by her calms me; it has always calmed me, even back when the reason I was nervous around Kimmer was that she was married to somebody else. "But, Misha, look at it from my point of view. You have what you want. You wanted a marriage and a child and tenure at a good law school. Well, guess what? You have all three." Kimmer begins to massage my fingers, one at a time, which she knows I like. "But what about me? I'm ambitious, okay? That's my sin. Fine. You've known since we were in law school that I wanted to be a judge, right? Well, now I have a chance. I used to think the . . . Well, okay, what happened with your father made it impossible. And maybe that's . . . that's maybe one reason I haven't been as good a wife to you as I should."

She drops her eyes briefly, a gesture so uncharacteristically coy I am sure it is feigned. When Kimmer and I finally married, my father wasn't even on the bench any more. Sensing that I have not bought her explanation, she tiptoes past it. "And I'm sorry about that. I really am. I want to do better for you, Misha. I really do. I've been trying." Caressing my hand now, as though Jerry Nathanson, probably the most prominent lawyer in Elm Harbor, does not exist. "But, Misha, then he . . . he *dies*. And I know you're aching and I'm sorry for that. I truly am. But, Misha, he's all over the papers again. Your father. Everybody's talking about him again. And I'm thinking, Okay, maybe I can still hold it together. So I go over and see the Senator, like a good little girl, and he just sits there with this . . . this supercilious grin, and I'm like, Why did I bother to come here? Because, you know, the whole thing is like fixed. Fixed so Marc wins, I mean. And then Ruthie won't tell me squat. And Jack

Ziegler at the cemetery, and then this FBI thing. What did those guys want? I mean, it's like this thing with your father . . . it's going to ruin it for me after all."

There are tears on Kimmer's cheeks. It has been years since she has opened herself to me this way; what she has said to others I don't want to know. Her pain is genuine, and I warm to her. Although we were law school classmates, my wife is three years younger than I—she skipped a grade somewhere along the way; I wasted twenty-four months as a graduate student in philosophy and semiotics before turning to law— and there are moments when the three years feels like thirty.

"Kimmer, darling, I had no idea," I whisper. And this is true. There are depths to my wife I am too often afraid to plumb; and my fears have done as much as her conduct to sour the sweetest parts of our marriage. I squeeze her hands. She squeezes back. As her tears reflect the candle-light, her face grows even more exquisite. "But none of it has to be ruined. The Judge was my father, not yours. And the Judge is not you. There isn't any . . . I mean, you don't have any scandals. They certainly can't hold your father-in-law against you."

Kimmer is miserable. "They can so," she says, all at once childlike. "They can. They will." A sniff. "They *do*."

"They won't," I insist, even though I am afraid she is right. "And you know I'm in your corner."

"I know *you* are," she says bleakly, as though nobody else would be so foolish.

"And Uncle Mal—"

"Oh, Misha, get real. Uncle Mal won't be able to do anything unless this goes away. You see what I'm saying? It has to go away."

"What does?"

"This thing with your father. Whatever it is, Misha. I don't know. The FBI. Jack Ziegler, all of it. It has to go away, and it has to go away fast, or folks will be like, 'No, uh-uh, not her, she's married to you-know-whose son.' So we can't do anything to keep it alive, Misha. Not me, not you, not Uncle Mal, nobody. We have to let it die, or I don't have a chance." Her mysterious, tormented brown eyes burrow into mine. "Do you understand, Misha? It has to die."

"I understand." Her fervor, as always, overwhelms my caution. Kimmer has long had a talent for coaxing promises out of me before I know what I am saying.

"*You* have to let it die."

"I hear what you're saying."

"But do you promise?"

She seems to think I have some choice. I am not sure I really do. Because love is a gift we deliver when we would rather not.

"I promise, darling."

She slumps back in her chair as though worn out from all this pleading. "Thank you, honey. Thank you so much."

"You're welcome." I smile. "I love you."

"Oh, Misha," she whispers, shaking her head.

The waiter brings a bottle of wine that I scarcely remember Kimmer ordering. I do not drink, given my father's history, but the Madisons consider the prudent consumption of high-priced alcohol a part of the sophistication of the palate. She takes a few sips and smiles at me, then leans back in her chair again and looks out over the room. Then she suddenly hops up. I know this routine. She has spotted somebody she knows. Kimmer loves to work a room: that's why she was president of her graduating class at Mount Holyoke and of our local bar association and might soon be a federal judge. As I watch, she hurries across the restaurant to greet an Asian American couple dining over by the far wall. They shake hands, and they all share a good laugh, and then she is back. The man writes editorials for the *Post*, she explains. She met him this morning, when she went to see her friend from college. His wife, Kimmer continues, is a producer for one of the Sunday-morning television talk shows. "You never know." She shrugs. Then she retakes my hand and plays with my fingers in the candlelight until our main course arrives. I would usually be willing to let Kimmer play with my fingers all night, but my brain refuses to cooperate. As I cut into my overpriced steak, a thought occurs to me, prompted by my wife's table-hopping.

"Darling?"

"Hmmm?"

"Do you remember the last time we saw my father? I mean, both of us, together?"

She nods. "Last year. He was in town for the alumni association or something." She will not concede he might have wanted to see Bentley, or me, still less *her*. She shifts in her seat. "About this time."

"And you said he looked . . . worried."

"Yeah, I remember. We'd be sitting at dinner at the Faculty Club or something and you'd ask him a question and he wouldn't say anything, he'd be looking into the middle of nowhere, and you'd ask again and he'd say, 'You don't have to shout.'" Her gaze softens. "Oh, Misha, I'm sorry. That's not a very happy memory, is it?"

I choose not to go there. "I've seen him since then. Once." When I was in Washington on business and we had dinner. He was distracted then, too. "I just wondered . . . did it seem to you . . . when you said he seemed 'worried,' did you mean . . ."

"Just tense, Misha. Stressed." Taking my hand again. "That's all."

I shake my head, wondering why the image of the Judge's last visit to Elm Harbor leaped so nimbly to mind. Maybe Mariah's creepy insistence that the causes were not natural is starting to get to me.

The talk turns to other things: gossip about the law school, chitchat about the firm, jockeying our vacation schedules. She tells me what her sister, Lindy, is up to these days, and I recycle old stories about Addison. I tell Kimmer what fun Bentley had on his first day on in-line skates, but not about the woman who flirted with me, or about my temptation to flirt back. Kimmer, perhaps detecting something in my eyes before I glance guiltily away, teases me about the crush everyone once thought I had on Lindy, the more solid and reliable of the Madison sisters, whom my parents fervently hoped I would marry. We banter on, as we used to in the old days, the good days, our courting days, and then, as dessert arrives, Kimmer, who has been watching the time, tells me that an hour has passed. She is all business again. I sigh, but dutifully summon the waiter and ask him where the telephones are, and he produces one with a flourish, plugging it into a jack underneath the table. I wink at my wife.

"You could have used my cell phone," she says glumly.

"I know, darling, but I've always wanted to do this. Just like in the movies." Her return smile is tight; I realize just how overwrought she is. I pat her hand and push buttons on the phone. Grace picks up and, as promised, puts me right through.

"Talcott," booms the great Mallory Corcoran, "I am so glad you called. I was just about to send out an all-points bulletin. Look, we have a serious problem. In the first place, Jack Ziegler is not currently under investigation by the Justice Department. They wish they had something on him, because, well, you know, it's every prosecutor's dream to put a powerful white guy away"—he barks these words with no sense of irony—"but right now they just don't. So they are busy frying other fish."

"I see," I say, although I do not. Kimmer, reading my face, looks fearful.

"That's not the problem, though. The problem is this. Morton Pearlman talked to the Attorney General and the AG talked to the director of the Federal Bureau and he talked to his people. And here's what they tell me. I heard it from the AG himself. The FBI did not know that you talked to Jack Ziegler in the cemetery yesterday, Talcott. There was no surveillance. And nobody from the FBI came to see you today, Talcott. Why would they? Nobody from the FBI has asked you anything about Jack Ziegler at all. And the background check on Kimberly hasn't really started yet."

"You're joking."

"I wish I were. Now, you're sure they said they were from the Bureau?"

"I'm sure."

"Did you see their credentials?"

"Of course I saw their credentials." But, thinking back, I realize that I gave their wallets only a glance: who studies photos and numbers and the rest in any detail?

"I figured you did." He hesitates, as though uncertain how to share an unpleasant truth. "Listen, Talcott, here's the thing. Somebody came to see you pretending to be from the Bureau. Well, that happens to be a major felony. That means they have to investigate it. As a courtesy, they are putting it off until tomorrow. But tomorrow morning, a couple of FBI agents, the real kind, want to interview you. Here, at the office, at eleven. I can't be there, because Edie and I are going to Hawaii for a few days, but Meadows and maybe a couple of my other people will. No charge," he adds, a considerable relief but also something of an insult. He senses my distress. "Sorry to dump all this on you, Talcott. Really sorry. But after it's resolved, I will make the calls for Kimberly. I promise."

After it's resolved, I am thinking as I hang up the phone. Meaning he will not lift a finger on Kimmer's behalf until he sees which way the wind is blowing.

"What's wrong, honey?" my wife asks, clutching my hand as though it can keep her from drowning. "Misha, what is it?"

I look at my wife, my beautiful, brilliant, disloyal, desperately if unhappily ambitious wife. The mother of our child. The only woman I will ever love. I want to make it right. I can't.

"It's not going to die," I tell her.

CHAPTER 9

A PEDAGOGICAL
DISAGREEMENT

(1)

THE FOLLOWING TUESDAY, twelve days after the death of my father, I return to my dreary classroom, populated, it often seems, by undereducated but deeply committed Phi Beta Kappa ideologues—leftists who believe in class warfare but have never opened *Das Kapital* and certainly have never perused Werner Sombart, hard-line capitalists who accept the inerrancy of the invisible hand but have never studied Adam Smith, third-generation feminists who know that sex roles are a trap but have never read Betty Friedan, social Darwinists who propose leaving the poor to sink or swim but have never heard of Herbert Spencer or William Sumner's essay on *The Challenge of Facts*, black separatists who mutter bleakly about institutional racism but are unaware of the work of Carmichael and Hamilton, who invented the term—all of them our students, all of them hopelessly young and hopelessly smart and thus hopelessly sure they alone are right, and nearly all of whom, whatever their espoused differences, will soon be espoused to huge corporate law firms, massive profit factories where they will bill clients at ridiculous rates for two thousand hours of work every year, quickly earning twice as much money as the best of their teachers, and at half the age, sacrificing all on the altar of career, moving relentlessly upward, as ideology and family life collapse equally around them, and at last arriving, a decade or two later, cynical and bitter, at their cherished career goals, partnerships, professorships, judgeships, whatever kind of ships they dream of sailing, and then looking around at the angry, empty waters and realizing that they have arrived with nothing, absolutely nothing, and wondering what to do with the rest of their wretched lives.

Or maybe I am just measuring their prospects by my own.

My family and I returned to Elm Harbor last Thursday after my brief interview at Corcoran & Klein with *real* agents of the Federal Bureau of Investigation, Cassie Meadows surprisingly mature and competent at my side. Kimmer went straight back to work, instantly resuming her manic pace and crazy hours, and has already made another trip to San Francisco, for the greater wealth and glory of EHP. The real FBI has had no success in tracking down the two men who confronted me at Shepard Street, but my wife has persuaded herself that they were reporters, looking for dirt. She does not care whether she persuades me.

Mariah, meanwhile, has a new theory. It is no longer Jack Ziegler who killed the Judge; it is a litigant who blames my father for rejecting some appeal; and she is undaunted by the fact that the Judge left the bench well over a decade ago. "Probably a big corporation," she insisted last night on the phone, her third call in five days. "You have no idea how amoral they are. Or how long they can hold a grudge." I wondered what Howard would say to that, but prudently bit my tongue. Mariah added that a friend of hers had agreed to search the Internet for possible hired killers. But when I challenged Mariah gently, she scolded me all over again for never standing by her in the clutch.

"Sisters are just like that," said Rob Saltpeter, the spindly constitutional-futurist who is my occasional basketball partner, when I related part of the story while we sat in the locker room yesterday morning at the Y, the two of us having been slaughtered by a couple of off-duty cops. His eyes, as always, were serene. "But, the thing is, you have to remember that *she* would stand by *you* in the clutch."

"What makes you say that?"

Rob smiled. At six feet five he has four inches on me, but I probably outweigh him by fifty pounds. Although not, yet, quite fat, I am more than a little bit overweight; he is terribly thin. Neither one of us is an impressive sight in Jockey shorts in a locker room.

"Just a sense that I get."

"You've never even met her."

"I have two sisters," objected Rob, whose fundamental warmth is tempered by a zealous certainty that all families are, or should be, like his own.

"Not like Mariah."

"It doesn't matter what she's like. Your obligation to be there for her is exactly the same no matter what. It doesn't come from her behavior.

It doesn't come from what you think of her. It comes from the fact that you are her brother."

"I thought we abolished status-based relationships about a century ago," I teased, a typically silly lawyer's inside joke. In a status-based relationship, the parties' obligations are determined by who they are (husband-wife, parent-child, master-servant, and so on), rather than by agreement.

"Man abolished them. God didn't."

Nothing much to say to that, and I suppose I agree. Rob is, by his own description, an observant Jew, and he talks about his faith more than any other professor I know, including, to the squirmy chagrin of many students, in the classroom. Perhaps it is this oracular side of Rob Saltpeter that keeps us from becoming closer friends. Or perhaps it is simply that I am not a friendly fellow. To cover an unexpected surge of pain, I asked him for advice.

"Nothing to do but go on," he shrugged, which is his answer for just about everything.

Well, fine. I am going on. Badly.

And so it is that on this, my first day back in the classroom, I find myself persecuting an unfortunate young man whose sin is to inform us all that the cases I expect my students to master are irrelevant, because the rich guys always win. Now, it is true that some poor fool announces this conclusion every fall, and it is also true that more than a few professors have earned tenure at some very fine law schools by pressing refined, jargon-chunky versions of precisely this thin theory, but I am in no mood for blather. I glare at the cocky student and see, for a horrible moment, the future, or maybe just the enemy: young, white, confident, foolish, skinny, sullen, multiply pierced, bejeweled, dressed in grunge, cornsilk hair in a ponytail, utterly the cynical conformist, although he thinks he is an iconoclast. A few generations ago, he would have been the fellow wearing his letterman's sweater inside out, to prove to everybody how little it meant to him. When I was in college, he would have been first to the barricades, and he would have made sure everybody saw him there. As he is sure everybody is looking at him now. His elbow is on his chair, his other fist is tucked under his chin, and I read in his posture insolence, challenge, perhaps even the unsubtle racism of the supposedly liberal white student who cannot quite bring himself to believe that his black professor could know more than he. About anything. A light frosty red dances around his face like a halo, and I catch myself thinking, *I could break him.* I remind myself to be gentle.

"Very interesting, Mr. Knowland," I smile, taking a few steps down the aisle toward the row in which he sits. I fold my arms. "Now, how does your very interesting thesis relate to the case at hand?"

Still leaning back, he shrugs, barely meeting my gaze. He tells me that my question is beside the point. It is not the legal rules that matter, he explains to the ceiling, but the fact that workers cannot expect justice from the capitalist courts. It is the structure of the society, not the content of the rules, that leads to oppression. He may even be half right, but none of it is remotely relevant, and his terminology seems as outdated as a powdered wig. I pull an old pedagogical trick, inching closer to crowd his field of vision, forcing him to remember which of us is in a position of authority. I ask him whether he recalls that the case at hand involves not an employee suing an employer but one motorist suing another. Mr. Knowland, twisted around in his chair, answers calmly that such details are distractions, a waste of our time. He remains unwilling to look at me. His posture screams disrespect, and everybody knows it. The classroom falls silent; even the usual sounds of pages turning and fingers clacking on laptop keyboards and chairs scraping disappear. The red deepens. I recall that I had to upbraid him three weeks ago for fooling around with his Palm Pilot during class. I was circumspect then, taking care to call him over after the hour ended. Still, he was angry, for he is of the generation that assumes that there are no rules but those each individual wills. Now, through the crimson haze, my student begins to resemble Agent McDermott as he sat, lying through his teeth, in the living room at Shepard Street . . . and, very suddenly, it is too late to stop. Smiling as insolently as Mr. Knowland, I ask him whether he has undertaken a study of the tort cases, sorting them by the relative wealth of the parties, to learn the truth or falsity of his theory. Glaring, he admits that he has not. I ask him whether he is aware of any such study performed by anybody else. He shrugs. "I will take that as a no," I say, boring into him now. Standing right in front of his table, I tell him that there is, in fact, a substantial literature on the effect of wealth on the outcome of cases. I ask him if he has read any of it. The antiquated fluorescent lights buzz and hiss uncertainly as we wait for Mr. Knowland's reply. He looks around the classroom at the pitying faces of his classmates, he looks up at the portraits of prominent white male graduates that line the walls, and at last he looks back at me.

"No," he says, his voice much smaller.

I nod as though to say I knew it all along. Then I cross the line. As every mildly competent law professor knows, this is the point at which I should segue smoothly back into the discussion of the case, perhaps teasing Mr. Knowland a little by asking another student to act as his co-counsel, in order to help him out of the jam into which he has so foolishly talked himself. Instead, I give him my back and move two paces away from his seat, then whirl and point and ask him whether he often offers opinions that have no basis in fact. His eyes widen, in frustration and childlike hurt. He says nothing, opens his mouth, then shuts it again, because he is trapped: no answer that he can give will help him. He looks away again as his classmates try to decide whether they should laugh. (Some do, some do not.) My head pounds redly and I ask: "Is that what they taught you at—Princeton, wasn't it?" This time, the students are too shocked to laugh. They do not really like the arrogant Mr. Avery Knowland, but now they like the arrogant Professor Talcott Garland even less. In the abrupt, nervous silence of the high-ceilinged classroom, it strikes me, far too late, that I, a tenured professor at one of the best law schools in the land, am in the process of humiliating a twenty-two-year-old who was, all of five years ago, in high school—the campus equivalent of a sixth-grade bully beating up a kindergartner. It does not matter if Avery Knowland is arrogant or ignorant or even if he is racist. My job is to teach him, not to embarrass him. I am not doing my job.

My rampant demons have chased me even into my classroom.

I soften once more. And try to clean up the mess. Of course, I continue, tweedily pacing the front of the room, lawyers are occasionally called upon to argue what they cannot prove. But—and here I spin and stiletto my finger again toward Mr. Knowland—*but*, when they offer these unsupported and unsupportable arguments, they must do so with verve. And they must have the confidence, when asked about the factual basis of their claims, to do the courtroom polka, which I demonstrate as I repeat the simple instructions: sidestep, sidestep, sidestep, stay on your toes, and never, ever face the music.

Relieved, jittery laughter from the students.

Except a glaring Avery Knowland.

I am able to finish the class, even to summon a bit of dignity, but I flee to my office the instant noon arrives, furious at myself for allowing my demons to drive me to embarrass a student in class. The incident will reinforce my reputation around the law school—*not a nice person*, the students tell each other, and Dana Worth, the faculty's foremost connoisseur of student gossip, cheerfully repeats it to me—and maybe the reputation is the reality.

(11)

My OFFICE is on the second floor of the main law school building, called Oldie by most of the faculty and all of the students, not because it is old, although it is, but because it was built with an endowment from and is named for the Oldham family. Merritt Oldham, who grew up with money—his grandfather invented some sort of firing pin during the Civil War and, according to legend, died when the faulty prototype of an improved version caused a gun to explode in his face—was graduated from the law school around the dawn of the twentieth century and went on to Wall Street glory as a founder of the law firm of Grace, Grand, Oldham & Fair. When I was a law student, Grace, Grand sat at the top of the New York heap, but it came down hard in the Drexel Burnham scandal in the eighties. Two of its hottest partners went to the penitentiary, three more were forced to resign, and the rest fell to squabbling over the corpse. The firm finally split in two. One half went under within a few years; the other, retaining the Oldham name, is still afloat, but barely, and our students, who memorize the relative rankings in prestige of every Manhattan law firm long before they master even the rudiments of tort law, would sooner go hungry than work there.

The firm may have collapsed, but our building is still Oldie—formally, the Veronica Oldham Law Center. Merritt adored his sainted mother, never married, never had children, and is claimed by our gay students as one of their own, probably with reason, if a fraction of the stories Theo Mountain tells are true. The Law Center sits on a grassy hill at the end of Town Street, looking down over the city. It comprises two square blocks, north and south of Eastern Avenue, joined by a pedestrian bridge. The southern block, with a view toward the main campus, is Oldie, a vaguely Gothic structure with three floors of offices on its east side and six floors of library on the west, joined by a row of classrooms to the south and a high stone wall to the north, all surrounding the lovely flagstone courtyard that is probably the school's greatest aesthetic attraction. The northern block of the Center, added twenty years ago on the site of an old Roman Catholic church that was devastated by fire and purchased by a clever dean, includes a large, rather spartan dormitory housing nearly half our students, and a low, ugly brick building (formerly the parish school) crammed with offices for all our student organizations except the most prestigious, the law review. This arrangement causes a bit of jealousy, but we have no choice: our alumni, like alumni everywhere, regard change as the enemy of memory, and would never allow us to evict the law review from its traditional warren of rooms on the first floor of the faculty wing.

To reach my office, one climbs the central marble staircase and, at the second floor, turns left, trudges to the end of the dreary corridor with its peeling linoleum floor, turns left again, and counts four doors down on the left. Immediately before my office is a large room housing four faculty secretaries, not including my own, who sits, thanks to some fascinating bit of administrative reasoning, on the third floor in another corner of the building. Beyond my office is the den of Amy Hefferman, the ageless Princess of Procedure, much beloved of the students, who talks every year or so of retirement, then relents when the graduating class votes her commencement speaker; directly across the hall is young Ethan Brinkley, who has the habit, without warning, of dropping by to share implausible stories of his three years as deputy counsel to the Senate Select Committee on Intelligence; next to him, in a room little larger than Kimmer's walk-in closet, sits the even younger Matthew Goffe, who teaches a course on corporations, a course on secured trans-actions, and a course on radical alternatives to the rule of law. Matt is one of our few untenured faculty members and, unless he discontinues his disconcerting habit of signing every student petition and joining every student boycott, is likely to remain in that category. Next along, in the northwest corner of the building, is the vast chamber occupied by Stuart Land, the former dean and, probably, the most widely respected intellect on the faculty, who teaches a little bit of everything, commands the services of two secretaries, and makes the reputation of the law school his special concern. Stuart, say the corridor gossips, has never quite recovered from the palace coup that led to his ouster and Dean Lynda's elevation, a revolution more about politics than about policies—for Stuart's unapologetic conservatism left him constantly at war with Theo Mountain and Marc Hadley and Tish Kirschbaum and many other powers on the faculty.

Or so it is rumored.

But that is the way of the place: down our many twisting corridors, one encounters story after story, some heroic, some villainous, some true, some false, some funny, some tragic, and all of them combining to form the mystical, undefinable entity we call *the school*. Not exactly the building, not exactly the faculty or the students or the alumni—more than all those things but also less, a paradox, an order, a mystery, a monster, an utter joy.

The hallways of Oldie are warm and familiar. I *like* it here.

Most of the time.

Today, however, when I turn the final corner toward my office after my unfortunate class, I encounter an agitated Dana Worth, rapping imperiously on my office door, as though irritated that I am not present to open it. She rattles the knob, pushes, then pulls. Cupping a hand above her eyes, she peers through the frosted glass, even though the darkness within is plainly visible.

I look on in amusement, then concern, for I have not seen Dana this upset since the day she told me she was leaving my friend Eddie . . . and then told me why.

Dana, who teaches contracts and intellectual property, is one of our stars, even though her diminutive stature invariably tempts a few unfortunate first-year students to think they can walk all over her. Dana comes from an old Virginia family that once had lots of money (read slaves) but lost it in what she laughingly calls "the late unpleasantness." She lives delightfully, even charmingly, in a world centered on herself. ("Your sister died in a car wreck? You know, back at the University of Virginia, I used to *date* a man who died in a car wreck. He was a McMichael, of the Rappahannock County McMichaels." Reminded that my father actually *knew* the senior McMichael, the Senator, knew him quite well once upon a time, Dana would be undeterred: "But not the way I knew his son, I'm willing to bet.")

Dana, three years older than I am, has survived, even transcended, the minor scandal of the way her marriage broke up. Eddie, whose life around the university was lived largely in his wife's shadow, left us last year to return to his native Texas, where, he insists, the kind of thing that happened to him in Elm Harbor would not be allowed. (He does not say who would stop it.) His departure reduced the law school's black faculty by twenty-five percent. Dana left him for a woman named Alison Frye, a nervous, fleshy New Yorker, all carroty hair and burning anger at the world. Alison is a novelist of slight accomplishment and runs a Web site full of airy but erudite social commentary, most with a "new economy" spin. Her courtship of Dana was a more or less public event, at least among the techie crowd. Three years ago, back when their affair was still secret, Alison posted on her site a composition entitled "Dear Dana Worth," a love letter of sorts, which was downloaded and e-mailed all over the world, and, more important, all over the campus—Dana likes to say that Alison mortified her into falling in love. Many of us have adopted the essay's title as a teasing nickname, although her husband understandably missed the humor. When Dana and Eddie were married, Kimmer and I hung around with them a lot, for Eddie and I played together as children. Eddie's parents are old family friends, and he may even be a distant cousin on my mother's side, although we never quite worked it out.

The end of the Dozier-Worth marriage two years ago soured my friendships with both partners. Eddie has become a stranger, his politics driven even further to the right. As for Dana, I truly like her, but she and I have serious differences on countless matters, the way she treated Eddie chief among them. *Misha, please, you have to try to look at it from my point of view,* she begged me in that last, hurtful argument before she left him. *No, I don't,* I stormed back at her, unable to be charitable. Perhaps I feared I might be seeing in the disintegration of her marriage a prefiguring of the end of my own. Nowadays, Dana and I try to be friends, but, to quote Casey Stengel, sometimes it doesn't always work.

Watching Dear Dana, I remember her tears at my father's funeral. She admired the Judge, her onetime boss, perhaps loved him a little, even though he never quite made his peace with the gay rights movement. But, then, neither has Dana, who likes to insist, in her pedantic way, that she is far more interested in her freedom than in her rights. Dana opposes rules to tell property owners whom to rent to or businesses whom to hire, for she is a radical libertarian right down to her pedicured toes. Except on the question of abortion. After the Judge's funeral, Dana joined the procession to the cemetery in her snazzy gold Lexus with its dual-meaning bumper sticker—ANOTHER LESBIAN FOR LIFE, it proclaims—which tends to confound people.

Dana likes to confound people.

"Dana," I say softly as she continues banging on the door. "Dana!"

She turns in my direction, one tiny hand to her throat in the familiar gesture of generations of wounded Southern ladies. Her short black hair glistens in the dim light of the hallway. But her face startles me. Dear Dana Worth is always pale, but today her whiteness is unusually . . . well, unusually white.

"Oh, Misha," she moans, shaking her head. "Oh, Misha, I'm so sorry."

"I'm betting this is more bad news," I say slowly, my speech inhibited by the block of ice that has formed around my heart.

"You don't know." Dana is surprised. Panicky. For a moment, she seems to be at a loss, which hardly ever happens. Sufficiently gutsy is Dear Dana that she spends most Sunday mornings at a small, conservative Methodist church twenty road miles and a thousand cultural ones away from the campus. *I need to be there*, she tells the few colleagues who dare question her.

"What don't I know?" I ask, a little panicky myself.

"Oh, Misha," Dana whispers again. Then she gathers herself. She grips my arm as I unlock the door, and we enter my office together. She points to the small, sleek CD player on the shelf above my computer. Kimmer bought it for me on one of her trips. My wife hates to spend money, so, whenever she buys me an expensive gift, I think of it as a second-place trophy, Kimmer's own version of guilt money. "Does that thing have a radio?" Dana asks.

"Well, yes. I don't use it much."

"Turn it on."

"What?"

"Turn on the news."

"Why can't you just tell me . . ."

Dana's gray eyes are troubled and sad. One of her great weaknesses has always been an inability to deal with the emotional pain of others. Which means that whatever she wants me to know is going to hurt. "Please. Just turn it on."

I swallow a retort about how much I hate these games because I can see that she is genuinely upset. I walk over to the CD player, always tuned to our local National Public Radio affiliate, which, when I switch it on, is playing insipid classical music—the *Fanfare for the Common Man*, I believe. I change to the all-news station, which comes in as clearly in Elm Harbor as it does in New York City. The anchor is waxing mournfully self-righteous about the latest act of racist violence, a black preacher who was tortured to death. My insides churn: stories of this kind are like a blow to my most sensitive parts. I always want to buy a couple of guns, grab my family, and run for the hills. And this time a preacher! I listen to sound clips, voices of national outrage: Jesse Jackson, Kweisi Mfume, the President of the United States. Two children discovered the body in the tall grass behind the swings in a playground earlier today.

I turn to Dana. "Is this what you wanted me to hear?"

She nods and perches on the edge of my desk, her voice faint. "Keep listening."

I frown. I do not get it. But I listen a bit longer. The man was found with cigarette burns on his arms and legs and several fingernails missing. He was tortured, the announcer explains. Death itself apparently came from a single gunshot to the head, and was probably a blessing. I close my eyes. A horrible story, true, but why does Dana think—

Wait.

The victim's body was found in a small town near Washington, D.C.

I turn the volume up.

A frightening lassitude begins in my toes and climbs slowly upward, until I am dizzy and swaying on my feet. The air grows heavy and oppressive, my stomach heaves, and my furniture begins to turn a ghastly, asphyxiating red.

Beware of the others. . . . I would not want to see you harmed.

The name of the murdered preacher is Freeman Bishop.

CHAPTER 10

A TRAGIC COINCIDENCE

(1)

"IT DOESN'T HAVE anything to do with your father," says Sergeant B. T. Ames, tapping a thick manila folder against the metal table.

"I don't see how you can be so sure," replies Mariah, sitting next to me on one of the hard wooden chairs in the small chamber off the police squad room. A single small window at about shoulder height lets in so little light that the day looks gruesome; it is hard for me to remember the bright autumn beauty I left behind just twenty minutes ago when we walked into the building. It is Thursday morning, one week and two days since the Judge's funeral, and both of us are scared . . . although both our spouses think their spouses are being silly. I think maybe our spouses are right, but Mariah begged me to accompany her. We met at LaGuardia Airport a few hours ago and flew down together on the shuttle. Mariah, who can better afford the expense, rented a car, and we drove out to the Maryland suburbs for this meeting.

"It's my job to be sure," the detective deadpans.

"Somebody killed one of them," Mariah says to the sergeant's raised eyebrow, "and then somebody killed the other."

Sergeant Ames smiles, but I can see the exhaustion. Obtaining this interview with a busy Montgomery County detective required Mallory Corcoran to make several calls from Hawaii, urged on by Meadows, who was badgered by me. The sergeant, leaning against the austere metal desk, has made clear that plenty of actual police work awaits; we can have only a few minutes.

We will take whatever time she can give.

"I've looked at all the reports on your father," says Sergeant Ames, waving a sheaf of faxes. "He died of a heart attack." She raises a large hand to forestall any protest. "I know you doubt it, and you are entitled to your doubts. I happen to think the reports are correct, but it isn't in my jurisdiction. The Reverend Freeman Bishop *is* in my jurisdiction. And he *was* murdered. Maybe he was murdered here, maybe he was murdered someplace else and then dumped here. Either way, Freeman Bishop is my case. Oliver Garland is not my case. And what I am telling you is that the cases do not have anything to do with each other."

I glance at my sister, but she is looking at the floor. Her designer pantsuit is black, as are her shoes and her scarf, and the choice strikes me as a little melodramatic. Well, that is Mariah's way. At least she appears relaxed. I am stiff and uncomfortable in the least seedy of my three tweed blazers, this one vaguely brown.

In any event, it now seems to be my turn. I throw what I hope is a congenial smile onto my face.

"I understand your point, Sergeant, but you have to understand ours. Father Bishop was an old friend of the family. He performed our father's funeral just a week ago. You can see how we'd be a little bit . . . shaken up."

Sergeant Ames puffs out a great gust of air. Then she stands up and walks around the wooden interrogation table to peer out the tiny window, where she blocks what little sunlight the window admits. She is a member of the paler nation, a broad yet graceful woman with a square, angry jaw and curly brown hair. Her size seems mostly muscle, not fat. Her dark blazer and cream-colored slacks are rumpled in the way that police fashions always are. A badge dangles from her breast pocket. Her florid face is chipped, from years of bad weather or years of bad diet or possibly both. She could be thirty. She could be fifty.

"We're all shaken up, Mr. Garland. Mrs. Denton. This was a brutal crime." She is still lecturing us from the window, giving us her back. "Kill a man this way, dump him in a public park." She shakes her head, but the facts don't change. "I don't like to have this kind of thing in my town. I grew up here. I have my family here. I like it here. One reason I like it here is that we don't have these problems." *Racial problems*, she means. Or maybe she just means black people: the town, after all, is nearly all white.

"I understand that—" I begin, but Sergeant B. T. Ames (we do not know her first name, only the initials) holds up her hand. First I think she has something to say, but then I realize that she has heard knocking that I missed, because she walks over to the door and opens it. A uniformed officer, also white, gleams at us suspiciously, then whispers to the sergeant and hands her another fax for her collection.

When the door is closed again, Sergeant Ames returns to her window. "They found his car," she says.

"Where?" Mariah asks before I have the chance.

"Southwest Washington. Not far from the Navy Yard."

"What was he doing down there?" Mariah persists. We are both frustrated. All the sergeant has really told us so far is what the newspapers reported: Father Bishop had a vestry meeting scheduled for seven on the night he died. He called to say he would be a little late because he had to visit a member of the parish who was having problems. He left home in his car about six-thirty, and his neighbors swear he was alone. He never made it to the church.

The detective swings toward us, but leans against the wall, crossing her arms. "I'm afraid I have to get back to work," she says. "Unless you have some information that you think will help us find Father Bishop's killer."

I spent my childhood being summarily dismissed, usually by the Judge, and have never been able to bear it as an adult. So I protest—as so often, without first thinking. "We told you we think there's a connection. . . ."

Sergeant Ames takes a step toward me, her heavy face unwelcoming. She seems to be growing larger, or perhaps I am shrinking. I am suddenly reminded that she is, after all, a police officer. She is not interested in our theories or our meddling.

"Mr. Garland, do you have any evidence of a connection between the murder of Freeman Bishop and the death of your father?"

"Well, that depends on what you mean by evidence—"

"Did anybody tell you that this crime was connected to the death of your father?"

"No, but I—"

"Do you know of your own knowledge who killed Freeman Bishop?"

"Of course not!" I am offended but also a little bit scared, the ambiguous relationship of black males to the nation's police departments being what it is. I remember that this tiny room is used for the interrogation of suspects. The furniture begins to emit a soft red glow. Mariah puts her hand on my arm, warning me to calm down. And I get the point: we are here, after all, and the sergeant has a job to do.

"Did anybody tell you who killed Freeman Bishop?" Sergeant Ames continues.

"No." I remember, far too late, what we used to tell clients facing depositions: Keep it simple, say yes or no, and never, ever volunteer anything, no matter how badly you want to explain.

And stay calm.

"Did anybody tell you that he or she knows who killed Freeman Bishop?"

"No."

"Did anybody tell you that anybody else knows who killed Freeman Bishop?"

"No."

"Then maybe you don't have any information for me."

"Well, I . . ."

"Wait." Spoken softly. The detective has taken command with remarkable ease. My intimidated students wouldn't recognize me, but Avery Knowland, I am sure, would have a grand time watching.

Mariah and I wait as instructed. Sergeant Ames, to my dismay, actually opens her manila folder. She pulls out a sheet of yellow lined paper and reads some handwritten notes, her tongue poking around her mouth as she concentrates. She grabs a ballpoint pen from the table and makes a couple of check marks in the margin. For the first time, I realize that the detective is not just questioning me for show. Mariah recognizes it too; her hand tightens on my arm. Sergeant Ames knows something, or thinks she knows something, that is leading her to ask these questions.

And she is asking only me, not my sister.

When the sergeant speaks again, she is looking at her notes, not at me. "Are you aware of any threats received by Freeman Bishop?"

"No."

"Are you aware of anybody with a strong dislike for Freeman Bishop?"

"No." Again I cannot help elaborating: "He was not the sort of man who generated, uh, strong emotions."

"No enemies of whom you are aware?"

"No."

"Have you had any recent conversations with Freeman Bishop?"

"Not since the funeral, no."

"Prior to the murder, but after the funeral, have you had any conversations with any person *about* Freeman Bishop?"

I hesitate. What is she driving at? What does she think happened? But hesitation in an interrogation is like a red flag to a bull. Sergeant Ames lifts her intense gaze from the manila folder and settles her eyes on me. She does not repeat the question. She waits, terrifying in her patience. As though expecting me to confess. To a conversation? To something more? Does she think that I . . . surely she doesn't think . . .

You're being ridiculous.

"Not that I can recall," I say at last.

She gazes at me a moment longer, letting me know that she recognizes the hedge, then looks down at her notes again.

"Have you recently noticed any peculiar behavior by Freeman Bishop?"

"I didn't know him that well."

She glances up. "I thought you saw him last week, at your father's funeral."

"Well, yes . . ."

"And did you notice any peculiar behavior?"

"No. No, I didn't."

"He seemed the same as always?"

"I guess so." I am puzzled by her questions now, not scared.

"Did anybody else recently tell you about any peculiar behavior by Freeman Bishop?"

"No."

"Did anybody tell you anything that could have a bearing on this murder?"

"I . . ."

"Don't hurry. Think hard. Go back a couple of weeks if you have to. Months."

"The answer is still no, Sergeant. No."

"You said you think there is a connection between your father's death and the murder of Freeman Bishop."

"I . . . we wondered, yes."

"Did your father ever talk about Freeman Bishop?"

This one puzzles me again. "I guess. Sure, lots of times."

"Recently?" All at once her voice grows gentle. "Go back, say, six months from your father's death?"

"No. Not that I remember."

"A year. Go back a year."

"Maybe. I don't recall."

"Was it your father's wish that Freeman Bishop perform his funeral?"

Mariah and I exchange a glance. Something is up. "I don't think he ever talked about his funeral," I say, once it becomes clear that Mariah is not going to speak. "Not to me."

Sergeant Ames turns her attention to the folder once more. I wonder what she could be reading in it. I wonder what she did when she learned that we were coming to see her, where she went for information, what information she found. I wonder where these questions are coming from. I am sorely tempted to violate the rules every lawyer lives by . . . and just ask.

Instead, I ask something else.

"Do you have any leads?"

"Mr. Garland, you have to understand the way this kind of thing works. The police usually are the ones who ask the questions."

Pushing my buttons: nothing galls me as much as being patronized.

"Look, Sergeant, I'm sorry. But, you know, this is the man who just did my father's funeral. Nine years ago he performed my wedding. Now, maybe you can see why I would be a little bit upset."

"I do understand why you are upset," Sergeant Ames says sternly, hardly bothering to glance up from her notes. "But I also have a murder to investigate, and as long as you have used your connections to barge in here on a very busy day, I expect you to try to help if you can. *Because* he did your father's funeral. *Because* he did your wedding."

Mariah tries to fix everything: "How can we be of assistance, Sergeant Ames?"

"Did you hear the questions I asked your brother?"

"Yes, ma'am."

Something registers in the sergeant's face: why didn't I think to say *ma'am*? Because she is white and I am black? Is rudeness the legacy of oppression? Downward, downward, civilization spirals, and all we Americans seem able to do about it is quarrel over the blame.

"Do you have any different answers to offer?"

"No, ma'am."

"You're sure?"

"Yes, ma'am." My sister has never sounded so contrite in her life. The tactic seems to have some effect.

"I want you to look at these," the detective says, her voice softer. She slides two glossy black-and-white photographs from her folder. "These are, mmm, the least horrible."

Mariah glances down and then looks away; but I do not want to lose face before the formidable B. T. Ames, so I force myself to stare, and force my protesting mind to process what it is seeing.

To look at the photographs is to realize immediately that whoever tortured Father Bishop did it, at least in part, for the fun of it. One picture is a close-up of a hand. If not for all the blood, you might not notice on first glance that three fingernails are missing. The second shot appears to show the meaty part of Freeman Bishop's thigh. Bright, almost bubbly circles are burned into his skin. Puckers of pain, like craters on the moon. I count them—five, no, six—and this is just one small area of his body. I try to imagine what kind of person could do this to another. And keep on doing it, because this took a while. And *where* somebody could do it, to ensure that nobody would hear his screams. I doubt that a gag over his mouth would have been enough.

"It's different when you see it, isn't it?" the detective asks.

"Do you—did you—" I am stuttering. This can't be what Jack Ziegler was talking about. It just can't. I start over. "Do you have any idea why somebody would do something like this?"

Sergeant Ames answers my question with one of her own. "Do you?" Her eyes are on me once more, watching as I examine the photographs. I sense an uneasy stirring in Mariah next to me, and I am not sure why.

"Do I what?"

"Do you have any idea why somebody might have done this?"

"Of course not!"

My protests do not interest Sergeant Ames. "Do you have any reason to think that Father Bishop had any information that somebody else would want?"

"I don't know what you mean. . . ."

"Well, he was tortured." The detective gestures at the photographs in what seems to be exasperation. "Usually, that means somebody wants information."

"Unless the torturing was just for show," Mariah interjects quietly.

Sergeant Ames turns toward my sister, her eyes alight with cautious re-evaluation—not of the case, but of Mariah.

"Or the work of a psychopath," I put in unwisely, not wanting to be left out if the detective is now ready to toss respect around.

"Right," says Sergeant Ames, her words made all the more scathing by the monotone in which they are delivered. "If it turns out that somebody cut out his liver and ate it with fava beans, I'll give you a call."

I bristle at this put-down, but, before I can think of a suitable riposte, the detective is making a little speech. "You're wondering why I am asking these questions. Let me try to explain what is going on here. You've read what was in the papers, I assume. So you know that Father

Bishop, may he rest in peace, died of a gunshot wound to the head. Well, that gunshot wound was to the base of the skull, angled slightly upward. No amateur would put a shot there. The amateur takes his cue from the movies and shoots people in the side of the head or maybe the throat. But if you want to be sure, you do the base of the skull. You also know that Father Bishop had cigarette burns on both of his arms and one of his legs and the side of his neck. You know he was missing three fingernails. You know that he was found with his hands tied behind his back. Other things were also done. You don't need all the details. But this man was tortured. Tortured viciously. The way that drug dealers, for instance, do it when they want something."

Hearing it put so starkly, and by a police officer, I almost cringe, for all I can think about is my family. The detective, however, has chosen her words with care. Mariah picks up on the little hint before I do, but Phi Beta Kappans tend to figure things out fast. Her head bobs up again.

"I thought it was a hate crime."

"Well, I can see why you would think that. The newspapers say it was a hate crime and the television says it was a hate crime and the NAACP says it was a hate crime and the governor of this fine state says it was a hate crime and I understand that the President of these wonderful United States even suggested it might be a hate crime. And so do the two busloads of protesters who are arriving this weekend to remind us all about how terribly the people of my town treat black people— never mind that there is absolutely no reason to think that the crime actually occurred here. But you know something? Hate crimes, even murders, tend to be committed by amateurs. This wasn't." She is watching our faces again. "Now, you have not heard *me* say it was a hate crime and you have not heard anybody from the police say it was a hate crime, have you?"

Mariah, the onetime journalist, keeps at it: "So was it a hate crime or wasn't it?"

Sergeant Ames fixes my sister with a baleful glare, as though she has recognized too late the species she has admitted to the inner sanctum. The detective's eyes are a flat, obsidian black, daring anybody to tell a lie in her presence. She plainly does not like being interrogated. But when she speaks, her voice is almost mechanical.

"Mrs. Denton, we do not know for sure what kind of crime it was except that it was a nasty one, and the person who did it is running around free. We will find who did it and then we will know what kind of crime it was."

"Wasn't there a note?" I ask.

"Evidently, we read the same newspapers, Mr. Garland. I read in one of them that there was a note pinned to Father Bishop's shirt, and somebody else had an exclusive report that the note was from a white supremacist group that wants to take the blame."

"In the papers," murmurs Mariah, the ghost of a smile on her lips. She did not read the detective's comment quite so contemptuously as I did.

"I am not confirming that," the sergeant agrees, smiling back. Now that each knows the other's agenda, they are comfortable together: more evidence, if any is needed, that the world would be better run by women.

"You are not confirming it," Mariah explains, probably for my benefit, "because, if there was a note and you don't tell anybody what it says, you can use it to sort the kooks who always call after a crime like this from people who might actually be able to help solve it."

"That's one of the reasons, yes."

I look from one of them to the other. There is something more here, some level of comprehension the two of them have already passed while I am still struggling to manage the first rung. It is rather like watching a chess game between two grandmasters, all the subtle maneuvers that make so little sense to the unschooled mind until, in a sudden flurry, one of them is defeated.

"The other reason," Mariah suggests in the same quiet tone, "is that the letter could be a fake."

"I didn't say that," the detective interposes immediately, her smile disappearing as though she has belatedly recalled that smiles are banned in this sad little room. I can feel the tension rising once more—and then, suddenly, I see where they are heading.

"Sergeant Ames," my sister says formally, "we are here because we have families, and we are worried about them." She rubs her ample belly to underline the point: she means we are worried about our *children*. "If you can persuade us that there is no relation between what happened to Father Bishop and what happened—what *might* have happened—to our father, we will go away and never bother you again. I promise you. We won't blab to the papers. I used to be a journalist, and I was always very good at keeping my mouth shut. I never revealed a source. My brother, as you know, is a lawyer, so he knows how to keep a confidence. I know you feel we used connections to barge in here. I'm sorry about that. But we did it for the sake of our families. And nothing you tell us will go any further than the two of us. I promise you that, too. And if we can ever do anything for you . . ."

She leaves the rest hanging in the air. Oh, but my sister is good! What a reporter she must have been! Without saying a word that can be held against her, Mariah has managed to threaten, indirectly, to make a nuisance of herself if she does not get what she wants. More important, she has also raised the specter of our supposed family influence—all of it, of course, actually the largesse of Mallory Corcoran.

Sergeant Ames gets the message. And is far too experienced to let herself get angry. Instead, she takes a nibble at the bait.

"Father Bishop's family," she says, "has not been very cooperative. They seem to think—well, the racial angle is giving them problems."

"I'll talk to them," Mariah says at once, as though she runs the Gold Coast, which our mother once hoped she would. "I was in Jack and Jill with Warner Bishop."

The detective nods as though she knows all about the various social organizations for the children of middle-class African America. "Warner Bishop seems to think we're all rednecks out here," she says.

"I'll talk to him," Mariah promises.

Sergeant Ames looks back at me briefly, but she addresses herself to my sister. "I won't show you the note," she says. "I can't do that. I'm sorry. But I can tell you, in the privacy of this room, that there is absolutely no reason for you to worry about the safety of your families. There really is no connection between this crime and your father. But you're right about the other part. There was a note, and we do think it was a fake. That is, we do *not* think this was a white supremacist thing."

She pauses, wanting us to take the next step. I am about to offer another question, but Mariah raises a hand and slips hers in ahead of mine.

"It was drugs, Sergeant, wasn't it?"

Sergeant Ames looks at her, then looks at me, then looks back at my sister. There is real respect there.

"Yes," the detective finally says. "Yes, we think it was drugs. Now, this also stays in this office. You cannot even tell Father Bishop's family, not just yet." A pause to let this sink in; police detectives can make threats too. "But we are quite confident that you and your father and your families are not involved. We have to wait a day or so for toxicology to be sure, but I already know from other evidence what they'll tell us: that Father Bishop was a fairly heavy user."

The detective stops. My jaw does not exactly drop, but I am pretty sure that time stands still and my heart skips a few beats, and lots of other clichés happen at the same time. So it was not simple incompetence that caused Freeman Bishop's sermons to meander into meaninglessness. I am astonished, and embarrassed, by the depth of my relief.

But Mariah sticks to the problem.

"How does that explain what happened to him?"

Sergeant Ames sighs. She hoped to get away with less, it seems, but now will have to tell us the rest. I am still wondering, however, what her purpose was in interrogating me. Was it just intimidation?

"We don't publicize this," she says, "because we are afraid of copycats. But, in the Washington area, I'm including the suburbs, we see a dozen or so of these cases a year. Most of them you never read about or see on television, because the victims are less prominent. The kind of torture Father Bishop suffered—well, it's horrible, but it's more common than you might think. In particular, it is used a lot by dealers to make their customers who are behind in their payments tell them where they have money stashed. They torture the information out of them and then shoot them in the back of the head. Or sometimes they get gratuitous about it, torturing for kicks. And we are pretty sure that is what happened here. Even a very tough man would have had a lot of trouble holding out against a fraction of what they did to him, and from what people tell me, Freeman Bishop, may he rest in peace, was not particularly tough. If they wanted information from him, I think they probably got it pretty fast. The rest of what they did to him was for kicks." A pause to let this sink in. The temperature in the room drops several degrees. "Still, the basic fact remains the same: Freeman Bishop, we are pretty sure, was killed because he used drugs and couldn't pay for them."

"Pretty sure?" I ask, just for something to say.

The sergeant glares at me. She would rather I shut up, her eyes say, so that she can pretend that I am not in the room. Mariah is the one she trusts. As far as Sergeant B. T. Ames is concerned, I am furniture.

I see my mistake an eyeblink later, but my sister sees it faster. She is already up on her feet, pulling me to mine, thanking the detective for her time, shaking hands as though closing a sale. Sergeant Ames steps around us and opens the door so that the rest of the squad can hear her dismiss us.

"Look, Mr. Garland. Mrs. Denton. I'm really sorry about your father. I am. But I have a murder on my hands and a lot of work to do. So, if you will excuse me, I have to get back to the job."

(11)

WE DRIVE TOGETHER to Shepard Street, where Mariah plans to spend the night; I am flying home on the shuttle a bit later this evening, but will return next week for the funeral of the man who, last week, officiated at the Judge's. The house is eerily silent after the hubbub of a week ago; it *sounds* like the house of a dead man. Our footsteps echo like gunfire on the parquet of the front hall. Mariah grimaces, explaining that she sent all the Judge's Oriental carpet runners out for cleaning right after the funeral. She raises her palm in half-apology, then turns on the CD player, but her kind of music this time, not my father's: *Reasons*, the long version, by Earth, Wind and Fire, which remains, in my sister's casual judgment, the single greatest pop recording ever made. The Judge would have been appalled. I remind myself that this is my sister's house now, that I am a guest, that she can do what she wants.

After Mariah visits the powder room, we find ourselves once again in the absurdly bright kitchen, sitting together at the table, sipping hot chocolate in companionable silence, almost—but not quite—friends again. I loosen my tie. Mariah kicks off her shoes.

"I wish you wouldn't stay here alone," I tell her.

"Why, Tal," laughs my sister, "I didn't know you cared."

Most siblings would identify this at once as the moment to say, *You know I love you;* but most siblings did not grow up in my family.

"I worry about you, that's all."

Mariah tilts her head to one side and wrinkles her nose. "You don't need to worry, Tal, I'm a big girl. I don't think anybody is going to break into the house tonight and burn me with cigarettes." Since that is exactly what I am scared of, I say nothing. "Besides," she adds, "I won't be alone."

"You won't?" This takes me by surprise.

"No. Szusza is bringing the kids down tomorrow." I assume this is the name of the latest unpronounceable au pair. "Well, some of the kids, anyway," she corrects herself, but maybe she has trouble keeping track. I would. "And Sally's staying with me tonight. So don't worry."

"Sally?" I didn't know my sister and our cousin were so close.

"She's been great, Tal. Really great. She's coming by right after work. We're going to start going through Daddy's papers." Mariah looks up at me sharply, as though I have objected to this plan. "Look, Tal, somebody has to do it. We have to know what's here. For all kinds of reasons. There are a lot of records and things that we might need. On the houses and stuff. And, who knows, maybe . . . maybe we can find some kind of clue."

"Clue to what?"

Mariah's russet gaze goes flinty. "Come on, Tal, you know what I'm talking about. You're the one who had Jack Ziegler screaming at you in the cemetery last week. He thinks there is something somewhere, some kind of . . . well, I don't know what." She closes her eyes for a moment, then opens them again. "I want to find what he is looking for, and I want to find it before he does."

I think this over. *The arrangements.* Well, she could be right. The Judge might have left a piece of paper, a diary, something to help us figure out what has Uncle Jack so worried. And what the fake FBI men evidently wanted. And maybe Sergeant B. T. Ames. *The arrangements.* Maybe a clue will turn up. I doubt it—but Mariah, ex-journalist, just could be right.

"Well, good luck," is all I can think of to say.

"Thanks. I have a feeling we'll find it." She sips her hot chocolate and makes a face: too cold.

"It could even be fun."

Mariah shrugs, somehow conveying her determination. "I'm not doing it for fun," she says to her cocoa, unconsciously rubbing her womb again. I find myself wondering what my wife is doing at this instant.

"Have you heard from Addison since the funeral?" I am making conversation.

"Nope. Not a word." She chuckles derisively. "Same old Addison."

"He's not so bad."

"Oh, he's great. Can you believe what he said about Daddy? In the *eulogy?* That maybe there was some reason to think he did something wrong?"

"That's not exactly what he said," murmurs Misha the peacemaker, a role into which I somehow stepped while trying to survive in the turbulent household of my adolescence, and one that I have never managed to relinquish.

"That's the way I heard it. I bet that's the way it sounded to most of the folks who were there."

"Well, maybe he did leave it . . . a little ambiguous."

"It was a funeral, Tal." Her eyes are flat. "You don't do that at a funeral."

"Oh, I see your point, kiddo."

Which is not precisely the same as agreeing with it, a nuance my sister catches at once. "You never want to take sides, do you? You like the view from the fence."

"Mariah, come on," I say, stung, but I offer no counterargument, not least because I do not have one.

We let the silence envelop us for a while, escaping into our own minds. I am adding up all the hours of work I have waiting for me back home, secretly furious that I allowed Mariah to spook me into this trip. Everything the detective said made sense; and none of my sister's theories are remotely plausible. I peek at my watch, hoping Mariah doesn't see, and lift my mug to my lips, only to put it down fast. My hot chocolate tastes as bad as hers.

"Did you believe her?" Mariah asks, as though in contact with my thoughts. "Sergeant Ames, I mean? About Father Bishop?"

"You mean, do I think she was lying?"

"I mean, do you think she was *right?* Please don't play word games with me, Tal, I'm not one of your students."

I have to answer this carefully; I do not want to make my sister my enemy all over again. "I know what you meant," I say slowly. "I think, if she *isn't* right, then the alternative is that he was tortured because of . . . because of something to do with the Judge. But that doesn't make any sense."

"Why not?" Her question is sharp; again I must pick the right words.

"Well, let's suppose—let's suppose that there is some bit of information that the Judge took to his grave with him, information that somebody wanted. I don't believe this, you understand, it's just a supposition."

Mariah gives a small, tight nod. I plunge on.

"Even if it's true—even if there *is* some bit of information—well, I doubt that the Judge would have confided anything important in Freeman Bishop. I don't mean to speak ill of the dead, but, come on."

"Nobody who knew Daddy would think he would tell Father Bishop anything."

"Nobody who knew Freeman Bishop would think the Judge would tell him anything."

My sister rubs her womb again, protecting her baby. "So he wasn't . . . tortured . . . for information about Daddy, was he?"

"I don't think so. If I thought anything else, I would grab my family and head for the hills."

"If your family would go." Mariah cannot help being mischievous when the subject of Kimmer comes up. I decide to ignore it.

"The point is, kiddo, the reason I think Sergeant Ames is right is that I can't think of any reason that anybody would have . . . done those things to him." *I promised to protect you, and so I shall.* I can repeat this mantra to myself, but reiteration does not make it feel true. Not completely. What feels true is that somebody is out there—Uncle Jack's *others*—playing a very long game, waiting for me to do . . . well, whatever it is that everybody expects me to do. I sense no danger, but I sense no peace.

Mariah nods. "Neither can I," she says. She runs a hand over her eyes. "She was really something, that detective. She was one tough lady."

"Well, you got her to admit that the note was most likely a fake. . . ."

"Oh, Tal, give it a rest." Mariah's voice has gone unexpectedly hard. I have stumbled into her realm of expertise. "I didn't get her to do anything. Cops don't ever admit anything they don't want to. She told us what she wanted us to know, and that's all."

"Well, that's my point." I am excited now. "She wanted us to hear all that stuff about drugs. Why? I bet the only reason she told us was that she doesn't believe we're going to keep it secret. She *wants* us to spread it around."

"I never knew you were such a cynic." Mariah shakes her head as though she has never been one. She shifts in her chair and her finger stabs toward me. "I *liked* Sergeant Ames."

"But did you believe her about the drug dealers?"

"Well, they did find his car by the Navy Yard."

"I bet there's about a hundred fifty thousand people down in Southwest who don't do drugs or sell them," I preach.

"Give it a rest," Mariah repeats. "Everybody knows Father Bishop does coke. Or he did, anyway. Everybody's known for years."

"Everybody knows *what?*"

"You're so innocent, Tal. Why are you the last to hear everything?" She laughs. At least we seem on relatively good terms again. "You really don't know?"

I shake my head.

"Well, it's an old story. Laurel St. Jacques caught him snorting three or four years ago, right in the sacristy. You remember Laurel, don't you? She married André Conway? I know you must remember André." A devilish smile, reminding me that I am Kimberly Madison's second husband. André was her first.

"I remember André," I say quietly. I also remember—although I never mention it—an irrational fury at André after he won the first round in our battle for Kimmer Madison, including a moment, in his apartment, when we nearly came to blows. At that time he was a local news producer named Artis. His new appellation came when he decided to make documentary films. "I even remember he married Laurel."

"Do you remember that they're divorced?"

"Rings a bell somewhere." I hope she is not hinting anything about André and my wife. Unbidden, my thoughts lead me down toward their usual obsessive fear: André is in Los Angeles these days, and Kimmer is often in San Francisco, and he could fly up to see her. . . .

Oh, stop it!

"I heard there was another woman involved," says Mariah, her old streak of cruelty unexpectedly manifesting itself.

"There usually is."

Mariah glances at me, perhaps trying to figure out if I am putting her down with what she disdains as my *Ivy League cleverness*, as though she has none of her own. I keep my poker face on. "Well, anyway," she finally continues, "Laurel caught Father Bishop at it a couple of years ago. And, Laurel being Laurel, she naturally told everybody. It's a wonder he wasn't fired on the spot. I think Daddy must have been off the vestry by then, or Father Bishop would have been gone. But they decided to keep him around. I guess they all must have felt sorry for him or something. You know us Episcopalians, Tal. We love to feel *compassion* for people. We're never happy unless we're ignoring somebody's sins to show how tolerant we are," adds my sister, who converted to Roman Catholicism in order to marry Howard and, Kimmer likes to say, has followed the Church's teaching on birth control ever since.

"I didn't know."

"Well, it was quite the little scandal, Tal." She flaps her hand for emphasis, tosses her head the way she used to when she wore her hair straight and long, then rushes eagerly on, happy for the chance to share gossip I seem to have missed. "Quite a few people left the church over it, as a matter of fact. The Cliftons left. Oh, they were furious! And Bruce and Harriet Yearwood left. Also Mary Raboteau. No, wait, she retired and went to Florida or something. I was thinking of Mrs. Lavelle—she's the other one who left. And you'd think Gigi Walker would have left, she's such a bluenose, but, well, I guess she had her reasons to stay." An odd little laugh. My sister loves being judgmental, even when nobody else in the room knows what she is judging. "I can't believe you didn't hear about it, Tal."

"No, I missed it."

"Daddy thought Father Bishop should quit voluntarily, you know, save everybody all the trouble? But he went in front of the congregation and did one of those God-isn't-finished-with-me-yet sermons, and that was pretty much the end of that. Oh, that reminds me." My sister is on her feet. "I promised Sergeant Ames that I would call Warner Bishop. Poor guy, he doesn't have anybody left." Mariah vanishes into the foyer. A moment later I hear her tread on the stairs, going up to the study to find the Judge's address book. I am amazed. I assumed that my sister was just talking when she said she would reassure Father Bishop's family, but I forgot how seriously she takes promises. When we were children, she used to run to our parents to complain whenever I (or, more frequently, Addison) went back on a promise. In the Garland household, promise-breaking was pretty much a court-martial offense. Our mother would punish us, usually confining us to our rooms for a couple of hours, but our father would do something far worse: he would call us into the little downstairs study he used in those days and deliver one of his excruciating lectures, letting the full force of his chilly, dispassionate disapproval wash over us as we stood before his desk at parade rest. *Promises are the bricks of life, Talcott, and trust is the mortar. We build nothing in life if we make no promises, and we tear down what others have built if we make them and break them.* Something like that. He struggled to make the same point to the Senate Judiciary Committee, explaining his relationship with Jack Ziegler: *Friendship is a promise of future loyalty, loyalty no matter what comes. Promises are the bricks of life. . . . I will never abandon a friend, and I expect that my friends will never abandon me.*

That's a very noble sentiment, Judge, but the fact remains that this particular friend of yours was under indictment for . . .

With respect, Senator, it isn't a matter of nobility. It's a matter of what kind of world you want to build. If you want to build at all—or just to tear down.

Lots of friends did abandon him, of course, once they calculated that the Judge was more likely to wind up in prison than on the Supreme Court.

I go to the sink and wash our cups. When the water stops running, I hear Mariah's voice drifting down the stairwell. Mariah, who can be warm and vivacious when she chooses, will probably be a considerable comfort to Warner Bishop, Freeman Bishop's hapless son, now some kind of advertising executive in New York, with whom my sister once put in time in Jack and Jill and all the other youth groups of our set. Homely, chunky, awkward Warner Bishop, who wanted desperately to date Mariah when they were teenagers, but never quite succeeded in drawing her interest. According to Addison, Warner has carried a distant torch for her ever since. Oh, our closed little world!

"Drug dealers," I mutter. Maybe, maybe not. Whoever it was, I do not even need to close my eyes to see the photos of what they did to Father Bishop. To his hand, to his thigh, and, easily imagined, to other parts of his anatomy that the detective chose, perhaps out of kindness, not to share.

Freeman Bishop, drug user, came to a drug user's end. How is it that I alone seem not to have known?

Maybe Mariah is right. Or maybe she is nuts. Or maybe I am.

Maybe I should make a peace offering.

Drying my hands on a kitchen towel of hideous red-and-black design, I dither for a moment, wondering if it is time to use the card Jack Ziegler gave me in the cemetery. But it isn't: after a murder, the last thing I need is to call in a monster for help. And then I know exactly what to give. The memory of my father's lectures reminded me. I think Mariah's hunt for a hidden clue will bear no fruit, but I do not want her to think I am her enemy. What I will offer is less a clue than a memento of the man our father was—a memento that might even persuade my sister to abandon her search. I stand up and head down the dark hallway to the claustrophobic first-floor library with its cherry cabinets. After a quick, covetous glance at the Miró, I sit behind the desk and roll the chair over to the bookshelf where my father kept his scrapbooks. I hunt through them for several minutes before giving up in puzzlement.

Mariah moved it, I am thinking. Or somebody else in the endless parade through the house after the funeral: Mariah's children, Howard Denton, Just Alma, the unpronounceable au pair, Mrs. Rose, Sally, Addison, his little white girlfriend, Uncle Mal, Dana Worth, Eddie Dozier, the woman who cleans the place, one of the numberless cousins, anybody.

The blue album with the newspaper clippings of hit-and-run accidents is gone.

A MODEST PROPOSAL

"YOUR WIFE and Marc Hadley are both up for the same judgeship," Stuart Land informs me as soon as I am seated in his capacious chamber around the corner from mine.

"I think I know that," I say, counterpunching but remaining respectful.

"In Europe, of course, this situation would be impossible."

"Which situation?"

"They have a professional judiciary. You rise through the ranks. They consider rather unseemly the American system, under which . . . amateurs . . . may be appointed to an appellate court."

"Well, we're stuck with our system." Although I am pretty sure my wife has just been insulted, I force a smile, not wanting to pick a fight with Stuart Land, the great Anglophile. I already have enough enemies around the building. "It's worked out pretty well so far. No more than one scandal per decade."

Stuart raises an eyebrow at my levity. Then he shrugs, as if to say responding to such nonsense is beneath his dignity. "Have you heard any news? About who might have the inside track?" Implying that my sources are better than his, which is unlikely. With the Republicans in the White House, Stuart probably could have had his pick of Washington jobs. Stuart Land, Lynda Wyatt's predecessor as dean, and the man who persuaded me to return to my alma mater to teach, is among the most conservative members of our faculty. In the four years since his fall from power, Stuart has shown no signs of bitterness toward Lynda or Marc Hadley or Ben Montoya or Tish Kirschbaum or any of the several other professors who conspired to oust him. He continues to crisscross the country in search of money for the law school, and our alumni, especially the older, wealthier ones, love him still and continue opening their wallets and checkbooks when Stuart calls. Indeed, many still refer to him as "the Dean," maybe because it once seemed he would hold the job until he died, and if Lynda is envious of their affection, she hides it well.

It is not possible to get close to Stuart, although the more conservative professors hang around with him, and Lemaster Carlyle, who seems to get along with everybody, is a pal. As for myself, I will confess that I have never quite liked Stuart. But I have always admired him, not least because he was the only member of the faculty actually to testify in favor of my father's confirmation to the Supreme Court. His integrity, moreover, is beyond question, which is why I was surprised and a little disturbed when he called me up just days after my return from Washington to suggest that I drop by for a chat.

Having nothing better to do at nine in the morning but sit in my office and feel sorry for myself, I agreed.

Stuart Land is a fussy little man whose vested suits with their pinstripes and broad lapels might be described as gangsta-like, except that he is white and crew-cut and somewhere north of sixty. His face is round and utterly without affect, his eyes are pale gray and glittering with fierce intelligence, and the half-glasses always perched on his nose make him look more censorious than professorial. His prim mouth is always ready with a word of sharp, witty disapproval. Nobody takes to him on first meeting, or second, but, somewhere along the way, a certain charisma emerges, and few of our students, even those on the left, manage to leave the law school without sharing in that general warm glow that everybody feels toward him.

This morning, however, Stuart is neither warm nor glowing. He exudes no charisma. He called me because he has a point to make, and, in true Stuart Land fashion, he chooses to make it through a series of gentle, indirect, yet very pointed assaults—the same style he uses in the classroom, and with which I was skewered more than once in the days when he taught me contracts.

"No, Stuart," I report dutifully. Half my attention is still focused on Washington, where Mariah, unable to reach Warner Bishop, left him a message. I said nothing to her about the missing scrapbook. "We haven't heard any news."

"Neither has Marc. I gather he's quite upset about the whole thing."

"I'm sorry to hear that." Which is vaguely true.

"Marc isn't a bad fellow, Talcott. You just have to get to know him."

"I don't have anything against Marc. I like him."

Stuart frowns as though suspecting a lie. He drums his fingers. "He hasn't been the scholar we hoped for when we hired him, of course. That writer's block. But he really is a fine colleague, Talcott. A wonderful teacher. A brilliant mind. And, you know, when we hired you, Marc was one of your keenest backers."

"I . . . had no idea," I say truthfully. Unlike some law faculties, ours makes a fetish of confidentiality, and talking to people about who voted for or against them is considered to be somewhere between unethical and outrageous. Still, I have heard that Theo Mountain was my biggest booster, and during my first few years on the faculty, he and I were quite close. He was never quite my mentor—I have never really had one—but, until my father's hard march to the right turned Theo into a carping critic, the two of us spent a lot of time together. Stuart Land, then the dean, was the man who actually persuaded me to quit the practice of law and come up to Elm Harbor to give teaching a try. He caught me at a good time: Kimmer and I were in the midst of one of our many estrangements. That she followed me to this city nine months later, and married me into the bargain, surprised me almost as much as it did our friends and families. And I have always wondered—although both parties deny it—whether Stuart might also have been responsible, somehow, for persuading my wife that the practice of law in Elm Harbor was not the hick job she imagined.

"Marc is a good man," Stuart repeats. "As your wife is a good woman."

"Yes," I murmur, taking mental exception to the comparison as I wait patiently for the rest. Stuart has asked me here for a reason, and I know he is about to tell me what it is. I do not, however, have much energy to spend worrying about Marc Hadley's feelings just now, even if he did back my appointment. The murder of Father Bishop, hard on the heels of the death of the Judge, has pretty much drained my wellspring of sympathy. Two nights of argument with Kimmer, whose position is still that there is nothing to worry about, exhausted the rest of my emotional self. Yet the main point I made to Stuart is correct: I do kind of like Marc Hadley, who is not much liked around the building. Marc, who has been teaching jurisprudence at the law school for eighteen years, is actually a fairly nice man. His son Miguel is one of Bentley's best preschool buddies, so we see Marc and his second wife, Dahlia, socially in the way that parents do: in the school parking lot, at birthday parties, on field trips to the fire station around the corner. We are not exactly intimates, Marc and I, but we always used to get along. And although Dear Dana considers Marc "over-reputed"—a famous Worthism—he is, in my judgment, every bit as brilliant as his legend insists; it takes only a minute or two in his presence to sense that fantastic brain pulsing forth its great ideas. But if his intellect is one legend, his inability to produce any scholarship is another. His academic standing rests on his single book, published quite early in his career. He has published almost nothing since. He seems to have read every book ever written, on every subject, and is ready with a quotation for any occasion, but Marc himself suffers from one of the great writer's blocks, a true monster of the species, and there are law reviews everywhere still waiting for articles he promised a decade ago. For a startling moment, I find myself sympathizing after all with Marc, who probably feels he needs the judgeship to prove his career has not been a waste. Then I shrug it off and am ready to fight for my wife again. "Two good people," I echo, just to show I have not lost my place.

Stuart nods, then leans back in his chair, steepling his long fingers, signaling that he is about to deliver a little sermon. I admire Stuart, but I hate his sermons.

"I don't like it when members of our faculty compete against one another," he says sadly, his tone proposing that his opinion matters. "It's not good for our collegiality. It's not good for the school." He points toward his wall of windows, through which one can see spires and towers and the huge, blocky library, the Gothic glory of the campus proper. "We are, first and foremost, a faculty. That's what it means to be in a university. We are scholars, and those of us who have tenure, what the university calls 'Permanent Officers,' are supposed to be leaders in our fields. Not politicians, Talcott, but Officers. Scholars. Every one of us is charged with precisely the same responsibility: to immerse himself in a chosen discipline, and then to teach his students what he happens to discover. Anything that distracts from that task is injurious to our common enterprise. You see that, don't you?"

I am somewhere between astonished and furious. Stuart is surely not taking the side of the man who orchestrated his own fall from power. I never thought Kimmer would have many supporters on the faculty, but I assumed that Stuart Land would be one.

"Do you see?" he says again. He does not wait to see whether I see. He continues his oration, raising an admonitory forefinger. "You know, Talcott, over my many years on this faculty, I have often been approached by this administration or that one, asking after my interest in some presidential appointment. A judgeship. Associate attorney general. Some post in an agency." He smiles in soft reminiscence. "Once, during a scandal, the Reagan people asked if I would be willing to come down and clean up a Cabinet department. But every time, Talcott, I have declined. Every single time. You see, it is my experience, my invariant observation, that a professor who is bitten by the political bug ceases to be effective as a scholar. No longer is he studying the world and teaching what he discovers. He is, in effect, running for office, and it affects everything from the subjects he chooses for his writing to the arguments he is willing to press in the classroom. He worries about leaving a paper trail and, if he has one, spends his time cleaning it up. As you can imagine, when two members of the faculty find themselves both bitten by the political bug at the same time, and both in competition for the same single slot on a court, well, the deleterious effects are . . . oh, geometrically increased. Quadrupled."

I cannot let this go on any longer. "Stuart, look. I appreciate what you're saying. But my wife is not a member of the faculty."

"Well, no, Talcott, you're right. She isn't." Nodding as though he knew this before and I, the slower thinker, have just realized it. "Not formally."

"Not even informally."

"Well, your wife may not be faculty, but she's family. Part of the law school family."

I almost laugh at that one. In Kimmer's ideal world, she would not even have to see the law school, much less think of herself as part of it. "Come on, Stuart. No matter what she is, the fact that she is in the running can't possibly affect how she does her job around the law school if she doesn't have a job around the law school." Refusing to fall into Stuart's cadences, in which the entire faculty is male.

The steely eyes hold mine. "Well, that isn't quite the end of the matter, Talcott. That your wife is, as you put it, in the running could have an effect on *you*."

"On me?"

"Oh, yes, Talcott, of course. Why is that so hard to believe? Your wife wanting to be a judge, you not wanting to spoil her chances—why couldn't such a situation lead to an excess of caution on your part?"

"An excess of . . ."

"Have you been yourself lately?" He chuckles to ease the blow. "The Talcott Garland we know and love? I think not."

Enough is enough. "Stuart, come on. My father just died. And then the preacher who did the funeral . . ."

"Was murdered. Yes, I know. And I am terribly sorry." He hunches forward, folds his small hands on the desk. "But, Talcott, listen to me. You've been distracted lately. A bit disorganized." Then, to my surprise, a shrug. "But this is wide of the point. . . ."

"Wide of the point! You just said the competition is affecting how I do my job!"

"And perhaps I was speaking out of school. Maybe it's none of my business. Maybe I was merely speculating. The truth is, I was not thinking about how you do your job. I was thinking about Marc."

"What about Marc?" I demand, anger still burning fiercely, even though I am utterly confused. A moment ago Stuart thought I was distracted and disorganized. Now it is none of his business.

"Marc is not doing his job well. I think the competition may be too much for him."

"Then why are you talking to me instead of to Marc?" Stuart says nothing, but only stares, scarcely blinking. I feel a little heady, an odd déjà vu, even though I cannot say what it is I am re-experiencing. I try again. "Did Marc put you up to this? Did he ask you to talk to me? Because if he did . . ."

"Nobody put me up to anything, Talcott. My only concern is this school." Talking as though he is still the dean. "And I know that, like me, you want what is best for the school."

"You're not suggesting . . . You don't think . . ." I stop, swallow the surging red anger, and try again. "I mean, if you're suggesting that I should tell my wife to drop out of the process, to give up her chance to be a federal judge, for the good of the law school or the good of Marc Hadley . . . well, Stuart, I'm sorry, but that isn't going to happen."

"It is just possible, Talcott, that the good of the school and the good of Marc Hadley are, in this case, identical."

"What do you mean by . . . Oh!" Did I happen to mention that Stuart Land is devious? I should have seen it earlier. Naturally he wants to help Marc obtain his treasured judgeship. Probably Marc could not have been a finalist without his help, for Stuart may be the only member of the faculty whom the administration would trust to vouch for the truth of Marc's own repeated assertion that he is a political liberal but a judicial reactionary. And why would Stuart assist the ambition of the man most responsible for his downfall? Because, if Marc were to become a judge, Stuart would be rid of him at last; and Dean Lynda, his rival, would lose the cornerstone on which her power base in the faculty is built.

Stuart has a hoary witticism to offer: "Perhaps Marc Hadley's departure from the law school to join the bench would enhance the quality of both institutions."

Again I choose my words with care. "I appreciate your point of view, Stuart. I really do. But Kimmer is more deserving of this seat than Marc is. I am not about to suggest to her that she withdraw her name."

Stuart nods slowly. He even finds a smile somewhere. "Very well. I had to give it a shot. I was fairly sure your answer would be what it was. And I respect you for it. But, you know, Talcott, there will be those around the building who will not."

"I beg your pardon."

"You have many friends on this faculty, Talcott, but you have . . . well, there are those who are not fond of you. Surely this comes as no surprise."

The curtain of red finally descends across my eyes. "What are you telling me, Stuart? Just spell it out."

"I wouldn't be surprised, Talcott, if certain . . . pressures . . . were brought to bear on you, to try to get you to convince your wife to drop out, to let Marc have the seat. That is a most unfortunate fact, but it is still a fact. I would prefer that the school be otherwise, that we retain our collegiality, but, when the political bug bites one of our own, we behave less like Permanent Officers than like Temporary Schoolchildren." He waits for me to grin at his small joke, but I do not. "I am afraid, Talcott, that some of the schoolchildren may try to . . . persuade you."

"I don't believe this. I don't *believe* this."

"I will not be a part of it, of course, and I will happily use my influence to protect you. But, Talcott, you have to realize that I, too, have enemies on the faculty. It may be that my influence is less than I might prefer." He sighs, contriving to suggest that the school would be a better place if he were still at the top of the heap. Perhaps it would. Say what you want about Stuart Land, his only ambitions, ever, have been for the school.

"I understand."

Stuart hesitates, and I realize he has not quite finished his sermon. "On the other hand, Talcott, if you are determined to go down this path, I think I might be rather helpful to you in Washington."

"Oh?"

"I believe I might have some influence there, and, if I do, I would gladly use it to help your wife along."

Which brings us, I see, to the point of the whole meeting. Tired of Stuart's subtle politicking, I try some directness: "And in return for your help, you want me to do what?"

Stuart frowns and steeples his fingers again. I brace for another speech, but he gets to his feet instead. "Not everything has a quid pro quo, Talcott. Don't be such a cynic. When you were young and untenured, you were more optimistic. I think the return of that peppy fellow would be a fine thing, for both you and the school." He picks up the volume of Holmes's collected papers he was reading when I came in, a signal of dismissal. But, before I have managed to excuse myself, he offers a revision of his point. "Of course, it is possible, Talcott, that you will have the chance later on to do the school a favor in return. If the opportunity arises, I assume you will take it."

"I . . . I'm not sure what you mean, Stuart."

"You'll be sure when the time comes."

Out in the hall, I feel a sudden chill. I realize now who it was that Stuart reminded me of during his lecture: Jack Ziegler, back in the cemetery, promising to protect my family, and asking me, in return, to tell him whatever I learn about *the arrangements*.

I wonder, uneasily, if Stuart is asking for the same thing.

CHAPTER 12

A SPECIAL DELIVERY

(1)

ELM HARBOR was founded in 1682, built around a trading post at the mouth of the State River. The original name of the town was Harbor-on-the-Hill, because the flatland near the water is so small and the ground slopes away from the harbor fast; and also because of the influence of John Winthrop's sermon half a century earlier about the shining city on the hill. The city fathers were dour Congregationalists who came down the coast seeking religious freedom and immediately set about adopting laws to prohibit it to everybody else. So they banned, among other things, blasphemy, popery, exposing one's ankles in public, idolatry, usury, disobeying one's father, and doing business on the Sabbath. Although they would have been aghast to think they might be worshiping a graven image, they laid out their city in the shape of a cross, building it around two long avenues, an east-west road known in those days as The East-West Road and now known as Eastern Avenue, and a north-south road called North Road, later changed to The King's Road, and now King Avenue.

The university opened its doors thirty years later, essentially a finishing school for dour Congregationalist men who wanted to study—along with their Bible—rhetoric, Greek and Latin, mathematics, and astronomy. The original campus was two wooden buildings in the long oval where King Avenue swings in a wide arc to follow the curve of the State River; that precious riverfront property is now owned by the medical school. Over the ensuing three centuries, the campus has spread like an aggressive cancer through the area west of King Avenue, invading one block, metastasizing on the next, demolishing whatever is in its way, or converting it to the university's purposes. Clapboard homes have come down, along with factories, schools, stores, flophouses, churches, mansions, warehouses, brothels, taverns, tanneries, and blocks upon blocks of tenements. In their place have risen libraries and laboratories and classrooms and offices and dormitories and administration buildings . . . and open space. Lots and lots of open space. The university likes to describe itself as Elm Harbor's number one builder of parkland, even if nobody from the city dares tread on any of the school's beautiful parks. The university has built museums and an aquarium and the region's leading performing arts center. Its hospital is one of the best in the world. The university invests in the community, providing capital to build new housing and start small businesses. No institution in the area provides more jobs.

Or so say our press releases.

The university also buys up entire streets, closing them to traffic, constructs massive edifices for parking cars, but only the cars of students and faculty, and, with its private security force with full powers of arrest, creates an island of relative tranquillity, surrounded by an almost visible wall to keep the townies out.

Elm Harbor itself is demographically complex. About thirty percent of the residents are black, another twenty percent are Hispanic, and the rest are white—but so diverse! We have Greek Americans and Italian Americans and Irish Americans and German Americans and Russian Americans. The residents whom the Census Bureau arbitrarily labels Hispanic are largely of Puerto Rican descent, but many others trace their families to Central America—as do many of our black residents, who are otherwise about equally divided between West Indians and those whose most distant identifiable roots are in the South. The city is hopelessly sundered along these many lines, as we learn every three years in municipal elections, where the city council is an endlessly bickering rainbow, and as many as five or six different ethnic groups often field mayoral candidates in the Democratic primary. (The local Republican Party is a joke.) Only two things unite the multi-original residents of Elm Harbor: a shared hatred of the university, and a shared dream that their own children will one day attend it.

Kimmer does not like living here, and the university, although an occasional client, is one of the reasons.

And my own view? I am a fan of no city, and Elm Harbor, with its many problems, seems to me no worse than any other. What I have learned over the years from my colleagues—especially the great conservative Stuart Land and the great liberal Theo Mountain—is that those of us who are members of the university community share a special responsibility for improving what Theo likes to call the metropole. The concept of responsibility, I know, is nowadays passé, especially the idea of obligation to those Eleanor Roosevelt used to call less fortunate than ourselves, but the Judge raised his children to it, and none of us can fully escape it. The Judge believed that his social conservatism demanded service: if the role of the state was going to be small, the role of volunteers had to be large. So Mariah holds parties for homeless children, Addison tutors inner-city high-school students . . . and I serve food.

(11)

THE SOUP KITCHEN where I sometimes volunteer serves hot lunches to women and children at half past twelve each weekday in the basement of a Congregationalist church a block east of the campus, and it is the perfect place to forget mystery and death, for the difficulties in which its customers find themselves are far more profound than my own. As I sat in my office preparing for my torts class following the baffling conversation with Stuart Land, I felt its call. Trying to explain to my wary students the intricacies of comparative negligence, I knew I was botching it, and sensed Avery Knowland looking daggers any time my back was turned. When the class ended, I dumped the books in my office and rushed out the front door of the building.

The soup kitchen, I decided, is the only place for me just now.

Service, I remind myself as I descend the steps to the church basement. We are all of us called to actual service. Not just giving money, Theo Mountain likes to preach, and not fighting to change the law, either, for Theo considers the law a lost cause. Service to real people, who ache and cry and challenge us.

The manager of the soup kitchen, a seventyish Teutonic widow who insists that we call her Dee Dee, greets me with a scowl as I bound through the door a few minutes shy of opening time. Her cane snapping against the vinyl floor, Dee Dee follows me into the kitchen, where the rest of the staff is slicing several donated pizzas, baked yesterday and now desert-dry. "Setup is at noon," she scolds me in her elegant voice as I pull on a pair of disposable latex gloves. "We expect everybody here by twelve-fifteen."

"I had a class, Dee Dee. I'm sorry."

"A *class*."

"Yes." Trying to think how my charming brother would handle Dee Dee. Badly, I bet.

Dee Dee, whose real name I have often been told and can never recall, is a small woman with carefully combed white-blond bangs and wide, solid shoulders. She wears floral-print shirtwaists and knee socks and sensible shoes. Her long, waxy face seems carved from some pallid stone, and her amazingly bright blue eyes often trick the uninitiated into thinking she can see. But Dee Dee is quite blind. She is also determined that our guests (as she calls them) will be treated with respect. We have colorful cotton tablecloths, which Dee Dee herself launders twice a week, vases of flowers on the tables, and strict rules that all food must be served from dishes, never from pots just off the stove or pans just out of the oven. Dee Dee insists that our guests say *Please* and *Thank you* and that the rest of us say *You're welcome*. Volunteers who are rude receive one warning, after which they are not welcome back. Dee Dee has no authority to bar guests for being rude to the volunteers, but her dead-eyed glare, disconcertingly direct, keeps all but the most schizophrenic in line. Dee Dee runs, by her own gleeful admission, a very tight ship. Her blindness does not affect her ability to know at once, as though through some sightless telepathy, which of her volunteers is being careless in measuring portions of lasagna and which of her guests is trying to stuff an extra apple or two inside her sweater.

Or who is late.

Dee Dee puts her large hands on her small hips and leans away, her thin lips turned down as she lets me have it: "Are you saying that your class is more important than feeding these unfortunate women?" Then she smiles and pats my shoulder with amazing accuracy, letting me know that she is mostly joking.

Mostly.

But today of all days, I welcome her wit.

I take my place behind the counter, at the salad station today. A few of the other volunteers say hello. *Professor*, they call me, a kind of inside joke, although I had the same nickname in high school. *Hey, Professor!* call volunteers and clients alike. *What's goin on, Pro?* I come to the soup kitchen for a million different reasons. One of them, the easiest to see, is service, the simple Christian duty to do for others. Another, always, is the need to be reminded of the diversity of the human race in general and the darker nation in particular: for the students and teachers who represent African America at the university tend to run the gamut mainly from Oak Bluffs to Sag Harbor. And perhaps I have also come here today in part to do penance for my browbeating of poor Avery Knowland, whose insolence is hardly his fault. But even that is still too thin an explanation. This may simply be one of those Tuesdays on which the company of this happy band is preferable to the company of my colleagues, not because of a flaw in my colleagues but because of a flaw in me. There are days when time at the office is like time with the Judge, and the fact that he is dead and buried is irrelevant. At Oldie I am surrounded by people who fondly remember my father as a student: Amy Hefferman, his classmate; Theo Mountain, his teacher; Stuart Land, who was two years behind him in school; a few others. Despite the scandal that wrecked his career, my father's portrait, like the portraits of all our graduates who have ascended to the bench, hangs on the wall in the vast reading room of the law library, which is one reason I spend little time there. Sometimes I feel suffocated by the role I am required to play: *Was Oliver Garland really your father? What did it feel like?* As though I am on campus principally to serve as an exhibit. I should never have allowed the Judge to persuade me to undertake the study of law where he had studied law before me; I cannot imagine what possessed me to decide that this was the right place to teach.

Maybe it was the fact that I had no other attractive offers.

Or that my father told me to do it.

I was a dutiful son in most things. My only act of rebellion was to marry Kimberly Madison, with whom I went to law school, when my family preferred her sister, Lindy, with whom I went to college. Kimmer, of course, is well aware of what my parents thought, as she reminded me two weeks ago in the steak house on K Street, and there are moments when the knowledge infuriates her, and other moments when she tells me she wishes I had done what I was expected to do. The trouble is I never loved Lindy, no matter what the Gold Coast seemed to think. And Lindy was never the least bit interested in me. If she had been, I suppose I would have married her, just as my parents wanted, and my life would have been different—not better, just different. I would not have Bentley, for example, which would be inestimably worse. On the other hand, some things would still be the same: the Judge would still be dead of a heart attack, and everybody would still be asking me what arrangements he made, and Freeman Bishop would still have been murdered, and Mariah would still be besotted with crazy theories.

And I would still be emotionally exhausted.

Kimmer and I quarreled yesterday morning, not over what she is or is not doing with Jerry, but over money. We have the same fight every autumn, because autumn seems to be the time when we realize that the budget we so carefully laid out in January has become a bad joke: in that respect, we do about as well, or as badly, as the federal government. Standing in the doorway to the walk-in closet while Kimmer, clad only in bra and half-slip, selected the day's power suit, I suggested to her that we cut back. She asked where, without turning. I pointed, somewhat gingerly, to her expenditures on clothes and jewelry. Exasperated, she explained that she is a corporate lawyer and must dress the part. So I mentioned the stifling lease payments on her Alpine white BMW M5, in which she zips around the city while I huff along in my boring but reliable Camry. The car, too, turned out to be more or less a requirement of her job. I proposed that we think about moving to a smaller house. Kimmer, shimmying into her skirt, said that our residence is also a part of her professional persona. As I shook my head in defeat, she glanced over her shoulder at me and smiled the way I like best. Then she raised the stakes, reminding me tartly that we now own the house in Oak Bluffs free and clear: we could sell it and fix all our financial woes at once. I unwisely answered in kind, asserting that the Vineyard place is necessary to *my* persona, and that selling it would be like rejecting my heritage. As it does every year, the argument ended inconclusively.

Rob Saltpeter scolded me yesterday when he and Theo Mountain and I lunched at a place called Cadaver's, a converted funeral home two blocks from the campus, a little pricey, with waiters who are paid to be weird. Rob proposed that I might have come back too soon, that I need some time to heal. He suggested I take a look at the Book of Job. Theo Mountain, never one to mince words, said it is not just exhaustion, and I didn't need "to read a bunch of Bible verses." He said I may be depressed.

And Theo is probably right. I *am* depressed. And I almost like it. Depression is seductive: it offends and teases, frightens you and draws you in, tempting you with its promise of sweet oblivion, then overwhelming you with a nearly sexual power, squirming past your defenses, dissolving your will, invading the tired spirit so utterly that it becomes difficult to recall that you ever lived without it . . . or to imagine that you might live that way again. With all the guile of Satan himself, depression persuades you that its invasion was all your own idea, that you wanted it all along. It fogs the part of the brain that reasons, that knows right and wrong. It captures you with its warm, guilty, hateful pleasures, and, worst of all, it becomes *familiar*. All at once, you find yourself in thrall to the very thing that most terrifies you. Your work slides, your friendships slide, your marriage slides, but you scarcely notice: to be depressed is to be half in love with disaster.

"So snap out of it," I say to the room, startling another volunteer, who is laying out week-old cookies at the station next to mine. I smile apologetically into her perplexity and turn back to my work. *Maybe you're depressed*, said Theo, who, it is whispered, has never missed a day of class in fifty years on the faculty. In the peculiar intermingling of old Elm Harbor families, Theo and Dee Dee are distant relatives, and it was Theo who first suggested, at a particularly difficult point in my marriage, that I volunteer at the soup kitchen as a way of raising my spirits. *It worked for me*, proclaimed Theo, whose wife has been in the ground since I was a student.

Measuring the salad onto small paper plates, I stand a little straighter; and, for a time, through service I manage to forget.

(111)

DEE DEE LEADS US in a brief prayer and we are open for business. She turns on music: a portable CD player with large, scratchy speakers. For a while she tried to push classical music (her tastes run only as far as the three B's), but she has yielded to the pressures of time and place and now plays smooth jazz and, occasionally, something harder-edged. We serve a hard, edgy crowd. Nearly all the women are black. Few make much effort with appearances any more. Most arrive with hair mashed and twisted, in unwashed sweatshirts and dirty jeans. There is grime under their cracked, badly painted nails. A handful have white teeth, but most passed long ago from yellow to brown. Several have problems with drugs. A few are quite obviously HIV-positive. The women drag themselves through the line like forgotten spirits shuffling off toward the River Styx. They are neither enthusiastic nor reluctant, neither fatalistic nor indignant. They are, for the most part, utterly without affect. They do not grin, cry, laugh, complain. They are merely present. In college, we would-be revolutionaries pretended that the oppressed would one day rise as a mighty army to smite the capitalists, overthrow the system, and establish a truly just society. Well, here are a couple of dozen of the most oppressed people in America, all lined up for their food, and the greatest passion they are able to summon is for brief but heated argument over who got the larger portion. Half may be dead in two years. If not for the hopeful, innocent beauty of their children, who still return a smile for a smile, I probably could not bear to come at all.

Few of the women want salad, although one of them propositions me quite openly as she passes by ("No salad, but, mmmm-*mmmm*, I'd sure like to get me a piece of *you*"). I want to weep.

This is what conservatives have spawned with their welfare cuts and their indifference to the plight of those not like themselves, say my colleagues at the university. This is what liberals have spawned with their fostering of the victim mentality and their indifference to the traditional values of hard work and family, my father used to tell his cheering audiences. In my sour moments, it strikes me that both sides seem much more interested in winning the argument than in alleviating these women's suffering. *Service*. Theo Mountain is right. No other answer but that one.

"Talcott?"

I turn around, the cracked wooden salad spoons still in my hands.

"Yes, Dee Dee?"

"Talcott, there's somebody at the door asking for you."

"He can't come in?"

"*She* doesn't want to." A teasing smile dances at the corner of Dee Dee's lips, and she flashes dimples that must once have been spectacular.

"One minute."

I return to the kitchen to find somebody to take over my unpopular station. I remove my apron and throw my gloves in the trash. After retrieving my jacket, I follow Dee Dee as she tap-taps her way up the concrete stairs to the entrance, where Romeo, the only other male volunteer, guards the door. Romeo's skin is the black-brown of a tree trunk on a moonless night. He is a man of no particular age, big in all directions. Although some of his heft is fat, most of it is not. Romeo's meaty hands are always wandering, the result of some nervous disorder, but a menacing effect. He is often a little slow, but his vaguely Southern patois is never hard to understand. I do not know where Romeo comes from or even his real name. He was once on the street, as he puts it— meaning he dealt drugs—but managed to find Jesus without the inconvenience of first going to prison. His round, clean-shaven face has a battered look. He is far more gentle than he appears; but it is his appearance on which the church relies to scare away anybody who thinks of breaking the women-and-children-only rule.

"She gone, Miss Dee Dee," he mumbles now, the immense hands rubbing each other furiously. "She say she can't wait."

"What did she look like?"

"A white girl," says Romeo as Dee Dee listens closely to us both. "Clean," he adds, meaning, *Not like the women inside.*

"A white woman," I repeat, wondering who, and also correcting him with the reflex born of life on a politically wary campus.

"Naw, naw," he disagrees, "a white *girl*." But his emphasis carries little information: in Romeo's typology, one must reach Dee Dee's age before becoming a woman. Romeo squints, searching for the right adjective. "Sweet," he says at last.

Sweet is one of Romeo's several words for *attractive*. Now I am thinking *student*, but I am at a loss to understand how one of my students would track me here—or why, having found me, she would not wait for me to come upstairs.

"Did you ever see her before, Romeo?" Dee Dee asks the question that should have occurred to me.

"No, Miss Dee Dee. Oh, yeah!" A sudden light comes into his eyes. One of those huge hands comes swinging up, offering a white legal-sized envelope. "She say somebody pay her to give this to the Pro." Meaning me.

"What is it?" asks Dee Dee, addressing the question to the Pro.

"I don't know," I admit. "Some kind of envelope." I take it from Romeo, examine the front. My full name and title and my correct law school address are typed neatly on the front. There is no stamp. There is no return address. I heft it, then squeeze it. Something small and hard is inside. Like a tube of lipstick. I frown. Every university in the country has warned its faculty about opening letters from unknown senders, but I have always been nosey.

Besides, you have to die of something.

"Did she say who paid her?" I ask, mostly to play for time.

"No."

My frown deepens. Somebody paid somebody else to deliver an envelope to me—at the soup kitchen. But how could anybody know I would be at the soup kitchen? I did not know myself until an hour ago.

Did I mention it to anybody? I don't think so. I didn't even see anybody as I left the building, other than a random student or two. Did somebody follow me? I shake my head. If Romeo doesn't even know who brought it, I certainly will never figure out who sent it. If the person who delivered it was a female student, well, there are only three thousand of them on the campus, five thousand more at the state university a few miles away.

"Huh," I say intelligently.

Dee Dee shrugs and wanders back downstairs: she has a lunch to run. So Romeo is my only company as I tear open the letter—from the side, not the flap, because there is no need to take chances—and tip the contents into my palm. A cylinder of paper, perhaps two inches long, spills out. No note, nothing written, just this tiny bundle. Adhesive tape winds around it in a sloppy spiral: somebody went to a lot of trouble to protect whatever the paper covers.

"Open it, Pro," says Romeo, like a child on Christmas morning.

I peel off the tape as gracefully as I am able, unwrap the paper, and find, inside, the missing white pawn from my father's hand-turned chess set.

CHAPTER 13

A FAMILIAR FACE

(1)

THE WEIRD PART is that there is nobody to tell. Walking back to the law school as the early November afternoon turns gray and brisk, I am struck by how . . . how *friendless* an existence I have managed to create. I pass the coffeehouses and photocopying shops and trendy little clothing stores that seem to border every campus in America. I pass flurries of undergrads who, despite their proudly proclaimed diversity, look more and more the same. And *think* more and more the same, too, for the range of acceptable campus opinion, on almost every subject, narrows depressingly with each passing year. I pass the jam-packed satellite lots that represent the university's passive-aggressive answer to the problem of campus traffic: make parking hopelessly inconvenient, some faceless bureaucrat has decreed, and most students and employees will leave their cars at home. The endless sea of automobiles parked overtime at the meters on Town Street and Eastern Avenue is the rebuttal of the idea, but a university administration is like an ocean liner: it does not turn swiftly or easily, even when there is ice ahead.

Come to think of it, neither do I.

Twice I take the pawn from my pocket and examine it closely, as though it is likely to mutate at any moment. I suppose I should call the FBI or Cassie Meadows to make some kind of official report, but I am oddly reluctant. I do not feel threatened in any way. The pawn is not a warning. It is a message. I would like some time to work out its meaning.

In whom might I confide? Not Addison. He is hunkering down, unreachable. Not Mariah, who is growing ever crazier on the subject of the Judge's death, and who, were I to call her, would transform the pawn into the symbol of a bullet or a vial of poison.

"Nobody to tell," I mutter to the air.

I cross the chilly campus, head down, hands in the pocket of my threadbare Burberry raincoat. As I reach the Original Quad, as it is called, where the oldest still-extant university buildings stand, I continue to review my meager options. I could talk to Kimmer, perhaps, when she is back from San Francisco, where she is once more doing due diligence with Gerald Nathanson, but I am supposed to be letting the matter die. Or perhaps I could talk to Dear Dana, who would turn it into a joke, or Rob Saltpeter, who would—

I am being followed.

At first I am not sure. The man in the green windbreaker, with the alarmingly familiar face, shows up just as I pass under one of the four stone arches that mark the boundaries of the Original Quad. I stop to say hello to a political scientist whose daughter attends preschool with Bentley. She says something about the construction of the new art museum on the corner, and we both turn to look, and there he is, a few dozen yards away, on the edge of a crowd of students. He makes no effort to hide, but just returns my scrutiny with a straight and watchful stare.

Even at this distance, I am depressingly sure I know who it is: McDermott, no first name offered, the man who pretended to be an FBI agent just two weeks ago in the living room of my father's house on Shepard Street.

First, however, I try to persuade myself that I might be mistaken, because, when I point him out to my friend, he has already disappeared, vanishing as neatly as my monthly paycheck. Just nerves, I tell myself when the political scientist has walked on, but then I spot him again as I reach the poured-concrete blandness of the Science Quad. This time he is in front of me, sitting placidly on the steps of the biology building, his windbreaker across his lap as he reads the campus paper. The strawberry birthmark glows from his hand as he turns a page. Okay, he briefly outwitted me. A nice trick, I admit, but I know the campus and he does not. Not sure what instinct is guiding me, but still thinking, probably, about Freeman Bishop, I decide to avoid him. I will take a shortcut back to the law school and call Cassie Meadows, or perhaps get in touch with the FBI directly. A narrow pedestrian mall between the biology building and the computer center connects the Science Quad to the administration buildings, and I turn sharply into the promenade, then dart between two students and hurry into the side entrance of the computer center, waving my faculty-identification card at the pimply guard, who hardly spares a glance from his *People* magazine. In my own student days, computer science was housed in a dilapidated warehouse on the uneasy border between the campus and the city's poor, before more enlightened (that is, entrepreneurial) university leadership raised a few tens of millions for this new facility. I glance over my shoulder: no McDermott. But he fooled me before. I rush down a false hallway created by shoulder-height partitions separating banks of terminals until I reach the fire stairs. I run up two floors, out of breath now, and emerge among the faculty offices. The professors I pass are all men, all white, and all either bald or wearing hair down to their shoulders—there seems to be no middle ground. They turn skeptical eyes as I hurry past: computer science is about as dark nation–free a major as the university offers (with the possible exception of Slavic literature), and not one of them imagines for an instant that I belong. I turn a corner and reach the glass-and-steel pedestrian bridge that crosses two stories above Lowe Street (the students call it the Low Road) to the physics department, where I take the elevator to the first floor, and emerge on the steps once more.

McDermott, as I predicted, is gone.

I straighten my coat, hitch up my pants, and lean forward for a moment, sucking deep, grateful gusts of clean autumn air. The muscles around my ribs are broadcasting a steady complaint. My thighs are not happy either. My shirt is drenched. It is hard to believe that I ran the 880 in high school—I ran it badly, but I ran it, driven, absurdly, by the need to compete with my athletic younger sister. What Kimmer keeps telling me is right: I have to get back into shape, and basketball once or twice a month with Rob Saltpeter is not enough. Still, although I cannot imagine what McDermott is doing here on campus, I manage a smile over my small victory as I trot down the steps.

But I have actually won nothing, because, as soon as I leave the Science Quad and hasten along Eastern Avenue toward the law school, where I fully intend to call at least the campus police, McDermott falls into stride next to me.

Not my imagination at all.

"I understand you've been looking for me," he says, and I can hear underneath his monotone the pride of a sixtyish man who easily kept pace with a quarry twenty years his junior.

"No, actually, I haven't," I mutter, using my longer legs to stay ahead of him. "It's the FBI—the real one—that's looking for you. They want to put you in prison."

"Yes, I know. I suppose I'm going to have to do something about that." And what scares me enough to make me stop walking is the seriousness of his tone, suggesting that he believes he *can* do something about it.

I turn and face him. "Look, Mr. McDermott, or whatever your name is. I don't want to talk to you. And, just so you know, when I get back to my office, I am going to call the university police and tell them you're dangerous. Then I'm going to call the FBI and tell them that you've been following me."

He nods soberly.

"That's fine," he says, as though giving me permission. "You can do that. But I'm not really following you. I just came to deliver a message."

"I'm not interested." I start to turn away. He puts his hand on my arm. I shake it off. But he has my attention again.

"Professor Garland, listen to me—"

"No, you listen to me." I move a step closer to him. I am at least three inches taller, but he does not seem the least bit intimidated. "You sent me that pawn, didn't you? You took it from my father's house and sent it to me. I want to know why."

"Pawn?"

"You sent me the pawn, and now you're following me to see what I do with it." But even as I say the words, the idea sounds implausible. Why would he think I would want, or know what to do with, a pawn from my father's chess set? I find myself almost persuaded. After all, if he stole the pawn and then had it delivered to me at the soup kitchen, why would he then call attention to himself by showing himself? It sounds like more paranoia, Mariah-style . . . except that the pawn is really in my pocket and McDermott is really here, in the flesh.

"I don't know what you're talking about." He seems sincere, but he seemed just as sincere when he made me believe he was a timeserver with the FBI. "I know there's nothing I can do to make you trust me, but I want you to understand that I'm not your enemy."

"Oh, no, anybody who comes into my house the day after my father's funeral and lies to me is my new best friend."

He closes his eyes briefly, huffs out a long breath, regards me again with that eerily empty gaze. "Professor Garland, I freely admit I am not as clever as you are, and you can no doubt stand here scoring points off me all day. Very well. You don't have to like me, but the fact is, we're on the same side. We both want the same thing."

"Good. Because what I want is for you to leave me alone." I am not usually this silly, or this dismissive, but, having overcome my fear of this man, I am a little bit out of control. I suppose this is what it feels like to be drunk.

He raises a finger into the air, wags it in admonition. "As I said, you are clever. But there is no need for your hostility. We do indeed have a common interest."

I bristle again. I have never liked being called *clever*, especially by residents of the paler nation. It never quite means the same thing as *intelligent* or even *bright*, but carries instead an intimation of a low animal cunning. Perhaps the semiotician in me overreacts in assuming that conversations are racially charged; but so many conversations are.

"I'm not hostile toward you," I flip back. "I just don't like you."

McDermott shrugs, as though to signal that he has survived the dislike of better men than me. "I didn't come all this way to argue with you," he announces. His speech is more fluent than it was at Shepard Street, but his accent is still hard to place. Southern, maybe, with an overlay of . . . something. "I came to tell you that I am sorry you had to get caught up in all this. I never met your father, but I admired him greatly. So I am sorry that my colleague and I had to come to your house with our deception so soon after you buried your father. But it was . . . necessary."

We are blocking the crumbly sidewalk. Students flow past us on either side, their groups breaking up and re-forming as they circumvent the obstacle.

"Necessary for what?"

McDermott puffs out his cheeks, then exhales slowly. His hands are in the pockets of his windbreaker, and he seems more frail than a few minutes ago; it occurs to me that he may be even older than I thought. Which makes it all the more embarrassing that he caught up with me so easily.

"I am a private investigator," he says at last. "I recover things for people. That is what I do for a living. People lose things, they hire me to get them back."

"What kind of things?" I interrupt, unwisely.

"Things like . . . *things*." He waves grandly, as though to encompass the campus in his professional world. "Jewelry, say. Missing persons.

Papers, maybe. That's what I was doing at your house." He nods, warming to his theme. "I was looking for papers."

"Papers."

McDermott glances down the street toward the law school, then focuses on me once more. "Yes, papers. You see, Professor, your father is . . . *was* . . . a lawyer. One of his clients entrusted him with some papers. Some very, very sensitive papers. Your father promised the client the papers would be safe, that he would arrange to have them returned if anything happened to him. That's what he said, that he had made arrangements to return them. Then he died. I'm sorry about that. But he died and the papers didn't come back. So his client hired me to find them. That's all."

"Why couldn't the client just call the firm and ask?"

"I have no idea." I wait, but that seems to be the entire explanation. The answer seems to satisfy him.

"Is your client aware that you broke the law to try to find the papers?"

"My clients do not inquire into my methods. And I am not admitting that I broke the law."

"Are the papers valuable?"

"Only to the client."

"What are they? What's in them?"

"I am not at liberty to say."

"So who's the client?"

"I can't tell you that either."

"You're working for Jack Ziegler, aren't you?"

At last a trace of emotion enters his voice. "Not everything I told you in Washington was untrue. Jack Ziegler *is* scum. And I don't work for scum." And the oddest thing is that, as he says these words, I pick up the faintest whiff, as though by telepathy, of the words *any more.*

"Okay, so why me? You were looking for papers a client gave to my father. Why not talk to my brother or my sister? Why did you come to me?"

"It was the client's suggestion," he says evenly.

"Your client told you to ask me? Why would your client think I would know anything about it?"

"I have no idea, Professor. But I had to give it a try."

I shake my head. "And why all the lying? Why not just come and tell me what you needed and why?"

"Perhaps it was a mistake," concedes the man whose name certainly is not McDermott. He does not seem even slightly uneasy. He even grins a crooked little grin that he has not shown before, and I see once more the pink scar at the corner of his lips, like a wound from a knife-fight. "Again, I am sorry you were bothered at such a sensitive time. But I promise you this. You and your family are perfectly safe. And you will never see me again."

Something in his tone strikes me amiss, as though he is conveying a double meaning. Why is he reassuring me when I have not inquired?

"What are we safe from?"

Again, he gives the matter long consideration, as though trying to figure out what he can reveal. He takes refuge in vaguaries: "From whatever might come."

I do not like this one bit. "And what exactly might come?"

"Anything." His pale, tired eyes are focused on the middle distance. Then his gaze settles on me once more. "Let me tell you something, Professor. You want to hear about pawns? We are small men, you and I. Great men are contesting, even at this moment, and *we* are their pawns. Our likes and dislikes have nothing to do with it. I have been manipulated. You have been manipulated."

"You're making me nervous," I confess.

"I'm trying to do the opposite. I'm trying to reassure you. So I suppose I should apologize again." Once more he flashes the crooked, pink grin. "I am sorry. Truly. I am not your enemy. In fact, we have a common interest, you and I—"

"No, we don't." Anger has finally rescued me from my initial intimidation. I remember my script. "We don't have anything in common. I don't have any reason to trust you. I don't even have any reason to talk to you. So, if you'll excuse me . . ."

"All right, all right." He raises both hands in surrender. "But I still have a job to do. I still have to find those papers."

"Not if I find them first," I snap, unwisely.

Not-McDermott's eyes widen with satisfaction, as though he has at last provoked the reaction he sought. "I hope you do find them, Professor. Truly." A brief nod. "Still, if I could, I would like to ask you one thing." And I know at once, as he means me to, that this entire visit has been for the purpose of raising this one question, whatever it is.

"I'm not interested in any questions you might have."

"It's about your friend Angela."

I pause for a moment, reviewing my rather short list of acquaintances.

"Off the top of my head, I don't think I have a friend Angela." I am still waiting for the question, thinking this is merely the premise; then I realize that the inquiry about Angela *was* the question.

"Thank you," says Not-McDermott. "Now I must go. I will not bother you again."

"Wait a minute—wait." I put a hand on his arm, registering the sudden alarm in his eyes. Like Dana Worth, he does not like to be touched.

"Yes?" He affects a patient tone, but the irritation is plain in his eyes. Having done what he came to do, the sham FBI agent is in a hurry to be free of me.

Well, I am irritated, too. He lies to me in my father's house, he shows up in the middle of the campus to ask me about somebody named Angela, and I still know nothing whatsoever about him.

"Look. I answered your question. If you're so sorry, maybe you can at least answer one for me."

"What question?"

"What's your real name?"

The man in the green jacket, the man whose job is finding lost things, the man whose age is no obstacle to keeping up with me, raises his thin eyebrows in surprise. "To tell you the truth," he says after another commercial break, "I don't think I have one."

He wags that finger at me again, then turns away, ducks into a crowd of students, and disappears.

(11)

I AM TREMBLING when I reach my office.

I am not particularly macho, but I do not scare easily: Garland men are noted, or maybe despised, for our cool.

McDermott scared me.

The reason, I know, is less the mystery surrounding him or his ability to turn up when least expected than what happened to Freeman Bishop. Sergeant Ames was confident that the murder is not connected in any way to my family, but . . .

But McDermott is here.

The fear that ripples through me as I sit at my desk, squeezing my hands together and trying to decide which call to place first, is not the physical fear of what might happen to me. I am worried about my wife and my son. The fact that McDermott went out of his way to assure me that my family is safe has only increased the level of my concern. I have, for the moment, put the magical pawn out of my mind. I have a family to protect.

I decide to pick up Bentley early from his preschool, and I call to ask them to get him ready. Under no circumstances, I add, should they allow him to leave with anybody but my wife or myself. The teachers, predictably, are insulted by my reminding them of their own rules, more attentive to their own egos than to the anxiety of a parent.

Still, one call down.

Next, I call one of the FBI agents who interviewed me the day after McDermott's visit to Shepard Street and told me to get in touch if I heard anything more, a thick, breezy man named Nunzio. I reach his voice mail and leave a message, then call his beeper and his cell phone, both of which he inked onto his card. There is no answer on the cell phone, and I leave my number on the beeper.

Think.

I consider and reject reaching the campus police: what exactly would I ask them to do?

The most sensible remaining option is to call Uncle Mal, but I am reluctant to do it. I have spoken to him twice in the last week, seeking updates on the Bishop investigation, and I have gained the strong impression that he has begun to tolerate me rather than listen to me: he does, after all, have actual paying work to do, and constantly indulging the implausible fears of the son of his dead partner has probably begun to press the limits of his beneficence. The second time I called, he suggested thinly that I might get in touch with Meadows for such "routine matters" as these. His time is tight just now, he said, and he will be handling only issues surrounding my wife's possible nomination. Perhaps it is just as well. I am tired of asking him for favors: one thing my father drummed into us repeatedly was that we must avoid the mistake of so many members of the darker nation who spend their lives going hat in hand to powerful white folks for help.

Yet I have no alternative.

I have just lifted the receiver to telephone Corcoran & Klein when Dorothy Dubček, my mothering secretary, buzzes me to say that Agent Nunzio is on the phone.

"Just talking to a friend of yours," he says in his gruff way, not bothering to ask what I called about. "Bonnie Ames."

I am a moment catching up. I have never been much good with names. Kimmer says I am just unfriendly; Dear Dana says it is genetic, calling it my "social orientation"; and Rob Saltpeter says remembering names is not so important if we honor God in everybody we meet.

Rob's answer is my favorite, but Kimmer knows me best.

"Bonnie Ames?" I repeat, stupidly.

"Sure, Sergeant Ames. You met her."

"Oh! Sure." A pause as each of us waits for the other. I blink first. "So, uh, what were you talking to her about?"

He lapses into cop-speak: "She informed me that they have apprehended a suspect."

"What?"

"In the murder of Freeman Bishop."

"Oh! Who was it?"

"Some drug dealer."

"You're kidding." Soothing relief unexpectedly flows through me at the realization that it was not after all McDermott who did the deed; a moment later, a shuddery wave of shame replaces it. Still: it was not McDermott.

"The Bureau does not allow kidding."

"Very funny."

"She wants you to call her. Wants to give you the details herself." He rattles off her number, which I already have. "What did you beep me about?"

The brusque change of subject sets me back for an instant. The urgency of my original call suddenly seems less—but not to Agent Nunzio. Once I tell him that I saw McDermott, he zips through a series of questions, nailing down everything from the color of the fake agent's shoes to the direction he took when he left. He is unsatisfied by my answers. He asks me if I really think McDermott traveled all the way to Elm Harbor just to ask me if I have a friend named Angela. I tell him it certainly seems that way. He asks me if I can think of any reason McDermott would think I have a friend named Angela, and I admit I am aware of none. He asks me if in fact I have a friend named Angela, and I tell him I cannot think of one. He asks me to call him if I happen to remember one, and I tell him I will.

"It could be important," Nunzio warns me.

"I figured that out for myself."

"I don't want you to worry, Professor Garland," he adds, unexpectedly expansive. "If McDermott is really some kind of private investigator, I'm sure we'll track him down, and we'll track his client down too. Those guys are a nuisance, but I'm sure he's harmless."

"How do you know that?" I ask, my earlier nervousness sharpening my tone. I am not reassured by the fact that McDermott said roughly the same thing: *You and your family are perfectly safe . . . from whatever might come.* I have the sense that everybody else shares some crucial bit of knowledge that I have been denied. Yet the fact that Freeman Bishop's murderer is under arrest makes me feel safer . . . safer for my family. A little bit, anyway. "If you haven't found him, how do you know he's harmless?"

"Because we see this type all the time. They lie to get information, they follow people, they weasel this and that. But that's all they do." A hesitation. "Unless, of course, you have some kind of evidence to the contrary. About McDermott, I mean."

"No."

"You've told me everything?"

"Yes." As I did in my meeting with Sergeant Ames, I have the sense of being under interrogation, but I have no idea for what.

"Well, then, it's like I said." Winding up. "You have nothing to worry about. You can go on with . . . well, whatever you're doing."

"Agent Nunzio . . ."

"Fred is fine."

"Fred. Fred, look. You're down in Washington. I'm up here. McDermott is here. I would be lying if I didn't admit, that, uh . . ."

"You're worried."

"Yes."

"I understand. But my resources are a little bit limited. And, well, it's not as if this McDermott character has threatened you. . . ."

"No, he just dropped by to impersonate an FBI agent."

I can almost hear him thinking, not only logistics, but politics: who owes what to whom and for what.

"Tell you what. I really don't think you should be worried. I want to emphasize that. But, if it will make you feel better, I'll make a couple of calls. We don't have much of an office up there, but I'll see what I can do. Maybe have the police take some extra cruises by your house till we track McDermott down."

I know I am being mollified, and I also know there is little reason to worry, but I am grateful all the same.

"I'd appreciate it."

"My pleasure, Professor." A pause. "Oh, and I hope things work out for your wife."

Only after we have hung up does it occur to me that I did not tell him about the pawn. But, then, perhaps I never meant to.

(III)

WHICH LEAVES ME BONNIE AMES.

Having acquired a first name, the sergeant is less daunting. Still, once I track her down, she is so brusque that I marvel she asked me to call in the first place. Either she is still feeling Uncle Mal's pressure or she is feeding a need to gloat over just how far wrong our suspicions were. The arrests in the "torture slaying" (as the reporters are calling it) of Father Freeman Bishop were made early this morning, she says: no Klansmen, no skinheads, no neo-Nazis, and no fake FBI agents either, but a Landover, Maryland, crack dealer, a small-timer—a nobody, the sergeant calls him—a twenty-two-year-old named Sharik Deveaux, street name Conan, and a member of his crew. Even as I listen to her account, I am skimming the story on the *USA Today* Web site. Sergeant Ames takes particular pleasure in informing me that Conan is black, which I already guessed. "So, no possible racial motive"—as though it was I, rather than the media, who proposed one. Mr. Deveaux, the detective continues, admits selling the precious little rocks to Father Bishop on a regular basis. Naturally, he denies the murder. But the other gangbanger—the sergeant's word—says he helped Conan dispose of the body once the ugly deed was done, and somebody else heard Conan bragging about it. "And he has a history of this kind of thing," she adds without elaboration.

For the barest instant, I see it happening: Freeman Bishop, bound or gagged or in some manner restrained as the two of them burn and cut and stab his twisting, helpless form, his desperate pain the very purpose of the exercise, his faith finally tested on the wretched rack of swiftly nearing oblivion: *Between thy judgment and our souls.* At that instant when the end is inexorable, we all of us, believers and agnostics, sinners and saints, discover what we truly embrace, what we truly know, what we truly *are*. What would I, with my shaky and intermittent faith, at that instant become? Better to suppress those thoughts.

"Is this going to stand up in court?" I ask timidly.

Sergeant Ames is more amused than annoyed. The case is overwhelming, she assures me, but it will never come to that. Sooner or later, she says, Deveaux will allow his lawyer to persuade him to plead guilty to avoid the death penalty.

"Does Maryland execute murderers?"

"Not often. But Mr. Deveaux was stupid enough to kill Father Bishop in Virginia. He just rolled into town to dump the body."

"Why?"

"You'd have to ask him that. And don't even think about actually trying."

"What sentence would he get? If he pleads guilty, I mean?"

"Life without parole is the best he can hope for. If he wants a trial down in Virginia? Something like this? They'll probably give him the needle."

Her casual confidence is chilling. "And you're sure he did it? You're very sure?"

"No, down here we try to arrest people at random. Especially for murder. We worry later on about making the evidence stick. Isn't that what they teach up in the Ivy League?"

"I didn't mean any disrespect . . ."

"He did it, Mr. Garland. He did it."

"Thank you for . . ."

"I have to run. Say hello to your sister for me."

I call Mariah to share my relief that the killing of Freeman Bishop had nothing to do with the Judge, and the housekeeper (not to be confused with either the au pair or the cook) tells me that my sister is back down in Washington. I call her cell phone and leave a message. I try Shepard Street, but there is no answer. Maybe it is just as well that I cannot reach her: she would likely tell me that the arrest is a setup, part of the conspiracy. So I try Addison in Chicago and, to my surprise, actually reach him at his townhouse in Lincoln Park. He is more saddened than delighted by the news. He whispers something I do not quite follow about the Hindu god Varuna, drops in a quotation from Eusebius, and warns me to take no pleasure in the pains of others, even those who sin. When it is finally my turn to speak, I assure him that I am taking no pleasure in any of this, but Addison tells me he has no more time to talk just now, because he has to catch a plane, which is probably a lie. I suspect, on no evidence other than history, that there is a woman in his bed. Maybe Beth Olin, although two weeks would be a long time for my brother to stick with the same girlfriend.

"We should get together soon," he murmurs so solemnly that I almost think he means it. "Call me next time you're in the Midwest."

"You never return my calls." The plaintive younger brother.

"My people must misplace the messages. I'm sorry, Misha." *My people*. If only Kimmer could hear that one.

"Actually, there are a few things I'd like to talk to you about," I persist.

"Right, right. Listen, my brother, I'm kind of in a hurry. I'll call you later."

Then Addison is gone—perhaps his people have arrived to take him to the airport. I have no opportunity to mention that most of the messages I leave are at his home.

CHAPTER 14

VARIOUS FREEDOMS OF SPEECH

(1)

AFTER LUNCH ON TUESDAYS, I meet with the members of my seminar on Legal Regulation of Institutional Structure. The seminar covers everything from securities regulation to canon law to the rules that govern student-council elections, always playing the semiotic game, trying to figure out not what each rule means, but what it signifies, and how that signal is related to the purpose of the institution. The course draws some of the brightest students in the law school, and probably I enjoy it more than any other class I teach. This afternoon features a delightful, good-natured clash between two of my favorites, brilliant if slightly addled Crysta Smallwood, still struggling to figure out when the paler nation race is going to expire, and the equally talented Victor Mendez, whose father, a Cuban émigré, is a power in Republican politics, which probably puts him to the left of Victor himself. I play referee as Victor and Crysta contend across the seminar table over the question of whether sexual harassment represents a failing of institutions or of individuals. When I finally call time as the class ends at four, I award the round to Crysta on points. Crysta grins. The dozen other students laugh and pound her on the back. I remind them that we will not meet next week because I will be in Washington at a conference, and admonish them to turn in the first drafts of their term papers to my secretary before I return. With students of this caliber, there is no whimper of complaint.

Oh, but there are days when I love teaching!

I trip happily up the stairs to Dorothy Dubček's office, where I collect messages and faxes, then bounce down to my own little corner of the law school. Outside my office, I trumpet a cheery hello to aging Amy Hefferman, my Oldie neighbor, who was in law school with my father. She blinks her tired eyes and tells me that Dean Lynda is looking for me, and I nod as though impressed. Safely inside, I toss everything onto my desk while I check my voice mail. Nothing important. A reporter, with a question, miraculously, about tort law, not the Judge. American Express—I am late again. And one of Lynda Wyatt's assistants: the Dean, as Amy mentioned, wants to speak to me, presumably about Kimmer's competition with Marc Hadley. No thanks. Instead, I call the day-care center to make sure Bentley is okay, and the head teacher's irritation blasts through the telephone. I smile at her annoyance: as long as she is angry, my son is doing fine.

My mood surprises me. I should, by rights, be dispirited. It is one week since my encounter with Not-McDermott, one week since the delivery of the pawn to me at the soup kitchen, one week since the arrest of Sharik Deveaux. Five days ago Kimmer came home from San Francisco and lovingly calmed me down. I am jumping at shadows, she murmured, kissing me gently. I have to look at things rationally, she said, cooking me a nice dinner. If the pawn was really a message and not somebody's tasteless joke, then whoever sent it will tell me sooner or later what it means, she whispered, head on my shoulder, as we sat up together and watched an old movie. What is there to be afraid of? she asked me softly as we lay in the darkness of our bedroom, surprisingly comfortable together. The murderer is in jail, and McDermott, who has come and gone, has been declared harmless by the Federal Bureau of Investigation. Day after day Kimmer has repeated the same arguments. She has been both comforting and persuasive. I have gone from frightened to worried to merely concerned. I have been trying to reach serene. I have been trying not to suspect that the real reason my wife wants me to relax is in order to keep her potential judgeship on track.

Nothing can quite drag me down. The weather has turned fair: temperatures in the fifties, and here it is the middle of a New England autumn. My mood has lifted along with the temperature. Today, for the first time since the death of the Judge, I am actually feeling like a law professor. I am enjoying the classroom; and so, it seems, are my students. (Except for Avery Knowland, whose attendance at my torts class has grown spotty and who has largely ceased to participate. I need to do something about him.) I remember that I chose this profession more than it chose me, and that I have been reasonably successful at it.

I am actually humming a bit of Ellington as I turn to the message slips and discover that one of my favorite people in the world, John Brown, has been trying to get in touch with me. John, a college classmate who now teaches engineering out at Ohio State, is the steadiest man I know. I call him back at once, hoping to hear the details of the visit he and his wife and children will be making to Elm Harbor in a few weeks. We exchange a few pleasantries, he tells me how much his family is looking forward to their stay with us, and then he discloses the reason for his call: an FBI agent dropped in yesterday, doing a background check for a possible "high-ranking federal appointment" for my wife. John wants to know what it is all about, and why he and his wife, Janice, have to be the last to know.

The only trouble is, Mallory Corcoran has assured me that the background check has not yet begun. The day that has been so peaceful and bright begins to turn dreary once more.

"John, listen. This is important. Please tell me that the agent who interviewed you was not named McDermott."

My old friend laughs. "Not to worry, Misha. It wasn't Mc-anything. I'm pretty sure he said his name was Foreman."

I try not to alarm him. I tease out a few details, suppressing the hollow feeling in the pit of my stomach. I cannot lie to John. I tell him that the man called Foreman is not really with the FBI, that he is some kind of private investigator, and that he is breaking the law by pretending otherwise. I tell him that the real FBI will probably want to talk to him, because they are looking for Foreman. I wait for John to turn chilly on me, but instead he asks if I am in some kind of trouble. I tell him I doubt it. I promise to explain what I can when he and his wife come visit. When we finally hang up, I put my face in my hands, feeling the weight of depression pressing down on my shoulders. I sit shaking my head, wondering how I could have been stupid enough to think it was all over.

And that is where Mariah tracks me down, still at my desk, to tell me the exciting news about the way the Judge was murdered.

(1 1)

"BULLET FRAGMENTS," I repeat, making sure I have heard my sister correctly.

"That's right, Tal."

"In the Judge's head."

"Right."

"Fragments that the autopsy somehow overlooked." I am clicking frantically with my mouse, trying to find the Web site Mariah is describing over the telephone with such gusto. This is the last thing I need. There are about eleven hundred things I would rather be doing just now, but, as Rob Saltpeter likes to say, obligation to family is non-refundable.

"On purpose, Tal." Mariah is suddenly impatient. "Not by accident. They didn't want us to know. They didn't want anybody to know."

"*They* in this case being . . ."

"I don't know. That's why I think we need some help."

"So why wasn't there any blood in the house?" I am proud of myself for asking a reasonably intelligent question. The quarrel with Mariah has at least distracted me from the possibility that McDermott and Foreman are still on the loose.

"They cleaned it up."

Of course.

"Or moved the body," I suggest facetiously, but Mariah takes it at face value.

"Exactly! There's lots of possibilities."

The university loves investing in its science departments, but the law school's cut-rate technology includes ancient computers, and the download of the supposed photographs of my father's autopsy is taking forever. I need to hurry, because it is almost time to pick up Bentley from his preschool. I mentioned this to Mariah, who told me that her news would only take a minute. Still waiting for the computer, I stand up and stretch. For the past two weeks, I have been listening to my big sister's ever-wilder theories about what actually happened. Despite an unambiguous autopsy result, Mariah continues to insist that so many powerful people wanted the Judge out of the way that some combination of them is bound to have brought him down. She has been reading up on drugs that can cause heart attacks. For a few days it was potassium-chloride poisoning: the medical examiner did not search properly for needle marks. Then it was prussic acid: the ME did not do an oxygen-saturation test. Each time it turns out that she is wrong, my sister comes up with something else. And, when pressed, she almost always concedes that her source is some Internet site. I remember something that Addison, proprietor of several sites, likes to say about the Web: *One-third retail, one-third porn, and one-third lies, all of our baser nature in one quick stop.*

"What kind of help do you think we need?" I ask her now.

"There are lots of people who want to help," Mariah proclaims happily, if cryptically. "Lots and lots of people." I grimace, wondering what has been going through her head as she sits all day with all those children in her palace, as Kimmer calls it, in Darien. Mariah has probably received the same bizarre calls I have, a variety of hard-right organizations dedicated to demonstrating conspiracies whenever they lose, and, certainly, when one of their most valuable assets is so prosaically struck down. Real men are murdered. Heart attacks are for wimps.

"What exactly do they want to do, kiddo?"

"Well, for one thing, they are going to run newspaper ads calling for an investigation."

"Great. When do they plan to go public with that brilliant idea?" Hoping that I can get Uncle Mal or some other of my father's wiser Washington acquaintances to prevent it.

"Don't take that tone, Tal. Wait until you see the pictures." A beat. "Have you looked at them yet?"

"In a minute." I return to my chair. "When is the announcement, Mariah?"

"Soon," she murmurs, no longer sure I am an ally.

"Mariah, you know . . . Okay, hold on." The download is at last complete, four rather gory photographs, and I see no reason to think that any one of them is authentic. Three of the four do not show the face of the corpse, but the build does not resemble the Judge. Nor does the skin color, in every case too dark. The one that clearly is my father is sufficiently grainy that it is not clear why it is even there, which conspiracy it is supposed to prove. I frown and lean closer, pushing my glasses up onto my nose with a finger. One of the nonfacial shots does indeed show the black specks that Mariah called to tell me about. I suppose they could be bullet fragments, if I knew how bullet fragments look. Only . . . wait . . .

"Mariah."

"Hmmm?"

"Mariah, I think . . . couldn't that just be dirt on the lens?"

"See? That's the same thing the medical examiner said."

I remind myself that Mariah is my big sister and I love her. "Mariah, kiddo, please tell me you didn't ask the ME about this."

"Oh, no, Tal, of course not."

"Good."

"I didn't have to ask. Her statement is in this morning's paper."

Oh, great. In the newspaper. The Judge must be spinning in his grave. I wonder if Kimmer has heard. "Well, if the ME says it was just dust . . ."

"You can't believe *her.*"

"Why not?"

"Well, for one thing, she's a Democrat."

The thing is, Mariah isn't joking.

So, glancing at my watch, I say what I know she wants me to say. "I'll call Uncle Mal and ask him to look into it." Not telling her that the great Mallory Corcoran hardly ever takes my calls any more, which means that I will be kicked down the ladder to Cassie Meadows. Or that Meadows herself is probably tired of me too, and will likely spend no more than one phone call on the matter.

I am hoping that is all it is worth.

(III)

To MY SURPRISE, not only is Meadows free to talk, but she has good news: the FBI has tracked down the mysterious McDermott. He is, indeed, a private investigator, based down in South Carolina. He has been bothering people who knew my father, especially around Washington, asking about a woman named Angela. He is well known to his local sheriff, who considers him persistent and perhaps a bit underhanded, but certainly not dangerous. He even has a real name, but the Bureau would not tell Meadows what it is.

"Why wouldn't they tell you?"

She hesitates, wanting to be a Washington player like Mallory Corcoran, and thus loath to admit that she is outside certain circles of knowledge. "They said we didn't need to know," she finally confesses.

"Did they say why?"

Another pause. "I didn't ask, to tell you the truth. Maybe I should have pressed. . . ."

"It doesn't matter." I sketch for her the substance of John Brown's call. "Did they tell you anything about Foreman?"

"Foreman works for him. He's some kind of private investigator too, and, yes, Mr. Garland, he is also considered harmless."

At last I allow myself a ripple of relief. "Anything else?"

"Only that the two of them have fled the jurisdiction. Left the United States. They apparently heard the FBI was looking for them and headed for Canada."

"Canada? What is the FBI after them for, that they would go to Canada?"

"That's what they told me."

Puzzled but relieved, I remember why I called in the first place. I tell Meadows about Mariah and her bullet fragments. Meadows laughs.

"What's funny?" I glance at my watch, worry about my son waiting.

"I'll add it to the file."

"What file?"

"Mr. Corcoran had me open a file for stuff like this. We've got every nutty letter, every Internet posting, every right-wing pamphlet, every wild talk-show host's theory about your father. It's a very thick file, Mr. Garland." Another chuckle. "We already have lots of alleged autopsy photographs in there."

"So what's the funny part?"

"Oh, well. I have a whole subfile full of e-mails from your sister." Meadows lowers her voice. "I haven't even bothered Mr. Corcoran with them."

"You've . . . heard from Mariah?"

"Would you believe twice a week?" Another laugh, except that this one is humorless. "I guess she figures, you know, being as how she's Mr. Corcoran's goddaughter and all . . ." Meadows trails off, then adopts a more serious tone: "Somebody has to do something about her, Mr. Garland. My friends on the Hill tell me that if she doesn't cut this stuff out . . . well, your wife won't stand a chance."

CHAPTER 15

TWO ENCOUNTERS

(1)

BENTLEY! HOME! Two of my favorite words!

I arrive twenty minutes late to pick up my son because of my time on the phone with my sister, and I endure the unemotive glares of the teachers—all women, all white—whose grim silence informs me that they are prepared to call the Department of Family Services to report the Garland-Madison team as far too frequently tardy and therefore unfit to parent. I take some solace, however, from the fact that Miguel Hadley is still there, too, his parents therefore every bit as unfit as Bentley's. Miguel, a pudgy little boy, is an amazingly bright child but never an ebullient one. He seems particularly solemn today. He hugs Bentley to say goodbye. The school encourages hugging between boys in the service of some unarticulated ideological goal—making sure they don't grow up to be the kind of men who drop bombs on innocent civilians, perhaps. But I am not sure why the teachers bother. University kids are far more likely to grow up to be the kind of men who sit in the White House ordering others to drop the bombs, in between hugging their constituents.

Standing off to the side, waiting for the two little boys to finish their embrace (the school preaches that we mere parents should never separate them by force), I gaze out the window toward the parking lot, hoping, through this device, to avoid having to make small talk with the teachers who staff the school. They are hopelessly well-meaning, in the manner of white liberals of their class, but because they believe they have transcended racism (which afflicts only conservatives) they remain blissfully unaware of how their disdainful elitism is perceived by the few black parents who can afford the school. Nor is there any point in enlightening them: their desperately sincere apologies would only make matters worse, signaling, as liberal apologies tend to, that the members of the darker nation are so weak of character that there can be no greater sin than insulting one.

White liberals, of course, believe themselves to be made of stronger stuff. That is why they so often support rules punishing nasty comments made by whites about blacks but readily forgive nasty comments made by blacks about whites.

I shake my head, struggling against the angry red direction of my musings. Does any of this diatribe actually represent what I believe? I scratch at the fading outline of a flower sticker in the corner of the window, wondering why these teachers, with their cultlike grins of welcome to every dark face, bring out the worst in me. And why I condemn liberals alone. The racial attitudes of conservatives are no better; often they are worse. These teachers, for all the arrogance of their sympathy, are not the ones scrawling *KKK* with cheap paint on the lockers of black high-school students or sending money to the National Association for the Advancement of White People. What is the source of my vitriol? Is it possible that I am just recalling, albeit dimly, some furious article or speech by the Judge? Odd how difficult it is becoming to tell the difference, as though my father, in death, owns more of my mind than he ever did in life.

I wonder whether I will ever escape him.

As I brood in the corner, waiting for the teachers to decide that Bentley has learned his anti-war, anti-macho, pro-hugging lesson for the day, I notice a trapezoidal black Mercedes minivan streaking and thumping across the potholes of the pitted lot. Dahlia Hadley, Miguel's mother, has arrived in her usual heedless rush. She bustles inside, a tiny, slender whirlwind of smile and energy, and the teachers, so unnerved by my presence, begin to beam again, because everybody loves Dahlia; it's like a rule.

"Talcott," she murmurs breathily, as soon as she has waved to her son, "I am *so* glad you are here. I was thinking of calling you. Do you have a minute?"

"Of course," I say, certain that something unpleasant is coming.

Dahlia takes my large hand in her small one and draws me off to another corner of the long room, where wooden blocks lie helter-skelter, sloppiness passing as juvenile creativity.

"It has to do with our *mutual* concern," she says, glancing around.

Her indigo jeans and matching sweater are a little showy, but that is Dahlia. "Do you know what I am talking about, Talcott?"

Of course I know, but I am still free to pretend that I do not, because the *Elm Harbor Clarion*, no whiz at digging up stories unrelated to municipal corruption (of which our fine city has plenty), has yet to run the obligatory article on the finalists for the seat on the court of appeals. But I decide not to play games.

"Ah . . . I think so."

She hesitates, then meets my eyes and smiles again. Dahlia Hadley is in her early thirties, a raucous, hennaed Bolivian even Kimmer, in spite of her best efforts, cannot help liking. Marc and Dahlia met, Dahlia points out whenever somebody will listen, *after* his first marriage was on the rocks. (But *before* he left his wife, Kimmer adds savagely.) Marc's first wife was Margaret Story, a very distinguished historian a year older than he, with whom he had two children, the younger of whom is Heather, now a student at the law school, and the older of whom is Rick, a poet often published in *The New Yorker*, who lives in California. Margaret was broad and quiet and distant, even forbidding, whereas Dahlia is slim and loud and gregarious and loves to tease. But she is no mere trophy. Although she lacks a full-time academic appointment (which, in a university, makes her a citizen of the second class), she possesses a doctorate in biochemistry from MIT and, supported by various corporate grants, labors in some obscure corner of the Science Quad, testing unlikely cures for unknown diseases, passionately killing lab rats by the hundreds. The greatest threats to the impoverished, according to Dahlia, who has been one of them, are neither political nor military nor economic but biological: scientific progress and nature alike are constantly releasing new microbes into the ecosystem, and it is the poor they usually kill first and fastest. Dahlia believes that justice will be found at the bottom of a test tube. Once a group of animal-rights activists invaded her laboratory, smashing reagents, releasing contagious rodents from their cages, and spreading dangerous germs. Most of the staff fled, but Dahlia stood her ground and called the protesters racists, which first confused and then defeated them. The leader of the group, struggling to respond, made things worse, drawing an awkward analogy between the situation of the rats and the situation of the people in the barrios. He evidently assumed that Dahlia, whose skin is the red-brown of desert clay, was Mexican American. She corrected him furiously in two languages. The campus police arrived while the leader was struggling to explain his solidarity with the oppressed people of Bolivia—which, unfortunately for his argument, happens to be a democracy.

Later, Dahlia testified at the trial. She talked about the experiments he wrecked, the people who might die: not testimony that would ordinarily be admissible, but the prosecutor pretended Dr. Hadley was merely describing the damage, and the judge went along. Dahlia drew plenty of hate mail from people who love animals more than they do human beings, but won a substantial increase in the grant from the pharmaceutical company that backs her research.

Dahlia is a wise woman.

"This is not an easy *time* for us," she says now, and I find myself wondering briefly, and foolishly, whether she might after all have pulled me aside to discuss another subject, whether perhaps Ruthie has kept confidential what is confidential and not told Marc that his main rival for the post he craves is my wife—or, if she has told him, whether Marc might have kept it secret from his wife. Dahlia herself answers my unspoken question, saying, almost casually: "You know, Tal, the FBI has started to bother all our friends. I guess it must be the same for you."

"Oh, yes, right," I mumble, quite taken by surprise, and now forced to wonder why no friends have called us to share the same news, other than John Brown's call about Foreman, which obviously doesn't count. Maybe the FBI has made no visits. Certainly no agents—no real agents—have been by to talk to Kimmer herself. Have they interviewed Marc? If so, the fight presumably is already over . . . and with it, possibly, my marriage.

"Marc is very tense just now," Dahlia whispers. "How is Kimberly holding up?"

"Hmmm? Oh, fine, fine."

Miguel calls out to his mother in Spanish. Dahlia half turns in his direction and says *"En un minuto, querido,"* but does not release my hand. She glances at the teachers, all of whom have been watching, all of whom now pointedly look away. She pulls me farther into the corner. She seems not to want to be overheard. The teachers are probably wondering what kind of tête-à-tête they are observing. Most people consider Dahlia quite an attractive woman, but I find her features too soft and undefined, and her ambition far too openly worn, for true beauty.

"It's just so hard to get any news," she pouts. "Have you heard anything?"

And then I have it—and am stunned. Marc doesn't know any more than we do. All of Dahlia's clumsy pumping is a fishing expedition on her husband's behalf. It isn't over at all! I want to laugh aloud, so great is my relief. But I control my instincts and, as usual, my facial expression.

"Not a word, Dahlia." I have seen very little of Marc these past weeks: nothing more than an occasional tense hello as we pass in the hallway. I decide to do a little investigating of my own. "I guess we'll all have to wait."

Dahlia does not seem to hear. She looks up at me again. She is no longer smiling. "Do you know Ruth Silverman?" Not *Ruthie*, I notice.

"Yes, I know her."

Dahlia closes her eyes briefly. There is a girlish innocence about the gesture. Out in the parking lot, a couple of fathers are in the midst of a loud dissing match over the relative merits of the Jets and the Giants. I want to be a part of their universe, not Dahlia's.

"Well, she was Marc's *student*. He got her her *job*. But she is so ungrateful. She will not tell us anything." She shakes her head. Across the room, the restless teachers are casting surreptitious glances in our direction and irritated glances at the clock. Very likely marveling at what they take to be our intimacy, in a hurry to get home to gossip to spouses, lovers, friends, because Elm Harbor, for all its Ivy League sophistication, is nothing but a small town. *You'll never guess who I saw together at school today!* I realize I am oversensitive to appearances, but my history with Kimmer has left me with that burden. "Marc keeps telling me that she has an obligation to keep quiet, but I was raised to believe you return a favor for a favor." She has released my hand. She is gritting her perfect teeth and making fists. I notice that her nails are bitten so deeply that the flesh is fiery pink.

"Marc is right, Dahlia. Ruthie—Ruth can't talk about her work."

"It is just all so sudden," she explains, which I take to mean that Ruthie revealed confidences to Marc earlier but, for some reason, has now stopped. Dahlia's next words confirm my suspicion. "Three weeks ago, Marc was the leading candidate. That is what Ruth Silverman said. Then she told us that the President was looking at other names, in the interest of *diversity*." Emphasizing the word in a way that suggests how little it should count when anything real is at stake. Last year, I greatly upset the students in my seminar on Law and Social Movements by suggesting to them the following proposition: *Any white person who truly believes in affirmative action should be willing to pledge that, if his or her child is admitted to a Harvard or a Princeton, he or she will at once write to the school saying, "My child will not be attending. Please hold the slot for a member of a minority group."* The consternation among my students confirmed my belief that few white people, even among the most liberal, support affirmative action when it actually costs them something. They like it precisely because they can tell themselves that they are working for racial justice while pretending that the costs do not exist. But it is not their fault: who believes in sacrifice these days?

Diversity, I am now thinking. Ordinarily a word so empty of content that everybody can sign on without agreeing to anything, but, in this case, doubtless a code for Kimberly Madison. Which Marc must realize and, obviously, Dahlia as well. My wife's chances are better than I thought, better than Kimmer hoped . . . if we can just manage to keep the lid on everything else. An image of Jerry Nathanson drifts across my mind, and I stifle a surge of anger at my wife, less for violating her vows than for taking such a risk with so much at stake.

"I'm sure the President will pick the person he thinks will be the best judge," I say, even though no President in history has actually selected judges that way.

"I don't know," says Dahlia—but, then, of course, she thinks that Marc would be the best judge. Never mind that he has never practiced law a day in his life. "To tell you the truth, Tal, Marc has . . . not been himself."

"I'm sorry, Dahlia."

"This is not like him, missing his son's party," she continues. She somewhere lapsed from the interrogative mode into the confessional, but I am not sure when. She notices my distraction. "You remember, last Sunday? Miguel's birthday?"

I do remember. I had to take Bentley to the party, because Kimmer, who had promised our son she would be there, had to fly to San Francisco on Sunday morning. My wife and I fought about that, as we fight about so many things. And I remember, too, that Marc was absent. Dahlia made excuses for him: he had to attend a conference in Miami, she said, something about Cardozo. I noticed even at the time that she did not seem particularly happy about it.

"I'm sorry." Just something to say.

Dahlia gazes at the dying brown carpet. Tears glisten in her dark eyes. "Usually Marc is so loving. With me and with Miguelito. But now the tension . . ." She shakes her head once more. "He has grown short-tempered. He will not talk to me."

I do not know what has prompted Dahlia to open this window on the private life of the Hadley family, but it is not a burden I want to bear. Unfortunately, I continue to take refuge in inanities: "It's a tough time for everybody," I disclose.

Dahlia is hardly listening. "You are lucky, Tal. Kimberly is young. If it does not happen for her this time, there is another time. But so much in Marc's life has not been what he hoped it would. All the writing he has not . . . managed to complete. I worry about what will happen to him if this position goes to somebody else. I'm scared for him."

So that's the game. *Marc is going to jump if he doesn't get it, and Kimmer will have another shot, so, pretty please, won't you make your wife withdraw?* Desperate indeed! I remember Stuart Land's complaint that Marc has not been attending to his work because he is so upset . . . and his comment that he could help Kimmer in Washington. Perhaps he did.

"It isn't easy for any of us. I'm sure it'll come out the way it's supposed to." A little unfeeling, I guess, but how can Dahlia Hadley think it is my job to reassure her?

Dahlia refuses to give up. "You do not understand, Talcott. This is not just jitters. Marc is worried. Yes, that is the word. He is worried, Talcott. He will not tell me what is on his mind. We have always shared everything, ever since we have been together, and now he is keeping something from me. And it is . . . eating him." She shakes her head, waving her hand vaguely toward her son, who is drawing a picture with Bentley. "It is wrecking my family, Talcott."

I am not sure how to respond, but I want to say the right thing, my sense that it is not my place to comfort her blasted from my mind by the sudden exposure of her pain. Maybe Dahlia is not manipulating me. Maybe she really is worried about her husband. Maybe there is really something to worry about.

"I'm sorry, Dahlia," I say at last, patting her shoulder. "I really am."

She clutches my jacket, and, for a scary moment, her head bobs forward, as though she is about to rest it on my chest. Then Dahlia stiffens, less in anger than in embarrassment: she let the conversation get away from her and, belatedly, is concerned about what the wide-eyed teachers must be thinking.

"Oh, Talcott, I am sorry too." Standing straight once more, no longer holding my hand, she is wiping her nose with a handkerchief. There are tears on her face, but I did not see them begin. "It is not right to burden you. Go and get your boy, take him home, and hug him. That makes everything better."

"You do the same, Dahlia. And don't worry."

"Or you. And thank you." Still sniffling. "You're a kind man." Spoken as though she does not meet a lot of them.

I walk heavily across the room to get my son. The teachers step away, making a path: my furtive chat with Dahlia has transformed me into a celebrity.

Strapping a sleepy Bentley into the car seat he has probably outgrown, I glance back at the school I am beginning to hate. Miguel and his mother are in the doorway, holding hands. Dahlia, evidently herself once more, is chatting with one of the teachers, making her laugh. Miguel waves haughtily, very much his father's son. As I steer around the potholes, bumping the undercarriage of the Camry no more than three or four times, I marvel at the vicissitudes of fortune. If McDermott has truly fled to Canada, and if Conan Deveaux truly killed Freeman Bishop, then Kimmer is right: it is time for me to stop worrying. It is just a matter of getting my sister to stop all the conspiracy nonsense. If Addison will help, maybe I can.

The skeleton, I remind myself exultantly, as sharp memories of Jack Ziegler's sickly face swim upward into my consciousness. Marc is worried about the skeleton.

(11)

FIVE MINUTES LATER, I pull the Camry into the driveway of our twelve-room Victorian in the heart of the faculty ghetto. We are, as Kimmer often reminds me, surrounded by the law school on all sides. Dear Dana Worth lives two blocks farther along Hobby Road, around the corner is Tish Kirschbaum, our token feminist, and Peter Van Dyke, our token fascist—these are Kimmer's nicknames, not mine—is right across the street. Theo Mountain's back yard abuts Peter's. Four more faculty members live within an additional three-block radius. Once the mansions of Hobby Hill were hideously expensive, available to only the most senior professors in the university, and only those among them who came from money. But the Elm Harbor housing market has been soft now for close to fifteen years running, and youngish professors in the financially advantaged schools—law, medicine, and business—have purchased the huge homes once reserved for the masters of Mencius and Shakespeare and the curvature of space.

Still—home! Number 41 Hobby Road is a massive house, built at the end of the nineteenth century, with wide rooms and high ceilings and graceful wainscoting. A house to entertain in, although we never entertain. A house to hold gaggles of children, although we will never have more than one. Everywhere floors are sagging and panels are cracked and pipes are groaning—but they are *our* floors and panels and pipes. We are only the third black family ever to live in the section of town called Hobby Hill, sixteen square blocks of elegance, and the other two deserted the cause long before we arrived. I do not know how many owners our particular house has had, but it has survived them all, has even thrived. Somebody turned the basement into a playroom, somebody renovated the kitchen, somebody added a cramped garage where Kimmer, despite my entreaties to protect the more expensive of our cars, refuses to park her BMW because she fears the narrow entry might scratch the blinding white paint, somebody updated all four full and two half baths, including the one for the maid in the attic, if we only had a maid and could afford to heat the attic; yet I like to think the house has hardly changed since being built. Eight years after we bought the place, I am still tickled to walk in the front door, because I know that the original owner was the longtime provost of the university, a fussy Latin and Greek scholar named Phineas Nimm, who died around the time of the First World War. Something over a hundred years ago, responding to a survey from an unknown Atlanta University professor named W.E.B. Du Bois, Provost Nimm wrote unapologetically that a colored man, whatever the level of his educational achievement, would not be welcome as a student. As an undergraduate, I discovered a copy of the letter in the university archives and nearly stole it. After all these years, the irony of owning Nimm's house still brings me a bitter satisfaction.

As the daylight fades, Bentley and I play kickball in the yard for half an hour, watched with approval by Don and Nina Felsenfeld, our elderly next-door neighbors, who are sitting on their screened porch, as they do every day around this time, sipping lemonade. Don was in his day one of the nation's leading experts on particle physics, and Nina remains an expert at welcoming strangers, the Jewish tradition of *hesed*: within an hour of the arrival of the moving truck eight years ago, she was at our door with a tray of cream-cheese-and-jelly sandwiches. She has brought us other trays over the years, including one three weeks ago, after my father died, because she grew up in the kind of family where, when somebody died, bringing food was what neighbors did. Don and Nina believe that nothing is more important than family, and Don, who often spends a friendly evening whomping me at chess, is fond of saying that nobody ever lay on his deathbed wishing he had spent a few more hours at work and a few less with the kids.

Kimmer thinks they are interfering busybodies.

And they are, evidently, about to interfere again, because, as soon as I judge that my son is too tired to play any longer and turn around to head inside, Don rises to his feet and opens the door to his porch. He beckons to me over the high, thick hedge that separates our lots. I nod, take Bentley by the hand, and wander toward the front of the house, which is the only way around the sprawling, prickly hedge. Don and I meet on his front lawn, and there is a moment while he plays around with his pipe.

"How's the little chap?" he asks at last, referring to Bentley.

"Bentley's doing great," I answer.

"Grape! Bemmy grape!" chirps my magnificent son, reaching out his free hand for Don's. "Dare you!"

"Yep," says Don with every appearance of seriousness, swallowing the tiny proffered fingers in his own. "Yep, you're quite a grape little chap."

Bentley giggles and hugs Don's bony leg.

Don Felsenfeld is a tall, awkwardly thin man, graceless and aloof, the son of a Jewish farmer from Vermont. In his heyday, it is said, he knew more about subatomic particles than anybody on the planet, and a favorite bromide on campus is that he should have had the Nobel Prize twice. A sometime socialist and full-time atheist, Don once wrote a popular book whose title made a joke of Einstein's famous and difficult line: *The Science of Unbelief: How the Universe Plays Dice with God*, he called it. Now he is close to eighty, dresses every day in khaki trousers and the same blue cardigan, and spends most of his time gardening or smoking his pipe or both.

"Been quite a couple of weeks for you," says Don. No smile, few words: Jewish he may be, but Don Felsenfeld is pure New England too.

"I suppose."

"Nina's cooking for you."

"She's sweet."

"That she is." For a moment, we both stand in silence, appreciating his wife. Then Don begins to fiddle with his pipe again, the way he does just after unleashing a devastating attack over the chessboard, and I know we are finally at the heart of the matter. "Talcott, listen." I do. I am. "Are you having some kind of trouble?"

"I don't know. I don't think so." I swallow with effort, thinking: McDermott has been skulking around asking questions. Or Foreman. Or the real FBI. "What makes you ask that?"

Don does not look at me. Still puffing his pipe, he seems to take great interest in a white-throated sparrow hopping along the sidewalk, somehow left behind when the great flocks migrated south.

"It's been a pretty nice autumn, don't you think?" Don asks slowly. Bewildered, I nod. Is he thinking about the bird? "Weather's been fair, not too cold. Pleasant."

"Yes, it's been nice."

"One of the warmest since you've been in town, as a matter of fact."

"I guess it could be."

"Kind of autumn weather where folks keep their windows open at night to catch the breeze."

"Uh, right." Over the years, Don and I have discussed, in detail, everything from the university's policies on patent ownership by faculty, to the relative merits of John Updike and John Irving, to the relationship between capital gains tax rates and capital formation, to how Bobby Fischer would have fared against the current crop of chess champions, to whether the Book of Isaiah, which Christians believe prefigures the birth and ministry of Jesus, predicts the arrival of one infant or two. But we have never once held a lengthy conversation about the weather . . . which leads me to believe something important is on the way.

"You know, Talcott, there are no perfect marriages."

"I never thought there were."

"Your windows are open at night in this weather. Ours too."

A sudden awareness dawns. I look at him hard, but his gentle gaze is still locked on something in the middle distance. I know what is coming, and I know that Nina has put him up to it—for Don, like the Judge, would never willingly discuss an emotion, or even admit to having any.

"Uh, Don, look—"

In his kindly but single-minded way, the old physicist rides right over me, just as he does when we play chess. "Voices carry, Talcott. Couldn't help overhearing the other night. You and your wife, I mean. Two of you had quite a set-to."

Three nights ago, I am remembering: Saturday. The one sour note in an otherwise loving week. Kimmer announced she was leaving for San Francisco in the morning, and I asked, stupidly, about her promise to take Bentley to Miguel Hadley's birthday party so that I could drive over to the campus after church to catch the tail end of Rob Saltpeter's conference on the implications of artificial intelligence for constitutional law. She told me that she had no choice, that this was work. I told her mine was work too. She said it wasn't the same. She had made a commitment. I asked her who to. She asked what that was supposed to mean. I said she knew. She asked what *that* was supposed to mean. I said I didn't want to talk about it. She said I was the one who brought it up in the first place. I can see how Don and Nina overheard: our voices were certainly raised. Kimmer's anyway.

"I'm sorry if we disturbed you."

"Don't give it a thought, Talcott." He puts a hand on my shoulder, man to man, the way my father used to. Bentley, sensing the seriousness of the conversation, has ambled away. He is stooping on the Felsenfelds' lawn, examining Don's carefully tended flowerbeds, now mostly covered over for the coming cold weather. I have tried to get my son to stop picking the buds, but Don and Nina do not seem to mind. "I just wanted you to know I'm here if you ever need to talk. Sometimes talking things through is the most important step. Nina and I, well, we've had a problem or two of our own over the years. We got through ours, you'll get through yours if you let your friends help."

For a moment I am too humiliated to speak: there are *standards*, after all, my mother used to preach, and nobody should ever get the idea you aren't living up to them. As for the talking-things-out idea, my father always mocked the idea of counseling, which was, he said, nothing more than coddling the weak of will. *You draw a line, Talcott. Put the past on one side, the future on the other, and decide which side you want to live on. Then stick to your decision.* In my family, problems were secrets; so none of us ever received training on what to do if some outsider discovered that we actually had one.

Yet I manage somehow to gather enough wit to respond lightly:

"Oh, Don, thanks, but Saturday night, that was nothing. You should hear Kimmer when she gets *mad*." I would wink, too, but I never actually learned how.

Don summons a smile and gazes at me the way the Judge used to, when I joked about grades or tenure or politics or anything else my father considered important and I chose not to discuss. Don's bright, intelligent eyes convey the pitiless judgment of a man who has spent his seven-plus decades on earth getting all the answers right. I adore Nina, but not Don, probably because he reminds me too much of the Judge. The fact that my father was, for lack of a better word, a Tory, and Don is very much the other thing, does not change the essential similarity of their natures, particularly the somber self-satisfaction that commands those foolish enough to hold wrong political opinions to go to hell.

"I'm here if you change your mind," Don tells me. Which is something else that the Judge used to say. Only I never did, and he never was.

CHAPTER 16

THE THREE FOOLS

(1)

WE TAKE FORMAL POSSESSION of the Vineyard house in the middle of the week after Thanksgiving, driving Kimmer's sleek BMW up to Massachusetts, then down the Cape to Woods Hole, and crossing on the auto ferry. The ferry, my father used to say, is two of the Island's blessings: one because the trip over the water is so pleasant and restful that you arrive on Martha's Vineyard in the mood to relax, and the other because the Steamship Authority, which operates the ferry service, holds a monopoly on the franchise and runs only a limited number of ships, which means that only a limited number of cars, and thus of people, can get to the Island, especially in the high season of July and August. Whenever one of the children, usually Addison, whispered that this joy smacked of elitism, the Judge would respond happily with one of his favorite *bons mots*, quite possibly original with him: "Being part of the elite is the reward for working hard and living right." (Implying, of course, that if you are not part of the elite you either did not work hard or did not live right.)

I have always loved the crossing, and today's journey is no different. As the Cape falls farther and farther behind, I can feel my fears and confusions fading with it, receding in importance as the Vineyard looms ever larger off the starboard bow, first a distant gray-green shimmer, next a dreamlike vision of trees and beaches, now near enough to make out the individual houses, all gray-brown and weathered and beautiful. I gulp down its image like an alcoholic tumbling gratefully off the wagon as the ferry thrums steadily across the waves, a few dozen automobiles waiting in the hold to explode onto the Island in a noxious rush of joy. (In season there would be a hundred or more.) Bentley and

I stand at the rail, my son calling to the gulls that soar in the salty autumn air, seeming to hang motionless as they match their speed to the speed of the boat, hoping to gorge on what we wastrel humans toss aside. A chilly, distant sun beams its indifference across the water. My son stretches his pudgy hands over the side and, rather than frustrating him, I hook a prudent finger in his belt and try to convince myself that he is indeed all of three years old, with four swimming toward us fast, no longer a baby, yet the last child I will ever father as well as the first. For Kimmer is through with pregnancy: she has made that icily clear, even as so much in our marriage remains hotly confused. Part of it, I know, is fear, after our near miss with Bentley; but fear is not the entire explanation. A new child would be a fresh commitment to a marriage about which Kimmer remains unsure. To my desire for a large family, she answers correctly that she, not I, must carry the baby—except that Kimmer always says *fetus*, and is at pains to make everybody else say it too. My wife, who is never political except when she is, can sniff out an anti-abortion plot before it is hatched. This past March, Dear Dana Worth, who loves children but will never bear one, gave Bentley for his third birthday *Horton Hears a Who* by Dr. Seuss, one of her favorites, she told us, when she was a child. Kimmer thanked Dana, leafed through the book in horror, and put it away in the attic without ever troubling to read it to our son. She forbade me to read it to him either. "An anti-choice tract," she huffed, and, when I asked what she was talking about, she smiled dismissively and quoted the book's recurring tag line, *A person's a person, no matter how small.* "What else could it be about?" she demanded.

My turn to smile now. No matter what faces me in the rest of the world, I am revived by my sojourns on the Vineyard. And I am determined to make this one peaceful. Last week I had a fight with Mariah, our worst yet. Spurred on by Meadows, I made the long drive to Darien and took my sister to lunch. I tried to suggest, as gently as I could, that maybe she could tone down her constant invention of new conspiracies. I told her about the possible judgeship, told her that her conduct was hurting Kimmer's chances, but did not tell her my source. She shot back that the whole thing—offering my wife a shot at the bench, threatening to take it back if Mariah kept speaking out—was itself a conspiracy, a way of shutting us up. I told her that seemed a little far-fetched, we had words, and, suddenly, it was the terrible days after the Woodward book all over again. Only worse this time, because the Judge is not around to draw us back together by the force of his will.

And so I ache instead. Unable to concentrate in the classroom, I have asked for a few weeks' leave from the law school, and Dean Lynda has happily granted it, both because she dislikes me and because she knows it will put me in her debt. Stuart Land has agreed to cover my torts class until I get back, and has already called three times, distressed by the disorganization of my lesson plan and my office, and offering to repair both. I have politely declined, not wanting anybody probing the shadowy nooks of my life.

Earlier this month, I attended Freeman Bishop's funeral, my second funeral at Trinity and St. Michael within two weeks. Some visiting priest, a member of the paler nation, performed the service, and few mourners attended. I noticed a face or two that I remembered from the Judge's service, and I strained unsuccessfully to call names into my tortured mind. Mariah skipped the service. Sergeant Ames was there, however, perhaps expecting more bad guys to show up. I chatted with her briefly before she slipped out a side door, and I learned only that Conan was still negotiating his plea bargain, which I already knew from the *Washington Post*'s Web site.

Then, last week, came our usual tense Thanksgiving with Kimmer's parents, still waiting impatiently for me to tame their incorrigible daughter; evidently they do not realize that Kimmer is not quite tamable. Vera and the Colonel glared down the table at me as Kimmer and her childless sister Lindy gossiped and Bentley made a mess. If my wife does not become a judge, I suspect that my in-laws will somehow heap the blame on me.

But mostly I have been looking forward, with growing eagerness, to today's journey.

The ferry at last!

Now, turning my face into the sea breeze as the ship breasts the surging waves, rushing me toward the island I love, I am able to smile at Kimmer's eccentricity—and even at Kimmer herself, who is huddled near the snack bar, carrying on a conversation of vital importance on her cell phone. Perhaps the colloquy concerns her work, perhaps it concerns her candidacy, perhaps it concerns something more intimate. For once I refuse to care. Ever since I shared the news of trepidation in the Hadley household, Kimmer has turned loving and warm, as though to compensate for other behavior, a stark metamorphosis that I have seen before, and which, unlike Gregor Samsa's, can reverse itself in an instant; but I am determined to enjoy it for as long as it lasts.

So, finally, here we are on the ferry, the day I have been awaiting. Kimmer has stolen forty-eight hours from the demands of litigating for her clients' advancement (and lobbying for her own) to cross with me the threshold of the house that now is ours, and for that small act of theft, I am grateful. She might have forced me to go with only Bentley, or even alone. The fact that she did not I take as a signal of continuing armistice. Nearing the glory of the Vineyard, I find myself believing, against every objective indicator, in the possibility of happiness. Even with my wife. Which is why, I suppose, fidelity in a sad marriage can fairly be described as an act of faith: faith in life's endless possibilities, which is another way, I am sure Rob Saltpeter would insist, of describing God's bounty. And so I smile as I stand at the rail, my finger tucked into my son's belt as he leans into the spray and calls to the gulls and laughs and laughs, and, as I glance around the deck at my fellow passengers, each, I am sure, as joyful as I as we rush on toward our island, my heart bursts with love: love for my child, love for my wife, love for the very idea of family, love for—

And suddenly she is there.

Right here, on the deck, long and nicely muscled, in jeans and a bomber jacket, not twenty paces away—the woman from the rollerdrome. It is not remotely possible, it is far too great a coincidence, I must be mistaken, my sullen libido is playing tricks on me . . . yet I know it is she. The roller woman. The woman who, a long month ago, flirted with me until she spied my wedding ring. The woman who haunted my dreams for the next couple of weeks. She is toward the prow, standing a little apart from the crowd, her face turned into the wind, so I see only a piece of her dark brown profile, but the smooth, broadly set jaw and the mass of impossible curls cannot belong to anyone else. A flamboyant purple overnight bag is slung over one shoulder and she is clutching a book: something genuine, hardcover, thick, the title in some other language, which my distant eye identifies tentatively as French. An edition of Molière, perhaps. *Student or teacher?* I wonder, suspecting that the answer is neither, for the text feels like a stage prop. I am thrilled to see her. I am appalled. I continue to stand at the rail, gazing in astonishment at this improbable apparition, far too shy to—

"I would kill to have her body," says Kimmer. So distracted have I been that I am not sure how long my wife has been next to me, but the wicked bemusement in her voice hurts as much as ever. On the other hand, I am guilty as charged. "She's gorgeous, isn't she?"

"Who?" I venture, careful not to turn around too suddenly, lest my wife conclude that I am actually staring where she thinks. I still have tight hold of Bentley's belt, and he is still hanging over the rail, hypnotized by the wake. The roller woman might be carved from stone.

"That giant *nzinga* over there," answers my learned Kimmer, who likes to pepper her conversation with the occasional Afrocentric non sequitur. She points with one hand, holds my arm with the other. The cellular phone is nowhere to be seen. "The one you can't seem to take your eyes off of." Kimmer laughs as I twist slowly back in her direction, then barks softly like a dog. "Down, boy," she says, not kindly. No peace treaty after all.

"Kimmer, I—"

"Hey, she's looking this way. Misha, she's looking. She's looking at *you*. Turn around and wave." She grabs my shoulders and tries physically to make me do it, but I resist.

"Kimmer, come on."

"Hurry up, honey, you'll miss your chance." Teasing, but also making her ancient point, that I should have affairs to balance hers; that I should fall in love with somebody else and leave, sparing her the necessity of hurting me any longer; that my constancy in the face of her dalliances marks not Christian virtue but secular wimpiness. We have argued this out so many times that she need raise only a hint of the long-standing quarrel to bring all the torment rushing back to my heart.

"Cut it out," I hiss, allowing an edge to come into my tone.

"Misha, go on!" my wife laughs, ignoring whatever I am feeling. "Go say hello, fast!" Then she stops pushing. Her hands fall from my shoulders. "Too late," she murmurs in mock sadness. "She's gone."

I cannot help myself. I do turn back now. The roller woman *is* gone. In her place are two plump white girls, stuffing Reese's Peanut Butter Cups into their mouths and dropping the wrappers into the sea. The gulls hover nearby, either protesting the pollution or hoping for a bite. The roller woman has vanished as silently as she materialized; had Kimmer not confirmed the evidence of my eyes, I might decide the roller woman was never there at all.

"I just thought she was somebody I knew," I say, knowing how lame it must sound.

"Or somebody you'd like to know," my wife suggests. It occurs to me, against all evidence of our recent years together, that Kimmer is jealous.

"I'm a one-woman man," I remind her, trying to keep it light.

"Yeah, but which one?"

I turn in her direction again. She likes to goad me into these arguments, and, although I try to keep my temper, she often succeeds. As she succeeds now: "Kimmer, I've told you before that really I don't appreciate jokes about . . . about my fidelity."

"Aw, honey, I'm only kidding." A playful kiss on my nose. "Although, you know, it's okay with me if you decide you want somebody else. . . ."

"I don't want somebody else. . . ."

"That's not how it looked to me a few minutes ago."

"Kimmer, I love you. Only you."

My wife shakes her head and smiles sadly. "Well, then, you're crazy or stupid . . ."

"That's entirely uncalled for," I say in the most wretched Garland tone.

". . . or maybe just some kind of masochist who gets his kicks from having a woman treat him like . . ."

This nonsense might go on forever, except that Bentley rescues us. Having spent a good twenty minutes simply watching the water go past, he has at last worked out what is happening. Grabbing both his mother's hand and my own, he swings around until his back is to the rail. When he is sure he has our full attention, he smiles up at us and proclaims with great glee, "I'm on *boat*."

The fight goes out of both of us, and we are, for an instant, united in pure and strong parental love for our son.

Then the moment passes, and we are competitors once more. And Kimmer, as usual, beats me to the punch. "Yes, you are on a boat, honeybunch, yes, you are," she murmurs, gathering a proud, wriggling Bentley to her breast. "Yes, you are, baby, you're on a boat, that's very good; now let's go inside and get warm. Mommy will get you a Coke."

"Hot chockut, Mommy, hot chockut!"

"Hot chocolate! Great idea, baby, great idea!"

Without a further word to her husband, my wife, the prospective judge, carries our son into the cabin. I watch her go, reading questionable messages in the sway of her hips and the set of her back. As so often happens at these moments of marital frustration, something primitive and ugly twists and furrows within me. A terrible red heat rises inside my head, a kind of indigestion of the brain; as always, a brisk but patient stroll helps me to wrestle my demons down. I make two complete circuits of the deck and one of the indoor seating down below before I feel sufficiently calm to join my family in the canteen; in all that walking, I see no sign of the roller woman. And this bothers me, not simply because I miss her already, but also because I am convinced that her presence on board is no accident. She is here for the same reason she was at the rollerdrome, because she was *sent*—and not by God either.

(11)

OCEAN PARK is a broad but irregular expanse of grass fronting on Seaview Avenue, the busy street one crosses to reach the rickety wooden stairways leading down to the slowly eroding beach known, unofficially, as the Inkwell, in whose gentle waters, for generations, the darker nation has frolicked. The house where I spent the summers of my youth is on the opposite side, where the neat Victorians are small and cramped together and too expensive. At one end of the park, to the right as one faces the water from our front porch, a line of fine old houses, all of them much larger than ours and topped with brightly colored turrets and fancy weather vanes, dominates the horizon. At the other end, to the left, just beyond the line of sight from our porch, stands the Steamship Authority dock, where some of the ferries unload in summer; during the off-months, all the ferries tie up a few miles up the coast in Vineyard Haven. A bit closer in are a lovely weather-beaten Episcopal church, its doors open in summer to the sea and so to every Sunday storm, and the city police station, which looks out on a tiny plaza featuring an aging bronze statue bearing a plaque that commemorates, for some arcane reason of Yankee logic, Confederate war dead. The statue guards the top of Lake Avenue, the narrow, crowded street leading down to the Flying Horses carousel, which is all that matters to Bentley.

Like many homes in Oak Bluffs, my family's summer place has a name, emblazoned on a faded wooden sign hanging from one of the posts along the front porch. Ours, unfortunately, is called VINERD HOWSE, a phrase selected by my sister Abby when she was small, quite by accident—she wrote it on a picture of the house she drew in the kitchen with crayons from the Crayola 64 box one rainy Oak Bluffs afternoon—and it was my unemotive father who surprised us a week later with the plaque. After Abby died, the family never had the heart to change the name. When we climb out of the white BMW on this bright fall day, however, the first thing my darling Kimmer says is that the time has come to get rid of it. As she pulls a sleeping Bentley from his car seat, I ask her which she means: the plaque or the name. "Either," my wife tells me, still showing me her back. "Or both."

My father once proposed changing the name to The Three Fools, one of his many obscure chess puns, but my mother put her foot down; my father, in all the years I remember, never acted against her wishes. Addison insists that it was Claire Garland who made the decision that it was time to end the confirmation battle, when the Judge was prepared to fight to the bitter end. Mariah whispers that it was Claire who argued that he should resign from the bench after the humiliation of the hearings, so that he could speak out publicly and clear his name. And all of us know that it was after Claire's death that my father's speeches became as wild and nasty as most people surely remember. Small surprise, then, that even after my mother died, my father honored her memory—and Abby's too—by retaining the sobriquet Vinerd Howse. But now that Vinerd Howse is mine, or, rather, ours, my wife has other ideas.

I stand for a long moment in the narrow front yard, the key dangling from limp fingers, remembering the glorious Martha's Vineyard summers of my childhood, when friends and family swirled constantly in and out of the double front doors with their tiny panes of glass, some rose, some azure, some clear, held fast in frames of involute leading; remembering the many sad and lonely visits to this house through those endless months when my mother sat dying, often alone, in the front bedroom on the first floor; and remembering, too, how easy it became to avoid coming back here once the Judge began his tumble toward megalomania. As Kimmer fusses with Bentley and I stare at the summer home of my youth, I find that I have difficulty recalling precisely why I was so filled with joy when I learned that the Judge left me this cramped and unhappy shell. With my parents both dead, the house should by rights be dead as well, quiet and neutral; instead, it seems almost a live thing, fiendishly sentient, brooding malevolently on the family's misfortunes as it awaits the new owners. Quite suddenly I am paralyzed with some emotion far more primal than terror, a clear and utterly persuasive knowledge, shivering through me from some unnatural source, that everything is about to go wretchedly wrong: I fear that my legs will not move me to the porch, or my hands will not work the key, or the key will break off in the lock. In that terrible moment, I want to reject this scary inheritance and all its ghosts, to grab my family and hurry back to the mainland.

As usual, it is worldly Kimmer who restores me to my senses.

"Can you hurry up and open the door?" she demands sweetly. "Sorry, but I have to piss in the worst way."

"No need to be vulgar."

"There is if nothing else will get you moving."

She is correct, after a fashion, and I am being foolish. I smile at her and she almost smiles back before she catches herself. I heft the heavy suitcase in my left hand and bounce the key in my right. Then I stride boldly up the steps, heedless of the demons who caper in the shadows of memory. Drawing a breath, I dismiss them like a veteran exorcist and rattle the key into the lock. Only as the lock begins to turn do I notice that one of the tiny panes of colored glass is missing—not broken, just not there, so that through the space defined by the narrow gray leading I can see into the darkness of the house. I frown, pushing the door wide open, and, standing frozen on the threshold of the house I have loved for thirty years, I realize that the goblins have not all retreated. I try to swallow but cannot seem to gather any moisture in my throat. My limbs refuse to move me forward. Through a slowly descending curtain of the deepest angry red, I see my handsome wife brushing past me with a whispered, "Sorry, but I gotta go," and I feel her transferring Bentley's hand to mine.

Kimmer is three steps into the house before she, too, stops and stands perfectly still.

"Oh, no," she whispers. "Oh Misha oh no."

The house is a disaster. Furniture is upended, books are strewn over the floor, cabinet doors broken, rugs sliced to ribbons. My father's papers are everywhere, the breeze from the open front door ruffling their edges. I peek into the kitchen. A few of the dishes are smashed on the floor, but the mess is not as bad, and most of the plates are simply stacked on the counter. While Kimmer waits in the front room with Bentley, I force myself to go upstairs. I discover that the four bedrooms are barely disturbed. As though there was no need to bother, I am thinking as I stand in the window of the master suite, telephone in hand, talking to the police dispatcher. As I explain what has happened, I look down at the BMW, parked illegally along the split-rail fence that guards the south side of Ocean Avenue, doors still open, baggage not yet unloaded. Something isn't right. They did not wreck the second floor. The thought keeps swirling through my mind. They left the second floor alone. As though ransacking the first floor was enough. As though—as though—

As though they found what they were looking for.

Now more puzzled than frightened, I go back downstairs to join my wife and son, who, wide-eyed, are hugging each other in the living room. The police, arriving in minutes from their quaint headquarters a block away, quickly pronounce the destruction the work of local vandals, teenagers who, unfortunately, spend much of the winter trashing the homes of the summer people. Not all the Vineyard's teenagers are vandals, or even very many: just enough to annoy. The very kind officers apologize to us on behalf of the Island and assure us that they will do their best, but they also warn us not to expect to catch the people who did it: vandalisms are nearly impossible to solve.

Vandals. Kimmer eagerly accepts this explanation, and I am quite sure the insurance company will too. And, more important, the White House. Kimmer promises to make plenty of trouble for the alarm company, and I have no doubt she will keep her word. Vandals, my wife and I agree over pizza and root beer at a nearby restaurant a couple of hours later, after the man who looks after the house in the off-season has dropped by to inspect the damage.

"I'll make some calls," he told us when he finished tut-tutting his way around the place.

Vandals. Of course they were vandals. The kind of vandals who destroy one floor of the house and ignore the other. The kind of vandals who steal neither stereo nor television. The kind of vandals who know how to circumvent my late paranoid father's state-of-the-art alarm system. And the kind of vandals who are in direct contact with the spirits of the departed. For I do not tell either my wife or the friendly police officers about the note I found upstairs while waiting, sealed in a plain white envelope left on top of the dresser in the master bedroom, my correct title and full name typed neatly on the outside, the perplexing message on the inside written in the crabbed, spiky hand I remember from my childhood, when we would proudly leave copies of our school essays on the Judge's desk and wait for him to return them, a day or so later, with his comments inked redly in the margins, demonstrating what idiots our teachers were to award us A's.

The note on the dresser is from my father.

CHAPTER 17

THE BRASS RING

(1)

MANY YEARS AGO, when as a child I first visited the town of Oak Bluffs, I at once became entranced by the grand old wooden building at the foot of Circuit Avenue housing the Flying Horses, which bills itself as the oldest carousel in America, having been in continuous operation now since 1876. The idea was to make riding a game. You sat astride your horse while leaning, each time around, toward a stationary wooden arm that dispensed tiny rings. As you passed, you would grab the ring on the end of the arm, and a new one would snap into its place. Nearly all of the rings were made of steel, but the last one in the arm was made of brass. A rider lucky enough to catch the brass ring won a free ride. During that first delirious summer, I would stay aboard the carousel for hours, spending my quarters one by one, forsaking even the beach to fill my days mastering the tricks of the older children (including how to catch two or sometimes three rings at once on my stubby brown fingers), paying for turn after turn, trying, almost always in vain, to grab the brass ring and earn a free ride.

As a child, I imagined that the Flying Horses was the only carousel in the world with the marvelous idea of awarding a free turn to the lucky rider who caught the brass ring. As I grew older, I learned that this was not so, that the idea of winning a prize for catching a brass ring was in fact rather ubiquitous, if not actually mundane. Intellectually, I have long ago made my peace with this development. Emotionally, I continue to feel that the brass ring on the Flying Horses in Oak Bluffs is the only one that really counts. Perhaps the reason is that our summer house on Ocean Park was little more than a child's hop-skip-and-jump from the carousel. I grew up with the Flying Horses around the corner, and with a child's freedom to visit whenever I pleased; and, having learned its lessons, I have been stretching for that brass ring ever since.

Of course, the Flying Horses of today are not the Flying Horses of my youth. The organ music, for example, now comes from compact discs, and the crowds push and jostle so that it is no longer possible to imagine riding all day. A couple of the wooden steeds have lost their genuine horsehair tails. But, then, so much of the Vineyard seems to need a coat of paint, the scrub of a brush, the whisk of a broom. The Island is neither as tidy nor as friendly as it once was. And it is all so sudden, so sudden. Blink once and a dusty road where you used to play tag is paved and clogged with traffic. Blink twice and the vacant lot where you had your ball games has a gigantic house on it. Blink again and the vast, dreamy beaches of your youth have lost half or more of their sand to the sea. Blink a fourth time and the pharmacy where your mother used to buy Coricidin when you were sick is a boutique. The Judge blamed the changes on demographics—the *new people* was his term for everybody who discovered the Island later than we did. I try to be wary of such generalizing sentiments, however, not least so that I do not sound too much like my father. So I look around and try to tell myself that little, after all, has really changed. And if a few more candy wrappers than I remember from my youth seem to be blowing along the streets, I like to think it is only because the new people have not yet learned how to love an island—not because they do not care.

Ordinarily, on the third afternoon of a Vineyard sojourn, I would be at the Flying Horses with my son. But our sojourns are usually in the summer. Now it is autumn, and the carousel is closed for the season. Fortunately, the Island offers other diversions. Yesterday, as a hastily assembled clean-up crew tried to put Vinerd Howse back in some kind of order, the three of us journeyed up-Island—that is, to the western-most end—and spent a marvelous afternoon walking the breathtaking ancient cliffs at Gay Head in the chilly November air, picnicking in our down parkas at the perfect pebbly beach in the fishing village of Men-emsha, and driving the wooded back roads of Chilmark, near the sprawl-ing property once owned by Jacqueline Onassis, pretending not to be on the lookout for the rich and famous. We had dinner at a fancy restaurant on the water in Edgartown, where Bentley charmed the waitresses with his patter. How many demons we exorcised I am not sure, but I saw no sign of the roller woman, who might be a phantom after all, and Kimmer did not mention the judgeship once and talked on her cell phone only twice. And she kissed me quite carefully this morning when Bentley and I dropped her at the airport for her flight back to the mainland in one of the little turboprops that serve the Island. Bentley and I are staying on because . . . well, because we need to. Kimmer has work to do, I have a week or so of leave left, and Bentley needs some rest and recreation. And there is another reason as well. In Oak Bluffs, unlike Elm Harbor, I will never be tempted for a moment to let my precious son out of my sight.

Right now my son and I are preparing to go to the playground; or, more precisely, Bentley is ready, waiting for me.

I am less ready.

I am sitting at the table in our newly cleaned kitchen (full of plastic plates and cups from one of the Island's two A&Ps), the note from my father flattened on the surface, willing its secrets to reveal themselves. In the next room, Bentley is watching the Disney Channel and occasionally waddling to the door of the kitchen and calling, "Dada, pay-grown now. You say paygrown!" in the plaintive, self-righteous tone that makes busy parents writhe with guilt. To which I respond with the familiar "Yes, okay, just a minute, sweetheart," which every busy parent uses with equal embarrassment.

Last night, as my family slept uneasily, Kimmer curled protectively around our son, I wandered Vinerd Howse from the foyer to the attic crawl space, searching for something, but I do not know what. I need to know what is going on. I need a clue.

Unfortunately, the most obvious clue, my father's note, remains gibberish:

> *My son,*
>
> *There is so much I wish I could share with you. Alas, at the present moment, I cannot. I have asked a good friend to deliver this note should anything befall me; if you are reading my words, one must assume that something has. I apologize for the complexity of this method of contact, but there are others who would also like to know that which is for your eyes only. So, know this much: Angela's boyfriend, despite his deteriorating condition, is in possession of that which I want you to know. You are in no danger, neither you nor your family, but you have little time. You are unlikely to be the only one who is searching for the arrangements that Angela's boyfriend alone can reveal. And you may not be the only one who knows who Angela's boyfriend is.*
>
> *Excelsior, my son! Excelsior! It begins!*
>
> > *Sincerely,*
> > *Your Father*

The handwriting is unmistakably the Judge's, as is the flowery, over-wrought, self-important prose, even the formality of the signature. Quite unexpectedly, my fury at my father threatens suddenly to over-whelm me. *If you want to tell me, tell me!* I rage against him in my tor-tured mind, a tone I would never have selected in life. *But don't play these games!* Jack Ziegler in the cemetery demanded to know about *the arrangements.* Now, at last, I know for certain that my father actually made some. But I do not know what they are, and this hint, this clue, this post-mortem letter from my paranoid father, whatever it is sup-posed to be, lends me no assistance at all.

Excelsior? Angela's boyfriend, despite his deteriorating condition? What is all this?

One point is clear: Not-McDermott's mission in Elm Harbor was neither to apologize nor to reassure but, as I suspected, to see whether I know an Angela or not—which means that he and, presumably, Fore-man are somehow privy to the contents of this letter. I wonder if the letter was the reason for the destruction of the first floor, except that I cannot quite fathom why they would break into the house, find the let-ter, and then leave it behind.

Or, for that matter, how the letter got here in the first place. Pre-sumably McDermott, if he was even here, would not have dropped it off. The Judge wrote that he asked *a good friend* to deliver it should any-thing *befall* him. But what good friend would break into Vinerd Howse to drop it off? Why not mail it to my house or bring it by my office? Why not deliver it to . . .

. . . *to the soup kitchen?*

Can the pawn be connected to the letter? Did my father arrange that delivery as well? I try to remember whether I ever mentioned to my father that I volunteer at the soup kitchen, but my mind offers every answer I could want: yes, I told him; no, I did not tell him; yes, I hinted at it; no, I kept it secret. I shake my head in rich red anger. If he wanted me to have the pawn, wouldn't he have delivered pawn and letter together?

Not that it matters. For my father's note is actually no help at all.

I have a terrible memory for names, but it is good enough for me to be sure that I do not know an Angela, and I have no idea who her boyfriend could possibly be.

"PAYGROWN NOW now *now!*" Bentley calls. "Dare *you!*"

"One minute!" I shout back, still puzzling over the letter. How am I to locate *Angela's boyfriend,* who is in *deteriorating condition?* Does that mean that the man I should be talking to is sick? Perhaps dying? Is that why I have *little time?* I know who the *others* are, who *would also like to know,* having met a pair of them, but I do not understand why the Judge is at such pains to assure me that my family is in no danger, the fourth such reassurance I have received in the past month: first Jack Ziegler, then McDermott, next Agent Nunzio, now my late father.

I shake my head.

I try to think of famous Angelas: Lansbury? Bassett? I do not know enough about them to know if they even have husbands, still less boyfriends—and, anyway, my father did not exactly run with the Hollywood crowd. I have already had my secretary search the student directory at the law school: three Angelas, one black, two white, none of whom I have ever had in class or have any reason to think my father knew. Maybe there is a way to put together a list of all the Angelas my father might have met, but not without involving somebody official— Uncle Mal, for instance—or somebody who knows lots of the Judge's friends—Mariah, for instance—and I cannot quite imagine sharing the note with either of them.

Not yet.

Little time.

I almost smile. The phrase explains nothing about Angela's boyfriend, but a good deal about the Judge. He used those words often in his speeches, in trying to explain to his friends in the Rightpacs why they needed . . . well, racial diversity. The median American, he loved to tell his eager audiences, is socially conservative. The median black American, the Judge would add, is even more conservative. *Look at the data on any question,* he would rumble. *School prayer? Black Americans favor it more than whites do. Abortion? Black Americans are more pro-life than whites. Vouchers? Black Americans support them more strongly than whites. Gay rights? Black Americans are more skeptical than whites.* The applause would roll across his (overwhelmingly white) audience. Then he would hit them with the big windup: *Conservatives are the last people who can afford to be racist. Because the future of conservatism is black America!* They would go wild for him. I never saw it in person, but I saw it, often, on C-SPAN. And whichever Rightpac he was speaking to would march out to try to recruit black members, because, he would insist, there is *little time* . . . and, almost always, the recruitment effort would fail . . . quite abysmally. Because there were a few little details the Judge always left out. Like the fact that it was conservatives who fought against just about every civil rights law ever proposed. Like the fact that many of the wealthy men who paid for his expensive speeches would not have him in their clubs. Like the fact that it was the great conservative hero Ronald Reagan who kicked off his campaign by talking about states' rights in Philadelphia, Mississippi, a location with a certain wicked resonance for the darker nation, and who, as President, backed tax exemptions for the South's many segregation academies. The Judge was surely right to insist that the time has come for black Americans to stop trusting white liberals, who are far more comfortable telling us what we need than asking us what we want, but he never did come up with a particularly persuasive reason for us to start trusting white conservatives instead.

My father trusted them, however, and they trusted him right back. I wander into the dining room, where the long wooden table could easily seat fourteen or more and, during my childhood, often did. On the long wall of the room is a crumbling brick fireplace which has been unusable for as long as I can remember. Above the hearth hangs an enlarged version of my father's treasured *Newsweek* cover the week after his nomination was announced. THE CONSERVATIVE HOUR, reads the caption, and, in smaller type, *A New Direction on the Court?* Well, yes, the answer might be—yes, there was a new direction on the Court, but my father was not destined to be one of its leaders. I examine the picture. The Judge looks bold, handsome, smart, ready for anything. He looks *alive*. In those days, for some reason, the press decided to like him; but you should never fall in love with your own press clippings, because it is very much the nature of the beast that the same journalists who build you up between Monday and Friday tear you down for weekend fun. And suddenly, instead of fame, you have infamy; instead of a life of public service, you have a life of private bitterness; and you turn your house into a museum of what might have been. Again I recall my father's nostalgic phrase: *the way it was before.* My family's habit of living in the past seems to me pathological, even dangerous. If all greatness lies in the past, what is the point of the future? There is no going back, and the Judge, of all people, should have known better than to change his vacation home, his hideaway, his place of respite, into a shrine to his shattered dreams. Kimmer, I know, is waiting for a suitable moment to let me know that it is time to remove this and the other self-congratulatory emblems scattered around Vinerd Howse, to bury them in the attic with my old baseball-card collection and Abby's stuffed animals—

"Paygrown *now!*" Bentley announces from the doorway to the kitchen, stomping his foot. I look up at him, ready to be angry, and smile instead. He is wearing his midnight-blue parka and has even pulled his sneakers onto the wrong feet. He is dragging my windbreaker behind him. Oh, how I love this child!

"Okay, sweetheart." I fold my father's letter, return it to the envelope, and slip it into my pocket. "Paygrown now."

Bentley jumps up and down. "Paygrown! Dare *you!* Wuv *you!*"

"Wuv you, too." I hug him and kneel down to fix his shoes, and, of course, the phone immediately starts to ring.

Don't answer it, Bentley tells me with his earnest, judgmental brown eyes, for he does not yet know how to say the words. *Please, Daddy, don't answer it.* And at first, I consider ignoring the phone. After all, it is most likely Cassie Meadows calling from Washington, or Mariah calling from Darien, or Not-McDermott calling from Canada. On the other hand, it might be Kimmer with good news, or Kimmer with bad, Kimmer to say she loves me, or Kimmer to say she doesn't.

It might be Kimmer.

"Just one quick minute," I say to my son, who eyes me with the sort of hopeless disappointment that some psychiatrist in his future will doubtless unearth. "It's probably Mommy."

Only it isn't.

(I I I)

"TALCOTT? Hi, it's Lynda Wyatt."

The Dean. Great.

"Hi, Lynda, how are you?" I am deflating fast, and I know my voice betrays my disappointment.

"*I'm* fine, Talcott. But how are *you?*"

"I'm just fine, Lynda, thanks."

"I hope that you're having lots of fun on the Vineyard. I love it up there in the fall, but Heaven knows when Norm and I will have a chance to get to our place." Serving to remind me that she and her husband own a huge, modern house on the pond in West Tisbury, the up-Island town where many artists and writers spend their summers. Actually, I know about the house only by the tales my law school colleagues tell, because, in all the years that Lynda Wyatt and I have both been vacationing on the Island, she has invited my family to her house exactly never. (I have reciprocated just as often, so perhaps the fault is mine.)

"We're having some fun," I concede, smiling desperately at my son. Bentley, glaring, toddles to a corner of the kitchen and sits on the floor.

"Well, that's great, just great. I hope you're getting some rest, too."

"Some," I say. "So, what's up?" I am rushing her, I am probably being rude, but I figure I have lots of excuses.

"Well, Talcott, I'm actually calling for two reasons. First of all—and I wouldn't make anything important of this"—meaning, of course, that she thinks it very important indeed—"first of all, I received the strangest call from one of our graduates who is a trustee of the university. Cameron Knowland. You must know Cameron?"

"No."

"Well, he has been a great friend of this school, Tal, a great friend. In fact, Cameron and his wife just pledged three million toward our new law library. Anyway, he says that his son got kind of a rough going-over in your class. Said you made fun of him or something."

I am already steaming.

"I assume you told Cameron to butt out."

Lynda Wyatt's voice is amiable. "What I told him, Tal, was that it was probably blown out of proportion, that all first-year students complain. I told him that you weren't the type to abuse a student in class."

"I see." I grip the telephone but sway on my feet. I am appalled by the weakness of this defense of a professor from the dean of the law school. I am growing hotter and the kitchen is growing redder. Bentley is watching me closely, a hand to his ear as he holds an imaginary receiver of his own. He is mouthing occasional words, too.

"I think it would be helpful," Dean Lynda continues soberly, "if you were to give Cameron a call. Just to reassure him."

"Reassure him of what?"

"Oh, Tal, you know how these alumni are." Offering me her charming side. "They need to be stroked all the time. I'm not trying to interfere with how you run your classroom"—meaning she is trying to do exactly that—"but I'm just saying that Cameron Knowland is concerned. As a father. Think of how you would feel if you heard that one of Bentley's teachers was beating up on him."

Red, red, red.

"I didn't *beat up on* Avery Knowland—"

"Then tell his father that, Tal. That's all I'm asking. Calm him down. As one father to another. For the good of the school."

For the three million dollars, she means. She seems to assume I care. In my current state, however, I would not object if the library sank into the earth. Gerald Nathanson is often there: it is quieter than his office, he says, and he can get more work done. Another reason I stay out of the place is to avoid running into him.

"I'll think about it," I mutter, not sure what I will do the next time I see young Avery Knowland's insolent face.

"Thank you, Tal," says my dean, knowing at once that this is as much as she will be able to get. "The school appreciates all that you do for us." For *us*—as though I am an outsider. Which I pretty much am. "And Cameron's a nice guy, Tal. You never know when you'll need a friend."

"I told you I'll think about it." Letting some ice slip into my voice. I am recalling what Stuart Land said to me about pressures being brought to bear, and I wonder if this call is a part of it. Which leads me to be ruder still: "You said there were two things."

"Yes." A pause. "Well." Another. I imagine that she is leading up to a comment of some kind about the competition between Marc and Kimmer, along the lines of what Stuart attempted. Except that Lynda is unlikely to back down.

I am right . . . but Lynda is more subtle than I am.

"Tal, I also had a call from another one of our graduates. Morton Pearlman. Do you know Mort?"

"I've heard the name."

"Well, he was four or five years ahead of you. Anyway, he works for the Attorney General these days. He called to see . . . he wanted to know . . . if you're doing okay."

"If I'm doing okay? What's that supposed to mean?"

Again Dean Lynda hesitates, and it occurs to me that she is trying to be kind, in the manner of a physician looking for the words to explain what the tests uncovered. "He said that you've been . . . well . . . that the FBI and various other agencies have received a lot of calls on your behalf recently. Most of them, I gather, at your behest. Calls about . . . oh, things related to your father. Questions about the autopsy, about that priest who got killed by the drug dealer, all sorts of things."

In the ensuing pause, I almost burst out that it was my sister, not me, who wanted those calls made, and sometimes who actually made them. But I am lawyer enough to wait for the rest. So I say only, "I see."

"Do you? I can't make any sense of it at all." Her voice is growing harder. "Now, we've known each other a long time, Tal, and I'm sure you have a good reason for just about everything you do." I register, with dismay, *just about.* "But I have a feeling that what Mort was trying to ask, in a nice way, was whether you might need a little rest."

"Wait a minute. Wait. The Deputy Attorney General of the United States thinks I'm crazy? Is that what you're telling me?"

"Calm down, Tal, okay? I'm only the messenger here. I don't know what you're up to, and I don't want to know. I'm just repeating what Mort asked me. And I probably shouldn't even be telling you, because he said it was confidential."

I unclench my fist, make myself speak slowly and clearly. I am not worried, now, about Kimmer and her judgeship. That can wait. I am worried about whether the FBI plans to stop taking my concerns seriously. "Lynda. This is important. What did you tell him?"

"I'm sorry?"

"What did you tell Morton Pearlman? When he implied that I needed a rest?"

"I told him I was sure you were fine, that I knew you were a little upset, and that you were away from the school for a few weeks."

"You didn't say that."

"I did. What did you expect me to say? I didn't want to mess anything up for you, but . . . well . . . Tal, I'm worried about you."

"Worried about me? Why are you worried about me?"

"I think maybe . . . Tal, look. If you want to rest for a couple of more weeks before you come back, I'm sure it would be no problem."

For a moment I can think of nothing to say. The implications of her machinations briefly overwhelm me. Put simply, if Morton Pearlman can be persuaded that Kimberly Madison's husband is a nutcase, then there is no way that she gets the seat on the court of appeals. Tagging me with that label, and thus helping Marc achieve his lifelong goal, is evidently Dean Lynda's purpose. And although I am impressed by the elegance with which she is trying to do it, I am infuriated that she would use the complications of my father's death this way—and that she would hold me in such low regard as to think she could get away with it. Well, Stuart tried to warn me.

"No, Lynda, but thank you. I'll be back next week, as planned."

"Tal, you really don't have to rush. You really should take as much rest as you need."

I wish I were more political. I wish I were smooth, like Kimmer: then I could find the words to defuse the situation. But I am neither political nor smooth. I am just angry, and I am one of those strange people who sometimes, in anger, allow the truth to slip out.

"Lynda, look. I appreciate your call. I understand why you don't want me to come back just yet. But I'll be back next week."

Her tone goes frosty at once. "Talcott, I value your friendship, but I resent your tone and your implication. I am trying to help you with a difficult situation. . . ."

"*Lynda*," I begin, wanting to make clear that we are not and have never been friends, and then I make myself stop, rubbing my temples and closing my eyes, because the world is bright red and I am probably shouting and my son, alarmed as he stands in the doorway, is shrinking back. I smile at him, with difficulty, and blow a kiss, then continue in what I hope is a more reasonable tone. "Lynda, thank you. Really. I appreciate your concern. But it's about time for me to get back to Elm Harbor anyway—"

"Your students are really enjoying Stuart Land," she interrupts cruelly.

I force myself to respond with grace. "Well, that's all the more reason for me to get back. They might forget about me."

"Oh, well, we wouldn't want that, would we?" She is furious. I am amazed. I am the one who should be enraged. I say nothing; even after all these years of living with mercurial Kimberly Madison—or perhaps because of them—I lack the confidence to deal with female anger. "Anyway," the Dean concludes, "we all look forward to having you back among us."

"Thank you," I lie.

(IV)

"I'm sorry, sweetheart," I am saying to Bentley as we sit in the booth, waiting for our cheeseburgers.

"Paygrown," moans my son. "Go *paygrown*."

"It's too late, buddy," I murmur, tousling his hair. He shrinks away. "See? It's dark outside."

"You say *pay*grown! Dare *you!*"

"I know, I know. I'm really sorry. Daddy got busy."

"Daddy say *pay*grown."

His tone is understandably accusatory, for I have committed one of those parental sins that children, in the innocence of their youthful integrity, find it all but impossible to forgive: I broke my promise to him. We never made it to the playground. Because, after my tussle with Dean Lynda, when I should have gathered up my son and rushed out the door, if only to remind myself of what really matters, I made the mistake of checking my office voice mail. I found two frantic messages from a lawyer at a New York firm that recently retained me as a consultant, to help some greedy corporation craft a constitutional argument to challenge new federal regulations concerning the disposal of toxic waste: not precisely the side of the angels, but law professors desperate to augment academic salaries take what work we can get. I sent a draft of the brief last week, and now, according to her message, one of the partners at the firm had a few questions. I decided to take a quick minute to call her back, forgetting that lawyers, particularly those at large law firms, prefer talking on the phone to any other activity. Her list of questions was about seven miles long, and some of them were genuinely tough ones. I was tied up for the next ninety minutes (two hours of billable time for both the lawyer and myself—her rates are higher, but I have no overhead), plying my poor son with cookies and fruit to keep him relatively quiet, watching the light fade from the November sky, promising myself every five minutes that I would be done in five more.

Telling myself lies.

When I informed Bentley that it was too late to swing by the playground, he literally fell to the floor in tears. Nothing theatrical or manipulative, nothing fake. He simply put a hand over his face and crumpled, like hope dying.

My efforts to comfort him were unavailing.

And so I pulled the other sad, spoiling trick of the contemporary parent: I bribed him. We bundled into our parkas and walked the two blocks from Vinerd Howse to Circuit Avenue, the commercial heart of Oak Bluffs, a few hundred yards of restaurants, boutiques, and shops offering the various knickknacks that one finds in any resort town. In the summer, we might have stopped in at Mad Martha's ice-cream par-lor for vanilla malts or strawberry cones, but the local outlet is closed for the season. Instead, we made our way down to Murdick's candy shop—my son's second-favorite place on the Island, ranking just be-hind the incomparable Flying Horses—to buy some of the cranberry fudge that is a specialty of the house. Then we meandered back up the street. I bought the local paper, the *Vineyard Gazette*, at the Corner Store, and we stopped in for dinner at Linda Jean's, a quietly popular restaurant of unassuming decor and remarkably inexpensive food, and, at one time, my father's favorite place to eat. In the summer, he used to drop in just about daily for a warm lobster roll, but only on the off-hours, never when Linda Jean's was crowded, because, after his fall, the Judge worried constantly about being recognized.

Some years ago, on the tenth anniversary of my father's humiliation, *Time* did a story about his life since leaving the bench. The two-page spread revisited his angry books, quoted some of his stump speeches, and, in the interest of journalistic balance, gave some of his old enemies the chance to take fresh shots at him. Jack Ziegler's name was men-tioned three times, Addison's twice, mine once, Mariah's not at all, although her husband's was, which seemed to displease her. A sidebar summarized the post-hearing life of Greg Haramoto, who, like my father, refused to be interviewed. But the main theme of the story was that, despite the frenetic activity that marked his days, my father was far lonelier than even many of his friends realized. The magazine noted that he was spending more and more time "at his summer home in Oak Bluffs," nearly always by himself, and although *Time* made the house sound far grander than it is ("a five-bedroom cottage on the water") and also got its name wrong ("known to friends and family as simply 'The Vineyard House'"), the article caught the tenor of his life exactly. The piece was titled, with faint, depressing irony, "The Emperor of Ocean Park." I was aghast and Mariah was furious. Addison, of course, could not be reached. As for my father, he shrugged it off, or pretended to: "The media," he said to me at Shepard Street, "are all run by liberals. *White* liberals. Of course they are out to destroy me, because I know them for what they are. You see, Talcott, white liberals disapprove of black people they cannot control. My very existence is an affront to them." And returned to the reassuring pages of his *National Review*.

As to my father's fear of being recognized, it was, I confess, no small concern. In the wake of his failed confirmation, he was occasionally accosted by strangers in airports or hotel lobbies or even on the street. Some of them wanted to tell him they were for him all along, some of them wanted to tell him the opposite, and I think he despised both kinds equally; for my father, whose income in his last years derived principally from public appearances, was forever a private man. He invited no one to share his life. A few years ago, when the Judge stayed a weekend with us in Elm Harbor, a lone protester somehow spotted him and spent the better part of two days patrolling the sidewalk in front of our house, his placard proclaiming to the world that JUDGE GARLEN SHOUD BE IN JAIL. I tried to cajole the man into leaving us alone. I even tried to bribe him. He refused to leave. The police told us they could do nothing as long as he remained off our property and did not block access, and my father stood in the window of my study, glaring his hatred and muttering that if this were an abortion clinic the protester would already have been arrested—not an accurate statement of the law but, certainly, an accurate statement of the Judge's desire to be left alone. Which helps explain why, in Oak Bluffs, he would take his public meals only at the slack hours. Linda Jean's has long been a favorite hangout of celebrity-watchers, especially during the summer: Spike Lee often stops in for breakfast, Bill Clinton used to drop by for brunch after church on Sunday, and, in the old days, there was always the chance that Jackie O would wander past the window, eating an ice-cream cone. Once my wife spotted Ellen Holly, the pioneering black actress who appeared for many years on the soap opera *One Life to Live*, and, in the best Kimmer Madison manner, popped over to her table for an introduction and a chat.

But the best thing of all about Linda Jean's is that it is open year-round, which many of the Island's trendier restaurants are not.

"Hey, buddy," I say now to my beautiful son. He eyes me uncomfortably. Nibbling his cranberry fudge, he seems content, even if not yet ready to forgive. The doggie my brother gave him is on the seat next to him, a paper napkin tucked daintily into the ribbon around its neck. Have I always, I wonder, loved my son so much, yet felt such pure and piercing unhappiness?

"You say," Bentley whispers. His big brown eyes are sleepy. Not only did I break my promise, but I forgot his nap, and I am feeding him too late. I am quite sure there must be good fathers in the world; if I could meet one, maybe he could show me how to do it right.

"I'm sorry," I begin, marveling at how craven parenting has become in our strange new century. I do not recall my parents ever apologizing for failing to take me someplace I expected to go. Kimmer and I seem to do it all the time. So do most of our friends. "Sorry, sweetheart."

"Dare *Mommy*," he replies—perhaps a hope, perhaps a preference, perhaps a threat. "Mommy *kiss.* Dare *you!*"

My heart twists and my face burns, for he has learned how to use what few words he knows to skewer his guilt-ridden parents, but I am saved from having to answer my son's riposte by the arrival of our cheeseburgers and lemonade. Bentley digs in eagerly, whatever he was trying to say quite forgotten, and, in my considerable relief, I take far too large a bite of my burger and begin at once to cough. Bentley laughs. Gazing at his smiling, ketchup-smeared face, I find myself wishing that Kimmer were here to see her son, to laugh along with us, the old Kimmer, the loving, gentle Kimmer, the witty Kimmer, the fun Kimmer, the Kimmer who still, now and then, wanders by for a visit; and, if my wife's becoming Judge Madison will make it easier for that Kimmer to pop in, then it is my duty to do everything I can to help her achieve her goal. All the more reason not to let Marc and Lynda win.

Duty. So old-fashioned a word. Yet I know I must do my duty, not just to my wife but to my son. And to that increasingly arcane concept known as family.

I love my family.

Love is an activity, not a feeling—didn't one of the great theologians say that? Or maybe it was the Judge, who never ceased to stress duty rather than choice as the foundation of a civilized morality. I do not remember who coined the phrase, but I am beginning to understand what it means. True love is not the helpless desire to possess the cherished object of one's fervent affection; true love is the disciplined generosity we require of ourselves for the sake of another when we would rather be selfish; that, at least, is how I have taught myself to love my wife.

I wink at Bentley again and he grins back, chewing thoughtfully on a french fry. I unfold the *Vineyard Gazette*—and nearly choke again: PRIVATE INVESTIGATOR DROWNS AT MENEMSHA BEACH, the headline blares. *Police Consider Death "Suspicious,"* the next line informs us. Staring up at me from the right-hand side of the page is a very bad photograph of a man the newspaper identifies as one Colin Scott; but I knew him somewhat better as Special Agent McDermott.

PART II

TURTON DOUBLING

Turton doubling—In the composition of chess problems, a theme in which one White piece withdraws, allowing a second White piece to move in front of it, so that the two of them can attack the Black king together along the same line.

CHAPTER 18

MORE NEWS BY PHONE

(1)

"You know, he really was from South Carolina," says Cassie Meadows. "And Scott really was his name."

"Oh, so now they're willing to tell us his name? Nice of them."

"I'm not sure why they wouldn't tell us before."

"Well, now that he's dead, they don't have a choice, do they? I mean, his name was all over the papers up there." It is Monday, four days since I opened the *Gazette* and saw the picture of Colin Scott, three days since I hopped the first ferry of the morning and rushed home to a frantic Kimmer. The three of us stood in the driveway hugging for so long I actually believed that my wife wanted a full explanation; but I was wrong. She was just happy, she said, to have her family back. The rest would have to wait. "I don't get the idea the FBI is actually being all that helpful on this," I tell Meadows bitterly.

"Mr. Corcoran thinks the Bureau is doing all it can."

"I see," I mutter, although I do not. I am standing in my study, gazing out the window as I love to, wishing the late November sky would clear sufficiently to spill a bit of sunshine on Hobby Road. I draw in a breath, let it out, concentrate on not placing blame. Yet. "So, if the FBI is being so helpful, have they explained what Scott was doing out in that boat?"

"Oh, he was keeping an eye on you, no question about that. He'd been following you for weeks, it sounds like."

"Swell."

Meadows laughs, but gently. "I don't think you have to worry about him any more, Mr. Garland. If you see what I mean."

I make a small sound of assent.

"The Bureau doesn't think his friends had anything to do with it," she continues, her tone conversational. She seems amused by the whole thing. "They were just fishing buddies from Charleston. One of them—let me check my notes—yep, ran a filling station. It seems Mr. Scott spun them some story about fishing in New England out of season, said he knew where they could get a boat. . . . Anyway, they went to the Island with him. They told the police that Scott had been drinking, and when he fell overboard and they couldn't find him, they kind of panicked. So they returned the boat and ran off."

"But they came back."

"Later, when they were a little less drunk. But I don't think that was until after they saw the story in the paper."

"So, did either one of them meet the description of . . . of Agent Foreman?"

"I'm afraid not." She actually laughs. "His friends were both white."

"Huh." I remind myself of a tiny bit of wisdom from my own days of practicing law, that there are times when the story that sounds too good to be true is the story that is true.

Meadows is still disgorging facts. "So, anyway, the Bureau raided Scott's office down in Charleston. And guess what? They found his diaries and some files, and it looks like he told you the truth. Somebody did hire him to recover papers that your father supposedly had in his possession when he died. Unfortunately, the diary doesn't say who hired him to do it, or what the papers were exactly."

"How convenient," I mutter, suddenly quite lonely. Bentley is back at his preschool, Kimmer is back in San Francisco with Jerry Nathanson, and I have yet to venture back into the classroom. But for my wife's possible judgeship, I would be tempted to take Dean Lynda up on her manipulative offer after all, and forgo a few more weeks. Of course, if Kimmer were not a candidate, the offer would never have been made.

"Hmmm?"

"If he wouldn't trust the name of the client to paper . . ."

"Oh. Oh, I see." Enthusiastic. "You're thinking about Jack Ziegler, I guess."

"That would be correct."

"Well, Mr. Garland, you shouldn't worry about Mr. Ziegler. Mr. Corcoran told me you would probably think Mr. Ziegler had something to do with . . . with hiring Mr. Scott. Mr. Corcoran asked me to tell you that he spoke to Mr. Ziegler, and that Mr. Ziegler denied hiring Mr. Scott, and Mr. Corcoran says he is inclined to believe him." I almost smile at the way Meadows is tripping over the need to call everybody "Mr.," but Uncle Mal runs a very old-fashioned law firm. I wonder how long he will be able to get away with insisting on these little formalities, whether the new breed of lawyers—the ones who skip ties because their dot-com clients do—will put up with the Corcoran & Klein style. "He also asked me to tell you that he defended Mr. Ziegler in his perjury trial in '83 and can usually tell if he is lying or not."

"How does he know he can tell?"

"I beg your pardon?"

"Never mind. Look. Could I speak to Mr. Corcoran myself?"

"He's in Brussels. But whatever you need, you can get through me."

I wonder whether Uncle Mal is avoiding me intentionally, foisting me off on Meadows in order to get rid of me, or if I am simply being my usual hypersensitive self.

"But, hey, I have some good news for you," says Meadows suddenly, ever chipper.

"I could use some."

"Mr. Corcoran says that the background check on your wife has started. In fact, the Bureau will be sending a couple of agents to interview her in the next few days. And to talk to you, too."

"She's out of town." I am being quarrelsome for the sake of being quarrelsome. By rights I should be happy for Kimmer.

"Oh, I think the Bureau will be able to track her down." Meadows seems to be waiting for me to say something—*thank you*, perhaps—but I am in one of my bright red moods and am having trouble with good manners. "Anyway, Mr. Corcoran just wanted you to know that," she concludes, deflated.

Despite my efforts to restrain it, Garland breeding asserts itself at last: "That's great news, Ms. Meadows. Thank you." Or maybe I am just being polite because it has occurred to me that I need more of her help.

"I had nothing to do with it. And, please, call me Cassie."

"Okay, Cassie."

"You're certainly an interesting client," she adds, and I can tell she is leading up to a hurried goodbye, to get back to serious work. "It's been an experience."

"Wait."

"Hmmm?"

I take a moment to select the right words. "Cassie, look, there's something I was wondering."

"Why am I not surprised?" She is trying, I know, to stay friendly, but her sarcasm cuts near the bone. I hate seeming needy.

"Because you're good at your job," I murmur, stroking her a little.

It does no good. "What is it you want to know, Misha?" Very businesslike. She has no reason to take me too seriously, for there is plenty I have yet to unveil. I have not quite told everything to anybody. Not Kimmer, not Meadows, not Uncle Mal. So Meadows knows nothing of *Angela's boyfriend*, let alone the peculiar repetition of the word *Excelsior*. The trouble is, I have to talk to somebody.

"Well . . . you remember that Colin Scott said he was looking for some papers that a client left with the . . . with my father?"

"Sure." I have the impression that Cassie Meadows's attention is on something else, work for a paying client, no doubt.

"And you told me the FBI thinks it's true?"

"Mmmm-hmmm."

"Well, did you ever find out who?"

"Sorry?"

"Did you ever find out which client left the papers?"

"Oh. Oh, well." I have the sense that I have touched upon a delicate matter. "Well, Misha, I can assure you, the firm is going through its records with some care." I wonder if she is the one who has been assigned to *go through* the records. So boring and thankless a task for a fast-track lawyer would certainly explain her irritation. "The process is pretty much complete. We haven't found any indication of anyone who might have given your father any papers. But you have to understand, your father was an extremely busy man who did not generally have, uh, the kind of relationship with the firm's clients that would lead to their entrusting him, and him alone, with sensitive documents." Her uneasiness, even across the telephone line, is contagious. I get the message, the one I half expected: as far as Corcoran & Klein knows, the Judge didn't *have* any clients. And I remember, suddenly and sadly, the moment at the funeral when Mallory Corcoran's turn to speak came round. Standing before the thin congregation, his voice cracked and teary, he kept referring to the Judge's *greatness*, repeating the word until I began to wonder whether he meant to imply that the greatness expired long ago, perhaps because the increasing wildness of my father's politics had become more and more an embarrassment for a firm that once thought his name would positively glow from a letter-head already bright with former Senators and Cabinet officers.

No clients, I register. The Judge had no clients. I make a little mental note, a knot in my memory handkerchief, and then I make another decision.

"Does the firm happen to have any clients with 'Excelsior' in the name?" I ask Cassie Meadows.

"Why do you ask?"

"Call it a hunch."

"Hold on," she says. I hear the sound of a keyboard tapping and a mouse clicking, and then that distinctive *blunk!* sound that Windows generates (unless you know how to change it) when it cannot find what you are looking for. "Nope." She pauses, clicks again, types, waits. Another *blunk!* "Not even in the confidential files."

"Well, it was just a hunch."

"Sure. The name just popped into your head."

"No, no, just something . . . something somebody mentioned about my dad." I never lie well, least of all when I have no time to think.

"Okay, if you say so."

Great. Now, where I was worried about generating irritation, I have created actual skepticism, if not distrust. Still, there is nowhere to go but forward, as the Judge loved to say. "I have one last favor to ask."

"I've heard that before."

"I'm serious this time."

"Okay, Misha, okay." Somewhere during the past few minutes, Meadows began using my nickname, but she never quite asked permission. Perhaps *Professor Garland* is a bit too formal, but even Mallory Corcoran, who has known me all my life, calls me *Talcott*. I have not corrected her, because contemporary norms of conversation do not provide any tools for asking someone to be more formal in addressing you, rather than less. "One last favor." She laughs briefly, high-pitched, reedy. "So, who do I pry information out of this time? The White House Situation Room? The CIA?"

"No information. I have to be in Washington the end of the week for a conference on tort reform. I'd like to come by the firm and take a look at my father's old office."

"There's no point, Misha. I don't know what you're looking for, but the room is completely empty. There's not even any furniture. I think one of the partners is getting ready to move in."

"I just need two minutes. But if you think it's going to be a problem,

I can call Uncle Mal." Using the nickname to remind her that I have some clout with her boss.

"No," she says at once, "I'm sure it'll be fine. Just call me in the morning whatever day you want to come up."

I tell her I will. Then, because I can tell she is getting worried, I assure her that I am through asking favors. This is probably a lie, and Meadows probably knows it. If only the dead bodies that are starting to pile up were not so conveniently and swiftly explained away, I might even leave her alone. Or maybe not. There is, after all, still the Judge's cryptic note to decipher, but I have yet to mention it to Meadows or Uncle Mal. "I'll try to behave," I promise her.

Meadows laughs.

After hanging up, I sit irresolutely, wondering how much I really want to know. But after what happened on the Vineyard the only reasonable answer is *everything I can.* So I call my basketball buddy Rob Saltpeter and ask him to try to set up an appointment for me when I am in Washington at the end of the week. His contacts, in this case, are better then mine.

"Sure, Misha," says Rob. "Whatever will help." But I detect in his voice, as in those of most of my friends lately, an emotion I have not previously encountered.

Doubt.

(11)

A GRAY AUTUMN DUSK is falling, and I am standing at the kitchen window, watching my son at play. A little while ago, it finally occurred to me to try to reach Just Alma, down in Philadelphia, who predicted, in her confusing way, that people would be coming after me. But nobody seems to know how to reach her. Even Mariah, who keeps in touch with everybody, has only a street address, not a telephone number. I wonder, briefly, whether our mad aunt even has a telephone. Finally, I try one of her children, a social worker, who tells me that his mother always goes to the islands from December to March. He refuses, rudely, to give me a number for her, but does agree to pass along the message that I would like to speak to her. If he hears from her, that is; he assures me gleefully that he may not.

I shake my head at the incivility of the world, even though I have shown the capacity to be a bit uncivil myself. In the old days, if I came upon my wife's address book sitting open on the little table in the front hall, I might begin flipping through it without troubling to obtain her permission, pausing here and there to ask myself whether a particular underlined name was a contact, related to her career . . . or whether it was something else. I might even scribble down a few. Recently, Kimmer has become "teched-up," abandoning her address book for a Visor Edge, and thus, intentionally or not, rendering her telephone list impervious to the scrutiny of her husband, who is irretrievably analog. (My wife sometimes accuses me, gently, of possessing "analog morality.")

Kimmer, whether she admits it or not, is a considerable star at the firm, and in the city's legal community. She works much longer hours than I do, but also brings in two-thirds of our family's income, which gives her a built-in advantage whenever I point out that her extravagant spending—clothing and jewelry and the car, mainly, but also fancy gifts for relatives back home—dents our already battered family fisc. She seems to think I should be quiet and uncomplaining as long as the money rolls in. Kimmer loves the practice of law, but our conversations about her job rarely extend any longer beyond *I have to stay late tonight* or *I have a filing due.* It pains me to realize how little I know of Kimmer's working life, and how much her excitement over what she does for a living has become an additional barrier between us. Perhaps that is one reason I am so suspicious of Jerry Nathanson, one of the leading lawyers in the city and generally considered above reproach: when my wife speaks of her work with him, her eyes sparkle and her breath quickens. I wonder whether she displays as much emotion when, at the office, she speaks of me.

Bentley, chasing a pigeon, stumbles over a tree branch. I stand very still, fighting the impulse to rush out the door to comfort him, and, sure enough, he comes up laughing. I smile, too. Back in September, over Kimmer's strenuous objections, I began allowing him to venture alone into the back yard. Bentley was delighted. His mother, not yet over the pain of nearly losing him the night he was born, points out that he could fall and injure himself, but I have always believed in letting children explore, another hard lesson from the Judge, who preached that a few fractures and bruises are a small price to pay for a sense of wonder and independence. One of my father's favorite applause lines was that the purpose of the state is not to create a society that is risk-free. His corporate audiences loved it because it implied less regulation of their products. His religious audiences loved it because it implied the fragility of our material lives. His college audiences loved it because it implied considerable freedom in their personal habits. None of his audiences quite realized, I suspect, how important a catharsis it was for my father to believe what he was telling them. And all of it, like his hard-edged conservatism itself, went back to the death of Abby.

Before Abby was killed, my father was already a favorite of conservatives, but only because he was, as somebody once said, to his fury, a "reasonable Negro"—the kind of black man you might be willing to negotiate with. In the sixties, the Judge was not yet the dour, distracted, somehow depressing man you no doubt remember from his regrettable confirmation hearings. Even after Abby's death, I have often thought, his career might not have taken the bizarre direction that it did, had he only experienced the emotional satisfaction of seeing her murderer— that was always the Judge's word for the hit-and-run driver, and, by his lights, a fair one—seeing her murderer caught and punished. But the police never found a suspect. My father being who he was, my parents were regularly briefed by a senior detective: a few leads, he would tell them month after grueling month, but nothing concrete. The law had been the anchor of my father's faith, as it was for so many civil rights lawyers of the fifties and sixties, and the inability of the vast machinery of American justice to find a sports car that killed one little girl first bewildered him, then angered him. He badgered journalists, belittled the police, and, at the recommendation of friends, hired a private investigator, an expensive one from Potomac, whose supposed leads the police scornfully dismissed, to my father's fury. He bearded friends in the White House, friends on Capitol Hill, even friends in the District Building, the shabby brown structure housing what there was in those days of the city's government, and received in response only pitying condolences. He posted ever-larger rewards, but all the calls were from cranks. According to Addison, the Judge even consulted a psychic or two—"but not the right ones," adds my brother, the radio talk-show king, who no doubt could have provided better names.

As his ideas evaporated and his wrath mounted, my father spent more and more time locked in his study at Shepard Street. (This was before he knocked down the walls upstairs.) I would listen fretfully at the closed door, soon joined by Mariah, home for the summer from Stanford, neither of us sure whether there was something we should be doing. We would hear him muttering to himself, possibly weeping, certainly drinking. He passed the midnight hours on the phone with his few remaining friends, who began to avoid his calls. He ate little. He fell behind in his judicial work. He stopped playing poker with his cronies. My mother soldiered on in the manner of her class, hosting her parties, often alone, and representing the family at a variety of functions, always alone, but we children were terrified.

When the time came for our annual trek to Oak Bluffs, Mariah, with a summer job in Washington, stayed behind, leaving me alone to suffer through what I truly thought was my father's madness. I worried that it might be contagious, or hereditary. My mother offered endless tearful hugs and desperate reassurances, but no explanations. September arrived. Mariah returned to Stanford and I began my final year of high school. The house on Shepard Street became a single vast silence. The family spiraled downhill, and nobody talked about it. I stopped inviting schoolmates home. I was too embarrassed. Some nights, I myself stayed away. To my chagrin, my parents scarcely noticed. A year passed, a year and a half. I made my own escape to college. Now my parents had only each other for comfort, and their marriage—so my brother later assured me—came as close as it ever would to sundering. I spent most of my vacations away from Washington. I had no sense of being missed. And then, quite suddenly, the sea of melancholy in which the Judge was drowning dried up. I never quite understood why. All I knew was that the will of which he had preached throughout our several childhoods reasserted itself: he drew a line, as Addison later explained it, and placed Abby and the mystery of her death on the side marked *Past*. He came roaring out of his study like a recently uncaged animal, alive once more to life and its possibilities. He began to laugh and joke. He reawakened to his old goal of being the fastest writer on the court of appeals. He stopped his frightening new habit of drinking, and resumed his boring old one of interfering in his children's lives. He seemed himself once more, and would not admit his momentary weakness had ever existed. So, when his old friend Oz McMichael, the cantankerous Virginia moderate who sat in the Senate forever, lost his own son to a hit-and-run driver, and dared suggest that my father join his support group of parents whose children had been killed the same way, the Judge curtly refused, and—this is still according to Addison—stopped speaking to the man altogether.

A support group, I am thinking, gazing at my contemplative, and now sleepy, little boy. Maybe, now that Scott is gone, I need to overcome my family's prejudice against counseling and get some. Last summer I gave it a try, pouring out my marital woes to a pastor—not my own, which would have been too risky, but a gentle man named Morris Young whom I met through my work in the community.

And Morris Young helped. A little.

Maybe, I am thinking now, maybe if I promise to stop tracking down the various mysteries my father left behind, Kimmer and I can go to counseling together, and make the marriage work. It will be easier, of course, if the President picks her for the court of appeals, but, I admit glumly, that prospect seems to fade with every online crank who spreads a theory just crazy enough to keep the story alive.

(III)

MARIAH CALLS while Bentley is in the bathtub. I am doing the night-time duty with our boy because Kimmer, who usually draws sustenance from caring for him, is away. Not that I mind spending this time with him. Oh, no! Ever since our return from the Vineyard, I have hardly been able to bear having Bentley out of my sight—although life and work make it necessary. Still, I could listen to his *Dare you* for hours on end, even as my heart twists with the hopeless pain of the failed desire to give him a normal childhood . . . whatever counts as normal these days. Two parents who actually love each other might be an interesting and radical beginning, but the mere suggestion that the traditional household might turn out to be good for children offends so many dif-ferent constituencies that hardly anybody is willing to raise it any longer. Which further suggests, as George Orwell knew, that within a generation or two nobody will think it either. What survives is only what we are able to communicate. Moral knowledge that remains secret eventually ceases to be knowledge.

Although it may still be moral.

When the telephone rings, Bentley is performing a delicate experi-ment in which he stuffs into his bright red plastic boat as many little Playmobil characters as it will hold and waits to see if it will sink. Some-times it sinks. Sometimes it doesn't. Sometimes he can pile on fifteen soldiers and the boat remains comfortably afloat. Sometimes fewer than a dozen will sink it. Bentley frowns, trying to reason out a princi-ple. I do not see one either, which pleases me: No matter how much of the universe the physical scientists are able to explain, some events remain chaotic, even random. The sinking or floating of Bentley's red boat seems to be one of them.

We live so much of our lives in chaos. Human history can be viewed as an endless search for greater order: everything from language to religion to law to science tries to impose a framework on chaotic existence. The existentialists, sometimes wrongly described as disbelieving in an underlying order, saw the risks and the foolishness of the obsession with creating one. Hitler showed the risk, as did any number of populist tyrants before him. I teach my students that law, too, shows the risk, when we try to regulate a phenomenon—human behavior—that we do not even understand. I am not arguing against law, I add as they scribble in furious confusion, but against the Panglossian assumption that we can ever do law particularly well. The darkness in which we live dooms us to do it badly.

Which is why, weighing up the balance of my life, I would rather be bathing my son at this moment than finishing any of the pointless work piled up in my small study down on the first floor. On my desk is the edited version of the overdue manuscript on mass tort litigation that I am publishing in the school's snooty law review. I sometimes wish I had the courage of my colleagues Lem Carlyle and Rob Saltpeter, two of our genuine superstars, who announced in a joint letter to the *American Lawyer* three years ago that they would no longer write for student-edited law reviews because they were tired of kids two or three years out of college purporting to know the law—to say nothing of how to write—better than their professors. As nearly all the nation's law reviews are edited by students, this means, in practice, that Lem and Rob, if they want to be taken seriously as scholars, are forced to write books, which neither one of them seems to have any trouble getting done. But most of us labor on in the trenches, filling the pages of the nation's law reviews with ideas that, to paraphrase what someone wrote about the great eighteenth-century chess theorist François-André Philidor, move at dizzying speed from being too far in advance of their time to be taken seriously to being too outmoded to matter.

Yes, there are days when I love being a law professor; but there are days when I hate it, too.

BENTLEY'S HEAD jerks up furiously at the sound of the telephone, for he knows that it commonly presages a parental abandonment. I carry the portable into the bathroom whenever he is in the tub, a habit I picked up from Kimmer, who does not want to miss the chance that a client might call, allowing her to dry Bentley and dress him for bed with the handset cocked in her neck, talking away, able to bill an hour or two while doing her maternal duties.

I try to compromise, picking up the receiver with one hand, piling Playmobil men and women onto the red boat with the other.

"Did I wake you?" Mariah begins, which has been her idea of a joke ever since the early days of my marriage to Kimmer, when calling after the dinner hour was always a risk: the chances were excellent that we were already in bed, although never asleep.

"No, no, I'm sitting here with Bentley. He's in the tub."

"Give him my love."

"Auntie Mariah says she loves you."

My son ignores me, shoving aside the Playmobil boat, plunging his face into the water, and blowing bubbles to the surface.

"He says he loves you, too."

"So how are you guys doing?"

"Oh, great, we're great," I enthuse, knowing Mariah did not call to chitchat. We have made peace from our fight of a few weeks ago, but I pay tribute in the form of listening whenever she wants to talk. I carry the portable phone over to the sink and fill a paper cup with water. This could take a while.

"Anyway, Tal, I'm in Washington, and I found something that might interest you."

"Why am I not surprised?"

We share a laugh, small and strained, like the forced hysterics that paper over pain. Early in her seventh month of pregnancy, my sister has made the round trip between Washington and Darien three times in the five weeks since we buried the Judge. After years of moody silence toward me, Mariah now phones every three or four days, probably because nobody else will listen to the theories she revises so fast that they now and then seem to switch identities in the middle of a sentence. Her husband is too busy, our big brother is too hard to track down, and her friends . . . well, her friends, I suspect, are not taking her calls.

As for myself, I do not mind the calls, as long as she talks only to me; if I can keep her speculations within reasonable bounds, or keep her from voicing them aloud, I can help Kimmer and my big sister at the same time.

Besides, Mariah could be on to something; Colin Scott, after all, did not go off to Canada; he followed my family to the Vineyard, and died there. Or maybe I am simply joining my sister in her headlong rush toward the far reaches of fantasy.

This evening's call is typical. Mariah is down at Shepard Street again, and was apparently awake for half the night, going through the papers in the attic. Her obsession ever since the night she and Sally began the search, after our meeting with Sergeant Ames. Mariah sits for hours on end, surrounded by mountains of contracts, letters, check stubs, drafts of essays and speeches, menus, folded press clippings tearing along their ancient creases, diagrams of chess positions, notes for the Judge's books, recipes, unframed awards and commendations, bills from the man who boards the window of Vinerd Howse every winter, condolence cards, *Playbills* from forgotten Broadway shows, deeds, drafts of long-forgotten opinions from his days on the bench, printed instructions from a long-vanished game called Totopoly, unused yellow legal pads, photographs of our mother, hardcover editions of Trollope, memoranda from various assistants, outdated maps of the Vineyard, credit card receipts, pocket diaries, and newspapers and magazines galore: back issues of the *Washington Post*, the *Wall Street Journal*, and the *National Review*, a handful of yellowing front pages from the *Vineyard Gazette*, even, astonishingly, two or three tattered copies of *Soldier of Fortune*. And, amidst it all, a grim sentinel guarding the debris, sits my big sister. Patiently examining the bits, one by one. Looking for a pattern. A clue. An answer. Hoping to finding something the police missed. And Mallory Corcoran's minions, who spent an afternoon in the house three days after the funeral, hunting for any confidential papers that belonged at the firm. Mariah believes she can outsearch them all. Real investigative journalism, I suppose, is like that: the sifting of details to find more details to find a muddle, and then discerning in the muddle an outline, and finally rendering the outline clear for one's readers.

I have lately seen the low-ceilinged attic of the house on Shepard Street, its dreary, dusty shadows lighted by the single skylight. I dropped in while Kimmer and Bentley and I were in D.C. for our miserable Thanksgiving. You have to climb a narrow staircase behind the bathroom to get up to what the Judge called the garret, but Mariah climbs it regularly, and scarcely a corner has been spared her researches. I have stood there, hunched over, letting my gaze wander across the stacks and sprays and crosses of papers, some lying underneath glass paperweights borrowed from our mother's collection downstairs, some shoved up against the single gabled window, some connected by pins and colored yarn—red for this, green for that. It is not right to call her creation a shambles. Mariah has explained the system to me, or tried to, during our late-night calls, and she has described for me the little black composition book where she has sketched her theories and drawn her connections. *My ledger,* she called it in one late-night call. *Next to my family, the most precious thing I own.* Looking around at the chaos that Mariah thinks is orderly, I worry. Surely Arthur Bremer's apartment once looked as the attic now does. And John Hinckley's. And Squeaky Fromme's. I have had a few chats with Howard, who tells me that he is starting to worry about his wife, that he never sees her, she is down in Washington nearly every weekend. She often takes the children, too, sometimes bundling all five of them, along with the au pair of the moment—she fires them fast—into the Navigator for the rumble down the New Jersey Turnpike. Marshall and Malcolm are old enough to help a little with the sorting, but the twins only play, and Marcus, soon to relinquish his role as the baby, naps in my sister's old bedroom on the second floor, watched over by the au pair, who rarely speaks English, at least to me.

Usually, when Mariah calls after a few days in the attic, we fight. The conversation always begins the same way. She whispers unhappily of her discoveries, always things I would rather not know—an ancient love letter to the Judge from a woman whose name neither of us quite recognizes, an award from his college fraternity for victory in a drinking contest, a note in his appointment book to meet some Senator whose politics make her ill. My sister sets great store by such artifacts. She believes that she is reconstructing our father, that she will learn from his simulacrum a deeper truth he kept hidden from us. That his shade lives on amidst the flotsam and jetsam of his written life, and that it will finally speak. I try to tell her that these are just worthless scraps of paper, that we should discard them, but I am speaking to a woman whose five-million-dollar home is decorated almost entirely with photographs of her unprepossessing children, and whose sentimentality, as

Kimmer once observed, would lead her to save her children's soiled diapers if she could only think of a way to do it neatly. I gently suggest to my stubborn sister that we did not understand our father when he was alive, and we will not understand him any better now that he is dead, but Mariah, alone among the children of Claire and Oliver Garland, has never conceded that there are things beyond her understanding, which is doubtless why she was the only one of us to earn straight A's in college. I try to tell her that we certainly will not come to know the Judge through his papers, but Mariah remains a journalist at her core, with a master's degree in history, and my words are a challenge to her faith. So, in the end, unable to bear another dramatic reading from a request for a zoning variance to enable installation of a nonconforming septic system at Vinerd Howse, I always tell her that I have problems of my own, and she snaps back that blood is thicker than water, which was one of our mother's favorite phrases, and which Mariah repeats often, even if she claimed as a child to hate it. My sister and I are talking more often than in the past, but, truce or no truce, we get along as badly as we ever did.

Consequently, when she tells me that she has found something we need to talk about, I brace myself for the worst—meaning the most useless, boring, trivial. Or the scariest—more talk of bullet fragments, which, lately, she has not mentioned. Or the most likely—she has heard about the death of McDermott/Scott, and wants to explain how it fits into the conspiracy.

What actually comes out of her mouth, therefore, takes me by surprise.

"Tal, did you know Daddy owned a gun?"

"A gun?"

"Yes, a gun. As in a handgun. I found it last night, in the bedroom, in the back of a drawer. I was just looking for papers, and I found this gun. It was in a box, with . . . well, with some bullets. But that's not why I called." She pauses, presumably for dramatic effect, but there is no need: she has my full attention. "Tal, I had somebody look at it this afternoon. An expert? It's been fired, Tal. Recently."

CHAPTER 19

TWO TALES ARE TOLD

(1)

"THE DISTRICT OF COLUMBIA probably has the strictest gun law in the country," Lemaster Carlyle assures me. "It's pretty much impossible to obtain a permit there." Pause. "On the other hand, Virginia is right across the river, and it is one of the easiest places in the civilized world to purchase a legal handgun. People buy them there and take them everywhere."

"Huh," is my thoughtful contribution.

"So, if a relative of *mine* who lived in D.C. died and left a gun behind"—in his teasing Barbadian lilt, he is tossing my transparent hypothetical back at me—"my guess would be that he purchased it in Virginia and simply ignored the District's laws. Plenty of people do."

I nod slowly, my half-finished grilled-chicken sandwich, the specialty of the house at Post, gone cold and chewy. Lemaster is a former prosecutor and knows about these things, but his information dovetails with my intuition. Once again, my father seems to have lived on the edge of the law. I would rather uncover fewer of these distressing tidbits of information, but I cannot seem to stop looking for them.

"You have to turn the gun in, of course."

"What?"

"The gun. It is still unregistered and unlicensed. Nobody can legally possess it. It has to be turned in."

"Oh." Lemaster Carlyle is a person of sufficient integrity that I suspect this would be his advice even had he not spent three years as an Assistant United States Attorney before turning to the academic world. I watch him pick at his shrimp salad. He never seems to eat very much, never seems to gain an ounce of weight. His suits always fit perfectly.

He is a small man with a huge mind, a few years older than I, a Harvard Law School graduate who was also in his day a divinity student before joining our ranks. His smooth, lean face, at once playful and wise, is a rich West Indian purple-black. His perfect wife, Julia, is as small and dark and cute as Lemaster himself. They live in one of our tonier suburbs with their four perfect children. He stands miles above me in the school's unwritten hierarchy, and is adored by everybody in the building, and most alumni as well, for he is also a nearly perfect politician. Although he calls himself a progressive, Lem has voted Republican the last few elections, citing the Democratic Party's opposition to school vouchers, which he sees as the only hope for the children of the inner city. He was cofounder and, for all I know, sole member of a forgotten organization called Liberals for Bush. His pithy, closely reasoned op-eds dot the pages of the *New York Times* and the *Washington Post*. He seems to be on television every five minutes. He is also said to be restless. Many of our colleagues are begging him to wait patiently to succeed Lynda Wyatt, becoming our first black dean, but the rumor mill reports that Lem has grown as bored with the academy as he has with most things he has conquered, and will soon be leaving us for a full-time position at one of the television networks. At the Judge's funeral, people made a great fuss over him. I often wish I could like Lemaster more, and envy him less.

"And if the person who found the gun didn't turn it in?" I press.

He sips his water—nobody claims ever to have seen him drink anything else—and shakes his slender head. His small eyes smile at me above a thin mustache. "Finding it is not a crime. Possessing it is a crime."

So I will advise my sister to turn it in. Case closed.

Except that Lemaster Carlyle levers it back open. "This relative of yours, Talcott—do you know why he thought he needed a gun?"

"No."

"Most people buy them for self-protection, even people who buy them illegally. But some of course are purchased in order to commit crimes."

"Okay."

He dabs at his lips with the paper napkin, then folds it carefully before depositing it on the table, next to his plate. He has eaten perhaps four bites. "If it were a relative of mine, I would not be interested in where he got the gun, or what could happen to me for possessing it. I would be interested in learning why he bought it in the first place."

BACK INSIDE OLDIE, heading for the central staircase, I pretend to myself for a silly moment that I want to put all of this behind me. But I am no longer chasing the truth; the truth seems to be chasing me. Why did my father want a gun? To protect himself or to commit a crime, Lemaster Carlyle suggested. Neither one is happy news. What was my father involved in? I think of Jack Ziegler in the cemetery. I think of McDermott-Scott, deemed harmless by his local sheriff, but dead nevertheless, the circumstances suspicious. My shoulders sag. Kimmer's judgeship seems miles and miles distant. I am struck by a sudden urge to rush upstairs to visit Theo Mountain, for I need to be cheered up, but I have to avoid making my onetime mentor my full-time crutch.

I pass a knot of students: Crysta Smallwood arguing heatedly with several other women of color, as they nowadays style themselves. A few words float outward from their confab: *dialectical interstices* and *outsider position* and *reconstructed other.* I long for the days when students argued over the rules of civil procedure or the statute of limitations, back when the nation's leading law schools thought their job was teaching law.

Nearing my office, I notice Arnold Rosen, one of the faculty's great liberal hard-liners, gliding toward me in his powered wheelchair. He smiles his thin, superior smile, and I smile back reluctantly, for we are not close. I admire Arnie's mind and his determination to stick to his principles, but I am not sure that he admires anything in me, especially given that I am the son of the great conservative hero. Arnie came to us from Harvard about a decade ago, Stuart Land's masterful recruiting coup, and is said to be Lem Carlyle's only competitor to succeed Dean Lynda when she one day steps down.

A flick of his finger on a control rod slows the chair. His pale eyes are distant and judgmental as he looks up at me. "Good afternoon, Talcott."

"Hi, Arnie." My key is in my hand, signaling, I hope, that I do not really feel much like talking just now.

"I don't think I've had the chance to tell you how sorry I am about your father."

"Thank you," I mutter, too tired to be annoyed by his hypocrisy. Arnie teaches legal ethics and a variety of commercial law courses and is a prodigious scholar, but saves his real enthusiasm for the three great causes of the contemporary left: abortion, gay rights, and a very strict separation of church and state. A few months ago, my former student Shirley Branch, the first black woman we have ever hired, gave a paper at the semi-weekly faculty lunch arguing that the form of separation we intellectuals today take for granted is too strict, that its application would have harmed, for example, the civil rights movement. Arnie disagreed, suggesting that Shirley's notion would lead us back to the days of America as a Christian nation. The two of them went at it quite heatedly, until Rob Saltpeter, the moderator, defused the situation with a wry observation: *The trouble with America is not that it is a Christian nation but that too often it isn't.*

Rob, like Lem, has style.

"You know, Talcott," Arnie murmurs, smiling up at me, "one of our colleagues came to talk to me about you the other day."

"About me? What about me?"

"Well, it was peculiar. He thought you might have violated a rule of ethics. I set him straight, I assure you."

I sway on my feet. "What rule? What are you talking about?"

"You're doing some consulting work for a corporation. Something to do with toxic torts, correct?"

"Uh . . . yes. Yes, I am. So?"

"Well, our colleague asked me if it was proper for you to continue to write in the area when you were getting paid as an advocate to take a particular view."

"What!"

"You see the problem, I'm sure. Legal scholarship is supposed to be objective. That's our myth and we cling to it. We have to, or we're in the wrong business. That's why the school frowns on professors' doing too much consulting work."

"I understand that, but—"

Arnie circles his chair backward an inch or two, waves a hand in dismissal. "Not to worry, Talcott. It's a common misconception. There is no rule against it—there aren't really any ethical rules about legal scholarship—and, besides—"

"And, besides, I would never slant my scholarship for the sake of a fee!"

"Well, that's what I said, too." Nodding his head. "But our colleague seemed pretty sure. I have the impression we haven't heard the end of this."

I make a small sound. Disbelief, maybe, or simply anger. Is this more of the pressure Stuart mentioned?

"Arnie, listen. Who was it that came to you? Who brought this up?"

His hand flaps again. "Ah, Talcott, I wish I could tell you, but I can't."

"You can't? Why not?"

"Attorney-client privilege." Still smiling, he sails off down the hall.

CHAPTER 20

THE HALLS OF JUSTICE

(1)

"MISHA, it is so good to see you." A hug, because I am a man and he is a man. Male judges nowadays are afraid to hug their female clerks, or so my father used to say. But some of his facts he made up. "Come in, come in."

Wallace Warrenton Wainwright steps to one side, beckoning me to join him in his inner office. The chubby black messenger who walked me in from the clerk's office has vanished. As the door to the anteroom closes, it is just me and Wallace Wainwright. He is a tall man, at least five inches over six feet, with shoulders more thick than muscular, thinning brown-white hair, and a pale, studied asceticism about his friendly face. He seems too happy to be as smart as he is. He looks less like a judge than a friar—Franciscan, to be sure—and if you sat next to him on an airplane, you would never take Wallace Wainwright for an Associate Justice of the Supreme Court of the United States. But that is how history will record him. Outside this spacious room, computers buzz and bleep, printers zip, law clerks rush about, telephones softly burr— the sounds, as Justice Wainwright would surely describe the tumult, of justice being done. And maybe, from time to time, the Court *has* done justice, but a good deal less than most people seem to assume, for it has been, for most of its history, a follower, not an agent, of change. We law professors like to speak and write as though the past is otherwise, as though the Justices have lately abandoned a traditional role of protecting the weak against the strong.

We speak and write nonsense.

Like every other social institution, the Court has mainly been the ally of the insiders, a proposition that should come as no surprise, because only the insiders become the Presidents who nominate the Justices, the Senators who confirm them—or the candidates from whom the nominees are chosen in the first place. Liberals point to *Brown v. Board of Education* and *Roe v. Wade* as though they have identified the Court's appropriate role in the nation's governance, whereas all they have really identified is a peculiar epoch in history, during which the Justices set about trying to change America rather than trying to keep it the same. The epoch died, and the Court swiftly faded as an engine of social evolution, which probably would have made the Framers of the Constitution very happy. After all, Madison and Hamilton were insiders too.

Justice Wainwright—Mr. Justice Wainwright, they would have said in the grand old sexist tradition—is very much an insider, for he knows everybody. Everybody, that is, who matters in Washington. Small wonder that he, alone among the Justices, attended my father's funeral. He attends every wedding in town, so why not every burial? As I look around the room at his grand blue carpet and grander wooden desk, my eyes light upon his ego wall, a montage of photographs of the Justice with everybody from Mikhail Gorbachev to Bob Dylan to the Pope. There is a photograph of a stern Wainwright in Marine dress uniform, and another frame holds his decorations. There is a photograph of a smiling Wainwright with a clutch of babies in his lap: grandchildren, I suppose. The remaining walls are lined with solid wooden bookshelves holding the hundreds of cream-colored volumes of the United States Reports, the official record of the decisions of the Supreme Court, even though, in this digital age, no lawyer under the age of thirty opens the books any more, for everything in the books is also online (or so, unfortunately, young lawyers believe). I shake my head, trying and failing to envision my father in this magnificent office, had things gone otherwise. A wave of fatalism sweeps over me, the sense that nothing anybody could have done would have changed the inevitable outcome.

Nothing.

Wallace Wainwright, with his fine political eye, notices my uneasiness, puts a hand on my elbow, and directs me to a plush blue sofa. He perches on a hard wooden chair standing catercorner to it. Over his shoulder, through the high window, is a view of the Capitol building, its massive dome dull gray in the unkempt drizzle that is so predictable a part of a Washington December. Despite the weather, I revel in the delicious independence of the truant. I am playing hooky this wet afternoon from the conference on tort reform that is paying the expenses for my visit to the city; I am insufficiently grand to be missed. Yet, now that I am seated in Wainwright's chambers, the appointment arranged by Rob Saltpeter, who clerked for Wainwright years ago, I try to figure out how to begin. I fidget like a nervous first-year student forced unwillingly to recite a case.

Wallace Wainwright waits. And waits. He can afford to wait, or not to wait, as he likes. He knows who he is. He sits at the summit of the legal world and has nobody left to impress. His suit is mousy and shapeless and brown, more what you find in the secondhand shops down in Southeast than what you expect a Supreme Court Justice to wear. His old narrow tie is askew. His blue shirt is poorly pressed and unevenly tucked. Despite his impressive name, Wallace Wainwright comes, as the Judge used to say in some astonishment, from no particular background. The Wainwright family, again according to my father, was Tennessee trailer trash. Wallace, the middle brother among five, lied and cajoled and borrowed his way through UT, attended Vanderbilt's law school on a scholarship, and, in his early years of law practice, sent half his paycheck home, sometimes more if somebody from his vastly extended family needed surgery or the down payment for a car. Yet nowadays he lives in a small but pricey row house in Georgetown, with a huge country place for the weekends, twenty-five acres with horses for his daughters to ride, out near the town of Washington, sometimes called "Little Washington," in the middle of the Virginia hunt country. My father used to shake his head, bemused that his onetime colleague married rather well.

Associate Justice Wallace Warrenton Wainwright, the intellectual giant.

The man of the people.

The darling of the legal academy.

The last of the great liberal judges.

And the closest thing my father had to a friend when they sat together on the United States Court of Appeals for the District of Columbia Circuit, which is the real reason I have come. Despite their marked ideological differences, the two men were united in the belief that their minds were greater than those of the other judges on the court, a condescension not infrequently reflected in their dissenting opinions. It occurs to me that a court can be a little like a law school, or at least like mine. There are tiers, at least in the minds of those who assign themselves to the highest one. Judges Garland and Wainwright believed themselves to occupy a tier of their own, much to the resentment, so I have heard from Eddie Dozier, of the rest of the court. Although my father was perhaps a decade older than Wainwright, they used to pal around outside the courthouse too, playing golf and poker and fishing a bit, back before scandal destroyed my father's career. Even afterward, Wainwright tried to keep in touch, but eventually—so Addison has told me—the strain on my father was too much. The Judge was sitting still, even tumbling downward, and his old friend Wallace was still climbing the ladder. When the Democrats recaptured the White House, everybody knew that Wainwright would fill the first vacancy on the Supreme Court.

Everybody was right.

We sit in silence a moment longer, as I try to force myself to press forward. But the depression that has characterized the past couple of months has seized me once more, slowing my reason, increasing my doubts and fears. This morning I dropped by Corcoran & Klein, where Meadows, as promised, let me look around my father's empty corner office just down the hall from Uncle Mal's. Mrs. Rose, who was the Judge's assistant forever, is long gone, retired and moved to Phoenix. The room itself was truly empty: after the new carpet, repainting, and drapes, not even the Judge's ghost would be hanging around. But the inspection was just for show. I really dropped in to buy Cassie Meadows a cup of coffee so that I could have her undivided attention and watch her spontaneous reaction when I asked her whether my father had left behind one of those if-anything-should-happen-to-me notes.

Meadows never flinched. She thought it over, tapping a long finger against nearly invisible lips. "If he did, I wouldn't be privy to it. That kind of thing would be more Mr. Corcoran's department than mine."

The response I expected. I knew the answer to my next question before I asked it: No, Mr. Corcoran isn't in. He's away in Europe for a few weeks.

(I I)

"IT'S GOOD OF YOU to see me," I begin, feeling awkward and childish in the face of this physical, human reminder of all my ambitious father sought to attain . . . and failed to achieve.

"Nonsense," Wallace Wainwright huffs, with a surreptitious look at his watch—a Timex for the man of the people—before settling in his uncomfortable chair, crossing his bony legs, folding his large hands on his knee, which he at once begins to jiggle. "I'm just sorry we haven't had the chance to sit down in so long."

"It has been a long time," I agree.

"How's your lovely wife?" the Justice asks, even though I am fairly sure he has never laid eyes on Kimmer in his life. He is famous for a twisted, kindly smile, and he displays it now. Learned articles have been written on its significance. "I understand you have a couple of children now. Or is it just the one?"

"Just Bentley. He's three."

"A wonderful age," he says, filling the time with these irrelevancies. I do not know whether he is trying to put me at my ease or to put me off. "I remember when mine were three. Well, not all at once," he adds pedantically. "But I remember each of them."

"You have three children? Is that what I remember?"

"Four," he corrects me gently, ending my effort to show that I, too, am a social being. "All girls," he muses. "An intriguing variety of ages."

Still he waits.

Nowhere to go but forward.

"Mr. Justice, I wanted to talk to you, if you are willing, about my father." He raises his eyebrows in gentle inquisition, and waits some more. "About those last couple of years he spent on the bench. Before . . . well, before what happened."

"Of course, Misha, of course." Charming as ever. Years ago, honoring his friendship with my father, I invited Wainwright to call me by my nickname, and he has never stopped. "Those were difficult years. I cannot imagine what it must have been like for you, and I am so sorry about it all."

"Thank you, Mr. Justice. I know what your friendship meant to the . . . to my father."

Justice Wainwright smiles again. "Oh, well, he was a very special man. He meant a great deal to me. A giant, an absolute giant. The finest judicial craftsman it has ever been my privilege to know. I suppose you would have to say he was my mentor on the bench. Yes. What happened . . . well, it does nothing to alter my admiration for him." A pause, now that he has made his little speech. "Yes. So. What would you like to know?"

Here goes. "Well, I was wondering . . . not about the days after what happened, but the days before. When he was nominated in the first place. Around then. What was going on. Including what was, or wasn't, going on with Jack Ziegler."

"You know, it's interesting. Interesting. Nobody has asked me about any of this, not even when the Congress"—*the* is his affectation, as are the studied repetitions and pauses that give him time to think—"was doing all those investigations. A few reporters, I guess, who somehow wangled my home number. Reporters. Of course I didn't talk to *them*." Like most judges, Wallace Wainwright regards journalists in the way that the human body probably views the *E. coli* bacterium: you know you need a little of it for everything to work right, but you still kind of keep hoping somebody will kill it off. "There's been a great silence about your father, Misha. A silence. Yes. I mean about what it was like in the courthouse in those days. And maybe that's best."

I hesitate. Is he warning me away or drawing me in? I do not know. I cannot read the signs. So I press my own agenda instead. "That's what I want to know, I guess. What it was like in the courthouse. What my father was like in those days."

"What it was like." Repeating my line, repeating his, the Justice recrosses his long legs and leans back in his chair. He is looking now not at me but at the ceiling, where, perhaps, he is reading the waves and currents of memory. "Well. Yes. You have to remember that, at the time all of this happened, your father was a nominee for the Supreme Court."

"I know that."

He catches my impatience and patiently corrects it. "Well, you know and you don't know. You have to have a sense of what a court is like when one of the judges is headed for the high bench—or when everybody thinks he is headed that way, anyway. I've been through that several times. Several times. I was there for Bob Bork. For Oliver Garland. For Doug Ginsburg." A wry smile. "Of course, when I list the names that way, I guess you could say the odds are not very good from the D.C. Circuit."

I smile back.

"But, still, even though none of those nominees . . . ah, none of them prevailed . . . even so, at the time of the announcement, the atmosphere was, well, special."

"Special how?" I prompt.

"Well," says the Justice again. "Well, now, at first, when Reagan announced that he was nominating your father? Nobody was entirely surprised, but, still, there was this . . . this excitement around the place. Your dad, well, he was always an impressive figure, but, after the news was out, he kind of . . . when he walked down the hall, into the courtroom, wherever, it was kind of . . . well, breathtaking, I suppose. Breathtaking. I mean that literally. It was as though he was incandescent, burning the oxygen right out of the air. I don't know what the word is. Magic, maybe. People did not exactly fawn over him. No. Come to think of it, it was just the opposite. People drew back a little bit, grew . . . mmmm, let's say diffident, as though he was being elevated to some higher plane of existence, and the rest of us mortals were no longer fit company. No longer fit. Not a king, but . . . a crown prince! That's the analogy. There was this . . . this glow. Incandescent," he repeats.

I nod, hoping he will get to the point. Wainwright's judicial opinions have this same scattered quality, full of weak allusions and awkward metaphors. Law professors reward him for this literary confusion by referring to his writing as stylish. But perhaps my own tendency to drabness makes me envious.

"Well. Your father handled it all beautifully. *We* might have been diffident, the other judges, and, especially, the law clerks, but your father was as friendly as always." Another smile, soft, reminiscing, and I wonder whether he is teasing, for the Judge was many things, some of them admirable, but none of them friendly. "You know, now that I think about it, I suppose your father had a lot of time to prepare himself, to think about how he would behave if lightning struck. You might remember that it was not exactly a surprise. Your dad was one of the finalists, it was in all the papers, and, besides, people were talking about your dad even back in '80, right after the election. Yes. Right after the election. Come to think of it, when Reagan was elected, some rightwinger or other—excuse me, no offense to your father—but somebody from one of those terribly conservative think tanks was quoted in the newspaper about your father as the possible successor to Justice Marshall. He said something offensive, something like, 'I hope Thurgood is keeping Oliver's seat warm.' Words to that effect."

I have forgotten the atmosphere of the time, but Justice Wainwright's tale brings it tumbling back. I even remember, for the first time in years, the quote he mentioned. I was outraged by it, and so was nearly everybody else I knew, including my father. Outraged by the presumption, for instance, that there could be only one black Justice at a time. And by the presumption that the speaker was on a first-name basis with both my father and the great Thurgood Marshall. And then the racist choice—there is no other way to put it—to call both jurists by their first names. I cannot recall any similar quote along the lines of "I hope Lewis is keeping Bob's seat warm"—not when the Justice and the potential nominee were both white. My father, for a strange, shining, sacrificial moment, pondered removing himself from all consideration as a future member of the Court, out of respect for Justice Marshall, before flaring ambition triumphed once more.

"I remember," is all I say now.

"It was a terrible thing to say, Misha, a terrible thing, and your father was furious. But, well, this Court . . . there's been a circus atmosphere around the nominations for decades. Longer. It goes back at least to Brandeis. Maybe even to Salmon Chase, or Roger Taney. Of course you know the storms their nominations caused! Well, this is getting far afield, and I know I'm boring you. You didn't want to know about the mood around the courthouse. You know it already. You wanted to know . . . well, about your dad around this time, right?"

"Yes. Whatever you feel you can share."

"Mmmm." Wainwright has unveiled a different nervous gesture. He is worrying his retreating hair with one hand, drumming the fingers of the other on the arm of the chair. Doing both at once is actually a rather impressive display of coordination, like the juggler who also dances on a ball. "I'll tell you, Misha, your father, as I said . . . he was incandescent. But not always. Even before the scandal broke, there were times, when I would catch Oliver at an unguarded moment, when he seemed . . . strained, I suppose, is the word. Worried about something. Yes. We would meet in the judges' elevator and he would look tense and I would ask him what was wrong. I would remind him he should be walking on air. Yes. And he would shrug and mutter about how anything can come out in these hearings. 'Look at Fortas,' he said one night when we went down to the garage together. 'The man takes perfectly legal money from a foundation and they destroy him for it.'" Wainwright twists his mouth in prim distaste. "Not that the problem with Fortas was legality, of course. He took money from . . . well, a shady character." Then he sits up straight. "I guess I see the comparison."

I am stunned. "You're not saying . . . my father didn't . . ."

"Take money? Oh, no, no, nothing like that. I'm sorry, Misha, I didn't mean to leave that impression." Wainwright actually laughs. "Your father taking money. That's a real joke. I know there were some nasty rumors about that, but I knew your father as well as anybody, I sat with him on, literally, hundreds of cases over the years. I would have known. We all would have known. No chance. None. What a silly idea. I am only trying to explain that your father was nervous, that he thought something would come out, something perfectly innocent that would be distorted into something completely different."

"Did you have any idea, at the time, what that something might be?"

"No, no. How could I? Your father was—what's the old phrase?—oh, yes, a man of transparent rectitude. An impeccable résumé, a wonderful marriage, fine children. An exemplary career. Nobody would have imagined that scandal could attach itself to such a man. Your father was a great man, Misha, no matter what happened. You have to bear his greatness in mind."

He is trying to reassure me, I know, but I find his cockiness off-putting. On the day of the funeral, Mallory Corcoran, too, spoke of my father's greatness, and I sensed he meant the past tense. I wonder now whether Wallace Wainwright means the same thing. For a difficult moment, it bothers me, Wainwright's smugness. Bothers me, I know full well, because he is white and untouchable. Was the Judge this smug? Would he have been as smug had he been confirmed? Yes, I suppose he was, and, yes, I suppose he would have been, except that he would have behaved even worse. But it would have been different. And not because he is—was—my father. After all the painful centuries, there is still a gap, a gulf, a yawning chasm between the smugness of a successful white man and the smugness of a successful black man. I suppose that white folk must find the first far easier to bear. Not black folk, however. Not this one, at least.

Yet I must press on to my point. I am not here to judge Wallace Wainwright. I am here to gather information. I am here because of *the arrangements*. Because there is *little time*. Because I have to know.

(III)

"JUSTICE WAINWRIGHT, if it's okay with you, I'd like to ask you about what happened . . . um, after the scandal broke."

"By all means." He settles his hands over his knee, looking for all the world like an alert schoolboy. But his generosity seems forced, as though I am opening a wound, and perhaps I am.

"Do you remember the security logs from the hearings? How they registered all those visits from Jack Ziegler?"

He nods slowly. "I wish I didn't. It was a sad moment."

If it was sad for you, I almost say, *think of how it felt for us.* Until the logs showed up, I suppose I mostly believed my father's denials, under oath, of Jack Ziegler's visits. I was quite ready to accept that Greg Haramoto was, whether out of bizarre mental illness or sheer perversity, a perjurer. Even after the Democrats sprung the logs, when my mother would no longer speak to us on the question, Mariah and I would sit around for hours in the evening, arguing over whether (as my sister proposed) the records might somehow have been forged.

I can say little of this to Wallace Wainwright. "Yes, it was. A very sad moment. But let me ask you a question. Do you believe my father was lying when he said he had not met Jack Ziegler at the courthouse?"

Wainwright is definitely nervous now; this is territory he would rather not cover; and it occurs to me, too late, how much he is like me, for I, too, hate to deliver unpleasant news in person. Waiting, I notice, to my surprise, a photograph I had overlooked before: Wainwright and my father, standing in a small boat, displaying the fish they have caught. That he would keep this picture hanging, in the Supreme Court yet, touches me deeply. I realize with a surge of warmth that his affection for my father is not feigned; that Wallace Wainwright never cut him off as other friends did; and that he came to the funeral because we were burying a man he admired. He will not, of his own free will, say a bad word about my father. So, even before the Justice speaks, I know roughly what he is going to say. "Misha, you have to understand, your father was in a difficult position. A difficult position. Yes. Obviously, he did not attach much attention to the courthouse visits. Forgive me. It was the first time I ever saw Oliver overwhelmed. He was not quite able to believe people were making such an issue over the matter. For him— for your father—the visits were simply acts of friendship, occasions to offer comfort to his college buddy who had gotten himself into trouble. You remember what your father used to say about friendship? Something to do with bricks . . ."

I have the words ready: *"Friendship is a promise of future loyalty, loyalty no matter what comes. Promises are the bricks of life and trust is the mortar."*

"Yes, that's it. Bricks and mortar." The twisted smile again, giving him the cherubic look his fans adore. "So you see the point. To your father, it was all so terribly unfair. On television, before the nation, in the scrutiny of the media, the visits looked sinister. To your father, they were innocent gestures of friendship. Innocent. Yes. I think he simply decided there was no sensible way of explaining them—that is, nothing that would make sense in that hearing room. So of course he denied the meetings. You're a semiotician. You know what I'm trying to say. Yes. Your father did not mean that there were no meetings. He was denying the meetings as his critics were constructing them, not as he himself understood them. Had the question been, 'And did you, out of loyalty and friendship, meet with Jack Ziegler and encourage him to keep his spirits up in his time of travail?'—something more like that—well, then, I think perhaps Oliver would have given a more acceptable answer." He notices something in my face. "I'm sorry, Misha, I know this is not exactly the answer you wanted."

"I just want to understand. You're saying my father lied. When you cut away all the underbrush, that's it, right? He lied under oath?"

Wainwright sighs. "Yes, Misha. I'm sorry. I do think your father lied."

"So Jack Ziegler was in the courthouse on . . . well, however many occasions it was."

"Three, I believe." Greg Haramoto only knew of one visit. The courthouse logs told the nation about the others.

"I think that's right. Three meetings, all after hours."

"Yes. After hours."

My turn to see something in his face. He drops his eyes briefly. I have no idea what could be troubling him. And then I do. "You knew," I say softly, wonderingly.

"I beg your pardon."

"Oh, no. You knew. You . . . you saw them in the hallway or something. Maybe you dropped by my father's chambers after hours, and there was Jack Ziegler. But somehow . . . somehow you knew, didn't you? You knew my father was meeting with Jack Ziegler."

He looks off toward the far window, as though the view of the Library of Congress down the hill will rescue him from the dilemma into which he has talked himself. "This is off the record. You're not writing a memoir or an essay for *The Atlantic* or something like that, are you?"

"It's off the record," I agree. I would agree to almost anything to get him to keep talking.

"I'll deny it if you quote me."

"I understand."

Wallace Wainwright sighs. "Yes, Misha, I knew," he says to the wall. "I saw them together, as you say. Not in the hallway. In the elevator. The private elevator for judges. Late one night. It must have been, oh, ten o'clock. Maybe later. I didn't notice the time, because I didn't attach so much . . . so much importance to it when it happened. Anyway, you will recall that my chambers and your father's were on the same floor. I rang for the elevator, and, when it arrived, there was your father and a man I did not recognize at first. Both of them seemed surprised to see me. In retrospect, I suppose your father thought all the other judges had left the building, so that taking the private elevator was a good way to whisk Mr. Ziegler in while minimizing the chances that anybody would see. I don't know. Anyway, they were, as I say, quite surprised. Quite surprised. But Oliver was never caught up short. He introduced us. He described his companion as his college roommate, I believe, and at first I attached no significance to the name."

"At first?"

"Perhaps I was a little slow that night. It hit me a couple of days later. That the man in the elevator was not just *a* Jack Ziegler—he was *the* Jack Ziegler. An accused murderer, extortionist, I don't know what else. Right in the courthouse, with a federal judge. Which left me, to say the least, uneasy. As well as unsure what to do. Quite unsure. Perhaps I should have talked to your father directly. Perhaps I should have raised the matter with the chief judge. In the event, I did not acquit myself admirably. I said nothing to anybody. I suppose I thought your father had his reasons. After all, I respected him, I considered him a man of enormous integrity. I still do."

"Even though he lied under oath."

"That was a terrible, terrible mistake on his part, Misha. To be perfectly honest with you, I considered it disqualifying. Lying under oath! I told you before that I understood it, but I do not want you to think for a moment that I approved of it. Not at all. Your father was right to withdraw. It was an honorable thing to do. Or would have been, that is, if your father had only shown . . . well, some contrition. Contrition. Yes. Your father . . . I know, Misha, that this is hard for you. But the fact is that he never seemed to accept that he had done anything wrong, either by bringing a man about to stand trial for murder into the courthouse or by lying about it under oath. Unfortunately, like a lot of defeated nominees, all your father could think about was the motives of the people who had ferreted out the visits in the first place. And now I have to apologize again. You have come seeking assurance and I have made a speech, and a painful one at that."

"No, that's okay. I know my father lied." A pause. "But there is one thing I don't understand. If you knew about Jack Ziegler from way back when it happened, why didn't you speak to anyone about it when the issue arose during the confirmation hearings?"

He answers so quickly I know he has anticipated me. "Nobody ever asked. The FBI never came around and interviewed the other judges, you know."

"You could have volunteered the information. You would have spared Greg Haramoto so much anguish."

"Oh, Misha, really! One judge ratting on another. Unthinkable. It simply isn't done. Nor is it in the spirit of the Constitution. The legislative branch passes upon the fitness of the nominees for the judiciary. It would not have been right for me, as a member of the third branch, to try to influence a confirmation hearing in any respect."

I like Wallace Wainwright, maybe because my father did, but his cocksureness astounds me, as much in person as in his opinions, where the implication, often, is that a law must be unconstitutional because he happens not to like it.

"I appreciate that," I say after a moment, not at all sure that I do. I wonder whether Wainwright stayed out of my father's mess precisely to protect his own chances. I do not know whether it is unthinkable for one judge to rat on another, but it surely would not help either one of them get to the Supreme Court. "However, I need to understand something else."

"Of course," says Wainwright, struggling against his impatience.

"When my father . . . when he met with Jack Ziegler. That was in the evening."

"Yes. Fairly late, as I said."

"That wasn't unusual, was it? For my father to be at the courthouse so late?"

"Unusual?" He smiles. "No, Misha, not at all. I worked long hours, too, but nothing like Oliver. You have to remember the kind of man your father was. The kind of judge. He was—you know the old phrase—a demon for details. I remember one oral argument, an appeal of some kind of criminal conviction, in which the lawyer for the convicted man made the mistake of playing to your father's vanity, quoting some dissenting opinion your father wrote in his early days on the bench. Your father asked him, 'Counsel, do you know how many times that issue has come before this court since I wrote those words?' The poor man didn't know. Your father said, 'Seventeen times. Do you know how many times the court has rejected that approach? Seventeen times. And do you know how many of those opinions I wrote?' Oh, the wretched lawyer! He did what every first-year law student learns never to do: he guessed. He said, 'Seventeen, Your Honor?' Walking right into the trap, you see. Your father said, 'None. I adhere to the views you quoted,' and the entire courtroom bursts out laughing. But not the lawyer and not your father. He was not making a joke, he was teaching a lesson. And he couldn't resist adding a second punch line. 'My views don't matter, counsel. In a federal appellate court, you have to cite the law of the circuit, not the views of the individual judges. Perhaps you remember that from law school.'"

I close my eyes briefly. I can easily imagine the Judge using his wit so nastily, because he did it all the time.

Wainwright isn't finished.

"But, Misha, most of the time, your father's penchant for details didn't hurt anybody that way. For instance, whenever a case came before us involving, say, an EPA standard, he would insist on reading the entire rulemaking record himself, instead of leaving it to his law clerks, as most of us would. And we're talking rulemaking records that could run to more than twenty thousand pages. He would say, 'If I can read Trollope I can read this.' Or say there was a case in which one of the parties was obviously a dummy corporation, registered in, say, the Cayman Islands or Netherlands Antilles? Your father would demand that the corporation file—under seal, of course—a list of its actual owners, not just the shells within shells where they were hidden. Or a public interest group? He would require a list of donors."

I am, in spite of my mission, fascinated. "He could do that?"

"Well, not by himself. It would take an order from the panel hearing the case. Since the panel had three judges, two would have to agree to the request. But it was unanimous, at least in every case I can remember. A matter of intrajudicial courtesy, I suppose."

"And would the corporations or whatever turn over the records?"

"What else was there to do? Appeal to the Supreme Court? Even assuming that the Justices paid any attention to a request for a stay—which is very unlikely—and assuming they granted it—which is even more unlikely—what would a corporation really have accomplished by the appeal? I'll tell you. It would have pissed off at least one judge, and maybe two or three. Even if the stay was granted, so the documents or whatever didn't have to be disclosed, the corporation would still have to go back to the same panel of three judges to have the case heard. So who wants to argue in front of three judges you've just made very angry by appealing what seemed to them a pretty innocuous order?" He chuckles softly in delighted reminiscence. "Oh, but he was fun on the bench, your father! And such a fine judge. Such a fine judge."

But I know what he is really thinking, as I am: *Such a waste. Such a waste.* Looking at Wainwright's sad face, I am tempted, for a moment, to ask him if he ever heard my father mention the word *Excelsior,* or perhaps a woman named *Angela*, who might have a *boyfriend.* I wonder if he knew my father owned a gun. Or why he would want one. I cannot quite bring myself to raise these questions, however, perhaps because I would feel too much like . . . well, the unnamed reporter in *Citizen Kane*, tracking down "Rosebud." So I skip to the single question I am really here to ask.

"Justice Wainwright"—I notice that, despite our long family friendship, he has not invited me to call him anything else—"this is . . . this isn't easy." He makes a magnanimous gesture. I continue. "A few minutes ago, you made a comment about . . . uh, money. . . ."

"Let me anticipate you, Misha. You're wondering the same thing the press wondered for a couple of years after the hearings, if there was anything other than friendship between your father and Jack Ziegler, right? The same thing all those congressional committees wanted to know. You're asking whether I think your father did little favors on the bench for his old roommate. You're asking, money aside, if he was a corrupt judge."

Now that the words have been spoken, they seem less frightening. I can handle the answer. "Yes, sir. Yes, that's exactly what I'm wondering."

Justice Wainwright frowns, drums his fingers on the table. He does not so much drop his eyes as cast them toward the right-hand wall, his ego wall, where that photograph of him and the Judge on a fishing trip continues to surprise me, for one would think that a political animal like Wallace Wainwright would have removed it long ago. Then I remember how he offered my father a character reference once the hearings took their painful turn, was willing, even, to testify in person to the Judge's honesty, no matter what the damage to his own career. My father, although grateful, turned him down flat. But my affection for Wallace Wainwright surges afresh at the recollection.

The Justice continues to ponder. I allow the moment to spin out. His balding head at last swivels in my direction once more, and a smile twitches at the corners of his mouth. "No, Misha. The answer is no. All those investigators, all those committees, all those journalists, none of them ever turned up anything. You have to remember that. They turned up nothing. Not one single thing. The reason is that there was nothing to turn up. Your father was a man of enormous integrity, Misha, as I told you. You mustn't lose sight of that, no matter what he might have done." I realize he is referring to his political views, his later career on the speaking circuit, not the scandal. "Please don't think for a moment that your father was doing anything contrary to judicial ethics. Please don't think of him as corrupt. Put that right out of your head. Your father would no more have sold his vote on a case than . . . than"—a pause while he searches for just the right simile, then a mischievous grin to tell me he has found it—"why, than I would," he finishes with a self-deprecating smile, realizing, perhaps, that he has played perfectly into his own image as moderately egomaniacal.

I am almost done. One last bit of confusion to clear up.

"So, if my father was a man of such integrity and such intelligence"—I hesitate here: did Wainwright actually say at any point that my father was smart? I cannot recall, and, when white intellectuals speak of black ones, the question is of no small importance—"if he was so honest and so smart, then why did he bring Jack Ziegler into the courthouse? He could have met with him anywhere. At home. At a golf resort. In a parking lot. Why take the risk?"

Wainwright's eyes grow soft and distant, and the sad little smile returns. When at last he speaks, I at first think he is answering a different question from the one I asked, before I realize that he needs to sketch the preamble.

"You know, Misha, I never raised the question of Jack Ziegler with your father. But he raised it with me. We had dinner together, it must have been six or eight months after he . . . resigned from the bench. Yes. He was, at that point, not yet the . . . um, angry polemicist he would soon become. He was still in despair. Confused, I think. Yes. Confused. He still could not see how things had turned around on him so swiftly. And he asked me—the only time he ever wanted my advice!—he asked me what I would have done in his place. About Jack Ziegler. I told him I did not know how I would have handled the questions. I guess I was trying to be political. Then I saw I had misunderstood him. 'No, no,' he said. 'Not the hearing. Earlier. If he was your friend. Would you have abandoned him?' I realized he was talking about the courthouse visits. And I wondered the same thing you did. I told him that, if I felt I had to meet with a friend who was in trouble, and if there was even a whiff of scandal about the friend, I would do it someplace private. Your father nodded. He seemed very sad. But this is what he said, Misha: 'I had no choice.' Something like that. I asked him what he meant, why he had to bring Jack Ziegler into his chambers, but he just shook his head and went on to another subject." A pause before he tells me the final piece of the truth. "He wasn't himself that night, Misha. He probably didn't know what he was saying." Wainwright stops abruptly. I wonder whether he was about to tell me that my father had started drinking again. He folds his hands over his mouth, then opens them and smiles sadly. "Remember his greatness, Misha. That's what I try to do."

Suddenly, unaccountably, I am furious. At the Judge for his cryptic note, at Uncle Mal for not taking my calls, at the late Colin Scott for harassing me, at Lynda Wyatt and Marc Hadley and Cameron Knowland and everybody else who has brought me to this moment. But, just now, I am mostly angry at Wallace Warrenton Wainwright.

"I want to remember my father as he actually was," I say calmly. I do not add: I just have to find out who he was first.

Ten minutes later, I leave the building by the main entrance, descending the steep marble stairs past shivering knots of tourists waiting for a peek inside the temple of our national oracle. Yes, Associate Justice Wallace Wainwright is an egomaniac, but it is that very ego on which I am counting. If Wainwright is willing to put my father in his own lofty company, then he surely believes what he says.

Bottom line: the Judge did not sell his vote to Jack Ziegler and his friends.

So what was he doing? I know what Wainwright was trying to tell me at the end, even if he could not quite say the words: he thinks the Judge brought Uncle Jack into his chambers because he wanted someone to see them together. He wanted, in short, to get caught. But, if the Justice is right, what did my father want to get caught *at?*

CHAPTER 21

A TRIP AROUND THE CIRCLE

THE TORT-REFORM CONFERENCE is at the Washington Hilton
Hotel and Towers, located on Connecticut Avenue, a few blocks north
of Dupont Circle. Following my meeting with Justice Wainwright, I do
not return to the hotel directly; I am searching, desperately, for distractions. Instead, I have the taxi drop me on Eye Street to see the book-
seller I visited the last time I was in the city; not only does the man
remember me, but he assures me that he is on the track of the Fischer
pamphlet I asked about. We chat about a few other matters, then I stroll
a few blocks up to L Street for a quick swing through Brooks Brothers,
in an unsuccessful search for the perfect tie to wear with a yellow silk
blazer that Kimmer bought me on her last trip to San Francisco—
another second-place trophy to add to my collection. I buy a couple of
pairs of socks, then flag down a taxi to return to the hotel to catch the
late-afternoon panels.

As the taxi driver goes around the block and heads north on Twentieth Street, I lean back and try to relax. Despite the tension in my muscles, I even manage to doze a bit, required in these tense days to grab a
nap where I can.

Then the taxi turns right onto New Hampshire Avenue, and the
driver suddenly says: "None my business, sir, but you know car behind
is following us?"

Fully awake, I spin in my seat.

"What car?"

"Little green car. There. You see?"

I see it. It is two or three cars behind us, some cookie-cutter American sedan.

"How do you know it's following us?"

"After I pick you up, I go around block to point taxi right way." To charge a higher fare, he means; in Washington, where there are no meters, all that matters in adding up the fare is how many fare zones the cab crosses, and drivers often choose one street rather than another to cross a zonal line. "Green car go around block also. I turn another right, he turn another right. I turn right again, he turn right again. In my country, I often see cars do this. Cars of secret police."

Great.

I think fast. I am not sure who might be following me now that Scott is dead, but, being back in Washington, I cannot quite clear from my mind's eye the photographs of what somebody did to Freeman Bishop. Conan or no Conan, arrest or no arrest, I feel a chill.

Think!

In about thirty seconds, my taxi will hit the nerve-blasting confusion of Dupont Circle, which only the most foolish out-of-towners and the most experienced Washington drivers ever dare, because you must change lanes rapidly and efficiently, depending on which of the many intersecting streets you plan to take, and, at the same time, steer counterclockwise around a circle rather than straight, all the while avoiding other motorists just as bewildered as you are, to say nothing of pedestrians darting from one misshapen concrete island to the next. I am still looking back at the green car. The driver is a gray smear in the window; there seems to be a passenger too, but it is hard to tell.

Probably my cabbie is mistaken.

But maybe he isn't. Maybe somebody wants to see where I am headed. Barely plausible, I know, but the green car is there just the same. And, no matter who it is, I find that I don't like it one bit.

"When you get to Dupont Circle, get in the lane for Massachusetts Avenue."

"Which way?"

"Uh, southbound, or east, whatever it is—toward the Capitol."

"You say Washington Hilton. On Connecticut Avenue." We are stopped at the last traffic light before the Circle. The green sedan is now just two cars back. The passenger seat is definitely occupied.

"How much is the fare to the Hilton?"

He names a figure.

I pore through my thin wallet, select a twenty-dollar bill, and, with a grimace, drop it over the seat. He understands at once that he is to keep the change.

"Turn on Massachusetts, then take the first right, behind that gray building. The one at the corner." I point. I know the building well, having once practiced law in a firm there, back in the days when Kimmer and I were fooling around behind her first husband's back, pretending to keep secret what everybody knew. The driver says nothing. He is wondering, no doubt, why I am running away from the green car. As a matter of fact, I am wondering too. But I lay my plans anyway, just in case I turn out to be sane. "Keep the change," I tell him. No response. "When you hit Massachusetts, go as fast as you can," I continue. "Then turn onto Eighteenth, also very, very fast." The driver's wary eyes meet mine in the mirror. He does not like this. He associates cars that follow other cars with the police. In his country, wherever that is, the police are the bad guys. Here in America . . . ?

"Listen," I say, adding another twenty from my dwindling supply of cash. "I am not a criminal, and the people in that car are not the police, okay?"

The driver shrugs. He will not make any commitment that he cannot deny later. But he does not offer to return my money.

The light changes, and the taxi surges forward so suddenly that I will probably be in the emergency room later tonight, being treated for whiplash. Crouching, I look back. As my driver weaves through traffic, the green car follows. I look forward. My driver is not in the Massachusetts Avenue lane! He has decided not to cooperate! I am trying to come up with another argument to offer when, without warning, the taxi bumps over the curb into the lane for Massachusetts Avenue before several startled, honking motorists. A clutch of pedestrians scurries for cover. As the green car falls farther behind, I wonder fleetingly what my driver did for a living that caused him to flee to America, bringing along such detailed knowledge of how the police of his country conduct surveillance.

And of how to escape it.

Probably better that I not know.

We fly through the complicated intersection and turn hard onto Massachusetts. The green car is stuck at a light, and in the wrong lane. Its passenger door whips open, just as we swing around the corner behind the gray building.

"Slow down for a second," I tell the driver as soon as the green car is out of sight. I know it will catch up momentarily, the passenger, who can slide between stopped cars, even faster. I have only seconds. I slip the driver another bill, a ten: I have no more twenties.

He is shaking his head, but he slows. I push open the door and climb, crouching, from the still-rolling car. "Now go!" I call, slamming the door.

I do not need to tell him twice.

As the taxi squeals around the next corner, I am already darting into the narrow alley separating the back of my former office building from an old townhouse next door, home to some private institute or other. The alley dead-ends at the building's service entrance. Cameras of doubtful working order guard the scene. I crouch behind a drab green Dumpster just as my pursuer, now on foot, hurries by. My eyes widen, and I fight down a sudden trembling in my extremities. I wait, instinct telling me that we are not through yet. I check my watch. Three minutes pass. Four. The alley stinks of old garbage and recent urine. I notice for the first time that I have company: a homeless man, his possessions heaped around him in plastic bags, is fast asleep near the loading dock of the office building. I keep watching the street. The green car finally slithers past, moving slowly, the invisible driver probably checking hedges and doorways—and alleys. I wonder why they are not chasing the taxi. They must have seen me get out. I sink farther back into the shadows. The green car is gone. I still wait. A flurry atop the Dumpster draws my attention, but it is only a mangy black cat, gnawing on something foul. I am not superstitious. At least I don't think I am. I wait. The homeless man mutters and snores, a fibrous alcoholic sound I remember from the days when the Judge used to lock the door of his study. Ten minutes pass. More. Sure enough, the passenger from the car passes me again, having evidently walked all the way around the block. The green car reappears. The door swings open. They appear to argue. The passenger points down the street, vaguely in the direction of my hideout, then shrugs and climbs in. The car drives away. Still I wait. I remain crouched in the alley for close to half an hour before I slide out and join the stream of pedestrians. Then I sneak back in and stuff my other ten-dollar bill into the homeless man's pocket.

More guilt money.

Back on the sidewalk, I cross Massachusetts Avenue and mosey into Dupont Circle, pausing at the stone chess tables, pretending to watch the games, but really craning my neck to see whether I spot the green car or its furtive passenger. I drift from one table to the next, glancing at the positions on the boards. The players are a true rainbow, a random mix of ages, races, languages. Few of them seem very strong, but, on the other hand, I am not giving their games much of my attention. A crazy old man yells at a younger woman who just defeated him. The woman, who looks about as healthy as my customers at the soup kitchen, wears a hairnet and glasses repaired at the temple with a Band-Aid. She points a quivering finger at her vanquished opponent. He slaps it aside, baring brownish teeth. The kibitzers take sides. Other games lose their audiences. The crowd around the stone table grows raucous. Lawyers with cell phones at their hips jostle with slender bicycle messengers as everybody seeks a better view of the hoped-for tussle. I lose myself inside the throng, trying to peek in every direction at once. I cannot remember when my senses have been so open, so absorbent. I am not even scared. I am exhilarated. Every color of every branch of every tree is so crisp and clear I can almost breathe its hue. I feel as though I can examine the face of every one of the hundreds of pedestrians who walk through the park every minute. Another half-hour elapses. No sign of the green car, no sign of the passenger. Forty-five minutes. Eventually, I slip away and walk north, toward the Hilton.

Then I change my mind. There is another stop I want to make first, for I have a new question to ask, and I know where to ask it. I look for a bank, find a cash machine, and withdraw another hundred dollars from our dwindling checking account. I will explain it to Kimmer somehow. I find a public telephone and make a quick call. Then I hail another cab and give the driver instructions.

We pass the Hilton and then cut east on Columbia Road, passing through the loud, colorful, ethnically complicated neighborhood of Adams-Morgan, where, following law school, I lived for several years in a tiny walkup apartment with my books and my chess set and an unadorned mattress on the floor, my diet consisting almost entirely of apple juice and Jamaican meat patties from a shop down the block, until, at Kimmer's urging, I moved to far more expensive quarters in a dreadfully modern building much further up Connecticut Avenue. Sitting in the back of my fourth taxi of the day, I shake my head ruefully, for she was still married to André Conway when she began complaining about how I lived. The cab passes my old building, and I soften with sentimentality. We hit Sixteenth Street, where we turn north toward the heart of the Gold Coast. Along the way, I remain alert for any sign of the green car or the passenger who searched for me on foot.

A very familiar passenger. The passenger of my dreams.

The roller woman.

CHAPTER 22

CONVERSATION WITH A COLONEL

(1)

VERA AND THE COLONEL were surprised to hear from me, not least because, despite ten years of entreaties, I hardly ever just drop in when I happen to be in the District on business. Their modest house on Six-teenth Street is set in the middle of the Gold Coast; the Judge's larger place, Mariah's now, lies on the border with the paler nation, as did his public career.

My in-laws welcome me effusively, banishing the dogs to the yard because they know I suffer from allergies, a fact that Kimmer's father holds against me, for he thinks it betrays a fundamental lack of tough-ness. From the number of hugs we exchange, I almost believe they are happy to see me. Then I remember the chilly Thanksgiving dinner two weeks ago in this very house; I remind myself of the tendency of Madi-son moods to swing, usually without warning. They lead me into the small family room at the back of the house, a converted sun porch, the decor a suffocating mix of cheap souvenirs from ports around the world and photographs and citations from the Colonel's days as a leader of men, as he likes to describe himself. Vera serves cheese and crackers and asks us what we want to drink. The Colonel scowls at the platter and sends her back to the kitchen for a bowl of nuts.

The shelves sport a whole series of pictures of Kimmer and her sis-ter, Lindy—Marilyn at birth—from infancy to the present, and you can see, even in the early teen years, a hint of smoky challenge in the way the fleshier Kimmer glares at the camera, whereas willowy Lindy is, early on, more remote, less giving. The Madisons, like the rest of our set, were always puzzled at my apparent preference for Kimmer. Her parents certainly remember that I dated both their daughters, albeit not at the same time. What they do not realize is that only Kimmer dated me back.

Vera returns with the nuts and our drinks.

We sit surrounded by bric-a-brac and chintz, the Madisons as nervous as I, pretending that we are having a grand time, that we do this every day. The Colonel is drinking Scotch straight. A cigar smolders in an ashtray pilfered from a cruise line, for the Madisons seem to be off sailing somewhere every five minutes. Vera sips white wine. I stick with my usual ginger ale. I am never sure how to begin a conversation with my in-laws, whose skeptical eyes and querulous manner often make me wonder whether they blame me for ruining Kimmer's marriage to André Conway. Perhaps they believe that, if not for the nefarious and wily Talcott Garland, their daughter would have been a faithful wife, and they would have a son-in-law who makes films and is always on television rather than one who professes law and is always in his office. They ask a question or two about Kimmer, just for form, but the subject is awkward and we hastily move on. The Colonel asks how Elm Harbor is doing these days, for he has heard that speculators are buying up the broken neighborhoods, and is wondering if he should get in on it; Miles Madison owns empty houses, to hear him tell it, in half the cities on the East Coast, waiting for real estate to take off. Some places it has. Kimmer is always at pains to explain that, since her father has no tenants in the dying areas where he buys, he is not a slumlord.

When we have exhausted the subject of Elm Harbor real estate, Vera, perfect hostess, makes polite inquiries about the law school—she has, of course, seen Lemaster Carlyle on television quite often, and asks what he is like, and I burn a bit but answer as politely. Then my in-laws grow effusive as they ask about the marvelous Bentley, for Lindy, the darling of the Gold Coast in her youth, made a single bad marriage and has yet to give them any grandchildren. Now she is just another unmarried black woman in her forties hoping for lightning to strike, a pattern all too common in the darker nation as intermarriage, violence, prison, drugs, and disease combine to decimate the pool of eligible males.

Then it is time to get down to business, and Vera can tell whom my business is with. "I'll leave you men alone," she murmurs and withdraws. She always defers to her husband, although, in other respects, she is like her daughter: no shrinking violet, few skills of self-effacement.

"So, Talcott," says the Colonel expansively, waving the Cuban cigar in his stout hand. He has offered me one, but I have declined. Unlike André, I neither smoke, drink, nor curse; the Colonel, accordingly, considers me less manly. His smooth, hairless dome glistens. "What can I do for you?"

I hesitate for a moment, my mind spinning back absurdly to my flight around Dupont Circle an hour ago. I wonder, for a silly moment, if the roller woman might be lurking in the bushes outside the window, perhaps holding a directional microphone that can pick up voices from vibrations in the pane. I force my concentration back into the room, meet the Colonel's challenging stare.

"My father owned a gun," I tell him flatly. His yellowing eyes widen slightly, the intricate motions of his cigar hand grow more extravagant, but he shows no other reaction. So I continue. "I checked. . . . I hear it's easy to buy them in Virginia."

"It is. I've bought a few."

"Well, that's the thing. I don't believe he bought it there."

"You don't."

"I just can't imagine my father sneaking over the Memorial Bridge in the dead of night with an illegal handgun hidden in the trunk. It just . . . wouldn't have been his kind of thing."

A faint smile creases his pudgy face. He finishes his drink, glances around for his wife to fix him another, then remembers she has left the room and goes to the wet bar to get his own. He waves the ginger ale bottle vaguely in my direction, but I shake my head. "You're probably right," he murmurs as he returns to his lounger.

"It's not that he wouldn't have kept an illegal handgun. It's more that he wouldn't have taken the chance of getting caught."

"Mmmm."

"On the other hand, you have quite a collection of guns down in the basement."

"It's not a bad one," agrees my host, who has failed many times to get me interested in his hobby.

"Well, this is what I was thinking. If my father wanted a gun, I guess I could see him borrowing one from you."

The smile broadens. "I could see that, too."

I finally exhale. "So I guess what I was wondering was . . . when exactly he asked you for a gun, and why he said he wanted one."

The Colonel shifts comfortably in his seat. He inhales, blows a few rings, but not at me. "I would say it was . . . oh, a year ago. Maybe a little more. Say, October a year ago, because we were just back from . . . from . . ." He turns his head slightly, shouts: "Vera! Where did we go last October?"

"St. Lucia!" she shouts from the next room, over the television. Vera's Jamaican accent has grown faint over the years; the Colonel's is all but impossible to detect.

"No, not this October. Last October."

"South Pacific!"

"Thanks, doll." He grins sheepishly. "Old gray cells aren't what they were. Yes, just back from the South Pacific. Seems to me we invited you folks to come. . . ."

"No."

"No? Maybe it was Marilyn. But I could have sworn we called Kimberly. Weren't you on leave from the law school or something? We thought you'd have free time." He sees the answer the same time I do: they invited Kimmer, and she declined without troubling to mention it to me. Maybe even lied to her parents and said I was the one who said no. Being cooped up on a ship for two weeks with her father, her mother, and her husband would be my wife's notion of hell on earth. He rushes on to cover his faux pas. "Well, we were back, oh, say four, five days when Oliver called. Came over at night, sat right where you're sitting, asked could he speak to me alone. He wasn't the sort to mince words"—looking right at me, as though implying that I am—"and he told me what he wanted."

"What did he say exactly?"

"Said he was getting a little worried about safety at his age, and could I help."

"Safety? His own safety?"

The Colonel nods, blows more rings. I am being brusque, in my half-remembered litigation mode, but it comes back to you, like riding a bicycle. Kimmer's father does not seem to mind being interrogated. He is having fun. His tiny eyes gleam. "That was my impression. He was kind of—" Suddenly he spins in his chair, the light selecting a different angle to reflect off his bald head. "Vera! Hey, Vera!"

She is in the room at once, hands folded at her waist. Probably she has been listening from the alcove.

"Yes, sweetie?"

"Damn cigar's no good. Be a doll, go down to my desk, get me another."

"Of course, dear." She heads for the basement stairs at once, and I am reminded, for the thousandth time, just what Kimmer was rebelling against. But I also know that there is nothing wrong with the cigar, that the Colonel is just sending her away.

"What a doll," he murmurs, watching her go. "You're a doll!" he calls, but she is out of earshot, which is what he is waiting for. He leans toward me, and suddenly is all business. "Look, Talcott, I don't know exactly what the hell was going on. I never saw your father scared in my life, and I've known him—sorry, I knew him—for twenty years. But he was white as a sheet, if you'll excuse the expression. He wouldn't tell me why he wanted the gun, just that he wanted it fast."

"You gave it to him? No questions asked?"

"I asked lots of questions, I just didn't get any answers." A guffaw. He has dealt with pipsqueaks before. Then the serious tone again. "Look, Talcott. I saw him before we left on our cruise and he was fine. Then I saw him when we came back and he was . . . oh, hell, he was terrified, Talcott, okay?"

I try to picture the Judge terrified. I draw a blank.

Miles Madison is still talking, his voice low and sure. "So whatever happened to scare him, it happened while we were away. I'm talking about last October, just about a year before he died, and it spooked the hell out of him. If you find out what happened, you'll know why he wanted a gun." His head jerks, for he is preternaturally alert, as he must have been in his days in the infantry. "Vera! Thanks for the cigar, doll!"

"The one you have looks just fine to me," she points out as she empties the ashtray into a wastebasket decorated with a map of the Caribbean.

He grins sheepishly up at her. "Damn imports. No quality control." He turns back to look at me, winks. "Talcott and I were just making a friendly wager on a game of pool."

But nobody beats the Colonel at pool. He cheats.

(11)

VERA AND THE COLONEL wind up giving me dinner. I want to escape, but declining their hospitality would be rude. By the time I return to the Hilton, almost four hours have slipped past. It is nearly eight, and the streets of Washington are full pre-winter dark. I have missed the final day of the conference, but I am sure I was not missed.

The lobby is crowded with citizens of the darker nation, most of them in evening attire: black tuxes with bright and distinctive cummerbunds for the men, glittering gowns of various lengths for the women. They glide up and down the escalators, striking poses for the absent cameras. The beautiful people! Nobody seems an ounce overweight. Every patent-leather shoe is perfectly shined. Every hair on every head appears to be perfectly in place. Every nose is in the air. My parents' kind of crowd. And the Madisons'.

I wonder what event they are attending. In my plain gray suit, sweaty from my brief run, sweatier still from my long walk, I feel out of place, as though I exist on a level far below the paradise inhabited by this radiant throng. From the skeptical looks they cast my way, some of the well-to-do folk gathered in the lobby have the same thought: that this disheveled man slinking along in the gray suit is not, as my mother used to say in the old days, our kind of Negro. Although the absurd American system of racial counting would consider all of these glitterati black, most of them are of hues pale enough to have passed the paper-bag test that so justifiably enraged Mariah back in college, when she flunked it, even though it is, supposedly, no longer in use: *If your skin is any darker than this paper bag, you can't join our sorority.* Oh, but we are sick people! A buried sentiment catches me by surprise, welling up from some putrefying source deep inside me, a wave of cold, brutal hatred for my parents' way of life, for their exclusive little circle and its usually cruel snap judgments about everybody on the outside. And hatred for myself, too, for all the times I actually answered their snide little questions about where this friend of mine went to school, who that one's parents were, and, sometimes, where the *parents* were educated. Addison, as he grew, began to talk back to our mother and father; Mariah and I never did; and perhaps he preserved an independence of being that my sister and I lost. The lobby reels redly about me for a moment, and I find myself wondering, as I did in my nationalistic college days, who the real enemy is, for those of us who considered ourselves the radical vanguard of the battle for a better future used to sit up half the night cursing the black bourgeoisie. E. Franklin Frazier was right: I see my father and his cold intellectual amusement at "the other Negroes," I see my mother and her elite sororities and social clubs as living a dark imitation of white society, ultimately mimicking, in their desperate quest for status, even the racial attitudes of the larger world. So stunned am I by the visions pulsing angrily through my mind that I am, briefly, unable to move or speak or do anything but watch these beautiful people swirl around me.

And then the part of me that lapped up the Judge's occasionally pompous wisdom reasserts itself. These thoughts, I remind myself, are unworthy, a distraction, and not entirely fair; besides, I have more immediate worries. So I wrestle the visions down.

For now.

I edge through the lobby, sucking in my belly, my eyes on the elevators, but I also find myself checking the exultant swarm, almost automatically, for any sign of the roller woman—or, for that matter, for the late Colin Scott's partner, the missing Foreman. I wonder why the roller woman was following me. I wonder why she searched for me so hard, and why I decided at once to run away. I was tempted, quite seriously, to leap from my concealment and confront her, for I was unable then, and am unable now, to believe that the roller woman could have meant me any harm. Perhaps I am kidding myself. I keep seeing her face, not suffused with the concentrated anger of this afternoon's failed search, but alight with the flirtatious, toothy grin of our first meeting. I shake my head. Trying to figure it out is like chewing on cotton.

Like trying to figure out why the Judge was scared enough to get a gun.

Off toward the gift shop, I spy two law professors from the symposium, members of the paler nation, looking rather lost in flannels and tweeds as they watch the dark conclave with apprehensive eyes. They wave to me as though relieved to come across a friendly face in a lobby that suddenly resembles the *Essence* fashion show, and I smile back but decide not to go over to join them for the usual evening round of post-conference academic gossip, which would feel, somehow, like rejecting my own. I decide instead to head upstairs to play chess on my laptop until I get sleepy, which is how I spend most evenings when I am away from home, and many when I am not. I weave through the happy multitude, trying not to bump into anybody and intermittently succeeding, now and then nodding at a vaguely familiar face. I have nearly reached the elevator bank when a pleasantly round shape, draped in an outrageously tight purple gown, detaches itself from a circle of laughing friends and strides purposefully in my direction.

"Tal! I had no idea you were in town!"

I stare in disbelief as Sarah Catherine Stillman née Garland materializes before me.

"Sally?" I manage. "What are you doing here?"

"What am I doing here?" Cousin Sally giggles and pats my cheek and takes my hand in both of hers. Her palm is moist. Her eyes are slightly wild from whatever substance she is abusing this week. She is wearing her hair in long, beaded braids now, some of which are black, some of which are light brown, most of which are quite fake. "*I'm* here for the fund-raiser. The real question, sweetie, is, what are *you* doing here? And where the hell's your tux?" Tapping my wool jacket with feigned disapproval.

"Uh, I'm not here for the fund-raiser. I'm here for the tort-reform conference." I am babbling but seem unable to stop. "It's just a bunch of law professors. I delivered a paper yesterday." I wave vaguely toward the stairway down to the room where we have been meeting. I am sure she has no clue what I am talking about.

Sally is peering at me closely. Her eyes shine wetly. "Are you all right, Talcott? You don't look so good."

"I'm fine. Listen, Sally, it's nice to see you, but I really have to go."

I wait for what seems an eternity but is probably two seconds, and then she answers me, ignoring my brisk effort to escape as she conveys her own message: "I'm so glad I ran into you, Tal. I've been thinking about calling you." Sally gets up on her toes—no easy trick in heels that high—to whisper in my ear: "Tal, listen. I need to talk to you about where I saw Agent McDermott before."

After the events of the past several hours, it takes me an awkward moment to recall that McDermott was the name used by the late Colin Scott; that Sally told me on the day I met him that she thought she knew him.

All at once I am tired of theories. My father is dead but leaving me notes, my wife is doing goodness-knows-what, and I am being followed by a mysterious woman who was on the Vineyard when Scott/McDermott drowned. The human mind, especially when under stress, can assimilate only so much information. And I am beyond my capacity.

"I appreciate it, Sally, but I don't think this is the time or the place—"

She cuts me off, her wine-soaked breath tickling the side of my face.

"I saw him in the house, Tal. On Shepard Street. Years ago." A pause. "*He knew your father.*"

CHAPTER 23

THE AMBIGUOUS FIGURE

(1)

"IT WAS SUMMER," Sally begins, sipping a bottle of beer from the mini-bar. I would rather have given her plain water, or maybe coffee, but standing up to tough women has never been my forte. "Maybe a year or two after Abby died. Mariah was in college. I think maybe you were, too, but I can't remember. But I know where I saw him. I'm sure of that part."

I wait for my cousin to get the story out. She is lounging on one of the two double beds in my hotel room. I am seated at the tiny desk, the chair turned in her direction. We have ordered food from room service, because Sally told me she has not eaten all day. I would rather not have this meeting in my room—she has a certain reputation, after all—but one look at her in the lobby made clear that she was in no shape to sit in a public place. Still, I tried a variety of excuses to avoid talking to her at all. Sally blew each of them away. A pile of work awaiting me? *Oh, this won't take too long.* Her children? *Oh, they're with my mom for a couple of days.* And the ever-jealous Bud? *Oh, he's not around so much any more.* So we came up here, where my stout, showy, overdressed cousin, the hem of whose flaming purple gown is several inches too short, immediately kicked off her shoes and demanded a drink.

If I am going to hear the story, this is the only way.

"I was at your house," she says. "On Shepard Street. It was night-time. I guess I was sort of asleep. Until . . . until the sound of an argument woke me up."

"Where was I?"

"I think you were probably on the Vineyard. You and your mom. Maybe Mariah. But not your father. And not Addison. That's why I was over at your house. I was, um, sort of with Addison." Sally is a very dark woman, but she blushes anyway. Lying on the bed, she twists physically away, as though it is easier to tell her story if she can pretend she is alone. And she at once launches a digression, in which Misha is the villain: "I know what I used to do with Addison was wrong, Tal, so I don't need you to tell me that. It's over, okay? It's been over like forever. I know you never approved. You always let me know. Oh, you never said a word, but you've always been, in the family, I mean, sort of like your father—you have all these rules and things, and when somebody doesn't follow them, you don't get mad, you get this disapproving look. Like everybody's morally smaller than you are. I *hate* that look. Everybody hates it, Tal. Your brother, your sister, everybody." I almost speak up, but remind myself that Sally is probably on something, that she certainly is not herself: knowledge that does nothing to reduce the sting of her words.

"My dad hated it, too," she is saying. "Your Uncle Derek, I mean"—as though I have some question about who her father is, or was. "He hated it when Uncle Oliver would look at him that way, and Uncle Oliver looked at him that way a lot. Because he hated my dad's, you know, his politics. He thought my dad was a Communist."

I venture my second interruption: "Sally, your dad *was* a Communist."

"I know, I know, but, what's that old joke? He made it sound so dirty." She laughs screechily as she repeats this line, although it cannot possibly be the whole joke, and then, suddenly, she is weeping. Whatever drug she is using, it seems to cause severe mood swings. Or perhaps there is no drug and she is simply unhappy. Either way, I decide to let her cry. There are no words of comfort I can offer, really, and putting my arms around her on the bed is out of the question.

"See, Tal," she resumes after a couple of minutes, "you think the world is made up of simple moral rules. You think there are just two kinds of people in the world, people who obey the rules and people who break them. You think you're so different from Uncle Oliver, but you're just like him. In some good ways, sure, but in some of the worst ways, too. You look down your nose at people you think are your moral inferiors. People like your brother. People like me."

Now I remember why Kimmer and I never socialize with Sally: you have to fight through ten minutes of her verbal abuse before you can have anything resembling a normal conversation. So I grit my teeth and keep silent, reminding myself that she is not a well woman.

Besides, what she says about me is probably right.

"So, anyway, that's why I didn't tell you before. About McDermott, I mean. I sort of pretended I didn't remember, but that wasn't true. I knew who McDermott was the minute I saw him. I probably should have said something, but I knew I would have to tell you why I was in the house that night, and I didn't want to see that disapproving look." She turns toward me long enough to glare, and I ponder the way belief in right and wrong can interfere with the project of human communication. "See, Tal, that's why we always had to sneak around, because people like you and Uncle Oliver . . ."

She stops. A shudder runs through her. Another sob? No, a memory, a recollection she prefers to hold at bay.

"It's ancient history," I murmur, trying to divert her. If Sally is seeking an apology, she is out of luck, for I cannot pretend there was nothing wrong with what she and Addison did.

Sally knows what I am thinking. "Even Mariah's not as bad as you are, Tal. You know what? When Mariah is in D.C., she always calls me up. We have some good times. . . ."

"She told me you've been helping her go through the Judge's papers."

Sally snickers. "Is that what she told you? Well, yeah, we do that sometimes, but that's not what I mean. I mean we have *good times*. We talk. She listens to me, Tal. We go to the clubs. You know. Your sister likes to get down sometimes. Not like you. And she isn't judging me all the time like you are. She takes people just the way they are. So that's why I didn't tell you, Talcott. Because of the way you are. Because it involves Addison, too. I mean, me and Addison. You're just like your father," she repeats. I am playing catch-up, stuck on the image of my sister in a club—the kind of club that Sally likes—*getting down*. You would not think, to look at Mariah, that she was the partying type; sole black member of the yacht club is more her style. My cousin, on the other hand, is a party and a half all by herself.

"You could never understand about Addison," Sally continues, her voice excited and angry and full of life's broken promises. "You could never understand what we had. Okay, it was wrong. But it was *special*"—as though I have disputed her. "We were lovers, Tal. It wasn't just sex, it was love. Now, is that crude enough for you?"

She is up on her elbow, eyes aglow with belligerence. Her mood is swinging, all right, and she is saying anything that comes to mind.

"I'm not judging you, Sally," I lie carefully, my tone as neutral as I can make it. "I just want to know what you remember about McDermott."

"You *are* judging me."

"I'm just glad it's over," I assure her. But I marvel at how a civilized world can make a virtue of having no judgment, teach it to kids, preach it from the pulpit.

"You know something, Tal? You're a fake. Misha. *Mikhail.* A fake." A harsher laugh. "My dad *gave* you that nickname, in case you forgot, and you still treat his daughter like trash." My cousin flops back onto the bed, her braids settling around her head like an ebon halo. The tirade seems to be over.

The room-service waiter wisely chooses that moment to arrive. When Sally makes no effort to get up from the bed, I sign the bill in the corridor, blocking the waiter's view of the room, and roll the cart in myself.

We eat in silence for a few minutes: mushroom soup and a club sandwich for me, shrimp cocktail and filet mignon for Sally. Having shared a healthy repast with my in-laws just an hour ago, I should not be eating again so soon, but I tend to find the self all too easy to indulge, which perhaps explains my burgeoning waistline. In short, I eat too much; when I am nervous or stressed, my will to resist is weaker still. I am, unfortunately, like Mark Twain, who once said that he ate more on some occasions than others, but never less. Sally and I sit facing each other on the two beds with the table between us. She eats fast and without any finesse, simply fulfilling a bodily desire. The food seems to revive her, or maybe the drug, if there is one, has worn off; whatever the reason, when she next opens her mouth, she is her old flirty self.

"I'm sorry I ordered the most expensive thing on the menu, Tal, but men don't buy me dinner very often any more, so I figured, what the hell, make the most of it."

"Don't mention it."

"Of course, sometimes a man expects something in return."

"All I expect is to hear about Mr. McDermott." Giving her my best stone face.

"Sure that's all you want?" Coy, as if the intimacy of sharing a secret dinner with a man in a hotel room has given her permission to misbehave. "Most men have other things in mind."

"I'm not most men."

"Come on, Tal, don't you *ever* relax and have fun?"

"Only on Tuesdays and alternate Saturdays."

This, at least, brings a genuine smile. "Okay, Tal," she says. "Let's be friends."

"Okay."

"Look, I'm sorry for what I said before." Although she does not sound *very* sorry. She curls her solid legs underneath her. "I just can't seem to help myself tonight. I guess that's my flaw, I always say what I'm thinking. At least, when I'm with a man."

"That's not necessarily a flaw." Not liking, however, her use of the word *with*.

"Well, no, not if the man I'm with happens to like what I'm thinking." A pause as she contemplates a punch line. "And if he doesn't? To hell with him."

Again she laughs, a light, trilling sound: there is nothing hateful in her words. Sally does not dislike men, even though she has not been well treated by them. She is amused by them. By us. It occurs to me that Sally, when she is not being melancholy, can probably be a lot of fun. I begin to see why Addison, and so many other men, have found my plump cousin attractive. Last year, I saw an exhibit at the university museum of some of those drawings that used to be popular early in the twentieth century, the ones that look like smiling dogs until you invert them, when they turn into angry cats, or change from a beautiful woman to an unhappy sultan, and so on. "Ambiguous Figures," the exhibit was called. Sally is like one of those ambiguous figures: at first glance she seems wild, overweight, hopeless, pill-popping, pathetic; catch her from another angle and she is bold, bright, sexy, scathingly witty. I am catching her, at this moment, from that second angle, which means that I need, quickly, to bring some discipline to our conversation.

"About McDermott—"

"Yes, *sir!*" She snaps off a mock salute. "At your service, *sir!*"

And then she tells me the story.

(1 1)

WE HAVE FINISHED DESSERT—the fruit cup for me, tiramisù for Sally. I have rolled the room-service cart back into the hallway. Sally is lounging on the bed, weight on her elbow, one toe touching the carpet.

I am at the desk once more, my hands folded in my lap, as I wait for her to begin.

"I was at the house on Shepard Street, like I said. I don't know if you remember or not, but in those days, Dad and Mom and I lived down in Southeast. He used to work for that little private library. You remember."

Indeed I do: *Were you aware, Judge Garland, that the library where your brother worked was a known Communist front?* And, inevitably: *No, Senator, I was not aware. My brother and I did not have much to do with each other.* Then the switch to maudlin mode: *That must have been a source of some pain, Judge.* My father at his coldest, yet his most disarming: *I loved my brother, Senator, but our differences were pretty strong. Communism is a terrible, terrible thing—at least as bad as racism. Maybe worse in some ways. I could not be a part of his world. He could not be a part of mine. I suppose I wasn't the best brother in the world, and if I hurt my brother, I'm very sorry. Each of us thought the other was pretty dangerous, I guess. But I admit I don't think about it much.* Absolutely destroying this line of questioning.

"I remember," I say softly.

"Well, anyway, in those days, I used to take a bus—was it the S4?—up to your house. You know, to see Addison? I mean, if he happened to be in town? I never went when your parents were there, or when you and Mariah were there either. I sort of only went to meet Addison alone." A small, sheepish grin. "The truth is, I never told my folks where I was going either. Dad was just as bad as Uncle Oliver—that disapproving look, I mean. Maybe all the guys in your family have that frown. I mean, except Addison."

I consider suggesting that we were disapproving because there was something to be disapproving *of*, that a sexual relationship between first cousins is incest. But Sally would probably remind me that she and Addison are not blood relations. Or perhaps she would cite Eleanor and FDR at me; and I would answer that they were actually first cousins once removed, contrary to popular understanding, which means that their family relationship was distant indeed, their last common ancestor something like five generations back; and Sally would accuse me of patronizing her; and the conversation would spiral downhill from there.

Besides, she has already admitted that what they did was wrong.

I say: "If I could just hear about McDermott . . ."

"You're so damn single-minded." She laughs and lies down on the bed again, this time with her heavy knees in the air. "The thing is, Tal, you have to understand, I would never have been in that house if I knew your father was going to be there. I was supposed to meet Addison, and we were supposed to be alone. Your father—well, he was supposed to be away." She closes her eyes, frowns. "Not on the Vineyard, though. I think—I think he was supposed to be at some judges' convention."

"Probably the Judicial Conference," I murmur.

"Huh?"

"The Judicial Conference. Federal judges' group. Meets during the summer. He was probably there."

She shakes her head. "Maybe he was *supposed* to be there, maybe he told *Aunt Claire* he would be there, but where he *was*, was in D.C."

I bite my tongue. If Sally is telling the truth, she has caught the Judge lying to my mother, which, I would have sworn until this moment, never happened once.

"Anyway, I didn't know your father was around. I was supposed to see Addison. We were both just out of college, both in town for the summer, and he was living at home. So was I. And he called me up and said everybody was away for a few days, so we could . . . we could spend some time together if I wanted. Well, I wanted."

As I nod and offer no comment, I see something behind Sally's words: Addison was the pursuer. He was a year younger than his cousin, but, from the start, even on the Vineyard, my brother was the seducer, not, as family folklore has it, the other way around; and a part of her hates him for it.

"So, anyway," Sally is saying, "I told my folks I was going out with some girlfriends or something and not to wait up for me, then I hopped on, let's see, must have been the 30 bus, or the 32, and then got on the S4"—wanting me to know, from all this, how hard she worked to see her love—"and, well, anyway, I got to Shepard Street and went up to the house, and Addison was there. . . ."

Pausing to see if I have any reaction. When I do not, she resumes.

"Anyway, after a while, I fell asleep. I don't know how late it was. I know it was dark when these voices woke me up. Not loud. Kind of whispery. But still angry. I mean, they were arguing, and maybe they were trying to argue quietly, but I still heard them. I realized there was somebody else in the house, and I sort of got scared. So I turned to wake up Addison, but he wasn't there. So I figured it must be Addison arguing with somebody. I thought it must be Uncle Oliver, which would probably mean we were caught, which would mean we were seriously up the creek. So I put my clothes on. I figured I would sneak out the back door. I've snuck out of a lot of back doors in my life, haven't I?" Another one of her mirthless laughs. There is no point in responding; the question is clearly rhetorical, and we both know what the answer is.

"Addison's bedroom was on the third floor," she continues, rolling onto her side, facing me now, except that her eyes are still closed. "At the end of that long hallway. The old servants' quarters, I guess. You know, low ceiling, gables, the Nathaniel Hawthorne thing." Actually, I know perfectly well what the house looks like, having grown up in it, but I have no intention of breaking the flow, now that she is telling the story. "The argument was way down in the foyer, two floors away, but I heard it anyway. I think it was some trick of the ducts or something."

Now it is my turn to smile in memory. The Shepard Street house has old-fashioned heating grates, metal screens covering what are basically holes in the wall with chutes behind them, left over, I suspect, from the days when the whole house was heated by a single stove. We had radiators, of course, but they were added sometime after the house was built. The ducts themselves were never removed. My parents never realized that sounds from the first floor, especially the foyer, routinely found their way to the top floor, where Addison and I slept. Perhaps there was some common vent: I never figured out how all the old ductwork ran. In any event, my brother and I were always able to hear what was going on down there.

"So, anyway," Sally resumes, "I got dressed and went on downstairs. I planned to sneak out, but first I wanted to see what all the fuss was about. Down the back stairs, I mean. The servants' stairs."

We both laugh, although nothing is funny. I glance at the digital clock on the nightstand. It is close to ten.

"So I went down to the second floor and then went out into the hall. You remember there's this long landing that runs all around the foyer, what do they call it?"

"The gallery."

"Oh, right. And the gallery has this, um, this balustrade, I think is the word, and the, uh, the wooden posts—what are they called? Spindles? Dowels? Whatever they are, the posts that hold the balustrade? They're very wide. Almost wide enough to hide behind."

"Especially for a child." I smile briefly, remembering how, when we were children, Addison and Mariah and Abby and I loved to play hide-and-seek, and I used to hide up in the gallery there all the time. One of the things I quickly discovered was that, if the lights were on in the foyer and off in the hall, and the one who was *it* was down in the foyer, he—or she—couldn't see me hiding in the gallery.

"Well," says Sally tartly, "I was never that tiny, but I could hide up there anyway. Or I did that night." She stirs: the memory is starting to bother her. Maybe her moral sense has kicked to life. But she does not stop talking. "Anyway, the only light that was on was in your father's study. That's the part I remember best. It was so dark in the foyer, like Uncle Oliver was . . . oh, like he was doing something that needed the darkness. I know that sounds crazy, Tal, but that's the way it felt. And the voices I heard were from inside the study. I couldn't make out what your father was saying, I think because he was trying to keep his voice down, but the other man was yelling: 'That's not how the game is played.' Something like that."

"He said 'the game'?"

"That's what I said he said." She pouts, not as prettily as she probably thinks, and continues. "Well, anyway, the other man, the man who was yelling, came out into the hallway, and he was pointing at your father, shaking his finger like he was angry or something. That's how I saw the birthmark, when his hand moved into the light. It was McDermott. Whatever his name is in real life. Was."

So Sally knows he is dead. Which means Mariah probably knows. Which means that everybody knows. Maybe that is why Sally has chosen to break her silence. I say, "His name was Colin Scott."

"Fine, Colin Scott. The same man who was in the living room the week after your father died, okay? He was right there in the foyer, talking to your father, twenty years ago. I swear he was. And he was saying something like, 'There are rules for this kind of thing.' Something like that. And then I heard Uncle Oliver's voice. You know, his lecturing tone: 'There are no rules where a'—and then he said some word I couldn't quite understand—'is involved.' He sort of dropped his voice on that word I missed. Not because he thought anybody was listening. It was sort of like a hiss. But I kind of heard it, Tal, and I think—I think it sounded like *dollar*. Like 'There are no rules where a dollar is involved.'"

"They were arguing about money?"

"I don't know. I might not have it exactly right. But it sounded like that. And the other man, he was shaking his head, like *No.* And then Uncle Oliver came into the light, and his face, his face was *wild,* it was scary. I figured he had been drinking."

"It's possible, I guess." I cannot, at the moment, imagine why McDermott/Scott and my father would have been arguing about money. "He drank a lot after Abby died."

"I know, Tal. I remember. I'm sorry."

"It's okay. It was a long time ago." I wonder how we got off on this tangent.

"My family had problems, too."

I only nod. Garlands do not talk about growing up, or about anything else that it is impossible to change. But Sally is undeterred.

"Nobody's childhood is what they want, you know? We don't choose our parents. We don't choose our parents' problems either. Once you recognize that, you're halfway home." A New Age feel-good comment, possessing no meaning I am able to identify.

"I just want to hear the story, Sally. I just want to know what happened with my father and . . . and the man he was arguing with."

Sally gives me a long look, provocative and disconcerting. I do not want this woman in my head. I do not even want her in my room. But I have to have the rest.

"Well, so, anyway, now they were staring at each other, like they were gonna have a fight or something. And then Uncle Oliver said, pretty loud, he almost shouted, 'I'm sick of following the rules.' The other man just shook his head. I think he wanted Uncle Oliver to be quiet. And he said something like, 'That's not the way it's done.' And then your father, his voice got real soft and cold, and he said, 'You'd do it for Jack.'"

"Meaning Jack Ziegler."

"I think so. I don't know for sure. He didn't say the whole name, but I think that's who he meant."

I rub a hand across my face. A few moments ago the room was too small. Now the walls seem to be receding, or maybe I am shrinking. I feel lost and giddy: this is a little too much, a little too fast. I rally, asking a lawyer's question to gain time.

"You're sure it was the same man? The same man who came to the house the day after the funeral?"

To my relief, my skepticism sparks no explosion. "I'm sure, Tal." She relaxes again, shifting her position on the bed. I can see she is about done. Still, like a good witness, she recites her reasons. "I remember his voice. It was so cold and so angry. I remember the birthmark on his hand from when he was shaking his finger at Uncle Oliver. I remember the big white scar on his lip. And I remember something else. I was uncomfortable kneeling on the ground up there, so I moved around, and one of the floorboards creaked? And that other man, McDermott, his head whipped around and he looked straight up at where I was hiding. His eyes were like, I don't know, some hunting animal. I was sure he was gonna see me. I was *scared*, Tal." She yawns, then shivers. "It was the same man, Tal. I'd swear on a stack of Bibles."

I take this in phlegmatically, calculating the possibilities of error, of wishful thinking, of false memories. Or of simple lying.

"'No rules where a dollar is concerned'? That's what he said?"

"That's what he said," Sally confirms. Her confidence in her recollection is growing with each passing second. Lawyers often see this in witnesses. Sometimes it means they really do have it right; sometimes it means they have become comfortable with a version manufactured on the spot.

Sally yawns again. I can tell she is fading.

"So, what happened next?"

"Hmm? What?"

"After the argument you heard."

"Oh. Well, that was about it. McDermott or Scott or whatever his name was, well, he stopped looking up at the gallery and looked back at your father and put a finger to his lips, and they whispered together a few minutes, and then they both nodded and shook hands. They . . . they didn't seem mad any more. Then Uncle Oliver walked him across the foyer and opened the door, and I went down the back stairs, and I guess your father went back into his study." She yawns again.

I sit silently for a couple of minutes. Sally's forearm is across her eyes. I have no reason to think she is making any of this up. Sally is not a liar; as she told me, she says whatever is on her mind. So Scott knew my father, knew him more than twenty years ago, visited our house one summer night when the Judge lied to my mother and said he was going to the Judicial Conference, argued with him in the foyer about dollars and rules and what he would do for Jack Ziegler. I find my irritation rising—not at my father, but at Sally, for holding this back. Not telling me earlier because she was worried about my disapproval. I glance at her now. My irritation melts away. She has had a rough life, has Sally, yet she somehow manages to find the energy for a smile or two. As she is smiling now, with her eyes closed, yet aware, I am sure, of my scrutiny. I do not like the way my feelings toward her are running. The Judge's words come drifting back: *Nobody can resist temptation all the time. The trick is to avoid it.*

Avoid it. Right. I have to think about easing Sally out of here. Her gown is badly rumpled, her expensively braided hair a brown wreck. She will be quite a sight going back downstairs. I find myself hoping that anyone who notices her will think she is sneaking out of somebody else's room.

And then I realize that a piece of the story is missing.

"So where was Addison?" I ask. No response. Louder: "Sally?"

"Mmmm?"

"Addison, Sally. Where was my brother when all this was happening?"

"Hmm? Addison?" She snickers. "See, well, that's the thing." She turns onto her other side, facing away from me. Her voice is slow. The drug? The drink? Exhaustion? All of them, I suspect. "That's the thing," she says again. "You know how the servants' stairs go down to that little hall behind the kitchen, right? Well, when I got down there, the kitchen was dark, but I was scared to turn on a light, because I didn't want Uncle Oliver, you know, to catch me. I was gonna go out through the mudroom? Well, I took about two steps, and then I bumped my shin on a stool, and I guess I was a little too loud or something, because the next thing I know, there's this hand over my mouth, I try to scream, I try to bite, I try to kick, I'm scared to death, and of course it's your damn brother." She stops for a moment. Shakes her head. "Addison," she mutters. "Addison, Addison, Addison." Her mantra. "*Addison.*" Then nothing.

"Sally? Sally, what about Addison? What happened in the kitchen?"

"Hmmm? Kitchen?"

"Of my father's house. When Addison put his hand over your mouth."

"Oh. Oh, yeah. Well. He told me to hush, and I asked him was he in the kitchen the whole time, and he asked me what whole time, and I said all the time your father was arguing with that white guy, and he said what white guy, and I said the guy who was talking to Uncle Oliver, and he said he didn't know what I was talking about, and I tried to argue with him, but then he said we had to get out of there, fast. So we went on out the kitchen door, and, well, that was the end of that."

I have the sense that I am missing something here.

"Sally, listen. Wake up. Sally, did you believe him? Did you believe Addison? About not hearing anything?"

Another snicker. "Believe *Addison?* Are you shitting me? That nigger never told the truth about anything in his life." Sally's speech is growing less cultured as fatigue claims her. "He would say any damn thing to get . . . to get what he wants. To get over." A small giggle.

"Sally. Sally, listen. Please. This is important, okay? Do you think Addison heard the argument?"

"Of course he did." A barking cackle. Sally possesses a remarkable repertoire of laughing sounds.

"Are you sure?"

"Sure I'm sure." Another yawn, longer. She has very little left. "He told me when I called to tell him what . . . that the same man was in your house the day after the funeral."

What!

"When was that?"

"Oh, I dunno." Sleepy. "A week later. Maybe two."

Of course.

He heard. And never said anything. Keeping his cards, as always, close to his chest. My family! All we know how to do is keep secrets! Addison heard the argument between my father and Colin Scott at Shepard Street twenty years ago; he knew it was the same man who pretended to be Special Agent McDermott because Sally, his former lover, told him a week or so after the funeral. And he never told me. I will bet he never told Mariah, either, who would have added that information to her conspiracy theory, and immediately blabbed it to me.

"Sally?"

Only snoring.

I sigh and settle in the chair. Exhausted, I immediately doze, a terrifying dream of perdition.

My eyes snap open. A moment's disorientation, and then everything comes flooding back in. I am still chewing on cotton, my cousin is still asleep on the bed, and it is now well past eleven.

"Sally, hey, wake up. Sally, you've got to go. Sally!"

More snoring. The hard, alcoholic kind. The kind I used to hear coming from the Judge's study at night in those terrible days after Abby died; maybe the kind that Addison heard when he got back to the house after seeing Sally home on the night Colin Scott fought with my father. Or maybe he just walked her to the S4 bus.

My brother, the late-night talk king. Oh, Sally has his number all right. Do anything, say anything.

"Sally? Sally, wake up. Come on, Sally!"

I stand up and cross to the bed. Asleep, breathing through her slightly open mouth, her small fists curled near her throat, Sally Stillman has a vulnerable look; it is easy, now, to see the cute teenager she once was, back when I spied her with Addison at Vinerd Howse. I touch Sally's bare shoulder, my fingers lingering a few seconds longer than they should. Her flesh is warm and dangerously alive.

"Hey, Sally, come on."

She mutters something and curls away from my hand. I doubt that I can wake her, not without physically shaking her, which I am not about to do. The events of the last few weeks have left me emotionally sick, and what I want to do most is snuggle close to Sally's ample body, wrap my arms around her, and lose myself in her warmth.

I am so, so tired. Of so, so much. Of worrying about conspiracies, of running from phantoms, of fighting with my wife. So tired. And so lonely.

I decide to let Sally stay. Even if I could wake her, I can hardly send her home like this. Which means she will have to stay here in my hotel room and sleep it off.

For her own good.

Temptation. The trick is to avoid it.

"It's not that easy, Dad," I mutter, sitting gingerly on the edge of the rumpled bed where my cousin slumbers on, oblivious to my distress. I remind myself that I am a married man, but the room feels so terribly small, the bed so terribly large. My throat is dry. My fingers, without my quite willing it, reach toward Sally's round, inviting shoulder once more.

Then they fall back.

Avoid it.

I go to the closet for an extra blanket, which I drape over Sally's somnolent form. I remove my tie, slip out of my shoes, and return to the desk chair to keep vigil.

What a mess.

CHAPTER 24

THE DIAGNOSIS

(1)

IF YOU DRIVE along Seventh Street near Howard University, you discover a little college town of remarkable complexity, buried in the heart of Washington, D.C. It is only a couple of blocks long, so it is easy to miss, but it is there. It features fast-food outlets instead of delis, Southern-style kitchens rather than pizza parlors, but you also find the usual scattering of small office buildings, apartment houses, and photocopying outlets. To be sure, this particular little college town also includes an unhealthy proportion of boarded-up windows, empty, weed-choked lots, and warehouses surrounded by razor wire. But, if one wants to look beyond the expensive brochures my own university sends out, Elm Harbor has many of the same sordid features; and if we disguise them better, it is only because we have that much more money with which to purchase camouflage.

It is to the tiny Seventh Street corridor that I go on the last day of the conference, to have lunch, as Kimmer teased me when I told her, with another woman. The woman in question is Lanie Cross—formally, Dr. Melanie Cross, F.A.C.O.G., but she always asked the Garland children to call her Lanie, much to my parents' chagrin. She and her late husband, Leander Cross, a prominent surgeon of the darker nation, were, in my childhood, perhaps the leading hosts of the Gold Coast party circuit, a circuit my parents traveled often, because it was, in those days, what one did: glittering dinner at one house on the Friday, champagne brunch at another on the Sunday, caterers, cooks, even temporary butlers at the ready as the best of black Washington charged about in mad imitation of white people's foolishness. Yet it was not, really, so mad. In the old days, my mother used to say, there were only a hundred black people who mattered in America, and they all knew each other. A bit of snobbery, but also an intriguing proposition. The social scene, so inexplicably wasteful and pretentious to its critics, refreshed and reinforced those who whirled through it, strengthening them to face another day, another week, another month, another year of expending their prodigious talents in a nation unprepared to reward them for their abilities.

As a child, I loved to come downstairs early Saturday morning when my parents had entertained the night before. I would wander through the not-yet-cleaned first-floor rooms, sniffing the glasses, handling the place cards, looking for fresh scratches on the huge polished rosewood table in the dining room. Sometimes, as my parents slept off their partying, my siblings and I would play, sitting around the table, raising our glasses in toasts we imagined were clever, trying through this little drama to figure out exactly what all those adults *did* so long into the night that kept them laughing raucously and shouting each other's names with such glee as we crouched in the stairwell, listening and trying to learn. More than thirty years have passed since those days, and I wonder still what the secret was, for the unspoken magic of integration is the way it has made the spirit of those long, happy nights disappear. True, there is still entertainment, and there are even still parties, but something of their character has been lost, their role in bolstering community has grown less certain, perhaps because community itself is beginning to die. Kimmer and I live in an otherwise all-white neighborhood, and few of the friends of my adolescence live anywhere near the Gold Coast, unless one counts the fancier suburbs of Washington itself.

Lanie Cross is a connection to that earlier era. She lives, in a sense, between the two worlds, then and now. Perhaps it is her age. Her husband was of my father's generation, but Lanie herself was something around fifteen years younger—nobody mentions that they married when she was his student at Howard—which puts her, today, in her late fifties. She is a tall, handsome woman, with long bones in every part of her body, from her legs to her cheeks, and skin that maintains its smooth brown beauty even as it begins to wrinkle around her face. Her gray eyes flash playfully with energy and intelligence. When I was a kid, all the boys had crushes on her.

Like all her working days, this one is busy, and when I hunt down her office in one of those whitewashed, blocky, low-rise professional buildings, her stern but polite receptionist, another woman of years, a

West Indian, commands me to wait. I sit on a hard wooden bench amidst her patients, women running in age from early teen years to significantly older than I. All are of the darker nation. Most seem, from their manner or their dress, comfortably middle-class, for Lanie Cross maintains a clientele from the old days. But a few display outward signs of impoverishment, and a couple seem little more than an economic rung or two above the patrons of the soup kitchen. Lanie, by reputation, treats all of them the same, and my affection for her is such that I would like to believe it is true.

Lanie was surprised to hear from me when I called a week ago, the way anybody would be at sudden protestations of friendship from an individual with whom she has not exchanged a word in probably five years except for a token hug at the funeral. I reached her at home, having obtained the unpublished number from gregarious Mariah, and I heard a child crying in the background. Lanie told me that her daughter and son-in-law were visiting, and I tried, and failed, to remember how many children she had. (The number turned out to be three, all adopted: Lanie and her husband could have no children the old-fashioned way.) When I explained that I wanted to talk about my father, she grew more cautious still. In the end, she agreed to see me for lunch, I suspect because she is as curious to learn what I can tell her as I am to learn what she can tell me. Her late husband, in addition to being a golf and poker buddy of many years' standing, was one of my father's two real confidants—the other was my mother—during the difficult days after Greg Haramoto stepped forward. Addison told me once that the two doctors Cross were extraordinarily close. I hope this turns out to be true.

(11)

I TOOK A TAXI to Lanie's office, so we drive over to Adams-Morgan, my old neighborhood, in her blocky and practical Volvo, which she was driving at the time of my father's confirmation hearings. She has picked out a Cuban place that she loves, and which she has not visited in a while. Lanie is, as always, well turned out, in a slimming navy pantsuit and an ankle-length vicuña coat that must have cost my monthly salary. She has to be back at the office by two, she tells me, so we will have to hurry.

During the painstaking journey across town—I forgot that Lanie drives as cautiously as her choice of car suggests—we exchange the expected pleasantries of two acquaintances who have not really talked in half a decade, and who were never particularly close. I also keep an eye out for a green sedan so ordinary it might stand out, but there are too many ordinary cars around. Lanie, oblivious to my vigilance, mentions that she saw my in-laws at a dinner party last month, and they looked fit enough to live forever, then realizes how I might take this and covers her slip with tales of her children: the oldest, her son, is rising in the Air Force, dragging his wife and three children all over the world; the second oldest, a daughter, is a freshly minted history professor right at Howard, divorced and raising a son on her own; and the youngest, another daughter, is a homemaker in New Rochelle, raising three children while her husband, who "does something with municipal bonds," commutes to Manhattan. Lanie is proud of her children and delighted to have seven grandchildren, and I remember, uneasily, the way that some of us used to tease the Cross kids for their unquestioning devotion to their parents, the Fifth Commandment being, for most of us, just a collection of silly words hanging on the wall of the Sunday-school classroom. But I suppose if I were adopted by two parents as loving and generous as the Crosses I would put them ahead of everything too.

Around the time our appetizers run out, it is Lanie, finally, who brings us around to our purpose. "So, anyway, you said you wanted to talk about your father."

"Well, about his relationship with your husband."

"Relationship?" Holding her water glass in her thin hand, Lanie seems amused.

I color a bit. "What I mean is, I want to know anything you're willing to tell me that your husband told you about my father."

"What Leander told me about your father?"

"Yes."

"All of it?" Her eyes twinkle. I have forgotten this about Melanie, her mischievous way of communicating with men by repeating back to them, as questions, whatever they say to her. I suppose I thought she would have outgrown it, but it is, perhaps, an instinct with her, not so much flirtatious as cautious. She likes to keep men off their guard, to enable her to stay on hers.

"Not all of it. But, thinking back to . . . well, when my father was nominated to the Supreme Court and had all that trouble. My dad didn't ask many people's advice, but I know he asked Dr. Cross's. Anything you can tell me about what your husband told you . . . well, that's what I'd like to know."

Lanie brushes her short bangs away from her face, eats a couple of bites of her *bistec empanizado*, pondering. I lean back and sip my Diet Pepsi, waiting for her to make up her mind. I don't know why everyone I talk to seems considerably less than forthcoming. Perhaps I am touching a common wound.

"There isn't that much to tell," she finally says. She smiles nervously, displaying perfectly capped teeth. "Leander confided in me about your dad less than everybody seems to think. A lot less."

I file away the odd word *everybody* as I nod my encouragement. "Anything you can remember."

"Those were not the easiest times," she warns.

"I understand that, but . . . well, there are things I have to know."

"Things you *have* to know?"

"When his nomination . . . when the whole thing fell apart, he didn't talk to a lot of people. I know he talked to Dr. Cross. To your husband. I just want to know what they talked about. And what . . . I guess you'd say, what my father's mood was."

Lanie is still fencing. Perhaps her husband instructed her not to tell. "Why is this so important to you, Talcott? Does this have something to do with Kimmer's judgeship?"

Ouch! I remember Mallory Corcoran: *Aren't there any secrets in this town?* Well, no, not really, as my father learned. I choose my words warily. "No, it's because of some other things that have been happening."

"That private detective, you mean? The one who drowned."

Ouch again! "Uh, yes. Maybe. I'm not sure."

"He tried to interview me, you know. He talked to a few people from the old days. I don't think any of them told him very much." About what? I want to ask, but Lanie does not pause in her narrative, and I do not want to interrupt. "Not that any of them had very much to tell him. He was looking for some papers or something. I don't know the details, because I refused to talk to him. The nerve!" She frowns, shakes her head. "From what I hear, he was worse than a policeman. Badgering elderly people in their homes, intimidating them. Grace Funderburke had to sic her dog on him, I heard. Carl Little told him he was going to get his shotgun, not that Carl has probably fired the thing in a quarter-century. And they say he gave poor Gigi Walker such a hard time she was in tears when he left."

"What was he giving them a hard time about?" I ask, fascinated.

Lanie seems irritated. "I told you, Talcott, I'm not sure. The FBI went around and interviewed all of them about it. I guess he must have broken some law. But, from what I understand, it was what I told you, papers. Some papers your father was supposed to have left behind when he passed. I don't know." Another shrug, elaborate now, closing the subject. "I didn't talk to him," she reminds me.

I take a moment, forking rice and beans into my mouth as a cover. If Lanie did not grant an interview to Colin Scott, then who is the *everybody* who thought her husband would have confided in her? Does she just mean her friends along Sixteenth Street? Or is there a level to which I have not penetrated?

I am sure of one thing: I am visiting the right person.

"Lanie, let's talk about my father, not about the detective."

"If you want."

"I need to know what your husband told you. Please. Anything you can remember."

"You haven't told me why, Talcott."

And, indeed, I have not. I realize that what I say has to be good. If Melanie Cross has not spoken of these matters in fifteen years or more, there is no reason for me to think she is ready to unburden herself now just because I ask her to.

"Because I think my father wanted you to tell me," I say.

This gets her attention. Her wise eyes flash at me, her thin brows rising in question, and in doubt.

"He left me a note," I explain.

(III)

LANIE CROSS DOES NOT ASK me what the note said. She merely nods her slim head, perhaps in resignation. "Tal, you know, this might not be easy for you to hear."

"I know that, but I think I need to hear it."

"You mean you want to."

"I don't think this is about wants any more."

She is unhappy. "Tal, you understand, my Leander was a surgeon, not a psychiatrist. But . . . well . . . okay. You want to talk about what happened after the hearings? Fine. I'll tell you." And she does, straight out, no frills. "Leander told me he thought your father had a breakdown."

"A breakdown? What does that mean, a breakdown?"

"You know what it means. A nervous breakdown. He . . . When all the stories about Jack Ziegler started to come out, Oliver would call up Leander in the middle of the night—probably, oh, two or three times during that first week. The phone would ring at two in the morning and Leander would grab it, and I would lie there watching him, and he would whisper a few words, and then his skin would go pale, and I could see he was trying to say the right thing, trying to soothe, but after a while, he couldn't get a word in edgewise. And later Leander would tell me that it was Oliver, and he was crying on the telephone. I'm sorry, but that's what he said. That he was crying and kept saying things like, 'How could he do this to me?' Meaning that law clerk, Leander said, the one who testified against him. Or he would say, 'I did everything I was supposed to do, I did my job right, how could he put me in this position? Whatever happened to loyalty?' Things like that. Leander got a little frightened for him. Because of the way he was raving about his law clerk, and also because . . . well, Leander thought he sounded drunk again."

"Drunk! But . . . but he stopped drinking back when . . . years before."

Lanie shakes her head, the gray eyes solemn and sympathetic, the way they must be when she tells a patient she has ovarian cancer. "I guess he started again. At least that's what my Leander thought. And . . ."

"Wait. Wait a minute. If he was drinking, I would have known about it."

"Why do you say that?"

"Well, for one thing, I came down from Elm Harbor when all this was going on. Now, my father didn't talk to me about any of it. I'm not even sure he wanted me around." A sudden, hot catch in my throat. I never wanted to remember this, never expected to. "He . . . he didn't talk to me about any of it," I repeat, trying to find my place. "Neither did . . . neither did my mother. I guess they weren't . . . they weren't the kind of people who talked much about, uh, feelings. Problems. So, when all this happened, when his nomination fell apart, we . . . the children . . . couldn't get them to open up. But, still, drinking . . . if he was drinking . . ." I trail off, my eyes misty and stinging. I remember Wallace Wainwright's unsubtle hints during our meeting yesterday: *He wasn't himself. He didn't know what he was saying.* Maybe I was the only one who didn't realize that my father, in his pain and humiliation, had crawled back into the bottle.

Melanie Cross is physician enough to know that there are times when you do not reach out to comfort your patients, and she says nothing. She waits. For a terrible moment, I relive the sudden plummet from joy to horror, from a household topsy-turvy with phone calls and friends and telegrams because the Judge was about to become the Justice, to the lonely, brave, hopeless death-watch as friends disappeared and the phone grew silent—except for the soulless media—once it became clear that not only the nomination but my father's career itself was doomed. At the time I was enduring my third and final year of law school, and I skipped classes for the first glorious days of the hearings, then returned, a little over two weeks later, to sit in the back of the room as Greg Haramoto's testimony and a tidal wave of corroborating evidence washed away my father's protestations of innocence. After that first, wonderful morning, I stayed on at the Shepard Street house, as well-wishers and social climbers swirled in and out of the door, and my parents, at their royal and charming best, accepted the adulation as their due. But, after the dam broke, when I wanted to help, it became clear that neither of my parents quite knew what to do with me.

"I didn't spend much time at the house," I say finally. "I was still in law school."

"I remember," says Lanie, smiling with warm reminiscence and gossipy mischief. "You and Kimmer had just started dating, right?"

I hesitate, for Lanie has, perhaps unintentionally, set me a little verbal trap. In 1986, at the time of my father's nomination, Kimmer and I were classmates, nothing more, each of us—technically, anyway—dating someone else. In truth, the two of us were in the *oh-no-we-better-stop-wait-what-about-Kathy* stage of rekindling what had once been a rather passionate relationship; like most young adults of that era—or, for that matter, this one—we were besotted with the notion, dangerously antithetical to civilized life, that obeying our instincts was not merely our right but our responsibility. Somehow that tendency has always been the leitmotif of our attraction: three times, maybe more, depending on how you count, we have wound up in each other's arms at a moment when at least one of us belonged to someone else.

Not ready to confess to Lanie what everybody already knows, I decide, as so often, that the best answer is a distraction. "I guess you could be right. About my father's drinking, I mean. I wasn't living in the house. If my father was drinking, say, at night . . . well, I wouldn't necessarily know about it."

"I'm sorry, Tal."

"No, it's okay. It's . . . believable."

"You know, Tal, my husband tried . . . the first time, after Abby . . . he tried to get your dad some help for his drinking. But Oliver kept saying no. And, of course, he stopped on his own." Drumming her nails on the table. "Leander said your father always seemed a little insulted when he brought up the idea of treatment."

"He would have been." I sigh, heart heavy with memory. "He considered counseling and therapy the final resort of the weak of will."

"Alcoholism is a disease . . ." the doctor in her begins, automatically.

Laughing, I put up my hands in surrender. "Hey, you don't have to convince me. I know it's a disease, and I know there's a genetic tendency to it, which are two reasons that I never touch the stuff." Then I grow sad again. "And if it's a disease and my father never had any treatment . . . well, yes, I can believe that he would have started again." I play with my food, my appetite fading. None of this is what I came for. All I have done is reopened the never-quite-healed wounds of those debilitating days. But I press on. "Is that all your husband told you? The drinking? The . . . the crazy phone calls?"

"Well, no. No, there was more." Lanie clucks her tongue thoughtfully. She is about to drop another veil and, obviously, wondering whether she should. "Like . . . the chess," she says at last.

"The chess? What chess?"

Lanie's strong brow furrows in thought. She brushes her hair back again, forks some salad into her mouth. I wait while she sips her water. "Leander used to drop by to see your father in the evenings, both while this was going on and . . . and afterward. He didn't always call first . . ."

"Because he wanted to see if my dad was drinking," I suggest.

"I suppose that was part of it. But also remember, Tal, they were from a different generation. Dropping by unannounced was what friends did. It wasn't like today, where nobody's house is ever neat or ready for company, so you call first so your friends can clean everything up. People's houses, people's lives were more . . . oh, more open in a way. Not that nobody had any secrets, but, you know, there was a kind of a sense that . . . that . . . that your friends could see you as you really are. Were. You know what I'm saying."

"Yes." I smile slightly, hoping Lanie will hurry, because it is quarter past one and I know she has a patient at two. Or perhaps my secret memories of the neighborhood itself are generating this unexpected urge to rush. A few blocks up Columbia Road is the apartment where I lived in the late 1980s, and where Kimmer, although married to André, sometimes slept. Probably we ate a furtive meal or two in this very restaurant.

"Anyway. So Leander would drop by and he would usually find your father down in his little study—you know the room I mean—and Oliver would have his chessboard out, the one he was so proud of, always showing off the pieces, and he would be playing chess with himself." She makes a face. "No, that's not right. Let me think. I don't know much about chess, so it's hard to remember. No. He wasn't playing. He was trying . . . he was making chess puzzles. . . ."

"Problems."

"Hmmm?"

"Chess problems. My father liked to . . . They call it *composing*. He liked to compose chess problems. I guess you'd call it his hobby."

"Right!" Her face brightens. "Because, I remember, Leander told me he thought it was great therapy, should be very relaxing for your father, except . . . except that . . ."

"Except what?" I am running out of patience as well as time and wish she would just say it right out.

She looks me straight in the eye. She has caught my mood and is ready to give me the unadorned truth. "Leander thought Oliver had grown obsessional about it. About the chess problems he was composing. He didn't even want to play golf any more, because he always was at his chessboard. He hardly went to the poker games. I'm talking about the months after the . . . after the problem with his nomination. So Leander would go to Shepard Street to visit him. And your mother would let him in, and he would find his way back to the study, and he would walk in the room, Oliver's best friend, and Oliver wouldn't even get up from the chessboard. Sometimes he wouldn't even look up. He kept talking about how even chess was fixed, white moved first, white usually won, black could only react to what white did, and even if black played a perfect game he still had to wait for white to make a mistake before he would have any hope of winning—that kind of thing." Lanie frowns, remembering another point. "But . . . but I think I remember that Leander said that was why Oliver liked to—what was that word?— to compose. He liked composing problems because there was some special kind of problem, where black moved first. . . ."

"Helpmate problems, they're called," I say, even though this was never the side of chess that intrigued me. But something is crawling upward in my memory. "Black moves first in a helpmate, and black and white cooperate to checkmate the black king."

Lanie raises a thin eyebrow to show what she thinks of this. "Okay, maybe so. But, Talcott, the thing is, your father, well, he kept saying that this would be his redemption, that he couldn't win in one field but he could win in another. And . . . now, I don't remember this so well . . . but Leander said your father had some kind of chess problem he was working on, something that had never been done before, and he somehow thought if he could solve it . . . or compose it, I guess . . . that it would make up for what happened to his nomination to the Supreme Court. Something about a knight? Double . . . something. I don't remember what it was called. Chess isn't my game. But Leander said your father seemed so . . . so desperate to do it, so obsessed about it, that, for a while anyway, he didn't seem to give much time to anything else. Even his work started to slip, so Leander told me. All so he could . . . could compose his chess problem. Which is why my husband thought Oliver had a . . . a kind of breakdown. That's what Leander said, anyway." She looks at her watch, and I know our time is up.

Back out on Columbia Road, good old Lanie is Dr. Melanie Cross once more, and she is also in a sudden hurry to be free of me. I want to ask her whether she ever heard anything about my father wanting a gun, or whether she knows what might have spooked him a year before he died, but I see no way to phrase the questions that does not sound absurd. I walk her to her Volvo. I am not riding back to Howard with her, because my hotel is right down the hill, a ten-minute stroll. I am holding the door for her, and she is chattering about how it would be nice to get Bentley together with her grandchildren, it's such a shame we don't see more of each other, and I am nodding at all the right places, when the thought that has been trying to jostle its way into my consciousness suddenly bursts free.

"Lanie?"

"Hmmm?" Half in the Volvo and half out, she looks up in surprise and just a smidgen of annoyance. In her mind she is already back in her office, free of conversation almost as painful for her as for me.

"Lanie, just one other thing. The chess problem your husband told you my father was working on . . . the one he thought would turn everything around if he could only solve it?"

"What about it?"

"Can you try again to remember what it was called. You said . . . Double something?"

"I don't know much about chess, Tal." Smiling to hide her impatience. "I told you."

"I know, I know, I'm sorry. But can you remember anything your husband might have said about it? Please. I know you're in a hurry, but this is important."

She does that brow-furrowing thing again, her eyes distant. Then she shakes her head. "I'm sorry, Tal, it's been too long. I don't know. I know Leander mentioned a name, he said your father kept calling it by name—the chess problem, I mean. But, I'm sorry, I honestly don't remember. I should remember the name, Leander talked about it so much, because your father talked about it so much. Let me see. Maybe 'Double Excellence'? Or 'The Triple Exception'? Something like that." She looks at me again, very much the doctor, very much in a hurry. "Thanks for lunch, Tal, but I really have to run."

"I know," I murmur, suddenly dispirited. I remember it all now. The problem the Judge hoped to compose. The one about which he talked to me from time to time when I was much younger, even though his explanations bored me stiff. I wish now that I remembered more about it. "Thanks for trying. And thanks for your time."

"My pleasure." Lanie Cross brightens as she slides into the car in a flurry of thin arms and legs. I close the door solidly behind her. She rolls down the window. "Oh, I do remember one other thing. Leander told me that your father kept saying he was tired of the way white won all the time. He was going to fix it so that black would win instead."

"You mean the chess problem? Black would win?"

"I think so. I'm sorry, I don't remember anything else." She gives me a harried smile. "So, Tal, let's definitely get the families together, maybe this next summer, on the Vineyard."

"That would be nice," I say softly, but my mind is elsewhere.

As I watch the Volvo disappear into the swarming traffic, I am thinking of my father, out of his mind with fear and fury after the collapse of his nomination, sitting alone night after night in his little study, ignoring the overtures of his oldest and dearest friend, getting drunk, letting the rest of his world collapse around him, as he tried to fix it all by composing a special kind of chess problem called the Double Excelsior.

CHAPTER 25

A MODEST REQUEST

(1)

"I'D LIKE TO ASK YOU A FAVOR," murmurs the Reverend Doctor Morris Young.

"Of course," I say softly, because Dr. Young exudes a peace that calms those around him, as well as a power that seems to make everybody say yes.

"I hope I will not embarrass you."

"That depends on what the favor is."

Morris Young smiles. When happy, his pocked, orange-brown face seems gently rounded, casting warm beams of sunlight on anybody nearby. When angry, the same face is all hard planes and square corners and final judgments. His hair is sparse and gray; his reddish eyes are no longer sharp, even aided by his thick glasses; his lips are insolently protrusive, although he is as humble as they come. Though large of girth, he wears nothing in public but vested suits of dark wool, white shirts, and dark ties, a throwback to an earlier generation of preachers. He is in his early seventies, but possessed of all the evangelizing energy of the era of "muscular" Christianity. He is the pastor of Temple Baptist Church, probably the most powerful institution of the darker nation's battered outpost in the divided city of Elm Harbor, which makes him, by many accounts, the most influential black man in town.

He is also, with the possible exception of my colleague Rob Saltpeter, the finest man it is my privilege to know. Which is why, last summer, mired in depression over the state of my marriage, I chose him for my counselor. And why I have decided I need to see him again.

Last weekend, I returned from Washington to face a buzz saw: *It's not enough for you to lust after my sister, you have to spend the night with your fat slut of a cousin!* Evidently, somebody saw me going upstairs with Sally and told somebody else who told somebody else, the word reaching Elm Harbor in less than half a day. And, like every married man in America who has found himself in this situation, I raised my palms for peace and insisted, *Nothing happened, darling, I promise*—which in my case happens to be true. Kimmer was quite unappeased: *So what? Everybody thinks something did, Misha, and that's almost as bad!* I was stung by the realization that Kimmer is less concerned about what I might have done than by what people believe I might have done; that my wife, who long ago liberated me from the stultifying prison of my parents' expectations, has locked me away in the tight dungeon of her own.

I spared Kimmer the details of the dreary denouement of my night with Sally. So I omitted, cravenly, any mention of how I sat awake half the night in the uncomfortable wooden chair, fighting the impulse to stretch out on the other bed, lest Sally wake and misinterpret the situation. I did not tell my wife that I woke abruptly in the morning, still in the same position, feeling as though I had spent the night with my body twisted in some medieval torture device, my mouth clogged and muzzy, my head pounding, the vague lust of the night before a distant, barely plausible memory. My cousin was still asleep, breathing regularly now, and in the hard glare of daylight she was just dull, overweight Sally Stillman again. I had no trouble shaking her shoulder to wake her. She was no longer witty or cute or bold: her eyes red and puffy, she was panicky and disheveled and worried about being late for work, as well as being caught by Bud, who apparently remains more present in her life than she admitted. She could not get out of the room fast enough. Her coat, unfortunately, was in the cloakroom downstairs. To cover her wrinkled gown, I loaned her my tattered Burberry, which she promised to send back by Federal Express. She spent a few minutes in the bathroom, fixing her face, as she put it, and then was gone. It remains to be seen whether she took my reputation with her.

Yet my life continues. Onward and upward, one might say, given my father's emphasis on the word *excelsior.* At Oldie earlier this morning I sat through a brief and respectful session with two quiet investigators from the FBI, this time in connection with my wife's background check. Kimmer, interviewed twice, is excited. She thinks the portents may yet be favorable if, as she puts it, we stay on the same page. Over breakfast, she rehearsed me carefully in what to say and what to omit. She wants nothing more about the *arrangements* on the official record. I was too worn out to argue, and, besides, I really do want her to get what she wants. So I followed the script.

"We've known each other a long time, Talcott," says Dr. Young now, leaning forward to fold his hands on his immaculate desk. His office in the basement of the church is cramped and airless, the heating vent noisy. I am sweating. Dr. Young is not. His tie is perfectly knotted, his shirt crisp and fresh, although it is late afternoon. "How many years is it?"

"Since the time the boys made a fool of me."

He chuckles. "They didn't make a fool of you, Talcott. A man can only make a fool of himself. All they did was treat you like they treat every other outsider. And"—he holds up a pudgy hand to forestall my interruption—"and, you can be sure, I gave them a difficult time for it. You know what we teach in the program. Understanding that every human being we meet, white or black or brown or yellow, rich or poor or in between, police officer or pusher, whether he helps us or hurts us, every person we meet is made in the image of God, and it is our task, therefore, to seek that image in each encounter."

"I think I've heard this one before, Dr. Young." My turn to smile.

"I know, I'm a bit of a broken record. But you see how it is with the boys."

"I do," I tell him, and, at this moment, I would rather talk about the boys in his Faith Life Skills program than almost anything else, although, at some point, we need to talk about . . . well, about my marriage. I am trying to be patient and calm, as Kimmer, desperate worry in her eyes, keeps urging me. And Dr. Young, in his jovial, evangelical way, is helping. His reminder about the boys in his Faith Life Skills program helps, too.

"We've made some progress," the pastor murmurs, and I am not sure, at first, if he is talking about me or the boys. He leans toward me once more, his brown eyes blazing. "But, you understand, Talcott, all that these young men have learned from the world is mistrust. You know how many of them ever see their fathers? About one out of ten. You know how many of them have brothers or best friends who deal drugs? About nine out of ten. Half have been arrested. Some have been to prison. Not one has held a real job for more than a few months. They have no idea what a job is. They think the boss is dissing them when he tells them what to do. They think customers are a pain in the rear. They have no education to speak of. The schools have failed them. Welfare has trapped their mothers, but what else are their mothers to do? So the boys fight back. They hate white people, and they're scared of them too. Successful black people"—he points a pudgy finger at my chest—"they also hate, but they do not fear. They hate the whole world, Talcott, for leaving them behind and leaving their mothers behind and leaving their mothers' mothers behind. How are they to see God in others? They do not even see God in themselves."

"I believe you've mentioned this before."

Morris Young nods, satisfied. His face relaxes once more into its usual expression of quiet serenity. I have known him for about six years, since he invited me to talk to some of the young black men in his program for at-risk kids. I prepared a half-hour lecture about some of the heroes of the civil rights movement. It was a disaster. The younger boys dozed off; the pre-adolescents whispered behind their hands; the older teens, burdened with gold and attitude, were ostentatiously bored. Not a single one of them seemed remotely interested in anything beyond his own immediate experience. When the time mercifully ran out, Dr. Young shook his head and said, *Welcome to the real world.* A few months later, I persuaded my colleague Lemaster Carlyle, the former prosecutor, to speak to the same boys about the criminal justice system. I stood in the back and watched him engage them on everything from the way the jury looks at them (*They'll vote you guilty in two minutes if you walk into the courtroom the same way you walked in here*) to how to avoid getting shot by police (*Just saying "Yes, sir," and "No, sir," and keeping your hands where he can see them will do a lot more to keep you alive than "Get out of my face," even if he's in your face*). I would not say Lem's performance was spellbinding, but the young men warmed to him as they never did to me. Since that time, I have spoken to the boys at least twice each year; Lem Carlyle, star of the nightly network news, only once more. But he is the one they remember.

Yes, okay, I am envious.

Now, sitting in the church basement, I exchange more pleasantries with Dr. Young and wait for him to get around to the point. He has been appropriately consoling about the loss of my father and about the death of Freeman Bishop, whom he knew for my family pastor, as he seems to know every fact about every African American in the city. He has asked after my wife and my son, and I have asked after his wife and three daughters, the eldest of whom is a first-year law student at the state university. I have always admired Dr. Young for not asking my help to get his daughter into our law school, and for the way he politely but firmly rebuffed the offer I made without his asking. *The Lord has given Patricia certain talents, and she will go as far as her talent and achievements take her, praise the Lord,* was all he said.

We turned her down.

"So," murmurs the good reverend, "I suppose we should get back to your fight with your wife."

"Please."

"You would agree, would you not, Talcott, that what you did was unwise?"

"Yes."

"A woman in your hotel room," he murmurs.

"I realize it was a mistake. I wasn't thinking too clearly."

He nods. "You know, Talcott, I know a man, a good Christian man, a pastor, a lifelong friend, who is never alone with a woman other than his wife. Not for a moment. If he is on a trip, he insists that a man pick him up from the airport. If he has to counsel a female parishioner, he always has his wife or a female deacon present. Always. That way, there is never even the hint of scandal."

I try not to smile. "I don't think that would work in my part of the world. People would call it sex discrimination."

"A strange part of the world." He seems about to say more, then decides not to pursue the point. "But, as I say, it is easy to understand your wife's anger, isn't it? You have hurt her, Talcott, you have hurt her reputation. . . ."

Suddenly I cannot contain myself. "Her reputation! She's the one who has affairs, not me! She has no right to get angry just because . . . just because people *think* I had one!"

"Talcott, Talcott. Anger is not a right. It is an emotion. It flows from our fear or our pain, of which we broken creatures possess a surfeit. Your wife's sins, her weaknesses, give you no right to impose further pain upon her. You are her *husband*, Talcott." He folds his hands and hunches over his desk, and I reciprocate, drawing closer. "You know, Talcott, I have asked you for quite a few favors on behalf of the boys, and you have always been more than generous."

I grimace. One of the favors was to accompany the boys, along with three or four other adults, on a trip to the beach, an event that confirmed my utter lack of influence over them. Another was to persuade my famous student Lionel Eldridge, the onetime basketball star known as Sweet Nellie, to talk to the boys last spring. I have been paying for that one ever since, for Lionel seems to think, having done me a good turn, he no longer needs to finish his seminar paper . . . from last spring.

"Thank you, Dr. Young, but it was the least I could do."

"You're storing up treasures in Heaven, praise God. You're a good man, and the Lord has important work for you."

I nod, saying nothing. Although every believing Christian understands that God guides our steps, fewer and fewer emphasize the point. A God working actively in the world makes us uneasy. We tend to like our God distant and a bit malleable, ready to bend to every new human idea. A God with a will of his own is too scary, and, besides, he might get in the way of our satisfaction of immediate desire. Or so my father wrote someplace or other.

"But this next favor . . . well, this is a favor I want you to do for yourself." Dr. Young leans back in his creaky chair once more. "You see, Talcott, when you first came to me for counseling, you said you thought your wife was having an affair. You wanted her to come for counseling with you, she refused, you finally came alone. Remember that? And yet, praise the Lord, the two of you are still together, and you, Talcott, you personally are committed to staying with your wife until you are parted by death, just as the Scriptures instruct."

"Yes."

"Or unless *she* leaves *you*."

I swallow. "Yes."

"You are one flesh, Talcott, you and your wife. That is Christian marriage."

"I know."

"So perhaps it is time you found it in your heart to forgive her."

"Forgive her for . . ."

"For her transgressions against you, Talcott. Real or imagined."

An unexpected shot. And he is grinning as he fires it. "What do you . . . when you say *imagined*, are you implying that I . . . uh . . ."

He folds his plump hands in his lap and swivels his chair, this way, that way. "Talcott, you came to me in the summer and said your wife was having an affair with a coworker. But, as far as I can tell, you have no actual evidence."

"Not evidence that would stand up in a court of law, but . . . well . . . a husband just knows these things. . . ."

"Talcott, Talcott. Listen. You have told me she often works late. You have told me she often is not at her desk when you call, sometimes for hours. She goes out of town a lot with her boss, and she seems to have lots of meetings with him when they travel. Why is it impossible, Talcott, that she is simply a hardworking lawyer, devoted to her job and trusted by her boss? If a man worked the same hours at the same firm and did the same things, would you, Talcott, assume that he was having an affair with the boss?"

I hate being hemmed in this way, but Dr. Young is an expert. "You're forgetting those furtive telephone calls. . . ."

"No, Talcott, I have not forgotten. You say you will be eating dinner or lying in bed and the phone will ring and your wife will answer it and she will say, 'Sorry, Jerry, I can't talk now.' And when you ask her what that was all about, she will say something like, 'Oh, I just didn't want to interrupt our time together.'"

"Exactly."

"One interpretation is that she and Jerry—or whoever was really on the other end of the line—are, indeed, engaging in an adulterous relationship. Another, however, is that she is simply telling you the truth. She does not want to ruin what precious time she has with you and your boy by getting into an extended telephone conversation."

I shake my head, certain it cannot be this simple, yet suddenly assailed by doubts. "I . . . you would have to know Kimmer. The kind of person she is. She's totally devoted to her work. She wouldn't hesitate to interrupt our time at home for a business call."

"Talcott, Talcott." Smiling in that avuncular way of his. "Perhaps your wife senses in your marriage the same strains as you do. Perhaps she thinks she is partly to blame, the way she works. Perhaps she is trying, in her own way, to fix it."

"I don't know. . . ."

"And there is the point, Talcott." Pouncing like an experienced litigator. "There is my very point. You don't know!" Excited now, he leans across the desk, no easy feat for a man of his bulk. "You don't know for sure she is running around with her boss. You don't know for sure if she has had *any* extramarital affair. Except the one, of course."

"Which one?"

"A little over a decade ago, Talcott, in Washington, D.C. When she was married to André. I mean the affair she had with you."

I blink. This shot hit me, as it was supposed to do. They say that Dr. Young boxed when he was in the Army, back in the fifties, and I can believe it, for he has the boxer's mind, the ability to weave and jab and jab and weave until, finally, he lands a straight right.

"I . . . I don't see what that has to do with anything."

"Maybe nothing. Maybe everything. Maybe you are just assuming that your wife will do to you with someone else what the two of you did to her first husband."

Another blow lands! I reel into the ropes, memories tumbling through my mind at a dizzying pace. Kimmer and I dated during our first year in law school, and then she broke up with me over the summer because she found one of our classmates more interesting. We dated during our third year in law school, but she broke up with me three months before graduation, again for another student, although not the same one. In Washington, she spent two years dating me along with two other men, and then she pared the number to two, of which I was not one. A year later, she married one of the finalists, André Conway, formerly Artis, a production assistant at a television station, with dreams of becoming a big documentary filmmaker. By then, I, too, had moved on. My new girlfriend, Melody Merriman, a journalist and member of the darker nation, expected to marry me. I suppose I expected to marry her. Then, a little more than a year into her marriage, Kimmer began a torrid extramarital affair . . . with me. Kimmer left Artis-André, I left Melody, scandal ensued, and when Stuart Land called a few months later to ask if I was interested in teaching yet, I decided to leave a law practice I loved in a city I hated. My father was delighted, but I was never sure I wanted to be a professor: I probably fled to Elm Harbor as much to escape the Gold Coast gossip mills as because of my desire for the academic life. But I also had the hope that Kimmer would follow me, demonstrating through this affirmative act on her part a commitment to our future.

To my astonishment, she came. To my astonishment, we married. Kimmer put off starting a family until she feared her biological clock might just stop ticking altogether. Then God gifted us with Bentley.

And, in what is about to be nine years of marriage, I have hardly given a thought to what Kimmer and I . . . *did*, that was the word Dr. Young used . . . what we *did* to André Conway. Or, for that matter, what I did to Melody Merriman, which I am sure Dr. Young will bring up momentarily.

I continue with difficulty. "So—you're suggesting that I . . . I'm just projecting . . ."

Dr. Young holds up a hand. "Talcott, listen to me. Listen carefully. Have you asked the Lord to forgive you and your wife for the wrong you did your wife's first husband?"

I nod slowly, admitting the truth. "Yes. Many times." I close my eyes briefly. The heating vent gives off a brief, angry whine. "But, to be honest with you, I don't know if I . . . if I've forgiven myself."

Morris Young is too old a hand to be sidetracked by a therapeutic confession. "We can certainly work on that, Talcott. But at the moment, I am more interested in whether you can forgive your wife."

"For these . . . imagined transgressions?"

He shakes his heavy head. The telephone on his desk begins to bray, but he ignores it. "For what she did to her first husband."

I open my mouth, close it again, then try once more. "You think I'm mad at Kimmer for . . . for cheating on André with me?"

"Mad? I wouldn't know. I do wonder, though, if you have somehow . . . frozen her in that moment of time. The only Kimberly you are able to perceive is, not to put too fine a point on it, the adulteress." The phone has stopped ringing. "In your eyes, she is stuck in a particular pattern of behavior. But the Christian life is a life of constant growth. Perhaps you need to give her the chance to show she has grown."

"You think she's changed that much?"

"Have you ever cheated on your wife?"

"No! You know I haven't."

"So you have changed, Talcott. Don't you see? And perhaps your wife is as capable of change as you are. Maybe not at the same rate. But the same capacity."

I am getting the message. Slowly, but I am getting it. "You think I . . . look down my nose at her?"

"I think, Talcott, that sometimes your marital fidelity is a wall between you. Perhaps you are right and she has been unfaithful. Very well, how have you responded? Perhaps you have used your own virtue to keep your wife at bay. Remember, Talcott, that her sins are only different from yours—not necessarily worse. And that you promised to love her for better or worse." He pauses to allow this to sink in. "Now, understand me. I am not exonerating your wife. She may indeed be engaging in an extramarital relationship with Mr. Nathanson. Or with someone else. But, Talcott, right now, what matters is your own conduct. If your wife is straying, the time will come when it is appropriate to deal with her behavior. For the moment, however, I wish to ask of you a simple favor: that you will, until the next time we meet, try to treat Kimberly as you would want to be treated. You do remember the Golden Rule? Good. You think your wife should give you the benefit of the doubt. Perhaps you should do her the same courtesy. Kimberly is your *wife*, Talcott, not a suspect in some crime. Your job is not to catch her in lies. Your job is not to prove you are better than she is. Your job is to love her as best you can. Scripture tells us that the husband is head of the wife, but we are also warned that the headship is of a special kind: 'as Christ is head of the church.' And how does Christ love his church, Talcott? Unquestioningly. Forgivingly. And sacrificially. That is the responsibility of the husband, Talcott, especially when you do not actually know that your wife has done you wrong. The two of you wronged her first husband, and it may be that you are wronging her now, by your suspicions. So the favor I wish to ask is that you try as hard as you can, until our next meeting, to love your wife that way. Unquestioningly. Forgivingly. Sacrificially. Can you say those words for me, Talcott?"

"Unquestioningly," I say, unwillingly. "Forgivingly," I say, unhappily. "Sacrificially," I say, resignedly.

Dr. Young's smile is wider than ever. "Never fear, Talcott. The Lord will strengthen you to do what you must do. Let's pray together."

Which we do.

(11)

DEAN LYNDA INTERCEPTS ME as I rush up the steps into Oldie. I have avoided her since my return from the Vineyard, although this has meant skipping faculty meetings, workshops, and lectures. I am not sure whether I am driven by embarrassment, anger, fear, or some emotion I have yet to detect. Whichever it is, its protection has just run out.

"Talcott. Good. I've been hoping to run into you."

I look up at her, she looks down at me. She is in the company of Ben Montoya, her tall, restless factotum, who has a joint appointment in the law school and the anthropology department. Ben was whispered to be the logistical genius behind the coup that toppled Stuart Land, and he remains Lynda's instrument, it is said, in the most ruthless tasks of her deanship. The three of us stand on the steps as the season's first snow flurries softly around us. Ben's suspicious eyes peer at me from the upturned collar of his mountainous parka.

"Hi, Lynda." I slow but do not stop. "Hi, Ben."

"Talcott, wait," my dean instructs.

"I have office hours."

"I just need a minute. Ben, you go ahead, I'll catch up with you." With a final glower, he rushes off as instructed, hands deep in his pockets.

Then it is just the two of us.

Dean Lynda, a vigorous woman who wears her graying hair unfashionably long, folds her arms, clucks her tongue, and shakes her head. She is wearing a light topcoat over one of her outdated granny dresses. A black beret perches at a jaunty angle. She enjoys her reputation as an eccentric.

"We're on our way to see the provost to talk about the budget," Lynda explains.

"I see. Well, good luck." I climb another step toward the building, but my dean freezes me with a gesture. I am suddenly sure she is going to ask me whether I have been slanting my scholarship for the benefit of a client.

"Talcott, Talcott, Talcott," she murmurs, intense blue eyes measuring me from behind steel-rimmed glasses. "What am I going to do with you?"

"What do you mean?"

"I understand you canceled another class last week."

"I was in Washington, Lynda. A torts conference. The students knew about it weeks in advance."

Unmollified, Dean Lynda purses her thin lips in disapproval, possibly of the weather but more likely of me. "How many classes does that make that you've missed this term? Ben tells me that it's something like seven or eight."

"Good old Ben."

"He's my deputy dean, Talcott. He's just doing his job." She brushes snow from her lapel. "If a member of my faculty is underperforming, I need to know." *My* deputy. *My* faculty. I have not previously realized how much she reminds me of Mallory Corcoran.

"Lynda, you . . . you're the one who told me to take time off."

"And you certainly did, didn't you?" She does that tongue-clucking thing again. "I have to tell you, Talcott, I am starting to get a little worried about you."

"Worried . . . about me?"

She nods silently, waiting for a group of laughing students to pass us. They are all white, the stars of the law review, the faculty favorites, who will get the most desirable judicial clerkships and the offers to come back and teach. "You must admit, Talcott, your behavior has become a little bit erratic."

To my dismay, I realize that she is continuing our conversation from the Vineyard, still building a case for Marc Hadley. I manage to hold my temper, but only because I have just left Dr. Young. "I'm not going to let you do this to me, Lynda."

The blue eyes, pale as morning, protest her innocence, as does the hand over her heart. "I'm not doing anything to you, Talcott. I'm worried about what you're doing to yourself." She pats my arm. "You're family, Talcott, you know that. I only want what's best for you."

"I see."

"You sound sarcastic. Now, why is that?"

"Because you're determined to find fault with whatever I say?"

Her eyes, suddenly diamond-hard, flash blue fire. Lynda Wyatt is not a woman to cross, and now I have done it twice. "That's uncalled for, Talcott. I'm trying to help."

I want to hold back, but the temptation is more than I can withstand: "Are you, Lynda? And who exactly are you trying to help?"

For the first time in all the years I have known her, Lynda is speechless. Her mouth forms a small red O of offense, and a furious flush rises in her cheeks. Her hands go to her hips. Not waiting for her riposte, I smile and dodge past her into the building.

Striding hurriedly through the lobby, dismayed at my own rudeness and half worried that Lynda Wyatt will come storming after me to inform me that my tenure is being revoked, I notice, off in a corner near the stairwell, my student Lionel Eldridge, the former basketballer, leaning against the wall, towering over a member of the paler nation who gazes up at him with adoring eyes. His admirer, I see in surprise, is Heather Hadley, Marc's daughter from his first marriage, usually found in the company of her droopy boyfriend, Paul. I blink to make sure I am seeing straight. I have never understood the magnetism of the man once known to millions of basketball fans as Sweet Nellie, although even Kimmer, whose firm I all but begged to hire him last summer, concedes that he is gorgeous. Rumor has it—that is, Dear Dana says— that young Mr. Eldridge has cut quite a sexual swath through the student body. Now, seeing Heather evidently in Lionel's thrall, I allow myself a moment of mean-spirited speculation, wondering how Marc, in his self-assured liberalism, would cope with an affair between his beloved, brilliant Heather and the married, academically marginal, and very black Sweet Nellie.

I curl around them, heading for the stairs. Lionel spies me and flashes the smile that, despite the knee injury that forced him to retire early after seven appearances on the NBA All-Star Team, is still worth millions of dollars in endorsements. I do not smile back. I do not wave. Sweet Nellie might have averaged nineteen points a game during his career—his application for admission said so, and his résumé does too—but around Oldie he is just a student who owes me a paper.

On the stairs, I encounter Rob Saltpeter and Lemaster Carlyle, books under their arms, on their way down to teach. Rob, who uses Powerpoint in the classroom, is also carrying his laptop. He offers his usual effusive greeting, but Lem only smiles briefly and ducks past me as swiftly as I ducked past Lionel. He is usually so friendly, even flowery. I stand looking after him for a second or two, uneasy thoughts crowding my brain, before forcing my mind back to the present problem of Lionel and Heather. Unlocking my office, I ponder whether this could be the rattling skeleton of which Jack Ziegler spoke, and which is obviously worrying Marc Hadley and, by extension, Dahlia. Are there whispers of a liaison between Heather and Lionel? Anything is possible, but this seems an unlikely candidate for scandal. Even in Washington, where nearly everything is fair game at confirmation time, nobody has yet hit upon the strategy of dredging up the love lives of the nominee's children. Still . . .

Oh, stop it.

I am too busy for this nonsense, I remind myself as I flop into my desk chair. I have important writing to finish. If I think really hard, I might even remember what it is. I am still busily dumping on myself when Cassie Meadows calls, wanting to bring me up to date.

"Mr. Corcoran estimates your wife's chances at about fifty-fifty," she says, which is not terribly helpful. The next part seems to give her trouble. "He thinks they could be improved if . . . well, if . . . if this *search* of yours comes to an end." She pauses, then blurts out the rest: "I'm actually kind of in the doghouse. He was mad that I've been . . . well, don't take this the wrong way . . . the way he put it . . . he said I've been treating your ideas too seriously. He said . . . I probably shouldn't tell you this . . . he said it makes the firm look bad."

I keep my voice very cool. "And why didn't *Mr.* Corcoran call me himself?"

"I don't know. Maybe he was busy." But I know. By delegating to Meadows the duty of telling me off, Uncle Mal can later deny, if he must, that he was ever the least bit perturbed. At the same time, he punishes Cassie by making her the bearer of bad news. "Anyway, he said the word on you is getting around, and . . . and, well, it isn't helping your wife any."

"I see."

"I think he wants you to say you'll stop."

"I'm sure."

She lets out a sigh, perhaps relief: she has delivered a tough message to the client, and lived to tell the tale. "So, what are you going to do?"

"I'm going to play chess," I tell her.

(I I I)

A COUPLE OF STUDENTS come to my office hours. Between meetings, I sit at my desk, willing the anger out of my soul. When I am finally ready to leave for the day, the telephone rings again, and I see from the caller ID that it is a Washington number. I almost do not answer, certain it is Uncle Mal; then I decide it makes no difference.

It is Special Agent Nunzio.

"I just wanted you to know, we traced that gun," he says after a few gruff pleasantries. Informing the Bureau about Mariah's discovery was my idea; persuading her to go along took a lot of cajoling. After my conversation with Kimmer's father, I wanted to call Nunzio off, but there was no good way to do so, so I have simply been hoping that the Colonel was wise enough to leave no traces when he gave the Judge the gun. "The gun is a Glock, a police special, part of a shipment that fell off a truck in New Jersey about four years ago."

"Fell off a truck?"

Nunzio laughs. "Just a cop's way of saying it was stolen, Professor. Three or four of the missing Glocks have turned up in the possession of various lowlifes. I don't suppose you would have any idea how one of them turned up in your father's bedroom. Didn't think so," he continues without a pause. I hear a keyboard clicking. "Prints. From what we can tell, the gun was new and clean when your father got it. Three sets of prints. Your father's. Your sister's, who found it. Third is an instructor at a gun club in Alexandria. Turns out your father joined the club about a year before he died, took shooting lessons. He was very serious about it for a while, then he kind of fell away, then started up again in September. The last time he was there was a couple of days before he died. That seems to be when the gun was fired last."

"I appreciate this," I tell him, although I am vaguely disappointed. I am not sure what I hoped for, but this is too prosaic.

"Incidentally, your father had no D.C. permit, which made his possession within the city limits illegal. But I guess that doesn't matter now." I say nothing. Nunzio fills the void with another question. "So, what are you and your sister up to, anyway? Are you taking this stuff seriously?"

"What stuff?"

"Tracking down the stuff about your father, all that."

I am suddenly wary, though also intrigued that he has lumped Mariah and me together. "I just want to know the truth," I say boldly, if a bit stupidly. "About my father, I mean."

"Yeah, well, I guess we all want to know our fathers better, don't we?" Agent Nunzio laughs, not unkindly. "I wish I'd known mine better, anyway. So, good luck."

Everyone else in the world is telling me to back off. But the Federal Bureau of Investigation seems to want me to go ahead. A good thing, too, because I am not about to stop.

CHAPTER 26

SAM LOYD'S CHALLENGE

The Elm Harbor Chess Club meets every Thursday night in an antiquarian bookstore owned by an evil old man named Karl. The establishment, which does business under the deceptively misdescriptive name of Webster & Sons—there never was a Webster, so he had no sons; Karl has always owned it, believing that New Englanders will more readily buy books from a shop that hints of an Anglo-Saxon provenance—rambles and zags through the second floor of a three-story brick-fronted building just beyond the northern edge of the campus, near Henley Street, the unmarked but widely accepted border between the overwhelmingly white university community and the unfamiliar, and thus, by definition, dangerous, black-and-brown world next door. On the first floor is an Indian restaurant that does a brisk student business, and one browses books or plays chess surrounded by the eye-scorching aroma of cheap curry. Cramped apartments, including Karl's, fill the third. Probably Karl owns the whole building, but nobody knows. One reaches the store by pushing the appropriate buzzer, then opening a glass door, being careful of the diagonal crack that has been there since I was a student, and finally climbing a narrow staircase that surely violates every safety rule enacted since the nineteenth century: no railings, uneven risers that tend to pop loose unexpectedly, an impossibly sharp turn at the halfway point, and the only useful illumination the uncovered bulb on the landing, with a wattage of, perhaps, forty.

I do not know where Karl is from, but I do know that his fundamental meanness, like a cancer, has always kept him thin and bald, evidently nourishing itself on his own flesh, for he eats everything in sight. His face is an odd inverted triangle, jowly at the bottom despite his otherwise entire lack of body fat. The pupils of his eyes are colorless and pale, like the eyes of an albino. What hair he has left is piled in thin snowy wings on either side of his flat head. In my student days, Karl was a terror, not over the board, as chess players like to say, for he boasted only moderate strength, but around the club itself. If you spilled a few drops of Coca-Cola on his grimy wooden tables, those pale, lidless eyes would darken and grow monstrous, and Karl would screech obscenities for a minute and a half, never mind the players trying to concentrate. If you happened to remark that a peanut-butter cookie seemed stale—he always provided refreshments, and they usually made you sick—he would mutter, "I see," then proceed to blunder around the rooms with a wastebasket under his arm, sweeping away everything edible or drinkable, even food you brought upstairs yourself. Karl's comments about the games in progress, or the games just finished, were always punctuated with his proudly offensive locker-room humor—male locker-room humor, that is, and the raunchier the better; he was the master of similes comparing chess pieces to body parts, and positions on the board with those same parts at work. As for women, they should not, in Karl's opinion, play chess at all; whenever a female student was sufficiently unfortunate to find her way to the club, Karl would be gracious and charming, the very picture of Old World courtliness. He would then proceed to rest his lustful gaze on her for the entire visit—but never on her face. Karl's crawling, creepy stare is like a live thing, a devouring force of nature; you can feel its greedy, envious insistence even when it is directed at somebody else. Of the very few women who happened by the club in my student days, almost none returned. One brave teen, a math major, a Russian émigrée whose younger brother is nowadays one of America's better players, actually withstood Karl's crude, unblinking scrutiny for eight weeks running before he finally managed to drive her away.

Yet there was, and still is, no other game in town.

As an undergraduate, I could hardly be kept from the chess club; during law school, I made a point of visiting at least monthly; in my ten years on the faculty, however, I have stopped in no more often than once or twice a year. Each time, Karl finds a way to treat me with the same viciously rude bonhomie I remember so painfully from my student days, for his racism, if not so deeply ingrained as his sexism, has nevertheless managed to survive the university's lurch through integration to ethnic tribalism to diversity to multiculturalism to whatever it is we call the unbridled celebration of the self with which the nation's campuses seem determined to welcome the new century. I am scarcely surprised, then, when I walk in the door just before meeting time and Karl, busily setting out last month's crackers, spins in place, hitches up his too-large pants, and booms, "Well, look who has darkened my doorway again! After all this time! You get it, Doctor? Darkened my doorway!"

I would stare him down, but Karl has no time for such games, and has already turned back to his work. Two local teenagers, one of them an authentic rising star, are playing blitz games—five minutes apiece—in the corner, punctuating their rapid moves with the patter of the Lower East Side of Manhattan, circa 1950, which has somehow become the established second language of chess players all over the United States: "You patzer! You nebbish! You fish! You didn't see that, did you? Sac, sac, mate! You should have left your king a little luft!" Actually, in the mouths of fourteen-year-old Ivy League faculty brats, it sounds very funny, and I sometimes join in just to keep the chatter going, but my business tonight is with Karl. So I say calmly: "Yes, Karl, I get it." And Karl turns and lifts a snow-white eyebrow, as though to say he expected better.

"Yes? So? Good. So, what do you want? A game? Yes? Liebman over there is available, or he will be as soon as Aidoo finishes cutting off his balls. Here, have a cracker, Doctor." Proffering the wicker bowl. *Doctor* is what he always calls me, his mocking tone another of his unsubtle insults, but ineffective because I know it for envy.

"No, thank you."

"You do not trust my crackers? They are maybe too old for you?"

"They're fine, Karl."

"Then have one, Doctor." Thrusting the bowl again. "Go ahead."

"Thank you, but no."

"I insist."

I shake my head. With Karl, everything is a fight. Everything has frustrated him. They say there is an angry ex-wife someplace, sullen sons and daughters someplace else, a grandchild or two whom he never sees, and a university chair in political economy left behind when he fled Eastern Europe thirty years ago, but Karl generates rumors the way the summer sun generates heat: you have to be careful, wearing skepticism like sunblock, or you are likely to get scorched.

"Thank you," I tell him, "but I'm not hungry." He stares, pale eyes waiting me out. He knows I want something; he can smell hope in others, and lives to squelch it. Still, no place to go but forward. "The truth is, I have a question that calls upon your expertise."

"My expertise," he repeats, rubbing his perfectly shaved chin with skinny fingers. "I was not aware I had any *expertise* that could be of use to a professor of your eminence."

His ridicule is unrelenting, but I refuse to be sidetracked. Karl is not much of a chess player, but he is a brilliant problemist, holding countless national and international titles for composing chess problems and solving them. He is the only person I know who is likely to possess the answer to the question that now troubles me.

Still, the simple experience of being in the chess club soothes my ragged nerves: the click of pieces being slammed down and the clack of the chess clocks and the hoots from the winners and the excuses from the losers, a splendid symphony of the titanic, tense, yet ultimately relaxing battle of mind versus mind. And relaxation I need, time away from . . . well, away from the very concerns that have brought me to Karl's door.

I ask him if we can sit down, and he leads me to a corner from which he can still see the entrance, in order to make fun of whoever walks in. We sit under a cheap blowup of a book-jacket photograph of Emanuel Lasker, bearing a sloppily forged version of the great champion's autograph—*To Karl*, and so forth—even though Karl would have been a toddler when Lasker died. Perhaps it was inscribed to some other Karl. I wonder whether he really believes anybody will be fooled, or whether he intends it as a joke.

"So—you need what?" Karl demands angrily, finally settling at the table after twice jumping from his chair to make members crossing the threshold feel unwelcome. He beckons me with his fingers. "What expertise?"

"It has to do with a chess problem," I begin.

"So! A problem! Please set it up for me," he commands, waving toward a board, and I sense his secret delight that I am actually inquiring about a subject on which he knows more than anybody else.

"No, no, it's not a problem I'm having trouble solving. It's—well, it's more like a *kind* of problem."

"What *kind* of problem?" he inquires sweetly, mimicry being the least of his misspent gifts.

"I need to know about—well, I seem to remember, years ago, when I was a student, you used to give these lectures about chess problems. . . ."

"Back when there were people who *cared* about chess problems. When chess was art, not the wretched computer-driven *science* it has become. In the old days, we cared more about beauty than victory. These *children*"—he waves toward the filling room, where the youngest child is in high school—"well, they have no concept. None. All they want to do is win. That is your culture. America spoils chess, as it spoils all things. Art? What art? Winning, all you Americans can think of is winning. Winning and getting rich. Your country is too young to have so much power. Too immature. Yet, because of your power, everybody pays attention. Everybody. You are teaching the whole world that only one thing matters!"

It occurs to me as I listen to this screed that Karl and my father probably would have gotten along, but I have to cut him off or he will preach to me the rest of the night.

"Yes, Karl, yes, exactly." Word by word, I raise my voice to make him listen. "I want to talk about chess as an art."

"Good! Good! At last I find a man of culture!" His words are filling the room, and a few of the players look up in irritation, but nobody admonishes him. Another rumor is that Karl once picked up a student who talked back and tossed him down the stairs.

"Thank you," I murmur, uncertain whether he expects a response.

"So, how is it that I can help you?" he demands, his lips curled in an ungracious sneer.

"One of those lectures you gave—it was about a kind of theme in problems called the Excelsior. Do you remember that?"

"The Excelsior," he snaps. "A helpmate. A silly idea. Sam Loyd's invention. He invented it as a joke, and now we all take it seriously. Because we have no memory." A shake of the wispy head. "So. The Excelsior. What about it?"

I hesitate, trying to frame my query in a way that will excite his interest rather than his ridicule. The helpmate is an unusual species of chess problem in which black moves first instead of white and the two sides cooperate so that, after a stated number of moves, black is checkmated. Sam Loyd, who lived and worked at the end of the nineteenth century, was a journalist and magician who invented many games and puzzles popular to this day. He was also one of the great developers of the art of the chess problem . . . and one of my father's heroes. *Sam Loyd turned everything upside down*, the Judge used to say, who now and again dreamed of doing the same thing, only in law, not chess. *He taught everybody that the pieces were smarter than anybody thought.*

"I remember that Sam Loyd invented the Excelsior," I tell Karl. "I remember that much from your fascinating lecture." Pouring on the butter. "But I admit I don't remember, um, just exactly what the Excelsior was. And, in particular"—finally selling the whole hog—"in particular, if somebody was working on a problem called the Double Excelsior with the knight. . . ."

Karl interrupts. He is tired of the sound of my voice, as he is tired of the sound of any voice not emanating from his mouth. He prefers his own answers to other people's questions, even when nobody has asked him anything. It is easy to believe that he used to be a professor; he would fit in perfectly over at the law school. When he speaks now, his pace is rapid and clipped, as though I am wasting his time.

"The Double Excelsior with the knight is a famous chess challenge, Doctor, and a lovely one. The only difficulty is that it happens to be impossible. Listen." He leans close to me, pointing a bony finger as though casting a spell. "The Excelsior theme has a very clear and very silly set of rules. In an Excelsior, a white pawn begins on its home square and makes exactly five moves, moving two squares on its first move, then one square on each of the next four, so that it ends on the eighth square. And even though you are no doubt rusty, Doctor, I am sure you remember what happens when a pawn reaches the eighth square? Mmmm?"

"It promotes," I mutter in irritation, like a child attending his first lesson.

"Exactly, exactly, it promotes, it becomes another piece—usually a queen, everybody knows this, but it can become any other piece, too, whatever the player wishes. That is the point of the Excelsior—the pawn may promote to any other piece. It does not become a queen. It becomes something else. We call this underpromotion. You have heard the term?"

"Yes."

"Good. Because you see, Doctor, the ordinary Excelsior is child's play, so easy that, if you are solving problems and you see the words *Helpmate in five moves*, the first thing you do is look for a pawn to start pushing. If the only way to force mate is for a pawn to make five moves and then underpromote—well, then you have your Excelsior."

"I understand." But his didacticism is beginning to wear on me, and I wonder if I am on a fool's errand.

"Good. Because, Doctor, the Double Excelsior—ah, well, that is a challenge for the sophisticated designer only."

"Why?"

"You have forgotten what I said before? That in a helpmate it is black who plays first and the two sides cooperate to checkmate black? The Excelsior requires five moves. So does the Double Excelsior. But there is a difference. In the Double Excelsior, each side must make all five moves with just one pawn, and, on the fifth move, both sides—first black, then white—must promote to the same piece. So, if we have a Double Excelsior with a rook, black moves first, makes five moves, and on the fifth move the pawn becomes a rook. And white moves second, makes five moves, and on the fifth move the pawn becomes a rook. And after white's fifth move, black is checkmated—but there must be no other possible line of play leading to mate except for each side to make five moves and promote to the same piece on the fifth move. You are with me, Doctor?"

"I'm with you."

"So, a Double Excelsior with the knight would mean that the only way for white to give mate in five moves is for both players to move a single pawn exactly five times, at the end of which both players promote to a knight, and black is checkmated."

"But you said it's impossible. . . ."

"That is correct." I have touched, finally, his pedagogic side, and he is almost patient, now that he has the opportunity to do some actual teaching. "You have to understand that the other Double Excelsiors have been demonstrated. Both players promote to a rook? Done. Both promote to a bishop? Yes. But nobody has managed to make it work with the knight. Thirty years ago, forty, something like that, a chess writer issued a challenge, and offered a significant money prize to anybody who could successfully demonstrate the Double Excelsior with the knight. But the challenge has never been answered. Lots of composers have tried, but nobody, even with the aid of computers, has managed to do it. So, most of us have come around to the view that it cannot be done."

I frown, trying to take this in. My father was trying to solve a chess problem that the composing world believes to be impossible. His immortality? I think not: his mind was more subtle than that, unless it was as simple as Lanie Cross suggested, that he suffered a nervous breakdown and was not thinking straight. But I am not so sure. I think the Judge would have wanted more. Oh, he might have possessed the raw ambition to compose the problem nobody had ever managed. He might have dreamed of being the one to do it. But the reason he put the word *Excelsior* in his note to me . . .

"Karl?"

"Yes, Doctor?" The mocking tone has returned. Karl's attention has wandered back to the suddenly crowded room, and therefore to his regular duty of making lives miserable. "Is there a problem? Was the explanation too complicated? Or do you perhaps resent that it is black instead of white who is checkmated at the end?" He laughs. "But in the chess problem it is always black who is checkmated at the end, is it not?" Cackling, he makes to rise.

"Wait," I say, more sharply than I intended, as though he is a student.

Karl's eyes widen. Very little surprises him, but my tone does. Now that I have his full attention once more, I take my time. Something he just said—*it is always black who is checkmated*—was that it? In the Double Excelsior, black is indeed checkmated, but . . . but Lanie Cross said . . . wait . . .

"Karl, look. In the Double Excelsior with the knight—I mean, if you yourself were to try to construct one—which pawn would you use?"

"Eh?"

"The pawn that becomes a knight at the end? The knight that gives checkmate? It has to start somewhere, right? So—what is it, a rook pawn, a bishop pawn, what?"

"Oh, I see. It is the white queen's knight pawn."

Meaning the pawn that, at the beginning of the game, is standing on the square right in front of the knight that is two squares to the left of the queen.

"Why is that?"

"In theory it should make no difference. You could use any pawn to demonstrate the theme. But when Sam Loyd developed the original, he used the queen's knight's pawn. So a serious composer of a Double Excelsior would honor the original by using the same pawn."

"The . . . uh, the *white* queen's knight's pawn."

"Of course the white."

"But the white queen knight's pawn would be the second piece to move. Black moves first."

"Again you are correct, Doctor. Of course, in the old days, some composers designed helpmates in which white moved first, and it was white who was mated at the end." He squeezes his jowls as though trying to shrink them. "But no true artist would do it that way. Not any more. A composer must follow the rules. It is black who must lose."

"Still, if someone wanted to design the problem so black would win—"

"That would be silly. A waste of time. Unartistic."

"But which pawn would move first?"

Despite himself, Karl is interested. He sighs to prove he isn't. "Any pawn would do, of course. The true artist, however, would again use the white queen knight's pawn. Only it would now be the black pawn, moving second, that would deliver mate on the fifth move." He is on his feet again, surprisingly light and gay, leaping toward the narrow wooden bookcase that stands in the corner. Nobody is allowed to touch the old books, many of them in German or Russian. He selects a volume and, to my surprise, thrusts it into my hands. "Take this." He nods with some enthusiasm. "It has many examples of the Excelsior theme. Keep it as long as you like." This astonishing and uncharacteristic act of generosity brings a solemn hush to the dozen or so members in attendance tonight.

I know at once the book will be unhelpful. I already have what I came to get.

"Thank you, Karl, but this . . . it's not necessary."

"Nonsense. But we must protect the book, of course. Here." He hands me an aged and torn manila envelope. "You will carry it in this."

"Karl, I . . ."

He holds up a warning finger. "I have loaned perhaps three or four books in all my years in your fair city. You owe me thanks."

And he is right. He is as controlling as ever, but he is trying to help. I do owe him thanks. "Thank you," I say, and I mean it.

Except that Karl is now embarrassed, perhaps not sure what impulse moved him to such a kindness. I suspect it was simply his delight at finding someone—in these uncultured days, as he would say—who actually showed an interest in the area of chess he knows best, an area about which almost nobody cares. I remind myself how empty a life he leads, and I smile my gratitude even as I watch his face turn sour again. I know he is going to send me off with a fresh insult, and I know how badly he needs to do it.

"Just remember what I told you, Doctor." His brutal laugh is back.

"The Excelsior must end with the white pawn promoting and giving mate. Black moves first in the helpmate, remember, but it is still white who gives mate at the end. Always white." He falls silent and regards me suspiciously, as though no longer sure I have come to his club on legitimate business. He leans close, his tiny fists pressing on the table in front of me. "We cannot change the way of the world over the chessboard, can we, Doctor?" Chuckling at his success in getting in the last word, Karl wanders off to torment somebody else.

I am glad to be rid of him. I hang around for another half-hour, watching a couple of games and playing a couple of games, and then, carrying Karl's book in its protective envelope, I slip out into the frosty night.

Excelsior, my father wrote, and he repeated the word. *It begins!* Neither the popular Addison nor the social Mariah had much interest in chess when we were children; only the bookish Talcott. Which means that the Judge wanted me, but only me, to know that he was referring to the Double Excelsior. Unfortunately, I still do not know why he wanted me to know. Karl has told me how the Excelsior should work, and Lanie said that my father wanted black to win. But I am still chewing on cotton. I am sure there is something there that should jump out at me, but nothing does. I do not know how the arcane chess problem the Judge wanted desperately to be the first to compose could possibly be related to *Angela's boyfriend* or *the arrangements*. Perhaps the white pawn delivered to me at the soup kitchen was a part of a composition, too, a composition with pieces that live and breathe and ache. If so, then my father was surely the composer. No doubt he was confident that I would see the connection, and the last elusive clue surely lies in that very confidence. Which leads to a question I have not heretofore considered: if I have the missing white pawn, who has the also-missing black one?

I am still turning these problems over in my mind when I realize I am being followed.

CHAPTER 27

A PAINFUL ENCOUNTER

(1)

THIS TIME there are two of them.

I have known for some while that I have shadows. Not just the roller woman in a green car in Washington, but other people, other times. How long have I known? Hours. Days. Weeks. Never anything concrete, just hints, impressions, a face glimpsed too often, the same car in the rearview mirror for blocks at a time in the middle of the night, a step matched too quickly to my own. When I could no longer put it down to paranoia, I consoled myself with the words of Jack Ziegler in the cemetery and the late Colin Scott two weeks later: that my family and I are safe from whatever might come. I have, in other words, allowed myself to be reassured.

Now I wonder whether I have made a mistake.

When I finally left the chess club, it was almost ten, and I hurried down the dangerous staircase, wondering what I would tell Kimmer.

By the time I reached the edge of the campus, the men were behind me.

Crossing the darkened Quad with Karl's package under my arm, scurrying toward my shortcut to the law school—the alley between the computer center and one of the dorms, a street, then the alley between the administration building and another dorm—I try to figure out why the two dimly seen figures a block or so behind me seem so much more ominous than the watchers of recent weeks, who have been little more than ghostly background impressions. Perhaps it is the very solidity of these new arrivals, the confident, aggressive tread that makes no effort to hide its purpose. Either they are not very good at remaining surreptitious or they want me to know they are behind me.

Both possibilities frighten me.

The campus is nearly deserted this time of night. I pass the occasional student, hear music faintly through the dormitory windows, closed against the weather. I quicken my pace, heading for the first of the two alleys. I sense rather than see the two men behind me speeding up to match me.

The computer center has a guarded entrance, courtesy of an unfortunate incident three years ago involving a fraternity prank and several gallons of orange juice, and I consider going to the guard and asking for help, but what would I say? That I, a tenured professor, think I am being followed? That I am frightened? No Garland could do such a thing, least of all on such scant evidence. Passing the building, emerging at the crosswalk for Montgomery Street, I glance over my shoulder. At the far end of the alley, I see, at most, one shadow moving in my direction. So perhaps my imagination is overactive after all.

I am on the other side of the street and heading for the second alley when I look down at the package in my hand. The book Karl gave me. The battered old envelope. Slowly, I begin to get the point.

The key word is *old*.

Somebody has jumped to the wrong conclusion.

I look back. My stalker is on the other side of the street, staring directly at me. He is standing under a streetlamp, and I can see him clearly. At first I suffer from a hallucination, both reassuring and startling, for the man who is after me looks like Avery Knowland. Only they have nothing in common but a sloppy ponytail, and, in the cone of light, I can see that my pursuer's hair is slicker and darker than my arrogant student's. Besides, the man who has followed me halfway across the campus is shorter and more muscular and thicker around the middle, and his ruddy face has been colonized by a disorder of dun-colored hair. His fierce red eyes are wild, as though he is high on something. He is wearing a leather jacket and I can envision him, easily, in a biker bar.

At the entrance to the alley, I hesitate. He is starting across the street, heading directly for me. Perhaps it is a coincidence. Perhaps he is not interested in me at all. On the other hand, the man who reminds me of Avery Knowland is now less than fifty feet away, and I have to make a decision.

He is still moving toward me, and his intentions do not seem honorable.

Adrenaline is pumping now.

For all my fevered imaginings, I could still be wrong. Or, if I am right, I can still make it through the alley and over to the law school before my follower can reach me, unless he is some sort of Olympic sprinter.

So I rush into the space between the administration building and two connected Gothic structures on the other side, first the university library, then a dormitory. The alley is really the side of a grassy hill, with the glass-walled solemnity of the administration building at the summit, and the library-dormitory complex at the base. The library is, as usual, undergoing renovation, and there is scaffolding all the way up the side that borders the alley. I slow my steps briefly, peering into the scaffolding, wondering whether some other watcher might be hiding there, but it is too dark down the hill, and I cannot see anything.

I turn my eyes forward again, and I stop.

There were two men following me before, then there was one. Now I have found his companion. He is at the far end of the alley, in the middle of my path to the law school, and he is moving toward me. I do not know how he knew I would be taking this alley, but, then, I do not know how they knew I would be at the chess club. There are plenty of blank spots, but this is not the time to fill them in.

I look back. The man with the sloppy facial hair is still approaching.

I glance around in dismay. The university has grown so security-conscious that its open spaces are utterly insecure. I cannot hide in a dormitory, because I lack the electronic key to open the door. I cannot hide in the library, because the only entrance open at night is around the front. I cannot hide in the administration building, because it is locked up until morning. Probably I should not have taken this short-cut, but campus crime is an exaggeration: all the official publications of the university say so.

The man at the far end of the alley, blocking my way, continues to inch closer, a dark smear against the traffic on Town Street beyond. Behind me, the footsteps of my pursuer grow more rapid. He knows I am trapped.

I remind myself that I am supposed to be immune from harm, but it occurs to me that Jack Ziegler might have less influence than everybody thinks he does; or that at least one of the several parties contending for whatever my father left behind might be unaware of his edict, or willing to defy it.

I spin in a small circle. One man ahead, one behind. On my right, the bulk of the library, covered in scaffolding. On my left, the administration building. And then I see . . .

. . . a blue light . . .

Next to the locked rear entrance to the library, right next to the scaffolding, is a police call box. The university has installed them all over. Open the front panel and the campus police will respond, whether you speak into the microphone or not.

I cut in that direction.

And hear the sound that frightens me most.

"Wait, Professor!" calls the man behind me. "Professor Garland! Stop!"

They know my name.

And then I hear something worse: "Don't let him get away!"

Suddenly both men are running toward me.

I reach the box and yank open the panel. Inside I see another blue light, a small key pad, and the microphone. A burst of static erupts from the speaker, probably a dispatcher asking a question. I am about to answer when my legs are kicked out from under me.

I hit the pavement, hard, and I am trying to roll over when a foot comes flying through the darkness and makes sharp, painful contact with my ribs. I groan but struggle to my knees, trying to recall my karate training from college. A fist smashes into my face. I reel backward, losing the package. The same fist strikes again, this time on my shoulder, which goes numb and flabby from the force of the blow. I hit the ground again. One of the men kneels next to me, yanks my head up by the hair, hisses, "What's in that package?" Then the fist whistles through the air again, striking my ear, which erupts in more pain than I imagined it was possible to feel. "What's in the package, Professor?"

"A book," I mumble, clawing at the dirt, trying to rise.

Another punch, right in the eye. The night flashes green. My face seems to split and splatter, and the pain is an icy blade down my cheek.

"Stand him up," the same hissing voice demands, and, obligingly, the other man pulls me to my feet.

"The police are coming," I mutter.

A pause as the two of them look at each other. Then that iron fist comes flying in once more, this time catching me in the ribs, the same spot as the kick, and my whole body sings a hymn of agony. Another punch, this one in the stomach. I fold over. A hand grabs for my shoulder. Using a barely remembered move from my old self-defense classes, I duck and shove upward and shrug free of the grip. Then I turn away, stumbling down the hill toward the base of the library scaffold. I hear the two men whispering to each other, maybe arguing over which is going to follow me onto the construction site. I do not look back. A low metal bar blocks my path to the scaffold, a sign warning me not to trespass. Considering the alternatives, however, I think I should. Beyond the bar is an angled ladder, precisely one story high. The scaffold is full of such ladders, running all the way up the side of the library, with landings at each floor for the construction workers. I hold on to the bar, because I am woozy and nauseous from the beating. Swallowing hard, fighting the waves of anguish, I glance back. One of the two men is coming down the slope. The other has disappeared, which would worry me if I had any time to worry. I climb awkwardly over the bar and reach the ladder just as my pursuer begins to run down the slope. My ribs are aching from the kicks and the punches, and my face feels squishy and twice its normal size, but I make it to the second level. My head pounds. I sag against the ladder leading up to level three, my arms suddenly on strike, refusing to pull me up any farther.

From below, a hand snakes out and grabs my left ankle. The hand yanks, very hard, and I tumble to a sitting position.

His head emerges, and I see something glinting in his hand: brass knuckles, perhaps, or a small knife. All of that fine talk about how I cannot be harmed, and now this! Gathering what strength I have left, I draw my right leg back, then brace myself against the ladder and kick out, putting all my weight into it. I strike flesh: his face? his hand? He cries out in pain and releases my ankle as his head pops down and out of sight once more. I force myself to my feet and, over the objections of my shoulders, resume my climb. My pursuer does not seem to be following, but I have been wrong too often lately. I keep my feet moving on will alone, one above the other, as I make the third level, then the fourth. I pause and look down. The fourth level of the scaffolding seems dizzyingly high. I support myself on the dark metal rail. I can see several blocks of the campus. I can see the law school. I do not see the man who was chasing me, even directly beneath. I am about out of energy but do not want to take any chances. He could, after all, be invisible on the ladder below. I force myself up one more level and then stop on the fifth landing, leaning against the rail, breathing hard. I hear voices, louder this time, and I see flashlights at the end of the alley. I cannot make out any details, for it is still dark down there, and the beams dazzle me as they advance, slowly, and then angle upward, toward the scaffolding.

I duck behind the ladder, but too late.

The lights have me.

Still I try to withdraw into the shadows, except that there are no shadows left, the illumination from below is too bright, almost blinding now, like a searchlight.

And, from below, an amplified voice: "This is the university police. Come down the ladder, very slowly, and keep your hands in sight."

Aching but relieved, I follow the instructions precisely, climbing carefully down the ladder, my trembling feet occasionally uncooperative, the light following me down, a second light, much brighter, joining the first, so I suppose a squad car must now be in the alley; or, from the sounds I hear, more than one. I cannot remember when I have been so happy to see the police.

Determined not to show weakness before my rescuers, I hop the last few rungs to the ground, nearly spilling again in the process, before turning into the glare. I blink hard, shielding my eyes, aware for the first time of how I must look: a disheveled black man in a dark windbreaker climbing up the side of the library in the middle of the night, obviously guilty of every crime on earth.

"All right, sir," says a heavy white voice from behind the light. The way the officer pronounces the word *sir*, although not quite mocking enough to constitute a clear insult, is definitely in the ballpark. "Let's just keep our hands in front of us, shall we?"

"Okay, but they're getting away. . . ."

"Please stand still, sir."

Evidently, the policeman does not know that I am a professor, so I decide to enlighten him.

"Officer, I should tell you that I teach . . ."

"Not a word, please, sir. Please walk toward me, slowly, hands out in front of you, palms toward me."

I point toward the end of the alley. "But I teach at the . . ."

"Keep your hands still!"

"But I'm not the one who . . ."

"Please stand where you are, sir. Hands out. Good. That's it."

I do as I am told, holding out my blameless, trembling hands for the officers to see. I want to be calm, in the best Garland manner. I am not.

I am frightened. I am seething. I am humiliated. The chilly Elm Harbor night burns bright red. I feel a peculiar weakness in my groin and, despite my many pains, an amazing surge of strength in my limbs: my fight-or-flight reflex seems fully activated. I can now make out the two officers, both variations on white, as they make wide half-circles toward me. Neither one has actually drawn a gun, but each has a hand on his hip and his holster unstrapped, and both are carrying those long police flashlights up high in the air, the barrels extended well past their fists, so that they can swing them as clubs without cocking. The officers move slowly, but not without vigor. I cannot take my eyes off the flashlights. I have heard stories about this kind of thing but have never experienced it. For a moment, I envision a second beating, this time by the campus police. A hot shame rises in my cheeks, as though I have been caught on the brink of a terrible deed. I actually feel *guilty*, of whatever they like. Not budging, I watch the two officers watching me. Their lassitude has a purpose, I decide: they are trying to wait me into a foolish move or a smart crack or a nervous laugh, maybe an excuse to use those flashlights. Or maybe they are only doing a tough and dangerous job and prefer to take no chances. Either way, I have never felt so helpless, so unable to influence my fate, as I do at this moment. At my father's feet, I learned to cherish will. He was always quite unforgiving of those who seemed to him to lack it. But now I face a moment when my will is quite irrelevant. I have never experienced our nation's ruthless racial divide with quite this vigor. I wonder what the Judge would have done.

One of the officers beckons. "Take a step forward. Good. Now lean forward, put your hands on the wall, right there, feet apart, good."

I comply. Light spills from a couple of windows of the dorm at the far end of the alley, and the electronically locked gate swings open: excited students coming out to watch with approval the ethnic purification of the campus.

"That's fine, sir, right, that's fine," says the officer who has, so far, been doing all the talking. "Now, let's see what we have here."

My voice is cold. "You have a tenured professor, that's what you have here. I'm the one who called in the alarm." I pause, breathing hard in my fury, wishing I could see their faces behind the blazing flashlights. "I was attacked."

"Can we see some identification, sir?" asks the same officer, and, this time, the *sir* sounds like he just might believe me.

"You may," I tell him with pedantic emphasis.

At that moment, as I am finally allowed to pull out my wallet and prove that I am who I say I am, my eyes fall on the spot where the assault took place. I realize that I will have to go back to the chess club and experience Karl's abuse all over again, as I explain to him how somebody beat me up in the middle of the campus and stole his old chess book.

(11)

TWO-THIRTY-THREE IN THE MORNING. I am sitting in my study overlooking Hobby Road, a baseball bat near my right hand, trying to figure out what went wrong. Once persuaded that they had erred, the police took me to the emergency room of the university hospital, where a young resident hummed an old Broadway tune while stitching up my face and taping my bruised ribs. An hour later, I left the hospital with Kimmer and Bentley. Already sick with worry, my wife was sobered— not to say frightened—by my appearance. She managed a certain grace nevertheless, and was gentle and solicitous all the way home, kissing my battered face and assuring me that all would be well, even though I never asked. But perhaps it is Kimmer herself who needs the reassurance, for having your husband beaten and nearly arrested outside the university library is not the sort of thing that helps your chances for the bench. I have not, yet, shared with my wife the details of the assault. I have told her only that they stole Karl's book of chess problems. She has, I think, enough worries. I suppose I will explain it all in time.

And Bentley! My happy, mischievous son, so shocked by his father's appearance that he curled up and went to sleep the instant we strapped him into his car seat. I would trade it all for the chance to give him back his childhood; the past few weeks have surely been harder on him than on Kimmer and myself. Right now, slouched at my desk with one eye on the street and one on the Internet, where I am lurching more than surfing from chat room to chat room, I wish I knew what my father had left behind and who precisely wanted to know, so that I could give them whatever it is and get myself and my family out of this mess.

The arrangements: what are they? The Excelsior: why chess?

The disappearing scrapbook, the reappearing pawn, the delivery at the soup kitchen, far too many mysteries for good health.

Or safety. *You and your family are perfectly safe.* Oh, sure. Tell that to the two men who went after me tonight. I would like to meet them again. On my terms. I stand up in the small room, grip the baseball bat like a hitter, swing it smoothly, as though to meet a fastball, and, on the follow-through, I come within inches of demolishing my computer. Actually, I have not struck a human being in anger since an inconclusive skirmish on the playground when I was in eighth grade and the school bully, furious at me for some witticism or other, made a serious effort to punch my lights out. Swinging the bat more carefully now, standing in the gloom, I let the memories flow, memories of a happier time, when Abby still lived. The bully, an angry white pre-teen whose name, I believe, was Alvin, aimed for my nose but missed, splitting my lip instead. Flailing in pain and fear, I hit him back, flush on the jaw, which astonished him more than hurt him, and then I threw a hard right into the center of his astonishment, and he went down with a grunt. I backed away, and then Alvin was up again, tackling me, and we were on the ground, striking each other with the short, pointless blows of many a schoolyard battle, until separated by a teacher. Oh, but the Judge got after me! Not for fighting, but for failing to finish what I started. He quoted me the old saw: If you strike at the king, you must kill him. Fighting a bully to a draw, he warned, is never enough. When my three-day suspension ended, I returned to school warily, wondering if Alvin was lying in wait somewhere. Alvin. Yes. I sit at my desk once more, laying the bat on the floor. That is what the fight may have been about, his name, for he required us all to call him Al, and I was never the sort to allow others to impose their will on me—other men, anyway. As it turned out, I did not have to fight Alvin again. He did not return to school, not then, not ever. I smile and swivel my chair away from the desk, toward the window, where the street is quiet and empty. It was one of my heroic moments, for a rumor spread through the school that it was Al's savage beating at the hands of the shrimpy Tal Garland, derisively nicknamed "Poindexter," that drove him away. The bully was gone, and, for about a week, I was even popular, an unaccustomed phenomenon that has not been repeated in my life. Of course, I had barely held my own in the fistfight, and the truth was more prosaic. It turned out that poor Al, during his own enforced vacation, had performed some egregious act involving an automobile that did not belong to his family, and was headed for a "special" school—the euphemism of the day for the vocational schools, many of which were little more than warehouses for the unwanted, the unwashed, the unwilling . . . the . . . the . . .

The telephone is ringing.

My eyes jerk open and, automatically, I grab for the baseball bat. I stare, disbelieving, at the instrument that woke me from my doze, then turn to look at the clock, its red digital readout barely visible behind a stack of books on my desk. Two-fifty-one. In the morning. Nobody has ever called at two-fifty-one in the morning with good news. The caller-ID screen tells me only that the number is blocked.

Not a happy indicator.

Still, I grab the receiver, on the second ring, so as not to wake my wife. My heart is beating too fast, my grip on the baseball bat is too tight, and I have shifted my gaze back to the street, as though the ringing is the signal for an assault on the house.

"Yes?" I demand softly, for I will not even pretend to be glad to get a call in the wee hours. Besides, my adrenaline is still pumping, and I am a little frightened . . . for my family.

"Is this Professor Garland?" asks a calm male voice.

"It is."

"The problem is taken care of," the voice assures me, the tone voluptuous, almost hypnotic. "I regret what happened earlier tonight, but now everything is fine. Nobody will bother you again. You and your family are safe, just as promised."

"What? Who is this?"

"And, of course, you should make no mention to anyone of this call." I can think of no one I would dare mention it to. On the other hand . . .

"Suppose my phone is tapped?"

"It isn't. Good night, Professor. Sleep well."

I hang up the phone, my mind a confused admixture of puzzlement, relief, and a fresh, more profound fear.

Everything is fine. The problem is taken care of. Nobody will bother you again.

Maybe a crank call, maybe a bad joke, or maybe, just maybe, it is something far worse.

Maybe it is the truth.

I am shuddering as I climb the stairs, wondering if I heard what I thought I did just before I hung up: the distant click as my wife, trying to be quiet, put the upstairs extension back in its cradle.

CHAPTER 28

TWO NEWS FLASHES

"I HEAR YOU HAD A LITTLE TROUBLE," says the great Mallory Corcoran, who has at last condescended to speak to me again. In fact, he called me this time, rather than the other way around.

"You could say that." Carrying the portable phone down the hallway, I rub my bruised face, smiling ruefully at my image in the narrow gilt-edged mirror that hangs across from the dining room, a hideous artifact given Kimmer by some distant aunt on the occasion of her first marriage. It is past eleven in the morning, but Bentley is still up in his bedroom, sleeping off the exhaustion of last night. One of the great advantages of the academic life is that it is possible to take a morning off for little things like loving a child.

"The police are faxing Meadows a copy of the report. Is there anything you'd like me to do? Any way I can help?"

"I don't think so, Uncle Mal. I'm fine. Just a little shaken up."

"You're sure?"

"I'm sure," I mutter as I stand in the kitchen window, looking out on the pummeling rain threatening to drown our small but family-friendly back yard. Hedges close it in on two sides, a high wooden fence on the third, and then there is our own house making the fourth wall. We let Bentley spend all the time he wants out there, often unsupervised. "I think I have things . . . pretty well under control."

"Do you have any idea what they wanted?"

I hesitate. I told the police that the two men took the package, but not that they kept on asking about *the arrangements* as they pummeled me. I have told nobody about the phone call that came in the middle of the night, and light-sleeping Kimmer has not asked.

For some reason, I believe the phone call. It just feels . . . plausible, maybe.

"I don't know, Uncle Mal," I sigh. The pain is back, weakening my voice, but it is not yet time to take another Advil. "I don't really know."

"You don't sound so good."

"Oh, that's just my jaw."

"They broke your jaw?" Alarm. Incredulity. But also some amusement, the tone of a man who has seen it all.

"No, no, nothing like that. It just hurts, that's all."

"Humph." Mallory Corcoran obviously doubts my claims to be okay. I do not really blame him, but the more important pains I am suffering are not physical. This morning, aching bones and all, I made breakfast for Kimmer and myself and then tried to get her to sit still and listen to the whole story. I planned to tell her everything, everything I know, everything I have guessed, everything I am worried about. Dressed beautifully for work in a navy chalk-stripe suit, my wife shook her head wearily. *I don't want to hear it, Misha, okay? I trust you, I really do, but I don't want to hear it.* I protested, but she shook her head again. She put her fingers gently over my lips. Her eyes, serious and questioning and worried, held mine. *I just want to ask you three questions,* she said. *First, is our son in any danger?* I had spent half the night, even after the telephone call, considering the same question, so I had my answer ready. I told her what is true, that I am sure he is not. She took this in and then asked, *Am I in any danger?* Again I told her no, of course not. Still regarding me solemnly, Kimmer asked what she really wanted to ask all along: *Are you in any danger?* I turned this over in my mind and then shook my head. *I don't think so.* She frowned. *You're not as certain.* I shrugged and told her that I was as certain as I could be. And Kimmer nodded and stepped into my arms and kissed me for a while and then put her head on my chest and told me to remember that I have a family who needs me. *You do what you think you have to do, Misha, but think about what happened last night and remember the rest of your obligations.*

Then she went off to work, leaving me with an unexpected smile on my face.

Later in the morning, Don and Nina Felsenfeld stopped by from next door, delivering casseroles and kindness, nearly smothering me with their fluttering worry, but warming me as well. How they found out what happened last night I have no idea, but Elm Harbor is, as my wife keeps pointing out, a very small town.

"Well, if you think of anything the firm can do to help," Uncle Mal is saying, with a forced bonhomie, "you be sure to get in touch."

He means get in touch with Meadows. He is tired of me again. I can tell.

"I will." I make myself say it. "And thanks for calling."

Mallory Corcoran actually laughs. "Oh, Talcott, wait a minute. Don't hang up. We haven't even gotten to why I called yet. I was going to call you anyway, even before I heard about what happened."

"Why? Is something wrong?"

Another potent laugh booms over the miles. "No, no, everything's just fine. Listen, Talcott, on this judge thing? Your wife must have a secret admirer."

"A secret admirer?"

"That's right."

"Meaning what?" I ask uneasily, no longer thinking about last night's assault, worrying now that the White House has discovered something about my wife's possible extramarital activities, the ones concerning which I promised Dr. Young I would give her the benefit of the doubt. Then I realize Uncle Mal is suggesting that Kimmer's chances are getting better, not worse.

"My sources tell me that the President's people are souring a bit on Professor Hadley. He isn't out of the running yet, but he's teetering. The Republicans had him down as a Felix Frankfurter type, this big political liberal who was also a judicial conservative, because that's what you can glean from what little he's written. They liked that combination, figured they could make the Democrats happy and warm their own right wing at the same time. That's the line somebody sold them, anyway."

"I see."

"Not a bad idea, either. The President has had some rocky confirmation fights, and I think he'd love a smooth one."

"I'm sure." I have carried the portable phone into my study, absently massaging my wounded ribs. The front window shows the same endless rain as the back. Hobby Road, as usual in mid-morning, is pretty much empty, for children are at school and parents are at work or the supermarket or aerobics or wherever parents go these days.

"That was the idea, anyway," he continues. "But I hear that somebody's been feeding them transcripts of these after-dinner talks Professor Hadley has given here and there, and now they're thinking they have a crypto-liberal at the top of their list. He may not publish this stuff, but, well, some of his ideas look pretty screwed up."

"I see," I say slowly.

"Whereas in Kimmer's case . . . well, Talcott, given your father . . . let's just say that the President has a right flank to please, and nominating the daughter-in-law of Oliver Garland would have a certain . . . cachet. Plus she's black. A black woman. A three-fer."

"Lest we forget."

"You sound upset, Talcott."

"No, no." There is no way to explain to Uncle Mal how his last comments have stung me, and how they would sting my wife even more were I to share them, which I will not. A Garland marriage without secrets would probably be too happy, and that the family could never abide. "No, but . . . you said somebody's feeding them the transcripts?"

"Somebody from Elm Harbor, I hear."

"From Elm Harbor?"

"From the university." His voice is harder now.

"Oh. Oh, I see." I keep my tone neutral. Plainly, Uncle Mal thinks I am the one doing the feeding, and his attitude tells me what bad taste he thinks it is for a man to use his Washington connections to promote his own wife's candidacy for the bench. Although, if he were to take a moment to consider the matter, he would remember that I have no Washington connections other than the one to whom I am currently speaking.

"But, Talcott, the thing is, shoveling dirt on somebody this way can backfire."

"Backfire?"

"What I mean is, whoever is feeding the White House those transcripts? Well, okay, maybe they can do Professor Hadley enough damage that he won't get the seat. But, you know, there isn't any kind of guarantee that the feeder's candidate will get it, either. This kind of thing can hurt. If A is slinging mud at B, sometimes A and B both get so dirty that they're knocked out of the . . ."

"I get the idea."

"And even if it doesn't backfire? Even if it works? Well, still, it's just plain wrong."

Wrong. Now, there's a word likely to die during the new century. "I agree."

"I'd find a way to put a stop to it if I were you."

"Uncle Mal, it isn't me!" I blurt, feeling just as I did last night, the innocent black man looking guilty in the eyes of white power.

"I never suggested that it was," he intones piously.

"Will you tell them?"

"Tell who what?"

"Tell the White House that it isn't me."

"Well, if you really want me to," he murmurs dubiously, implying that he is not sure they would believe him, or that they should.

"Please."

"I will," he says, but he means he won't. "So, anyway, stay tuned."

"Right."

"Good. That's what we're here for. Oh, and let us know if there is anything the firm can do."

"Of course," I tell him.

Stuart, I am thinking as I hang up. That pompous idiot, Stuart Land.

CHAPTER 29

AN ENJOYABLE EVENING

(1)

"ARE YOU OKAY, TAL?" asks Shirley Branch, pecking me on the cheek as I step across the threshold of her condo. She peers sympathetically at the still-visible bruise under my eye. Outside, the wet New England winter wind carries on its annual December argument with those who prefer warmth. "I heard you almost got arrested. Let me have your coat. Where's your wife?" One question stumbling over another, because Shirley possesses the kind of disordered brilliance that cannot keep up with itself.

I shake my head and hand Shirley my parka, answering the first question for about the tenth time in the past two days and the second for about the hundredth time in the past year. No, I was not almost arrested, I tell her; a minor misunderstanding, nothing more. And Kimmer could not attend the dinner party because the sitter came down with the flu, which is true enough, even though, had the sitter been well, Kimmer would have found some other excuse. Dinner with law school faculty is, for my wife, a little bit like being stretched on the rack, only without the health benefits. Kimmer, who at surprising moments decides she likes my company, suggested that I should stay home, but when I told her I thought that was a very good idea, she changed her mind, citing the very arguments that persuaded us to accept Shirley's invitation to Saturday dinner in the first place: Shirley is the school's first black female professor, and there is such a thing as solidarity, even in these fractured times. Shirley is my former student and research assistant, and there is such a thing as loyalty, even in these selfish times.

But I think the real reason Kimmer wanted at least one of us to go was in order to spy on Marc Hadley, who is also on the guest list. Kimmer and Marc have not been in the same room since they became contenders for the vacancy on the court of appeals, and my path and Marc's have barely crossed at the law school, not least because I have spent so much time away. I think Kimmer, who is a good deal less intimidated by my colleagues than she thinks she is, decided that it is time to take his measure.

Until it turned out we had no sitter: then she sent me on alone.

"Have you seen Cinque?" Shirley asks hopefully in her gentle Mississippi accent—Cinque being the quite formidable name of the quite unformidable terrier which now and then accompanies her to her small office in violation of numerous university rules. "He got out somehow."

"I'm afraid not," I tell her.

"Are you really okay, Tal? I'm not sure you actually know everybody. You've met Reverend Young, right? No? Oh, you have? He's my pastor. Your eye looks terrible. Are you sure you didn't see Cinque out there? He's not really a winter dog."

"I'm sure he's fine, Shirley," I murmur, and she shrugs and tries to smile.

I smile back as best I can. The pain in my ribs is less, but the stitches in my cheek itch terrifically. Stuart Land turns out to be away for a few days—in Washington, no less—so I have been unable to upbraid him for his efforts to sabotage Marc Hadley, if, indeed, Stuart is the one who is doing it. The stranger with the voluptuous voice has not called back with any further reassurances, but I no longer sense that I am being followed. Were things otherwise, I suppose I would have skipped the party.

I am among the last of the guests to arrive. Marc and Dahlia Hadley are already here, as are Lynda Wyatt and her sleepy husband, Norm, the architect. And crafty old Ben Montoya, Lynda's strong right hand, whose wife, like mine, is substituting for a babysitter sick with flu. Lem Carlyle and *his* wife are expected a little later, after their daughter's ballet recital. Four of the most powerful members of the faculty, plus me. Shirley was my student ten years ago in the first torts class I ever taught. She is three years away from a tenure vote, but she already knows whose good opinions matter. And she is sufficiently street-wise to understand that evaluations of her scholarship, no matter how we try to fight it, will always be influenced, at least a little, by how much the evaluators like her as a person.

Three guests have no direct university connections. My sometime counselor, Reverend Dr. Morris Young, is accompanied by his quiet wife, Martha, who is nearly as pudgy as he is—quiet, that is, outside of church, for her voice is the loudest, if not perhaps the best, in the choir, which sings all over the state. The other is rail-thin Kwame Kennerly, a shamelessly calculating politico with prematurely thinning hair and a magnificent goatee, along with a reputation as a rabble-rouser, implicated but never quite caught in several municipal scandals, who currently serves, as Kimmer likes to say, as the mayor's special assistant in charge of keeping the minority community domesticated, although his job title reads "deputy chief of staff." He is also, I realize as he slips his arm around her slim waist, Shirley's boyfriend. And it occurs to me that Shirley is strengthening her ties not only with the most influential professors at the law school, but with two of the most influential figures in the city's black community.

In short, she is fitting in; I, her ex-teacher, beam.

Kwame Kennerly, standing right behind Shirley with a wineglass in his hand, is quite rude as Shirley introduces me, presumably because he blames me for being my father's son, an attitude I frequently encounter from activists of the left. (Those on the right are always in a great hurry to shake my hand, with as little reason.) I often see Kwame's name in the *Clarion*, for he is one of those rising politicians who manage to be everyplace at once, but I have never met him. He is a long, sinewy man whose wide, blinking eyes disagree with you before you have opened your mouth. For this occasion, perhaps because Shirley lives on the water, he is sporting a navy blazer with brass buttons even though it is out of season, the sort of offense against which my mother used to rage. As if for balance, he wears a round hat of bright orange kente cloth. The riot of color—the hat, the blazer, his dark skin, his ebon beard—is likely to be of quite intimidating effect on the white liberals present. If he feels out of place he is determined not to let on.

Shirley Branch lives in a sprawling condominium complex fronting on Elm Harbor's narrow and seaweed-clogged beach. Her one-story unit is not very large: a bedroom that apparently doubles as her study, a kitchen the size of a closet, a single bathroom, and a long area that does duty as both living room and dining room, although the dining table, which seats twelve, takes up half the space. For the same money (so she has told me more times than I can remember), she could have bought a three-bedroom townhouse on the other side of the complex, but she would not have had her spectacular view of the water. "I don't need much space," she likes to say, "because it's only just me and Cinque." Cinque, I should explain, is Shirley's third dog of the same name, stretching all the way back into college: she makes sure we all know she selected the appellation long before Steven Spielberg made it famous.

To sit in Shirley's condo, to gaze out the glass doors, across the balcony, to beach and smooth black water not fifty yards away, is almost to be transported back to Oak Bluffs.

Almost.

Shirley is a slim, flat-footed woman with a long, sad face and prominent teeth—what we used to call a horsey face when I was a child. Her eyes are a little bit too sincere, her flip hairdo is a little bit too pressed, her movements are a little bit too frenetic: even as a student, she had a tendency to overdo. Her work is principally about race, and she is determinedly, aggressively, almost palpably leftish. To hear Shirley tell it, no problem facing America or the world has any cause but white racism. Her mind is keen and energetic, she loves to write, but her scholarship lacks, I suppose, a certain subtlety, an attention to nuance, studied consideration of alternatives—she is, in a word, pigheaded, which is probably one reason we almost decided not to hire her. Marc Hadley led the opposition.

I wonder whether Shirley knows that.

I wander into the area that serves as both living room and dining room—sofa and loveseat at one end, glass-topped dining-room table at the other—and find Marc already holding forth, for he can no more resist an audience than the press can resist a scandal. Shirley shrugs in what might almost be apology as she hangs my coat in the crowded closet by the front door. Lynda Wyatt smiles merrily as I enter, raising her glass in ironic salute: she does *try* to like me, I must give her that. Marc's greeting is so perfunctory that it is really a dismissal, but he is busy lecturing, into it now, tweedy arms pumping madly as he entertains the guests with his latest theory. Gregarious Dahlia does her best to make up for his rudeness, hugging me like a long-lost brother and asking after my family. Old Ben Montoya, scrawny yet still strong, puts a powerful hand on my shoulder and whispers that he heard I'd been arrested. I turn and glare, not at Ben, but at Shirley, who grins nervously and shrugs as if to say, *It's not my fault—I don't start rumors, I just spread them.*

My gaze finally settles on Marc himself, my wife's rival, a man to whom I once felt reasonably close: Brother Hadley, as Dear Dana Worth likes to call him, or Young Marc, as the mischievous Theo Mountain prefers, for Marc possesses the kind of presence that inspires facetiousness. He smells, as always, of the rather pleasant raspberry tobacco he favors, for a battered old pipe is one of his many affectations. He pays no attention to the state's recently enacted law forbidding smoking in the common areas of office buildings, having already decided for himself that it is unconstitutional, and nobody seems ready to challenge him, so the pipe travels with him everywhere around Oldie, although I notice he has not lit it at Shirley's home. Marc is esteemed, quite properly, as one of the best brains on the faculty, a reputation, it seems, which justifies his failure to cut or even comb the gray-blond hair that falls past his ears, as well as his failure to shave more than once or twice a week, or to put on a tie, or to polish his shoes. He teaches jurisprudence and he teaches criminal law and he teaches learned seminars on the lives of the great judges and the coming death of law itself. Students are in awe of him. Most of his colleagues admire him. Some of us like him. Despite his ego, he is a kind man, always willing to give of his time and talent to those just starting out, and would be a considerable academic star but for the single failing I mentioned earlier: he simply does not write. His scholarly reputation rests not only on his single book—*The Constitutional Mind*, published almost twenty years ago—but on a single scintillating chapter of the book, Chapter Three, always written that way, capitalized, sometimes with no further citation: *But Hadley's Chapter Three has already refuted that argument*, a sympathetic scholar might contend. In the famous Chapter Three, Marc presented what is commonly accepted as the best analysis ever of Benjamin Cardozo's judicial style, and used it to present a critique of constitutional theory that remains in vogue today. Even Dana Worth, who despises Marc, concedes in her sober moments that she knows of no book as influential—no chapter as influential—written by a legal scholar in the past half-century. The book was a blistering attack on what has come to be called judicial activism, written by a professed liberal, but one who calls himself old-style, preferring what he calls the democratic liberalism of grass-roots organizing to the bureaucratic liberalism of litigation and legislation.

A dazzling thinker and fine teacher, my former friend Marc Hadley, but I hope he remains a law professor.

At last I tune in Marc's lecture. He is talking, as usual, too fast, but I capture the gist. "You see, if *Griswold* is correct—if decisions about birth control are to be made by women and their doctors—then marriage itself is obsolete. I mean *constitutionally* obsolete. Just look at the findings of history and anthropology and you will discover that Freud turns out to have been right all along. Defenders of traditional marriage, especially those who argue that the marital relationship is somehow *natural*, point out that it exists in some form in just about every culture we have ever discovered. But what does that prove? Only that every culture has faced the same problem. Marriage evolved to solve the problem of how society would cabin the human urge to reproduce, which is the strongest urge humans possess, except for the urge among the weak-minded to invent supernatural beings to worship because they're so afraid of dying." A chuckle to soften the blow he believes he has dealt. Then he resumes. "You see, marriage is, historically, about nothing but reproduction and economics—that is, children and money. Married couples bear and raise children. The marital unit earns and consumes and acquires property. That's it. All the rest of marriage law is surplusage. But now, with the evolution of technology and of culture, reproduction is no longer a matter of marriage. Unmarried women reproduce and there is no social sanction. Married women decline to reproduce and there is no social sanction. And not only is there no social sanction—there is a constitutional right. So, you see, we have this area of law that is built entirely on a social understanding that no longer exists. Once severed from reproduction, marriage becomes irrational. The law of marriage, then, is not reasonably related to any legitimate state purpose, which is the fundamental standard that any statute must meet under the Constitution. And there we have it. Marriage law is unconstitutional."

He stops and looks around the cramped room as though awaiting applause.

Everybody is quiet. Marc looks pleased, perhaps imagining he has so impressed us that we are too awestruck to answer. I cannot speak for anybody else, but I am silent because I am considering whether to ask my doctor for a hearing test: I do not believe I could possibly have heard all this nonsense right. Marc will never write any of this down, and this is where his block disserves him: it seems to have made him reckless, for the fact that nothing he says will be recorded in some permanent medium will allow him, if ever asked, to deny his words, to insist his argument was misinterpreted, or to claim to have been engaging in mere speculation. Marriage as unconstitutional! I wonder if the White House is privy to this mad theory, if it is one of the tales that

Stuart has passed along—assuming that it is Stuart who is trying to sabotage him, for I have yet to track him down. I wonder how it would play in the press. (Not that I would ever talk to a reporter, but Marc has enemies. For instance, I could tell Dana Worth about Marc's idea, and she would have no compunction about sharing it with as many journalists as she and Alison can find in their digital pocket planners.)

Marc continues.

"I do not say that private institutions, such as religious organizations, cannot, if they so choose, continue to perform their quaint ceremonies and announce to the faithful that this or that couple, of whatever description, is married in the sight of their particular God. But that is just an exercise of their basic religious freedom, guaranteed by the First Amendment. The point is that the state should not be involved in any way, whether by licensing these so-called marriages, or by granting particular state benefits to those who enter into them, or by purporting to decide in the place of these private institutions how and whether the marriages end. *Griswold* tells us that reproduction is not the state's business. Therefore, marriage is not the state's business."

Ben Montoya, the great liberal, winks at me, a bemused grin on his face. He is Marc's occasional sparring partner, for they are very much on opposite sides of such decisions as *Roe v. Wade*. (Marc would say he is personally pro-choice but believes the state has the authority to disagree.) Tonight, however, Ben does not argue with Marc. Neither does Lynda Wyatt, although she is standing right next to him. Lynda in her day has taught both family law and constitutional law and thus might be able to correct a few of Marc's errors, but she is looking down at the sea-green carpet. I have never understood this effect that Marc has on people. Kwame Kennerly, who has given much of his considerable energy to encouraging marriage among the young African American men of the inner city, most of whom seem to have forgotten how it is done, looks furious. On the other hand, he remains a relative newcomer to the town of Elm Harbor, still building his political base, and is not quite ready to challenge a representative of the hated and envied university, especially one who raises so much money for Democratic candidates. Dr. Young looks troubled, but not intimidated. He shakes his head a few times, his fleshy lips pursed in disapproval. He does not say a word. I have the impression that he is biding his time, letting Marc punch himself out: the rope-a-dope. As for me, well, I would not dream of opening my mouth; so I content myself with wishing Dana were here to shut Marc up. Norm Wyatt alone has the impertinence to roll his eyes in open disbelief, but he feels about the law faculty roughly the same way that Kimmer does.

"Now, if you apply my theory to same-sex marriage—" Marc hurries on, but Shirley wisely chooses this moment to announce that dinner is served.

Marc's audience happily deserts him, to his apparent puzzlement, because his hands are still waving even when most of the guests have turned toward the table. Shirley points out our various seats. Before sitting down, I take a moment to glance out the sliding glass doors, past her balcony, down to the beach and the gently throbbing surf, and I wonder whether Kimmer and I, too, should have sacrificed space for this gorgeous proximity.

I am seated in the middle of one of the long sides of the table, squeezed between Dr. Young on my right and Dahlia Hadley on my left. Across from me is Dean Lynda, flanked by Kwame Kennerly on one side and an empty chair for Lem Carlyle on the other.

"The cops give you that black eye?" Kwame Kennerly inquires without any preamble, tipping his head away from me as though to get a better view. I wonder if this tale will ever go away.

"No."

"So who did?"

"Somebody else," I mutter, rudely. Truly my father's son tonight.

Kwame is undeterred. "*Not* the cops? You sure?"

"I'm sure, Kwame. I was there when it happened."

Irony gets me nowhere. "I heard you got arrested."

"No, I didn't."

"They didn't pull their guns on you?" Blinking furiously.

"Nobody pulled any guns."

Kwame Kennerly strokes his small beard as he works out his next move. He is not to be put off by a little impudence. I may be the son of the late and hated Oliver Garland, but I am also a black man who might have been beaten by the cops; besides, the story is too juicy to ignore. Dean Lynda is listening with more than half an ear.

"But you did have some trouble with the police, right? *White* police?"

"It was all a misunderstanding," I sigh. "I was mugged, I called in an alarm, and when they came they just thought I was the mugger instead of the muggee. But I showed them my university ID and then they apologized and let me go."

"*City* police?"

"Campus police."

"I knew it. That's what they do." He does not wait for my answer. "A black man in the middle of the campus, right? Two blocks from the law school, where you *work*. If you were white, there would never have been any *misunderstanding*."

I do not waste time wondering where Kwame got the details of my encounter, because getting the details is his job. I do, however, waste time arguing with him, even though his analysis is precisely correct. "I wasn't walking, I was . . ." I hesitate and glance at my dean, but there is nowhere to go except forward. "I was climbing on the scaffolding outside the library. You can see why they were suspicious."

"But on your own campus, right?" he persists, nodding his bearded head as if he sees it every day, which I suppose he does.

"Yes."

"And the muggers were white. If the police got there and you were fighting with the muggers, they would still think *you* were the bad guy."

"I guess they might."

"That's what I'm talking about!" he exclaims to Lynda Wyatt, perhaps picking up on some earlier argument.

"I know, I know," my dean says hastily.

"It's his *own* campus, but it's a *white* campus! See, this is the main thing the police are *for* in a town like this one—keeping us in our place."

"Mmmm," says Dean Lynda, eating fast.

"Black men are an *endangered species* in this country." He pronounces it like a quote from an encyclopedia, then points his finger at me as the number-one exhibit. "No matter who their *fathers* are."

The mashed potatoes are coming in our direction, and Kwame has to pause to spoon a healthy portion onto his plate. He adds some gravy from a small tureen, then leaps nimbly back onto the track.

"It's *open season* on our young men!"

"I'm not so young," I interrupt, struggling for a light tone.

"But you're still lucky to be alive. No, I mean it. We all know what the police can do." Still nodding with vigor. He turns back to Dean Lynda. "See what I mean?"

"Oh, yes. And we're all very glad you weren't hurt, Talcott." She smiles with every sign of genuine concern. I realize that they are both thinking about a case in the neighboring all-white town of Canner's Point two years ago, just about the time Kwame Kennerly arrived in

Elm Harbor. A black teenager was shot to death by two police officers when he exited his stolen car with his hands in the air after a fifteen-minute chase ended with a crash into a convenience store.

But that was different, I want to say in the Judge's voice, biting my tongue just in time, because the Judge would be mostly wrong.

"Everything worked out fine," I tell Kwame instead, wishing he would stop.

"You should let me handle it."

"No, thank you."

"I mean, I could call the commissioner, okay? This kind of harassment happens to be an important issue right now. The mayor is very concerned."

The last thing I need: some kind of official investigation. I cannot afford to become an *issue*. Not only would it be just the kind of thing that might tilt the scale back from Kimmer to Marc—*See? We told you her husband is unstable!*—but, worse, it might uncover much that I am not ready to reveal.

"That won't be necessary."

"I think the commissioner should look into it," Kwame says stubbornly.

"No, thank you," I repeat, "and, besides, I told you, they were campus police, not city."

"I *know* that. But the commissioner is in charge of both. It's in the state law."

Right. And the university has to obey the city zoning laws too, but it doesn't when it doesn't want to.

"I just want to put it behind me," I tell Kwame, deliberately turning away to talk to the enchanting Dahlia Hadley. In his clumsy race-baiting, Kwame actually means well, and, worse, he is beginning to make sense. Shirley, at the far end of the table, notices the tension and frowns, for she loves controversy at her dinners as long as it does not get personal.

Dahlia seems more serene than the last time I saw her, perhaps because she and Marc have calculated that the little incident outside the library can only help his chances for the nomination. Marc comes from money—lots of money. One of his great-aunts was supposedly half a Vanderbilt or Rockefeller or something—the rumors vary—and a state park is named after his long-dead Uncle Edmund, whose charity was legendary. Marc has grown accustomed to getting what he wants.

"I'm glad you weren't seriously hurt," Dahlia murmurs in her syrupy voice.

"Thanks."

"You have to take care of yourself, Talcott. Your family needs you."

"I know, I know."

"They need you to defend a pawn."

My eyes widen. There is an epiphany in every paranoid fantasy, a moment when the truth suddenly blazes whitely around you: yes, the world is united, and, yes, everybody is on the other side.

"What did you say?" My voice is tight, almost a gasp.

Dahlia cringes. "I . . . I said they need you to depend upon."

I realize I am sweating. I cover my eyes for a moment. "Oh. Okay. Sorry. I guess . . . I guess I misheard you."

"I guess you did."

"I'm sorry, Dahlia."

Dahlia draws back a few inches, as though I have made an indecent proposition. Her face remains hard and offended as she says sternly, "I think perhaps you need more rest than you are getting, Talcott."

"I'm sorry. I didn't mean to . . . to raise my voice."

"You seem tired. You should not be so swift to anger," she adds helpfully, then turns to her left to chat with Norm Wyatt.

When I look up toward the far end of the table, my former friend Marc Hadley is glaring at me.

(11)

THROUGH MOST OF THE MEAL, almost everybody around me seems to find somebody else far more interesting to talk to. Lynda Wyatt, whose conceit is that she can charm anybody into anything, seems to have her hands full with Kwame Kennerly, and Dahlia Hadley, who has not said another word to me since I raised my voice to her, is arguing historic preservation with Lynda's husband, Norm. (She's pro-, he's anti-.) Marc Hadley is instructing Shirley on the finer points of separation of church and state, about which she has written and he has not. Lemaster and Julia Carlyle, both slim and pert, finally arrived, their daughter's recital having gone well; seated on opposite sides of the table, the two of them have eyes, as usual, mainly for each other. I have tried to say a word to Lem, usually a sparkling conversationalist, but he has responded with little more than grunts, as though he cannot bear talking to me; and I wonder anew whether his changed attitude is my imagination, or whether my stock around the law school has really fallen so far, so fast.

But Dr. Young, who earlier prayed over the food with no pretense of ecumenism, has decided to bend my ear about the murder of Freeman Bishop, which has not come up in our counseling sessions. He has been relating a rather long story about a lynching that his granddaddy told him about, back in Georgia around about nineteen-ought-six, in which a black preacher was burned with a hot coal all over his arms and legs and then shot in the back of the head when he refused to talk about his efforts to organize the mill workers.

"You see," says Dr. Young, rolling into his theme, "Satan never changes. That is his great weakness. That is where the believer has the advantage over him, praise God. Satan is a creature of habit. He is clever but he is not intelligent. Satan is always the same, and his subjects, those souls who are lost to him, always behave the same. If Hitler marched the Jews off to the extermination camps, you can be sure that some other wicked leader, in times out of mind, slaughtered the innocents because they were different. You see leaders today, all over the world, doing it again! Black, white, yellow, brown, people of every color slaughtering people of every color! Because Satan is always the same. Always! Satan is stupid. Clever, you see, but not intelligent, praise God. This is God's gift to us, requiring Satan to remain stupid. Why is Satan stupid? So that, if we are alert, we can recognize him. By his signs shall we know him! For Satan, stupid Satan, always attacks us in the same ways. If the old methods fail, he can think of nothing new, praise God. So he just goes on to attack somebody else. He attacks us with sexual desire and other temptations that distract the body. He attacks us with drink and drugs and other temptations that addle the brain. He attacks us with racial hatred and love of money and other temptations that distort the soul."

Dr. Young's sermon is louder now, and the whole table is paying attention, even Marc, who cannot stand to have the attention of a room focused on anybody but himself.

"You see, then, what Satan does. He attacks the body. He attacks the brain. He attacks the soul. Body, mind, and soul—those are the only parts of the human being that Satan understands how to attack, praise God. If you guard them from Satan, you are safe. If you guard your body, you are guarding the *temple* of the Lord, for you are made in God's image. If you guard your mind, you are guarding the *toolhouse* of the Lord, for God works his will here on earth through mortal human beings. And if you guard your spirit, you are guarding the *storehouse* of the Lord, for God fills our souls with his power to help us to do his work on earth."

Marc Hadley, author of the famous Chapter Three, can stand this no longer. He interrupts.

"Morris . . ." he begins.

"Dr. Young is fine," says Dr. Young equably.

"Dr. Young"—it burns Marc to address him this way when his doctorate is surely in divinity, probably from some unknown seminary—"first, let me tell you that my wife and I are freethinkers. We are religious skeptics," he translates unnecessarily. Most of the table is watching Marc, but I am watching Dahlia, whose small mouth curls in distaste just before she turns to gaze out the window toward the surf. I wonder whether she is mad at her husband for entering into the argument in the first place, or for his use of *we*, while neglecting to mention that she is a very serious Roman Catholic who takes her son to mass every Sunday. "We are not atheists," Marc presses on, "because there is no proof that God does not exist, but we are skeptical of the truth claims of all religions, because there is no proof that God does. Or that Satan does. Second—"

"Well, let us deal with the first first." The pastor smiles. "You know, a very great thinker named Martin Buber once wrote that there are no atheists, because the atheist has to struggle with God every day. Maybe that is why the Scripture tells us, 'The fool has said in his heart there is no God.'"

"I don't remember that in Buber," says Marc Hadley, who hates to be told anything he does not already know.

"It was in *Between Man and Man*," Lemaster Carlyle, the onetime divinity student, intervenes quietly, taking the whole table by surprise. "A marvelous book. People who have read *I and Thou* and think they know Buber have not even scratched the surface." A dig at poor Marc, something of an insider's sport around the law school.

Dr. Young points a gray finger at Lem. "You are right, Professor Carlyle, but you are also wrong. The important question is not whether or not you have read Buber, nor is the important question which Buber you have read. The important question is whether you know what the stakes are. When I was at Harvard getting my doctorate, I had a philosophy professor, an atheist, who used to remind us what religion was all about: 'It is not your mind that God wants,' he used to say, 'but your soul.' Because God invented the human mind, but enters that mind through the human heart. My professor used to say, 'God does not want you to read the Bible and say, *What a beautiful book!* He wants you to read the Bible and say, *Hallelujah, I believe!*'"

I enjoy watching Marc's jaw drop, which does not happen often, but his mouth has been hanging open since the Reverend strung together the words *doctorate* and *Harvard*. Morris Young has depths that Marc Hadley, in his genteel liberal racism, never imagined.

Meanwhile, the preacher's pocked face arranges itself into a smile of reminiscence. "This was back in the fifties, of course, a time when philosophers, even atheist philosophers, were expected to know their Bible. After all, the Bible has been by far the most influential book in Western history, praise God, probably in the history of the whole world. Well, how can anybody pretend to understand or to explain that world without understanding the book that built it? But when you come to know the Bible, you come to know God. So the atheist who has truly tried to understand the world will already be closer to God than many Christians, because he will know God's word. The Lord creates many paths to his house, and he will, in the fullness of time, gather in even many of those who believe that they do not believe; for, in struggling with God, they are halfway to belief already."

"Amen, Reverend," says Kwame Kennerly. Shirley beams at him.

Meanwhile, Dahlia Hadley is taking her turn. "But isn't the atheist at risk? He *might* come to God, but, then again, he might *not*." I glance up just in time to see her smile prettily at Marc, but the surging anger is there, just below the surface of her girlish face, for those who care to look.

Dr. Young notices her fury. He notices everything. He nods his heavy head. "That is true, my dear, that is true, that is true." His rolling voice has developed a musical lilt. "The Lord opens the door to Heaven to the most miserable sinner, but the sinner still has to step through it. And the human mind, that glorious creation, has a way of throwing up obstacles. Oh, yes. The Lord holds the door open and the mind says, 'That's not the Lord!' or 'That's not the door!' or 'I'd rather store up treasures on earth!' Those are the counsels of Satan, who is always the same, remember, praise God, clever but not intelligent. Many a man would rather listen to Satan's counsels, would rather win what the sinful world gives grudgingly than accept what God offers freely. And we all know what the Gospel says about such men: 'They have their reward.'"

Marc Hadley wants to interrupt again, but Shirley Branch, sitting next to him at the head of the table, has the temerity to put a hand on his arm to make him shush.

Ben Montoya speaks up instead: "Some people don't happen to share your religious beliefs, Reverend," he declares, rudely but correctly. "Have you thought about their rights?"

Dr. Morris Young smiles down the table at him. "Oh, Professor Montoya, I have no concern for such matters. Rights are a thing of men. God is a God of love. You do not love your neighbor by giving your neighbor a right. You give the poor man or the black man a right and you feel you have done your duty to him. You may even feel that he now owes you a debt of gratitude. But if you had loved him to begin with, the question of right would never have arisen."

Lem Carlyle again intervenes gently, seeking common ground, as a future dean must. "But Christianity teaches that human beings are fallen. That we are sinful by nature. So Christianity justifies the state itself as ordained by God to keep order among these fallen creatures. Isn't that why we have rights, in Christian thought—because we know that we are too weak to live in love for each other, as God would prefer?"

Dr. Young nods benignly, but not in agreement. "The trouble with rights," he says, "is that, as soon as you have them, you think you have something of value. But all that has true value comes from the Lord. When you give a man a right, it is too easy to forget to love him."

Lynda Wyatt catches the drift: "So compassion is more important than rights."

"Rights are a thing of man," Dr. Young agrees. "Loving our neighbor, turning to one another in charity and humility, is a gift we give back to the Lord."

And then I see it. The chance of escape from the web my clever father, in death, has woven around me and my family. Everyone seeks the treasures of the earth, just as Morris Young suggested. The treasures of the earth. The *earth*. A memory tugs at me, an uncomfortable afternoon with the Judge many years ago, right on the campus. The white pawn. The Excelsior. The earth. Possibly, just possibly, I can make it all fit together.

"Amen, Reverend," I echo, a glimmer of hope finally flashing in my tortured mind.

BEN MONTOYA AND I leave the dinner at the same time, picking our way through the crusty snow toward the parking lot. He has timed his departure so perfectly that I am sure he wants to talk to me about something.

I am right.

Ben begins with a feint. "Do you think he really believes all that stuff?"

"Who? What stuff?"

"Reverend Young. All that stuff about Satan."

I look at him. "I don't have any doubt that Dr. Young believes every word of it. I believe it, too."

Ben shakes his head but says nothing. A silence descends as we crunch through the snow, each of us alone with his thoughts: Ben no doubt confirmed in his opinion that I am out of my mind, and me recognizing the deep truth of what I have just reported. But Ben's true purpose in following me out has nothing to do with theology or metaphysics.

"Ah, Talcott," he murmurs officiously, after a few seconds of silence, and I know we have reached the main event.

"Hmmm?" I do not look in his direction. The walkway to the visitors' lot leads between two rows of cookie-cutter units. Around the edges of drawn curtains or blinds, television images flash colorfully. I hear bursts of laughter, argument, music. But my attention is mainly on the sidewalk in front of me, from which this afternoon's freezing rain has not yet been cleared. The condominium association is begging for a lawsuit, should somebody trip and fall.

"Talcott, can I talk to you for a minute?"

"We are talking, Ben. That's what this is, talking." I suppose I would like Ben more were he not Dean Lynda's tool in so many of the various unseemly things a dean must do; or if I, too, were an insider; or if I were simply a better man.

Ben laughs shortly. He is, I suppose, about sixty, his hair thin on top and quite gray, his pouchy eyes wary yet accusatory behind thick glasses. His walk is the assertive lurch of a man in a great and irritated hurry. He is an anthropologist by training and has done important work on the way that contracts and property are handled in certain Pacific Islander societies that lack a tradition of making promises.

"Talcott, ah, you know, the Dean, well, she would never say anything, but . . ."

"But?"

"Lynda's very upset with you, Talcott. You have to realize that."

We have emerged at the poorly plowed visitors' parking lot. My shabby Camry is off in a corner, but we are standing and facing each other, maybe because we are right next to Ben's classic Jaguar XKE, or maybe because of what he just said to me.

"Upset about what?"

He blinks behind those powerful lenses. "Oh, well, you know. The way you've been acting lately. And this business with you and Marc . . ."

"There is no business with me and Marc."

"You know what I mean."

"I'm not sure I do." I look him up and down, my temper flares redly, and Ben steps hastily back as though expecting a blow. "If Lynda wants to talk to me, she knows where to find me."

"I'm not sure she does want to talk to you, Talcott." The officious tone is back. Ben is expert at looking down on others, not only because of his height. "The Dean is too polite to say anything to you, but I understand you were abusive to her the last time you talked."

"Abusive? We . . . we just had a disagreement, I wasn't . . ."

He rolls right over me. "Then there is this business with the police earlier this week. I know you didn't almost get arrested, but the situation was, ah, a little bit messy. We have to think of the law school's image, Talcott. We can't have a professor pouring gasoline on the racial fires in this town—"

"Ben—"

"No, no, I'm not saying you're doing it intentionally. But people are likely to exploit what happened for political gain"—he means Kwame Kennerly—"and, well, we can't have faculty members abetting this sort of thing, even unintentionally. And that's not all, Talcott. Lynda also says you're costing the school three million dollars. . . ."

"Now, wait a minute! Wait just a minute!" Fresh snow is beginning to fall, and the wind is picking up. Road conditions will soon be treacherous, and we both should be hurrying home, but I want to make sure I have the message straight, because I know it is coming from Lynda, not from Ben. "Are you telling me that Cameron Knowland is really taking his money back? Because his spoiled brat of a son is mad at a professor?"

Ben has his palms toward me, a gesture of surrender. He has backed all the way to the door of his Jag. "I don't know what Cameron is doing. I'm not privy to everything the Dean knows. I just want you to know that she's upset with you, and . . . and, well, I think it would be a good idea if you were . . . um, on your best behavior. . . ."

"Are you trying to warn me of something, Ben? Am I in some kind of actual trouble, or is this just a matter of ruffled feathers?"

Ben has the door of his car open. Having delivered his message, he seems to want no more conversation. "I just think you should be careful, that's all. You should think of the good of the school."

"As opposed to thinking of what? I don't get it. Ben, wait." He is sitting now, ready to close the door behind him. "What are you trying to tell me? Is this really about me, or is it about Kimmer and Marc?" I remember Stuart Land's warning that pressures would be brought to bear. "Come on, Ben, tell me."

"There isn't anything to tell, Talcott." His fierce eyes are looking straight ahead, as though he is angry at me for some offense I have yet to commit.

"But wait a minute. Wait. I don't understand what you're telling me." I put my hand on the door, not allowing him to close it. "Am I in trouble?" I ask again.

"I don't know, Talcott. *Are* you in trouble?" As I struggle for a clever response, he points with his chin. "Would you mind taking your hand off my car?"

"Ben . . ."

"Good night, Talcott. Love to your family."

He is gone.

Reeling, I nearly storm back into the party to confront Lynda Wyatt, to ask her what the real message is. But there would be no point. Lynda would deny everything. That is the reason to have a hatchet man in the first place: she can disavow whatever he says, and the message can still get across.

There are days when I hate this place.

I hurry through the snow to my own car, wishing for a way to put the whole pack of them behind me. Not only Lynda Wyatt and Ben Montoya and the others at the law school, but Uncle Mal and the Washington pack, too. I wish I could grab my family and head for the hills—or, failing that, for Oak Bluffs. A few thousand people live there year-round, after all. We could find a way to do it. We could run a bed and breakfast. Or hang out a shingle and practice law together. We could do it.

Not that Kimmer would go.

Still shaking with anger over my confrontation with Ben, I stab my key at the lock—my tough little Camry is too old to have a keyless entry system or an alarm—and then I notice that the door is already unlocked.

I must have left it that way, because nobody goes to the trouble of picking the lock of a car and then leaves the car. And nobody would steal a twelve-year-old car in the first place.

Except that, when I open the door and the dome light comes on, I realize that there are people after all who break into cars and take nothing, just as there are people who break into vacation homes and do the same thing.

Some people pick locks to make deliveries.

Lying squarely in the middle of the driver's seat is the chess book that was stolen by the two men who beat me up.

CHAPTER 30

THE USUAL SUSPECTS

(1)

"I HEAR YOU HAD A FIGHT with Stuart Land," says Dear Dana Worth, who is the first to hear about most things that happen around Oldie, including some that didn't. She is perching on the edge of her desk, palms on the top, the soles of her shoes pressed flat against the side, her small body set in a posture that has become so Worthian a trademark that the students have somebody mimic it most years in the satirical show they put on just before graduation. I am sitting on the long, solid sofa she found at a used-furniture store and reupholstered.

"Not a fight exactly. More . . . a free and frank exchange of views."

"About what?"

"I accused him of trying to wreck Marc's candidacy. I told him it was backfiring, that it might hurt Kimmer, too." I rub my itching cheek, remembering the look on his face, the surprise I would almost swear was genuine. "He said he wasn't doing any such thing."

"Maybe he wasn't."

"He just got back from Washington, Dana."

"Don't be silly, Misha, darling. I'm sure he wasn't there on behalf of your wife. He was just there cooking up some constitutional mischief with his right-wing buddies. Stuart never goes anywhere on behalf of anybody else but Stuart."

"And the law school."

"And the law school," she agrees, less certainly. She hops off the desk and begins to stride around the room. Her spacious office is on the second floor of Oldie, right next to Theo Mountain's, and it is said that the two of them share gossip incessantly. Everything about her office is just right, from the obsessively neat desk to the collection of plants along the windowsill to the shelves where her books are arranged in alphabetical order by author. I stand up as well, crossing to the window, where I look down on the front steps of the building and the granite wall of the main campus across the street. I can see the alley where I was beaten up a few days ago. It is Monday, nine days before Christmas. Classes are finally over, and the faculty is starting to scatter, but the students are stuck in town for another few days, taking their final exams. As for me, I have been keeping my head down, and dithering over what to do next. I have the terrible sense of time running out.

"So, Dana, anyway, you called. . . ."

"I know." A pause. "I wanted to make sure you're okay."

I nod my head without turning around. Our friendship has been maturing over the weeks since Freeman Bishop's murder. I am not sure I will ever be as close to her as Kimmer and I were, jointly, to Dana and Eddie in the old days, but Dana seems determined to patch up what she can. I am moved by her efforts. Unlike other members of the faculty, who seem to view my recent behavior roughly the way Dean Lynda does, Dana has drifted closer. Outcasts, she told me a few days ago, have to stick together. When I pointed out to Dana that she is no outcast, she reminded me that she runs the local branch of the Pro-Life Alliance of Gays and Lesbians. *Everybody hates us for something or other,* she told me, quite pleased.

"I'm okay," I assure her.

"Nice stitches. Very becoming."

"Thanks."

"I've been thinking about what happened to you."

"What happened to me?"

"Your near arrest—"

I finally turn back into the room. "I didn't get nearly arrested."

"I don't know what else to call it."

"It was a misunderstanding, that's all."

The great libertarian grins. "Oh, right, the kind of misunderstanding where they come within an inch of beating you to death."

"Nobody beat me," I say sharply, suddenly worried about what rumors my old friend might be spreading, for Dana, as she likes to say, can be trusted absolutely to repeat what you tell her to no more people than you have told.

"The guys who were chasing you did."

"True."

"Well, Misha, that's what I wanted to talk to you about." Still in constant motion, her arms swinging as though for balance. I wonder if she is ever tranquil. "The guys who were chasing you."

"What about them?"

"Well, they stole the chess book, right?"

"Uh, right." I have not told her it rematerialized. Nevertheless, I have told Dana more of the story than I have told anyone else, maybe because Dana, unlike my other acquaintances, keeps asking me to.

"And do you see why?" She is standing next to me at the window now, looking out across the campus as students trudge raggedly through the cold rain. She is smiling. Dear Dana Worth loves this job.

I turn to watch the scene with her. I have guessed the answer; has she? "You tell me."

"Because, Misha, darling, they thought it was what they were looking for."

"Huh?"

"My, but we're slow today, aren't we? Number one, you said they were following you. Number two, you said they knew your name." Dana is a great one for making lists, usually on the spur of the moment. "Number three, they asked you what was in the package. And, number four, they beat you up and made off with the book."

"Right."

"So, why that particular night? Of all the nights they could have gone after you, why did they pick that one?"

"I don't know."

"Because you did something, or said something, that made them think that this was it, this was the real thing." She weaves her head like a boxer, pleased with her own deduction. "So all you have to do is figure out what you did to set them off."

But I already know what I did. I went to the chess club. The men who followed me must have worked for somebody who, like the late Colin Scott, knew what was in the Judge's letter. Somebody who figured out what Excelsior meant, which means somebody who knew my father was a chess problemist. Somebody who might have said, *If he ever goes near anyplace having to do with chess, keep a particularly close eye on him. If he brings anything out, get it from him, any way you can.* Somebody . . . somebody . . .

"What about Jack Ziegler's promise that nobody would hurt me?"

"Somebody hasn't heard the news," she says.

I frown. I have not told her about the phone call at two-fifty-one. I have not, yet, told anybody. Sooner or later, I will have to. As soon as I figure out who around the building could be keeping tabs on me. It occurs to me, for a worrisome moment, that it could be Dear Dana herself.

"Penny for your thoughts," she murmurs.

"I'm compiling an enemies list," I answer.

"Oh, Misha, don't say that. It sounds positively Nixonian."

"Doesn't it, though?" I wink at her. "Nixon was my father's hero."

"Nobody's perfect. Except Lemaster Carlyle." Dana chuckles. She has used this line before. But I find it less funny than in the past.

"Speaking of Lem," I hear myself asking, "has he seemed . . . a little *strange* lately?"

"He's always strange."

"No, I mean . . . I don't know, I've been finding him . . . distant."

"He's always distant."

"What I'm saying is, he is less friendly. Like he's trying to avoid me."

"Gee, I can't think why. He only wants to be dean."

I surrender, quite frustrated. In her teasingly direct way, Dana is reminding me that I am nobody's favorite around the law school just now, except maybe hers. It hurts to hear it, but she might be right about Lem. Then another thought strikes me. Dana the gossip knows everything, surely. "By the way, and I know it isn't any of my business, but have you heard any rumors about, um, some kind of relationship between Lionel Eldridge and Heather Hadley?"

Dear Dana seems startled. Then a slow, almost feline smile softens her face. "No, I seem to have missed that one. But that would be so delicious! I really must ask around."

There's more than one way to start a rumor, I tell myself sourly.

(11)

LEAVING DANA'S OFFICE, I run into Theophilus Mountain, who is unlocking his door with the same laborious attention he gives to driving, walking, and teaching, none of which he any longer does particularly well. Under his arm are an ancient binder and a red-and-black casebook, so he has just returned from class. I greet him as he finally manages to work the latch.

The aging Theo swivels stiffly, like a mannikin on a stand, smiling benignly.

"Well, hello, Talcott."

"Hi, Theo. Do you have a minute?"

He frowns as though this is a difficult question. "I suppose I might," he concedes, his hand still on the doorknob. At eighty-two, Theo is not what he was in my father's student days, or even in mine. A few days ago, he finally got around to offering his condolences on the Judge's passing, oddly late, but he has never quite been subject to the expectations of others. He is the only survivor among the famous Mountain brothers, the other two being Pericles, who taught at UCLA, and Herodotus, who taught at Columbia. They were, once upon a time, considered the three great constitutional scholars of the age. Perry died a couple of decades go, Hero just last year. All three were among the century's celebrated liberals, and Theo tends the flame. In his constitutional law class, Theo covers few cases decided after 1981, "when that son of a bitch Reagan took over and everything went to hell." He teaches his bewildered students not what the law is, or even what it should be, but what he wishes it still were. A few years ago, he wrote to a Supreme Court Justice who was once his student, accusing him of "idiotic reasoning in service of your immoral reactionary campaign." He then released the letter to the press, an act which earned him an invective-filled appearance on *Larry King Live.* Theo has always been willing to say anything to anybody. And so he does to me now: "You look terrible. Did the police do that to you?"

"Of course not."

"I heard you were almost arrested."

I wonder whether I will be stuck with the story for the remainder of my career. "No, Theo, I was not almost arrested. It was just a misunderstanding."

"Oh." Spoken dubiously.

"Theo, I wanted to ask you about my father."

"What about your father?"

I hesitate as a couple of students pass us, deep in argument over what Hegel would have said about some rule of the Securities and Exchange Commission. When they are out of earshot, I continue. "You knew him when he was a student. And after."

Theo nods, still standing in the doorway. "We were pretty good friends, till he went off the deep end. Excuse me."

"By the deep end, you mean . . ."

"After his hearings." He waves a vague hand. "Lots of people in this building signed petitions against his confirmation, Talcott. Well, you know that. You weren't here at the time, but you remember."

"I was a student, Theo, so I remember."

"Well, also remember that I didn't sign." Splaying his hand on his chest. His shirt, as usual, seems incompletely laundered. "I didn't agree with him about very much, but we were friends. Like I said, until he went off the deep end."

"Well, what I'm wondering is . . . after the two of you weren't close any more . . . if, uh, if there's anybody here on the faculty my father would have been close to. Somebody he would have trusted." I pause. It is so typical of my family that I must ask an outsider who my father's friends were on the very faculty where I teach. "Somebody he might have trusted with confidences."

Theo's disordered beard splits in a grin. "Well, Stuart Land is certainly a Reaganite prick."

Is this the non sequitur it seems? Maybe not. "So he trusted Stuart, you're saying."

"I don't know if your father even knew Stuart, but it wouldn't surprise me. All those neo-cons stick together. Excuse me." He tips his head back momentarily and frowns, gazing at the ceiling. "Who else? I guess he must have known Lynda Wyatt, from all his alumni work. And I think he knew Amy Hefferman pretty well. Amy was his classmate."

I shake my head. Poor Amy, the much-beloved Princess of Procedure. I have almost forgotten that she and my father were in law school together. Over the years, my father seemed never to tire of cruel jokes at her expense, all of them about her intellect. *The second-best third-rate mind in the building*, he would say of her student days, shaking his head in wonder that she was invited back to teach. His evaluation of her work on the faculty was little different, bordering at times on misogyny. *Dizzy*, he would call her writing, or *not serious*. As so often, the Judge was frightfully unfair; but whatever devils drove him to dismiss Amy Hefferman would also prevent him from trusting her with whatever elaborate secrets he wanted me to uncover. "Not Amy," I say sadly.

Theo squints. He is not as quick as he was, but he is no fool. "Not Amy what? Are you up to something, Talcott?" He does not sound disapproving. If I am up to something, he probably wants in on it. He leans close, his breath hideous, and whispers, "Is it about Stuart? Is he in some kind of trouble?"

"Uh, not that I know of."

"Too bad." Theo finally opens his door and steps into his office, which, although long and high-ceilinged, is so thick with huge piles of books and papers that a trip inside can be like a spelunking expedition. He does not invite me to follow. "I haven't really been keeping close track of your father, Talcott. Not since . . ."

"He went off the deep end," I finish for him.

"Oh, so you noticed too?" Theo's tone is somber. "He was a good man, your father. Not my kind of politics, but a good man. Until your sister died. Then it all went downhill."

"Wait a minute, Theo. Wait. After my sister died?"

"Right."

"But before you said he went off the deep end after the hearings."

Theo blinks. Has he forgotten what he said? Is he confused or clever? "Well, I don't know exactly when it happened, but he did go off the deep end." Then his eyes brighten once more. "But if it's not Stuart you're looking for, then I guess you must be looking for Lynda."

"Do you seriously think my father would have trusted Lynda Wyatt?" Even as I say the words, it occurs to me that Lynda knew I was going to be at Shirley's party. Could she have noticed, from her office window, that I was headed for the soup kitchen all those weeks ago? Could she have known I was planning to go to the chess club last Thursday? I cannot see how, but I cannot see a lot of things that are true, like why Kimmer married me.

"More than he would have trusted me, I'll tell you that." A grin makes its way to the surface of his thick white beard, and he is laughing aloud by the time he closes the door in my face.

(111)

BACK IN MY OFFICE, I field a telephone call from a woman named Valerie Bing, who was two years behind Kimmer and myself in law school and now practices with a firm in Washington. She and Kimmer grew up a few blocks apart and have remained friends as well as professional colleagues, handling a number of matters together. Valerie says that the FBI has been in to talk to her as part of the background check. No doubt the investigators swore her to silence, but Valerie, for whom gossip is nutrition, gives me a line-by-line account of the interview. No questions about *the arrangements*, but they did ask Valerie if she ever heard my wife mention Jack Ziegler, a fact I immediately decide not to pass on to Kimmer.

As soon as I hang up, the phone rings again, and I find myself fending off a representative of the agency that used to book the Judge's speaking tours. If I will keep some of his dates with the Rightpacs, it seems, the agency will guarantee me half my father's fee. I glare at the telephone for a moment, then tell him I am not interested. He interrupts to point out that my father received forty thousand dollars per engagement, sometimes more. I am stunned. Like so many boomers, Kimmer and I live beyond our means, chronically in debt, our credit cards maxed out, our payments late. Twenty thousand dollars may be an afternoon's income for Howard Denton, Mariah's investment banker-husband, but it is all the money in the world to me. The man keeps talking. He says there could be television appearances, a book contract, the works.

All I would have to do is say the things my father would have said.

I'm afraid I'm not available just now for a meretricious relationship, I want to tell him, but I settle instead for a simple "No, thank you."

He says he might be able to get me three-fourths of my father's fee.

I repeat my refusal.

But he will not give up. He says I wouldn't really need to speak for my father. I could talk about whatever I wanted, express any views I wanted. A couple of his clients, he adds, are very excited at the thought of having me come. All they ask is a lecture to a small group, a dinner with people who are great fans of my father, some reminiscences about the Judge, insights into his thinking. Just two or three dates, he murmurs.

At twenty to thirty thousand dollars apiece.

A debilitating worm of temptation is inching through me, thrilling and warm, as I think again of our debts. Then I remember what Morris Young said the other night about Satan, and I call a halt, rather rudely, to the conversation. "My *no* means *no*," I tell him.

He says he will try me again in a month or two.

An hour later, Just Alma finally calls me back. She is still in the islands, whatever that means. I have forgotten why I called her in the first place, so I ask her how she is enjoying herself instead. She complains that the men can't keep up with her. I imagine this is true.

Then I remember and say: "Alma? Do you remember when we were down at Shepard Street? Right after the funeral?"

Over the scratchy line, she acknowledges that she does.

"You told me people would . . . come after me. Remember?"

"Your daddy told me. He said folks always came after the head of the Garland family."

"Did he say . . . which folks?"

"Sure. The white folks," she says at once, and my theory goes to pieces. I thought perhaps the Judge had shared with Just Alma a piece of his secret. Instead, more ramblings of his tortured mind in which everything that happened to him was somebody else's fault.

"I see."

Alma is not finished. "The way the white folks went after Derek."

"Derek as in his brother? The Communist?"

"You know some other Derek? Lemme tell you something, Talcott. Your daddy, he never liked his brother, not till after he was dead. Even when they were kids, he never liked him. Never."

"I know, Alma." I am trying to bring the conversation to an end, but Alma rides right over me.

"Main thing was, Talcott, your daddy thought Derek complained too much about the white folks. Well, turned out the white folks got your daddy too. So he started to think maybe Derek had a point. Used to say he wished old Derek was still around, so he could tell him how sorry he was."

"My father said he was sorry?" I try, and fail, to recall a single instance of the Judge's ever apologizing. "What was he sorry about?"

"He was sorry they split up. Said everything went bad after that."

"Everything like what?"

"Goodness, Talcott, *I* don't know. He just said he was sorry. Because of what the white folks did. I guess maybe he just missed his brother."

A question occurs to me. "Alma? When my father talked about splitting up with his brother—was there something particular he meant?"

"I guess when your daddy decided to be a judge and all that. He kind of had to leave all the baggage behind."

"Derek was baggage?"

"Your daddy just missed him, Talcott, that's all."

This is getting me nowhere. I have to go. Fortunately, so does Alma. We talk about seeing each other over the summer, but we won't.

NIGHT ON HOBBY ROAD. Once more I keep my lonely vigil from the front window. I do not know what I am looking for. Around eleven, I imagine that I see a man across the street in the darkness, watching the house, a very tall man who could be black, although the shadows make it hard to tell: Foreman? Perhaps a hallucination, because, when I look again, he is gone. Half an hour later, a pickup truck jolts down the street, and I fantasize a detailed story of surveillance, alternating vehicles, legions of watchers.

Silly, of course, but I really did get beaten up a few nights ago, and somebody really did call and tell me not to worry, that everything was taken care of.

So stop worrying!

I have tried to talk to Kimmer about what has been happening, but she still refuses to listen beyond wanting to make sure I really believe we are all safe. I cannot seem to breach the wall that has arisen between us. It is as though, by being assaulted, I have become hard evidence of what my wife, still hoping for judicial office, prefers to pretend is not true: that something is going on, and that dropping it, letting it die, is no longer an option.

I shake my head. I log on to the Internet Chess Club and play four quick games with somebody from Denmark, losing three. And still I have the sense, with me now for weeks, that my efforts to reason my way through are like chewing on cotton: I chomp and chomp and chomp, but I make no progress.

Sleep is suddenly very attractive.

I hurry upstairs and look in on Bentley, whose bedroom is decorated principally with various Disneyesque images of Hercules, who was, it seems, a smiling blond Aryan with the world's largest teeth. *Herkes* is our son's word for his favorite hero. I adjust his Herkes blankets by the light of the streetlamp, check his Herkes nightlight, kiss his warm forehead, and then head down the hall to join my slumbering wife in the master bedroom at the back of the house. I undress in the bathroom, remembering with some pain the days when Kimmer and I used to leave each other little notes, and sometimes a flower, atop the vanity; WAKE ME, we would write in amorous invitation. I do not remember when we stopped, but I do know that Kimmer ignored my notes for several weeks before I realized that she wasn't leaving them any more. I wonder whether my father, in his last years, had anybody to leave him a flower or a note at bedtime, and it occurs to me that I know nothing of his romantic life, if he even had one after my mother died. Alma implied that the Judge was lonely, and, looking back, I can see that he probably was. Now and then he would show up at an important dinner or theater opening, some famous conservative woman on his arm, invariably a citizen of the paler nation, but he always managed to convey the impression that these were mutually useful escortings, nothing romantic or sexual. I am aware of no girlfriend: if he had one, he kept her well hidden.

I decide that I do not want to know.

The notes: nowadays, Kimmer leaves on my pillow only articles torn from popular magazines, offering assistance in dealing with the death of a loved one, for she believes I have grieved insufficiently, or perhaps incorrectly. There is no serious scientific evidence that grieving in fact possesses the famous five stages, but an entire industry of counselors makes a fortune insisting that it is so.

"Go to bed," I remind myself, lest I forget why I came upstairs.

I glance out the bathroom window into the yard. All seems to be at peace. At last I return to the bedroom and crawl between the sheets. *I am so, so sorry*, I whisper to my sleeping wife, but only in my mind. *I didn't mean it to go this way*. I lie still, I say my prayers, and then I gaze at the ceiling in the darkness, sensing more than feeling my wife a few feet away, not daring to reach out to her for the comfort I crave to give, and to get. My mind refuses to settle into sleep, still besieging itself with all the guilt I can heap on my own head, which is quite a bit. I turn toward Kimmer again. *Where did you go for three hours this afternoon?* I ask her in my mind: for she was not at her office and did not answer her cell phone. It has happened before. It will happen again. *How did we get here, darling?*

I try another position, but sleep refuses to come, and the answers I crave remain as elusive as ever. I am doing little work. My reputation is crumbling around me. I am becoming known as the mad law professor who skips classes, makes nutty accusations, and gets beaten up in the middle of the Quad.

And no human being, certainly no wife, to comfort me in my depression and distress.

Ah, Kimmer, Kimmer! Why do you do . . . what you do? Again I remember, uneasily, our relationship in its youth, when opening my eyes each morning to Kimmer's smiling face was all I asked of the world. I hear the rumbling of a train passing, but it is only the blood pounding in my head. I open my eyes, but my wife's face is hidden. The bed is suddenly too vast, the distance from Kimmer too great. I turn onto one side, then the other, then back again, as my wife rolls over and mumbles something unintelligible. I wish I could believe she was telling me, in her half-sleep, that she loves me. I wish I dared reach out to her for comfort. I wish I knew why I have the sense that I have been played for a fool by forces larger than myself.

You and your family are perfectly safe.

Well, he said nothing about humiliation or the ruin of my career.

Longing for my wife's unyielding body, I know the despair of the stateless refugee, praying that he might, against all expectations, reach once more his war-torn home, a cold, unfriendly territory from which he has been excluded. But out there in the darkness, I sense the forbidding barricades I cannot see. When one of my feet touches one of hers, Kimmer stirs and shifts her leg away, even in sleep rejecting my presence. For a long moment, I consider waking her, to argue my way back to my homeland, or perhaps to beg. Instead, I turn away from the border of the lush and sensuous land that once welcomed me, close my eyes, and hope not to dream.

CHAPTER 31

BROWN WEEK

(1)

"THAT'S AN INTERESTING STORY," says John Brown.

"It's not a *story*."

"It's still interesting." He sets himself in the middle of the driveway, shoots the basketball, misses badly. I grab the rebound, dribble to the edge of the grass, try a jumper.

Swish. I point my finger at him. He laughs and slaps it away, then high-fives me.

It is Friday afternoon, three days after Christmas, although Kimmer sometimes insists on celebrating Kwanzaa, too. Two nights ago it snowed three inches, but the unpredictable Elm Harbor weather has once again turned fair, warm enough for this Saturday barbecue. The slushy remainder of the storm splashes and runs under our feet. Not quite a white Christmas, but we didn't miss it by much.

The Christmases of my childhood were grand and joyous affairs, the Shepard Street house decorated by my mother with freshly cut garlands and poinsettias and mistletoe, a tree of intimidating size glowing in the two-story foyer, the downstairs full of boisterous relatives and friends, with more reciprocal visits to come in the days to follow. We children dozed through midnight mass at Trinity and St. Michael and rose early the next morning to find the gigantic tree surrounded, as if through wizardry, by a small mountain of gifts. Even though we knew the greater part of the festively wrapped packages would turn out to hold clothing and books, we always imagined them full of beautiful toys, which some of them were. And the Judge—in those early days, merely Daddy—would sit in his favorite armchair in slippers and robe, the pipe he smoked back then held fast between his teeth, relishing our love and gratitude, rubbing our backs as we hugged his strong legs.

At Number 41 Hobby Road, Christmas has always been a more staid affair, as Kimmer and I exchange token gifts in front of the small artificial tree on which my practical wife insists, pointing to the time, trouble, and what she calls the risk—*Water and electricity together? Forget it!*—of the real thing. With Bentley, at three years and nine months, old enough to appreciate what is going on (although it is Santa, not Jesus, he seems to appreciate), Kimmer and I both tried to be a little more upbeat this year. Wrapping our son's gifts together on Christmas Eve was actually a joy, and, in bed later on, as we lay awake listening to the wind, my wife kissed my cheek and told me she is glad we are still together. I told her I am glad, too, which is the truth. I have worked hard over the past couple of weeks to keep my promise to Morris Young by treating my wife to love rather than suspicion, and she has responded with a lighter, happier mood. I have the unexpected but reassuring sense that whatever man she was involved with she has put behind her, perhaps as a New Year's resolution, or even a Christmas gift to her husband. At the same time, belowdecks, I have tried to think of a way to move forward on cleaning up the mess into which the Judge has drawn me.

Telling John Brown a little of what has been going on, as I promised last month I would, seems to me a sensible start.

"So, what do you think I should do?" I ask John as I shoot again. The ball clangs off the rim and crashes down on his dark blue Town & Country minivan. He scoops up the ball before it has the chance to knock over my rusty but trusty grill, where orange flames frolic over freshly lighted charcoal.

"Nothing. Leave it to the FBI. There's nothing to be done. Interesting shot." As laconic as always. John does not believe in using two words when one will do, and will never substitute three syllables when two are sufficient. We have been shooting hoops so that we can talk without fear of interruption. John has been urging me to tell the authorities about everything, but I have not committed myself to anything. "You need an expert, Misha. And they're the experts."

I nod thoughtfully. I am not the sort of man who easily befriends other men, but my relationship with John has been an oddly enduring thing. I have known him and his wife, Janice, since we were all college freshmen together, Janice the most sought-after among the black women in the class, John easily the most studious of the black men. Today John is an electrical engineer, which is what he always planned, and Janice is a full-time mother, which is what she always wanted. Now that he is at Ohio State, they live in Columbus, we see them only once or twice a year, usually just after classes end for the holiday. They are wonderful people. Kimmer likes them, too: *Even though you brought them into the marriage*, she likes to quip.

"I don't know," I say finally, the Hamlet of Hobby Road.

John's eyebrows go up. "What, you don't trust the FBI?" Another shot. Bumps around the rim, then drops through, bounces on the pavement, and rolls into the wet snow that still obscures most of the lawn.

"What if the FBI is part of it?" asks Mariah sharply from behind us, taking us by surprise. "How can we leave it to the FBI?"

I smile uneasily. I do not know how long my sister has been listening. I have not told her about the pawn or the note, both of which I have just finished disclosing to John. He nods slightly: he will keep his mouth shut.

John turns to Mariah. "You gotta trust somebody," he says, which is likely a code for: *Once you go down that road, you might as well move to one of those survivalist compounds in Montana.* John possesses a respect for authority that I wish I still shared, but the events of the past few weeks have shaken my faith in many human institutions.

I toss the basketball to my sister: "Come on, kiddo, take a shot."

She catches it smoothly and throws it back hard enough to wind me at this close distance.

"No, thanks."

"You used to love to play."

"I used to love a lot of things."

I glance over at John, who has developed a sudden interest in the little paper sticker glued to the side of the post holding the hoop, filled with small-print warnings in the fruitless hope that the manufacturer will be protected from liability in the event that some child manages to topple the thing over. John once protected the university hospital from possible liability too: when Kimmer and Bentley both almost died, John and Janice flew out at once. Janice held me while I cried, but it was John who talked me around, both as a scientist and as a Christian, to the view that I should be grateful to the doctors for saving my family, not angry that they almost didn't.

"Come on, Mariah," I say softly, extending a hand. "Don't be down."

"Don't be down," she repeats. "Like there's nothing to be down about."

I manage not to groan. In her current mood, Mariah will ruin everything.

John and Janice and their children are in Elm Harbor for our regular time together, always during the quiet week before the New Year dawns, sometimes out in Ohio, usually here. Kimmer and I celebrated, if that is the word, our ninth anniversary yesterday; John and Janice, who have been married seven years longer, will celebrate theirs tomorrow; the nearly common wedding dates are what got the tradition started five or six years ago. Our annual get-together tends to be a delightfully rambunctious affair, but this time it is quite solemn, acknowledging not only the death of my father but also the mood in my household, for, if Kimmer is no longer sneaking out, she is not precisely loving her husband either. The Browns believe that every marriage can be as perfect as theirs and are often uncomfortable in the presence of living refutation of their theory; but they are good friends and refuse to abandon the dream that our marriage is reparable.

My sister is a last-minute addition to Brown Week, as we like to call these occasions. Kimmer was surprisingly gentle in responding to the news that Mariah would be joining us, but it was the gentleness we reserve for the mentally ill. *Of course, Misha, she is your sister after all,* she murmured, patting my hand. *I understand, I do*—contriving, through this emphasis, to make clear that she does not. I am not sure I do either. The truth is that I would rather not have Mariah visiting during Brown Week, even if just for the day. (She is alone, having left her brood in Darien with the au pair. Howard, I believe, is in Tokyo.) Her fidgety presence is bound to wreck the comfortable chemistry of our two families, the Browns and the Madison-Garlands. I would rather have met Mariah at some other time, alone, but she refuses to discuss her news, whatever it is, on the telephone, perhaps afraid of a tap, and today turns out to be the earliest date on which we can make our calendars match.

Janice and Kimmer are in the kitchen, cooking and conspiring and snubbing Mariah. John and I are splitting our time between the driveway and the yard, fiddling with the grill on which we shortly plan to burn some expensive steaks, and, just now, listening with every appearance of credulity to Mariah's ramblings. Over by the high hedge wall separating our property from the Felsenfelds', Bentley is playing happily with John's younger daughter, Faith, three years older than he, and together they are doing something clever and mysterious with Faith's Nigerian Barbie and her hot-pink Barbie sports car, which is missing a wheel. Faith's sister, Constance, has reached the age of nine, and is therefore above such pursuits; the last time I saw her, she was at the kitchen table, listlessly playing Boggle on her mother's laptop. She clamors for the new version of Riven, which everybody else at school has, but her evangelical parents forbid it. Their oldest child, Luke, is fifteen, and he is somewhere in the house with his nose in an Agatha Christie novel.

"Sometimes the FBI is on the wrong side," Mariah insists. "I mean, look at what they did to Dr. King."

John and I exchange a glance. John is a small, tough man who grew up in a housing project in the state capital and scholarshipped his way to Elm Harbor. His dusky skin seems darker in the sinking light, but his eyes are bright and concerned.

"That's one part of what I wanted to talk to you about, Tal," my sister continues, walking between us so that we cannot continue the game until we have heard her out. She drove up today not in the Navigator, but in her Mercedes—hubby has his own—and is wearing a fancy brown tweed pantsuit with an Anne Klein air about it, probably the right attire for an autumn cocktail party in Darien, but not precisely what we tend to don for December backyard barbecues in Elm Harbor. I have no doubt that Kimmer is making this very point to Janice in the kitchen. "We need to decide what we're gonna do."

"About what, kiddo?" I ask gently.

"About the whole thing."

John takes another shot and misses. The rebound arches into my hands. I lift the ball as though to shoot, but Mariah takes the ball from me and tucks it under her arm, a parent correcting a child. No more basketball, she is signaling, until we have heard her out.

"You remember that Sally and I have been going through Daddy's papers, right? So let me tell you what we've found, and you'll see why we have to do something."

I almost interrupt, but I catch John's look and subside. He plainly wants her to get it all out, and I decide to follow his example. Like a good lawyer, John knows when to avoid leading questions and let the client ramble.

"Okay, shoot."

Tossing the basketball onto the snow-crusted grass, Mariah walks to her sparkling sea-green car and rummages in the front seat, pulling out a shiny brown briefcase, which she proceeds to set on the hood. "Wait a second," she adds, setting the combination and opening the lid. A locked briefcase, I register, half amused and half alarmed. I glance at the back yard, worrying about the coals. Mariah returns with several folders. As she shuffles through the files, I remember the black-and-white covered ledger where she used to record the evidence of conspiracy. I tease her about the volume of her discoveries in the attic outgrowing the book.

"No, I just can't find it," she says, distracted.

"Maybe the bad guys stole it."

Taking the point seriously, Mariah points to the briefcase. "That's why I have a lock now." Before I can digest this, she is holding one of the folders out. "Look at this," she orders.

I take the folder, and John and I examine the neatly typed but fading label: DETECTIVE'S REPORT—ABIGAIL, it reads. I am suddenly excited. Except that the folder is empty.

"Where's the report?" I ask.

"That's what I'm trying to tell you, Tal. It isn't there. Doesn't that strike you as a little weird?"

"A little." But I am thinking that there are about two million reasons the report could be missing, one of them being that Mariah took it herself, or even created the empty folder as a prop for her fantasy.

On the other hand, that scrapbook did disappear, and an enchanted pawn made its way from the heart of the Gold Coast to an Elm Harbor soup kitchen, and a book that was stolen by the men who beat me up rematerialized on the seat of my car. So lots of things are possible.

"Then I remembered. When Daddy got the report from the detective, he turned it over to the police. You remember? Hoping they would do something."

I do remember, with fresh pain. The Judge was so pleased with himself: hiring a private investigator, producing new leads. He had engaged somebody fancy, he assured us, from out in Potomac, even in those days an exclusive little town. Somebody, said the Judge, who was highly recommended and very expensive. He seemed proud to be paying so much.

"Villard," I murmur. "That was his name, wasn't it? Something-or-other Villard."

"That's right." Mariah smiles. "Jonathan Villard." I shake my head, for I was half hoping she would correct me, telling me the PI's name was really Scott. But my memory has no trouble supplying the rest of the story. When the Judge received the report, he came out of his funk, told the family that he was sure we would soon see the killer punished. That was what he always said, *the killer.* And then he settled back to wait. And wait. And wait. As despair settled in once more.

"The police never followed up his leads," I say softly, as much to myself as to John or my sister. I am far behind her, still wondering what really happened to her ledger. First the scrapbook vanishes, then the ledger. A chilly breeze stirs the hedges. "Or, if they did, they never found anything."

"Right," says Mariah, congratulating a slow pupil on finally getting it. "But they had a copy of the report. So I called up Uncle Mal and talked to that woman, Meadows. I asked her if she could get a copy from the police files. She said it might take a while, because they would have to go look in the archives or something. Then she called me back a few days ago, and, guess what? The police don't have a copy of the report either."

"Curiouser and curiouser," I admit. John might be a statue, for all his contribution to the conversation. Then a thought strikes me. "But I'll bet you can get a copy from Villard himself. He has to be around somewhere."

Mariah seems almost gleeful. "I guess all you lawyers think alike. Meadows tried that, Tal, and—guess what?—Villard died of colon cancer fifteen years ago."

The words escape me before I can think: "Are you sure?"

"Of course I'm sure, Tal, I'm not stupid. Meadows even got a copy of his medical records. He really was sick, and he really is dead."

"Oh." I am a bit deflated: until the cancer news, I was still ready to bet that Villard was another alias of Colin Scott. Then I brighten: "But even if he's dead, his investigative files have to be somewhere. . . ."

"I'm sure they do, but nobody knows where. That's my point. Now, look at this," Mariah continues, like a lawyer building a case, or a magician pleasing a crowd. From another folder, she draws a couple of pages torn from a yellow legal pad. I immediately recognize my father's cramped handwriting. She handles the papers carefully, as though worried they might ignite. "This is all I can find about the report," she explains.

I scan the pages, which are creased as though folded several times.

The ink is old and smeary; *V'S REPORT* is scribbled at the top, followed by a column of seemingly random notations: *Virginia plate? . . . Must be front-end damage, V checked shops already . . . V says police work shoddy re paint etc . . . No ID driver, no ID passenger . . .* I stop, go back, look at the last line again.

"Passenger?" I ask.

Mariah nods. "There was somebody else in the car that killed Abby. Interesting, huh?"

"The Judge never mentioned it," I say distantly, remembering something else. "And neither did Mom."

Mariah is excited now. "The notes were folded up in the back of one of his chess books. I guess whoever took the report didn't know that." I am about to ask which book, wondering about secret messages, but Mariah is already dealing the next card. "And look at this." A manila envelope emerges from her briefcase. She hands it over. I open the flap and pull out a sheaf of check registers. A quick glance confirms what I have already guessed: they are from the period when the private detective was working on the case. "Look at it," she instructs me.

"And what exactly am I looking for?" I ask as John watches in interested silence.

"The name Villard! Daddy said he was expensive, right?"

"Uh, right. Yes." Said it with pride: nothing but the best to track down Abby's killer, he was suggesting.

"Right. Now, look at the list of checks." I look, still not sure where this is going. "Tal, these are all the checks Daddy wrote for the four years after Abby died. There is not a single check written to anybody named Villard, and there is not a single check written to anything that sounds like a detective agency."

"So he was careless. He didn't record the check."

"I have all the canceled checks, Tal. And you know how Daddy was. Everything is perfectly organized. Just to make sure, I did the math. There isn't a single one missing."

I have a disturbing vision of Mariah hunched over a calculator in the attic, punching in numbers, obsessively checking the Judge's subtraction as her kids run all over the house and Sally does . . . well, whatever Sally does when they are together.

"So he paid cash." Yet this seems odd to me as well.

"No," says Mariah, flourishing another folder. She has lost none of her investigative skill. "This is a list of every single cash withdrawal

Daddy made from his accounts during those years, and not a one of them, Tal, not a one of them is enough to pay for anything more than groceries."

"His brokerage accounts—"

"Come on, Tal. He didn't *have* any brokerage accounts in those days. He didn't have enough money. That came later." After he left the bench, she means.

"So what are you saying? That there never was a detective?" I shake my head, trying to escape the mists of painful memory. John is looking on like a bystander at a car wreck, fascinated by the carnage but unable to help. "That Villard was . . . some kind of figment of the Judge's imagination?"

"No, Tal. Listen to me. Of course Villard was real. No, what I'm telling you is that *somebody else paid for the detective.* Don't you see? Either Daddy borrowed the money or—well, I don't know what. But the money came from somebody else. And if we find out who that somebody else is, we'll find out who killed Daddy."

I am not quite believing any of this, but not quite rejecting it either. Emotionally, I am in no fit state for rational judgments just now.

"And you think that the somebody was . . ." I leave the rest hanging, inviting the response we both know is coming.

"It was Jack Ziegler, Tal—who else? Come on. It had to be Uncle Jack. I was right the first time, Tal. Daddy was afraid of Uncle Jack. That's why he had the gun. But it didn't do him any good. Jack Ziegler killed him and took the report."

So the Mariahan conspiracy theory, as I suspected, has not changed. Yet it occurs to me that my sister might be on to something, whether or not she knows it. Because at the heart of her reconstruction is a simple truth that frightens me . . . frightens me because I know some facts that she does not.

"But wait a minute. I still don't see why Jack Ziegler would do it." I do, of course. I am objecting, probably, just to keep the conversation going.

"Yes, you do! There was something in the report he didn't want anybody to know, so he had to get the only copy. Why else would he have killed Daddy in the house?"

"Then why did he leave the empty folder?" I object.

"I don't know all of it! That's why I need your help!"

A thought strikes me. "That public call for an investigation you mentioned . . ."

"Somebody talked them out of it, Tal. Somebody got to them, don't you see? And Addison's useless," she adds, mysteriously, while I am still busily exulting over the fact that somebody talked them out of it. "You and I are the only ones left who care. So you and I have to prove what really happened."

"We don't have enough information."

"Exactly! That's why we need to work together! Oh, Tal, can't you see?" She turns to John Brown. "You understand, John. I know you do. Explain it to him."

"Well," John begins. "Maybe it would be better if . . ."

An interruption. The other two women, broad, fair Kimmer and dark, slender Janice, come outside with the steaks, all seasoned and ready for the grill. There is corn on the cob, wrapped in foil, and a small plate of sliced greens, which will also receive a light touch of flame. And two Cokes, because neither John nor I drink alcohol: John out of religious conviction, I out of simple fear, given my father's history. We dutifully exclaim over the food, which does look awfully good. There is some ritual teasing about how the men are so busy playing basketball that we do not yet have a decent fire going. Kimmer is still irritated at me about Mariah's presence, but with our friends around, she is being a good sport. Last night I told her finally about the call from the agency about my father's speaking dates; she was furious at their presumption, and I loved her more for it. *You're not your father, and they have no right to pretend you are!* I told her I had already said no, and she told me I did the right thing. If they ever call me back, I will say no again.

"You want me to put them on the grill?" Kimmer asks, hands on her hips in mock irritation.

"No, darling."

"Then you guys get to work." She swats my bottom playfully. Surprised, I tickle her. She grins and pushes me away. "Work!" she repeats.

"Mariah, we could use some help in the kitchen," adds Janice, to my sister's astonishment, for she has been feeling like a fifth wheel.

Mariah turns her sullen gaze toward me. "Just think about it," she says. Kimmer and Janice return to the house, Mariah sulking in their wake.

"Your sister's a trip," John murmurs as we walk back into the yard.

"Hmmm? Oh. I'm sorry about that." Taking a second or two to find my place in the conversation once more, because I am still a bit dazed to be on such good terms with my wife, even if it is just for show.

"Mariah has—well, she hasn't been herself since our father died. I want to thank you, you and Janice, for being so nice to her."

"Janice is nice to everybody." As though he himself is not.

"That's true."

"I don't know how she does it." He shakes his head, but there is pride in his voice: he loves his wife so, and she obviously loves him right back. I try to remember exactly how that sensation feels, only to decide I have never felt it. "Mariah could be right, though," John adds thoughtfully.

"Oh, come on. You don't think the autopsy results were faked."

"No, not about the autopsy. And not about your father being murdered." John shrugs. "But what I'm saying is, she could be right about the private detective. That somebody else paid him."

"You're not serious."

"You think he worked for free? Mariah said he was expensive."

"Hmmmph." My usual intelligent response.

John waits while I examine the steaks and lay them, one by one, on the long grill. He is wearing loose, clean blue jeans and a New York Athletic Club windbreaker over a white dress-shirt. His shoulders are remarkably broad for so short a man, but the start of a paunch is evidence that he no longer works out regularly.

"Add her story to yours, Misha." John balances on the balls of his feet, his hands behind his back, letting me do the work. "The combination is interesting."

"Hmmmph," I repeat, not wanting John to take Mariah seriously.

"Maybe the report is what the fake FBI guys were looking for." When I do not rise to this, John murmurs: "You haven't told her everything, have you?"

"No."

"She doesn't know about the note from your dad, right? Or the pawn?"

"No."

"She's your sister, Misha. You really should share that stuff."

I give him a look. "The way she's been acting?"

John is hardly interested. He is no longer looking at either me or the steaks, but instead is gazing off toward the trees beyond the fence marking the border of our property and the beginning of the two acres owned by the president of the First Bank of Elm Harbor. Can I be boring my friend? "John?"

"Oh, I'm sorry. I'm listening. Go on."

"You have to understand about Mariah. It isn't just this one thing. She, um, she has always been . . . excitable. She has always had a tendency to jump to conclusions. I mean, okay, she's smarter than I am, but she's not always, um, reasonable. She . . . I guess she's a little bit passionate, you know?"

"Yes." Absently. He continues to study the fence.

"I have this friend. Eddie Dozier. You remember Dana? Dana Worth? I've told you about her, right? Well, Eddie is her ex-husband. He's black, but he's pretty far to the right. Into all this anti-government stuff. Anyway, Dana told me the other day that Eddie and Mariah have been talking, that he's the one who convinced her that the autopsy results were faked. You know, those specks in the photo? I've tried to convince her not to talk to him any more, but she just—"

"Misha." Softly.

"—won't listen to anything I tell her. I don't know. I have to find some way to get her to back off, to stop all of this before it gets out of—"

"Misha!"

"What?" Annoyed that John, who never interrupts, has broken in.

"Misha, there's somebody in the woods. On the hill. Don't turn around."

From what seems a very great distance, I hear my voice, answering calmly with the Gospel according to Kimmer: "It's just my neighbor. I told you, the president of the bank lives over there—"

John's laugh is cold. "Not unless the president of the bank is tall and black. And, besides, he has a pair of binoculars. He's watching us." Pause. "It could be that Foreman guy."

I turn around at last. I cannot help myself.

"I don't see anybody," I whisper.

"He's gone. We must have spooked him."

(11)

JOHN BROWN is as level-headed a man as I know. He is not given to hallucinations. If he says somebody was there, somebody was there.

We warn our mystified wives that we have to go check something out. Then we leave the steaks and go into the woods. I suppose I should be worried—the watcher, if there was one, had to be Foreman—but if the late Mr. Scott turned out to be harmless, how dangerous can his sidekick be? Besides, being part of a team increases courage remarkably.

"Over here," John murmurs, pointing to the spot where he thinks the man he saw was standing, between two barren trees. But we find only a few tracks in the melting snow, neither one of us outdoorsman enough to know how long they have been there, or even where they lead, for they vanish quickly in the brambles. My old friend and I look at each other. He shakes his head and shrugs, the message clear. We are trespassing and cannot linger long.

"What do you think?" I ask.

"I think we missed him."

"I think so, too."

"But if he scares so easily, Misha, I don't think he's dangerous."

"Neither do I. I'd still like to know who he is." I do not want to remain up here. A neighbor could see two black men creeping through the woods and get the wrong idea, and I have already had my obligatory once-a-decade encounter with the law.

"You don't think it was that Foreman guy?"

I turn toward him. "You saw him. I didn't."

John frowns. He is disappointed in me. "I don't think you're telling me everything, Misha."

"I don't know what you think I'm leaving out."

His voice remains milder than mine. "You can't play games with your friends."

"I'm not," I snap. John shrugs. As we prepare to return to my property, we hear a car growl into life on the adjoining street, which runs parallel to Hobby Road. Racing over the slushy ground, we reach the sidewalk in time to see a powder-blue Porsche disappear into the distance. But this is the ritzy part of town, and it could belong to anybody.

Although the driver looks black, and we are the only black family on Hobby Hill.

"I think you should call somebody," says John.

"I'm going to sound silly," I sigh, thinking of Meadows's warning about the risk to my wife's potential nomination. But I know that on Monday I will make the call anyway, just to be on the safe side, and that Cassie Meadows, down in Washington, will roll her eyes and make another note in the conspiracy file.

I also know something else, which I do not share with my friend as we trudge back down the snowy, leaf-strewn hill. Hidden within Mariah's ramblings was a tiny nugget of hard information, a new and troubling fact over which she skipped too lightly because she was searching for an epic conspiracy to end our father's life.

I know who has read the missing report.

CHAPTER 32

A PIECE OF THE ANSWER

(1)

THE CLEAR, ICY WATERS lap at my sneakers as I sit on the sand, my arms encircling my knees, gazing out across the mists of Menemsha Bight to Vineyard Sound. The afternoon sun, hanging low in the sky, sparks bright golden triangles in the swells before me. Off to my left is a long jetty built of huge stones, a favorite spot for summer people who like to fish. On the right, the headland presses far out into the water, and a handful of homes, from this distance stolid, secluded, and spacious, dot the point. Their shingles are weathered to that wonderful New England gray-brown. A clutch of fishing boats bobs along the horizon, sailing in with the day's catch, their labor finally done. And somewhere out there is the spot where Colin Scott, whom I knew as Agent McDermott, went overboard.

The question is who pushed him, for I no longer believe that he fell. If I ever did.

After John and I chased Foreman through the woods, I made my decision. I waited for the Browns to depart and then, on the first workday of the new year, I picked up the telephone and fought my way through Cassie Meadows and various secretaries until I finally reached Mallory Corcoran. I told him about the chess book being taken and returned. I told him about the pawn being delivered to the soup kitchen. And I asked him point-blank if he knew anything about these matters.

He asked a perfect lawyer's question: *Why do you say "these matters"? Are you telling me you think they're related somehow?* Not an answer, just a question.

And I knew I couldn't trust him any more. Bizarre. I trust an unidentified voice on the phone at two-fifty-one in the morning that assures me there is no more danger, but not my father's law partner, who sat behind him in the hearing room for two days when things began to go sour, then gave him a job and a healthy stipend after he left the bench.

So, why am I back here? Goodness knows, my trips are stretching our budget. Worrying about money again, I did not, after all, say no to the man from my father's speakers' bureau when, persistent as ever, he called back much sooner than he had promised. I did not say yes, either, but I allowed him to fill my head once more with the beguiling vision of earning close to a hundred thousand dollars for three days' work. Plus first-class air travel, he added.

I told him I would think about it.

I creak to my feet and shuffle down to the water, yearning for the delicious shock of cold spray on my face. I have been on this pebbly beach for a little over an hour, walking, sitting, praying, thinking, skipping stones, but mostly worrying the facts around in my mind. I have spotted a couple of beachcombers, year-round people, but have stayed clear of them. I need to think—and to work up my courage.

The truth is, I am not quite sure what I am doing back on the Vineyard. I only know that I woke very early on Thursday quite clear in the conviction that I had to return, even if only for one day. Kimmer, already up, was sitting at the kitchen table in a long tee shirt and nothing else, working on a brief. Standing in the arched doorway, I watched her strong body move under the loose white cotton. I allowed myself ten or twenty seconds of fantasy, then crept up behind her and kissed her on the back of the head. Kimmer pushed her glasses up on her nose and smiled but did not offer her lips. I sat down next to her and took her hand and told her I had to go. She did not seem sad. She did not throw a tantrum. She did not even argue. She just nodded solemnly and asked when.

Today, I told her. This afternoon.

"You'll miss the Citywide Lamentation," Kimmer deadpanned— this being our shared slang for an interfaith service held on the first Sunday in January, where the leaders of the Elm Harbor community come together and pray to be reconciled across the divisions of race and sex and class and religion and sexual orientation and nationality and language-spoken-at-home and disability and educational level and marital status and neighborhood-of-residence and whatever else is popular this week. Recently the organizers have tossed in "institutional affiliation"—evidently a reference to the widespread belief in the community that university types look down their (our) noses at everybody else. Kimmer goes because everybody who is anybody in town goes, including a good chunk of the faculty, and several of her partners at Newhall & Vann; she goes, in short, for the networking. I go because Kimmer does.

"Well, that's true—"

Kimmer shushed me. She stood up and spread her arms, at first, I thought happily, for a hug. But then she closed her eyes and turned her palms toward me, splaying her fingers wide, and leaned her head back and intoned solemnly: "May Whoever or Whatever might have been involved in our creation . . ."—an eerily precise imitation of last year's inclusive yet surely blasphemous invocation by the new university chaplain, who came to us from a West Coast college where her studied caution on the question of God's actual existence apparently went over somewhat better than it does here.

Then my wife's somber look vanished and she broke into giggles. I laughed too, and, for a silly moment, it was old times. Kimmer stepped into my arms and actually hugged me, quite hard, and kissed the corner of my mouth and told me she understood what was driving me, and if I had to go, I had to go. Usually when my wife kisses me with softly open lips, I get a little goofy, but this time I bristled, for Kimmer was sweetly affirming, the way we are with the mentally ill. She believes only in my compulsion, not in my version of the facts.

I went upstairs to pack, leaving a still-twittering Kimmer down in the kitchen.

Bentley nodded gravely when I told him Daddy was going away for a day or two, and he offered only one piece of parting advice just before I went out the door: "Dare you," he whispered.

I'm trying, son.

(11)

EVENTUALLY, it is time to move. I walk along the single sandy street leading from the beach to the quiet village of Menemsha, peeking behind every shuttered restaurant and fish store until I stumble across Manny's Menemsha Marine, which turns out to be no more than a battered wooden shack, once painted white, a few dozen paces from the nearest dock. The two small windows are sealed. The sagging roof is made of tin. The building looks just about big enough to turn around in. No wires for telephone or electricity run anywhere near it. But Manny's is the place, according to the *Gazette*, where Colin Scott and his two friends rented their boat. I wonder why they chose it. It is quite indistinguishable from any number of other boat-rental operations scattered around the harbor; and every one of them, including Manny's, seems to feature a painfully hand-lettered black-and-white sign, prominently displayed across the door, reading CLOSED FOR THE SEASON.

Perhaps their choice was random, except that I do not envision Colin Scott doing anything at random.

I knock. The whole edifice shakes. I tug the ancient padlock, then walk completely around the shack twice, first clockwise, then counterclockwise, straining my eyes to peer into the single grimy window. I step back and put my gloved hands on my hips and try to figure out whether I actually have a plan. What did I think, that Manny himself would be here to welcome me with a broad smile of relief? *Yes, I've been waiting for somebody to ask me about that birthmark!* Well, he isn't—but if the rental service is closed for the season, how did Scott/McDermott and his friends get a boat? I turn awkwardly in a circle, trying to think what to do, and that is when I notice a skinny white man in his twenties, much in need of a shave, wearing old khakis and a heavy sweater against the January cold, watching me from the hard dirt path between the shack and the road. He carries a small backpack. I have no idea how long he has been standing there, and I experience, briefly, the secret fear of false arrest that every black male in America nurtures somewhere deep within, especially those who have nearly been falsely arrested: did he see me yanking on the lock?

"They're not there," the man says helpfully, and grins to show me his very bad teeth. It actually sounds a little more like *Theyah not theah.* As though he is as much Maine as Cape.

"Where's Manny?" I ask.

"Gone."

"When will he be back?"

"Oh, April. May." He starts to walk away.

"Wait!" I call, hurrying after him. "Wait a second, please."

He turns slowly back to look at me. He eyes my clothes. No smile this time. His dark green turtleneck sweater looks like a hand-me-down. His sneakers are bursting. I am wearing a fleece-lined jacket with the little Polo logo on it and designer jeans. I feel suddenly, weirdly out of place, and out of time, a black capitalist come to call on the white working class. Everything is upside down, as though all the nation's tortured racial history has undergone an inversion. The young man's gaze is disdainful. His colorless hair is pulled back in an unwashed clump. The dirt under his broken nails looks permanent, a proclamation to the world that he works for a living. I chafe under his scrutiny. I have earned what I possess, I have stolen no bread from his table, this fellow has no right to disapprove of me—yet I can think of nothing to say in my own defense.

"What?" he inquires.

"How long has Manny been gone?"

"He always goes away this time of year." *Of yeeah.* Answering a slightly different question, and wanting me to know it.

"Listen. I'm sorry." Not sure why I am apologizing, but it seems appropriate. "Uh, isn't this the place where, uh, that man who drowned back in November rented his boat?"

He makes me wait.

"You a reporter?"

"No."

"Cop?"

"No." I search for the words. Yankee reserve has always driven me nuts, but this man is ridiculous. "I wanted to talk to Manny because I saw the story in the paper, and I think . . . I think the man who drowned was somebody I knew."

"You could call him up." *Cahl im uh-upp.*

"Do you know his number?" I ask eagerly.

"Why would I know your friend's number?"

Okay, so I'm the village idiot. I thought he meant Manny. A pickup bounces past, some kind of maritime equipment jostling in the back, and the young man leaps nimbly out of its path. But I notice the start of a smile on his bronzed face and I realize he is putting me on.

A little.

"Look, I'm sorry. The man I think drowned . . . I didn't know him that well. He and I, uh, had some dealings. I just want to see if it's the same man. All I'm trying to find out is if there's any way to get in touch with Manny."

He scratches his arm, then returns us to start: "Manny's gone."

"Gone? You mean off-Island?"

"Florida, I think."

"Do you know where in Florida?"

"Nope."

For a few seconds, we listen together to the calling gulls.

"Would anybody around here know where?"

"Have to ask them, I guess."

"Any idea who I should ask?"

"No."

Like pulling teeth. From a pit bull. With no anesthetic.

And then I put together his reserve and his disdain and his likely belief in my wealth and the fact that he has not yet walked away and I realize what he is waiting for. Well, why not? I don't give my knowledge away for free either. As I reach inside my jacket for my wallet and examine the paltry sum inside, I feel his interest quicken. I have just over one hundred dollars in cash. I pull out three twenties, wondering how to explain it to Kimmer when she goes over our accounts this month, for she has lately become meticulous with money, trying to put aside enough to replace her luxurious BMW M5 with an even more luxurious Mercedes SL600, which is, she says, more appropriate to her position.

"Look," I say, fanning the bills so he can see them clearly, "this means a lot to me."

"Guess it does." He takes the cash at once. He does not seem offended, as I feared he might be. "You're a lawyer, right?"

"Sort of."

"Figured you were." *You wu-uh.* But at least he's on my side now. The bills have disappeared, although I never saw his hand move toward his pocket.

"When did Manny leave?" I ask.

"Three weeks ago. Maybe four. Right after all the ruckus."

"And you're sure he went to Florida?"

"That's where he said he was going."

He waits. There is something he expects me to ask him; he took the money so fast because he knew the value of what he was selling. I look over at Manny's shack, and at the others along the water, all of them closed, the boats grounded and covered with tarpaulins. A few gulls peck at the sand, searching for breakfast.

"Does he usually go to Florida this time of year?" I ask, just to keep punching.

"Don't know. Don't think so."

Okay, that wasn't the right question.

"Did you see the men who rented the boat?"

"Afraid not."

Okay, that wasn't it either. I let my eyes wander over Manny's tiny shack again. Maybe I'm wrong. Maybe he doesn't have any—

Wait.

. . . *all of them closed* . . .

I have it.

"Listen," I say, "was Manny's closed five weeks ago? When that man drowned?"

"Yep."

"I mean, it was closed when, um, when the man who died and his friends rented the boat?"

"Yep." I detect the faint smile again. We have finally arrived where my new friend expected to go from the moment he saw me peering in Manny's window.

"So—what happened? Did he open the shop for them specially?"

"The way I heard it, they paid him a lot of money. Drove up to his house—he lives down that way—oh, say around noon. Told him they needed one of his boats, promised to pay him a nice chunk of cash to open for them specially. And so he did."

"Why did they go to his house?"

"Because the shop was closed."

Oh, these Vineyarders!

"No, I mean, how did they know where he lived?"

"Oh. Well, the way I heard it, one of the fellers who rented the boat comes up every summer and rents from Manny."

Now this, at last, is something new.

"Do you know which one?"

"Way I heard it, 'twas the tall feller, looked sort of like you."

"Like me?"

"Sure, like you." Now the smile is wide. "Black feller."

(111)

THE DRIVE FROM MENEMSHA to Oak Bluffs is overlong and rather dull even in the high season, as miles of thick trees flash by, punctuated by the occasional unpaved driveway, usually complete with a battered mailbox and a spanking-new NO TRESPASSING sign. In late autumn, the trees are considerably thinner, the vistas more brown than green, and the journey itself is even more lonely and bleak. This time of year, one can see many of the houses ordinarily hidden in the woods, but they are shuttered and empty, an easy mark for any burglar or vandal, except for the sophisticated alarm systems that will bring the Island's small but efficient police force running.

Not that our alarm helped protect Vinerd Howse from the late Mr. Scott's invasion.

My father's alarm, I correct myself silently—at least at that time, for the house was invaded before Kimmer and I took possession.

Wait.

My *father's* alarm.

I tie another small knot in my memory handkerchief, knowing that I am straying very close to an important clue I will never quite reach if I search for it, but confident that it will drop into my mind unexpectedly if I just think about something else.

So I pay attention to the scenery, although it is not particularly scenic. The sky is a misery of gray. Empty trees rush past the car like a skeletal army marching at double time. And Meadows gave me bad information, either because she lied or because she was lied to. She told me that Scott's companions were white. My new friend, with nothing to gain by manufacturing a clever story, says that one of them was black. Moving pictures on the screen of my imagination: a mysterious dispute between the man whose name was not McDermott and the one whose name presumably is not Foreman, a fight in the boat, the third man—whoever he was!—takes Foreman's side, and Scott goes over the side. And what disagreement could possibly lead to murder?

The arrangements, of course.

Something my father had, or organized, scared somebody sufficiently that he, or she, or it, or they, would be willing to kill to . . .

No, no, no, it is too much, I am beginning to think like Mariah. Besides, a stranger in the middle of the night called to tell me that my family and I are safe.

Maybe poor Colin Scott obtained no such guarantee.

On the other hand, my father was obviously worried about something. He owned a gun. And had an instructor. Taking target practice.

I shake my head as the loneliness of North Road in the winter crowds in on me. I pass a handful of very determined cyclists in brightly colored jerseys, then two rugged women on horseback, even a car or two headed in the opposite direction, but, basically, I have the road to myself.

And then I do not.

Coming up behind me on the narrow road, moving very fast, is some sort of sports-utility vehicle, large and intimidating, deep blue, tinted windows. A Chevy Suburban, I register as it roars up to my bumper. I might have seen the same car in Menemsha. I might not have. It hangs annoyingly close. I hate being tailgated, but there is no passing on this stretch of road, so I am stuck. I try speeding up, topping sixty on the winding road, but the driver sticks to my rear. I try slowing down, but the Suburban's horn brays in irritation and the headlights flash.

"What do you want me to do?" I mutter, the way we talk to other drivers, as though they can hear us but, usually, secretly relieved that they cannot.

I decide to get off the road and let the fool pass me. The trouble is that there is no shoulder, so I have to wait for a side turning. I slow down, because if a crossroad should emerge I do not want to miss it.

The Suburban flashes its lights again but does not leave my tail.

For reasons I cannot quite explain, I feel myself slipping from annoyance toward fear, although I would be a lot more frightened if the car that is chasing me were a green sedan. Perhaps I have become over-watchful, an aftereffect of the beating I suffered.

I notice a couple of large ponds on the right-hand side of the road, meaning I am now in the town of West Tisbury, site of the Island's summer agricultural fair, where Abby won all those prizes a million years back, when everybody was still alive. Thinking about my baby sister awakens in me an image of a fiery crash, and a desire, perhaps irrational, to get the Suburban off my tail. I try to recall the Island's geography. Most traffic this time of year will bear left, in the direction of Vineyard Haven. So will the Suburban, I suspect, if it is not following me. Only one way to find out. There is a sharp right-hand turn coming up: the South Road, which I can take to the Edgartown Road, where a left turn will take me toward the airport, and, ultimately, Edgartown . . . a crowded part of the Island. And crowds are what I suddenly crave.

I see the intersection ahead. I accelerate, flipping on my left-turn indicator, and then, at the last possible second, I turn a hard right onto South Road. The rear end fishtails, the front wheels whine in complaint, and then the little Camry is under control again.

Behind me, the hulking Suburban duplicates my maneuver with contemptuous ease.

For a foolish instant, visions of Freeman Bishop's mutilated body dance in my head. And of Colin Scott, pitched over the side of a boat. Then I remind myself that I am on the Vineyard, for goodness' sake, where I have summered for over thirty years. Maybe the leviathan behind me is only a rude driver, not . . . well, whatever else I was worried about.

Two minutes later, with the Suburban still on my tail, I streak past the tiny clutch of stores and houses that mark the center of West Tisbury, but there is nobody on the street. The sun is sinking, the trees are casting long, unhappy shadows, and the empty town looks like a movie set. I turn left onto the Edgartown Road, and the Suburban remains a few car lengths behind me.

Once more the trees close in on either side. The day is suddenly darker: perhaps a storm is gathering. The Suburban still hangs on my bumper. I am not quite sure how far the airport is. Three miles, I suppose, maybe four. The Martha's Vineyard airport is a tiny affair, but there are bound to be people there, and people sound good right now.

The airport, then, is my new goal.

I never get there.

As I top a small rise, the Suburban roars up close to the Camry's tail once more, and now it is mere feet behind me.

The road falls off into a steep gully, we are momentarily invisible from both directions, and that is when my irritation causes me to make a mistake. Trying to prove I will not be intimidated, and also trying to avoid leaving the road when I reach the bottom of the hill, I slow down further, letting the speedometer drop below twenty.

The Suburban hits me from behind.

The bump is not hard, but it is jarring enough to snap my neck to the rear. As my head whips forward again, my teeth close on my tongue.

As instinct makes me press the brake, the Suburban strokes my car again, this time at an angle, so that the rear end slews a little and the front wheels slide, almost as though the larger car is trying to force me off the road and into the woods.

I manage to remember to steer in the direction of the skid instead of fighting it, and so I avoid spinning the Camry completely around, but I still travel another twenty or thirty feet, all the way to the bottom of the little valley between the last hill and the next, before I regain control.

The Suburban glides down the hill behind me. We both stop, right there in the road.

I take a moment to make sure that all my body's working parts are in good order. I taste blood in my mouth. My neck is singing with pain. My fear is gone. I am furious, the daylight is all fading to red, but I make myself control the rage, keeping my Garland cool, rooting in the glove compartment, thinking: *Rear-end collision, always the fault of the driver in the back, and a good thing, because bashed bumpers are expensive, especially on foreign makes, and where in the world is that insurance card?*

The other driver is already out of his vehicle, leaning over, inspecting the damage to our bumpers. I open the door and walk back to join him, reminding myself to remain calm, and I discover that the driver who hit me is female. She does not even glance up, and I find myself looking down at the back of a very tall woman in a yellow cashmere overcoat. I notice for the first time that she is a member of the darker nation, a fact which, through some bizarre trick of racial psychology, actually reassures me. The semiotician in me takes a brief interest in this symbology, but I shut him up.

"Excuse me," I say, with a little less force than I intended, but it has never been easy for me to be tough with women. "Hey," I add when I am ignored. And then I notice the familiar shock of hideously flat brown curls.

The driver of the Suburban straightens up, turns slowly in my direction, and smiles toothily as I gape in astonishment.

"Hello, handsome," says the roller woman. "We have to stop meeting like this."

CHAPTER 33

A HELPFUL CHAT

(1)

THE ROLLER WOMAN TURNS OUT to have a first name, but apparently no surname, because Maxine is all she is willing to tell me. She also has made luncheon reservations for two at a cozy inn I have never heard of down one of the confusing little side streets of Vineyard Haven. I can think of no particular reason to turn down her invitation, especially because I make no effort to come up with one. So Maxine drives the Suburban, which seems unscratched by our collision, and I follow in the Camry, whose rear bumper is badly mangled.

Vineyard Haven is the common but unofficial name of the town of Tisbury, or else it is the other way around—more than thirty summers on the Island and still I cannot keep them straight. The word *picturesque* tends toward overuse, especially to describe New England shore towns, but the narrow, neatly tangled lanes of Vineyard Haven, each lined with tiny white clapboard homes, stores, and churches, actually deserve the accolade. The town looks like a film set, except that no director would dare to create a town so perky, full of bustling energy, amidst gorgeous leafy trees and magnificent views of the water from . . . well, just about everywhere. Ordinarily, a trip to Tisbury brings a smile to my face, because it is so shamelessly perfect. But today, dragging my bumper along Main Street, I am too busy wondering what is going on.

I assume I am about to find out.

"Sorry about your car," Maxine murmurs as soon as we are seated. The dining room only has about a dozen tables, and all of them look out on a grim churchyard, the rooftops of houses down the hill, and the inevitable blue water beyond. Ten tables are empty.

"Not as sorry as I am."

"Aw, come on, handsome, lighten up."

She grins the same infectious smile I first saw at the rollerdrome the day after we buried the Judge. She is wearing a brown jumpsuit and a multicolored scarf, her clothing every bit as unconventional as her hair. I find that I like her a lot more now that she has a name, even though I expect to discover sooner or later that Maxine, like just about everybody else I have met since my father died, has as many different names as she needs.

"I wish you'd stop calling me that," I mutter, refusing to be drawn.

"Why? You *are* handsome." Although I'm not, really.

"Because I *are* married."

Maxine puffs her lips in amusement but lets this go, for which small mercy I am grateful. I usually hate being out with women other than my wife, out of a holy terror that somebody will see us together and draw the wrong conclusion. I value my reputation for fidelity, and I believe in the old-fashioned notion that adults have a responsibility to live up to their commitments—something I learned as much from my mother as from the Judge. Yet, sitting here with the mysterious Maxine, I find myself unable to worry about whether anybody will think we are a couple.

Which is why I must tread carefully.

"So, if I can't call you handsome," she sighs, "what would you *rather* have me call you?"

I want no intimacy with this woman. Or, rather, what I want is irrelevant, since I *are* married. "Well, given the difference in our ages, you should probably call me Professor Garland, or Mr. Garland."

"Yucch."

"What?"

"I said . . . yucch, Professor Garland." Flashing those dimples at me. "And you're not *that* much older than I am." Smiling.

I am tempted to smile back. "Why are you following me?" I ask, trying to stay on track.

"In case you change your mind about that skating lesson."

She laughs. I don't.

"Come on. I'm serious, Maxine. I need to know what's going on."

"You'll figure it out sooner or later." Her wide, lively face is buried in the menu. "I hear the crab cakes are the best on the Vineyard," she adds as the waiter nears, but half the restaurants on the Island make the same claim.

We both order the crab cakes nevertheless, we both choose the rice, we both ask for salad with the house dressing, we both decide to stay with the sparkling water we are already sipping. I am not sure which one of us is copying the other, but I wish he or she would stop.

"Maxine," I ask as soon as the waiter is gone, "what are we doing here?"

"Having an early dinner."

"Why?"

"Because we need to talk, handsome. Sorry, sorry. I mean Professor Garland. No, I mean Misha. Or I could say Talcott. Tal? Isn't that what they call you? By the way, did anybody ever tell you that you have too many names?" More laughter. Maxine, however many names *she* may have, is far too easy to be with.

I stay on message. "You just thought you'd run into my car so we could have a talk?"

That fun-loving grin again. "Well, it got your attention, didn't it? Oh, yeah, before I forget." Maxine opens her large brown purse, and although my exhausted eyes might be playing tricks, I am pretty sure I see a holstered gun before she pulls out an envelope and snaps the bag closed again. Still smiling, she drops the envelope on the table. It is as thick as a telephone book. "Here."

"What is that?" I have no particular desire to touch it, not yet.

"Well, I did wreck your bumper, and I can't exactly give you my insurance card."

Shaking my head at the unreality of the moment, I pick up the envelope and peek inside. I see a sheaf of hundred-dollar bills. Lots of them. Not new, either: well used.

"How much money is this?"

"Um, twenty-five thousand dollars, I think." Not managing to sound quite as casual as she wants to. "Around that, anyway. Mostly hundreds." The pixie grin again. "I know foreign-car repairs can be expensive."

I drop the money back on the table. Something truly weird is going on. "Twenty-five . . . thousand?"

"Why, it's not enough?"

"Maxine, I would *sell* you my car for maybe one-tenth of that."

"I don't want your car." Deliberately missing my point. She taps the envelope. Her unpainted nails are trimmed very short. "I *have* a car. Take the money, honey."

I shake my head, leaving the cash exactly where it is.

"What's the money really for?"

"The damage, handsome. Take it." She tilts her head to the side. "Besides, you never know when you'll need some extra cash."

Somebody obviously knows about our debts, a fact that irritates me.

"Maxine . . . whose money is this?"

"Yours, silly." Oh, but Maxine has a smile! I struggle to keep my composure.

"What I mean is, where did you get it?"

She points. "Out of my purse."

"How did it get into your purse?"

"I put it there. Do you think I let just anybody go through my purse?"

I pause, remembering the lessons from my years of law practice. In a deposition, formulate the questions with care. Most of them should be capable of *Yes* and *No* answers. Lead the witness, through her *Yes*es, to where you want to be.

"Somebody gave you that money, right?"

"Right."

"Gave it to you to give to me?"

"Maybe." She is being playful, not cautious, which is scarcely surprising, given that I have no means of compelling her to answer.

"Who was the person who gave you the money?"

"I'd rather not say." But a toothy grin to make it friendly.

"Was it Jack Ziegler?"

"Nope. Sorry."

I ponder, watching Maxine sip her Perrier. "Did the person who gave you the money tell you what it was really for?"

"Uh-huh."

"And what was the money really for?"

"For your car." Pointing toward the window. "If anything happened to it."

Okay, I admit I was never a very good lawyer. Maybe that is why I became a law professor.

"You planned all along to hit my car?"

"Well, yeah. Probably. I mean, sure, I could have been more dainty about it." She shrugs, a significant movement in a woman six feet tall, signaling me, perhaps, that there is nothing dainty about her at all. "I mean, you know what they say. Accidents can bring people together, right?" Tilting her head now to the other side and fluttering her eye-lashes. Playacting, but not ineffectively.

"Sure, that's the way I always meet people. Crash into their cars and take them to lunch."

"Well, it worked."

Okay, I am still a married man and the mystery is still too much, and we have done enough flirting. I lean across the table. "Maxine, that's nuts and you know it. Now, I need to know what's going on. I need to know who you are. I need to know *what* you are."

"What I am?" Her eyes glitter. "What do you think I am?"

"You're somebody who . . . who keeps turning up. It's like you know where I'm going to be before I do." I fork some salad into my mouth, chew a bit, swallow. "For instance, you were waiting for me at the skat-ing rink."

"Maybe."

"Well, you got there first. I'd be very interested to know how you knew I was going there." A horrible thought occurs to me. "Did you bug my father's house?"

Maxine's response is leisurely. "Maybe I didn't get to the rink first. Maybe I just got my skates on first." She takes a small bite from a bread-stick. "Think about it. How long were you at the rink before you saw me? Twenty minutes? Half an hour? Plenty of time for me to follow you there, rent some skates, and lose myself in the crowd."

"So you did follow me there."

To my surprise, she gives what I take to be an honest answer. "Sure. You're pretty easy to follow."

This irritates me for some reason. But just briefly. "You should know. You followed me—my family and myself—to the Vineyard back in November. And you followed me in Washington."

"Not very well." She giggles, and this time the corners of my lips twitch. "I lost you at Dupont Circle. That was a neat trick, what you did with the taxi. If I can't do any better than that, I'm not gonna have a job."

An opening large enough for a truck. And intended, I have no doubt, for me to drive straight through.

"Exactly what *is* your job?"

All the fun goes out of Maxine's expression, although her eyes are passionate and alert. "Persuading you," she says.

"Persuading me of what?"

She pauses, and I can see that she has played the whole game to get to this precise point. "Sooner or later, you're gonna find out what arrangements your father made. When you do, it's my job to persuade you to give us what you find."

"Who's *us?*"

"We're kinda like the good guys. I mean, not the *great* guys, we're not saints or anything like that, but we're better than some people you might give it to."

"Yeah, but who are you?"

"Let's just say . . . an interested party."

"Interested party? Interested in what?"

She answers a slightly different question. "Whatever you do, don't give it to your Uncle Jack. In his hands, it's a weapon. It's dangerous. In ours—it disappears, and everybody is happy."

(11)

MAXINE TURNS OUT TO BE RIGHT. The crab cakes are delicious, for the chef has managed to keep them flaky and light without leaving them with the fishy taste that is a sure sign of undercooking. The sauce is peppy but unintrusive. On the side are long serrated wedges of baked potato that fool the eye, but not the palate, into thinking they are fried. The waiter is helpful and present when needed without seeming to hover, and he evidently feels no need to share his name with us. It is, in short, a good place, of which the Vineyard has many, some, like this one, hidden away on side roads, far away from Oak Bluffs and Edgartown, known mainly to the well-to-do folks who own second homes up-Island but invisible to tourists and, just as important, to tourist guidebooks.

Maxine and I are talking, improbably, about our childhoods. The envelope full of cash has disappeared back into her bottomless bag, just like a conjuring trick. Maxine has declined, so far, to improve on her brief statement of her purpose in following me, parrying my every dialectical thrust with her hearty grin and contagious laughter. Yet, unlike my similarly hopeless effort to pry information out of the late Mr. Scott, this one rouses in me principally a sense of play; and possibly something more. I am having a far better time with this mysterious woman than a married man really should, particularly when you factor in the intelligence that she just ran into my car to get my attention, that she tried to bribe me, that she is carrying a gun in her shoulder bag, and that she was on the Island when my other pursuer, Colin Scott, went into the water.

"Even in high school, I was always taller than most of the guys," she is saying, "so I never got many dates, because most guys don't like taller girls." Inviting a compliment that I elect not to bestow. So she talks on.

Maxine, it turns out, was a faculty brat, her parents both professors at old black colleges in the South. She refuses to specify which.

"So I was kind of happy to get an assignment that involved another academic."

"I'm an assignment?"

"Well, you're not an assignation, Misha."

Using my nickname again. Then she startles me by asking how I got it. I startle myself by answering. I do not tell the story often, but I tell it now. I tell her how my parents, in their wisdom, named me Talcott, after my mother's father. And how I changed it because of chess. My father taught me to play during some early Vineyard summer. He tried to teach all of us, insisting it would improve our minds, but the other children were less interested, perhaps because they were already in rebellion. Chess was one of the few things the Judge and I had in common when I was younger, and maybe when I was older, too; for we never seemed to agree on very much.

I do not remember my precise age at the time of my first lessons, but I do remember the event that led to my rechristening. I was playing chess with my big brother on the creaky porch of Vinerd Howse when my Uncle Derek, the big Communist whom my father more or less denied at his hearings, stumbled drunkenly from within, shading his rheumy eyes from the morning sunlight with his thick fingers, stained a tobacco yellow. The Judge used to lecture Derek for his weakness, not realizing that the same tendency to alcoholism, perhaps an inherited trait, would later snare him, too, at a moment of depression. For Derek, having soured by then on the possibility of a revolutionary movement among American workers, was terribly unhappy, as we could always detect in the worried glances of his wife, Thera. Now, swaying on his feet, my uncle looked down at the chessboard. Despite the difference in our ages, I was beating Addison soundly, for this was the only arena in which I usually bested him. Uncle Derek squinted at the two of us, puffed out his sallow cheeks, exhaling alcohol fumes strong enough to make us children dizzy, grinned unpleasantly, and mumbled, "So, I guess you're *Mikhail* Tal now"—the Latvian wizard Mikhail Tal having been, for the briefest of historical moments, the chess champion of the world, and Uncle Derek having been, for nearly all of his life, an admirer of most things Soviet and, in consequence, an enduring embarrassment to my father. But Addison and I knew nothing of the larger chess world, and certainly had never heard of the great Tal. We looked at each other in confusion. We were always a little bit scared of Uncle Derek, and my father, who thought he was crazy, would have preferred to have no contact with him at all, but my mother, who believed in family, insisted. "No," said my uncle, squinting against the glare. Our heads swung back in his direction. "No, not *Mikhail*—just *Misha*. That's what the Russians call Tal. You're a kid, so let's call you Misha." He laughed, an ugly, liquid sound, accompanied by a gurgling deep in his chest, because he was already ill, although he would linger, in declining health, for another few years. He shuffled to the edge of the porch, coughing helplessly, the timbre thick and wet and physically disgusting to my child's ear, for it takes many years on God's earth to learn that what is truly human is never truly ugly.

I would have let the name go, but Addison, who hated chess, liked the sound of it and began to call me Misha, especially once he discovered how much it annoyed me; so did his many friends. I learned to love the nickname in self-defense. By the time I got to college, I rarely identified myself as anything else.

"But most people still call you Tal," says the roller woman when I am done. "You reserve the name Misha for . . . mmmm, your very close friends."

"What do you have, a file on me?"

"Something like that."

"You being the good guys? Just not the great guys?"

She nods, and this time I laugh with her, and quite easily, not because anything either of us has said is amusing, but because the situation itself is absurd.

The waiter is back. Dessert orders occupy us: Pêches Ninon for the lady, plain vanilla ice cream for the gentleman. He nods at Maxine's order, frowns at mine. Maxine grins conspiratorially, as if to say, *I know a nerd when I see one, but I like you just the way you are.* Maybe her grin does not signify all that, but I still blush.

We talk on. Maxine's previously raucous face grows somberly sympathetic. She has led me, somehow, to the night Abby died, and I am reliving the wretched moment when my elegant mother, her hand shaking, answered the telephone in the kitchen, let out that horrible moan, and collapsed against the wall. I tell her how I stood alone in the hall, peering in the kitchen door, watching my mother wail and beat the phone against the counter, far too terrified to comfort her, because Claire Garland, like her husband, encouraged a certain emotional distance. In my adult lifetime, I have shared the story only with Kimmer and, in less detail, with Dana and Eddie, years ago, when the two of them were still married, and Kimmer and I were still happy. I have scarcely told it to myself. I am surprised, and a little annoyed, to find a catch in my voice and moisture on my cheeks.

(111)

WE ARE WALKING NOW, the two of us, a pleasant stroll in the brisk air of an autumn evening on the Vineyard. We are sauntering along the deserted Oak Bluffs waterfront, for all the world a happy couple, passing the empty slips across from the Wesley Hotel, a gracefully sprawling Victorian behemoth built on the site of an earlier hotel of the same name, which perished by fire. The flat January water laps comfortably at the seawall. A few pedestrians pass us, headed toward town, but the harbor, like the rest of the Island in the off-season, has the texture of an uncompleted painting.

"I can't tell you everything, Misha," says Maxine, her handbag, gun and all, swinging gaily from her shoulder. Her arm is linked in mine. I am pretty sure she would let me hold her hand if I tried.

"Tell me what you can."

"It might be easier if you tell me what you think. Maybe I can tell you if you're hot or cold. And what I can't tell you, you might be able to figure out for yourself."

I think this over as we walk. After dinner, we stood a little too close to each other in the parking lot, sharing that odd reluctance to part that characterizes new lovers, as well as people who follow other people for a living. It was Maxine who suggested we drive to Oak Bluffs, although she refuses to tell me where she is staying. And so we did, the Suburban following me once more, along the Vineyard Haven Harbor, over the hill separating the two towns, and down again to the center of town.

We both parked on the waterfront, across the street from the Wesley. I have no doubt that Maxine knows exactly where I live, but I do not want her anywhere near Vinerd Howse.

Call it an excess of marital caution.

"Well, handsome?" she prompts. "Are we gonna play or not?"

"Okay." I take a breath. With darkness, the air has turned icy. "The first thing is, I think my father was involved in . . . something he shouldn't have been." I risk a glance at Maxine, but she is looking at the water. "I think that, somehow, he arranged for me to get some information about it after he died. Or somebody thinks he did."

"I agree," she says softly, and, for the first time in this mad search, I own an actual fact.

"I think that Colin Scott was looking for that information. I think he followed me because he hoped I would find my father's . . . arrangements."

"I agree."

We walk on, headed toward East Chop, a wide outcropping dotted with shingled homes, more Cape Cod style than Victorian, many of them on high bluffs overlooking the water, most of them considerably more expensive than the houses closer to town. Kimmer and I briefly fell in love with a gorgeous house up there, three large bedrooms and a back yard opening onto the beach, but we did not have two million dollars to buy it. Probably it is just as well, given what has happened to us in the years since.

"Other people are also interested in the arrangements," I suggest.

"I agree," Maxine murmurs, but when I press her, she declines to be more specific.

I stare at East Chop Drive, which leads up to the old lighthouse and what used to be called the Highlands. At the foot of the bluffs is a private beach club. In the middle of the Chop is a private tennis club. East Chop, for all its crisp New England beauty, has a whiter feel than the rest of Oak Bluffs. Not many of the summer residents seem aware that East Chop was once the heart of the Island's black colony.

"Colin Scott knew my father."

"I agree."

"He worked for my father. My father . . . paid him to do something."

Silence.

I am disappointed, for I was trying, one last time, to discover that

Colin Scott and Jonathan Villard were the same person, which would explain what Scott was doing in the foyer at Shepard Street, arguing with my father. But evidently not.

I hesitate, then try another tack. "Do you know what my father left for me?"

"No."

"But you're familiar somehow with the . . . clues."

"Yes. But we aren't sure what they mean."

I try to think of another intelligent question to ask. We are in a little park full of brown grass, East Chop rising before us, downtown Oak Bluffs off to our right. The occasional car passes on East Chop Drive, which separates the park from the harbor.

"This island is lovely," Maxine says unexpectedly, gripping my arm lightly with both her hands, her gaze on the distant shimmering water.

"I think so."

"You've been coming here for how long? Thirty years? I can't imagine—I mean, we didn't have that kind of money."

"We've always really been just summer people," I explain, wondering whether Maxine appreciates the distinction. "And it wasn't so expensive in the old days."

"Your family had money, though."

"We were just middle-class. But you were, too. A couple of professors."

"They never got paid very much. And, besides, my father used to be what you'd call a high-stakes gambler. Only he wasn't very good at it."

"I'm sorry."

"Don't be. He loved us. We lived in a big old house on the campus with about five dogs and ten cats. Sometimes we had birds. Our folks loved animals. And, like I said, they loved us."

"Us?"

She wrinkles her nose. "Four brothers, one sister, nosey. I'm the youngest and the tallest."

"The one who didn't get any dates."

"Well, I didn't have my own car, so I couldn't crash into anyone." Not a great joke, but we both laugh anyway.

A companionable pause as we look out toward the water together. A yacht, an unexpected sight this time of year, is just motoring out, moving much too fast, but boat owners are like that. Few of the houses are showing any lights. Most are closed for the season. The promised storm never quite arrived, and the night sky is clear and cold and perfect.

The need to take Maxine in my arms has been creeping up on me all afternoon, and is suddenly very strong. I cover it with a shower of pointless questions.

"You don't have much of an accent for somebody from the South."

"Oh." She nods but does not turn toward me. "I was educated in France, too, and I think I've said enough about that, thank you."

Suggesting the need to propose a different subject. I feel like an incompetent gigolo at a cocktail party.

"So how did you get into this business?"

Maxine eyes me sideways again. "What business is that?"

"You know. Following people around."

She shrugs, glancing at me in irritation, upset, perhaps, that I have broken the mood. Sometimes spouses must protect their marriages from their own baser instincts. "Please don't think of it as *following*, Misha. Think of it as *helping*."

"Helping? How are you helping?"

Maxine lets go of my jacket and turns to face me. "Well, for one thing, I can tell you when other people are following you."

"Other people? You mean, like Colin Scott?"

"That's correct."

I think this over for a moment, then toss out the obvious objection. "But he's dead."

"Correct," she agrees, then adds the most chilling words possible: "But, remember, he had a partner." The silence resumes. We are walking back toward the Wesley again, an unspoken decision having turned us around, in more ways than one. Then Maxine raises the stakes higher still. "And there could be others, too."

"Others?"

She points up the hill the way we came. "The same man passed us twice on a bicycle while we were back there. Maybe he was just riding up the hill and back down. Or maybe he was following us. No way to tell." She turns and points back toward Vineyard Haven. "And there was a dark brown Chrysler minivan parked a block from the restaurant. Another car of the same description is parked down at the harbor, right now. It isn't the same car, because it doesn't have the same license plate and there was a nice little dent in the bumper of the one at the restaurant. You can change the plates, you can put in dents as a disguise, but it's really hard to take them out that fast. So it isn't the same car. But it easily could have been. Do you see what I mean? You won't notice things like that. You're not trained for it. I am."

This viciously detailed recital has left me dizzy. Does Maxine suppose that she is reassuring me? I look out toward the water, where the yacht I noticed a moment ago is rounding the point. One rarely finds boats in the Oak Bluffs harbor once the Island shuts down, and I wonder whose side this one is on.

"What are you saying? Are we supposed to be a team?"

"I'm just showing you how I can help."

"And so you'll be watching my back?" I do not quite manage to hit the superior tone I am attempting. "Keeping me safe from all the bad guys?"

Maxine does not like this at all. She turns toward me, grips my shoulders once more in her strong hands. "Misha, listen to me. A lot of people might be interested in what arrangements your father left. And not all of them will settle for bumping into your car and taking you to lunch. They can't do anything to hurt you. But they can certainly scare you."

We both wait for this to sink in.

"Is my family in any danger?" I am thinking, *Jamaica, call Kimmer and tell her to take Bentley and go stay with her relatives in Jamaica.*

"No, Misha, no. Believe me, nobody is going to hurt you. Nobody is going to hurt your family. Mr. Ziegler has guaranteed it."

"That's all it takes?"

"In my world, yes."

I knew this, of course. I just never quite believed it before. It is one thing to read about Uncle Jack's power in the newspapers; it is something else to feel it in action, a protective cocoon around me and my family.

"Then what are you trying to say?"

"It's the *information* that's dangerous, Misha." The conversation has returned to its starting point. "If it falls into the wrong hands—that's the danger."

"Which is why you think I should give it to you—whoever you are—instead of to Jack Ziegler."

"Yes."

"Do you work for . . . well, the government?" She shakes her head, smiling. "No, that's right, you work for the good-but-not-great guys."

"In a contest between us and Jack Ziegler, nobody is going to Heaven, but, yes, that's still about right."

"Except that you're following me surreptitiously, and Uncle Jack is protecting me."

"Maybe he's following you too. Maybe I'm protecting you too."

"I haven't seen any sign—"

"Remember how he acted in the cemetery, Misha? Was that the way a man behaves when he has no stake in the outcome?"

"In the cemetery? You weren't at the cemetery—"

"Yes, I was," Maxine smiles, delighted to be one up on me again. "I was at the funeral too, sitting in the back row with a bunch of your relatives. They all thought I was somebody's cousin." The smile dims a bit, and I sense weariness now: she is tired of playing a role, tired of flirting, tired of the job. "You even hugged me over by the grave," she adds softly. "It was a nice hug."

I am a little surprised, as Maxine means me to be. But I am also undeterred.

"You still haven't given me a reason to give the . . . the information to you. That is, if I ever find it."

"You won't take my word for it? I mean, I did buy you crab cakes."

"*And* wrecked my car."

"Just the bumper. And I offered to pay for it."

When I remain silent, Maxine stops walking and grabs my arm again. We are in the parking lot of a tiny store that sells just about everything, from breakfast cereal to fine wine to the little stickers that allow you to put your trash at the curb for collection.

"Listen to me, Misha. I am not your enemy. You have to believe that. I told you that the people I'm working with aren't saints. You might not invite them to dinner. But believe me when I say that, if they get their hands on what Angela's boyfriend knows, whatever it turns out to be, they will destroy it. If Jack Ziegler gets his hands on it, he will use it. It's as simple as that." Her eyes seem to glow in the darkness. "You have to go back and find it, Misha. The clues are all there. It's just that nobody else can figure them out. I think your father thought you would know right off who Angela's boyfriend was. Your father was an intelligent man. A careful man. If he thought you knew, then you know. You just don't know what you know."

I shake my head in frustration. "Maxine, I have to tell you, I don't have any idea what my father was talking about. I think he made a mistake."

"Don't say that! Don't you *ever* say that!" Maxine seems fearful, looking around as though she expects to find somebody is listening in. "You *do* have an idea. Your father did *not* make a mistake." Almost shouting as she corrects me.

I remove her hand from my wrist. "I'm too tired for all this. I think I might . . . I've been thinking of giving up the search."

Her eyes grow wider and, if anything, more alarmed. "You can't stop now, Misha. You just can't. Nobody else can figure out the arrangements but you. So you have to do it. You *have* to. Please."

Please?

"I see." I keep my tone neutral. I do not want her to realize that this sudden lapse into supplication is more terrifying than anything else she has said. But Maxine detects my mood; I can see it in her intelligent face; and I can see her decide to let it go.

"I don't think we'll see each other again, Misha. That is, I don't think you'll see me. Not if I do my job right. I'll be watching you, but you won't know when. So just act natural, and assume I'm there to help."

"Maxine, I—"

"I'm sorry about the money," she hurries on. "That was clumsy. And it was insulting. It wasn't to fix your bumper. And I had a lot more of it in my bag, just in case. I still do." Her tone is wistful.

"In case what?"

"We heard somebody else was trying to buy the arrangements from you. Disguising it, maybe, as fees for speaking engagements, something like that." I feel a chill but do not say a word. "So, anyway, I was actually supposed to . . . well, I was supposed to bribe you, Misha. I'm sorry, but it's true. We know you've had certain financial pressures. And, um, domestic pressures, too. I was supposed to bribe you with money or . . . or, well, with whatever else it took." Now it is her turn to blush and drop her eyes, and mine to feel a rising warmth I would rather keep at bay.

"Bribe me to do what?" I ask after a moment. We have arrived back at our cars. She takes her keys from her pocket and presses the button. The Suburban's lights flash, the alarm bleeps off, and the doors unlock. I grab her arm. "Maxine, bribe me to do what?"

She stiffens at my touch. She is suddenly quite unhappy. I do not know whether it is just coincidence that every woman I meet seems to be depressed, or whether I make them that way.

"Bribe me to do what?" I ask a third time, dropping my hand. "To give whatever it is to you instead of Uncle Jack?"

Maxine has the door open and a foot on the running board. She answers me without turning around.

"I know your life has been difficult lately, Misha. I know some scary things have happened. A lot of people would decide to give up the hunt at this point. We heard you might be thinking about it." She hesitates. "I guess the best way to put it is that I was supposed to do whatever it took to get you not to give up. To convince you to keep looking. But I don't think you need to be bribed. I think you're the kind who can't let go. You'll keep looking for him because you need to."

"Looking for whom?"

"For Angela's boyfriend."

"And then what? Maxine, wait. Then what? If I find him, and if he tells me what my father wanted him to tell me, what am I supposed to do? I mean, suppose I agree with you? How do I get the information to you?"

Maxine is up in the seat of the Suburban now, ready to close the door on me. But she turns and looks straight into my eyes. I can see the mixture of exhaustion, irritation, even a little sadness. This day did not go precisely as she planned.

"First, handsome, you have to find him," she says.

"And then?"

"Then I'll find you. I promise."

"But wait a minute. Wait. I'm out of ideas. I don't know where to look."

The roller woman shrugs and turns the key. The engine explodes into life. She looks at me again, her gaze clear and direct. "You might start with Freeman Bishop."

"Freeman Bishop?"

"I think he was a mistake."

"Wait. A mistake? What kind of mistake?"

"The bad kind, handsome. The bad kind." Maxine closes the door and throws the Suburban into reverse. The car accelerates up the hill toward Vineyard Haven. I watch until the taillights vanish around the bend.

I am alone.

CHAPTER 34

A STORY UNRAVELS

(I)

I WAKE EARLY THE NEXT MORNING, alone in Vinerd Howse, ashamed of how much of the night I spent tossing restlessly, unable to sleep, wishing for company but not my wife. I pull on my robe and step out onto the little balcony off the master bedroom. The streets are empty. Most of the other houses on Ocean Park are closed for the season, but one or two show signs of activity, and a jogger, out early in the crisp air, waves cheerily.

I wave back.

Down in the kitchen I toast an English muffin and pour some juice, for I did not fill the larder when I arrived, expecting to be here only a day or two. I carry my breakfast into the little television nook by the front hall where, three decades ago, I saw Addison and Sally tussling away. Simpler times.

You might start with Freeman Bishop. . . . I think he was a mistake.

A mistake? What kind of mistake? Whose mistake? Mine? My father's? Questions I throw at the roller woman, even though she is not present to answer them.

And how can a dead man help me find Angela's boyfriend?

I cannot sit still. I wander from room to room, poking my head into the guest room, done up in red wallpaper and red fabric on bed and chairs, the room where my mother died; and into the bathroom that doubles as a laundry room, with the cheap linoleum floor that was already old when my parents bought the house; back into the small kitchen, where I pour more juice; and, finally, into the dining room, where that blowup of my father's *Newsweek* cover still hangs over the unusable fireplace. THE CONSERVATIVE HOUR. The way it was before, as the Judge would say. When life seemed golden. I remember how my father's nomination tested the unity of the Gold Coast, how lifelong friends stopped speaking to each other as they came down on opposite sides. But perhaps splintering was more common than I suspected in our happy little community. Didn't Mariah tell me that the congregation at Trinity and St. Michael split down the middle when Freeman Bishop's cocaine use came to light? And if—

Wait.

What was it Mariah said? Somebody who would have left except—except—

I hurry back into the kitchen, snatch up the telephone. For once I reach Mariah on my first try. Battling back her efforts to fill my ears with the latest conspiracy news gleaned from the Internet, I throw in the crucial question:

"Listen, kiddo, wasn't there somebody you said would have left the church over Father Bishop's drug use, except she had her reasons?"

"Sure. Gigi Walker. You remember Gigi. Addison used to date her little sister? Of course, Addison used to date everybody, so I guess that isn't much of a—"

"Mariah, listen. What did you mean when you said she had her reasons?"

"Oh, Tal, why are you the last to hear everything? Gigi and Father Bishop were an item for *years*. This was after his wife died, and after her husband left, so it wasn't quite the scandal it could have been. But, still, Daddy said he didn't think a man of the cloth—"

Again I interrupt. "Okay, okay. Listen. Gigi. That's a nickname, right?"

"Right."

"And her real name is . . ."

Even before my sister answers, I know what she is going to say. "Angela. Angela Walker. Why do you want to know?"

Mariah babbles on, but I am not listening. The telephone is trembling in my hand.

No wonder Colin Scott, according to Lanie Cross's tale, gave Gigi Walker such a hard time that she cried. He knew what I now know, but he knew it first.

I have found Angela's boyfriend.

But somebody else found him first, which is why he is dead and can tell me nothing.

I CANNOT REACH AGENT NUNZIO. Sergeant Ames refuses to listen to my theories, and I can hardly blame her. If I have actual evidence that she has the wrong man in custody, she suggests that I should share it with her. If I do not, then I should leave her alone and let her do her job. The trouble is, I am in the dangerous middle ground. Sitting in the kitchen of Vinerd Howse, trying to figure out how to get her to take me seriously, I run up against a wall. I think I know who tortured Freeman Bishop to death and what he wanted, but I am certainly in no position to prove it. Bonnie Ames, on the other hand, has a witness willing to testify that Conan bragged about what he did, a history of violent behavior on the part of her suspect, and evidence that Freeman Bishop was behind in money he owed Conan for drugs.

I do not know how Colin Scott manufactured all that evidence, but I have no doubt that he did so. Poor Freeman Bishop was not included in Jack Ziegler's command that the family not be harmed. So Scott tortured him to learn what he was supposed to tell me, and, as the sergeant pointed out grimly when Mariah and I visited her, it is unlikely that the priest held anything back. And there is the problem, I reflect as I hang up the telephone and begin once more to wander the house. If Father Bishop told Colin Scott everything, why did Scott still see a need to follow me? If he was following me, he obviously had not learned where my father hid . . . whatever he hid.

Which means that Freeman Bishop never told him.

Which means that Freeman Bishop never knew.

I think he was a mistake. The bad kind.

Now I understand what Maxine was talking about. Freeman Bishop was murdered because Colin Scott thought he was Angela's boyfriend. And he was, indeed, Angela's boyfriend. He just wasn't the Angela's boyfriend my father meant.

Nevertheless, as far as I am concerned, it was the Judge who got him killed.

CHAPTER 35

THE SKELETON

(1)

"You'll never guess what happened," announces a gleeful Dana Worth, striding into my office uninvited.

"That's right," I tell her crossly, barely looking up from the galley proofs I am busily correcting with a broken red pencil. I have not had the emotional energy to do a lot of work since my return from the Vineyard. It is the end of the second week of January and Elm Harbor's streets are choked with dirty snow. The spring semester formally begins on Monday, but the minutiae of law school life cannot hold my attention. Students have been coming in with excuses for not having their papers done on time. I have not wasted words scolding them. The library still wants the book I have misplaced. Earlier today, Shirley Branch called, still depressed about her missing dog. I tried to be comforting, as a mentor should, even though I was tempted to tell her—it was a near thing—that I can only look for one missing item at a time. On the Vineyard, Maxine begged me to continue the search for *the arrangements*, but I am not sure I will be able to do it. Too many ghosts now haunt me.

Last night around eleven-thirty, the telephone woke us, and Kimmer, who sleeps on that side of the bed, picked up the receiver, listened for about three seconds, and handed it to me without a word: Mariah again, calling to disclose a fact she had previously hidden. As my wife pulled the blanket over her head, my sister told me what she had wheedled out of poor Warner Bishop when the two of them finally talked over a cozy dinner in New York. In the telling, Mariah confirmed my fears. Warner, it seems, lied to the police. On the night Freeman Bishop died, just as Sergeant Ames said, he informed his vestry that he would be a little late for the meeting because he had to stop and comfort a distraught parishioner. But he told his son, who happened to call just before he left, a different story. Father Bishop said he would be late because he had to see an FBI agent who had dropped by the church earlier in the day, set up a clandestine meeting to talk about an unnamed congregant, and sworn him to silence. Why did Warner keep this fact from the police? *Because he was scared,* said Mariah. Of whom? *Of whoever killed his father.* She grew enthusiastic. *I wanted to tell you earlier, Tal, when I was over at your house. But you spent so much time dissing me that I didn't really trust you. Now I do.* I tried to remember whether I was really so cruel. Before I could figure out whether Mariah expected me to apologize, she was on to the next point in her brief. *See why I don't trust the FBI?* But she knew as well as I did that the real FBI had nothing to do with what happened to Freeman Bishop.

"Misha, come on, pay attention." Dear Dana brushes aside a stack of papers—never mind where *I* want them to be—and hops onto the corner of my desk. Her feet do not reach the floor. She strikes her famous pose again, soles flat on the side. "This is good news. This is *important.*"

I lean back in my aged chair and hear the familiar crack of the broken bearings. In my experience, nothing but faculty politics ever arouses such exuberance in my occasional friend, so I steel myself for an interminable tale of triumph or tragedy, related somehow to the question of who will or will not be appointed to the faculty, an issue, although I have not informed Dana, about which I no longer actually care.

"I'm listening," I tell her.

Dana flashes her pixie grin, the one she reserves for teasing old friends and baiting new students. She is wearing a dark sweater and a pair of beige pants that would fit a twelve-year-old, but the sharp crease suggests a product affordable only by twelve-year-olds who live in Beverly Hills. "It actually has more to do with that wife of yours than with you."

"I'm still listening." I cannot imagine what aspect of Kimmer's life Dana would find so fascinating, but I am always willing to learn.

"This is a good one, Misha."

"No doubt."

"You're no fun, you know that?"

"Dana, are you going to tell me or not?"

She pouts briefly, unaccustomed to this new, less playful Misha Garland, but decides, as Dana always will, that her gossip is too juicy to remain unconfided.

"Well, you'll never guess who spent the last two hours in Dean Lynda's office."

"True." I turn my attention back to the proofs.

"True?"

"True, I will never guess. So why don't you just tell me."

Dana makes a face and waits for me to notice, then plunges on. "I'll give you a hint, Misha. They were using both of her telephone lines—this person and Lynda, I mean—and they were on the telephone to just about everybody in Washington, trying to persuade them that he didn't plagiarize the world-famous Chapter Three of his one and only book."

My chair tilts forward with a surprised crunch. For a marvelous instant, the worries about my father and his arrangements and Freeman Bishop and the roller woman evaporate.

"You don't mean . . ."

"I do mean. Brother Hadley."

"You're kidding. You're *kidding*."

"I'm not kidding. Chapter Three? The one he's always quoting? The one *everybody* is always quoting? Well, it turns out he copied it from an unpublished paper by none other than Perry Mountain."

"Marc plagiarized Theo's brother? *Marc?* I don't believe it."

Dana is disappointed by my skepticism; she wanted my cheers. "Why do you find it so hard to believe? You think Marc is some kind of paragon? You think he doesn't cheat and steal like everybody else?"

"Well, no, it's just that I can't believe Marc would ever think that somebody else's ideas were good enough to call his own."

This wins me the coveted Dear Dana Worth grin of approval.

"Well, in case you've forgotten, Brother Hadley also has the greatest writer's block in the history of Western civilization. So maybe stealing somebody else's ideas is better than never publishing at all, huh?"

I shake my head. This is happening too fast. Kimmer's path is suddenly clear—

Except—except—

"Dana, what exactly is Marc supposed to have done?"

"Well, this is the good part, my dear." She hops off my desk and begins to wear the familiar circle in my carpet. "It seems that some student was going through the archives out at UCLA, you know, throwing away old files—"

"—AND HE COMES ACROSS SOME PAPERS of none other than Pericles Mountain," I tell Kimmer on the telephone minutes later, having had her secretary call her out of a meeting as soon as Dana went on to spread the bad news along the corridor. I sense my wife's growing impatience as I repeat the story Dana told me. Impatience, but excitement too. "And so now he's sitting there in some subbasement of the UCLA Law School, reading through this stuff, the way students do when they'd rather not be working, and it happens that he just read Marc's book in one of his classes, and he notices this draft, and the language is very similar, and he gets to wondering if this is maybe an early draft of the book. Like maybe he can show it off next week in the seminar, surprise everybody by telling them what the great Marc Hadley *thought* about writing before he changed his mind." We both laugh. Kimmer is so delighted by this news that we are almost happy together. "Only, when he looks at it a little more closely, it turns out not to be a draft of *The Constitutional Mind*. It's just a draft of some paper that Perry Mountain wrote. He's about to throw it away, but the similarity of the language sticks in his mind. So he saves it from the recycling bin and takes it back to his apartment and a couple of days later he compares it with the book and, sure enough, it's almost word for word the same. So the next day he tells his professor, and one professor tells another, and, well, here we are."

"I don't believe it," my wife marvels, although she plainly does. "Do you know what this means, Misha? I can't believe it."

"I know what it means, darling."

"He'll have to withdraw, won't he? He'll have to."

She is almost giddy, a Kimmer I have never seen.

"I think you're right. He'll have to withdraw. Congratulations, Your Honor."

"Oh, honey, this is so wonderful." It strikes me suddenly that Kimmer is taking a little too much pleasure in her rival's misfortune—or, rather, misfeasance—and it seems to strike her, too. "I mean, I'm sorry for Marc and all, and, if I'm gonna get it, I didn't want to get it this way. This is just . . ." A pause. I can almost hear her mood beginning to shift, even if for no other reason than that she is moody. "Have you talked to Mallory?"

"Nobody but you."

"I'd love to know what folks are saying in D.C."

"I'll call him as soon as we're done," I promise.

"I think I'll make a few calls of my own." I am not sure why this strikes me as more ominous than optimistic.

"It's pretty amazing," I say, just to keep the conversation going.

"But I don't get it." Kimmer throws in an objection because she thinks human beings are rational. "I don't understand why he would be so stupid. Marc, I mean."

"Well, we all make mistakes."

"This is a pretty big one." As she thinks it through, her mood shift continues, clouds of doubt forming. I can hear it in her voice. "It doesn't make any sense, Misha. Why would Marc copy it? Wouldn't he be afraid of getting caught?"

"Well, here's the interesting part. It turns out that Perry Mountain got sick and never published the article. *The Constitutional Mind* came out three years after Perry Mountain died."

Skeptical Kimmer remains unpersuaded. Her good humor is definitely beginning to fade. "And nobody noticed? Perry didn't send a draft to anybody else? Maybe Theo, for instance? I mean, I'd have thought Theo would be screaming from the day the book was published."

I frown. I did not consider this possibility. I tell her I will call Dana and see.

"*Dana* is your source for all this?" Kimmer splutters. Thinking to bring my wife the news she most wants to hear, I have instead managed to anger her. "I mean, come on, Misha, I know she's your buddy and all, but it's not like she always has her facts right."

"Kimmer—"

"And she can't stand Marc," my wife adds, as though she herself can. "So maybe she's a little biased."

"On the other hand, she always knows what's going on around here."

"I'm sorry, Misha." My wife is her old, cold self again, suspicious of everyone and everything. "It's just that I have the feeling I'm being set up."

I try to keep it light. "This would be an awful lot of trouble to go to just to set you up, darling."

A silence while she thinks this over. "I guess you're right," she grudges. "But I gotta tell you, honey, it sounds awfully weird."

It is only after I glumly hang up the phone and return to my unfinished galley proofs that I realize Kimmer may be half right.

It does look like a setup.

But my wife is not the one being set up.

(III)

"SURE I KNEW ABOUT IT," Theophilus Mountain tells me, a broad smile materializing from some unexpected valley in his acres of beard. "You think I wouldn't have noticed?"

As usual after arguing with my wife, I am feeling logy, my head filled with fuzz rather than thought. I do not quite get Theo's point.

"You knew Marc copied Chapter Three from . . . from your brother? You knew it all these years? And you didn't do anything about it?"

Theo laughs, shifting his round body in his wooden desk chair. He is delighted to be present at the rout of Marc Hadley, one of his many enemies. Most of those Theo despises he hates for their politics; Stuart Land, for example. But the ambitious Marc Hadley carefully cultivates the image of a scholar not driven by politics; Marc he hates for his arrogance. From the day he arrived in Elm Harbor a quarter century ago to teach constitutional law, Marc Hadley has never kowtowed to Theophilus Mountain in the way that the youngsters in his field used to do . . . and the way nobody does any longer. Nowadays, they kowtow to Marc Hadley instead. Theo has never forgiven Marc for changing the rules.

"I never saw the point," says Theo. He begins to pace his huge office, located all the way at the end of the second floor, overlooking the main entrance of Oldie. Theo Mountain, say the wits, watches the new faculty come in the door and watches the old ones get carried out; but Theo himself seems eternal. The office he inhabits is eternal, too, a law school legend, an incredible mess, featuring stacks of papers halfway to the ceiling, covering just about every surface. My office is cluttered, true, as many around the building are, but Theo's is awesome, a masterpiece, a monument to a true genius of disorganization. The only way to sit down is to move some of the junk aside. Theo never seems to care where you put what you move or which stacks you knock over in the process of emptying a chair; he never throws anything away but never looks at anything he keeps. It is said that he has copies of every faculty memo going back to the dawn of the twentieth century. Sometimes I think he might.

"I never saw the point," he repeats, striding over to his file cabinet and yanking open drawers in apparently random order. "Marc was younger then, and a bigger idiot than he is now, and he was convinced, the way you all are when you first arrive, that he knew pretty much everything there was to know. So one day we had lunch and talked about Cardozo. And it turned out he didn't know much about Cardozo at all." Theo has found something to fascinate him in the back of one of the drawers. He leans over and pokes his head in, just like a cartoon character, and I half expect his upper body to disappear, with his feet tumbling in just behind.

"Do you need any help?"

"Are you kidding?" He is among the living again, a thick manila folder clutched in his meaty hands. His laugh makes his beard flutter. "So, anyway," he resumes, "I told him about this paper my brother had written, arguing, um, that Cardozo's judicial method was really the model for just about all the important constitutional adjudication since the 1940s."

"Marc's theory," I murmur.

"*Perry's* theory," Theo corrects me with gentle good humor. "Marc asked me if he could see a copy of the paper. Well, my brother was never one for sharing his papers, except with me and Hero, of course. So it wouldn't have done any good to ask Perry. But I liked Marc, I thought he had some promise, and I loaned him my copy." He spins the folder across his desktop in my direction, and, even before I open it, I know I am holding in my hand the evidence of Marc Hadley's plagiarism: Pericles Mountain's unpublished manuscript on Cardozo, the uncited source for the third chapter of Marc's book, the single great idea for which he won every prize the legal academy can offer.

I flip through the yellowed pages. I see occasional notes in Theo's hand, cross-outs, question marks, inserts, coffee stains. "Are you sure . . ."

"That Marc copied it? Sure I am. You read it, you'll see for yourself."

"And you knew at the time? When his book came out?"

"Sure did."

I ask Kimmer's question: "So why didn't you do something about it?"

"Like what?"

"Like . . . go public."

Theo frowns briefly, as though he does not know the answer himself. Except that he does. I can read it in his cautious, calculating eyes. Theo has seen it all, yet life never seems to bore him. When he smiles again, his look is so devious it scares me. "Well, I wouldn't say I did *nothing* exactly."

"What *would* you say you did?"

"I would say I told *Marc*."

"Why would you just tell Marc and not tell anybody . . ." I begin. Then I stop. I see it. Oh, this is so Theo! Of course he told Marc! He told Marc so that he would have the plagiarism to hold over the head of his young, arrogant colleague for the next couple of decades. He told nobody else because he wanted Marc beholden to him. And because, as I now realize, Theo, my onetime mentor, is the kind of secret, envious hater who would prefer to own the knowledge of Marc's perfidy, rather than sharing it with the world. If everybody else realized that the great Marc Hadley was a liar and a cheat, that would actually have reduced rather than enhanced Theo's pleasure.

Besides, by keeping the secret to himself, he could wait until this perfectly delicious moment to tip over Marc Hadley's house of cards. If, indeed, he was involved in the tipping.

"I didn't want Marc to get in trouble," says Theo in the pious tone of a man who has never despised a colleague in his life. His brother's memory, it seems, mattered to Theo not a smidgen; what he cared about was making Marc suffer. "But I wanted him to know that ideas are not all that easy to disguise. I wanted him to know that I knew. I wanted him not to do it again. And, well, you know what happened, I suppose. Everybody knows."

I do not see it. Then I do. "His writer's block."

"Exactly." Theo almost cackles with glee. "I guess I scared him into never writing another book."

Or ordered him not to, so that his arrogant colleague would have to suffer years of listening to people mutter about his wasted potential.

"Why would you do something like that?" The words jump out of me.

"People like Marc Hadley deserve what they get."

"But why would he imagine he could get away with it?"

"Marc thought he was clever. He asked me, maybe half a year after Perry died, if I remembered his paper on Cardozo. I told him I didn't remember a word of it, that I never even read it." Theo's merry eyes twinkle. "That was a lie."

I am ready to go. I have had enough of Theo. I suspected his capacity for hate, but never imagined this streak of cruelty. Poor Marc is finished as a judicial nominee: that is the one nugget of actual news in this stream of reminiscence. Dana's story is right on the money. The allegation of plagiarism is not survivable in today's climate, even if it turns out not to be true—and, not having read Perry Mountain's manuscript, I warn myself cautiously, I have no way to be sure. The whole tale could turn out to be fiction. Or a misunderstanding. But I doubt it. The lines of worry in Dahlia Hadley's face that afternoon at the preschool were too stark; when she said something was eating away at her husband, she spoke the simple truth. Marc was not worried about people discovering that his daughter was sleeping with Lionel Eldridge; he was worried about his own terrible error of two decades back. Sitting in Theo Mountain's paper-strewn office, I find myself growing lightheaded. Marc is out. Kimmer is in. The President wants quality and diversity, according to Ruthie Silverman, and my wife brings both: unless something pops up in her background check, my wife is going to become a federal judge.

And maybe our marriage will be saved, despite my late father's machinations.

I hand back Theo's battered old folder and thank him for his time. Theo snatches it from my hand and buries it afresh in his file cabinet, although not in the same drawer from which he initially pulled it.

At the door, another thought strikes me.

"Theo, don't you think it's awfully convenient, all of this coming up at just the right moment to knock Marc out of the box?"

"Yes, I do." A smile of reminiscence. "I'm reminded of what Mr. Justice Frankfurter supposedly said when he heard the news of Mr. Chief Justice Vinson's death just before the reargument of *Brown v. Board of Education* in the Supreme Court: 'This is the first indication that I have ever had that there is a God.'"

Theo chortles madly. I wait until he settles down and then ask the other question that is burning in my mind: "Theo, you wouldn't happen to know how the news really got out, would you? I mean, about the . . . alleged plagiarism."

"Believe me, Talcott, it's genuine plagiarism." He smiles at his own turn of a phrase. "What, you think I let the cat out of the bag? Well, you're wrong. From what I hear, it was a student at UCLA. I told you."

"But do you believe that story?"

Theo is finally exasperated. "Tal, come on. Sometimes you get actual, genuine good news. Try to appreciate those moments. They don't come often."

"I suppose not," I murmur, shaking his hand as I go, because Theo is of the generation that appreciates such niceties. But my mind is not in this office, or even in this building. My thoughts are back at the cemetery on the day we buried my father, when a sickly old man named Jack Ziegler told me to tell Kimmer not to worry about Marc Hadley. *I do not think he has the staying power. Weren't those the words? A fairly large skeleton is rattling around in his closet. Sooner or later, it is bound to tumble out.*

I'll say.

CHAPTER 36

A BROTHER'S TALE

(1)

I FINALLY REACH ADDISON on the quiet Sunday afternoon before classes resume. I have been calling him, on and off, since Mariah's visit, and tried him on both Christmas Day and New Year's Eve. I have left messages on his machine at home and with his producer at the studio. I have tried his cell phone. I have sent e-mail. I have received, in response, nothing. In a fearful burst of inspiration, I even tracked down Beth Olin, the poet, who turns out to live in Jamestown, New York, but when she heard who I was and what I wanted she hung up on me, which answered the question of whether they are still together. I even thought of calling one of his ex-wives, but my boldness has its limits.

"I've been away," he tells me now, as I sit in my study eating a tuna sandwich and watching a fresh flurry of midwinter snow blowing around the street. Another four to six inches are forecast, but Kimmer went to the office anyway. Addison sounds exhausted. "Sorry."

"Away where your cell phone doesn't work?" I ask peevishly.

"Argentina."

"Argentina?"

"I never told you? I was looking at land. I've been there, I don't know, seven or eight times in the past two years. I'm thinking I might build a house down there." To live in until the Democrats are back in the White House, maybe. "And I had such a good time I thought I'd stay a few days. The days became weeks and . . . well, anyway, I'm back."

Days became weeks?

"So—what did you do? Took time off from the show?"

"The show is getting a little old, to tell you the truth. I think it's time for me to get back to work on the book." Addison says something like this every few years, but all it ever means is that he is about to change jobs. Nobody I know has ever actually seen him write a line.

"That would be great," I offer loyally. "To do the book, I mean."

"Yeah."

"It's a history that needs to be written."

"Yeah." It isn't just exhaustion that is depressing my brother's voice, I realize. There is a sense of resignation. I wonder what it is to which he is resigned. "Hey, guess what, bro? The FBI was out talking to me. About *your wife.*" A small chuckle. "Like, sure, I know anything about her."

"It's her background check, Addison. They have to talk to everybody."

"I know that. I just don't know why *her* damn background check has to include so many questions about *my* damn money." But I am sure Addison remembers, as I do, the embarrassingly cursory investigation of the Judge. Procedures, it is said, have been tightened since those days. "So, anyway, you left lots of messages. Must be something important."

I have had plenty of time to think about how to handle this moment. I work around to the more urgent issue by starting with the lesser one.

So I tell my brother about Mariah's visit and the missing report from Jonathan Villard. I explain that there is no copy to be found anywhere, including the police files, where Meadows drew a blank. I tell him about the two pages of notes in the Judge's handwriting. All we can glean from the notes, I add, is that the car that killed Abby had two people in it.

"Huh," is Addison's only comment. Then he adds, surprised, "You guys have made a lot of progress," and I know, at that moment, that I am right. My brother pauses again, but I wait him out. Finally, he asks the question that surely troubles him most: "So, why are you telling me this?"

"You know why," I say softly. Waiting for his answer, I can hear the television in the family room, where Bentley is watching a squeaky-clean video that John and Janice Brown, his godparents, gave him for Christmas. Two nights ago, Kimmer and I attended the annual post-holiday bash of Lemaster Carlyle's fraternity, joining a couple of hundred other well-to-do members of the darker nation, dancing the electric slide, the cha-cha slide, and a brand-new invention known as the dot-com slide into the wee hours of the morning. Maybe we do have a bit of a social life after all.

"No, I don't know why," says my big brother, his voice now peevish.

"Because you know where the report is."

"I *what?*"

"You know where it is. Or you know what was in it."

"What makes you think that?" Addison sounds more frightened than irritated. "I don't know anything about it."

"I think you do. Remember the day we buried the Judge? You were up there by the grave, and I came over to talk to you? Remember what you said? You said you wondered if we'd ever find *the folks* who were in the car that killed Abby. That's what you said, *the folks.*"

"You heard me wrong," he says after a pause.

"I don't think so. There isn't any word I could mistake for *folks.* No word that's singular." Silence. "All these years, Addison, everybody in the family has talked about finding the *driver* of the car. Mom used to say it before she died. And Dad. And me and Mariah, and you, too. But at the cemetery you knew there were two people in the car. I think you knew because you read the report."

"That's a little thin," Addison announces, but I can tell his heart is not in the quarrel he is trying to provoke. "Maybe I just misspoke. Maybe I was guessing. You can't make anything out of it."

"Come on, Addison, don't play games. You know I'm right. Either the Judge gave you a copy or you just took it from his files. But I know you've read it. And I'd like to know what's in it."

Another pause, longer this time. I hear what might be a voice in the background, then Addison's whispered reply. He seems to be telling somebody to give him a minute. Maybe somebody he took to Argentina with him. Or somebody he didn't.

Then my brother is back.

"Shit," he says.

(11)

ADDISON IS UNHAPPY. I am complicating his life. He would rather be off lecturing on a college campus or looking at property in South America or doing his talk show, even if it is getting a little old—anything other than spending emotionally costly time with a member of his family. All three Garland children have spent our adulthoods fleeing from our father, but Addison fled the furthest, which might be why he was the one the Judge loved best. Until the last couple of months, I have always admired Addison, but the way he has been avoiding me has tested my fraternal commitment.

"Look, my brother, I don't actually have a copy of the report. I never had a copy. I just read it once." Another pause, but he can find no escape. "Dad showed it to me."

I draw in a breath. Addison sounds so nervous that I am not sure whether to believe a word he says. "Okay. So, what was in it?"

"You don't want to know any more about it, Misha." Addison's voice hardens. "You really don't."

"Actually, I do."

"You're crazy. You're as crazy as he was."

Probably he means the Judge, but I suppose there are plenty of other candidates as well. A week and a half ago, I finally got a call back from Special Agent Nunzio. Without mentioning Maxine, I told him I thought Father Bishop was murdered by mistake. He thanked me coolly for my idea and promised unenthusiastically to look into it. Could have been worse.

"I just want to know the truth," I tell my brother calmly.

Addison sighs. "I don't understand you, Tal. You're a Christian, right? And I think it says somewhere you're supposed to make your life a work of forgiveness, not a work of vengeance."

This sets me back even further. I thought Maxine left me at sea, but this must set some kind of record for the most Delphic reply.

"I'm not seeking any vengeance."

"Well, yeah, that's what you say. But maybe it's bullshit." Addison loves vulgarity, believing, I suspect, that it makes his otherwise cultured Garland speech more authentically black. Actually it sounds forced, like a child playing with a new vocabulary. "You might *think* you don't want vengeance, but you might be wrong. You don't really know what's in your heart making you act this way. You need to ask God to heal your heart, bro."

I have long since stopped eating. I am ruining my appetite trying to fight through all the verbal smoke Addison is blowing across the miles; and to understand why he is doing it.

Addison, meanwhile, is quoting Scripture. "'Bless those who persecute you,' Paul tells us in Romans 12. Remember? 'Do not repay anyone evil for evil.' And if you read the story of Samson . . ."

I cut him off, something I have hardly ever done since childhood. "I'm not trying to return evil for evil, Addison. Come on. I'm not trying to do anything to anybody. I'm just trying to find out what's going on."

"Yeah, you *say* that. But, see, it could be that there's shit that, if you knew, you *would* want a piece of somebody."

"Addison, please. I'm not trying to hurt anybody." Because it has occurred to me that the vengeance my brother is discussing might have something to do with himself. "I just need to know what was in the report."

"No, you don't. Believe me. You don't need to know, you don't want to know. You want to leave the past in the past, bro, and move on to the future. You want to love your wife and family and take care of business at home. You want to face the world with a whole lot of forgiveness in your heart. But you absolutely do not want to know what was in that report."

"Why not?"

"Temptation. Do you want to be led into temptation? Because that report was full of temptation to sin, believe me."

Setting me back even more. But I have made it this far. I press on.

"Addison, please. At least tell me when Dad showed it to you."

Another pause as the wheels go round in that subtle, manipulative mind. "Say a year ago. A little more. Yeah. Last fall."

I have the sense that he is coloring the truth, shading it, shifting it in a comfortable direction, the way witnesses often do. I decide to settle in for a long game, concealing my own impatience while allowing his to grow. Having taken a deposition or two in my time, I understand the virtue of circling gradually to the main point, and pretending to be bored when you get there.

"Do you know why he showed it to you?"

"Not exactly."

"Well, can you tell me how he came to show it to you?"

Again my brother makes me wait. I do not understand what is worrying him so, but I can feel its effects through the telephone line. "Like I said," he begins, "it was maybe a year and a half ago. Dad called. He was coming to Chicago to give some speech, and he wanted to know if we could get together for dinner or something. I said yeah, sure, whatever. I mean, you know, I'm not into his kind of politics, but he was my father, okay? So we had dinner, over at his hotel. One of those elegant little private places downtown. Not in the dining room, up in his suite. Naturally he had a suite. Huge. Two bedrooms, like he needed them, right? But, you know, all those right-wing crazies he always used to speak to, they loved him. They never spared any expense. Listen. He got these huge fees, right? Thirty thousand dollars a pop? Forty? Sometimes more. How come? So his audience could go back to the country club and tell their golf buddies that a black man agreed with their right-wing craziness, which meant that it was true, right?" I have never heard such hostility in his voice. Or maybe I just never realized quite how much Addison hated the Judge.

"So, anyway, we have dinner up in his suite. He says he doesn't want anybody to hear what we're talking about. So I'm joking around, okay, and I say, 'Well, what if they bugged your suite?' And he doesn't laugh. He takes it very seriously. He looks at me and he says, 'Do you think they might have?' Or something like that. And I'm, like, uh-oh. So I tell him I was only joking and he says he changed suites once already just to be on the safe side. And I tell him yeah, that was a smart move, but I'm thinking that he's, you know, maybe he's . . . well, you know. Maybe there's some kind of problem. Are you sure you wanna hear this?"

"Yes." My voice is tight.

"Okay. You asked for it. We sit down to dinner at the table—the suite had like a dining area. And he has a couple of folders, and I'm thinking we're gonna talk about the family finances. You know, like, *Here's where all the money is if anything happens to me?* And he has that really serious look on his face, the one he used to use when he was gonna give us one of his lectures, you know, about right and wrong, keeping your promises, all the bullshit he used to talk to us about. And he gets real excited and he says to me, he says, 'Son, we have to talk about something important,' and I'm, like, yes, I was right. He says it might be a little tough to take, and I just sit up straight and nod, and he says there's a part of his life he's never really talked to the family about, and I nod, and he says he's coming to me because I'm the eldest child, and I nod my head again."

My face burns at this—the old, familiar jealousy over Addison's favored place in the Judge's heart—but I have the wit, for once, to remain silent.

"And so now I think he's gonna tell me about the money, but, instead, he opens the folder and he pulls out a sheaf of papers, five or six pages, and he says to me, 'I want you to read this. You need to know.' I ask him what it is. I'm thinking it's like an investment plan or something. And he says to me, 'This is Villard's report.' And so I ask him who Villard is. I wasn't goofing, I really didn't remember. And he gets mad and he says, 'Son, I told you to read it, so just read it.' You know what he could be like. 'Just read it.' So I did."

Addison clams up. He has no sense of leaving a story unfinished. I asked how he came to read the report and he has told me.

"Did he say why he wanted you to read it?"

"He had some story. I don't know. Something had spooked him."

"Spooked him?"

"I don't know, okay? I mean, I really didn't listen that closely. I wasn't interested."

"Not interested? Addison, he was our father!"

"So what? Listen. I could tell you a few things you don't wanna know about . . . about our father. That confirmation thing, it just about wiped him out. You never realized that, you and Mariah, but you weren't the ones he used to call up at night, drunk—yeah, he started drinking again. You didn't know that, did you?"

I do know, of course, because Lanie Cross told me, but, now that my brother seems to want to talk, I am not about to break his narrative flow.

"So, yeah, he used to call me up in the middle of the night, crying about this or that. Because I was the *eldest*. 'I wouldn't share this with anybody but you, son.' That's what he used to say. Like it was some great honor, having him wake me up at two in the morning to tell me how he deserved to die for his sins, how they were gonna kill him one day, never mind worrying about who *they* were. So, yeah, Dad was a paranoid, okay? He thought everybody in the world was coming after him. The truth is, he was as crazy as a bedbug. Is that what you want to hear, bro? Is that straight enough for you? Yeah, great, so he had some kind of story about how somebody came to see him and now he was in real trouble and he needed me to look at these papers. And me, I'm sitting there in his hotel trying to figure out how me reading this report is gonna get him out of trouble. Not that I completely cared. I was so sick of him, so sick of all the crap I took from him over the years—"

Addison makes himself stop. Garland men can do that, like turning a switch. Surely that is one of the reasons that our women always grow to loathe us.

"Maybe I was wrong," he continues in a milder tone. "The Judge came to me for help and I turned him away. That was wrong in every religion I know. And to talk about him the way I am now, that's wrong, too." Another pause. I imagine him in his house in Chicago, eyes closed, for he is whispering what sounds like a prayer, maybe for forgiveness, maybe for strength, maybe for show.

"Addison." The whispering continues. "Addison!"

"You don't have to yell, Misha." The cocky big brother is back. The furious, nearly inarticulate Addison of two minutes ago is gone, a demon driven out. "There's this great new invention, the telephone?

And you can talk in a normal tone and the person at the other end can be all the way in Chicago and he can still hear you just fine."

"Okay, okay, I'm sorry. But look. What was the story? Who came to see him? You said somebody spooked him. . . ."

"Well, you know, I don't think I should talk about that part. I mean, the Judge kind of made me promise not to tell."

I ponder. I am close, so close, and Addison has never been any good at keeping secrets, except when he has to hide one girlfriend from another. There must be a way to pry this one loose. Certainly I am determined to try. Somewhere deep down, in that place that Garland men never reveal, my anger is beginning to burn. A degree of anger at my brother, for playing these games, but mostly anger at my father, for confiding in his first son, the fly-by-night activist, instead of his second son, the lawyer. *If you wanted to confide in Addison,* I wish I could shout at him, *then why in the world didn't you arrange to have the pawn and the note delivered to him instead of to me?*

Not that I would ever shout at the Judge.

Then I remember how Addison, alone among the children, argued with our father. When the Judge would take over the dinner table for one of his lectures on what to do and what to avoid doing, Mariah and I would sit dutifully, mouthing all the right responses, *Yessir, No sir, Whatever you say, sir*—and Addison, even as a teenager, would look him dead in the eye and say, *Bullshit, Dad.* He would be grounded for a week, of course, but we could see the pride in his handsome eyes, and even in the Judge's. *I like the boy's chutzpah,* he would tell our mother, *even if it's misdirected.*

Well, his chutzpah has carried him a good long way. Let's see how far.

"So, what happened to the report?"

"What do you mean, what happened to it?" Combative.

"Did you read it? Did Dad take it with him?"

Addison's voice is suddenly slow. "No, I took it with me. I promised him I would look at it." I hear his ragged breathing as he tries to control his anger. "And it's gone, Misha. Don't even ask. I got rid of it."

"How? You mean, you threw it away?"

"It's gone. That's all."

I believe him. Whatever was in Villard's report, Addison did not want anybody seeing it. And he is not about to tell me why.

"Okay, Addison. Forget about what happened to the report. Forget about why the Judge was spooked. Let me tell you the other reason I've been trying to reach you." Addison, likely relieved that I am changing topics, offers no objection. "I want to ask you about something the Judge could not have sworn you to silence about, because he didn't know about it."

"Fire away," he says indulgently, guessing that I have no ammunition left.

And so I tell him about my meeting with Sally. I describe the night the two of them were in the house together, making love, and were interrupted by the Judge's furious argument with Colin Scott.

"Yeah," he says when I am done. "Yeah, Sally told me she talked to you and that she kind of let the cat out of the bag. Poor kid."

"Addison . . ."

"You have to understand, Misha, Sally's been through some rough times. You have any idea how many times she's been in and out of rehab? Sometimes she embellishes things a little bit, okay? It wasn't necessarily the way she makes it sound."

The sex, he is talking about, not the argument.

"Addison, that's fine. I don't care about you and Sally. I really don't." A lie, but I see no reason to remind him how wrong it was, especially when I have him cornered. "What I care about is what the Judge and Colin Scott were talking about. Sally said you overheard part of the conversation. That's what I need to know about. What you overheard."

Silence.

"Come on, Addison. You heard the whole thing, I bet. Or most of it."

"I heard most of it," he finally concedes, "but I can't tell you about it, Misha. Really. I just can't."

"You can't? What do you mean, you can't? Addison, the Judge isn't your property. He was my father, too."

"Yeah, but there are things about a father that . . ." He hesitates, then tries again. "Look, Misha. There's stuff you don't really wanna know, believe me. About Dad. I know you think you wanna know, but you don't. I mean—look, bro, he did some bad shit, okay? We all do, but Dad—well, you wouldn't believe it if I told you, and I'm not gonna tell you. No way." Another pause. He is sensing my pain, perhaps. Or my bewilderment. Or my simple need. He grunts: Addison really cannot bear the pain of another human being, which is an element of his personality I have always loved and envied. I sometimes think it is this aspect of his character, not mere carnal desire, that has led my brother to rampant promiscuity. He cannot bear to say no. Perhaps that explains his frequent mysterious disappearances from the family for months or years at a time: in order to stay sane, he has to find a path to refuse what others, through their neediness, demand of him.

I play, shamelessly, to his weakness.

"Addison, come on. You have to tell me something. I'm going to go crazy if I don't have some hint of what's going on. Of what happened that night." I lower my voice. "Look, Addison, I can't go into the details now, but this is destroying my life."

"Get serious, bro."

"Seriously. Remember when Uncle Jack came to the cemetery? Ever since then . . . well, you wouldn't believe what's been going on. But it's wrecking my marriage, Addison, and it's driving me nuts. So, please, anything you can tell me. I have to know."

My brother goes into another long think. I am supposed to be finishing another article, trying to work my way back into the respect of my colleagues, but I am prepared to wait all afternoon to get this one answer. And Addison, bless him, seems to sense the truth of my need, and so compassion draws out of him what argument would not.

"Well, okay, Misha, okay. You've got a point. Listen. Tell you what. I can maybe tell you one little fact, but that's gotta be it, bro. Seriously. This is, like, a sacred trust."

"I know, Addison, I know. And I respect that."

My brother's silence bespeaks a certain suspicion, and why not? I am lying through my teeth. Addison continues to make me wait. Even sitting a thousand miles away in his Chicago townhouse, holding my sanity in his large hands, he has a way with silence. I try to be patient, try not to put a word wrong, try not to speak at all, because I respect the fragility of the moment. Underneath my brother's silence, I sense bewilderment, even fury. He never wanted to tell me anything; he wanted to talk me out of my search. He failed, and he is furious about it.

I sense something else, too, something I faintly scented at the beginning of our call and can now confirm. My brother is afraid. I only wish I knew what of.

At last he deigns to speak: "One fact, Misha, that's all. Please don't ask me to tell you any more, because I won't. One fact, and then I'm not answering any more questions." He sounds like a politician refusing to talk about his personal life.

"One fact. I understand."

"Okay. Listen. When Colin Scott was at Shepard Street that night? Yeah, Sally is right, I heard the whole thing. Every word." My brother lets out a long sigh. "Sally told you she heard Dad say, 'There are no rules where a dollar is involved,' right?"

"Right."

"Well, I heard it too. And I was a lot closer." A final pause, perhaps trying to find a way out of this, a phrase, an argument, a warning that will make me stop. Evidently, he cannot come up with one. "Sally got it wrong as usual, bro. The word Dad used wasn't *dollar*. The word was *daughter*."

Click. Dial tone.

(III)

MORRIS YOUNG MAKES TIME FOR ME later that night, because he can tell that I am desperate. We meet at his church around eight, and he hears me out patiently. When I am done, he offers no advice. Instead, he tells me a story.

"In the Old Testament—in Genesis—there's the tale of Noah."

"The flood?"

His pocked face softens. "No, no, of course not the flood. There is much more to the tale of Noah than the flood, Talcott."

"I know." As though I do.

"I am sure you do. I am sure you remember the account, in Genesis 9, of the time when Noah got drunk and was lying naked in his tent. His son Ham went looking for him and found him naked and went and told his brothers, Shem and Japheth—remember? And Shem and Japheth went into the tent backward, so they wouldn't see their father naked, and covered him up. Noah, when he awakened, cursed his son Ham. Ham, you see, did not respect his father. He wanted to see his father naked. Wanted his brothers to see. What kind of son is that, Talcott? Do you understand the story? Sons are not supposed to see their fathers naked. A son is not supposed to know all his father's secrets . . . or all his father's sins. And if he does know, he is not supposed to tell. Do you understand, Talcott?"

"You think I should stop? I shouldn't try to find out what my father was really up to?"

"I cannot tell you what to do, Talcott. I can tell you, however, that the Lord requires you to honor your father. I can tell you that sons who go looking for their father's sins are bound to find them. And I can tell you that the Bible teaches us that such sons will almost always come to grief."

CHAPTER 37

SOME HISTORICAL NOTES

THE LARGEST EGO ON THE FACULTY is owned not by Dana Worth or Lemaster Carlyle or Arnie Rosen or even the recently humiliated Marc Hadley; no, it is the sole possession of my Oldie neighbor Ethan Brinkley. Little Ethan takes enormous pride in his achievements in advance, according to Dear Dana Worth, the faculty wit. That way, says Dana, he avoids the stress of worrying about whether he ever actually achieves them or not.

Over the years, Ethan has told everybody who will listen, and quite a few who would rather not, about the secret appendices he has stored around his office: photocopies of hundreds of files and reports that he somehow neglected to turn in when he ended his stint on the staff of the Intelligence Committee. Little Ethan, as Theo Mountain derisively calls him, likes to pepper conversations with delectable tidbits from the files, the identities of John Kennedy's lovers, for instance, or the brand of Fidel Castro's cologne. At times, it is a little like living with a budding J. Edgar Hoover. Stuart Land has told Ethan to his face that he should be in prison, and Lem Carlyle, the ex-prosecutor, has contemplated turning him in, but, so far, nobody has quite gotten up the nerve to do anything, even when Little Ethan, beguiling sprite that he can be, was a regular television guest during the Clinton impeachment proceedings, issuing vehement calls for a return of integrity to the federal government.

Ethan possesses considerable ambition, but no scintilla of either irony or shame. And so it is, on the first afternoon of the spring term, less than a week after the collapse of Marc's hopes for the judgeship that now seems Kimmer's for the taking, and one day after my debilitating conversation with Addison, that I stand in front of Ethan's door, right across the dim hallway from mine. I am nervous, partly because Ethan and I are not remotely friends, but mostly because what I plan to ask of him is somewhat tricky. No, let me be truthful: what I plan to ask of him is probably against the law.

Not that mere illegality will bother Ethan Brinkley.

"Misha!" he booms when I step into his office. The little man bounds from behind his desk to give my hand a practiced pump. I have never invited Ethan to address me by my nickname, which is reserved for a handful of intimates, but he has heard Dana use it and adopted it as his own, assuming, in the manner of salesmen and politicians everywhere, that his choice to call me what he wants rather than what I want somehow cements our intimacy.

Actually, it offends me, but, as so often, I keep that fact to myself, confident that a secret time of reckoning will come.

A few pleasantries as Ethan waves me to a hard wooden chair. His office is the size of a large closet, and his two smallish windows on the longer wall look out on nothing except the next wing of the building. But the vista and the square footage will come with time, believes Ethan, whose ambition knows a certain patience, thus enabling him to take the long view. *The day will arrive*, Ethan told me in a careless moment well before he was voted tenure, *when I am a power in this place.*

He already has the swagger, muttered Dana when I shared this *bon mot*.

Ethan reads my mood. His face is composed and sympathetic as he settles himself on the chair next to mine. Another politician's move: he does not sit across the desk from me, perhaps believing that it lends too much formality. Everything Ethan does is purposeful, designed to make people like him, and most people do. Some say he is already running for dean, ready to tilt against Arnie Rosen and Lem Carlyle for the job when Lynda Wyatt decides to retire. I am surprised that people think he is aiming so low.

Ethan is an athletic and clever little man, with untidy brown hair and innocent brown eyes. He favors scuffed shoes and tweed blazers just rumpled enough to assure the people that he is one of them, except that his rumpled blazers cost a thousand dollars a throw. His gaze never wavers from the face of the person he is talking to, or listening to, but you have the sense from the set of his small mouth and the deep frowning lines on his forehead that it is all show, that behind the ingenuous eyes he is calculating, move and countermove, like a chess player working out his response while your clock is ticking.

"So, Misha, what can I do for you?" Ethan asks, brown eyes twinkling, as though I do not have five years of seniority on him.

"I need some information that I think you might have."

He almost smiles: Ethan is happiest when helping others, not because it excites his passion for charitable works, but because it leaves the people he helps in his debt. Little Ethan is spreading markers around the law school as fast as he can, teaching extra courses, attending every workshop, volunteering to write the committee reports no sane professor would touch, even showing up at the endless receptions for visiting assistant attorneys general from brand-new countries of which nobody has ever heard.

"Misha, you know me—anything for a buddy."

I nod, then gather my courage, for I am making a leap, one I have been pondering ever since my return from the Vineyard, and one that was cemented by what my brother told me. So, with a silent prayer, I voice the name: "Colin Scott."

Ethan frowns for a moment, not in distaste, but in concentration. His memory is part of his fast-growing legend. Our students are astonished by his ability to quote long passages from cases without troubling to look at a book or notes, a trick that most academics can do, but which Ethan renders with a certain implike flourish. And, if the truth is told, he has mastered the illusion far earlier in his career than most of us did.

"Rings a bell," Ethan concedes. The sympathetic look is back. "What about him?"

I wave my hand toward his painstakingly organized and carefully locked cabinets. "I need to know whatever you know about him."

"He's dead."

"I know that. I was on the Vineyard when it happened."

"Were you, now? Were you? Well!" He stands up to head to the cabinet, but claps me on the back as he passes, somehow implying that we have been to war together, but only I have seen combat. I do not even mind the gesture, for it signals what I have been half hoping, half hating: that Colin Scott is mentioned somewhere deep in the files of the Select Committee on Intelligence. Which explains, among other things, why the FBI was so reluctant to give Meadows his name.

"Colin Scott," he mutters, twirling the combination lock on one of the black metal monstrosities that line the far wall. "Colin Scott. You're around here somewhere." He makes a show of leafing slowly through the files, although I have no doubt that he knows exactly where to find whatever he knows about Mr. Scott, maybe because of his memory, or maybe because he would have had the folder out recently in order to add the information on Scott's death.

"What do you think of this business about Marc?" Ethan asks over his shoulder as he piddles around in the drawer. "Think it's true?"

"I don't know." I keep my voice neutral. Having spoken to Theo, I have little doubt that Marc did exactly what he is accused of doing, even though he has not yet formally taken his name out of the hat. But I am interested to see which way Ethan the great politician plans to jump. Ethan, who probably knows nothing of my wife's candidacy, is noncommittal by nature. Since joining our ranks, he has avoided controversy the way a cat avoids water. He enjoys debating proposals of only two kinds: those that pass unanimously, and those that are withdrawn without a vote.

"It's a sticky wicket," Ethan agrees, for he decided somewhere along the way that the occasional Britishism, even if a mere cliché, makes him sound statesmanlike. "I suppose one wants to see all the evidence first, hmmm?"

"I suppose."

"Mustn't leap to conclusions. Very unscientific," he admonishes. "Gotcha," he adds, straightening up with a thin manila folder in his hand, and, for a silly instant, I imagine I am still in Theo's office as he pulls out the proof of Marc Hadley's sin.

"Colin Scott?"

Ethan nods. "The very same." He walks back toward me, but this time he perches on the corner of his desk, which, like the rest of the office, is so neat that a casual visitor might be excused for supposing that no work goes on here. The obligatory photographs of his wife and infant daughter are so perfectly aligned that he must have used a ruler. The signed photographs of prominent Washington figures are quite a bit larger.

"Now, Misha, we have something of a problem here," he begins apologetically, and I know a lecture on confidentiality is coming, for, although Ethan Brinkley possesses no ethics to speak of, he has the politician's knack of talking as though he has plenty. "This information is technically the property of the federal government. If I were to show you this piece of paper, we could both wind up in prison." Ethan's bland face puffs up with pride at the idea that he controls so sensitive a document, even if he did steal it.

"I understand."

"But I can *tell* you the contents."

"Okay." I see no legal difference between the two scenarios, and I doubt that Ethan does either, although he would doubtless swear under oath to a grand jury that he thought he was within the rules: *If I don't read the actual words on the page, if I only summarize or paraphrase, I am not precisely divulging the contents of the document, and so I'm outside the statutory prohibitions.* Legal hairsplitting of that kind tends to make the public angry, but it is often a good way to escape responsibility for breaking the law. Politicians are fond of it, except when a member of the other party does it. We law professors teach it to our students every day as though it is a virtue.

"Colin Scott, Colin Scott," he muses, pretending to read it all for the first time. "Not a very nice man, our Colin."

"Oh? Not nice in what way?"

Ethan will not be hurried. He hates to relinquish center stage, even for a second, and is constantly rehearsing for the big chance that is on its way.

"He was with the Agency, of course. Well, you knew that." I didn't know, not for sure, and not even Uncle Mal, who knows everything, saw fit to tell me, but if the fact were a complete surprise, I would not be here. Still, the confirmation is a second strike against Mallory Corcoran. "A long time," Ethan continues. "Mmmm. Foreign postings . . . Well, I don't suppose I can tell you that. He was there in the old days, when they used to have what was known as the Plans Directorate. I see you never heard of it. Nice euphemism, isn't it? They call it Operations now. The people who are out there, overseas, *doing* things. Well, well." Still examining his pages. "This was back in the sixties, Misha. Large blank areas, pretty large. Not unusual with the gentlemen from Plans. Don't know the full scope of his activities. But he was dirty, and the Agency dumped him. This must have been . . . yes, after the Church hearings. New broom and all that. He was old-school. A dangerous man to have around."

"Why dangerous?"

But elfin Ethan prefers to dole out his precious little surprises one by one and wait for a reaction. "Colin Scott is not his real name, you know."

"As a matter of fact I didn't know, but I can't exactly say I'm astonished." When I am around Ethan, I seem to lapse into the same portentous constructions that are his only means of communication.

"It's one of his names, of course," Ethan presses on. "He has several. Look at this. Mmmm, yes. You see, Scott was a name they gave him, along with a new identity, after he was drummed out of the Agency. Set him up, let's see, yes, he opened a little detective agency in South Carolina. Well, you knew that. But South Carolina was not his first stop post-Agency, and Scott was his second new name. Seems some old friends, not the friendly kind, rumbled to his old one. His old new one, I mean."

"You mean enemies."

"Well, yes." Ethan is annoyed that I have broken into his narrative. He is having fun teasing me.

"What was his real name?"

"Oh, Misha, naturally, if it were up to me I would tell you, but, you know, national security and all that. Sorry, but rules are rules." Apologizing self-importantly. All at once this mystery is awash in people who could help me understand what is going on but climb up on their principles to explain their refusal.

"What did he do in the Agency?" I ask, really just to keep the conversation going; in truth, I have just about run out of ideas.

"He floated." Ethan smiles at my blank look. He loves jargon. "He was in Plans, as I told you, but he also worked for Angleton, who ran counterintelligence until he cracked up. Later on he did a little of the paramilitary thing in Laos, had lots of contacts up in the Shans—well, let me not bore you with any of these details. Point is, if there was a whiff of Communism, a fire to be put out, Mr. Scott was the kind they called. Not a fanatic, mind you. Not a Bircher or some such. That kind tends to go into politics, not intelligence, and, in truth, intelligence doesn't really want them. No, our Mr. Scott was more your spear-carrier. One of your technocrats, let's call him that. Totally devoted to getting the job done. The kind who followed orders, even if the orders were, shall we say, not the sort of thing that should ever see the light of day. A dangerous man, as I said, for just that reason. Past his time, of course. Dinosaur. Relic of an era the passing of which we do not exactly lament." Implying that *we* do not exactly lament his death, either, whoever *we* are.

And implying something else, something I have feared but buried almost from the night when Uncle Mal first told me that Agent McDermott was a fraud; a fear that wakened rudely when I heard Sally's story; a fear that clawed its way to the surface once Addison explained that *dollar* was really *daughter*.

"You're saying he . . . uh, he killed people."

"I cannot confirm that, of course," says Ethan primly. "Let us just say that he is, or, rather, was, a dangerous man."

I mull this over. A dangerous relic, a dinosaur, drummed out of the Agency, talking to my father in his study in the middle of the night, the Judge telling him that there are no rules where a daughter is concerned. A daughter, not a dollar. Then showing up a quarter-century later, pretending to be in the FBI, looking frantically for something or other, maybe trashing Vinerd Howse, then drowning at Menemsha Beach.

I am overlooking something, and I have a hunch it is something obvious.

Then I have it.

"Just one more question, Ethan. When exactly was Mr. Scott, or whatever his name was, thrown out of the Agency?"

Ethan assumes a pious pose. "Oh, well, I hardly think it would be proper for me to share actual *dates* with you, Misha. The law, is, well, the law is what it is."

"But it was after the Church hearings, right? And the Church hearings were—when?—'74? '75?"

"Around then, yes."

So Colin Scott was already out of the Agency by the time Sally and Addison heard him arguing with the Judge. About daughters, not dollars.

Already out of the Agency. *Recently* out of the Agency. Bitter? Desperate? Ready to be seduced by Jack Ziegler's rantings? And by the chance to—

"Ethan, one last thing."

"Anything, Misha. Anything within the law, that is."

"When the Agency first set him up as a private detective, where was that?"

"Maryland. Potomac, Maryland. Right across the river from Langley, you see."

"And what name did he use then?"

"Oh, well, I hardly think—"

"Never mind." I am on my feet. I cannot sit here for another second. "Thank you, Ethan. You've been helpful. If you ever need anything."

"I appreciate that, Misha, I really do," he murmurs, all the sympathy back on his face as he offers that practiced political handshake once more.

I cross the hall on rubbery legs, unlock my office, slam the door behind me, and collapse into one of the shaky side chairs. I lack the strength to make it to my desk, so I will have to weep here.

For now I know what should have been obvious, what I should have understood all along but suddenly can see with a horrid crystal clarity. Colin Scott, also known as Special Agent McDermott, indeed used the name, sometime earlier in life, of Jonathan Villard. When he had to disappear, the Agency created the story of Villard's death from cancer.

No wonder the police have no copy of Villard's report. Maybe the Judge never gave it to them. Maybe he never intended to. Maybe he lied to the family when he said otherwise.

My father's opponents were right from the start. He did not deserve a seat on the Supreme Court. But not for the reasons they thought: not because he had too many lunches with Jack Ziegler or, their true motive, because of his disagreeable political views.

They were right because the Judge knew Colin Scott.

They were right because, when Abby died and the police failed, the Judge did not simply hire a detective.

He hired a killer.

PART III

UNPROVIDED FLIGHT

Unprovided flight—In the composition of two-move chess problems, a square to which the Black king can move without immediately suffering a checkmate. The would-be solver will naturally focus on finding a way to checkmate on this square, making the problem too easy. *Unprovided flight* is considered a serious and perhaps fatal aesthetic defect in composition.

CHAPTER 38

A DOMESTIC INTERLUDE

(1)

TUESDAY IS TRASH DAY. I drag the cans down to the curb underneath a wrathful sky, then take a short jog along Hobby Road, which is all my body can bear: three blocks west, which takes me toward the campus, three blocks back, then three blocks the other way, which takes me to the edge of the Italian working-class neighborhood that borders Hobby Hill, and then, just as the cold winter rain begins to spatter, three blocks home. Twelve blocks total, probably less than a mile.

I have slept poorly during the week since my conversation with the diminutive Ethan Brinkley. I know what has to be done next, but I am loath to do it. And not only because my wife is all but begging me to stop. The truth is, I am afraid of learning anything else about my father. I have discovered that the Judge paid somebody to do murder, and hiring a killer is a capital offense in most of the United States. The rest can amount to no more than variations on a theme.

For several seconds, I try very hard to hate my father, but I lack the capacity.

Instead, I run harder. My muscles, considerably out of shape, set fire to my tendons in protest, but I press on. Nice and easy, nothing too strenuous, but keep moving, keep moving, you can run for miles if you just forget to stop! I pass my house again, cozy and warm, and temptation yawns before me, but I decide to run on. The air is crisp, good jogging weather, with little hints of distant spring on every breeze. I run and I think.

A sedan—not green and muddy like the one in Dupont Circle, not a Porsche like the one John Brown and I saw behind the house—zips through a puddle and sprays me with dirty water. I hardly notice. I am reviewing my colleagues in my mind, face by face, the kind ones and the haughty ones, the bright ones and the dim ones, the ones who respect me and the ones who despise me, trying, with no success, to figure out who among them might have betrayed me—if you call it betrayal when the only obligation broken is the obligation of humanity. For someone around the building seems to be keeping a close eye on me, knowing when I am off to the soup kitchen and when I am heading for the chess club. Who is the unseen enemy? An ambitious youngster on the rise, like Ethan Brinkley? A member of the old guard, like Theo Mountain or Arnie Rosen? Why not Marc Hadley, my wife's rival? We were friends once, but that has been a while. Or the great Stuart Land, who thinks he still runs the law school? Goodness knows what fantastic calculations are masked by his plastic smile. Must the spy be male? Dean Lynda seems to have taken a powerful dislike to me . . . although I have made it easy for her. Must the spy be white? The distant Lem Carlyle, in the best Barbadian tradition, keeps his true opinions to himself . . . and he has been evasive around me lately. But guesswork will solve nothing.

My wife spent the entire weekend in San Francisco: the deal, she says, is coming to a crucial point. I spent the entire weekend with my son. I did no work of any description, just cared for my boy. When a weary Kimmer returned yesterday afternoon, she sat in the kitchen sipping Chardonnay while I tried to talk to her about the events of the past week, but she cut me off: *Please, not now, Misha, I have a headache.* Smiling at her own witticism to hide the basic truth that she is tired of listening to me on this theme. Instead of hearing me out, Kimmer walked around the counter and kissed me for a while to shut me up, then rummaged in her bag and handed me my latest second-place trophy, a gold-rimmed quartz desk clock, signaling me that her latest transgression was huge. I thanked her unhappily and hurried out the door, rushing to make an evening lecture by a law school classmate who now teaches at Emory, where she has become the nation's leading expert—possibly, the nation's only expert—on the Third Amendment. I returned home three hours later to discover that Kimmer, despite her exhaustion, had waited up for me, and we made the hopeless, passionate love of clandestine paramours who might never see each other again. Later on, just before falling asleep, my wife told me she was sorry, but she never said for what.

MY LUNGS ARE SIGNALING that they have had enough. Running more slowly now, I cut through a side street four blocks from my house. This route takes me past the sprawling campus of Hilltop, the stuffiest of the city's several private elementary schools, and I remind myself that just about a year from now we will be making an appointment so that Bentley can have his interview. To see if he is good enough for the Hilltop kindergarten. *Interview.* At all of four years old! I jog onward, not quite believing that we are going to put our little boy through this nonsense. Once upon a time, all the university kids got in, but that was before rising costs, and their eternal partners, tuition hikes, forced Hilltop to go in search of the children of the region's commercial class. Last year the school rejected the youngest of my colleague Betsy Gucciardini's three shy daughters, and for the next month Betsy wore her frustration and despair like twin veils of mourning, seeming to equate failure to gain a place at Hilltop with the end of her child's productive life. I wonder, not for the first time, what has happened to America, and then I remember that my old buddy Eddie Dozier, Dana's ex, is about to publish a book advocating the abolition of the public schools and rebates of all the tax dollars that support them. The market, he assures us, will provide a plentiful supply of private replacements. So every child in America can have an interview before starting kindergarten. Swell.

"Focus on what matters," I wheeze, slowing finally to a walk.

By the time I stumble through the door, it is past seven. Kimmer has bacon and eggs ready—usually my job—and she even kisses me lightly on the lips. She is so sweet that the last few months might never have happened. She apologizes: not for refusing to listen to me last night, but for the fact that she has to go to the office this morning. She hoped to work from home today, but too many things have come up. I smile and shrug and tell my wife I understand. I do not tell her that I am wounded. I do not tell her how sure I am that the main thing that has come up is that I told her that I might work from home, too, so we could spend the day together.

Instead, I smile.

"What are you so happy about?" Kimmer asks, her arm surprisingly around my waist. In response, I kiss her forehead. There is no safe answer to her question, even though there are many true ones. I realize that I have finally bested the Judge: I am his equal at hiding my feelings, and his superior in pretending to be delighted when I am miserable.

Over breakfast, we leaf through our two daily newspapers, the *New York Times* and the *Elm Harbor Clarion*, each of us, for very different reasons, searching for articles about my father. I am deep inside the *Clarion* sports page, mulling over the latest injuries to players on the university's hapless basketball team, when I decide that the time has come to tell my wife the one last thing I must do. I do not expect her to like it.

I fold the newspaper carefully and look at her exquisite face, the bright brown eyes intense behind her glasses, the lines of middle age deepening above her cheeks with every passing month. Her mouth is drawn up in a little bow. I know she knows I am watching her.

"Kimmer, darling," I begin.

She flicks her gaze at me, then drops it once more to the *Times* editorial page. "Wanna hear a funny op-ed about the President's tax plan?"

"No, thanks."

"It's really clever, though."

"No, Kimmer. I mean, not just now. We need to talk."

Eyes rolling in my direction, rolling back to the paper. "Is it important? Can it wait?"

"Yes. And, no, I don't think so."

My wife, looking splendid as always in a robe, glances up and blows me a kiss. "You've found her? Your *nzinga* from the ferry?"

At first I am nonplussed, thinking that she has somehow discovered my tête-à-tête with Maxine on the Vineyard, but then I see that she is only joking, or maybe hoping.

"Nothing that interesting."

"Too bad."

"No, not too bad. I love you, Kimmer."

"Yeah, but only because you're a glutton for punishment."

Smiling as she says it, putting me off, not wanting to hear what I am going to say. But I have to make my point and, seeing no way to sugarcoat it, I decide to say it right out.

"Kimmer, I have to go see Jack Ziegler."

The paper closes with a snap. I have all of her attention. When my wife speaks, her voice is dangerously low. "Oh, no, you don't."

"I do."

"You *don't*."

"I would just call him," I propose, pretending that our disagreement is on a slightly different subject, "but he doesn't really talk on the telephone much."

"Fear of wiretaps, no doubt."

"Probably."

Kimmer's gaze is unwavering. "Misha, honey, I love you, and I also trust you, but, in case you've forgotten, I am being considered for a seat on the United States Court of Appeals. If my hubby traipses off to visit a Jack Ziegler, it is not going to do my chances any good."

"Nobody has to know," I say, but I am reaching.

"I think a whole lot of people would know, and most of them happen to work for the Federal Bureau of Investigation."

I have considered this, of course. "I would clear it with Uncle Mal first."

"Oh, goody. Then he can tell everybody else in Washington."

"Kimmer, please. You know what's been going on. Some of it. As much as you've let me tell you." Her eyes widen at that one, but I cannot stop now. "I've learned a lot of . . . of ugly things about my father in the past few weeks. Now I have to know if they are as ugly as I think they are. And I think Jack Ziegler knows."

"If the facts are ugly, there's no question that Jack Ziegler knows them."

"Well, that's why I have to go. People will understand."

"People will *not* understand."

"I have to know what's going on." But I think of Morris Young and the story of Noah and wonder if I am mistaken.

"I don't think there *is* anything going on, Misha. Not like what you seem to think, anyway."

"You're probably right, darling, but . . ."

"If you talk to him, there is going to be more trouble. You know there is." She does not say from whom, so I suppose it could be a threat.

"Kimmer, come on." My tone is gentle. I am concerned that Kimmer will start shouting, as she sometimes does, and wake Bentley. Or the neighbors. Neither of which would be a first. "Come on," I say again, still softly, hoping Kimmer will be soft in reply.

"You're the one who always says Jack Ziegler is a monster." Her tone is indeed soft, but more in hiss than compromise.

"I know, but—"

"He's a murderer, Misha."

"Well, he was never convicted of *murder*." She has me sounding like one of Uncle Jack's countless lawyers now, and I don't much like it. "Other crimes, but not murder."

"Except he killed his wife, right?"

"Well, there were rumors." I try to remember the way the Judge answered that one before the Judiciary Committee, for it was that single question from Senator Biden, and my father's unhelpful response, that cost him more than any other. *I don't judge my friends based on rumors*, my father said—something like that. And he folded his arms across his chest in a gesture that even the most incompetent public relations coach could have warned him never, ever, to make on national television. Although understandably angry at what he considered an unfair line of inquiry, my father came off as haughty and disdainful. One columnist wrote that Judge Garland seemed to be dismissing a man's possible murder of his wife as a triviality—a ridiculous assertion, but one my father invited by losing his temper before tens of millions of viewers. I knew, at that horrible televised instant, that the fight was lost; that, no matter how the Judge might duck and weave, his opponents had backed him into the corner of the ring; that the knockout punch would, at any moment, come flashing into his vision, just before it laid him flat. And I felt a rampant anger, not at the Senate or at the press, but at my father: *How could he be so stupid?* There were about six thousand possible answers to Biden's perfectly reasonable question, and the Judge picked the worst of them. Yet now, under Kimmer's cross-examination, I find myself following my father's lead.

"But he was never indicted, darling. He was never even arrested. As far as I know, what happened to his wife was an accident." Almost letter-perfect, I am sure: exactly what the Judge said to Senator Biden. Except for the *darling*.

"She fell off her horse after twenty years of riding and broke her neck by accident?"

"It's not a very good way to murder somebody," I point out. "You could fall off and walk away with a few scratches and live to tell everybody who pushed you."

Kimmer gives me a look. "You're joking, right?"

"No, I'm serious. I'm saying we don't know exactly what happened to Jack Ziegler's wife, but murder doesn't seem very likely. Am I supposed to hang him on rumors?"

Oh, I hate this side of myself, I truly do, the same way I hated this side of the Judge, but I cannot seem to stop.

"Rumors!"

"Well, since he was never charged . . ."

"Oh, Misha, listen to yourself. I mean, how legalistic can you get?" *You sound just like your father,* she is saying. Which is true.

"It's just a visit, Kimmer. One hour, maybe thirty minutes."

"He's a nut, Misha. A *dangerous* nut. I don't want us to have anything to do with him." Her voice is growing louder, and a clear edge of hysteria is creeping in.

"Kimmer, come on. Look at the facts. Freeman Bishop is dead—"

"The police say it was drugs—"

"And Colin Scott impersonated an FBI agent to get information on the Judge, and now he's dead—"

"*It was an accident!*" So much for soft.

"An accident while he was following me. Following *us.*"

"Well, it was still an accident. He got drunk and he drowned and he's dead now, okay? So you can drop it."

"And you don't think we should be a little bit worried?"

The wrong thing to say. Absolutely wrong. I know it at once. I feel like a chess player who has just advanced his knight, only to notice, an instant too late, that his queen is about to fall.

"No, Misha. No, I'm not worried. Why should I be worried? Because I'm married to a man who has gone off the deep end? Whose sister has turned into some kind of . . . of conspiracy theorist? A man who now thinks that the solution to all his problems lies in flying up to Aspen to drop in on a thug who murdered his wife? Inviting that thug into our life? No, Misha, no, I am most certainly not worried. There is nothing to be worried about."

I try to mollify her. "Kimmer, please. The Judge was my father."

"And I'm your wife! Remember?" She is holding on to the sides of the doorway as though worried that her anger might blow her away.

"Yes, but—"

"Yes, *but!* You're the one who always talks about loyalty. Well, be loyal to *me* for once! I don't mean loyal like never even looking hard at another woman so you can feel holier than thou. Than me. I mean loyal like you're doing something *for* me. Something that makes a difference."

"I've done plenty for you," I tell her in the calmest tone I can manage. I like to think I have developed an immunity to my wife's taunts, but her words sting.

"The stuff you do for me is the stuff *you* want, not the stuff *I* want."

I am trying to remember how close I felt to Kimmer last night as I held her in my arms, stroking her back, listening to her apologize before she fell asleep.

Last night. Last year. Last decade. All equally vanished.

"Kimmer, if—"

"And it's not like I've never done anything for you!"

As my wife's eyes continue to flame, I am astonished by her passion, magnified in the cramped space of the kitchen. Standing there in her bathrobe, her Afro awry, Kimmer remains the most desirable woman I have ever known, yet I have the eerie sense that if I make a move she doesn't like she will knock me down. This fury has been percolating ever since my return from the Vineyard. Despite the news about Marc Hadley, Kimmer seems to think her chances of appointment are slipping away. I do not know exactly why she believes this; I do know she blames me for it. As she blames me for much else. I have heard the litany a hundred times, a hundred different tales about how Talcott Garland ruined her life. How she married me to please her parents when there were far more exciting men interested in her. How she left her lively practice with one of Washington's most prestigious firms to follow me to this deadly-dull New England town. How most of our acquaintances (we have few friends here, Kimmer will note accusingly) are university types who look down their noses at her because she isn't one of them. How she easily earned a partnership at an unimportant law firm that nobody has ever heard of. How she had a baby to make her husband happy without really thinking about what she was getting into and is now stuck in a bad marriage because of it. How her life ever since has been a slow race between boredom and insanity. Kimmer made all the choices. But I take all the blame.

"I'm sorry," I say, raising my hands to make peace.

"Misha, please. For my sake. For the sake of our marriage. Our son. Promise me you will not invite that man into our life. That you won't visit him. Or call him."

And I discern something else, a version of the same screechy timbre I detected in Jack Ziegler's voice in the cemetery, as unexpected now as it was then: Kimmer is afraid. Not the physical fear of the soul for its fleeting mortal life, nor the desperate protectiveness of mother for child. No, this is her career fear. She is at the edge of what she has always wanted, and does not want Uncle Jack to spoil it for her—and how can I blame her?

I decide that there is no good reason to feed her fear. Not just now.

"Okay, darling. Okay. I'll stay away from Uncle Jack. I won't do anything to . . . to cause embarrassment. But . . . well . . ."

"You're not going to give up looking. Is that what you were going to say?"

"You have to understand, darling."

"Oh, I do, I do." Her smile is warm again. She comes around the counter and hugs me from behind. We have returned to last night's intimacy, just like that. "But no Jack Ziegler."

"No Jack Ziegler."

"Thanks, honey." Kissing me again, grinning. She hops up to clear the table. I tell her I will do it. She does not object. We talk as though we have no conflict. We have grown quite skillful at pretending that there are no issues between us. So we talk of other things. We decide not to drag Bentley off to his Montessori school today. We will let him sleep late, for once, since I will be at home anyway. She reminds me that we are due for dinner tomorrow night at the home of one of her partners and asks me to confirm the sitter, a Japanese American teen from the next block who enthralls Bentley by playing her flute. I ask her in return if she will swing by the post office on the way in, to drop off two postal chess cards that I finished last night, both of which must be postmarked today. (Each player has three days per move.) When we have completed all the complex negotiations of a typical morning in a two-career family, Kimmer disappears to dress for work. She is back twenty minutes later in a dark chalk-striped suit and blue silk blouse, kisses me again, this time on the cheek, and is off, leaving, as always, promptly at eight-fifteen.

I watch through the bay window in the living room as the gleaming white BMW hurries off along Hobby Road, swallowed almost at once in the sheets of rain. I put both hands in front of me and lean on the glass. Woody Allen once wrote something, tongue firmly in cheek, about loving the rain because it washes memories away, but I still remember the photograph of Freeman Bishop's bloody hand. I still remember the face of Special Agent McDermott glaring at me from the pages of the *Vineyard Gazette*. I see him on a boat with his buddy Foreman, and some disagreement, and McDermott/Scott tossed overboard. I see my father, arguing with a cautious Colin Scott a quarter-century ago, trying to convince him to kill the man who killed his daughter.

Yet, in the fresh light of day, even a day as rainy as this one, the images are a lot less scary. Not as scary, for instance, as the thought that one day my wife will drive off down Hobby Road and decide to keep on going.

Gazing out at the empty street, I remember, from a long-ago college course, a snippet from Tadeusz Rozewicz, something about a poet being someone who tries to leave and is unable to leave.

That is my wife: Kimmer the poet. Only nowadays she keeps all the best lines to herself.

Or shares them with somebody else.

CHAPTER 39

UNEXPECTED VISITORS

(1)

Mallory Corcoran calls just past ten with the news that Conan Deveaux has decided to plead guilty to a single count of second-degree murder in the death of Freeman Bishop. He and his lawyer looked at the evidence and decided the stack was too high. Under the plea agreement, Conan will escape the needle, but he will remain in prison for the rest of his life. "He's just nineteen," Uncle Mal adds gruffly, "so that's likely to be a very long time."

"So he did it," I whisper, wonderingly. I am at the kitchen counter, where I have been leafing through *Chess Life* while making hot chocolate for Bentley. How could I have misunderstood Maxine's hint so badly? *A mistake.* Could she have meant something else?

"Probably."

"Probably? He just volunteered for fifty years in the penitentiary!"

Uncle Mal insists on a seasoned lawyer's pedantry: "If the choice is life in prison or execution, you take what you can get." Then he is an old friend once more: "But, seriously, Talcott, I'm sure he did it. Please put your mind at rest. From what I hear, the case was a prosecutor's dream. They had a witness, they had forensics to place him at the scene, they had a print or two, they had him bragging about it later. I know you thought maybe it was a frame-up, one of your sister's conspiracies or something, but this is a little too much evidence for somebody to manufacture."

Still marveling, I say goodbye and carry two mugs of cocoa into the family room, where Bentley is sitting at the computer, playing with a math game in which he collects little pictures of candy if he can zap the numbers that correctly answer the questions dancing around the screen. So we can teach him the virtues of gluttony, greed, and violence all at once, while also improving his score on the math SAT he will have to take in about twelve years.

Watching him now, so engrossed he does not realize his father is near, I settle myself on the sofa and put the cups down on the coffee table. We all enjoy this room. The furniture is leather, a sofa and a loveseat and a chair, drawn together by a fake Oriental carpet—it is really from Sears. Built-in bookshelves of solid maple, painted white, surround a crumbling fieldstone fireplace; another shelf snuggles beneath the window to the back yard. There are books on politics and books on jazz and books on travel and books on black history and books reflecting our eclectic taste in contemporary fiction: Morrison, Updike, Doctorow, Smiley, Turow. There are children's books. There is a Bible, the blandly inoffensive New Revised Standard Version, and the Book of Common Prayer. There is a collection of C. S. Lewis. There are home-improvement books and back issues of *Architectural Digest*. There are a few chess books. There are no law books.

The telephone rings again.

Bentley looks up. I point to the hot chocolate. "Mint, Daddy, Bemmy drink mint." In a minute, he means.

The phone is not ringing any more. I realize that I picked up the receiver but, because of the byplay with my son, have not actually put it to my ear. I do so now, and immediately hear the static of a cell phone with a low battery. And a male voice:

"Kimmer? Kimmer? Hello? You there, baby?"

"She isn't home right now." My tone is as frosty as I know how to make it. "Would you care to leave a message?"

A long pause. Then a click.

I close my eyes, swaying a bit on my feet as my skillful son zaps numbers faster and faster. The years peel away, as does my confidence, and most of my hope. How many times over the course of our marriage have I fielded calls like this one—a mysterious man asking for my wife, then hanging up when I answer? Probably fewer than I think, but more than I would like to recall. Oh, Kimmer, how can you do this again!

You there, baby?

I fight down a wave of mind-blanking despair. Concentrate, I tell myself. In the first place, the cadence of the voice tells me that it was a black man—in other words, not Gerald Nathanson. A new affair? Two at the same time? Or my mistake, as Dr. Young suggested? No way to tell, not till my wife and I fight this one out, as, sooner or later, we will.

I cross to my study, looking for a distraction. The voice was familiar, that's the other thing. I cannot quite place it, but I know it will come.

You there, baby?

Odd the way the immediate concerns about a dying marriage can knock worries about torture and murder and mysterious chess pieces right out of the box, but priorities are funny that way. I plop down in front of my computer. Who would be so arrogant, I wonder, and so stupid as to say the word *baby* when calling a married woman he is not even sure is home? I shake my head again, the mixture of fury and fear and sheer nerve-racking pain momentarily crowding out every rational thought. I want to scream, I want to throw a tantrum, maybe even break something, but I am a Garland, so I will probably write something instead. I am zipping through my files, trying to decide which unfinished essay to exhume for a little pointless polishing, when my eyes are drawn to a car sitting across the street.

The blue Porsche.

The driver, a shadow behind the windshield, is unmistakably staring right at our house.

(11)

I RUN DOWN A MENU OF OPTIONS but choose the one that, in my current mood, I like the best. From beside my desk I take the baseball bat I hid there on the night I was attacked. I poke my head into the family room and tell my son to stay put. He nods, fingers clittering furiously at the mouse, winning huge piles of candy as he solves math problems. He may not talk much, but he certainly can add, subtract, point, and click.

I pull a light jacket from the closet, then yank open the front door, brandishing the bat, swinging it against my palm, so that the driver, whoever he is, can hardly miss it. I cannot do what I really want, which is to cross the street and smash up his Porsche, because I would not, even for an instant, leave my son alone. But I get my message across. The driver, a member of the darker nation, just as I expected, stares for a moment through the window. I see mirrored glasses on an ebon face, and little else. Then, very smoothly, showing no sign of panic, he puts the car in gear and cruises off down the street.

I wave the bat exultantly in the air but deny myself the victory shout.

Instead, I go inside and shut the door and put the bat away and ask myself what in the world I thought I was doing. The red haze of fury sometimes twists me in strange directions, but it has rarely led me quite so close to violence. Thoughts tumble through my disordered mind. The driver of the car is innocent, he lives or works nearby, and now he is going to tell everybody that I am crazy. The driver of the car is the man who called looking for Kimmer, and Kimmer is having an affair with him. The driver of the car is the man who pretended to be Agent Foreman. The driver of the car is the man who returned the chess book stolen by the men who assaulted me. All of the above. None of the above.

"You're a sick man, Misha," I mutter as I stand in my study. Nobody is on the street now except one of our neighbors walking her three-month-old twins in a stroller. "You need help. Lots and lots of help."

I imagine my wife would agree. So would the man in the blue Porsche.

And, for a hateful, envious moment, I entertain a truly horrendous thought: *The man in the Porsche is Lemaster Carlyle.* Perfect Lemaster Carlyle, spying on me and cheating on his wife, seeing Kimmer behind Julia's back. Calling Kimmer *baby*. Maybe leaving the stolen chess book in my car when he was late for Shirley's party. It would explain why he has lately been so distant. But the voice on the phone sounded nothing like his: no Barbadian accent, for example. Besides, Lem is short, and the man John Brown saw in the woods was tall. There could be two unknown black men around, but Occam's Razor, on which the Judge loved to rely, warns us not to multiply entities unnecessarily.

Anyway, the whole thing is a typically stupid Misha Garland idea.

I remain at the window, railing against myself the way manic depressives do, until I remember that I am supposed to be having hot chocolate with my son. I hurry back into the family room and find him still hard at work, the cocoa forgotten, his father forgotten, hooting gleefully to himself as he zaps the right answers and piles up his loot. My childhood must have produced such shining moments of joy, but what I mostly remember is the shadows.

The doorbell rings.

I swing around uncertainly, wondering if I should grab the bat again, or sweep my son out the back way, through the hedge, and into hiding with the Felsenfelds, for perhaps the driver of the Porsche has returned with friends. But the Garland training proves too strong to allow me to panic. I simply open the door, as I would on any other day.

Two men are standing there, one of whom I have met before. "Professor Garland, I wonder if you could spare us a minute?" asks Special Agent Fred Nunzio of the Federal Bureau of Investigation. He looks grim.

CHAPTER 40

ANOTHER DISCOVERY

FRED NUNZIO introduces his companion as Rick Chrebet, a city detective. They make an odd couple. Nunzio is a short, fleshy man, perky and confident, with smooth black hair combed straight back. The scrawny Chrebet is thin of both hair and affect: his manner is sufficiently distant that I catch myself wanting to confess to something just to gain his interest for a minute or two. His teeth are bright and even, his lips pale, his jaw pugnacious. His fair eyes are deep-set and wary. Dizzy with déjà vu, I lead them into the sunny living room, which we never use except for company. Across the hall, Bentley happily zaps away, oblivious to his father's sudden distress, and uninterested in the visitors. He is never interested in strangers, having perhaps inherited from me a tendency toward introspection.

"We won't need much of your time," says Nunzio, sleepy-eyed and nearly apologetic. "We wouldn't bother you if it wasn't important."

I mumble something appropriate, waiting for the ax to fall. Has something happened to Kimmer? Then why would the FBI be here? Is there news from Washington? Then why would a city cop be here?

"My colleague here wanted to talk to you about something," Nunzio continues, "and I kind of came along for the ride."

Detective Chrebet, meanwhile, has opened his slim briefcase on the coffee table and is leafing through the contents. He withdraws a glossy color photograph and slides it across to me: heavyset white man with an unruly shock of brown facial hair, staring at the camera, a plaque with a bunch of numbers held across his chest. A mug shot. I shudder with memory.

"Do you recognize the person depicted in the photograph?" the detective asks in his reedy, expressionless voice, the question phrased as carefully as an instruction book.

"Yes." I look hard at Nunzio but address myself to Chrebet. "You know I do."

Without missing a beat, he slips me another shot, a black-and-white, and this time I barely need a glance and I do not wait for the question. "Yes, I recognize him, too. These are the two men who assaulted me in the middle of the campus a few weeks ago."

Nunzio smiles slightly, but Chrebet's pale face is stone. "Are you absolutely certain?"

I dutifully study the pictures again, just in case they have changed over the last few seconds. "Yes, I am absolutely certain. I got a very good look at them both." I point to the photos. "Does this mean you found them? They're under arrest?"

The detective answers my question with a question. "Had you ever seen these men before the night they attacked you?"

"No. I never saw them before. I told the police that already."

Before Chrebet can ask another question, Nunzio speaks up. "Professor Garland, is there anything you want to share with me?"

"I beg your pardon?"

"Anything related to . . . well, the research you've been involved in?" I notice his careful euphemism and wonder if he is trying to hide something from Chrebet or if he thinks I am. "Anything you would prefer to discuss privately?"

"No, there isn't."

"Are you sure?"

"I already asked you about the possibility that Freeman Bishop . . ."

"We've looked into that." He speaks quickly, and again I have the sense he does not want the detective to understand. "Your source was wrong. There's nothing to worry about." Reassuring me when I have not asked. I am growing more puzzled by the minute.

Nunzio subsides. The ball is back in Chrebet's court. He resumes his interrogation as though the federal agent never opened his mouth. "Have you seen either of these men since the time of the attack?"

As my worry grows, my legal skills return: "Not that I can recall."

"Do you know whether anyone else has seen them?"

"No." I have waited long enough, so I throw in my own question again. "Now, tell me, please. Do you know who they are?"

"Small-timers," Nunzio puts in. "Hoods. Hired help. They're nobody."

"So are they under arrest? You've found them? Is that why you're here?" Because I am thinking that if I can find out who hired them I will be halfway home. "Do you know who they worked for?"

Chrebet again, pedantically: "No, Professor, we do not know whom they worked for. They are not under arrest. And, yes, we've found them. Or, rather, they were found."

"What are you telling me? Are they dead?"

He is relentless, like a machine. "A troop of Boy Scouts out hiking in Henley State Park found them over the weekend. They were lying in the bushes, bound and gagged. Alive, but just barely."

"They're not talking," Nunzio slips in, perhaps reading my mind. "As a matter of fact, they're scared shitless. I would be, too." An easy, mocking smile. "Somebody seems to have cut off all their fingers."

CHAPTER 41

CONFRONTATION

(1)

I DO NOT TELL KIMMER. Not just yet. Instead, on Thursday afternoon, I drop in to see Dr. Young. He listens with patience and concern, hands folded over his ample belly, shaking his heavy head unhappily, then talks to me about Daniel in the lion's den. He says the Lord will see me through. He does not have to ask me how my attackers came to lose their fingers. Chrebet asked, in his rat-a-tat style, whether I had any idea what might have happened, but he did not expect an answer and did not get one. Chrebet knew, as Nunzio did, as Dr. Young does, as I do, that the strong hand of Jack Ziegler has struck in Elm Harbor. The voice on the telephone at two-fifty-one in the morning—a voice I still have not mentioned to a soul—has delivered on its promise.

Before I leave the pastor's office, he warns me against taking pleasure in harm that befalls others. I assure him that I feel no joy at what happened to the men who assaulted me. Dr. Young says he is not talking about them. As I try to work this out, he counsels me to do what I can to repair human connection with those from whom I feel estranged. Uneasily, I agree. That same afternoon, I encounter Dahlia Hadley at the preschool and tell her how sorry I am for the scandal that has engulfed Marc, but she grows chilly and refuses to talk to me. Still, the need to make amends grows into a compulsion, perhaps because I believe I can in this way exorcise my demons. Feeling Jack Ziegler's smothering breath will make you crazy that way.

On Friday morning, I seek out Stuart Land and apologize for accusing him of trying to sabotage Marc's candidacy, but he professes to be untroubled, since he is not guilty. He is good enough to tell me that Marc has not yet taken his name out of the hat. When I ask him why,

Stuart looks at me coldly and says: "Probably because he thinks there is a better-than-even chance that you'll find a way to blow it for your wife." Stunned, I creep out of his capacious office, more determined than ever to behave. After lunch, I finally attempt to get in touch with the estimable Cameron Knowland, whose son never said another word in class after our little skirmish, but when I call the private investment firm Cameron runs in Los Angeles, he refuses to take my call; or, rather, his senior secretary, once I fight my way that far, tells me that Mr. Knowland has never heard of me.

Rob Saltpeter, upon hearing this news when we meet for basketball at the gym Monday morning, tells me that Cameron Knowland is playing games with me, but I have more or less figured that out for myself. We play one-on-one today, and Rob beats me badly, twice in a row, but only because he is taller and faster than I am, or maybe because his reflexes and coordination are better than mine.

It is now Friday, and my moods will not stop swinging. I continue to behave, but my self-control is brittle. Any small jolt will split it in two. I try to pray, but cannot concentrate. I sit at my desk, unable to work, furious at my father, wondering what would have happened if I had refused to talk to Jack Ziegler that day in the cemetery. Probably I would have been stuck with my father's note anyway, I would still be wondering who Angela's boyfriend was, and the dead would still be dead, so there is no point in wondering. . . .

The dead would still be dead. . . .

My mood brightens. I remember the idea that came to me at Shirley Branch's dinner party. In the light of day, I pooh-poohed it, but now I am desperate. And it just might offer me and my family a way out of this mess. The dead. The cemetery. Maybe, just maybe. I do not know if it will work, but there is no harm in preparing, in case I decide to give it a try. I start by calling Karl at his bookstore to ask him a question about the Double Excelsior. He is patient if not exactly friendly, and he thanks me for returning his book. As a result of his answer, I decide to keep planning. Only I will need some help. Later in the afternoon, after my administrative law class, I scurry down to the second floor to look for Dana Worth, but the sign on her door says that she is in the Faculty Reading Room. She always leaves a sign, because she always wants people to be able to find her: talking to people seems to be her favorite thing. And so it is that I make a huge mistake. In my eagerness to find Dana, I go into the library I usually avoid, and everything goes to pieces.

MOST PROFESSORS SIT IN THEIR OFFICES, buzzing the faculty librarian to bring them books they want, or even having their secretaries do the buzzing, but I now and then like to go and soak up the feel of the place, or I used to, before the first hints that Kimmer might be having an affair with Jerry Nathanson. At ten minutes to five, I use my faculty key to open the side entrance to the law library, on the third floor, away from the hubbub of the students. The key admits me to the back of the periodical room, two dozen parallel rows of gunmetal shelves stuffed with painfully organized, dog-eared law reviews. Hesitating to go forward, I look for a chance to hang back. If I am going to proceed, I need help urgently, and Dana is the only one I can think of who might be crazy enough to do it. Rob Saltpeter is too much the straight arrow, Lem Carlyle too much the politician. I have considered and rejected enlisting the help of a student. It is Dana or nobody. Striding uncertainly through the periodical room, I hear some students coming and decide to disguise my purpose, for, although I would never hesitate to enter Dana's office alone, I am uncomfortable at the thought that I might be observed chasing her down in the library. But my need is sufficiently pressing that I must get the answer immediately, or I will go out of my mind. I pull at random an old bound volume of the *Columbia Law Review*, leafing through it as though hunting ancient treasure. Walking along the aisles, carrying the heavy book as camouflage, I stop near the noisy old machine that makes blurred photocopies, and steel myself. Then I leave the periodical room and enter the main reading room, deliberately refusing to look up at the wall where the portrait of my father in his robes still hangs. If you examine the painting carefully, you can detect the poorly painted restoration work covering the nasty language with which somebody defaced the canvas during his confirmation hearings: UNCLE TOM was the least of it, with various comments about the Judge's ancestry appended by some political commentator too modest to sign his name to his work.

I never examine it carefully.

As I cross the wide room, a few bold students say hello, but most of them are far too savvy. They can read the faces of the faculty, they know when to interrupt and when to hang back. I pass a clutch of black students, a gaggle of white ones. I wave to Shirley Branch, who is standing next to a bank of computers, hands in frenetic motion as she makes some point, quite vehemently, to Matt Goffe, her fellow untenured professor, and fellow leftie. I spot Avery Knowland at the other end of the room, bending hopelessly over a casebook, but my path, fortunately, is not taking me in that direction. I wonder how angry his father really is. Maybe Cameron Knowland and his trophy wife will take their three million dollars back and we can keep the gloriously seedy library we have now. The Dean wants us to have a building worthy of the twenty-first century, but I think libraries should remain firmly planted in the nineteenth, when the stability of the printed word, not the ephemeron of the fiber-optic cable, was the method through which information was transmitted over long distances. I adore this room. Some of the long tables where students sit studying are more than half a century old. The ceiling is almost three stories high, but the brass chandeliers have been reduced to mere decorations: banks of hideous fluorescents now provide the light, in tandem with the sun that prisms through the clerestory windows high up above the intricately carved wooden shelves of law books. For those with the patience to follow, each window's stained-glass picture adds a frame to a story that begins just above the main entrance to the library, chases around all four outer walls, and winds up back in the same place: a violent crime, a witness signaling a police officer, the arrest of a suspect, a trial, a jury deliberating, a conviction, a punishment, a new lawyer, an appeal, a release, and, in the end, back to the same life of crime, a pessimistically unbroken cycle that drove me half mad when I was a student.

I smile at the reference librarian as I circle his long desk. He does not smile back: he is on the phone and, if the rumors are true, is probably placing a bet. On the other side of the desk is the Faculty Reading Room, as my destination is pompously called. I am about to use my faculty key to unlock the FARR when the double doors of frosted glass open in front of me and Lemaster Carlyle and Dana Worth saunter out, laughing together, evidently at some Worthism, because Lem is laughing harder.

"Hello, Tal," says Lem quietly. He is his usual dapper self, sporting a medium-gray sports jacket and a crimson Harvard tie.

"Lem."

"Misha, darling," murmurs Dear Dana, and I remind myself to tell her not to call me that in public. She, too, is nicely turned out, in a dark business suit.

"Dana, do you have a minute?"

"That depends on how you plan to vote on Bonnie Ziffren," Dana smiles, naming one in the endless stream of candidates recommended by the faculty appointments committee to whom Dear Dana, on one ground or another, objects. "I know Marc thinks she's the next Catherine McKinnon, but, in my opinion? She's a zircon in the rough."

"You shouldn't talk about potential faculty appointments in public," Lem reminds her piously. He is, once more, avoiding my gaze. "By university rule, personnel matters are confidential."

"Then come into my parlor." She points to the FARR.

"No, thanks," murmurs Lemaster. In fact, he remembers that he has to run: dinner with some visiting potentate from the American Law Institute. You can always count on faculty politics to drive Lemaster Carlyle away. He yearns for the law school's lost golden age, which he missed entirely but nevertheless loves, when the professors all got along with each other, even if those who were there, such as Theo Mountain and Amy Hefferman, recall it differently. He rushes off without a farewell, still unable to look me in the eye.

What is going on with him? Kimmer's lover? The deliverer of the pawn? I rub my forehead, furious again, not at Lem but at the Judge. Dear Dana Worth, noticing the sudden change in my mood, lays a gentle hand on my arm. She waits until she is sure Lem is out of earshot and then asks me softly what I want.

"We better discuss this in private," I tell her, still wondering what might be wrong with Lemaster, and whether it has to do with . . . well, with everything.

"Come into my parlor," she teases again. I hesitate, not wanting to be seen sneaking into the FARR with a female colleague, especially a white one, even if she has no interest in men, and my hesitation ruins everything. Dana is already smiling over my shoulder, greeting a new arrival, when the sharply spoken words rattle from behind me like bullets:

"I think we need to talk, Tal."

I turn in surprise to find myself staring into the angry face of Gerald Nathanson.

(111)

"HELLO, JERRY," I say quietly.

"We need to talk," he says again.

Jerry Nathanson, probably the most prominent lawyer in the city, was in law school with Kimmer and myself, married back then to the same unprepossessing woman who is his wife today. He is perhaps five foot eight, a trifle overweight, with a fleshy chin not quite able to spoil his 1950s-style boyish good looks. His features are clear and even and a little soft. His dark hair is curly, and he is balding, just a bit, in the middle of his head. He is an impressive figure in his light gray suit and dark blue tie. His hands are folded over his chest as though he is waiting for an apology.

"I don't think we have anything to talk about," I tell him, forgetting every lesson that Morris Young has tried to teach me. I might as well be one of the boys he tries to save from the corner, doing my macho styling for the sake of macho styling.

"Misha, I'll see you," says Dana, still grinning, but weakly now. She wants no part of what is about to occur. "Call me."

"Dana, wait . . ."

"Let her go," Jerry Nathanson commands. "We need to talk alone."

I look him up and down, moving the *Columbia Law Review* to my left hand, perhaps to free up my right. Then I force myself to calm down. I shake my head. "No, Jerry. I can't just now. I'm busy." Showing him the book. "Maybe some other time."

As I try to walk around him, he grabs my arm. "Don't you walk away from me."

My fury is about to boil over. "Let go of my arm, please," I whisper without turning around. I am aware that a couple of students are jostling and pointing, which means that a crowd will shortly be gathering.

"I just want to talk," mutters Jerry, also noticing the attention we are drawing.

"I don't know how many different ways I can say that I don't want to talk to you."

"Don't make a scene, Talcott."

"*You're* telling *me* not to make a scene?" I glare, wondering if I am supposed to punch him. Surely there exists somewhere a rule book for the behavior of a cuckolded husband upon meeting the likely object of his wife's affection.

"Calm down, Talcott."

"Don't tell me to calm down!" I am about to say more, but I restrain myself, for his fifties movie-star features no longer look angry. Instead, he looks puzzled.

"I have to go," I tell him, walking around him and striding for the exit. I can hear him hurrying behind me, and I begin to move faster. Now half the students in the law school seem to be watching, along with a faculty colleague or two. Still, nothing to do but get out and worry about the rest later.

Jerry catches up with me just outside the ornate double doors marking the main entrance to the library. "What's the matter with you, Talcott? I just wanted to talk to you."

I have had enough of self-restraint. I swing around in bright red fury. "What is it, Jerry? What exactly do you want?"

"Here? You want to talk here?"

"Why not? You've been chasing me all over the law school."

He draws himself up. "Well, in the first place, I wanted to tell you congratulations, in advance. About your wife, I mean. She told me"— he glances around, but now that we are outside the library, the few students standing around pretend not to be listening—"she told me, uh, about Professor Hadley."

In bed? On your office sofa? Despite the promise I made to Dr. Young, I am not able to shake off my anger—or perhaps my anguish— now that I am face to face with Jerry Nathanson. "Professor Hadley has not taken his name out of the hat," I snap.

"Oh. Oh. I didn't know that."

We have somehow started walking again, down the dimly lighted corridor toward my office. No students have dared follow, but a few office doors are standing open, and we might still be overheard.

"Well, it's true," I mutter. "It seems that Professor Hadley thinks he can explain it all away, that it's all a big misunderstanding."

"I see." Jerry's voice is small and hesitant. He tries a smile. We are standing outside my door. "Well, I'm sure your wife will get the job."

And it pours out of me. "My wife. *My* wife. My *wife!*"

He tilts his head to one side, eyes narrowed. "Yes. Your wife."

"I want you to stay away from her."

"Stay away from her? We work together."

"You know exactly what I mean, Jerry. Don't play games with me."

"I *do* know what you mean, Talcott, and . . . and it's completely ridiculous." Jerry's astonishment seems so genuine that I am sure he is playing me. "I don't know how you could think . . . I mean, me and Kimberly? What would give you an idea like that?"

"Maybe the fact that it's true."

"It isn't true. Please don't think that." He rubs his hands over his face. "Your wife . . . Kimberly . . . she, uh, she told me a few months ago that you seemed to think that there was something, uh, between us. I thought she was joking. Please, Talcott, believe me." His eyes grow earnest, and, for a second time, he puts an uninvited hand on my arm. "I happen to be a happily married man, Talcott. My relationship with your wife is nothing but professional. It has never been anything but professional. And it never will be anything but professional." Waiting for this to sink in. "Your wife is the best lawyer in the firm, the best lawyer in the city, the best lawyer in this part of the state. Maybe I . . . maybe we work her too hard, maybe we keep her away from home too much, but, Talcott, please believe me when I say that it is only work that is keeping her away."

"I don't know why I should believe you," I sneer, but I am on less certain ground now, and we both know it. I have shot off my ammunition, but all my powder was wet. Maybe it is Jack Ziegler, or the Judge, at whom I should be venting my fury.

Jerry Nathanson steps back again. He is no longer nervous. He is a fine lawyer and knows when he has the advantage. When he speaks again, his voice is cold. "Your wife also told me you were behaving in what she called an irrational manner. I told her not to worry, but I guess she was right as usual."

"She told you *what?*"

"That your behavior is starting to frighten her."

This is too much. I step close to him. It is all I can do not to grab him by the front of his hand-tailored shirt. "I don't want you discussing me with my wife." I do not realize how absurd this sounds until I have said it. "I don't want you discussing *anything* with my wife."

"I have a news flash for you, Talcott." Jerry's own anger rises afresh. He jabs a finger at me. "You need some serious medical help. Maybe a psychiatrist."

Ah, but men are horrible! I slap his finger away and say something equally useful: "If you don't stay away from my wife, Jerry, you're going to need some serious medical help yourself."

His face reddens. "That's a threat, Talcott. Do you hear yourself? That's just the sort of thing Kimberly was talking about."

"You've got a lot of nerve, Jerry."

"Oh, yeah?" He taps the front of my sweater, goading me. "And what do you intend to do about it?"

"Don't push it," I snarl. He laughs. Were we not a couple of intellectuals in an Ivy League town, we would no doubt come to blows. As it is, we shove a bit. Probably I shove harder. Even though I can see we are attracting a fresh audience, I cannot make myself back down, the world is too red around me. "Just stay away from my wife."

"You're crazy, Talcott." He composes himself with an effort, backs away, breathing hard. "Get some help."

When Jerry has gone, all of Oldie is staring at me.

CHAPTER 42

DEADLINE

"We're a little concerned about you," says Lynda Wyatt without preamble.

"I know."

I am determined to be contrite. Dean Lynda called me on Tuesday afternoon and asked me—told me, really—to be in her office on Wednesday at three, and her tone told me I am in serious trouble.

"You're family, Talcott," she continues, her eyes hard. "Naturally, when a member of the family is having problems, we want to help."

By *we*, she means herself, and Stuart Land, and Arnie Rosen, the three most influential members of the faculty and, by coincidence, the current dean, the former dean, and a strong candidate to be the next dean. The seriousness of the occasion is signaled by the absence of Ben Montoya, who usually does her dirty work. For this meeting, Lynda wants the heavy guns.

We are sitting in Lynda's office on the furniture arranged for conversation. I am in a wooden armchair, Lynda and Stuart are on the plush sofa that runs off at a right angle from my spot, and Arnie's wheelchair is right next to me. I can see where the mate to my chair has been pushed aside to make room. Usually Lynda has coffee and donuts on a side table, but not today.

Stuart takes his turn. He has less patience with circumlocutions, which is why he was a very bad dean and is a very good man. "Let's look at the evidence, Talcott. The reasons we are worried. Number one, we have the increasingly wild conspiracy theories you have been busily pursuing, even though some of us have warned you. Number two, we have that bizarre incident with the police, not what we need with the racial tension in this town. Those are old problems, of course, so let us put them aside for a moment. Number three"—ticking them off on his fingers—"you haven't been meeting your classes regularly. Number four . . ."

"Now, wait a minute," I interject, displaying my usual lack of feel for the nuance of a conversation. As a lawyer, I should know enough to let them lay out the charges first, take the time to think it through, and then rebut it all at once. But remember what they say about those who can't do. "You know I had a good reason to miss those classes. . . ."

"My father died on a Monday morning and I taught that afternoon and the next day and the day after that," Stuart says coldly. "Besides, your family difficulties would explain only the classes you missed in the fall. Not in the current semester, which is only a month old."

Arnie Rosen lays a restraining hand on my wrist before I can offer an ill-considered response. "Tal, please, just listen first. Nobody here is out to get you."

I decide to hold my tongue.

"Number four," Stuart resumes, "we have what I suppose we would have to call your little shoving match with Gerald Nathanson, a graduate of this law school and a prominent member of this community. Do you have any idea how many people overheard you? And, number five . . ."

"Just a minute," I interrupt, forgetting my resolution. Having been through this with a livid and chagrined Kimmer, I do not want to do it again. "Just a *minute!* If you're about to blame me for that argument, I'll have you know . . ."

Stuart has no capacity for retreat: "None of this has anything to do with blame. We are talking about what is happening to you, Talcott." Steepling his fingers. "Months ago, I told you that we needed the old, lively, optimistic Talcott Garland back. But you ignored that warning, as you have ignored the rest of my warnings." He pauses. "And we have not even begun to discuss your efforts to sabotage Marc Hadley's chances for judicial appointment."

"I had nothing to do with that!"

"Number five," Stuart resumes, relentlessly, "there is some talk around the place that you have written scholarship that is biased toward the needs of a paying client. . . ."

"That's completely ridiculous!" I sputter, having all but forgotten my interview with Arnie back a million years ago.

"Calm down, Talcott," says Lynda in her steely voice, and it occurs to me that Theo Mountain, if we were still on the close terms that once marked our relationship, or if he were a few years younger, would be in this room, trying to protect me, for he used to be a power on the faculty and would never have countenanced this ganging up on his protégé. "Stuart is simply explaining how things look from the law school's point of view."

"Gerald Nathanson was thinking of filing some sort of complaint," says Stuart, "but I talked him out of it."

"I'm glad to hear it," I mutter, my head swimming.

"There is a pertinent university rule," Stuart continues in his blunt fashion. "Officers of the faculty do not go around abusing prominent citizens this way."

"I didn't abuse anybody," I protest, hopelessly. "He started it."

"The ethics of the kindergarten." Shaking his head as though I am beyond redemption.

"What we're saying," says Arnie Rosen with plain reluctance, "is that it is time for the institution to think about how to protect itself." Behind the small, round lenses his eyes are soft with sympathy. He is not the sort of liberal who can easily criticize a black man.

"Are you . . . are you firing me?" I blurt, my gaze leaping from one impassive Caucasian face to the next.

"No," says Stuart icily. "We're warning you."

"Which means what, exactly?"

Stuart is about to speak again, but Dean Lynda holds up her hand. "Stuart, Arnie, will you excuse us for a moment?" Arnie immediately gets his wheelchair moving, and Stuart leaps to his feet with such alacrity that I am certain the entire display was orchestrated in advance, for no dean, not even the scary Lynda Wyatt, could ever make Arnie Rosen and Stuart Land jump if they didn't want to.

A moment later we are alone.

"I've always liked you," Dean Lynda begins, which is probably a lie, except that her definitions of words, in good decanal fashion, do not always match what others understand. Deans must have that trait to survive, for they must be able to say to some student activist, with the utmost compassion and sincerity, *Oh, did you think what I said before was a promise of action? I just said I would look into it, but as Dean my hands are pretty much tied. It's really up to the university provost.* Good deans not only say these things every day or two, they have the trick of making the students, and sometimes the faculty, believe that they are telling the truth.

"Thank you, Lynda," I say calmly, waiting for her to get to the point.

"You aren't being fired, Tal. We couldn't do it if we wanted to. You have tenure, so only the trustees of the university can dismiss you, and only for cause. I don't think that there is cause to revoke your tenure. Not at this time. But you have to know that there are people on campus, and some in this building, who think otherwise. A few members of this faculty have suggested to me that I ask for your resignation." I sit very still. I am stuck all the way back on *Not at this time.* "I wouldn't want you to give them any more reasons for action. If you behave yourself from now on—don't look at me like that, you know perfectly well what I mean—if you behave yourself, we can protect you. But if you keep on getting into fights in the hallways and canceling classes for no good reason and running all over the place searching for your conspiracy, and, especially, if you come anyplace close to another run-in with the police . . . well, if you do that, I'm not sure how long I can hold off the dogs. I'm not sure I would even try. Is that clear enough for you?"

"Yes, but . . ."

"I don't want to hear the word *but,* Tal. I don't want to hear you tell me you *have to think about it.* All I want to hear is your promise, your solemn word, that all this nonsense is over. I want you to say you'll go back to being the serious scholar and hardworking teacher we all know and love, or did until October. I don't want you to get so much as a traffic ticket for the next five years. That's what I want."

"Or what?"

Lynda brushes curly gray hair away from her long neck and shrugs.

"You wouldn't dare," I whisper.

"I wouldn't dare what? Get rid of a professor who makes insane accusations, conducts a whispering campaign against a colleague, screams at people in the hallways, and abuses students in class?"

I hardly know where to start, so I pick the silliest charge of all. "I didn't abuse Avery Knowland."

"That depends on how you look at it. Or, more to the point, it depends on how I look at it. Right now, I imagine you're thinking that it wouldn't matter so much if we were to ask you to leave, that you have something of a reputation, that you could always get a position at another law school. But that depends a great deal on what I decide to say about you to the dean of whatever school considers hiring you. I could sink you with a word, and you know it. Theo couldn't protect you. If you keep carrying on the way you have been, I doubt he would even try."

I reflect again on my friendlessness. Suddenly my allies on the faculty seem very few indeed. Who would speak up for me? Lem Carlyle? Not if it would hurt his impeccable reputation. Arnie Rosen? Not with his run for the deanship coming up. Dear Dana Worth? Certainly, but nobody listens to her. Rob Saltpeter, perhaps. But he is a very long way from the top of the heap. I imagine the knives being sharpened even now up there in the top tier, where those who possess influence and reputation gather: Peter Van Dyke, Tish Kirschbaum, and, of course, the estimable Marc Hadley, not so long ago a friend, would all be delighted by my departure.

"Lynda," I say at last, "I need time."

"That sounds like a *but* to me."

"Not time to think over what you've said. What you've said makes perfect sense." I am not very good at obsequiousness, but I have to try. "I want to go back to that old Talcott Garland—the one everybody loves, you said—I want that very much. I just need a little time to figure out what's going on."

"That sounds like the conspiracy again." Her voice is hard. When a dean's voice is hard, the pressures are immense. Probably Lynda Wyatt is following somebody else's script, which suggests that a part of what she says is true: she has gone to bat for me. The university administration may be pushing her to get rid of me, and perhaps she has persuaded them to give me one last chance. The administration, in turn, has dictated terms which she dares not vary. Still, if I am right, if she has gone to bat for me, then . . . maybe . . .

"I'm not seeing any conspiracy anywhere, Lynda. I don't think anybody is out to get me. But it is a fact, not a fantasy, that the man who was asking me questions about my father is dead. It is a fact, not a fantasy, that somebody trashed my father's house in Oak Bluffs. It is a fact, not a fantasy, that I was beaten up in the middle of the campus by somebody who asked questions about my father. And it is a fact"—I stop suddenly. Lynda is watching me closely. I was about to mention the pawn. Which would persuade her absolutely that I have gone round the bend.

Lynda sighs. "Well, then, Tal, your turn to listen. It is a fact, not a fantasy, that you were almost arrested. No, don't say anything. It is a fact, not a fantasy, that somebody from up here sabotaged Marc, and a lot of people think it was you. It is a fact, not a fantasy, that you were shoving and screaming at Jerry Nathanson in the hallway day before yesterday. It is a fact, not a fantasy, that lots of people on this campus think you are beginning to lose it. It is a fact, not a fantasy, that I think . . ."

"Two weeks," I say suddenly.

"I beg your pardon."

"Give me two weeks. Two weeks to wrap everything up. If I—"

"I can't let you miss more classes."

"I'll teach my classes. I won't miss a class. I promise you. But I have to have a little more time."

"Time for what?"

I take a breath, force myself to stay calm. What am I supposed to say? That whoever is on the outside trying to ruin me is being helped by someone on the inside, somebody here at the law school? Somebody who knows where I am going to be almost before I do—and is in a position to smear my ethics as well, perhaps to make it even less likely that anyone will listen to whatever I might discover?

I say quietly, "Just time, Lynda. That's all. I won't miss any classes, but I need to work things out." She just waits. "I won't hurt the law school or the university. This school has been good to me. And, right now, this school is all I have." I hesitate, wanting to say more, but not daring to open the painful subject of my waning marriage. "I've asked you for very few favors since you've been dean, Lynda. Now, you know that's true. There are people who are in your office every week, complaining about their salaries or their committee assignments or their teaching loads or the size of their offices. I've never done any of those things, have I?"

"No, you haven't. That's true." The ghost of a smile dances over her face.

"So I'm asking this one thing. To hold off those pressures just two weeks more. And then, after two weeks, I promise you, either I'll be a good little boy or . . . or I'll resign from the faculty and save everybody the trouble."

My dean shakes her head. Her look is unhappy. "I'm really not trying to get rid of you, Tal. I respect you and I like you. I know you don't believe it, but it's true. What Stuart said about biased scholarship, for instance. You didn't hear me say it. I know you wouldn't do it, and even if I thought you would, there's no way to prove it. It's ridiculous. Besides, we live in a world of only"—a wan, cheerless grin—"imperfect objectivity. Scholarship is argument, isn't it? And argument is advocacy. Were we to take the claim of bias seriously, any one of us might be open to the same charge. But . . ."

"But you have to think of the school," I finish for her.

"You'll have to apologize to Jerry Nathanson. No way out of that one. And Cameron Knowland, bless his heart, is still waiting to hear from you."

More pain. "I'll call Jerry. I tried to call Cameron but he wouldn't talk to me."

"Then try again," she says crisply. Professors are not ordinarily subject to the dean's orders, not at a school as eminent as ours. But these are no ordinary times.

"I will. I promise."

Lynda conjures a small smile. She stands up. So do I. We shake. We both know our meeting is over, and that the deal has been made. Probably it falls within whatever parameters she was given by the university. But, just to make sure, she repeats the agreement as she escorts me to the door: "Two weeks, Talcott. No more."

"Two weeks," I echo.

Hurrying back to my office, I am weak with relief: after all, I might have been asked to resign on the spot. By the time I am behind my desk, however, the burden of reality has settled once more upon my shoulders. I still do not know what the arrangements are. Or what my father meant by his cryptic note. Or which one of my colleagues is trying to ruin my career. I do not even know whether I will still have a job tomorrow or the next day . . . or, for that matter, a wife.

All I know for sure is that I have fourteen days to figure it all out.

CHAPTER 43

A CHOICE IS MADE

"WHERE HAVE YOU BEEN?" asks Kimmer in a tone that I cannot at first identify. I have been home perhaps five minutes. Finding no one on the first floor, I came upstairs, kissed a slumbering Bentley good night, and walked into a storm.

"I . . . had a meeting with Dean Lynda. And then, well, I told you I might have to work late. The draft of my paper is overdue, remember?"

"I called your office, Misha. Three times."

"Maybe I was in the library." I do not know why I am being so cagey.

"You never go to the library." My wife is sitting up in bed, extra pillows propped behind her, work strewn over the blankets as she flips through the channels with the remote. Her eyes seem puffy, as though she has been crying, but she does not look at me. "Or, when you do, you get in trouble," she adds.

"The truth is . . . I went for a walk."

"A walk? For two hours?"

"I had a lot to think about."

"I'm sure." But there is a catch in her voice. What is going on?

"Kimmer, are you okay?"

"No, I am not okay!" she flares, rounding on me at last. "My husband, who has lately been acting crazy, can't be found for two whole hours! Two hours, Misha! Did it ever occur to you that I might worry?"

I cross to the bed, sit next to her, try to take her hand. She snatches it back. "No, I guess not. I'm sorry."

"You're sorry. You're *sorry*."

"What do you want me to say, Kimmer? Tell me, and I'll say it."

"I shouldn't have to tell you what to say."

"Look, darling, I'll apologize to Jerry. I was out of line. I know that."

"There's nothing going on with Jerry. There never was! Why can't you just believe me when I tell you these things?"

Because you have lied to me before. Because a man called the house looking for you and said *baby*, a fact I have yet to mention to you. Because you and I once cheated on André, so you and somebody else could be cheating on me. Dr. Young is right, so right!

"I believe you," I whisper.

"Oh, Misha." Her voice breaks. And, quite suddenly, the tears flow. I am stunned. I have not seen my wife cry since the night Bentley was born. At first I am not sure how to react. I put my arms around her. She writhes free. I hold her again, pulling her close, and her head finally settles against my chest.

"Kimmer, what is it? What's wrong?"

"Were you . . . were you with somebody else, Misha? Because I could understand it if you were. I'm such a bitch." Jealousy? From Kimmer?

"No, darling, no. Of course not. I told you, I went for a walk." Which is the truth but not the whole truth. Even now, I am not ready to tell her where I walked. I do not want her to think I am crazy.

"Misha, Misha," she whispers, lightly punching my chest. "Misha, what happened to us? It was so good. It was so good."

I shake my head. I have no answer. "I love you," I breathe. I am stroking the back of her neck, the way she used to like, and her pain seems to be subsiding. "You know there's nobody else in my life but you and Bentley. And please don't call yourself names."

"Why? I *am* a bitch. I'm horrible to you. You should leave me. You would if you had any sense." And then more tears. I think of my encounter with Gerald Nathanson, his anger arguably previous to mine. Maybe he and Kimmer ended their affair (if there was one, if there ever was one), and she is unhappy about it. But my wife's pain at this moment seems more profound, and, besides, the little slice of macho competitiveness I usually try to cover up is unwilling to accept that she would weep over Jerry when she has me.

"Come on, darling, what is it? Tell me."

Kimmer shakes her head. I stroke her neck some more. She whispers something. I can't quite hear it. She says it again, louder. And, for a moment, I am as crushed as she is.

"Ruthie called. She . . . she said the President picked somebody else."

"Oh, Kimmer. Oh, honey, I'm so sorry."

"It's okay." She sniffles, wipes her face on the sleeve of her long nightdress. "I guess it wasn't meant to be."

"You still have me and Bentley," I murmur. "It's not your fault the President didn't pick the best candidate."

"That's right." Kimmer tries to smile. "I knew I shouldn't have voted for him."

My eyes widen. "You voted for him?"

She manages a shaky grin. "I told you I flipped a coin."

"I thought you were joking."

"Well, I wasn't." She kisses me suddenly, then whispers something inaudible against my lips. She says it again, louder: "Don't you want to know who he picked?"

"Uh, sure. Okay." Actually, I do not, especially if, somehow, the resilient Marc Hadley has found a way to rescue his candidacy. But I am bound to hear sooner or later, so I might as well hear from my wife.

"Lemaster Carlyle."

"What!"

"Lemaster Carlyle." She laughs, harshly this time, then coughs, and a few more tears burst through her self-control. "Oh, that snake. That snake! I know you think he's like the best thing since sliced bread, but I think he's just a snake in the grass!"

Despite my wife's pain, I have to smile at the way the rest of us out-smarted ourselves. When Ruthie told Kimmer that two or three of my colleagues were in the running, we stopped at Marc Hadley. When Ruthie told Marc that the President was interested in diversity, Dahlia and Marc stopped at Kimmer. And there all the time was Lem Carlyle, at the intersection, a colleague and diverse, fitting both descriptions yet unexpected; good old Lem, waiting patiently on the sidelines for something to go awry—a charge of plagiarism, a crazy husband, anything—lurking and lurking like . . . well, like a snake in the grass. At least now I know why he has lately seemed so nervous around me.

"I can't believe it," I finally whisper.

"Liberals for Bush," Kimmer reminds me.

"Oh, right."

"Maybe it's for the best," my wife suggests, but neither of us can think of a reason why. So we do what used to be one of our favorite things instead. We walk down the hall with our arms around each other and stand in the doorway of Bentley's bedroom, gazing at him in wonder. We say a little prayer of thanksgiving. Then we go back to our room and put *Casablanca* in the VCR, and Kimmer eventually brightens a bit as she gets into reciting her favorite lines. But her eyes have closed by the time Ingrid Bergman goes to the bar to beg Humphrey Bogart for the letters of transit. I turn off the tape and Kimmer opens her eyes at once. "Are you sure there's not another woman?" she asks. "Because I need you right now, Misha. I really do need you."

"I'm sure." Maxine flits briefly through my mind, but I push her away. "I only love my wife," I tell both women, truthfully. "And my son."

"And your father."

"Huh?"

Although my wife's tired eyelids have resumed their droop, her full lips curve into a smile. "You love that old man, Misha. That's why you keep searching so hard."

Love? Love the Judge? This is, tragically, a concept I have not previously considered. Maxine said she knew I couldn't stop chasing the arrangements. Now Kimmer is saying the same thing. "Maybe so," I finally say. "I'm sorry. I just want to know what happened."

My wife seems to understand. "No, no, it's okay, honey. It's okay." Her eyes have drifted closed again, and her voice is starting to slur. "I understand, Misha. I do. But promise you'll come back to us."

"Come back to you from where?"

"From Aspen," Kimmer murmurs. She yawns.

"Aspen?"

"Oh, come on, Misha. I'm not gonna be a federal judge. That's over. So you might as well go see your Uncle Jack." She opens one eye, winks, then closes it again. "Just say hello to the FBI for me, okay?"

"Uh, okay."

"Bastards," she mutters, and is asleep. I sit awake for a while, stroking her back, on the one hand confident that she loves me after all, on the other wondering who phoned the house and called her *baby*.

Two weeks.

CHAPTER 44

STORMY WEATHER

(1)

I HAVE VISITED the small and stunningly rich community of Aspen, Colorado, three times in my life, the first time on a ski vacation with my old college friends John and Janice Brown, back before Bentley was born, a misbegotten expedition in which I sprained my ankle quite badly on the very first day, in the very first hour of my very first lesson, and so spent the remaining four days alone in the tiny condo, the world's thickest snowflakes swirling outside, the television cable failing intermittently, and the fireplace too grimy to be of use, as John and Janice, veterans of the sport, went streaking down the slopes, and Kimmer, who used to ski in her college days at Mount Holyoke but hardly ever since meeting dull me, reconnected with her lost skill. On that first visit, the bumpy, prayer-inducing descent in the turboprop persuaded me that the four-hour drive from Denver up through the Rockies, high, winding, fenceless passes and all, was the less intimidating choice. Indeed, I swore at the time that I would never fly to Aspen again. So, for my next two trips, both to attend excellent seminars at the Aspen Institute—one with Kimmer, one without—I rented a car at the Denver airport and drove up.

But there are such things as blizzards that bury mountain highways, and the only way to be sure the roads are always open is to stay away from the mountains unless it is summer. Since that first trip, John and Janice have often invited us to join them on the slopes, or even to use their time-share when they can't. Kimmer has gone twice, once with the Browns and once, just last year, ostensibly alone: "Some time apart to think will do us both some good, Misha, honey." I have stayed home both times, honoring my oath never again to try to get into Aspen in the winter. But the Lord, we all know, has ways of confounding proud mortals who swear oaths too lightly. So here it is February, and here I am on my way to Aspen in another snowstorm, flying in defiance of my own rules, the small jet buffeted by the gusty Rocky Mountain winds, the skiers drinking hard, the rest of us turning green.

The plane lands safely, and, by the time we roll to a stop, the mid-afternoon sky even begins to clear. It occurs to me, as I scurry across the tarmac to the small but modern terminal building, that the people who live here year-round are not as crazy as I have always thought. The snow-dappled mountains are gorgeous in the winter sunlight, which picks out the details with a crystal clarity. The evergreens marching toward the summit are, if anything, more dramatic in February than in August, like winter-weather troops wearing green-and-white alpine uniforms. Most of my fellow passengers are wearing uniforms too, after a fashion, and their brightly colored ski parkas look very serious indeed.

I have time to savor this vision only until I turn toward the baggage claim area and find waiting there the lean bodyguard I remember from the cemetery, whom I know only as Mr. Henderson. The temperature is in the teens—the very low teens—but he is wearing only a light wind-breaker. He summons a dazzling smile and even a few words: "Wel-come to Aspen, Professor," delivered in an eerily familiar voice, a voice so sleek, so velvetly delicious, that I can readily imagine anybody he tries to seduce sliding willingly downward to oblivion. Yet there is nothing of the voluptuary about Mr. Henderson. He is, instead, rather standoffish—as a good sentinel surely must be—as well as alert, ener-getic, feline in his compact grace, somehow complete.

"Thank you for meeting me," I reply.

Mr. Henderson nods politely. He does not offer to take my bag.

Moving on remarkably light feet, he leads me out to the car, which, this being Aspen in winter, is a silver Range Rover. He reminds me to buckle my seat belt. He tells me in his sinuous voice that Mr. Ziegler has been looking forward to renewing our acquaintance. All of this while, apologizing for the necessity, he runs a hand-held metal detector over my clothes and then, when I assume the indignities are done, repeats this activity with a small rectangular device complete with LED digital readout, perhaps to discover whether I am broadcasting. I keep my tongue in check: the meeting, after all, was my idea. "It will take us half an hour or so to get up to the property," Mr. Henderson says as we pull out of the parking lot. Not the *house*, I register. Not the *estate*. The *property*. A good Rocky Mountain word.

I nod. We exit the airport onto Route 82, which parallels the Roaring Fork River into the town of Aspen. At first the scenery is broad white fields and scattered houses and the occasional gas station or convenience store, always against the backdrop of some of the most glorious mountains in North America, which frame the valley on every side. Then the clusters of dwellings grow thicker . . . and, on the distant highlands, noticeably larger. Bunched townhouses announce the city limits. Even before entering the town, one can see, to the north, the garish homes along the ridges of Red Mountain, looming over the town like a kitschy reminder of the yawning chasm between money and taste. Then we are inside Aspen proper, home to what might be the most expensive real estate in the United States. I watch the town pass by, almost too neat and picturesque in its bright frame of sun and snow. As always, I gawk at the tiny, perfect Victorians of the West End, painted a happy variety of earth tones, each selling at probably ten times what the same building, on a larger lot, would bring in Elm Harbor. Realtors refer to the Aspen housing market as "sticker shock for the rich," swapping gleeful stories of well-to-do couples who break down in tears upon realizing how little a four- or five-million-dollar nest egg will buy. It is said that one of every eleven year-round residents works at least part-time selling real estate, and no wonder. A single six-percent commission can make your year. The *median* price of a home in Aspen is more than two million dollars, which is perhaps a fifth of what the medium-sized estates on Red Mountain fetch. On the mountain, prices of twenty million or more are not uncommon.

Jack Ziegler lives on Red Mountain.

The Range Rover sails into downtown Aspen, where every pedestrian seems to be carrying skis. The police wear jeans and drive sport-utility vehicles or sky-blue Saabs. Mr. Henderson steers swiftly and confidently through the snow. The only American cars I see are Jeeps and Explorers and Navigators. We pass a couple of filling stations, then three or four short blocks of restaurants, town offices, and shops. In the center of town, we hang a sharp left, turning north. (For some reason, maps of Aspen are usually drawn upside down, with Red Mountain, which lies to the north, at the bottom, and Aspen Mountain, which lies to the south, at the top.) We pass one of the town's two supermarkets, cross a short bridge, take another sharp left, and, suddenly, we are climbing the winding road that is the only way up Red Mountain.

"I assume the meeting is just the two of us," I say.

"As far as I know." His battle-hard gray eyes never leave the road. I realize that Mr. Henderson has not given me quite the reassurance I need, perhaps because I did not ask quite the right question.

"Nobody else knows I'm coming?"

"Oh, I would guess that everybody does."

"Everybody?"

"Mr. Ziegler is a popular man," he says cryptically, and I realize that I am not going to get any more information than I already have, but what I already know is enough to keep my nerves humming.

The Range Rover corners hard to the right at a switchback and then, moments later, hard to the left at another. All around us lies the tawdry evidence of the madness of the *nouveaux riches*. To describe the mansions surrounding us as large does not quite capture the phenomenon of Red Mountain. They are immense testaments to misspent wealth, decorated with enough multi-tiered fountains, tennis courts under all-weather bubbles, four-car garages, turrets, indoor pools, and terrorist-proof gates to fill several museums, as perhaps in the future they will—the Museum of American Waste, our grandchildren's grandchildren might decide to call it. Further confirmation, my favorite student, Crysta Smallwood, would likely say, of the determination of the white race to destroy itself—in this case, by spending itself to death.

The Range Rover makes another sharp turn, and suddenly we are facing a heavy gate and Mr. Henderson is whispering seductively into a speaker along the side of the road. A tiny light turns green, and the gate rolls back. A wide, unmarked road stretches upward. At first, I imagine that we are entering Jack Ziegler's estate, which I have never seen but have always imagined to be sprawling and walled. I realize a moment later that I am mistaken. We are inside a private development, a subdivision for people whose wealth is in nine figures. Mailboxes are all clustered together near the entrance, and, moments later, individual driveways appear. The houses are no smaller than elsewhere on the mountain, but they are quieter somehow, less gaudy, their residents concerned more with privacy than showing off. Turning a wide corner, we pass a Grand Cherokee marked with the logo of a private security firm, and the two hard white faces inside look more like Green Berets than ordinary rent-a-cops.

We are in a cul-de-sac. The second driveway on the right is Jack Ziegler's.

Uncle Jack lives in what is sometimes called an upside-down house, because you enter on the top floor. From the outside, it is rather unpretentious, flat and rectangular with unassuming stucco walls and a garage that holds a mere three cars. But the secret, it turns out, is on the inside. We are admitted to the house by another quiet bodyguard, this one named Harrison, who is very nearly Henderson's twin, not in appearance but in behavior, for their affects are as confusingly similar as their names. The marble-floored entry hall is actually a balcony from which one looks down into the main part of the house; the dwelling is built into the side of Red Mountain, and to descend the stairs to the lower level, which is where they lead me, is to descend the mountain itself. The windows looking out on the town below and Aspen Mountain beyond are two stories high. The view is alarmingly beautiful.

I do not generally suffer from vertigo, but as I pick my way down the stairs I cannot resist the sensation that I am strolling into thin air, right off the side of the cliff, and one of the interchangeable bodyguards seizes my upper arm because I begin to sway.

"Everyone has that reaction at first," Mr. Henderson says kindly.

"Almost everyone," corrects his partner, who looks like a man who has never been dizzy in his life. Harrison is skinny, the wide receiver to Henderson's linebacker. I would figure Henderson as the intimidator, Harrison as the silent killer. They share the same dead eyes and cold, pale stare. But my imagination is running away with me: Uncle Jack is, after all, retired.

From whatever.

"Don't let the illusion deceive you," adds Henderson in his smooth voice, as though reciting to a group of tourists. "There is plenty of solid rock underneath us, and the ground outside is mostly flat." He points toward the window, probably to indicate a lawn, but I am unable to follow his gesture without having my head begin to reel.

"Mr. Ziegler will be with you momentarily," Harrison grumbles before trudging off down one of the two hallways that run from the immense ground-floor room into the wings of the house.

"Perhaps you should sit down," Henderson suggests, gesturing toward the several seating arrangements in the vast room: one white leather, another some brown tweed fabric, a third a bright floral print, all sharply distinct, yet blending somehow into a harmonious whole.

"No, I'm fine," I assure him, speaking for the first time since entering the house, and pleased that my voice is steady.

"May I offer you something to drink?"

"I'm fine," I repeat.

"At altitude, it is important to stay hydrated, especially the first few days."

I look up at him, wondering if he is after all, as I first suspected on the day we buried the Judge, not a bodyguard but a nurse.

"Nothing, thank you."

"Very well," says Henderson, withdrawing down a different hallway from the one that swallowed Harrison, and suddenly I am alone in the lair of the beast. For Jack Ziegler, I have come to realize, is not simply a source of information about the misery that has overtaken my family; he is, in some sense, its author. Where, after all, would my father turn if he wanted to hire a killer? There was really only one possibility, and that is the reason I am here.

I circle the room, admiring the art, pausing here and there, waiting. In the air is the scent of something zesty—paprika, perhaps—and I wonder whether Uncle Jack plans to offer me lunch. I sigh. I do not want to stay very long in this house. I do not want to stay very long in this town. My preference would be to talk to Uncle Jack and immediately leave again, but the depressing magic of time zones and the mundane obstacle of finding a flight out have combined to make that impossible. Uncle Jack, fortunately, made no offer to put me up for the night, and our rickety family budget would never bear the price of an Aspen hotel room in the high winter season, even were one available. So I have arranged to use John and Janice's time-share for this one night; it isn't their week, but they ascertained that it would be vacant and switched with whoever is scheduled to occupy it.

Other than my wife, nobody in Elm Harbor knows that I have made this trip. I hope to keep it that way. I am not technically exceeding the rules Dean Lynda laid down—it is Friday, so I am missing no classes—but I do not imagine she would be thrilled to discover that I have flown off to visit . . . the man I have flown off to visit. Being the helpful fellow I am, I would rather not add needless complications to Lynda's job. So I am not planning to tell her.

I glance at the window again, but the view is as disturbing as ever, and I hastily turn away to continue my circuit of the room. I pause in front of the fireplace, where the wall is dominated by a huge oil painting of Uncle Jack's late wife, Camilla, the one he is supposed to have killed, or had killed. The portrait is at least seven feet high. Camilla wears a flowing white gown, her jet-black hair piled on her head, her pale face surrounded by an unearthly light, probably in an effort to suggest an angelic nature. It reminds me of those idealized paintings of the Renaissance, when the artists took care to make their patrons' wives glow. I am willing to bet that the portrait was done after Camilla's violent death, for the artist appears to have worked from a blown-up photograph, so that the result appears not so much ethereal as fake.

"Not one of his better works, is it?" sighs Jack Ziegler from behind me.

(11)

I DO NOT STARTLE EASILY. I do not startle now. I do not even turn around. I lean over to squint at the artist's name, but it is an illegible scrawl.

"It's not bad," I murmur generously, pivoting to face Abby's godfather, and recalling the answer that ended my father's chance for the Supreme Court. *I don't judge my friends based on rumors,* he said when they asked about Camilla; then he folded his arms, signaling his contempt for the audience.

Jack Ziegler's arms are folded, too.

"He's not a real artist anyway," Jack Ziegler continues, dismissing the painting with a flap of one trembling hand. "So famous, so honored, yet he paints my wife for *money.*"

I nod, not sure, now that I am facing Uncle Jack, quite how to proceed. He stands before me in bathrobe and bedroom slippers, his face thinner and grayer than before, and I wonder whether he has more than a few months left. But his eyes remain bright—mad and gleeful and alert.

Jack Ziegler slips his skinny arm into mine and conducts me slowly around the room, evidently assuming that in my desperation, or perhaps my fear, I will be fascinated by what his illicitly obtained wealth has purchased. He points to a lighted display case holding his small but impressive collection of incunabula, some of them doubtless on Interpol watch lists. He shows me a small tray of magnificent Mayan artifacts that the government of Belize certainly does not know have left the country. He turns me to look back the way I came in. The wall below the balcony is covered by a huge fabric hanging, all multicolored vertical lines that attract and confuse the eye. There is a pattern hidden there, and the brain's stubborn determination to work it out holds the gaze. The piece is enormously beautiful. Uncle Jack tells me with unfeigned pride that it is a genuine Gunta Stölzl, and I nod admiringly, even though I have no earthly idea who, or even what sex, Gunta Stölzl is, or was.

"So, Talcott," he wheezes when our guided tour of his little museum is over. We are standing before the window once more, neither of us wanting to be the one to begin. As we measure each other, recessed ceiling speakers bark the hard musical edges of Sibelius's *Finlandia*, which has always struck me, despite its energetic pretensions, as one of the most depressing compositions in the classical repertoire. But it is perfect for the moment.

When I say nothing, Uncle Jack coughs twice, then moves swiftly onward: "So, you are here, you have made it, I am pleased to see you, but time is short. So, what can I do for you? You said on the telephone that the matter was urgent."

At first, I can manage only a nervous "Yes." To see Jack Ziegler so close up, his near-twin bodyguards waiting in the wings, his eyes glittering, not quite mad but not quite sane, waiting impatiently for me to explain myself, is quite different from sitting on an airplane planning how the dialogue will go.

"You said you had some trouble."

"You could say that."

"*You* said that."

Again I hesitate. What I am experiencing is not so much fear as a reluctance to commit myself; for, once I enter upon a serious conversation with Uncle Jack, I am not sure I can pull free of him.

"As you might or might not know, I've been looking into my father's past. What I've found has been . . . disturbing. And then there are other things, things that have happened over the past couple of months, which are also disturbing."

Jack Ziegler stares silently. He is prepared, it would seem, to wait all afternoon and into the night. He does not feel threatened. He does not feel afraid. He does not seem to feel *anything*—which is part of his power. I wonder afresh whether he really murdered his own wife, and whether he felt anything at all if he did it.

"People have been following me," I blurt out, feeling idiotic, and when Uncle Jack still refuses to be drawn, I simply tell the whole story, from the moment he left me in the cemetery to the fake FBI agents to the white pawn to Freeman Bishop's murder to Colin Scott's drowning at Menemsha to the book that mysteriously reappeared. I omit Maxine, perhaps because keeping at least one secret in the face of Jack Ziegler's demanding glare is all the victory I am likely to win.

When he is sure that I am finished, Uncle Jack shrugs his shoulders.

"I do not know why you are telling me this," he says gloomily. "I assured you on the day of your father's burial that you are in no danger. I will protect you as I promised Oliver I would. You and your family both. I keep my promises. Nobody will harm you. Nobody will harm your family. It is impossible. Completely impossible. I have seen to it." He shifts his weight, evidently from physical pain. "Chess pieces? A missing book? Men hiding in the woods?" He shakes his head. "These are not disturbing, Talcott. I had frankly hoped for better from you."

"But the men who got their fingers cut off . . ."

"I will protect *you*," he emphasizes, flapping a hand, and I comprehend instantly that I may not step another inch down that road. For a harrowing instant, I know true fear. "You and your family. As long as I live."

"I understand."

"If these men truly accosted you, I would think their misfortune was a sign that you are truly safe." Jack Ziegler lets his meaning sink in. Then his bleary eyes find mine. "I had hoped you were here with news of the arrangements."

I pause. There is opportunity here, I can sense it, if I can only get my creaky brain back into operation. "Not *news* exactly. But I think I might be on the track."

Once more I hesitate to press forward. If I complete the thought, I am committed to my path. I made my decision long before landing in Aspen, but between the decision and the act God has placed the will; and the will is quite sensitive to terror.

Still Abby's godfather waits.

"But, well, if you could just explain a couple of things to me—well, things would be so much easier." I am annoyed at myself. Just as in the cemetery, I am tongue-tied in Uncle Jack's presence. I suppose I have reason: Jack Ziegler is a murderer many times over, an efficient broker in just about every illegal substance, a middleman to the underworld, with connections to organized crime so complex, so neatly obscured, that nobody has ever quite succeeded in tracking them down.

Yet everybody knows they are there.

"A couple of things," he repeats, promising nothing. I notice a line of perspiration along his forehead. His hands as he brushes it away betray a slight tremor, and his eyes intermittently lose their focus. An attack of nerves? His illness? "A couple of things," he says again.

I nod, swallow, steal a glance out the window, this time without quite feeling like I am tumbling off the mountain—but still I cannot figure out how the house stays up.

I look back at Jack Ziegler again, and I realize, from the fact that he is waiting with so much patience, from the fact that he agreed to see me at all, that he is every bit as needy as I am. So my voice is calmer and more certain when I say: "First, I was wondering if you saw my father, oh, about a year and a half ago. A year ago last October. Around then."

His eyes cloud again, and I realize he is actually trying to remember. "No," he says at length. "No, I think not. At that time I would still have been in Mexico for my treatments." He sounds uncertain, not deceptive. Still, it is hard to be sure. "Why?"

"I just wondered." Realizing this sounds ridiculous, I reinterpret it. "I . . . heard a rumor, I guess."

"And is that why you came all this way, Talcott? To chase down a rumor?"

"No." Time to roll the dice. "No, Uncle Jack, I came because I want to ask you about Colin Scott."

"And who, please, is Colin Scott?"

I hesitate. Colin Scott, I know from Ethan Brinkley, had several names, and there is no reason to think Jack Ziegler knows them all. On the other hand, if, as I suspect, he has been keeping tabs on my life these last few months, he can hardly have failed to hear the name once or twice.

"Colin Scott," I repeat. "He used to be called Villard. Jonathan Villard. He was a private detective. My father hired him to find out who was in the car that killed Abby. Your goddaughter."

Now it is Jack Ziegler's turn to hesitate. He is trying to work out how much I know and how much I am guessing and how much he can hide. He does not like being vulnerable to me, and his willingness to show me this calculating side suggests that he wants my help.

"And?" he asks.

"I think you used to know him in the CIA."

"And?"

"And you had to be the one who put my father in contact with him."

"And?" Not even telling me if I am hot or cold. There is a wheeze in his voice, wet and sickly. He puts a hand flat over his chest, then bursts into a fit of phlegmy coughing, doubling over. Instinctively, I take his arm, which, beneath the bathrobe, has melted away almost to the bone. Harrison is next to us in an instant, gently removing my fingers, guiding Uncle Jack to the sofa, handing him a tall glass of water.

Jack Ziegler gulps the water, and the coughing subsides.

"Please sit down, Professor," the wiry Harrison orders gravely. His voice is a reedy chirp, and I look twice to make sure he really is the tough guy he obviously wants to appear. I examine his shoulders and decide that he is.

I sit as commanded, on a spindly chair across from the scariest man I know. Harrison proffers a pill, which Uncle Jack waves peevishly away. Harrison's outstretched hand might be carved from stone. Uncle Jack glares but finally yields, swallowing the pill, swigging the water.

Harrison withdraws.

Could he, too, be a nurse? Am I imagining too much? I glance at the infamous Jack Ziegler, slumped on the gorgeous sofa, spittle on his dry lips, his hand waving feebly, but not in time to the music. Why was I so afraid of him? He is sick, he is dying, he is scared. I look around the room. Not a museum, a mausoleum. My heart is seized with an unexpected wave of pity for the man huddled across from me. We sit in silence for a few minutes, or, rather, we sit without talking: *Finlandia* has been replaced by what sounds like Wagner, although I am unable to identify the piece. Jack Ziegler leans back on the sofa, his eyes closed.

"Please excuse me, Talcott," he whispers without moving. "I am not yet recovered." He does not say from what.

"I understand." I pause, but I am too well bred to avoid what I must say next: "If it would be easier for you, I can come back another time."

"Nonsense." Another cough, not as loud, but dry and rattling and obviously painful. He opens his eyes. "You are here, you have come this great distance, you have questions. You may ask." *Although I may not answer,* he is telling me.

"Colin Scott," I say again.

Jack Ziegler blinks, his eyes watery and ancient and mildly confused. I try to remember all the crimes he is supposed to have committed, all the connections with the Mafia, with the arms dealers and the drug lords and other people whose livelihood depends on the misery of others. But I am finding it difficult to recall why this doddering old man seemed so scary a moment ago. I remind myself about the men whose hands were mutilated after they attacked me, but it stirs less horror than before.

"What about him?" Uncle Jack finally says, blinking hard.

"I don't think my father paid him. There don't seem to be any canceled checks in my father's papers." I decided before I ever set foot in this house to leave Mariah out of it. Best that Abby's godfather find it necessary to kill no more than one of Abby's siblings.

"What was it for which your father failed to pay?"

"For the work he did. Tracking down the sports car." I swallow, my uneasiness building afresh as his face strengthens once more, but the time for caution was before I lifted the receiver to call Jack Ziegler in the first place. "My father didn't pay him for his work."

"So?"

This single syllable possesses an affect heretofore missing: a sleeping beast seems to be slowly waking, and Jack Ziegler does not seem nearly so doddering.

"I don't imagine he worked for free," I say carefully.

"So?"

My fear is creeping back, stroking my back and thighs with chilly fingers. Somehow, Uncle Jack has altered the temperature of our conversation.

"I think . . . I think you paid him. Paid the detective."

"I paid him?" The coal-black eyes are sharper now, and my stomach is touched by the same twisting unease I felt when I was a child on the Vineyard and my father gave me a torch and ordered me to burn a hornets' nest Mariah had discovered in the eaves above the porch. I knew then that unless I got every one of them I was going to be stung. A lot.

"That's what I think."

"That I paid this Scott for his work for your father." Jack Ziegler enunciates the words slowly and clearly, as though offering me the opportunity to retract my testimony.

"Yes." I may be stirring the hornets, but at least my voice is calm.

"Why would I do that?"

"I don't know. Maybe because you and my father were old friends. Because you were his daughter's godfather." I force the next words out, knowing he will never tell me which version is true. "Or maybe you helped him because you . . . you wanted my father to owe you a favor. A favor you could later ask him to repay."

Jack Ziegler makes the spitting sound I recall from the cemetery. His long fingers stroke the dying flesh of his chin.

"Maybe there are no checks to the late Mr. Scott because your father did not pay him anything. Maybe he did not pay him anything because Mr. Scott did not work for him."

"I don't think that's it. I think there are reasons why my father could not write him checks. I think that Mr. Scott . . . well, let's say he didn't exactly have the kind of background with which a federal judge could afford to be associated."

"So?"

"So my father had to avoid even the appearance of impropriety. Maybe, even then, he was thinking about the Supreme Court." When this evokes nothing but the same hard-eyed stare, I continue. "Besides, I'm not even sure my father could have afforded to pay him. Not on a federal judge's salary, especially in those days."

Jack Ziegler is wonderfully relaxed. "What else do you think, Talcott? This is really quite intriguing."

I hesitate, but it is a little late to turn back.

"I think Colin Scott did do a report about the accident. I think he figured out who did it. I think he gave it to my father. But I don't think my father ever took it to the police, did he? I think, when he saw what was in it, he asked Mr. Scott to do something for him, and, when he said no, my father brought the report to you and asked for your help."

I stop. The next words simply will not emerge. It is not that I am too frightened to speak them; it is that I am less sure than I was two hours ago that I want to know the answer.

But Jack Ziegler refuses to let me avoid the rest. "You say your father came to me for my help? I see. And what is it that you suppose happened then?"

Well, this is what I flew up the mountain to discuss. This is the moment toward which I have been working, through all the conversations with Wallace Wainwright and Lanie Cross and all the memories I have teased from Sally and Addison and even Mariah, through all the evidence I have assembled, with and without their help, up to and including the missing scrapbook. If I am not going to say it, all the months of work are wasted. So is the trip to Aspen.

To be sure, if I do say it, there is a nontrivial possibility that I will never see my wife and child again. But I have, as so often, the courage of the fool.

"I think, somehow, you got Colin Scott to . . . to take care of the problem for him."

So there, finally, it is out in the open.

Jack Ziegler shakes his head slowly, and a bit sadly, but his eyes angle away from me, gazing out on the vertiginous view. "Take care of it?" He snickers. Then coughs. "You sound like a bad movie. Take care of what?"

"You know what I mean, Uncle Jack."

"I know what you mean, Talcott, and, frankly, I am insulted by it."

His tone is low, almost caressing, and it chills me. Once again, something vaguely threatening thickens the air between us.

"I'm not trying to—"

"You are accusing your father of a crime, Talcott. You use silly euphemisms, but that is what you are doing, eh? You think your father paid this man Scott to do a murder." He is growing less and less simple by the moment. "That is bad enough. But now you are accusing me of helping him."

Once you stir the nest, the Judge told me, *you had better keep on burning, because you can never outrun the hornets if they get loose.*

"Look, Uncle Jack, I know how you make your living."

"No, I don't think you do." His mouth puckers and he holds up a twisted hand. He pokes a shriveled finger in my face. "Oh, I know, I know, you *think* you know. Everybody *thinks* they know. They read the newspapers and those imbecilic books and whatnot. Those fool committee reports. But nobody really knows. Nobody." He struggles to his feet. I have the good sense, for once, not to offer to help. "Come with me, Talcott, I want to show you something."

I follow him as he pads in his slippers across the long room, passing in front of that amazing window with the dizzying, panoramic view of Aspen, and out into the stainless-steel kitchen, where a stout Slavic woman is preparing lunch. Now I see the source of that zesty smell, for she is pouring powder into a pot. My host snarls at her in some language I do not recognize, and she smiles thinly and disappears. The back wall of the kitchen shares the same view through huge windows. On the far side, the room opens into a greenhouse. I follow Jack Ziegler inside, where a bewildering variety of plants perfume the air. I wonder how the intermixing aromas affect the taste of the food.

"Look," says Uncle Jack, pointing at something on the other side of the glass wall. "See what I mean? Everybody."

Now it is my turn to be confused. "Uh, everybody what?"

"Everybody thinks they know. Look!"

I look. I throw a serious expression on my face, hoping Uncle Jack will mistake my befuddlement for concentration, as I have not the faintest idea what he is talking about. I follow the path of his trembling finger. I see his sweeping lawn, the crisp snow sparkling in the rich mountain sun, I see high hedges, and the narrow road winding upward toward the ever-more-ostentatious homes of film producers and software entrepreneurs even wealthier than my baby sister's godfather. A minivan rumbles by: Kimmer hates them, considering them matronly, and refuses to let us buy one. A power company truck is parked a hundred yards up the hill as the uniformed crew, one male, one female, does something clever up on the pole. A bit closer in, a muscular woman in black boots and yellow spandex, evidently heedless of the cold, walks what my untutored eye decides is a Doberman. A battered red pickup bearing the logo of a lawn-care firm wheezes past, ferrying a trio of snow-blowers.

Jack Ziegler stands next to me like a statue, his finger pressed to the glass. I do not know what he is pointing at. I do know that the plants are starting to make me gag.

"Okay," I say carefully. "I'm looking."

"Well, do you see them?" His senility has made a sudden return, and I wonder again whether it is feigned. "Do you see them watching us?"

"See who?"

He grabs my shoulder. His fingers, hot with fever, dig into the muscle like talons. "There! The truck!"

"The truck? You mean the one over by the pole?"

"Yes, yes, do you see it?"

"Okay, yes. I see the truck."

"Well, then, you understand. You have no idea how they harass me—"

"Who? The power company?"

Uncle Jack looks at me hard, and for an instant the clouds seem to dissipate. "Not the power company," he says in a reasonable tone. "The FBI."

I look again. "It's a power company truck—"

"It is only a cover. They are here to harass me." He laughs unexpectedly, and his eyes darken and roll. His gleeful madness has returned. "The power goes out up here at least twice a month. Do you know why?" I shake my head. "So they can send their trucks and listen in on my telephone. So my alarm systems won't work and they can plant their bugs."

"Bugs—"

"Right here, in my house, in my *kitchen*, there are bugs!" To my astonishment, he produces a fly swatter from somewhere and whacks a spot on the wall. "Take that!" he cackles with such glee that for a moment I think that I might have misunderstood him, that he really is talking about insects. "And that!" he cries, turning away to smack the refrigerator, then one of the dark green granite countertops. "That'll rattle their earphones!" he hoots.

He tosses the fly swatter vaguely toward a closet, slips an arm around my shoulders, and leads me back into the great room, as he calls it. "They want to know what I do for a living. They think I am a criminal, for goodness' sake!" He pauses at his immaculate desk and scribbles something on a pad. "Like you do," he mutters. "Like you do." Then he coughs wetly, not bothering to cover his mouth.

Embarrassed, I make my typical retreat. "Uncle Jack, I, uh, I didn't mean—"

"But I'm on to them," he giggles, talking right through me. "And so, when the power goes out, do you know what I do?"

"No."

"I'll tell you what I do," he says, his expression crafty as he slips his arm around me once more. "*I go around with a flashlight and kill their bugs!*"

"I see," I say, wondering whether I have come on a fool's errand.

"No, I don't think you do see," he mumbles. Then he tilts his face sharply upward and bellows: "Harrison!"

The skinny bodyguard materializes at once. "Yes, sir?"

This is it. They are throwing me off the side of the mountain. Kimmer, I forgive you. Take good care of our boy.

"Is this house bugged, Harrison?" Abby's godfather demands.

"Occasionally, sir."

"And do we kill the bugs?"

"Whenever we can, sir."

"Thank you, Mr. Harrison, that will be all." Uncle Jack hands him the scribbled note, and the butler-valet-nurse-bodyguard withdraws. I begin to breathe normally once more. This is how they communicate in a house where any word might be overheard: they write each other notes. Now I understand what Henderson meant about Uncle Jack's popularity—and how everybody would know I am coming to visit. "Bugs everywhere," says Jack Ziegler, shaking his head sadly.

(III)

JACK ZIEGLER IS FADING. His lips quiver. The excitement seems to have worn him out, for his face has grown slack, the energy depleted. "Let me lean on you, Talcott," he murmurs, slipping a thin, feverish arm around my shoulders. We walk back into the main part of the house, Uncle Jack's feet sliding on the floor. He feels as light as a child against my body.

"Listen, Talcott," he says. "Are you listening?"

"I'm listening, Uncle Jack."

"I am not a hero, Talcott. I know that. I have done things in my life for which I am sorry. I have some associates who are sorry as well. Do you understand?"

"Not really . . ."

"I have made choices, Talcott. Hard choices. And choices have consequences. That is, I think, the very first rule of any just morality. Choices have consequences. All choices. I have always accepted that. I have made good choices and benefited from them. I have made bad choices and suffered for it. All of us have." He lets this sink in, too. I realize that he is truly angry underneath the politesse. The hornets are buzzing away.

"I understand what you—" I begin, but he interrupts swiftly.

"Consequences, Talcott. An underused word. We live today in a world in which nobody believes choices should have consequences. But may I tell you the great secret that our culture seeks to deny? You cannot escape the consequences of your choices. Time runs in only one direction."

"I suppose so," I assure him, although I do not.

Jack Ziegler's wet, tired gaze flicks over my face, bounds off toward the wall—is he thinking about the bugs again?—then settles on the giddying vista of Aspen beyond the two-story window. He begins a fresh lecture: "None of us who are fathers are quite what we wanted to be for our sons. You will learn that, I think." I remember that he has a son of his own, Jack Junior, a currency trader who lives halfway around the world—Hong Kong, maybe—to escape his father.

I wonder whether that is far enough.

Jack Ziegler continues to wax philosophical, as though the purpose of my trip is to comprehend his notion of the life well lived. "A father, a son—this is a sacred bond. All through history, the headship of the family is passed on that way, father to son to son of the son, and so on. Head of the family, Talcott! That is a mission, you see. A responsibility that a man may not shirk, even should he so desire. Nowadays, on the campuses, I know, such ideas are dismissed. Sexist, they say. You know the words better than I. Patriarchy. Male domination. Pah! My generation, we lacked the luxuries of yours. We had no time to wallow in such arguments. We had to *live*, Talcott. We had to *act*. Let others worry about why God spoke to Moses from inside a burning bush instead of a sycamore tree or a Wal-Mart store or a television set. Who had time to care? Yours is the generation of talkers, and I wish you well of it. Ours was the generation of doers, Talcott, the last the nation has seen. Doers! You do not understand this, I know. You have never lived a life in which there is no time to discuss, to debate, to litigate, to *analyze your policy options*—isn't that what they say now? We did not go on the radio and moan about the difficulties in our lives. We did not derive our self-worth from establishing how badly others had treated us. We did not complain. We had no time. My generation, we actually had things that we had to do, Talcott. Decisions to make. Do you see?" He does not care whether I see. He does not care whether I agree. He is determined to make his point . . . and, at this instant, sounds exactly like the Judge. "And this was the generation that spawned your father, Talcott. Your father and myself both. We were the same. We were heads of families, Talcott. Men. The old-fashioned kind, you would say. We knew what our responsibilities were. Provide for the family, yes. Nurture it, certainly. Guide it. But, above all, protect it."

The sun is setting over the town of Aspen, the snow turning a magnificent orange-red. Down below, the skiers will begin on the nightlife phase of their day; I wonder when they sleep.

"I know you are angry, Talcott. I know you are disappointed in your father." He casts his moist eyes toward me, then slides them swiftly away. "You think you have caught him at something terrible. Well, tell me, then, what would you have done? Your daughter is dead, the police do nothing—and you think perhaps you know who killed her. What would you have done?"

Now he waits. I have turned the same question over and over in my mind ever since Mariah's visit started me thinking along this road. Were someone to do harm to Bentley, and were the law to offer no justice, would I go out and hire a killer? Or do the job myself? Maybe. Maybe not. No one, I suspect, can answer with confidence as long as the question is abstract. Only when something is at stake do we test the principles we so proudly parade.

"I know what *he* did," I finally say.

Jack Ziegler shakes his thin head. "You think you know. But what do you know, really? Tell me, Talcott: what do you really *know?*"

His sudden directness takes me by surprise. His eyes are boring into me now. I look away. I wonder why Uncle Jack is not worried about the bugs any more, but as I replay our conversation in my mind, I realize that the only incriminating lines have come from me, and they all involve the Judge, who is already dead . . . and that Uncle Jack has maneuvered me into a position in which I am smearing my own father's memory for the benefit of the FBI's listeners.

So be it.

"He hired a killer," I finally say, wanting to match Uncle Jack's directness with some of my own.

"Pah! A killer! The man who mangled your sister was a killer, Talcott. And yet he was walking around free."

"The man my father *thought* did it. He was never convicted."

"Convicted? Pah! He was never arrested, never charged, never truly investigated." His chilly eyes never waver.

"Then how could my father know for sure that he had the right man?"

"It is an error, Talcott, to think of this matter as a proposition, true or false." A moist, ragged cough. "To be a man is to act. Sometimes you must act on the information available at the time. Perhaps it is accurate. Perhaps it is erroneous. Still you must act."

"I am not quite following you."

"And I am not able to enlighten you further."

Except that he has not enlightened me at all. I almost say this, but he has resumed the tone and didactic style of the lecturer. "Some of your questions have no answers, Talcott, and some of them have answers that you will never know. That is the way of the world, and our inability to discover all that we wish we could is what makes us mortals." The oracular side of Jack Ziegler bothers me, perhaps for ethical reasons: What right has a murderer to lecture on the meaning of life? Does he perhaps know things we weaker mortals do not? Or is all of this oratory simply obfuscation, so that the bugs, if there are any, will never catch him admitting a crime? "And some of your questions do have answers to which you are entitled. I believe that your father wanted you, more than the other children, to have the answers. Because he always lived in some awe of you, Talcott. Some awe, some envy. And, always, he wanted your approval. More than he wanted Addison's, more than he wanted Mariah's." I am not sure if I believe any of this. I am quite sure I do not want to hear it. "And so your father arranged for you to receive some of the answers. But you must also find them for yourself."

"Which means what?"

"The arrangements, Talcott. You must discover the arrangements." He frowns. "I do not know where your father buried the answers, but he buried them so deeply that only you would know where to look. That is why so many people have bothered you. But remember always that none of them can harm you." A curt nod. "And that you must not abandon the search, Talcott. You must not."

"But why is the search so important?" The question I tried to ask Maxine, whose real name is unlikely to be Maxine.

"Let us say . . . for your peace of mind."

I think this over. That cannot be quite all of it. Uncle Jack wants me to find whatever there is to find. It may even be, from his insistence, and Maxine's, that somehow his . . . his ability to protect me . . . is linked to a promise that the search will succeed. Frowning again, wanting to escape this horrible room, I fire off my last shot.

"And if I do discover the arrangements? What then?"

"Why, then, everybody will be satisfied." He falls silent, but I understand it is merely a pause: I even know what is coming next. And I am even right. "Perhaps, when you find what your father left, you should not examine it yourself. That would be a mistake. I think it would be best . . . yes. I shall expect you to share it with me first. Naturally."

"Naturally," I mutter, but too softly for him to hear. Mallory Corcoran, Maxine of no last name, now Uncle Jack: *When you find it, bring it to me!* Yet Jack Ziegler, unlike the others, pronounces his demand with a sense of entitlement. Suggesting, perhaps, that I will simply be returning to him his own.

"That is a fair exchange, I think." Meaning, in return for his promise to protect me and my family.

"Uh, sure. Yes." His tone suggests that I am about to be dismissed. I have the frantic sense of having omitted something important. Before I can control my voice, I hear myself raising the one subject I had buried deep inside, covered with the heavy earth of other mysteries, and promised myself I would not mention. "Uncle Jack, my father told . . . someone . . . that he talked to you the week before he died."

"And?"

"And I would like to know if he did."

I hold my breath, waiting for the hornets to attack, but the answer comes back so fluently that he has probably been planning it for months. "Yes, I saw Oliver. Why do you ask?"

"Did he call you or did you call him?"

"You sound like a prosecutor, Talcott." He smiles peacefully, so I know he is annoyed. "But, since you ask, your father called me a few weeks before and said he would like to see me. I told him I would be in Virginia in the middle of September and we could meet then. We had a nice dinner, purely social."

"I see." I have no doubt that his recitation matches precisely what the FBI has on its tapes of my father's telephone call. But there are no recordings of the dinner conversation: Uncle Jack would have seen to that. I sense a growing unease in Abby's godfather; I have struck close to the heart of what he most wishes to keep from me. Something happened at that dinner. Something that sent my father back to his shooting lessons? I know Jack Ziegler will never tell me. "I see," I repeat, mystified.

"And now our time is up, Talcott." He coughs wetly.

"If I could just ask one more—"

He holds up a restraining hand and bellows for Henderson. I wonder how he decides which bodyguard to summon for which purposes.

"Wait, Uncle Jack. Wait a minute."

Jack Ziegler's head swivels slowly back toward me, and I can almost hear the creaking. His pale eyebrows are elevated, his sable eyes wary. He is not accustomed to being told to wait.

"Yes, Talcott?" he says quietly as Henderson appears.

I glance at the bodyguard, then incline my head and lower my voice. "You know that the man who was competing with my wife for that judgeship . . . that, um, a scandal killed off his chances."

That look of hot glee. "I told you there was a skeleton rattling around."

"Yes. Well. But I don't quite understand . . . how you knew." This is not all that I was going to ask, but as Henderson floats closer, the room seems to close in, the view from the window dizzying me once more, and I am suddenly sure I must not press further. "About the skeleton, I mean."

"It doesn't matter," Jack Ziegler whispers after a moment. "You must concentrate on the future, Talcott, not the past."

"But wait. How did you know? Only two people knew. And neither of them would ever . . ." *Tell somebody like you,* I do not quite say.

Jack Ziegler knows exactly what I am thinking. I can read it in his tired face as he lays a wizened hand on my shoulder. "Nothing is ever known to only two people, Talcott."

"Are you saying somebody else knew? Somebody else told you?"

He has lost interest. "Mr. Garland is leaving us, Henderson. Drive him to the condo where he will spend the night. One of the older ones down by the library, the ones with the blue doors. I do not recall the number, but Mr. Garland will show you which."

"I didn't tell you where I was staying." My objection comes out slowly, for a sudden thrill of fear has made me lethargic.

"No, you did not," agrees Abby's godfather. He does not smile, his feeble voice and clouded expression never waver, and yet I know he has chosen, just for an instant, to show me the tiniest corner of his power. Maybe his goal is to persuade me to trust him, to believe he will protect me, and to bring him what I learn. If, on the other hand, his goal is to frighten me . . . well, in that he has succeeded.

Henderson is standing on the stairs to the entryway, my coat draped over his arm. I thank Uncle Jack for seeing me. He offers his hand and I take it. He does not let go.

"Talcott, listen to me. Listen with care. I am not a well man. And yet there are many who are interested in the state of my health. I take my measures, but they send their trucks and plant their bugs. I do not believe that you should try to get in touch with me again. Not unless you have uncovered your father's arrangements."

"Why not? Wait. Why not?"

Jack Ziegler almost smiles. It is a near thing. I do not think he is fighting the urge exactly; he simply lacks the energy. He waves to me instead, not speaking, then collapses in a fit of coughing. Mr. Harrison, instantly at his side, takes his arm and leads him away.

On the way down the mountain, I glimpse headlights in the side mirror, but that need mean nothing: everybody in Aspen has a car. I wonder whether Jack Ziegler was right about the power company truck. I wonder how long it will be before Agent Nunzio learns of my visit, or if, perhaps, he was listening in all along. I glance at the mirror again as we turn sharply through a switchback, but the lights are gone.

Henderson asks me if I had a good visit . . . and, all at once, I know where I have heard his velvety voice before. I could kick myself for not realizing the truth earlier. Mr. Henderson spoke to me on the telephone at two-fifty-one in the morning, sitting up after my beating, as he assured me with quiet confidence that my family and I would not be bothered again. Because his job is protecting Uncle Jack, he most likely called me from Aspen. But Elm Harbor is only a plane ride away, and the tools needed to cut off two men's fingers are surely available at any hardware store.

CHAPTER 45

A CALL TO ARMS

(1)

THROUGH THE LIVING-ROOM WINDOW of John and Janice Brown's small time-share, I watch the Range Rover glide deftly out of the parking lot. I walk around the place, turning on plenty of lights, and remembering the last time I was here, all those years ago, when my marriage was reasonably happy. I wonder whether there is any hope it can be happy again; if, for example, the man who telephoned that drizzly morning to call my wife *baby* is going to ruin our lives, or whether he is simply going to disappear, as, in the past, Kimmer's men have always done.

Or whether, this time, she will make me disappear instead.

The condo is two floors, the first a narrow living–dining room with attached kitchen, the second two bedrooms, each with its own bath. I rummage in the refrigerator and find nothing but bottled water, and I decide that whoever left it will not mind if I treat myself to some. I have not eaten, and there is no food, so I check the telephone book and call a pizza delivery service and discover, on this exciting Aspen winter night, that the wait is ninety minutes or more.

I tell them ninety minutes will be just fine.

I return to the front window, wondering, as I did on the drive down the mountain, whether the breath I sensed on the back of my neck was imagination or a shadow, somebody tailing me. On Red Mountain, with only a couple of roads, it is not easy to tell. Another car can follow you all the way up or all the way down, and there is no real way to sort the sinister driver who means you ill from the resident of the place who is simply heading in the same direction that you are.

I console myself that Henderson seemed unworried.

I prod the lacy curtain to one side and peer out into the lot. A few drunken revelers stumble about, an occasional car swishes in or out, but I have no idea whether I am being watched—or, if I am, who is doing the watching. A defiant, tangled part of my imagination hopes that Maxine will stride boldly up to the door, but the more rational part of my mind proposes it is far more likely to be an agent of the FBI, even a fake one, like Foreman, who is, as Maxine reminded me on the Vineyard, very much alive.

As there is no way to tell, I determine not to worry.

Instead, I return to the kitchen and call home to tell Kimmer I am safe.

I reach only the answering machine.

There could be a thousand reasons for her absence, I warn myself. It is just past six here, so it is just past eight there, and my wife could be out shopping, Bentley of course with her. Naturally. Shopping, running some other errand: it has never been in Kimmer's nature to share the details of her schedule with me.

So I plug in my laptop and play online chess for half an hour or so, then check my e-mail, but find, as usual, nothing of consequence. My office voice mail reveals that Visa, too, is now interested in when precisely the next payment will be received, and I wonder how long I will be able to balance all these trips on a budget stretched thin to keep us in a house we cannot really afford.

Seven o'clock, nine in the East. I unplug the laptop and call home again, and once more am treated to the answering machine. Odd, because it is Bentley's bedtime. Maybe he is in the bath, I tell myself, and Kimmer cannot hear the phone ring or does not want to leave him. Except that she always takes the portable into the bathroom.

The errand ran late, I decide.

When, half an hour later, there is still no answer, I can no longer hold back the more ominous musings that have been clamoring for attention.

For example, the fact that Colin Scott may be dead but Foreman is still alive.

My family is in no danger, Uncle Jack just assured me again, and I believe that he believes it, but I am not supposed to be in any danger either, and somebody assaulted me in the middle of the campus. True, somebody who sounded just like Henderson called later to apologize, but he called *later.*

Eight o'clock, ten in the East. I try Kimmer's cell phone. I try her office. Then I try my home number again. When there is still no answer, I do something I almost never do, which is to call Dear Dana Worth at her house, two blocks from mine on Hobby Road. I suppose I do not call because Alison makes me uneasy, or maybe I am the one who makes her uneasy. Either way, we do not get along. So it is Alison, of course, who answers the phone.

When I apologize for calling so late, Alison trots out the tired old joke, that she had to get up anyway because the phone was ringing. Her tone tells me that she is half serious, that she is annoyed that I called, so perhaps it is an awkward moment, a proposition on which I would as soon not speculate.

When I ask for Dana, Alison asks why.

"Because I need to talk to her."

"About what?"

"It's . . . it's private."

A brief, furious silence over the line. "Well, she's not here right now."

"Do you expect her soon?"

"I have no idea," Alison grumbles, and the anger in her tone tells me that the two of them have been fighting again, as they often do.

I can hardly ask Alison, who has no reason to like me, to do what I had planned to ask of Dana—to go by the house and see if Kimmer and Bentley are home and safe—so I make my excuses and hang up.

Another call home. Still the answering machine.

I cross to the living-room window again. There is little furniture in the place: a glass-topped dinette with six imitation leather chairs, an ugly green sofa and matching loveseat, two beanbag chairs on which, in a pinch, someone could sleep. The sofa, I suppose, also folds out into a bed. I push the curtain aside once more. Dark in Aspen. Dark on Hobby Road. More worried than ever, I return to the kitchen and try Don and Nina Felsenfeld, next door.

No answer. No machine. I remember that they have gone to visit a daughter down in North Carolina for a few days. And it is ticking fast toward ten-thirty back East.

I am beginning to tremble.

Who else can I call in the neighborhood? Peter Van Dyke, who lives right across the street, scarcely knows I am alive. Tish Kirschbaum, my next-nearest neighbor from the law school, has a house right around the corner, but we are not close. Theo Mountain, who resides one street over, is surely asleep. Within a couple of blocks are Ethan Brinkley and Arnie Rosen and a few other colleagues, but on all of Hobby Hill, there is nobody, with the exception of Dear Dana, fellow outcast, I can imagine waking to help me scare away the bogeyman. If there is a bogeyman.

Nothing is wrong, I keep telling myself. Everything is fine. Kimmer is asleep, I try. But the answering machine is right next to the bed. So she fell asleep downstairs, maybe in the family room, watching television and drinking wine. Except that Kimmer never drinks herself to sleep: it was the Judge who used to do that. She is at the office, then, finishing some urgent project, Bentley sleeping on the floor as she works, but the notion is insane, and, besides, I tried there already. So she is stuck in a traffic jam. Dead in a traffic accident. Maybe I should try the university hospital? She is out in the yard, being tortured by Foreman.

Who is still alive.

Enough!

I do what I should have done in the first place and call the Elm Harbor police. As I hang up the telephone after five minutes with a skeptical desk sergeant, the doorbell rings and I jump, but it is only the delivery man with the food I ordered.

(11)

I MUNCH MOROSELY ON THE RAPIDLY COOLING PIZZA and sip the rapidly warming Diet Coke and wonder when I should call back. The sergeant promised to send a car over to the house as soon as one was free. Nothing I was able to say persuaded him to hurry. Perhaps he gets calls like this all the time. I sit in Aspen in the little condo, my face in my hands, as I wait for some word. Is there a protocol? An established interval between calls to the police? I do not remember when I have felt so impotent, even when I was nearly arrested the night the two men beat me up: there, at least, I knew it would all be straightened out in the end. But now, two thousand miles from home, I am utterly helpless to do exactly what Jack Ziegler was just telling me was my duty, to protect my family. . . .

Jack Ziegler?

Should I?

Nothing to lose, not now. I pick up the phone and call the house on Red Mountain, and the telephone barely has time to ring before I hear the voluptuous voice of Henderson.

"Yes, Professor?" he murmurs before I can speak, and I am stunned only until I realize that Uncle Jack would naturally have caller ID.

"I . . . I need some help," I say, not bothering with pleasantries.

"In what way, Professor?" Patient, calm, but not quite eager.

"Is Mr. Ziegler available?"

"I am afraid that he is asleep and cannot be disturbed. May I help in some way?"

"I . . . I can't reach my wife," I blurt.

"Yes?" The same quiet monotone, proclaiming a readiness to kill or be killed with no whisper of objection.

"She's back home, in, uh, in Elm Harbor. It's awfully late, and she's not answering the telephone, and if . . . if there's anything . . ."

"Let me call you back," he says, and the line goes dead.

Again I am forced to wait. Now I outline a different scenario. Kimmer is not dead, and she is not running an errand or at the office. She is at another man's house, in another man's bed, her recent protestations of love notwithstanding. She is sleeping somewhere in Elm Harbor, not with my fellow pugilist Gerald Nathanson, but with a black man who calls her *baby*, although where our own baby would be during all this, my fevered imaginings are not ready to supply.

The telephone finally rings.

"Kimmer?"

"Professor Garland," says Henderson, "I am sorry to say that we have no coverage at this time."

"Can you give me that again in English?"

"I have no immediate means of checking on your wife. I apologize. I suggest, if you are worried, that you call the police."

"I already did," I mutter, hanging up, dizzy now, unreasonably shattered to discover that Uncle Jack, with all his supposed power, is unable to reach into the heart of Elm Harbor with a word, talk to some spy stationed along Hobby Road, and find out whether my wife is dead or alive or sleeping in another man's bed.

I sit up very straight, panic starting to take me: if Jack Ziegler has no . . . coverage at this time . . . then who exactly is enforcing the edict that says my wife and child cannot be harmed?

I snatch up the telephone and call the Elm Harbor police again, and the same sergeant tells me he gave the request to the dispatcher, and he will call me when he has something.

"It wasn't a *request*," I nearly shout across the miles as everything boils over. "Didn't you hear me? I said my wife is in danger!"

"No, sir, you said she *might* be in danger."

"Well, I think she *is* in danger! Right now. I think . . . Please, send somebody over now, right now, okay?"

"Can you say what kind of danger?" He sounds only mildly more interested than he was before.

I try to think what will catch his interest. "There could be . . . uh, an intruder in the house."

"Do you know for a fact that there is an intruder, or are you just saying that so we'll skip all the calls ahead of yours?"

"Sergeant . . ."

"Mr. Garland, look. We only have six patrol cars on duty at night. That's for a city of a little over ninety thousand people. That's one car for every fifteen thousand people." I groan at the thought of what havoc income inequalities can wreak on real lives: I am willing to bet that there are six patrol cars, all of them private, up on Red Mountain alone. "Now, we'll get to your call as soon as we can."

He hangs up.

It is well past eleven in the East. I call home and there is, once more, no answer. I am shaking all over now.

One last idea.

I pull Fred Nunzio's card from my wallet and use his beeper number. And I add, at the end, the two-digit code he told me to include if the matter was urgent.

He calls three minutes later.

And sounds concerned, or at least willing to play along. "I'm sure everything is fine, but, if it will make you feel better, I'll call this sergeant myself, okay?"

"Thank you, Agent Nunzio."

"Fred, I keep telling you to call me Fred."

"Fred. Thanks. And you'll call me right back?"

"Of course."

The wait is no more than ten minutes, which I spend pacing the first floor, wishing I had a punching bag. "Okay, Professor, there's people on the way to your house right now. I'll clear this line so they can call you. I'm sure everything's fine, but call me back."

"I will."

Again I settle down to wait. Ten minutes. Fifteen. It is almost midnight back home, and my resources have run out. I simply have no ideas. Are matters as bleak as they seem? Surely there is a rational explanation: the telephone is not working right at Hobby Road. I should have called the operator. Except, if the telephone is malfunctioning, how could I have reached the answering machine? Midnight in Elm Harbor. No call. I want to throw things through the window, I want to grab a gun somewhere and ride to my family's rescue, I want to pull the Judge out of the ground and shake him until he explains why he has done this terrible thing to us.

I want my family, safe and sound.

Finally, I do the one thing left to me. I kneel in front of the living-room sofa and pray that Kimmer and Bentley are safe, or, if not safe, then resting in God's arms.

As I rise, the telephone rings immediately.

I steel myself.

(111)

"WHAT THE HELL IS THE MATTER WITH YOU?" demands Kimmer, incandescent with rage. "We're fast asleep, and all of a sudden, there's, like, this banging on the door, and I nearly jump out of my skin, and I'm scared half to death, nobody knocks on the door at midnight, and I put on my robe and I go down there and it's like storm-trooper city, half the cops in the world are out there, and they say you called them and the FBI called them and—"

"I was worried," I put in, sagging in the chair as decompression hits.

"Worried! So you just thought you'd wake up the whole neighborhood!"

"You didn't answer the phone when I called, and I thought . . ."

"Because I didn't hear it! We were asleep, I told you!"

I rub my temples. Yes, she said the word twice. "Who's *we?*"

"Who the hell do you think? Me and Bentley. He missed you, he was crying, so I lay down with him in his bed, and we fell asleep. There's no phone in there, Misha," she adds, just in case I forgot.

"But how was I supposed to know . . ."

"I don't know, Misha, but you could have come up with a better idea! I mean, I can't take this shit all the time! You disappear for hours and don't tell me where you are, you get into fistfights at your office, you almost get arrested"—suddenly, unaccountably, my wife is crying—"it's too much for me, Misha, it's too much, I can't take this!"

"Kimmer, I'm sorry . . . I didn't . . ."

"Sorry! I don't want you to be sorry! I want you to *stop acting so crazy!*"

"I was worried . . ."

"No, Misha, no! I don't want to hear it, okay? I don't want any more stories or any more excuses or any more explanations. You say you love us, but you keep thinking about you. You, you, you! Well, *you* have to stop acting crazy. *You* have to stop all the nutty theories and calling the police from Colorado and getting crazy telephone calls at two in the morning"— yes, I now see, Kimmer *was* listening in the night I was beaten near the library— "and just getting into trouble. It has to stop, Misha. I can't take any more of this. It's not fair. You have to go back to the way you used to be. Because, if you don't, I can promise you, Misha, one day you're gonna come home from one of your crazy trips and we won't be here!"

Hanging up on me.

She calls me back six minutes later to apologize, but the damage, I fear, might this time be too great.

(I V)

IN THE MORNING, waiting for the taxi to take me to the airport, I feel foolish for last night's terrors. In the light of a crisp Aspen day, the larger terror is losing my family. Now that I have had some sleep, I realize that Kimmer is right. I have been acting crazy, and I do have to stop. The only trouble is, I cannot stop yet, no matter what threats my wife might make. We are not yet free: that was the message Jack Ziegler tried to impart last night. He will continue to protect us because he promised my father he would, but he can carry out his promise only if I continue my search. Presumably, that was his deal with . . . well, whomever a man like Jack Ziegler has to deal with. *Leave him alone and he'll find the arrangements. I guarantee it.* Quid pro quo. If I give my furious spouse what she wants, if I abandon the search for the arrangements, then Uncle Jack might be unable to protect my family.

Everything is still a mess.

And it is all the Judge's fault.

The beep of a horn announces that my taxi has arrived. I peek out the window and see the white van idling, the driver reading the newspaper. I go to the front hall, turn off the alarm, grab my overnight bag and my coat, and take a last look around. Have I left it all as neat as I found it? I hope so.

There is a way out of this. Morris Young would probably say that God will show it to me in time, and I think perhaps he has. A way to keep my wife and also keep the family safe. I believe I can do it, but I know I cannot do it without help, and I am running out of people who might be willing to . . . well, to take a chance for the sake of friendship. Really, there is only one. So I had better hurry back to Elm Harbor and ask.

With a shrug, I reset the alarm with the proper code, which will cause it to re-engage ninety seconds after I exit. I pause, my memory unexpectedly jogged by this simple act. A secret conviction that has been growing in my mind leaps once more to the surface. Frowning in worry, I open the door. And stop short.

In the middle of the doormat is a manila envelope with my name printed on the front in black felt-tip, block letters so big I could read them fifty yards away.

I wave to the driver, then stoop and pick it up with trembling fingers.

It is a little larger than the envelope that held the white pawn delivered to me at the soup kitchen, and I can feel something hard and flat inside. It does not feel like the missing black pawn I guessed it might be. I close my eyes, swaying slightly in the crisp mountain air. For a silly moment, I imagine myself reliving the past, frozen forever in an instant of time, forced to open the same envelope over and over again.

But this envelope holds no pawn.

Instead, I tear it open to find a hard metal disk, no more than an inch across, brass in color but smudged an ugly brown in places. I rub the disk. The stain flecks off. I turn it over, but even before I read the letters engraved on the other side, I realize what I am holding in my hand: a tag from a dog's collar. I do not have to read the name to know the tag belongs—or belonged—to Shirley Branch's dog, Cinque.

The brown stain is dried blood.

A note, generically word-processed and printed on plain white paper, provides the punch line: DO NOT STOP LOOKING. No translation necessary. The blood tells a story of its own.

They can't hurt me, the well-connected Jack Ziegler assured me; can't hurt me, can't hurt my family. Uncle Jack promised it, and I believe him; I have never for an instant doubted his power.

But nobody has mentioned a prohibition on scaring me half to death.

CHAPTER 46

RESTING PLACES

(1)

THE LAW SCHOOL STANDS at the corner of Town Street and Eastern Avenue. If you follow Town Street away from the university, past the aging sandstone pile shared by the music and fine arts departments, past the low, nondescript building that holds, improbably, the catering, parking, and public relations offices, you come to the eastern edge of the campus, marked by a poorly fenced, bumpy parking lot full of cheery red-and-white University Transit buses, all purchased second-hand from school districts looking to upgrade. Here you cross Monitor Boulevard (named not for the Civil War gunship but for a local kid who had a brief, uninspired professional football career in the sixties), and, suddenly, you are no longer on university property.

The difference is immediately apparent.

On the other side of Monitor from the parking lot is a disused park containing the muddy, grassless remnant of a softball field at one end and, at the other, what might pass for a playground among parents not picky about broken glass, splintered wooden swings, and seesaws missing a crucial bolt or two. Usually a couple of crackheads lounge harmlessly on what is left of the benches, nodding and smiling in their secret dreams. Today the park is deserted. Few students or professors venture out too far to the east, because of the crime rate—or, as Arnie Rosen likes to say, the perceived crime rate. The remnants of a public housing project lie a few more blocks in this direction, aging gray towers with the ubiquitous cream-colored window shades, and public housing, in the minds of most people, signals danger.

One wintry afternoon four or five years ago, I stood at the edge of this park with the Judge, who was in town for some alumni function, and he simply shook his head, wordlessly, as tears welled in his eyes—

whether for his lost youth (when the park, if it existed at all, was no doubt vibrant), or the lost lives of those members of the darker nation who suffer here, or some fugitive memory of his Claire, or of Abby, or of his shattered career, I dared not ask. "You know, Talcott," he pronounced in his preacher's voice, "we humans are capable of so much joy. But we are born unto trouble . . ."

". . . as the sparks fly upward," I completed for him.

He smiled a bit, probably thought about hugging me, then thrust his hands more deeply into the pockets of his camel's hair coat and pressed onward—for the park was, on that snowy day, not our destination, but a way station, a marker on our road. As it is for me today, as I repeat the journey I made with my father, past the park, past an elementary school that looks like a casualty of some Balkan war but is, in fact, still in use. Graffiti mark the walls. So do black burn marks, as though from an explosion in the yard. An armed police officer stands near the front door, scuffing the dirt with his toe as he sneaks a cigarette. Lonely sepia faces challenge me from the barred windows. Are the bars to keep them in or to keep me out? I shake my head, wondering how many of my faculty colleagues would remain so adamantly opposed to voucher programs if their children were required to attend a school like this one. Alas, the education of the darker nation has become a side issue in contemporary liberalism, which has found more fashionable problems about which to obsess.

Before continuing my journey, I turn slowly in a complete circle, looking for any sign that I am being followed. I see nothing suspicious, but, unlike Maxine, I have not been trained in figuring out what to suspect. Somebody is out there. Somebody is always out there. Somebody always will be out there, I remind myself as I begin walking once more. So Jack Ziegler implied: somebody will always be out there, until I dig up what my father buried.

Nice metaphor. Catchy.

A block farther on I reach my goal, which is the Old Town Cemetery. Over the years, the name has given rise to some silly campus rumors, such as the tale that the cemetery was once surrounded by a historical site—the eponymous "old town"—that the university plowed under in its manic, eternal, and ruthless quest for space. The truth is that the cemetery was once known as the Town Street Burial Ground, and then, when a newer cemetery was built at the other end of campus, the Old Town Street Burial Ground, and the name over the years grew clipped, as names will, its several metamorphoses signaling the gradual obscuring of history. Rumor is rarely more interesting than fact, but it is always more readily available.

I step through the single gated opening in the high wall and wave to the sexton, a guileless old man named Samuel, whose principal job seems to be to sit on an overpainted metal bench near the neat little stone cottage just inside the cemetery gates, smiling vacuously at every person who enters the grounds. The cottage is just one room, an office to keep all the records, with an ancient bathroom attached. Now and then Samuel vanishes inside, perhaps to relieve himself, although he never seems to eat or drink. And six nights out of the week, every week out of the year, promptly at half past five, Samuel locks the heavy iron gates and disappears to wherever it is that he lives. (On Wednesdays, for some odd reason, the cemetery is open late.) In my student days, when Samuel had the same job and looked every bit as worn as he does now, the wits used to claim that Samuel locked the gates from the *inside*, turned his body to vapor, and drifted into the nearest available grave. I knew this to be untrue, because once, as a law student, I was locked inside by accident, walking in the cemetery with my future wife, who sought me out because she was in the process of deciding between two men, neither one of whom happened to be me. She came to me for advice, not particularly interested in whether I found it painful to listen to her troubles. It was May, a few weeks before graduation, the weather balmy, and Kimmer was looking particularly ravishing, as she always does in the spring. We talked for a very long time but did not kiss or hold hands or any of the other things that had been, for the ten sizzling months of our middle year of law school, as natural to us as breathing. When at last we reached the entrance once more, Kimmer had resolved to dump both men and find somebody better, which I hoped was a reference to me—although, as matters turned out, it was not—and she was in a gay mood. Until we discovered that the gate was locked, and no apparition appeared with a key. The sandstone walls of the cemetery are eight feet high, and the front gate is higher still. As Kimmer alternated between giggling and growling, I peered through the bars, hoping to flag down a passerby. Nobody passed. I banged on the door of the cottage. Nobody banged back. Finally, I told Kimmer that we had only one choice. She glared, hands on her hips, and told me she was not about to spend the night with me in the cemetery. I spared a few seconds to wonder if she meant the conjunctive or the disjunctive—with me, just not in the cemetery? in the cemetery, just not with me?—and then I shook my head and told her that when I was an undergraduate some of us used to sneak in and out of the cemetery through a drainage tunnel at the other end. *Did you say drainage?* she gaped. *From a cemetery?* I assured her that it was perfectly safe. I asked her to trust me.

Kimmer hesitated, perhaps wondering whether somebody else might be available to trust instead, then said okay.

So we plunged back into the cemetery. It was twilight, but we could see just fine. I led her along the main path, which runs a winding quarter-mile or so to the back wall, where the ground begins to slope downward, toward the Interstate and the river beyond. We passed soaring obelisks and marble angels and grim mausoleums. A tiny animal, probably a squirrel, skittered across the gravel path. Kimmer's hand finally crept into mine. The temperature was falling, and both of us were wearing only shorts, and I began to wonder whether hanging out at the front gate might not after all have been the better idea. I led her down the hill, circling the headstones, many of them toppled with the heaving of the ground over the years, for this was the oldest section of the cemetery. And there it was, the old drainage tunnel, covered with the same wire mesh I remembered, which was still merely leaning in place, not actually attached. I kicked it aside. Kimmer released my hand. She asked if I seriously expected to get out of the cemetery this way. I said yes. She pointed out that the tunnel was no more than three feet high. I said we would have to crawl. She crossed her arms and stepped back. *Uh-uh, mister, no way am I going to crawl through that. We don't have any idea what could be running out of these graves. No.* I spread my arms. I told her we had no choice. I told her it wasn't bad, the tunnel was always dry, it was just a big metal pipe that came out down under the highway. I told her it was only twenty feet long, that we could make it in three or four minutes. I told her that I had probably done it five times as an undergraduate. She gave me that Kimmer look. *And I slept with you for a year?* But at least she smiled.

In the end, Kimmer gave in and we crawled through the tunnel. I wanted her to go first, but she flatly refused, suspecting that I just wanted to look at her backside, which was not actually true, not because I would not care to, but because it would be impossible—for one thing that I had omitted, but which Kimmer quickly discovered, was that the tunnel, no more than twenty feet long, was, once you got away from the entrance, pitch-black inside. At first she joked about it, then she got mad, and then, just past the middle of the tunnel, I realized that Kimmer was no longer right behind me. Turning around was impossible. I called her name and heard her curse at me. I backed up until my foot touched her hand. I told her that it was perfectly safe, that we were almost out, that there was light up ahead. She just sobbed. I knew the exit was perhaps ninety seconds away, but ninety seconds, as anybody who has ridden one of those roller-coasters-in-the-dark can affirm, is an eternity when you're frightened—and my precious Kimmer was terrified. She was stuck there, immobile. She did not respond to reassurance or cajoling. Now I was getting a little scared myself in the hot, dusty darkness. I had no space to turn around, but I did the best I could. I rolled onto my back so that I could look in her direction, then drew my legs up to my chest and shimmied closer. Still lying on my back, I stretched out my hand and caught her wrist. I called her name. She said nothing. I tugged. Kimmer resisted. I tugged harder and, all at once, she came tumbling downward, her body pushing mine, and, suddenly the two of us were sliding along the metal, both screaming, and I was scrabbling for a handhold, any handhold, and my fingers exploded with pain and then I popped neatly out the other end of the tunnel, knocking the mesh away, sprawling on the rocky slope with the cemetery wall up the hill behind me, the highway on its concrete supports looming above me, and the docks and warehouses and oil tanks of industrial Elm Harbor sprawled below. I saw all of this as I lay flat on my back, my feet pointing toward the tunnel, my head tilted so that my chin pointed skyward, my hair full of mud.

Kimmer, incredibly but characteristically, landed on her feet. Her tears were gone, her clothes filthy but not torn, and her expression was more amused than concerned as she crouched next to me.

Are you alive? she asked softly.

I assured her I was okay, although, in actual fact, no part of me was free of aches, and my fingers were swollen and my leg felt wrong. It was plain that I had no hope of standing. Kimmer kissed my forehead, brushed off her clothes, and walked down the hill to a convenience store, where she used a pay phone to call a friend to come pick us up— one of the men she had just decided to dump, as a matter of fact. Her beau helped me down the hill. The two of them drove me over to the university health center, where we learned that I had managed to break two fingers, twist my ankle, and open a messy gash on my leg. In my mind, it was a worthy sacrifice to help Kimmer, who emerged unscathed. In her mind, I was an idiot who lacked the common sense to wait at the front gate, who had to find some spectacularly stupid way to do something simple. *We should have broken into the office,* Kimmer pointed out as a nurse took my blood pressure. *I'm sure they had a phone.*

She left with her friend while they were stitching me up, promising to be back in thirty minutes in her own car to drive me to my apartment. The two of them looked very cuddly all of a sudden. In the event, she took more than two hours to return, as I sat in the lobby and suffered, not daring to call her, for fear of what I might interrupt, not daring to leave on my own, for fear of making her angry should her excuse turn out to be innocent. Kimmer finally showed up looking radiant and replete, having showered and changed, and she brought me a pair of sunglasses to hide a black eye I did not remember receiving. She made me sit in the back seat of her car, explaining that she thought I should stretch out my injured leg. She took my crutches up front. Driving over to the western end of campus, where I lived in an untidy apartment, she chattered happily about everything except where she had been for the past two hours, or where we had been for the two hours before. Dropping me at my front door, Kimmer thanked me for getting her out of the Burial Ground, brushed soft lips over my cheek, and was gone into the night.

Some metaphors need no interpretation.

I told my father the story of escaping through the tunnel with Kimmer, I have been reminding myself over and over, ever since my meeting with Dean Lynda. I hold that fact in my mind. I told my father the story, I repeat, even though I didn't. I tell myself again and again, hoping that I will not forget.

(11)

I EXPLAIN TO SAMUEL WHAT I WANT, taking care to be clear, yet, at the same time, going on at length. He nods vigorously and tries several times to end the conversation, but I am a law professor, and therefore not so easy to shut up. Samuel at last stops trying and just listens, which is fine with me. Today's is my fourth visit to the Old Town Cemetery in the past seven days. The first came a few hours after Dean Lynda's ultimatum: the "walk" I was not prepared to explain to Kimmer. Two days later I was in Aspen. The next evening I was home. I have been here twice since. All my visits have had the same structure: a review of the records, followed by a cautious amble around the grounds. Nevertheless, I remind Samuel once more of the reason for my presence. I want him to remember our conversation. I want him to remember what I need. I want it to be the first thing that comes to mind when he thinks about me. Because I will require his help in the days or weeks to come if I am to bring this whole mess to an end, and his help will be useless if he forgets what I am looking for.

So Samuel busies himself at one end of the room and allows me to draw the dusty old registers from the shelves. For the third time since my chat with Uncle Jack, I sit at a hard wooden table that probably stood in this very spot when Lincoln was assassinated. I study the lists of the dead, turning pages two hundred years old to reach pages just filled in last month, adding to the copious (but, I hope, perfectly clear and easy-to-follow) notes on a small pad that I have been hiding in plain sight in the top drawer of the unlocked desk in my office. I sit, probably, for forty-five minutes, most of which Samuel spends watching me with unfocused eyes. Watching me is exactly what I want him to do—watching and remembering, in case he is ever asked. When I am done, I thank the smiling Samuel, who pumps my hand in both of his as though I have just won the grand prize. After extricating myself, I proceed out onto the cemetery grounds, where, for the fourth time, I brave the springlike drizzle to stroll the paths among the headstones, scrutinizing the map I have drawn on my pad, adding notes when necessary to be sure I have followed the proper route. I pass the mausoleum of the Hadley family, which has had a presence in Elm Harbor and around the university for well over a century; Marc is the family's fourth professor here. I pass a small plot of old stones that was once a little Jim Crow cemetery-within-a-cemetery. The abolitionist town fathers of one hundred fifty years ago voted to allow free blacks to be interred, but not next to everybody else.

From time to time I look over my shoulder, a habit I suspect I will not shake for some while; I never see anyone but the occasional mourner, standing alone in the misty rain. I wonder if all of them are truly mourning, if any one of them might be following me, and how I would know.

I suppose that everybody is mourning somebody.

Several times I pause, making check marks on my pad as I read various tombstones, or noting where the gravel lanes intersect. I copy the names of the dead and the dates of their deaths. I draw squares within squares.

My notes finally completed, I leave the cemetery by the main entrance. None of the mourners stir. I wave farewell to the grinning Samuel on his bench and head back along Town Street toward campus, watching all the while for the invisible shadow I know is there.

Almost ready.

CHAPTER 47

A DECISION AT POST

(1)

"DANA?"

"Yes, my love?" Smiling girlishly over the lunch table at Post, pretending a bit, even though I could never, ever, be her love, for about six hundred reasons, even putting aside the obvious ones.

"Dana, look. I kind of need a favor."

"As usual."

"Seriously. I mean, it's important, and . . . and I don't know who else to ask."

"Mmmm-hmmm." Dana is cautious, certain, I have no doubt, that I am about to ask her for money.

It is Wednesday, four days since my return from Aspen, and twelve days since my blow-up in the hallway with Jerry Nathanson, an event that has shrunk even further my already shaky standing around Oldie. I am lunching with Dana today because it is the first chance we have had to get our schedules synchronized. And also because I am running out of options. Earlier I planned to ask her help as a contingency. Now my need is urgent. If Dear Dana says yes, and all goes well, I will be able to get everybody off my back, and my family's life back to normal, within a week, two at the most. My plan could put me outside Dean Lynda's deadline, but close enough that I should be able to fudge it. If Dana says no, or if things go badly . . . well, then, so be it.

Munching my cheeseburger, I try to think how to put it. Over in Darien, Mariah is coming up on a deadline of her own, for her baby is due in less than a month. No more trips down to Shepard Street, but she is happy in her distraction. We speak on the phone almost nightly as the big day nears, and even Kimmer now and then gets in on the fun.

I envy my sister her joy.

Three tables away, Norm Wyatt, the architect, Dean Lynda's blab-bermouth husband, is lunching with a prosperous but somehow furtive client. I get a bit furtive myself, hunching down to get closer to Dear Dana. Correctly interpreting my motion, Dana shifts her head a bit closer to mine. As usual, I wonder what the gossip-mongers will think. I wonder why I chose to ask my favor at Post in the first place. Dana's office would have been safer. Maybe I decided to come here because she tends to be more indulgent after meals. Or maybe because I am all at once worried about being bugged.

"Dana, look. What I'm going to ask . . . if you want to say no . . ."

"If I want to say no, Misha, I'll say no. I'm very good at it." A beat. "Except, now that I think of it, I'm not very good at saying no to *you*. You always seem to be asking me favors, and I always seem to say yes." She smiles nervously. She glares at Norm's broad back. She senses something amiss, and does not like the situation any more than I do. "I don't know what it is about you. It's not like you're particularly charm-ing or anything. . . ."

"Gee, you're sweet."

"Seriously, Misha. When I think about it, it's too weird. I can't say why, but I never seem to be able to say no. You know what? It's a good thing I'm not into men or we'd probably have had an affair by now."

"If I weren't married." A smile. "And if I were into white women."

"Touché." She smiles back. "So, what's the big favor? You want me to break Jerry Nathanson's kneecaps? Sorry, I'm retired from that line of work."

"No, but . . . well, when you hear it, it might seem kind of shocking. Scary, even. Not that there's any real risk, it's just not going to be easy to do. But it's something that . . . well, it has to be done, and I can't do it myself. And, if it gets done, maybe I can . . . um, put a stop to . . . well, whatever's going on."

"Well, thanks, my love, that certainly clears everything up for me."

"And, the thing is, I won't . . . I won't be able to tell you *why* I need you to do it. Not now. I can explain later, but not now."

Her smile slowly fades. "I'm beginning to wonder if maybe I should be scared."

"No, no, of course not. There's nothing to be afraid of."

"As Anthony Perkins said to Janet Leigh."

"I don't think there was any such line in the movie."

"Okay, Misha, okay." Laughing, holding up her hands. "So, tell me what you want already."

"Look, Dana, I wouldn't ask except . . ."

"Except you don't know where else to turn, I'm your best friend in the world, and blah-blah-blah. Just ask. I told you, I'm very good at saying no."

I draw in a breath, recognizing that I have never imposed on a friend as mightily as I am about to. But I am nearly out of choices. So I tell Dana Worth what I need done. It takes me five minutes.

And she *is* shocked. She tells me so, but I can see it anyway, in the widening of her coal black eyes, and hear it in the hissing of air over her teeth. She considers. She leans back in her chair. Norm Wyatt and his client are leaving. Norm waves from a safe distance, and we both wave back. A knot of students brushes past the table, chattering about Lemaster Carlyle, whom he will pick as his first law clerks, how long before he moves on to the Supreme Court.

Dear Dana turns to me once more. She tells me I am out of my mind, completely out of my mind. She tells me I am going to lose both my job and my wife. She tells me I am going to wind up in jail. She tells me that if she helps me she could wind up in jail too.

Then she tells me she will do it.

(11)

OUT ON THE SIDEWALK, Dana starts to tell me about the message her pastor preached last Sunday, something about the parable of the shrewd manager. I am only half listening. "You see the point, don't you, Misha? It doesn't matter whether things are going the way you want them to, but only how you manage the things God puts in your—"

I grab her arm. She struggles free, because she hates to be touched.

"Misha, what's wrong with you?"

"Dana, look." I physically turn her. Again she shakes me off, maybe worrying that the Dean is right about my mental state. I point. "Do you see that car?"

"What car?"

"There! Right there!" For it is right in front of me, as large as life, at a meter across the street, a block from the law school. "The blue Porsche!"

My old or maybe new friend smiles. "Yes, Misha, of course I see it. Now, listen to me. This is important. Please don't call it a Porsche. That car is not a Porsche."

"It isn't?"

"No, darling. It happens to be a powder-blue Porsche Carrera Cabriolet, this year's model, and it looks like the special order with all the options, retailing for something over a hundred thousand dollars, and cash only, please, no deadbeat law professors who need financing." Dana waits a beat. Ordinarily, this kind of Worthism makes me howl with laughter. Not today. "Misha, I think there is something seriously wrong with you, do you know that?"

"Dana . . . Dana, that car . . . it was outside my house a couple of weeks ago. And once back in December, too. And I think the man who was driving it . . . well, he was spying on us. On my family." I remember rushing through the woods with John Brown. "Dana, I think it was the other man who pretended to be an FBI agent in my house. The black man. Foreman. You know, right after the funeral."

She is laughing. Very hard, the sound almost screechy as she leans over, hands on her knees. She finally pulls herself up by using a lamp-post for support. "Oh, Misha, Misha!"

I fail to see the humor. Or maybe I have slipped off the deep end and this entire scene is my imagination, because nothing is making sense.

"What's the matter with you?" I demand.

"Oh, Misha, you are too funny!"

"What's funny?"

"A spy? A secret agent? You mean, you seriously don't know whose car that is?"

Anger begins to replace my befuddlement. Garland men can bear anything except the embarrassment of not knowing something. "No, Dana, I don't."

"I'll give you a hint." Still grinning, Dana actually wipes away a tear or two. "He's more famous than your father."

"Okay, that narrows it down to a few million people."

"Oh, come on, don't be like that. Listen. He lives out in Tyler's Landing, in a big house right on the water, probably cost him four million bucks, which I suspect he paid in cash, just like he did for the car. He's a student at the law school, and you're right that he's black, but that's about all you're right about."

I turn and look at the car. "Are you . . . are you telling me that the Porsche belongs to Lionel Eldridge? As in the basketball player?"

"The *former* basketball player. He's an ordinary student now." Her tone is singsong, playful. "He just wants to be an ordinary lawyer, like his hero Johnnie Cochran. I heard him say it on *Oprah*. And also on *48 Hours*. And Leno. And . . ."

I keep staring as Dana keeps laughing. Lionel Eldridge. Sweet Nellie, as they used to call him back when he made the National Basketball Association All-Star Team seven times. Six foot six or so: that would certainly qualify him as the tall black man John Brown spotted in the woods behind my house. An earnest student but not a great one, not here, although he did better at Duke in his undergraduate days. Sweet Nellie, whose famous smile still earns him millions of dollars every year in endorsements. Sweet Nellie, who still owes me a paper from last spring. Last spring, when he struggled through my difficult seminar. Last spring, when I helped him get his job at Kimmer's firm. Last spring, when I surprised the ladies at the soup kitchen and brought him with me one day to serve lunch.

I have found my enemy.

(111)

ARRIVING AT MY OFFICE A FEW MINUTES LATER, I find something else, too: an envelope leaning against the door with my name and proper title typed on the front. It is identical to a package I received at the soup kitchen a thousand years ago, or maybe in October. When I tear open the top, I find exactly what I expect: the missing black pawn from my father's chess set. I put it on top of the file cabinet, lining it up neatly, right next to the white one.

One white pawn, one black. The only pieces on the chessboard that move in the course of the Double Excelsior. The white pawn arrived first to tell me that white moves first, and if white moves first in a help-mate, then black wins. *It begins*, my father wrote in his note to me. But, if it's all the same to you, Dad, I would rather bring it to an end.

With Dana's help, I am about to make that happen. If all goes according to plan, I will be able to get rid of the burden my father bequeathed to me.

Or so I foolishly imagine. But another disaster is in store.

CHAPTER 48

ZWISCHENZUG

(1)

I DID NOT EXPECT TO BE RETURNING to Washington so soon. The bad news reached me this time through Mariah rather than Mallory Corcoran, but I half expect to find Uncle Mal at George Washington University Hospital when I arrive, even though, as far as I am aware, he has exchanged perhaps five sentences with Sally Stillman in his life. In the brightly colored waiting room just off the elevator, I find instead my eight-and-a-half-months pregnant sister, along with Sally's boyfriend, Bud, looking sullen and helpless, as strong men in despair do, and a tiny clutch of strangers, presumably waiting for news on other loved ones who have attempted suicide. Then a tall, nervous, terribly skinny woman, a representative of the paler nation, steps forward to introduce herself as Paula, Sally's Alcoholics Anonymous sponsor. I did not even know my cousin was in it.

"She's going to make it," Paula assures me with a ghastly smile.

I nod and clasp her arm and lay a hand, briefly, on Bud's shoulder. Then I hurry over to sit next to Mariah, who is alone in the middle seat of a rack of three, shaking her head, elegant in another tailored pantsuit, having managed somehow to create around herself a secret space which nobody dares try to penetrate, other than such obtuse fools as myself. "You okay, kiddo?" I ask, taking her hand.

"I don't understand. I don't know why she would do it." Mariah rubs her belly, a gentle, loving circle, as though reassuring her unborn child that, contrary to appearances, the world is a safe enough place. My sister does not look at me. In her lap is one of her manila folders, the corner of a photograph peeking out. I wonder whether this is another view of the autopsy, or whether Mariah is up to something new. "She's been doing so well. So well."

"At what?"

"She was fighting it, Tal. She'd been sober for . . . oh, almost two months. Since just before Christmas. Giving her kids a present, she said. So she's been going to all her AA meetings, going to church, working hard to stay sober."

"What exactly happened?"

"I don't know. She called Paula"—Mariah inclines her head toward Sally's sponsor—"and said she couldn't do it any more, she was taking pills. Paula did what she was supposed to do. When she realized she couldn't talk Sally out of it, she called 911, then got over there herself, just in time to see them carry her out. Paula called me. I called you. And here we are."

"Where are Sally's kids?"

"They were with Thera when . . . when it happened. Sally took them to her mom's house, then went home and took pills. I guess she didn't want them to be the ones to find her."

I try to think of another useful question. "Did you call Addison?"

Mariah gives me a look. "I'm sure he'll be along when he can." Then a return to the original theme: "I still don't understand why she would do it."

"Was she depressed?"

"How the hell should I know?" Unsatisfied, Mariah offers another variation: "I mean, Tal, she's *always* depressed."

"Have you seen her?"

"They won't let me. She . . . the doctor said she has to be isolated. Some kind of rule, I guess. Because of what she did. Tried to do. No visitors allowed for a couple of days or something."

I go over and check with the nurse and get the same information I already have: yes, it looks like Ms. Stillman is going to make it; no, we cannot see her for forty-eight to seventy-two hours. I allow myself the fantasy that Uncle Mal could get us in, but even superlawyers have limits. So Mariah and I sit side by side, hand in hand, bewildered, fearful, trying to be to each other what siblings should. My sister sheds no tears, although she seems on the verge a time or two. I reflect on God's mysterious purposes, and marvel that my own problems, just this morning, seemed so huge.

Paula is standing in front of us again.

"Uh, excuse me."

We look up at her as though she has the wisdom of the ages on her tongue.

"You're Misha, right?" Paula asks slowly. Before I can answer, she turns to Mariah: "He's Misha?"

My sister manages to find a smile somewhere: "That's one of his names. He has a whole bunch of them."

Paula looks confused. She is wearing a suit nearly as expensive as Mariah's. Probably a lawyer, I decide, a specialist of some kind: she is too high-strung to be a lobbyist, and I cannot quite envision her in a courtroom, arguing cases. I see her chain-smoking while she designs complex tax straddles for overseas clients.

"But you are Misha, right?"

"Some people call me that," I confirm. "My name is Talcott Garland. I'm Sally's cousin."

"Can I talk to you for a minute? Privately?"

Mariah is about to object, but I ask her with my eyes to let it be. Paula leads me off to another corner. I lean close because she wants to whisper. Paula explains that when Sally called, weeping, she just kept repeating that she couldn't stand to know what she knew. When Paula asked what she meant, Sally mumbled, *Poor Misha, poor, poor Misha.* Paula pauses, perhaps to give me the chance to confess, and I assure her that I do not have the slightest idea what my cousin was talking about. Paula nods glumly, then adds that Sally told her one more thing before hanging up the phone: *I don't know why he had to get them both.*

I frown. "Who had to get both of what?"

"I assumed she meant you. Because she started *Poor, poor Misha* again."

"That *I* had to get them both?"

A curt yet inoffensive nod. "And she didn't know why."

(11)

MARIAH AND I SPEND THE NIGHT AT SHEPARD STREET. I am astonished that she has made this trip with her due date so near, but she turns out to have arranged a car and a driver for the six-hour trek each way. "It's not that much more expensive than first-class air travel," she explains.

In the morning, we have a quick breakfast before I hurry home. Mariah wants to know why I am rushing, what I think of Conan pleading guilty, is it true that I punched out my wife's boyfriend in the law library like she heard from Valerie Bing, what I am going to do about what she told me Warner said, a thousand other things. I tell her it will all be over soon and I will explain it all when I can. I brace for an acid commentary on my selfishness, but the approaching birth of her sixth child seems to have made my sister serene.

"You be careful," she says when the taxi arrives to take me to the train station.

I promise her I will. I have to be. Despite this detour, the concrete situation, as chess coaches like to say, has not changed. When I am back in Elm Harbor, I will have one shot at ending it all and setting my family free.

"Time's up," I whisper as the cab pulls away from the curb. The driver raises his eyebrows, perhaps thinking I want him to hurry. As we head down Sixteenth Street, picking up speed, I turn my head repeatedly, searching for the tail that has to be there.

CHAPTER 49

A PLAN IS CARRIED OUT

(1)

"I THINK I'VE FIGURED IT ALL OUT," I tell an ostentatiously bored Mallory Corcoran on the telephone the following Monday. "The arrangements and everything. Tomorrow night I'll have the answer." He is delighted at the news and even more delighted to tell me he has another call that just can't wait. He suggests I share the details with Meadows.

"It's all over," I assure Lynda Wyatt when I encounter her, more or less on purpose, in the faculty parking lot that same afternoon. She tries to avoid speaking to me, but I am too fast for her. "By Wednesday morning, I'll have all the answers." There are still two days until her deadline, so she smiles and pats my arm, all the while looking around for the men in the white coats. On Tuesday, I continue my campaign. "I've solved the mystery," I murmur to a bored Lemaster Carlyle, soon to be an ex-colleague, peeking over his shoulder in the library as he hunts for a periodical. He is sufficiently politic to force a smile and clap me on the back. "I know the whole story," I announce to a startled Marc Hadley outside a classroom, where he stands happily, surrounded by a cloud of acolytes, their unswerving adulation having helped put his public humiliation behind him. "I think I can finally put it behind me," I promise Stuart Land when we pass on the central staircase. "I want to thank you for your help," I confide to little Ethan Brinkley during a chance encounter down in the courtyard. Only it is not really chance. "I'm on the verge of working out the whole thing."

I impart the same glad tidings, in more or less similar words, to Rob Saltpeter and Theo Mountain and Ben Montoya and Shirley Branch and Arnie Rosen and every other member of the law school faculty who might, even remotely, be connected to . . . to . . .

... to the *thing that's going on* ...

I don't even have the words for it, but I know that it is there. As long as Dear Dana does her part, I will not even be a liar: I *will* know all the answers. I will even know who has betrayed me. Unless the betrayer is Dana, in which case I'm in serious trouble.

I shake myself free of the feeling. I have to trust somebody.

From my office, waiting for the right moment to act, I put in a call to Mariah, meaning to check on Sally, only to learn from Howard that my sister seems to be in the early stages of labor. They are timing the contractions. An ultrasound a month or so ago confirmed that the baby is a girl, and they have finally settled on a name: Mary, after Mary McLeod Bethune—an "Ma-" name like the other five, and just in the nick of time. Howard adds quietly that the lifelong Roman Catholic in him also approves. I laugh jaggedly. When Mariah gets on, I offer cheery best wishes. She thanks me, then groans, then recovers long enough to tell me that she and Howard have reserved space for Sally at a rehab center in Delaware, one of the best in the country. "We are *not* going to lose her again," Mariah declares, grimly. For the first time in years, I realize how much I love my sister.

Then it is time to get moving. I have to trust somebody, I tell myself over and over.

(11)

BUT I CANNOT TRUST MY WIFE.

The day of my return from Washington, two days after discovering that Lionel Eldridge owns the ubiquitous Porsche—excuse me, Dana, the Porsche Carrera Cabriolet—I tracked down the owner himself, looking up his class schedule in the Registrar's office, then stationing myself in the hallway outside Joe Janowsky's employment discrimination class, waiting for Lionel to emerge. I had already tried the more traditional methods of summoning students—my secretary sent him e-mail, posted his name on what students call the "See me" board, called his house and left a message with his wife—but Lionel ignored them all. So I went to gather him in after his class.

And I did, spotting him easily, because he towered over the other eighty or ninety students flowing out of the room at eleven. As usual, half a dozen surrounded him like a posse, awaiting the next precious pearl from his lips. When Lionel saw me, his eyes widened in what I knew to be fear. I gestured imperiously, the way professors do. He backed away, resplendent in navy blue leather and shiny gold. Just an ordinary law student. Worried about what Lynda would say if I shouted, I made my way delicately through the knot of admirers, took him gently by the arm, and whispered that I would like a few minutes. He may be Sweet Nellie, but I am still a professor of law, and one to whom he owes a paper, so he had little choice. We walked together to a quiet alcove near the Dean's office. Other students gave us a wide berth. I noticed that Lionel kept his gaze mostly on the floor.

First I asked him about his paper. A hopeful look flashed in his famous dark eyes. He began to make excuses—travel, his wife giving him problems, the culture shock of being at a white law school, as he called it, which, I suppose, makes Lem and Shirley and me white professors, sort of—but I cut him off. I told him coolly that he could have another month. If the paper was not in, I would flunk him. Lionel nodded and started to move off down the hall, certain, no doubt, that this threat was subject to later negotiation, as, these days, most things are. I held him in place with a light touch, the way police officers do, and he began to look alarmed. Glaring up at Lionel, I noticed the words DUKE UNIVERSITY stitched into the black leather of his jacket and remembered how he twice took his college team to the Final Four a decade or so ago. Although he has had his troubles in law school, I recalled from ages past the broadcasters' reminding us all that he was an honor student.

Then I pressed on.

I told Lionel we had another matter to discuss. I asked him, point-blank, why he was following me around. I waited for him to confess that his secret girlfriend, Heather, asked him to do it, some kind of bizarre favor for her father. His response was puzzlement. He assured me he would never do such a thing, so I rephrased the question. What was he doing in front of my house last week? And in the woods out back a few weeks ago?

Now Lionel met my eyes, and even before he spoke, I knew I had guessed wrong, so terribly wrong. He was not my enemy after all, not, at least, in the way I had assumed. And he had obviously been in this situation before, because he knew exactly what to say, the worst words imaginable: *It isn't personal, Professor Garland. I like you. I admire you.* Then he followed it with: *I just like your wife, too.* And the million-dollar smile at last.

But by that time I already knew that Lionel had nothing to do with the arrangements or the pawn delivered to the soup kitchen or my beating in the middle of the Quad. I knew I was coming late to knowledge widely shared. I knew whose voice it had been on the telephone, calling my wife *baby* on the day she was supposed to be working at home and I was supposed to go to my office. I knew he called because he didn't see the BMW in the driveway, where she always leaves it, and he wanted to know if their rendezvous was on. I knew why the students gave us a wide berth just now, allowing us to discuss our business in privacy. I knew what Dean Lynda must have thought was the unmentioned and unmentionable explanation for my irrational behavior, and why she decided to cut me a little slack. I realized that even Dear Dana Worth, from whom no gossip can quite be concealed, must have been aware of the truth, which was why she was so startled when I asked her about Lionel and Heather, and why she tried to pass it off as a joke when we saw the Porsche on the street outside of Post, so that her screechy, slightly wild laughter was meant to cover her pain at realizing that I had no idea, and she was not about to tell me, that it was the world-famous Lionel Eldridge, and not Gerald Nathanson, who was having an affair with my wife.

CHAPTER 50

AGAIN OLD TOWN

(1)

I AM ENDING MY MYSTERY WHERE IT BEGAN: in a cemetery. Was it really four months ago that Jack Ziegler emerged from the shadows on the day of the Judge's burial to tempt me into this nightmare? Or was it only last week? In my recent confusion, not only truth and justice but time has seemed to turn in on itself, curving dutifully in the direction of gravitational pull—the pull, in this case, exerted by the mission, the desperate need to know.

I am once more on the grounds of the Old Town Cemetery, but not to see Samuel, for it is after eight and after dark, and Samuel is long gone. I did not scale the wall or the gates. I did not crawl through the tunnel. I simply strolled in around five, headed off to one of the marble benches in a far corner—invisible from the entrance—and waited. I brought along a backpack, from which I withdrew a copy of Keegan's book on the history of warfare, and I read about the way armies used to be organized, when the soldiers in the front lines knew they were going to die but marched off to battle anyway. Pawns, expendable pawns. I read and pondered and waited. Samuel locked the gates and disappeared and I kept on waiting. From my perch next to a mausoleum, I cannot see the gate, but I can see the only path that leads to my little corner of the cemetery. If anybody came in after I did, he has not followed me to the bench. Yet I am certain I am not alone.

As darkness gathers, I continue to ponder.

A cemetery is an affront to the rational mind. One reason is its eerily wasted space, this tribute to the dead that inevitably degenerates into ancestor worship as, on birthdays and anniversaries, humans of every faith and no faith at all brave whatever weather may that day threaten, in order to stand before these rows of silent stone markers, praying, yes, and remembering, of course, but very often actually speaking to the deceased, an oddly pagan ritual in which we engage, this shared pretense that the rotted corpses in warped wooden boxes are able to hear and understand us if we stand before their graves—and would not hear these same messages ("One day soon I'll be with you, darling" or "I'm doing everything you told me, Mom") if we merely took the time while, say, driving a car to project our thoughts into the next world. Unless we are here present, facing the appropriate gravestone, the messages do not get through—or so our behavior signals.

The other reason a cemetery appeals to the irrational side is its obtrusive, irresistible habit of sneaking past the civilized veneer with which we cover the primitive planks of our childhood fears. When we are children, we know that what our parents insist is merely a tree branch blowing in the wind is really the gnarled fingertip of some horrific creature of the night, waiting outside the window, tapping, tapping, tapping, to let us know that, as soon as our parents close the door and sentence us to the gloom which they insist builds character, he will lift the sash and dart inside and . . .

And there childhood imagination usually runs out, unable to give shape to the precise fears that have kept us awake and that will, in a few months, be forgotten entirely. Until we next visit a cemetery, that is, when, suddenly, the possibility of some terrifying creature of the night seems remarkably real.

Tonight, for instance. Tonight, I know some terrifying creature is abroad. I pause, my flashlight pointed down at the ground, and raise my head, listening, sniffing the air. The creature is nearby. I can sense it. Probably, the creature is human; possibly, the creature has done violence; certainly, the creature has betrayed me.

As has my wife. I do not even know if I am married any longer. After church on Sunday, the day before I began spreading around the law school the intelligence that I was about to put an end to the search, I finally confronted Kimmer with Lionel, sitting with her in the kitchen while Bentley played with his computer in the next room. She sat there for a while in a light-blue dress, lovely against her maple skin, and then said what spouses always say: *I never meant to hurt you.* We were very civilized. She told me bits and pieces of the story—*yes, it began last summer, yes, I tried to stop it, no, he wouldn't go away, and we were just supposed to talk that day when you saw him at the house*—but it swiftly dawned on me that Kimmer was talking around the actual issue at stake. So I stopped her and forced her to look at me and asked one of two relevant questions. *Is it over between you?* She said she didn't know. So I asked the other. *Are you leaving?* She held my gaze and told me she thought some time apart might be the best thing for us. We had, she said, a lot of issues to work through. When I had my voice back, I mentioned Bentley, and how hard this would be on him. She nodded sadly and said, *But you can come and see him whenever you want.* It took me a moment to get the point. I asked her if she was taking our son. *He needs his mother*, she answered. *And, besides, he is accustomed to this house.* As I sat there, flummoxed, Kimmer just shook her head unhappily. I asked if she was really leaving me for Lionel. She told me no, I was missing the point. Lionel wasn't the issue. My behavior was. *I didn't want it to come to this, Misha, I really didn't. I do love you. But you've been too weird lately, and I can't deal with it any more. We just need some time.* Time apart, she meant. Time during which she gets the house and I move out. *It's not an ideal answer, but custody fights can be hard on children.*

She gave me one week. That was two days ago.

I went to see Morris Young. I was unreasonably accusatory. He waited for me to calm down and reminded me that my wife's fidelity was never the issue. The promise I made to him was a promise of Christian duty, my obligation to treat her with love as long as we were married. I asked if the promise still holds. He asked if we are still married.

I keep walking.

I am angry still, but not at Dr. Young, for he is not the cause of my pain. No, I am angry at myself, and furious, finally, at my wife. I have passed from *How could she do this?* to *How dare she do this!* I am old-fashioned enough to think of the marriage vow not as a promise to stay as long as you want to, but a promise to stay whatever happens. Kimmer, obviously, believes otherwise—yet I love her still. There lies the true absurdity: if love is an activity, I find myself unable, or perhaps unwilling, to stop acting.

Still seething, I shake my head. I cannot be distracted now, even by the wreck of my marriage. Maybe, when this is over, Kimmer will have a change of heart. I have five days left to persuade her, and perhaps I can start tonight. I have calculated the moves as a chess player must. I am reasonably confident that my gambit will defeat the unknown but omnipresent adversary who sits, wraithlike, on the other side of the board. When that battle ends, I will be able to focus on saving my marriage. I know that my own actions have helped drive Kimmer away from me. I will apologize, bring flowers, and, best of all, bring her the news that the search is finally over, no more craziness. I persuaded her to marry me a decade ago, surely I can persuade her to stay.

Surely.

Or else I cannot. A wave of fatalism sweeps over me, and I wonder whether I could have done anything differently, or if, once the Judge died, setting his awful plan in motion, and Jack Ziegler showed up demanding to know about the arrangements, everything else was fixed. Whether my marriage, even, was doomed from the day of the funeral.

I remind myself to concentrate on the moment.

In my notebook are several genealogies and a handful of carefully drawn maps. Each is a map of a part of the cemetery, each points the way to a different plot. A casual reader who came across my notebook and leafed through it would probably think I was trying to figure out which plot was the one I wanted. This would be literally correct, but not at all accurate. During my visits, I have studied the great majority of plots in the cemetery—not in person, but in the ancient books entrusted to Samuel's care. I have been testing theories. I have been narrowing things down. Rob Saltpeter, the constitutional futurist, likes to refer to Supreme Court decisions as creating "plausible opportunities for dialogue and discovery." That is the purpose of my map: to create plausible opportunities. I have held plenty of dialogues.

The discovery part will have to take care of itself.

The cemetery is divided by a series of straight lanes crossing at right angles, forming a pattern of squares, each square holding a number of plots.

Kind of like a chessboard.

Following the map in my notebook, the carefully drawn grid, I walk along the main road, passing shadowy headstones, some stark, some ornate, some with angels or crosses, and many no more than tiny plaques at ground level. I keep my flashlight beam low, pointed at the gravel path before me. I walk all the way to the far wall of the cemetery, opposite the main gate, not far from the tunnel through which Kimmer and I made our silly escape back when we were of the age when everything was yet ahead of us. I wait, listening to the sounds of the night. A crunch of gravel: a human being far away, or a small animal much closer? I strain my eyes looking for other flashlights. Here and there a glimmer: somebody searching for me, or the headlight of a distant automobile, glimpsed briefly through the gate?

No way to tell.

THE EMPEROR OF OCEAN PARK

I have done this walk enough times now that I no longer need the map. I am in the southwestern corner, the right-hand corner from the perspective of the front gate. I stroll to my right—to the east—left as seen from the gate, passing one lane, then turning north along the second. The squares of a chessboard are numbered on an eight-by-eight grid, from A1 in the lower left corner on white's side of the board to H8 in the upper right. Were the cemetery grid a chessboard, with the gate on the black side, the lane I am now walking would be the B file. I pass three crossing lanes, labeled in my notes as B1, B2, and B3, although they are actually named for various founders of the city. At the fourth lane I stop.

B4, according to my notes.

B4, if one accepts the cemetery as a chessboard, even though it does not have sixty-four squares, and if one arbitrarily takes the gate as the black side.

Plausible.

B4, the first move of the Double Excelsior, with the knight, if black wins and white loses. I called Karl on the day of my argument with Jerry, because I wanted to be absolutely sure. He said yes, if the composer is an artist and a romantic. My father fancied himself both. *Excelsior! It begins!* If white loses, then *it begins* with the white queen's knight pawn sliding two squares forward. That is why my father arranged for me to receive the white pawn first. Lanie Cross was surely right: the Judge wanted to fix it so black would finally win. The move is b4, the square is b4, the move is written b4, and I am here, at B4. Thin, but plausible, at least if I told my father the story of my escape with Kimmer from the cemetery years ago. Thin, but plausible, and plausible is all I have just now.

I step off the path, following the cone of the flashlight beam, until I find the spot I am seeking, a family plot. I illuminate the headstones. Large ones for adults, smaller ones for those who died young. I range over the names and dates: most of the stones are from the nineteenth century, a few from the early twentieth.

I find the headstone I am looking for. This is my fourth observation of it, but my first while in possession of a shovel. I might have come earlier armed to dig. But I had my reasons for waiting.

I lift the light briefly to examine the marble headstone, confirming the identity of the person buried in the grave: ANGELA, BELOVED DAUGHTER. I look at the dates of her too-short life: 1906–1919. She died too young, but I already knew that, too.

I step to the left, away from this family plot, and on to the next. Once more, a low iron fence surrounds it. Once more, a long granite wall in the back bears a family name. And, best of all, once more, a smaller marker appears in front. In the right front corner, quite close to Angela's.

Perfectly placed.

ALOYSIUS, TREASURED SON. I examine the dates: 1904–1923.

Right next to Angela.

Perfectly placed.

Almost certainly not Angela's boyfriend. Not in real life. But close enough for a plausible opportunity for discovery. *To be a man is to act.*

I check my map, check the name again, then examine the ground. It takes two or three minutes, but I find what I am looking for. In the shielded spill of my flashlight, a patch of dark brown earth next to the grave looks freshly turned. There is not even any grass on it. I am astonished that nobody has disturbed it, but things always seem more obvious when you already know they are there.

Perfectly placed.

I bend to my pack to remove the shovel, then pause, straighten, and look into the dark, distant mists. Too many sounds in the quiet. A foot on icy gravel, or a squirrel in a tree? I have no objective way to tell if anybody is out there, yet I am certain that somebody is. Somebody has to be. But I do not know which side of the cemetery wall he—or she—is on, or, for that matter, which side of the grave. Perhaps there *are* ghosts. But I cannot let them stop me.

I put the flashlight on the ground, illuminating the muddy, grassless patch, and, with the spade I brought along, I begin to dig. The work is surprisingly light and easy. The earth is heavy, sodden with water on top and crisp with frost below, but it is not difficult to slide the shovel in. The harder part is lifting the soil out. Nevertheless, within four or five minutes I have made a shallow trench at least eight inches wide. It occurs to me that this hole took time to make, and I find it remarkable that nobody noticed the original act. I shrug. Not my problem, not now. I bend to my work. After two minutes, I strike metal.

Crunch.

I stop again, this time swinging my light in a wide circle, probing the fog. Somebody is out there. Definitely. And there is no point in hiding the flashlight any longer, because the one thing I know is that the somebody who is out there already knows where to find me. For a second, I consider replacing the earth I have dug, refusing to follow the game to its end. But I have gone too far. I had gone too far when I got into the shoving match with Jerry Nathanson, when I visited Jack Ziegler, and when I asked Dana Worth for a favor.

I had gone too far when I behaved in a way that may have cost me my wife.

Dig.

I widen the hole until I can see what I take to be the edges of the blue metal box, then I get down on my knees and try to pull it out. But my fingers can find no purchase in the wet earth, and I know I have to dig more. It never occurred to me that it would be easier to dig the hole than to remove the box. Perhaps there is some special tool that people use for tasks like this one.

I decide to dig further out from the edges. I stand up and grip the shovel, and that is when a slight, pale ghost materializes from the darkness, and I cry out and raise the tool as though to strike.

"Let me help, Misha," whispers the ghost, but it is really Dear Dana Worth.

(11)

FOR A MOMENT I CAN THINK OF NOTHING TO SAY. Dana stands before me, smiling shyly, and also trembling a bit, for prowling the cemetery at night is no fun for anybody. I should have known she would figure it out. She is dressed for the weather, in a dark ski parka and heavy jeans, and has even brought her own shovel.

"What are you doing here?" I demand, still shivering from the fright she gave me.

"Oh, come on, Misha. After what you asked me to do? Did you really think I would miss it?"

I let this go. "How did you get in?"

"Through the gate, the same way you did."

"I've been here since closing."

"The gate isn't closed."

"It what? It is. I saw Samuel close it."

Dana shrugs. "Well, it isn't closed now. I just walked in. So, are you going to let me help you or not?"

I put it together. The gate isn't closed. Somebody unlocked it. And why leave it ajar? Because this is not just about the arrangements any more, and it is not just about following me until I find them, either.

If the gate was left open, it was left that way in invitation. Which means that now this is about Dana, too.

Bad news. Very bad news. If Dana had left it at doing as I asked, if she had not come here tonight, what I said to her in Post would have been true: she would have been perfectly safe.

"Dana, you have to get out of here. You have to go, fast."

"I'm not leaving you here, Misha. Uh-uh, no way."

"Will you quit being so loyal?" I am shouting as best I can without raising my voice above a whisper.

Despite her fear, she responds tartly: "Gee, is this the guy who was lecturing me about loyalty two years ago?" When she left Eddie, she means.

"Come on, Dana, I'm serious. You have to get out of here." I wave a hand toward the rest of the cemetery. "It's dangerous."

"Then you shouldn't be here either."

"Dana, come on. . . ."

"You come on. Don't give me any of this me-man, you-woman stuff, okay? I know you're primitive, but you're not that primitive. Now, get serious, Misha. I'm not going to abandon you. I'm *not*. If we leave, we leave together. But if you stay, I'm staying, too. So, please, Misha, quit wasting time."

Well, the truth is, it's less spooky with Dana here. And I might need the help.

"Okay. Let's get to work."

I dig. Dana pulls. Dana digs. I pull.

Then we get it right. We both dig, clearing the dirt from all four sides. We both pull at the same time. And, just like that, the box is free of the earth, clods falling away from its shiny blue surface. The metal is at first so cold that my fingers stick. It is a box of the sort in which one keeps canceled checks or passports. A strongbox, which would usually be locked. But I am sure that this one . . .

Yes.

As Dana stands next to me, beaming, I brush away a few loose clods of earth and lift the top. It opens on its hinges, quite freely.

I glance around, then sit on the low stone wall, setting the box next to me. I leave it open but make no effort to remove the oilcloth package I have already spotted inside. A grin tugs at my lips as I consider all the people who would like to be holding what we have dug up.

"What now?" asks Dana, growing nervous again, shifting her weight from one foot to the other. "Is that it? Are we done?"

"I'm not sure."

"Misha, look, this has been fun, okay, but I want to get out of here."

I look around again, puzzled. "Okay. You're right. Let's go."

I close up the box, still leaving the contents undisturbed. I pack up my shovel and my notebook, haul the knapsack onto my back once more, and, with Dear Dana Worth at my side, stride toward the gate. This time my route is more direct, but the shadowy headstones here look like the headstones everyplace else. Dana practically skips along. She seems almost giddy at the thought that we are leaving this place, and I am rather pleased myself. I cradle the box in my arms, still worried about whether somebody else is in here with us.

As we hike, I listen. Was that a footstep? The sloughing of metal over stone? I fall back and listen harder. Nothing but silence now. We reach the second crossroads, turn right onto the direct path toward the gate. Dana's stride quickens. She is tough, the terror of the law school, but I know this sojourn among the remains of the dead has spooked her. She will be relieved to escape.

So will I.

I allow her to walk on ahead. I slow down. Cock my head to the side.

"Okay, Misha, what is it this time?" Dana's voice is impatient as she circles back in my direction. She folds her arms and clucks her tongue. No matter what evidence might have brought us to this point, the only conspiracies she really cares about are those perpetrated by the faculty appointments committee. Yet I note the hysterical edge to her voice; my erstwhile buddy is as frightened as I am.

"Hush," I murmur, listening.

"Misha, I really think we should—"

"Dana, will you please shut up?"

In the harsh white gleam of my flashlight, Dear Dana's face is twisted in anger and hurt, the face of a little girl. She has already declared our comradeship, her furious expression signals, by coming here in the first place. She does not have to accept my verbal abuse too.

"I'm sorry," I whisper.

"You know, Misha," she hisses, "there are times when I don't know what I see in you."

"I understand. But hush anyway."

"Why?"

"Because I'm trying to listen."

To my relief, Dana cooperates this time. She steps away, standing off to the side of the path, shaking her head at my foolishness, but she does it quietly. She puts a hand on the side of a mausoleum, pressing as though expecting to find a hidden doorway, then pulls it back, her fingers having touched something she would rather not name. She wraps her arms around herself, puffs out air. Her bluster, I know, hides a disquiet as great as mine.

I walk a few steps down the path in the direction from which we came. Nothing.

"I'm going to turn off my light for a minute," I tell her, and do it. "Point yours the other way."

Dana, her expression now uneasy, nods her head. I wait until the beam from Dana's lantern swings out of my line of sight. Then I move farther down the path and glare into the graying darkness. Nothing.

Something.

A small metallic click. Repeated, but not regularly enough to represent some broken valve on a truck idling outside the walls. It is made by a human being. A human being carrying something that clanks and jangles. But trying to be quiet about it.

Silence falls again, but I am not fooled. It was a click. A human click. Maybe more than one click. Maybe more than one human. And not far away.

Still clutching the box, I pull Dana close.

"Why, Misha," she says, "I didn't know you cared." But she says it in irritation, for Dana, as I believe I have mentioned, does not like to be touched.

I lean toward her ear and whisper, "Somebody else is in here."

Dear Dana shudders and pulls away from me. "That's ridiculous. Number one, I think we would have heard him. Number two, nobody else is as crazy as you—"

"Dana—"

"Number three, please don't grab me like that. *Ever.* Okay?"

"I'm sorry, but I was trying to—"

"Misha, look. We're friends and all. But, number one, grabbing me like that is disrespectful of my space. Number two, it's such an aggressive, male—"

This time Dana has to end her list inconclusively, because we both hear, very close behind us, the crunch of what can only be a human being crossing gravel, followed by a soft exclamation as said human stumbles.

Finally spooked, we take off, no longer trying to be quiet. We reach the front gate in less than a minute.

It is closed.

"Give it a shove," I suggest to Dana.

She pushes, pushes harder, then turns to me and shakes her head.

"What is it?"

"Look." Her voice trembles as she points. The padlock and chain are firmly in place. Now I know what was clanking in the darkness.

We are trapped in the cemetery.

"Okay," I mutter, thinking fast. Maybe Samuel simply forgot, then came back and put the chain on as usual. Maybe. On the other hand, he has done nothing else for the past quarter-century but open this gate in the morning and lock it at night. From force of habit alone, he would surely have chained it up. Somebody picked the lock and opened the gate to see if anybody else came in. Anybody who was helping me, for instance. Then the same somebody chained it again.

Dana, always prepared, reaches toward her belt. "I'll use my phone."

"To call whom?"

She frowns. "I don't know. The police or somebody. You have a better idea?"

Recalling my previous encounter with the police, I shake my head. "We can get out the other way."

"What other way?"

I find a grin somewhere, then turn to look toward the rear of the cemetery again. I do not want to plunge back into that awful darkness, easy prey for whoever or whatever lurks in the shadows of the dead, but we have no choice. "It's a long story, Dana. Believe me, there is another way out. A drainage tunnel in the south wall. Seriously. I'll show you." I take a couple of steps down the path. "Come with me."

She does not answer.

I turn back. "Dana? It'll be fine, I promise."

She is a couple of paces behind me, her wide-eyed gaze in the other direction, toward the gate. I follow her line of sight.

"Misha," she gasps, then drops her shovel on the ground and raises her hands slowly. Looking past her, I shut up at once.

He must have been hiding behind one of the mausoleums, I realize, for he appeared as though by magic. I congratulate myself on this deduction to avoid crying out. For the man who is standing just off the path, easily picked out in the glare of my flashlight, has obviously been waiting at the gate for us to return. He is a tough-looking man, blocky and loose-limbed, a wall of flesh barring our path. A scraggly beard encircles his wrathful face. His eyes are hard. A coldly efficient gun clutched lightly in his right hand is pointing in our direction. The air seems suddenly slushy and cold, an impediment through which I must swim to move any part of my body. Dana has already put her hands up, just like a character in a movie, and I decide to do the same, especially because the man holding the gun motions with the barrel, making it plain what he wants us to do. Moving slowly, to show that I am no threat, I put the flashlight on the ground. I straighten again. He gives me another signal with the gun. Reluctantly, I put the strongbox down too.

"Very good," says the bearded man in a terrifyingly familiar voice. His hair is a bright, fiery red.

"No," I breathe. "It isn't possible."

But it is.

Because my attention is naturally on the blue-black gun with its bulbous silencer, it has taken a few seconds for my terrified brain to register a simple, stunning fact: the man blocking our path is no stranger. Behind the reddish-brown hair and reddish-brown beard is the ruddy, self-satisfied face of Colin Scott.

CHAPTER 51

AN OLD FRIEND RETURNS

As so often, I am the first to speak, and what I say is utterly stupid: "You're dead."

Colin Scott seems to give this problem serious consideration, stroking his bushy new beard. A car passes by outside the gate, but it might as well be on the other side of the world. The hand holding the gun remains very steady, aiming at a spot midway between Dana and myself.

"He doesn't look very dead to me, Misha," whispers Dana, pretending that she is not frightened out of her wits. But I find myself growing calmer by the second. Either we will die here or we will not die here. The Judge always emphasized free will; I hunt around for the opportunity to exercise some.

"Keep your hands very still," says Colin Scott at last. My hands, like Dana's, are well up toward the stratosphere. All four are trembling. "Use your foot to push the box over to me."

I do it. He makes no move to pick it up.

"I knew you must have a helper, Professor." He turns to Dana. "We have not been introduced."

I realize he is serious. I say awkwardly, "Dana, this is, uh, Agent— that is, Colin Scott, also known as Jonathan Villard. Mr. Scott, this is Professor Dana Worth."

He nods, no longer interested, then cocks his head, listening. He frowns. He has the gun, so we wait for him to speak.

"Is somebody else here with you? Please don't waste my time lying."

"No, it's just the two of us," I assure him. Dana and I glance at each other, passing telepathic messages, trying to coordinate a lie. If telepathy only existed, we might even get away with it.

"Do you know what is in the box?"

"I opened it. It isn't locked. I saw a package inside, that's all."

"That's all." He crouches, the gun holding us in place, and slowly lifts the lid. In the movies, this would be the moment when I would spin around and kick the gun out of his hand while the bad guy stood still and let me do it, watching in amazement.

I can no longer restrain myself: "They said you drowned."

"It wasn't me," he answers calmly. "A man drowned, but it wasn't me. I told you I would have to do something about the Bureau. Being dead is an excellent way to forestall an investigation."

"I saw the photograph—"

"Yes, from the license. Well, that *was* me. The photograph. But a body from the water? Even a few hours with the fish can change the countenance to the point where it is difficult to tell."

I feel a leaden chill. *A few hours with the fish can change the countenance.* Is that where Dana and I are headed?

Dana's turn: "But the body was identified—"

"No. No, it was not. This is a common misperception." He tilts his head the other way and purses his thick lips as though measuring us for a casket. "No *body* is ever really identified. Certainly no body that has suffered any decomposition. The fingerprints are identified. The dental work is identified. We assume that, if we know the owner of the fingerprints, we know the identity of the body. But that assumption is only as good as the quality of the underlying records."

Even though I am likely to be dead in about ninety seconds, the semiotician in me is impressed. All of forensic science is, in this sense, based on a classic misapprehension of cognition: the inability to distinguish between the signifier and the signified. Fingerprints are the signifiers. Dental records are the signifiers. They are the coded messages to which we assign significance. The identity of the body, the person we decide is dead, is the signified. We all act as though knowledge of the first necessarily implies knowledge of the second. But the implication is only a convention. It is not celestial mechanics. It is not the healing of an illness. It works because we *decide* that it works. We make that decision by accepting, without question, the accuracy of the records themselves.

"You fiddled with the records," Dana murmurs, for she never has any trouble keeping up. "Or somebody did."

Colin Scott says nothing. This is not the time for true confessions. His silence is itself a menace . . . and an opportunity. His look is pensive. Not all, evidently, has gone as he planned. He is trying to decide what to do.

"So, you have the box," I point out, fighting for time. "You're safe now."

"The box was never for me, Professor. That much of what I told you was true. I was . . . engaged . . . to recover it for someone else."

"Who?"

Another long silence, weighing what to tell. His face is drawn, reminding me that he was already middle-aged when kicked out of the Agency almost thirty years ago. At last he says: "I am not here to offer you explanations, Professor. But do not assume that I was the only one hoping you would find this box. I am simply the only one who was present when you found it."

Dana's turn: "But why couldn't you find the box on your own?"

Colin Scott's yellow eyes turn toward her, flash dismissively, and return to me. Yet, in speaking to me, he is answering her question. "Your father was a brilliant man. He wanted you to find the box, but he also knew there would be somebody in the way. Me or somebody like me. He couldn't take any chances."

"What?"

"We knew what the Excelsior was, that was child's play. And we knew we had the wrong boyfriend for Angela, or he would have told us what we needed to find out. But the cemetery . . . that was clever, Professor. Very clever."

A silence. I break it. "Okay, so what do we do now?"

His thin, scarred lips curl into a slight smile, but he does not bother to answer. Instead, he gestures with the gun, moving us further away from the gate and along the path into the cemetery. Where he can kill us more easily. He points toward Dana's belt. With trembling fingers, she detaches her cell phone and hands it to him. He glances at it briefly, then drops it onto the gravel and, without seeming to aim, fires two quick bullets into it. Dana flinches at the muted sound. So do I.

"You don't have to be afraid, Professor," he declares. His eyes appear to be watching us, the path behind us, and, impossibly, the paths off to either side, without any movement of his head. "I have what I came for, and you will never see me again. So I am not going to kill you."

"You're not?" I ask with my usual incisiveness.

"I have no compunction against killing. Killing is a tool one must be prepared to use in my profession." He lets this sink in. "But there are such things as orders, and, as I once had occasion to tell your father, there are rules for this kind of thing."

"Rules? What rules?"

Colin Scott shrugs, without moving the gun a millimeter. "Let us simply say that your friend Jack Ziegler, scum of the earth though he may be, is a very vindictive man."

Yet he does not lower the gun, and I begin to see his problem. He is concerned about the promise Jack Ziegler made—the one of which he spoke in the cemetery on the day we buried my father, the one of which Maxine reminded me on the Vineyard, the one Uncle Jack told me in Aspen he intended to keep. The promise to protect my family. And this little drama is the result: Uncle Jack gave his orders, and even this professional killer, who has every reason to hate Jack Ziegler and to fear what I can tell the police, dares not disobey.

"He can't hurt us," says Dana, the relief evident in her voice. Her hands come down.

Colin Scott's baleful eyes move, and the gun, too, swivels, ever so slightly.

"My orders are not to harm Professor Garland or any of his family. But I am afraid, Professor Worth, that nobody said anything about his friends."

Dana sounds suddenly very small. "You're going to kill *me*?"

"It is necessary," he sighs, and now the gun is pointed at the bridge of her nose. "And it has a certain . . . symmetry."

"Wait," say both Dana and myself at the same time, our brains working full-bore to come up with the right words to slow him down.

"Please stand clear of Professor Garland," he says reasonably, as though keeping me from accidental harm would be her number-one concern at the moment. A graveyard rat materializes from the shadows, white and gross and huge, and sits on its hind legs, maybe sensing that dinner will soon be available. "Just close your eyes, Professor Worth, and you will not even have time to feel any pain. You, Professor Garland, will move aside and turn your face to the wall of the mausoleum."

"Don't do this," I protest.

"Professor Garland, I must ask you to turn away. You have heard enough to send me to death row. But you will not act on it, no matter what I do tonight, because, if you do, the orders regarding protection for you and your family are no longer binding. You might risk your own life, but you have a wife and a son to think of. Do you understand me?"

I thought I knew terror, but now it is alive within me, flapping about on mad, conscience-stealing wings. "Yes, but, you can't just . . ."

"Turn around, Professor."

"You're going to *kill* me," Dana repeats, her voice trembling.

In that instant, I commit the boldest and stupidest act of my four decades on this planet. I lower my hands and step between Dana Worth and Colin Scott.

"No, he isn't," I say, my voice shaking worse than Dana's.

"Step out of the way, please, Professor," says the man who killed the man who killed Abby.

"No."

Mr. Scott hesitates. I can almost hear the wheels going round: He does not want Dana to escape and does not really want me to escape either, and maybe the best thing is to kill us both and trust in his ability to escape Jack Ziegler's wrath. Or he may think he can blame my murder on somebody else. Or he may bet that Uncle Jack is so sick that his word does not carry the force it once did. Or his new client, whoever it is, might be even more powerful than the dreaded Jack Ziegler. Or he may have another theory, one I could neither imagine nor comprehend, for I do not live in his world. But, whatever the reason, I know an instant later that the former intelligence officer has made up his mind. He is going to kill us both, right here in the Old Town Burial Ground. His unbothered gaze carries the message as firmly as if it were chiseled in granite.

The gun barrel flicks up an inch or two and seems to grow very wide and dark, ready to swallow me up, and, even as I prepare to fling myself forward, I know I will never reach him in time to stop him from shooting, so I use my last seconds to pray instead and I wish I had a chance to say goodbye to my son and even my wife who is no longer fully my wife and I notice that Dana's small hand is in mine and I hear the Twenty-third Psalm on her lips and I wonder where her fabled martial arts training has gone and my senses are brightly alive, I can see, almost, the individual hairs on Colin Scott's red-dyed head, I can feel the pressure of his finger closing on the trigger, and then that deep and abiding instinct to live overwhelms my natural fatalism. I jerk free of Dana's hand and leap across the small distance toward Colin Scott.

Then everything happens at once.

Colin Scott is very fast. In the fraction of an instant between the time I leave the ground and the time I come down on top of him, he squeezes the trigger, not once but twice, and the entire cemetery rocks with the sound of the gun's report as my body goes suddenly icy, then numb, and I spin to one side, stumbling against an alabaster angel standing guard atop a headstone. I am amazed at the reverberations—his gun has a silencer, it should not be so loud—but I also realize that he was right, that I feel nothing at all, and then I realize that Dana is yelling something I am unable to hear, and also that I am not dead, the bullets must have missed, and Colin Scott is down on his knees and there is an awful lot of blood on the upper half of his shirt and the frozen gravel seems slick and my first thought is that somehow his gun has misfired, that it has exploded in his hand, and I am still on my feet, although woozy, and I push Dana back into the darkness toward the drainage pipe. She is clutching her shovel again, and it occurs to me that she must have hit Colin Scott with it, because there is a bloody gash on his forehead. Still trying to make Dana move, I keep my eye on Mr. Scott, who is swiveling around, one hand pressed to the ground, trying to point the gun behind him at something out in the darkness, and he fires twice more, very fast, two quick spits lighting up the cemetery and then vanishing in the flooding black, and then there is a loud cry from the shadows and Dana and I decide to hunker down and an instant later comes the sharp explosion of another gunshot and Colin Scott is flat on the ground now, the gun inches from his twitching hand, and his neck is very bloody and he is trying to say something, words are forming on his lips even as the light of life dies in his tear-filled, unseeing eyes, and I dare not go any closer because I do not know who is out there in the darkness waiting, but I see the shape of the simple sounds he is making and I know that his last living thought is of his mother.

Dana and I are flat on the ground.

Waiting.

Listening.

Footsteps crunching on the gravel. Moving slowly. Cautiously. Wary of a trap.

Dana is weeping. I don't know why. We are the survivors. I am holding her close to me on the grass along the side of the path. I feel chilly despite my parka. Dana is shivering and light as a feather in my arms. Mr. Scott is a bloody mess.

We are too frightened to move.

A flashlight flicks over us, picks out what is left of Colin Scott, slices the air above our heads as dancing specks cloud my vision.

We lie still. I sense that there is something I should be doing, but a lethargy has stolen over me. My body no longer wants to move. Perhaps it is the aftereffect of mortal terror.

The light is very close, almost blinding. I see what might be sneakers. Jeans. But whoever shot Colin Scott does not say a word, and Dana and I cannot see a thing. We hear a metallic scrape, then the light clicks off.

The footsteps begin to recede, and Dana vaults to her feet with an angry cry. Grabs Colin Scott's gun from the ground. Runs. Not toward the exit. Into the darkness.

"Dana!" I cry, scrambling after her, stepping around what is left of Mr. Scott. My voice is faint, tinny, an echo of an echo. "Dana, wait!" But my cry is a whimper. "Dana!"

I start to sway. The darkness swirls from black-black to black-gray to gray-gray, and the ground spins up to meet me once more. Dana disappears. I start to pick myself up again. I want to tell her that she is being foolish, that we should take the box and head for the gate or the drainpipe, but I lack the strength to call out. I slump against the headstone. I see the alabaster angel towering above me. Dana is gone. But it all seems very unimportant. My hands grow numb. Leaning against the stone is like clutching water. No, ice. I slide to the ground. One of my feet is twitching horribly. My stomach itches but I cannot lift a finger to scratch. In the glow of my fallen flashlight, I see why Dana ran. The metal box is gone; whoever shot Colin Scott must have taken it while we were blinded by the flashlight. That was the metallic scrape I heard.

I try to pray. *Our Father who . . . who art . . . who art in . . .*

I gather my energy, trying again to rise, to think, to focus.

God, please . . . please . . .

But sustaining these thoughts requires too much energy. I need to rest. The grass is sticky red underneath my cheek. Just before the shadows close in, I realize that not all the blood belongs to Mr. Scott.

I was shot after all.

CHAPTER 52

OLD FRIENDS VISIT

(1)

"THE KIDS ALL WANT TO SEE YOU," gushes Mariah, sitting next to my hospital bed. "It's like you're some kind of hero to them."

I smile reassuringly from deep inside my undignified tangle of bandages and sensors and sutures and tubes. My doctors have assured me happily that I lost so much blood in the Burial Ground that I nearly died. I have had sufficient pain since awakening that I have wondered once or twice whether I might have been better off had the paramedics taken a little longer to find me. Not all the pain has been physical. Yesterday afternoon, I opened my eyes to find Kimmer dozing in the armchair, a thick legal memo on her lap, then opened them again to find her gone. I decided I might have dreamed her presence. When the nurse dropped in to see whether I was dead yet, or at least whether there might be a reason to call in a code and have everybody come running, I asked if my wife had been in to visit. My voice did not come out right, but the nurse was very patient and, eventually, we managed to make contact. Yes, I was told, your wife *was* here for a while, but she had to go to a meeting. Which is when the pain settled in as a permanent companion. Same old Kimmer. Dutiful enough to visit me despite our estrangement, but not at the risk of losing billable hours.

I asked the nurse if I could have something for the pain. She flipped coolly through my chart, then fiddled with my IV for a few minutes, and when I opened my eyes again it was night and I had two detectives as company.

Dr. Serra, my surgeon, bustled in and told them I was too weak to talk.

Lots of flowers, but nobody from the law school on the first day, because I was not allowed visitors other than my wife. One of the critical care nurses, a robust black woman named White, turned the television on and surfed through the channels for me, but I paid little attention to the programs. She finally settled on a movie, something involving Jean-Claude Van Damme and lots and lots of guns. I turned my face to the pale green ceiling, remembered those last moments in the cemetery, and wondered when I could see my son.

I slept some more.

At some point I asked Dr. Serra how it was that I came to be in a private room, but he only shrugged, his palms turning upward as his shoulders sashayed, suggesting through this ornate Mediterranean gesture that his concern was the state of my health, not the state of my finances. I asked for a phone and was refused. A hospital can be like a prison. I wanted to make this point to Dr. Serra, but he rushed off to see his other almost-dead patients. Then Nurse White was back, explaining to me that, because of my guarded condition, I could have only a few visitors, which I had to list for her; once she told me that children were barred from Intensive Care, I lost interest in the exercise.

Five names, she told me, plus family.

I quickly listed Dana Worth and Rob Saltpeter. I listed John Brown. After a moment's desperate thought, I listed my next-door neighbor Don Felsenfeld. And I asked Nurse White, as a favor to me, to call the Reverend Morris Young, the fifth name on my list. She smiled, impressed. As Nurse White left, I noticed a man in dark blue serge sitting outside the door, and I wondered before falling asleep again whether I was under guard or under arrest.

When I next awakened, there was a Bible on the table next to the bed, a large-print King James Version, along with a note from Dr. Young in an old man's shaky hand. *Call me anytime*, he had written. Another nurse came in, and I asked her if she would read to me from Genesis 9.

She was too busy.

The police came back, with Dr. Serra's grudging permission, and one of them was my old friend Chrebet. I told them what I remembered, but they had talked to the FBI and Dana Worth and Uncle Mal and Sergeant Ames, and seemed to know an awful lot already. They asked me only one question that really seemed to matter: whether I had seen my assailant. That was the word they used, *assailant*. A word from the newspapers and the movies. I found I liked it. Despite pain and muzziness, the semiotician awakened, wondering why officialdom would choose so impressive-sounding a term to describe a brutal criminal. Perhaps because it made their job seem to lie higher on the social scale than it really did. They were not catching petty hoods, the uneducated and desperate detritus who had been, in the lovely coinage of Marx and Engels, "precipitated" into the *Lumpenproletariat,* they were chasing down assailants. Well, I had been assailed, all right. I had been struck by an assail of gunfire. Croaking out the words, I explained to the two patient officers that Colin Scott, the man who had done the assailing, was dead. They looked at each other and then shook their heads and told me that the three bullets that struck my abdomen, my thigh, and my neck were recovered, and only two of them were fired from the gun of the late Mr. Scott. Meaning that I was also shot by a fourth person in the cemetery that night.

The person Dana tried to catch. Now I knew why. Because, certainly, there was no need to recover the stolen box.

"We're not sure yet whether it was an accident," one of the detectives said. It was that third bullet, they added, that did most of the damage, catching me low in the chest. In the movies, they told me, people shoot for the heart, not a bad idea, but the heart has ribs around it; in real life, you often do more damage aiming for the belly, hoping to smash a kidney or, better still, the liver. And even if you miss those organs, they went on, you cause so much bleeding that there is a good chance that the victim will die long before help arrives.

Trying to scare me. Worked pretty well, too.

Then they told me the rest. Colin Scott was also hit three times. But only the final shot, the one that killed him, was from the same mysterious gun that pinpointed my abdomen from the darkness. The first two bullets to strike him were fired from yet another weapon. Two slugs dug out of headstones near the site of our confrontation also matched this gun. One possibility, the detectives said, is that the secret shooter out there in the mist ran out of bullets and pulled a second gun. Another is that there were not four but five people in the cemetery that night: Dana, myself, Scott, and two unknowns.

Stunned, I told them part of the truth: that I saw nothing except the muzzle flash, that I never knew I had been shot until I collapsed.

They shrugged and went away, never asking me the right question. I dozed, worrying about accident versus intention.

The next time I awakened, Mariah was at my bedside, and I gaze at her now, pert and mature and decidedly rich in designer jeans and ski sweater, a breath of royalty come to call on the commoners' wing. Crying for me, and telling me that her children think I am a hero.

"What are you doing here?" I manage to croak.

"Your dean tracked me down."

"No, I mean . . . I mean, you're a new mommy."

"And I can't leave you alone for a minute," she sobs, but laughing at the same time. "I go into labor and you go and get yourself shot."

"How's the baby?"

"The baby is beautiful. The baby is perfect."

"And, what? Two days old?"

"Four. She's fine, Tal. She's perfect. She's downstairs in the van with Szusza. Matter of fact, Mommy has to go feed her in a few minutes." Mariah is smiling as she weeps. "But look at you," she whispers, twisting her hands in her lap. "Just look at you."

"I'm fine. You should have stayed home. Really." I stifle a cough, because coughing hurts. A lot. "I mean, I'm glad you're here, kiddo, but . . . well, you really didn't have to leave the baby for this." I do not want her to know how touched I am. Nor could I form the words if I wanted to. I may be in Intensive Care, but I am still a Garland.

"Well, no, maybe if they just shot you once. Or even twice. For that I would have stayed in Darien. But, Tal, you've always been an over-achiever. You have to go and get yourself shot *three times!*"

I manage a smile, more for Mariah's sake than mine. I remember, when my mother was dying, how she seemed to think it her role to offer some word of comfort to every tongue-tied visitor who dropped by Vinerd Howse to pay next-to-last respects. I spend a moment's thought on my brother, wondering why only Mariah is here, but he never came to the Judge's confirmation hearings either: Addison only likes happy endings.

"I guess you have enough to do," says Mariah, pointing. My pocket chess set and my laptop computer are lined up neatly next to the bed. I smile like a kid on Christmas. Resting my voice, I gesture. My sister opens my laptop for me on the little table arm that swivels over the bed and turns it on.

Thank you, I mouth as Windows toots its cheery hello.

Kimberly brought them, says Mariah. "She thought you might want them."

Kind of her, but infuriating too.

"Kimmer's leaving me," I tell my sister in a flat tone, but I have to say it three times before my words are clear.

Mariah has the good grace to look embarrassed by her answer. "I think everybody on the East Coast knows that," she says gently. She turns chipper. "But you're better off without her. You know what Mom used to tell me when some guy broke my heart? There are many fish in the sea."

I close my eyes for a moment. If a hospital is a prison, this is my sentence: listening to my sister telling me that I am better off living without the mother of my child.

"I love her," I say, but so softly that I doubt Mariah hears. "It hurts," I add, but far beneath the range of sound detectable by the human ear.

"I never liked her," my sister continues, too distracted to heed any voice but her own. "She wasn't good for you, Tal."

We are, for a moment, alone together, for my family has no real emotional tools to support those in need, at least if those in need are relatives. Then I open my eyes and glance up at my sister. She is looking down at her lap, where her fingers are picking nervously at each other.

There is something else on her mind.

"What is it, kiddo?" I whisper, because whispers are the only tune my voice will sing just now.

"Maybe this isn't a good time . . ."

"Mariah, what is it?" My swiftly rising fear puts some energy into my voice. "You can't just come in here and not tell me. What?"

"Addison is gone."

"Gone?" Panic. Memories of gunshots. And a spike, no doubt, in the blue machine that monitors my heart. I would probably sit up were I not half dead and strapped down besides. "What do you mean, *gone?* You don't mean . . . he isn't . . ."

"No, Tal, no. Nothing like that. They say he fled the country. He's down in Latin America somewhere. They were going to arrest him, Tal."

"*Arrest* him? Arrest him for what?" But I am exhausted again, my voice is faint and dry, and I have to repeat this several times, with Mariah leaning close, before she knows what I am asking.

"Fraud. Taxes. I'm not actually sure. A whole lot of money was involved. I don't know the details. But Uncle Mal says that, whatever it was, they only found out about it from doing the background check."

"Background check?"

"You know, Tal. On Kimberly."

Biting the name off, suggesting through her tone that, had my wife not pressed so hard in her quest for a judicial appointment, Addison's financial shenanigans, whatever they are, would never have been found out. It is my wife's fault that Addison was ruined, just as it was Greg Haramoto's fault that the Judge was ruined. Neither man was brought down by his own demons. In today's America, and certainly in the Garland family, nothing is the fault of the person who does it. Everything is the fault of the person who blows the whistle.

"Oh, Addison," I whisper. At least I know now why he was looking at property in Argentina. And what was scaring him.

"Just Alma says he has a girlfriend down there. Only, the way Alma says it, I think maybe she's his wife."

Perhaps it is the medication, but I have to chuckle at that one. Poor Beth Olin! Poor Sally! Poor whoever-it-was-last-week! Then I realize it may be years before I see my brother again, and my face sags. Oh, what wreckage the Judge left behind him.

"Are you okay, Tal? Want me to call the nurse?"

I shake my head, but I do let her give me some water. Then: "Has anybody heard . . . from him? From Addison?"

"No," says Mariah, but the manner in which she cuts her eyes away from me conveys the opposite message.

Then, suddenly cheery, she changes the subject: "Oh, hey, guess what? We got the most incredible offer on the house."

"The house?"

"On Shepard Street."

I am fading fast, which might explain my confusion. "I . . . I didn't know it was, um, on the market."

"Oh, it isn't, but you know how these brokers are. They hear somebody died, and they're lining up buyers before the will has even been read." Mariah misunderstands the concern she reads in my face. "Don't worry, kiddo, I turned it down. I still have lots and lots of papers to go through."

I signal her to lean close. "Who . . . who made the offer?" I manage.

"Oh, I don't know. Brokers never tell. You know how it is."

Although too weak to say so, I view this development more ominously than Mariah does. "Have to find out who," I whisper, too softly for my sister to understand.

Mariah begins to talk about Sally, who is now in rehab at the fancy place in Delaware, but I cannot connect the dots. My mind wants some rest. The nurse comes in unapologetically to add some pain medication to the IV line. After that, things are hazy for a while.

The next time I awaken, Mariah is gone, but Dear Dana Worth is there, my first sight of her since—when was the cemetery? Three nights ago? Four? Hospitals, like prisons, erase the body's natural sense of time's steady passage. She is wearing a dress, which she rarely does, and looks rather cross. Perhaps it is Sunday, and she has stopped in on her way from that conservative church she so adores. She is wearing a white cardigan over her dress, and white shoes: she looks terribly small-town Southern. Her right arm is in a sling: a bone, she explains, was chipped by the ricochet of a bullet. "How many law schools have two faculty members who were shot on the same night?" she teases.

I struggle to smile back.

"I never caught up with him," Dear Dana says, her tiny fists clenched. I realize that it is herself at whom she is angry. "I'm sorry, Misha."

"It's okay," I mutter, but my voice is even weaker than before, and I wonder whether Dana even hears me.

"Then I came back to see how you were doing, and there was all this blood—"

I wave this away. I do not want to hear about her heroic rush down through the very drainage pipe I was looking for, or how she commandeered a telephone at a convenience store—maybe the same one!—and waited for the paramedics and the police and Samuel, to open the gate, and led them back into the cemetery, quieting their doubts and questions as the parade twisted and turned along the dark paths, or how they worked frantically to save me, carrying me out of the Burial Ground more dead than alive. I do not want to hear it in part because I have heard pieces of it already—from Mariah, from Dr. Serra—and in part because I cannot bear to think of Dana's heroism, when it has become important to deceive her.

And Dana, with her swift empathy, understands my reluctance at once, and so veers off on another path.

"Everybody at the law school is rooting for you," she insists, squeezing my fingers in the way that people do when they want you to know they are sincerely sad. Maybe the word is out that Professor Garland is not going to make it. "The students all want to know what they can do. Give blood, whatever. And the Dean wants to visit."

Just what I need. I shake my head wearily. "What about . . . about the deadline?" I manage.

"Are you kidding? They won't dare fire you now. We're famous, Misha, we've been in all the papers." She smiles, but it is forced. I gesture at her arm, whisper that I'm sorry.

"It's okay." She pats my hand. "My life is never this exciting."

"You shouldn't . . . shouldn't have . . ."

"Forget it, Misha."

"I . . . did they . . . did they . . ."

I can manage no more, but Dana gets the message. She glances toward the door before hazarding an answer. "Yes, Misha, it worked. As far as I know, they bought the story. And it's a good thing." She wags a tiny finger at me. "You owe me big-time, mister, and when you're out of here . . ." She trails off. She smiles. The truth is, Dear Dana is complete. She has nearly everything she wants. There is nothing she can think to demand of me, even in jest. Whatever she lacks, she goes to her little Methodist church to find, and providing it is God's problem, not mine. Dana sighs and shrugs. "Anyway, Misha, it worked."

I mouth the words *Thank you*, and I try to add, though I am fading, *I hope you're right.*

Dana is embarrassed now, or maybe she is sick of trying to cheer me up. For whatever reason, she is on her feet, brushing her lips against my forehead, pressing my hand, shrugging into her coat. At the door, she turns to look at me once more. "I'm sorry I didn't catch him," she repeats into my fading consciousness.

I try to tell Dana, although I doubt that I actually form the words, that I am pretty sure that the *him* she keeps apologizing for not catching, the person who fired the third bullet into me, was actually a *her.* I do not know her real name, but the first time I saw her, she was wearing Rollerblades.

(11)

"YOU'RE LOOKING A LOT BETTER TODAY, honey," burbles my wife of nine years, even though she no longer thinks of me as her husband.

"Must be all the push-ups," I manage through parched lips. But I am sitting up and can even drink liquids through a straw. My aching jaw is wired shut. Dr. Serra says I fractured it, but I do not remember when.

Kimmer smiles one of her slow, warming, secret smiles. She pours me some water from a carafe and snaps the plastic top onto the cup.

Then she leans over and puts the straw to my mouth so that I can sip. It hurts to watch her move. The sharp professional cut of her inky-black suit and ecru blouse do nothing to disguise her lazy sensuality. Since shutting me out of her life a week ago, Kimmer seems to have blossomed. She is, at this moment, a remarkably happy woman. And why not? She is free.

"Had enough?" asks my wife, sitting down again. I nod. She smiles. "The doctor says they'll have you up and walking soon."

"Great."

"When they let you out, you can come home if you want," she tells me, smiling, but even in the midst of my drug-induced torpor I recognize the trap. Kimmer is not proposing that we try to rebuild our marriage; she is simply suggesting a place for me to recuperate, *her* house, by *her* sufferance, placing me in *her* debt. "I could nurse you back to health, like in the movies."

She is trying hard, I must grant her that, but the offer is hardly one I can accept, as she well knows. So I merely stare, and eventually my wife loses her smile and drops her eyes and searches for a less controversial topic.

"You wouldn't recognize Bentley. He's getting so tall. And talking so much." As though I have been away for months or years, rather than hospitalized for four or five days.

"Mmmm," I acknowledge.

"Nellie hasn't been around the house," she adds softly, instinct telling her where my fears lie. "I wouldn't do that to you, Misha. Or to our son."

I wonder whether any particular word of this is true. Kimmer is a fine lawyer: how, I ask myself cleverly, is she defining *around?*

"I'm so sorry about how things worked out," Kimmer says a little later, her eyes teary as she holds my hand in both of hers. I pat her fingers.

"Me, too," I assure her.

"You don't understand." She seems ready to resume the argument she has already won, although I cannot imagine why.

"Not now," I plead, closing my eyes. All I can see is Bentley's glowing face.

"It's not that I don't love you, Misha," she continues unhappily, shoving my heart closer and closer to the precipice. "I do. I really do. I just . . . I can't . . . I don't know."

"Kimmer, please. Don't do this, okay?"

She shakes her head. "It's just so complicated!" she bursts out, as though my life is the simpler of the two. But maybe poor Sally was right all along. Maybe it is. "You don't know what it's like to be me!"

"It's okay, Kimmer," I whisper, to no apparent purpose. "It's okay."

"It's *not* okay! I tried, Misha, I really tried!" Pointing a slender finger at me. "I wanted to do it right, Misha, I really did. For you, for my folks, for our son—for everybody. I tried to be what you wanted, Misha, but you got too crazy on me. Or I got too crazy. Either way, I couldn't be that person any more. I'm sorry."

"It's okay," I tell her for the third time, or the thirtieth.

She nods. The silence stretches out.

The nurse comes in to do some of those invasive but necessary things that nurses do and asks my soon-to-be-ex-wife to wait outside. Kimmer dries her tears and stands up and says she has to be going anyway. She kisses me gently on the corner of my mouth and walks proudly to the door, where she turns and offers a half-smile and a quarter-wave, all the while looking tall and strong and incredibly desirable and not at all mine.

"You're a lucky man," says the nurse.

The odd thing is that, from the depths of my several pains, I agree.

CHAPTER 53

ANOTHER OLD FRIEND ARRIVES

(1)

ON THE FIFTH DAY FOLLOWING MY SURGERY, I am able to stand and walk around for a few minutes a day. Three days later, I trade in the assistance of the nurses for the support of two metal crutches. Then the harridans of physical therapy have their turn at adding to my medical torture, laughing and cajoling as I suffer and half die all over again. After nine days of their ungentle tutelage, the doctors reluctantly concede that I am about ready to go home.

This is the part I have dreaded. How can I tell my doctors that I have no place to go home to? I have no intention of setting foot in the house on Hobby Hill, trying to live under the same roof, even temporarily, with a wife who has not only thrown me out but who had, and may still be having, an affair with one of my students. Dana has offered to put me up for as long as necessary, but I can tell from the way she says it that Alison is opposed. Rob Saltpeter invites me to stay with his family, and I am tempted by the simple stability of his household, but I do not want to burden Rob and his extraordinary wife, Sara. Don and Nina Felsenfeld, still practicing the art of *chesed*, offer me their guest room, but living next door to the wife who no longer wants me would be slow torture. Uncle Mal leaves word that I am welcome at his house down in Vienna, Virginia, but I do not return the call. Dean Lynda does not offer me a place to stay, but she does suggest by phone that I take the rest of the semester off. And this time she says it nicely.

With Nurse White's occasional assistance, I finally turn to the get-well-soon cards stacked on the windowsill. Many of them are from the usual suspects—faculty and students and bits of family—but there are also a few surprises, including a couple from college friends I have not seen in years who must have heard about the shooting on the news, because it was reported everywhere. There are flowers from Mallory Corcoran and the law school, and cards from Wallace Wainwright and even Sergeant Bonnie Ames. And another card, postmarked at Miami International Airport, probably while its sender was on the way out of the country, brings me up short, for it is signed at the bottom, in a strong but feminine script, *Sorry, Misha. A job is a job. Glad you're OK. Love, M.* Somehow I doubt it is from Meadows. I gaze out the window and try to reconcile two images, a gentle evening stroll on the Vineyard, and a third bullet that almost killed me in the Old Town Burial Ground.

Morris Young stops by several times to see me, talking to me about God's providence and what the Bible has to say about how marriages end. God prefers that marriages last until death, he says, but also forgives us, if we are repentant, when we fail in the quest to do as he would like.

His message does not reduce my pain.

Three days before I am to be released, somebody from Accounting comes down with a thick sheaf of papers for me to sign. At last I have the opportunity to find out how it is that I came to spend my entire stay in a private room. She shows me the intake form: Howard and Mariah Denton are paying for it. I suppose I should have known. I am about to call Howard with my grudging thanks when Mariah bustles in again, telling me I look ready to travel and informing me that the Navigator will be downstairs when the "big day" comes, plenty of room for me to stretch out on the trip to Darien.

I consider. A private guest house, space to walk on their seven wooded acres, a housekeeper to wait on me, probably a private-duty nurse and an occupational therapist to get me going again. And Mariah to listen to, all day long, and five—no, six now—children to stumble over. And so many miles away from my boy.

"Thank you," I tell my sister, bewildered at the way my options have managed so swiftly to shrink.

The next afternoon, Special Agent Nunzio comes by, and I know they are about to shrink further.

"I CAN'T TELL YOU EVERYTHING," he says sadly, as though he wishes he could.

"Can you tell me anything?"

"That depends on what you want to know."

"Start with all the lying," I suggest.

Nunzio runs a rugged hand through shiny black hair. When he speaks, his face is turned partly away. He does not want to be here. Mallory Corcoran must have pulled the string of all strings to get the Bureau to send an agent up from Washington to brief me. But, then, Uncle Mal owes me, several times over. Oh, does he owe me!

"Nobody lied to you exactly, Professor Garland," Nunzio begins. We are on formal terms once more.

"Oh, no? Well, you did, for one."

"I did?"

I nod. I am sitting in my chair by the window again, the sun warming the back of my neck. "It wasn't coincidence that you were the one who came to interview me about the fake FBI agents who came to Shepard Street. If I hadn't been so busy worrying about everything else, I would have figured that out for myself. The Bureau moved awfully fast, didn't it? But it wasn't because of the impersonation. It was because you already suspected that one of the fake agents was Colin Scott. You had lost track of him, hadn't you? And you needed me to help you find him again."

Nunzio gazes at the various medical devices lined up next to my bed. "Perhaps it was something like that."

"No, it was exactly like that. I must be some kind of idiot to have missed it. You never even tried to discourage me. You never said I was nuts. You never told me to go away. I would call you with the wildest theories, and you would take them seriously. Because you wanted me to keep looking. You wanted me to find Scott for you."

"Maybe."

"That's why Bonnie Ames asked me all those questions about the arrangements. They were your questions, not hers, but you didn't want to interview me formally about my father's arrangements because I might get suspicious. So you let her do it."

"Possibly."

"Possibly. Right. All that because you wanted me to flush out Colin Scott. A murderer."

"You were never in any danger," he sighs, finally conceding the main point.

"That's what everybody keeps telling me. But look at this." I lift my hospital gown to show him the bandages all over my abdomen. He does not flinch. He has seen worse.

"I'm sorry about that, Professor. Truly sorry. Maybe we should have given you more formal protection. We did look in on you from time to time. You didn't know we were there, but we kept an eye out. Then, after Scott died—after everybody thought he died—we thought you were safe. I guess we miscalculated."

"Somebody did, anyway." I gather my waning strength. "Now, tell me about Ruthie Silverman."

"Ms. Silverman? What about her?"

"She's the deputy White House counsel. She helps pick judges."

"I know that. But I'm not sure why you're bringing up her name."

"You know what I'm talking about. My wife was never going to be a federal judge, was she? That was just a cover. A cover that let you investigate my family's life while you pretended that you were collecting data on Kimmer. A cover that was conveniently yanked away as soon as it looked like it was going to keep me from going to see Jack Ziegler."

"Exactly what are we supposed to have been covering?"

"No, you tell me." I want to keep punching, but I am wearing out. "I'm tired of guessing."

Special Agent Fred Nunzio stretches out his strong arms, links his fingers, cracks his knuckles. His shoulders seem too broad for his dark suit. Another agent, similarly attired, is waiting out in the hall—I saw him—and I suspect that it is contrary to Bureau policy for Nunzio to talk to me alone. Which means that Washington wants everything he tells me to be deniable.

"You have it wrong, Professor. Ms. Silverman never lied to you. Nobody from the White House lied. They weren't involved, not the way you seem to think. Your wife really was a candidate for that judgeship. We didn't manipulate that. I doubt we could have. The White House runs us, remember, not the other way around. But we took advantage of it, no question. It allowed us to . . . well, to delve into various things we could not otherwise have investigated."

"Such as my brother's finances."

He is more uncomfortable than ever. "This was not about your brother, Professor. I would call that . . . coincidence."

"Oh, really? The Bureau is doing a background check on one Kimberly Madison and, by coincidence, turns up information about the financial problems of her brother-in-law?"

"We have to look at every lead," he says unctuously.

"No. There's something more here. This wasn't even just about Colin Scott. He was . . . he was . . ." I cannot find the word. Then I have it, thanks to my father. "He was a pawn, wasn't he? Just like me. One black pawn, one white pawn."

Nunzio ignores the last part of my comment. "Colin Scott was a bad man, Mr. Garland. That's what we do down at the Bureau, we catch bad men."

"Oh, really? So was it the Bureau that shot him in the cemetery?"

"No, of course not," says Nunzio, too quickly. I do not think he is lying exactly. He is just telling less than the whole truth. The FBI may not have killed Mr. Scott, but it has a pretty good idea who did. And will never tell me. Which is okay: I have secrets I will never share, too. I just wonder if the Bureau could tell me where she is.

I am tired, and so many parts of my body are aching that my nervous system cannot decide which pain signal to send along first. So it sends them all at once. The sutures in my belly itch horribly, but I cannot scratch them. I have been warned by Dr. Serra, who says he does not intend to do all that work over again.

"Tell me about Foreman," I say quietly. "He's one of yours, isn't he?"

The agent closes his eyes briefly, sighs. "He wasn't from the Bureau. He was from . . . a cooperating agency."

"Was?"

"A hunter found what was left of him in some woods upstate. It wasn't pretty. You saw the pictures of Freeman Bishop, right? Well, this was a thousand times worse."

"I'm sorry," I mumble, resolutely refusing to imagine what could be a thousand times worse than what happened to Father Bishop.

"Foreman was a good man. He joined up with Scott to do an arms deal. It doesn't matter where. The point is, he managed to win Scott's confidence. Or so we thought. When Scott came back from overseas to track down your father's arrangements, he brought Foreman along to help."

"Or to keep an eye on him." Nunzio's earlier euphemism implied that Foreman was from the Central Intelligence Agency, which makes legal sense, if the operation against Scott began overseas. "Scott might have suspected him from the start. . . ."

"Yes. That's possible." He shrugs again. "Anyway, he obviously suspected him at some point."

"Now I see. You didn't just lose track of Scott. You lost track of Foreman. That's why . . . that's why . . ."

That's why you panicked, I decide not to say. *That's why you kept encouraging me to keep looking. That's why you kept telling me I was safe. You knew Foreman was in trouble, so you waited for me to lead you to Colin Scott.*

I allow my eyes to close. The pain is overwhelming me now, and I yearn to get back into the bed. But I have to raise a last subject. "And that was the goal, wasn't it? To get Scott back into the United States? That was the point of the operation?"

"I'm not sure what you mean, Professor," he fences.

"Yes, you are. The Judge . . . my father . . . died, and somebody had to persuade Scott that there was now a risk that something would come out that he didn't want to come out."

"Oh, I see. Yes, that's right."

Spoken quickly again, evasion in his tone. What is going on here? One more question that I will never have a better chance to ask.

"So, then, my father . . . was he murdered or not?"

The way Fred Nunzio ponders before answering, rubbing his chin and squinting, is a terror in itself. "No, Professor," he says at last. "No, we don't think so."

Even through my sedative-clouded mind, his words are a bolt of lightning. "You don't . . . *think* so?"

"No evidence of murder. Nobody with anything to gain by it. So, no, we're pretty sure it was a heart attack, just like the autopsy said."

"Pretty sure?"

He spreads his hands. "Life is probability, Professor, not certainty."

Maybe. Maybe. Nothing ever seems to be a hundred percent certain any more. All this time, and I am still chewing on cotton.

"Agent Nunzio?"

"Yes, Professor?"

"The two men who attacked me that night? The ones who got . . . who got their fingers cut off?"

"What about them?"

"You think Jack Ziegler did it, don't you?"

"Who else? He was protecting you and your family, remember? Mutilating the men who attacked you was probably his way of sending a message."

"To whom? A message to whom?"

For the second time I have the sense I have brushed up against knowledge he would prefer to keep from me. "Anybody who was paying attention," he says finally.

"But didn't everybody already know about his . . . his edict?"

"Evidently not." Again the evasion.

"If you . . . if you know Jack Ziegler did it, why don't you arrest him?"

Fred Nunzio's eyes go flinty. "I don't *know* he did it, Professor Garland. Nobody ever *knows* Jack Ziegler does anything. No, that's not it. Everybody knows, but nobody knows how they know. No proof, ever, where your Uncle Jack is concerned."

Probably I grunt. Nunzio doesn't like it.

"How much do you know, exactly, about your Uncle Jack?"

"What I read in the papers."

"Well, let me explain something to you. Let me tell you why his word was enough to protect you. Do you know what Jack Ziegler actually does for a living?"

"I can guess."

"You can't guess. So let me tell you. He's what you would call a broker, a man who could manage, say, a friendly takeover by interests in, oh, Cali, Colombia, of an operation in Turkey. Everybody trusts him to tell the truth, because he pays in blood if he ever lies. His fee is a percentage of the value of deal. I guess you would call him an underworld investment banker. We figure his annual income at between twenty and twenty-five million dollars."

"So why isn't he in prison?" Still counterpunching.

"Because we can't prove any of it."

I try to process this image, a man who lives by his word in a dangerous world, a man whose promises are so honored that he . . . he can . . .

Oh!

In spite of everything, a grin tugs at my mouth.

"What is it, Professor? What's funny?"

"Nothing, nothing. I . . . Look, this has been a little rough. I have to lie down. Will you help me back to bed?"

"Huh? Oh, sure."

Nunzio allows me to sling an arm over his well-muscled shoulder, and half sturdies, half carries me back to the glorified crib that the hospital has provided me.

On the way, I throw out another question: "So what was the big deal with Colin Scott? Why mount an operation to get him to come back to the States?" He hesitates. "Let me guess. I don't need to know that, either, right?"

"Sorry, Professor."

"No problem." I stretch out and buzz for the nurse, who shows up a moment later and begins to straighten the sheets and plug in all the right sensors.

"The box," I whisper as the nurse does her work. "Have you found out who took it?"

"Not yet." His tone is grim and determined. He has been embarrassed, I realize, by the way things turned out. "But we will."

"I hope so."

He looks at me. Something in my voice, I worry for a moment, has given away the game. "How did you figure it out?" he asks. "Your father's message, I mean? What made you think of the cemetery?"

"I had told him . . . told my father, I mean . . . a story about the cemetery. A long time ago. A personal story. Maybe he thought I would realize at once that the . . . the cemetery was what he meant. I don't know. I just . . . I guess I forgot it for a while."

I do not like the look on Agent Nunzio's hard face. He thinks I am hiding something, which is true. "What made you remember?" he asks sharply, just the right question to catch me lying, except that I have my answer ready.

"The two pawns," I say tiredly. "One delivered inside the law school, one outside."

"So?"

"A white pawn, a black pawn . . . separated by the walls of the law school. My father used to say all the time . . ." I yawn. My exhaustion is not feigned. "He used to say the wall separated us . . . separated the two nations, even in death."

"I don't understand."

"The Old Town Burial Ground. It used to have a segregated area in the back . . . a kind of black cemetery within a cemetery . . . and the . . . my father liked to walk there."

Nunzio gives me a law-enforcement stare, skeptical and scary. But I lack the energy to be properly intimidated. I peer up at him through the mists of pain and exhaustion. "You did well, Professor," he says at last.

"Thank you," I murmur, relaxing once more. "And thank you for coming."

"Oh. Oh, you're welcome. My pleasure." And he is pleased, I know he is: pleased that I have let him off so lightly.

I watch him go, smiling to myself as my body sneaks toward sleep. He doesn't know, I tell myself, delighted at my own cleverness. Nobody knows except Dana. We fooled Colin Scott, we fooled Maxine, we even fooled the FBI.

The box for which Colin Scott died and Dear Dana and I were nearly killed is worthless. The pouch inside is empty. I know because those were my instructions a month ago when, unable to act myself because I was being followed, I asked Dana over lunch at Post if she would buy a metal box and bury it for me.

CHAPTER 54

AN UNSTEADY RETURN

(1)

YOU DON'T QUITE REALIZE how busy a family keeps you until you don't have one any more. On the day of my release, I visit with Bentley for a couple of hours, playing in the back yard of the house on Hobby Hill while Kimmer works at the kitchen table. My bags are neatly packed in the front hall: Kimmer and Mariah did it together, a rare moment of truce as each eagerly anticipated getting what she wanted. The Felsenfelds drop by to say hello, but also, I am sure, to keep things calm. When our neighbors have gone, my wife and I have one last argument, for old times' sake. I probably start it, but Kimmer certainly finishes it.

We are in the kitchen, chatting, as though this is any other day, when we run out of conversation, and I finally say what every spouse in my position finally must: "I just don't get it, Kimmer. I really don't."

"What don't you get?" I sense her simmering hostility, which has grown since the first day she visited me in the hospital, perhaps because my approaching departure makes all our decisions suddenly real.

"What you see in him. In Lionel."

"For one thing," she says calmly, "he has me doing things that would never even occur to you."

"Like what?" I ask, stupidly, the wrong answer, blowing my last chance, my very last chance to win her back, but it is probably way too late anyway. Besides, my mind is too busy for caution. I am thinking: Bizarre sexual practices. Barefoot walks in the snow. Drugs.

"Like reading!" she spits out, to my astonishment. "Nellie isn't like you, Misha. He doesn't think he's twice as smart as I am!"

I almost ask her—it is a very near thing, but I restrain myself—why, if I am twice as smart as she is, she earns twice as much money as I do.

The truth is, I have never thought I was smarter than Kimmer; but Kimmer has always thought I do. When she first fell in love with me (or whatever it was she fell in), she told me that she admired what she called my brilliance. When I told her that I am not particularly brilliant, she grew irritated and accused me of false modesty.

Besides, she was smart enough to realize that she couldn't quite hide her affair, and smart enough to fool me into thinking that her paramour was Jerry Nathanson.

"And you really think this, um, relationship is . . . uh, serious?"

"It's not a *relationship*," Kimmer corrects me with the connoisseur's precision. "It's just something that happened. One of those things. He says he loves me, but I think it's probably over." Her voice is soft again, complacent, and I have the sense that she does not quite love him back, but sees Nellie instead as a conquest. The great Lionel Eldridge, who can have half the women in the city, winds up with a woman nearly a decade his senior. Yet I know even this is not the entire story. I envision Lionel, smoldering with anger against me for what he perceived as mistreatment in the seminar last year, working at Kimmer's firm, seeing her every day in her snazzy pinstriped suits, watching her stride confidently through the world where she is the superstar and he is the rookie, the world he is unlikely ever to master, the world Kimmer and I have already conquered. How could he resist the temptation to try? Here is Professor Garland, infuriatingly strict, pointedly unimpressed by Sweet Nellie's celebrity, and there is Professor Garland's wife, Kimberly, tall and sexy and seemingly unattainable. I see Lionel brooding at his desk in some quiet cubbyhole, turning the idea over and over in his mind, speculating, plotting, wondering whether my wife might not be the tool through which he could gain a measure of revenge. I imagine his initial overtures, most likely rebuffed, but perhaps not all that forcefully, because Kimmer, as she warned me back when we were courting, is always on the lookout for something new.

Or maybe my theory is too self-centered. Maybe my wife was the aggressor. Maybe there is no theory. Maybe, as Kimmer says, it was just one of those things.

"He's a married man," I point out.

"He doesn't love *her*," Kimmer sniffs, *her* being Lionel's wife, Pony, formerly a model or an actress or something, and the mother of his two children.

"So, is he leaving her, too?"

"Who knows? It'll work itself out."

The argument is inconclusive, because there is no point to concluding it. I return to the yard to play catch with Bentley, and my wife returns to the work she has spread over the kitchen table. In the early evening, my sister arrives in the Navigator to pick me up. Me and my bags. In the hallway, I say goodbye to Bentley. To my surprise, he does not cry, little Garland man that he is, and I wonder what, precisely, his mother told him. He is not pretending to be brave: he seems genuinely unconcerned.

Kimmer does not kiss me or hug me or smile. Standing in the foyer in her blue jeans and dark sweater, not far from the threshold over which I laughingly carried her on the day we moved in, she reminds me calmly that I can see my son any time I like, I only need to call—the real message being that she is in charge of my contact with him and wants me to know it. She has yet to forgive me, although it is not clear precisely for what. Kimmer has not had her hair cut in several weeks, and her Afro has grown in a bit, so that now, a sturdy blockade to any further penetration of the house, anger beaming from her dark, sensual face, she reminds me of one of the black militants from the old days. She should have a fist raised in the air, a placard, a chant: *Sufficient power to the appropriate people!* Not what any of the marchers ever said, but certainly what most of them actually meant. Or so the Judge used to proclaim, in his furious dismissals of the steaming rhetoric of the radicals of my youth. *They don't really know what they want*, he would accuse. *They only know they want it now, and they're willing to use "any means necessary" to get it.*

Well, Kimmer certainly knows what she wants, and she is willing to destroy her family to get it. She would probably answer that staying in this marriage a moment longer would have killed *her*; and, given my antics in recent months, I could scarcely blame her. Perhaps we were ill-matched from the start, just as my family always suspected. The marriage was my idea to begin with: having made so bad a fit with her first husband, Kimmer wanted less, not more. She argued at the time that ours was a "transitional relationship," a cruel yet convenient phrase left over from the self-indulgent sixties. She insisted that we were not right for each other, that each of us would, in time, meet somebody better. Even when I finally persuaded her to be my wife, she remained pessimistic. "Now you're stuck with me," she whispered after the ceremony as we snuggled together in the white limousine. "This was a big mistake," she told me dozens of times over the years, meaning our decision to marry—usually in the middle of a fight. Yet, whatever might be the virtues of choosing not to marry because you know you and your partner are a poor fit, it is not obvious that they transfer automatically to a marriage almost a decade old, with a child in the middle of it.

We should have tried harder, I realize as my stomach churns. My failings are surely as great as Kimmer's—but we should have tried harder. I consider saying this, even suggesting that we try again, but the hard set of my wife's lovely face tells me that she has already locked that proposition out of her mind.

Our marriage is truly over.

"We'd better go," Mariah whispers, tugging at my arm, when I just stand there staring at my wife, who returns the stare unflinchingly.

"Okay," I say softly, tearing my gaze away, fighting the hot mist on my eyes, willing myself to act as the Judge would have acted, even though the Judge would never have been in this predicament in the first place.

Wait.

I sense the edge of something: the Judge, who would never have been in this mess, and my wife, defiant in the hall, the images running together, fitting in with that last conversation with Alma, as the final, astonishing piece of the puzzle clicks into place.

Mariah and I drive down Hobby Road, away from the elegant old house where, until the night I was shot, I lived with my family. I do not look into the rearview mirror, because my father would not have done it. I am trying, already, to draw the line he always preached. The process will be as much fun as having an organ removed, but it is never too early to start planning. Yet, through it all, buried in the deepest crevice of my mind, is a tiny exaltation.

I know who Angela's boyfriend is.

(11)

WE MAKE THE NERVOUS DRIVE OVER TO DARIEN, and I move into Mariah's guest house. By the next day, I am a member of her household. For two weeks, I eat healthy meals prepared by her cook, walk the well-tended grounds, and swim in the heated indoor free-form pool, the rest and food and exercise building up my strength. I coo sincerely over the new arrival. I telephone Bentley every morning and every night. I play with my sister's disorderly children and, in the evenings, listen to her disorderly theories as she flips through the channels looking for another game show. Howard is almost never around, either spending the night in the city or flying off to the other side of the world. So we sit there, Mariah and I, on the imported brushed-leather sofa in the forty-foot family room of the nine-thousand-square-foot manor house. All the furnishings are so perfectly arranged that the children are allowed to visit very little of the first floor. It is like living in a magazine layout, and, indeed, Mariah says sadly that the designer submitted photographs to *Architectural Digest*, but nothing came of it. Her tone suggests that this is a genuine defeat.

I watch my sister, the best of us all, soldier her way through her loneliness in the midst of all this wealth while the au pair raises the children and the cook prepares the meals and cleans up afterward and the gardener comes by every other day to tend the plants and cut the grass and the cleaning service drops in twice a week so everything sparkles and the accountant calls every few days to discuss a bill that just came in—it occurs to me that Mariah really has nothing to do. She and Howard have purchased every service that middle-class folk like myself assume adults are supposed to perform. Apart from regular breast-feedings of little Mary, shopping and watching television and decorating are all she has left. So I start taking her out: to the movies, to the mall, hobbling on my cane around an art exhibit in the city while we push Mary in a stroller and two or three more of her children gambol in our wake. Mariah is too restless to take much interest. I try to talk to her: about the latest Washington scandal or the new Toni Morrison, because Toni Morrison has been her favorite author ever since *The Bluest Eye*. I ask after her children, but she shrugs and says they are right there if I want to see how they are doing. I ask how her golf lessons are going, and she shrugs and says it is still way too cold. Recalling what Sally said about how she and Mariah liked to go to clubs together, I offer to take my sister out to listen to some jazz, but she says she is not in the mood. Nothing draws her. She seems too unhappy to bother being depressed.

One afternoon, a couple of my sister's Fairfield County friends drop by, wealthy white wives she knows from one country club or another, with the coerced skinniness of personal training and the gossipy languor of lives as empty as Mariah's. Sitting listlessly in the sunroom, with its shiny silver-and-white tiles, sipping lemonade because it is there, they gaze at me in frank curiosity, even a little uneasiness—not, I finally realize, because I have been shot, but because I am a member of the darker nation. It is as though, in order to accept Mariah into their secret circle, they have schooled themselves to forget that she is black, and I am playing the role of the ghost at their elegant little banquet, calling them to remember an inconvenient fact they have cast aside.

I wonder whether their lapse into agnosia counts as racial progress.

Sometimes, late at night, Mariah sits in the library and logs on to AOL—the response time is very fast, for she and Howard have invested in a T-1 line—and chats with friends around the world. I watch as instant messages pop up: in cyberspace, at least, she does not appear to be lonely, and perhaps the very anonymity of the chat room is a part of what attracts her to it. She knows a few conspiracy theorists, it seems, and although she has never told them who she is, they have shared all manner of "information" about the way the Judge "really" died. She shows me a chat room dedicated to nothing else. I try to follow the conversation, which ranges over witnesses I know were not present and evidence I know does not exist. I nod sagely and wish I could see inside her tortured brain. Mariah is pressing, her refusal to face facts intentional. She continues to babble about the autopsy, even though she knows as well as I that two pathologists and a photographic analyst hired by Corcoran & Klein agreed with the medical examiner that the specks are only dirt on the lens. Mariah tells me she has e-mailed the photographs to cyberfriends around the world. It occurs to me to ask whether any of those friends are hiding out in Argentina, but she only smiles.

Howard is home for dinner once or twice a week, and as I get to know him, I warm to him. He seems incompetent at dealing with their many children, but his complete devotion to my sister reassures me. After dinner, Howard usually works out in a room set aside for that purpose, full of all the latest equipment, and he invites me to join him. Watching him pump, I realize that Howard Denton is, after all, nothing but a grown-up child with a talent for making money. He talks about his work because he does not know what else one talks about. Mariah is plainly tired of his stories of merger fights; I find them fascinating. Listening, I remember, with more sentiment than I would have guessed, my days as a practicing lawyer. I wonder whether Kimmer and I would have married had I remained in D.C. rather than fleeing to Elm Harbor.

In my plentiful spare time, I hunt through the boxes of notes and documents Mariah has stored in one of the six bedrooms of the main house, the fruits of her many trips to Shepard Street. Almost everything is useless junk, but a couple of items catch and hold my interest. In a file she has labeled UNFINISHED CORRESPONDENCE? I discover handwritten drafts of several letters, including four efforts at a note to Uncle Mal resigning from the firm, dated around the last Thanksgiving of the Judge's life, eleven months before he died, and a fragment of a note of apology addressed only to "G"—*I do not know whether you will believe me when I tell you I am heartily sorry for the pain you have endured because of your simple and unadorned love of*—at which point the note simply stops. I show this one to my sister, who, pleased by my interest, explains that it was intended for Gigi Walker, which I do not believe for a second. I do not think Mariah believes it either. If the Judge intended to follow the *of* by *the truth* or by *justice*, the letter could as well be addressed to Greg Haramoto. But when I call his family's importing firm in Los Angeles, I am told that Greg is on an extended overseas trip and cannot be reached. I ask for his voice mail and his e-mail address. After checking with somebody, the receptionist refuses to give me either.

As we sit up watching Letterman late one night, I tell Mariah what I am thinking and she agrees, reluctantly, to share with me her own speculations: that Wallace Wainwright may have been correct, that our father wanted to get caught at whatever he was up to. Nothing else could explain why he would invite Jack Ziegler, facing trial for murder and extortion, to meet him at the federal courthouse, where, even in the dead of night, witnesses were bound to see him and records were bound to be kept. Maybe he just wanted out at any price. Maybe, says Mariah, he hoped that if he was hanged for meeting with his old roommate nobody would look deeply enough to penetrate to what was really going on. If the second was true, the grand juries that were convened probably shook him severely.

"Suppose he was fixing cases," says Mariah, sadly.

"Justice Wainwright says he wasn't," I point out, the last ray of hope.

"Justice Wainwright isn't psychic. Suppose Daddy was fixing cases and found a way to hide it from his buddy. Maybe, after the hearings, he went to Jack Ziegler and said he could not continue to do . . . whatever he was doing . . . under these conditions, and Jack talked to his partners, and they agreed to let him resign. Or maybe he resigned on his own. Either way, he finally had an out."

I consider this. "If Greg's testimony was no surprise, the letter might make sense."

My sister nods. "If it was intended for Greg, then Daddy was a superb actor. If it was intended for Gigi, well, we're better off not knowing."

True enough. But, thinking about it, I am sure Mariah is right about Greg. Then all those long nights of deep depression that Lanie Cross reported, when my father would talk about the wreck of his career, when he asked whatever happened to loyalty, he was not blaming Greg: he was blaming Jack. He allowed Greg to take the fall, in effect, but that, too, was part of the fiction. If Mariah is right, if the Judge was fixing cases for Jack Ziegler and friends after all, then to admit that Greg was telling the truth might have been the signature on his death warrant, or his family's. But that answer seems insufficiently to capture what must have been the complexity of the moment. The Judge probably wondered whether he should have given it all up, whether he did the right thing when he sabotaged his own nomination to the Supreme Court. Some of his hatred for Greg Haramoto was probably genuine.

Then the baby starts to cry, and Mariah has to run off. In the morning, she will talk of the Judge no more. How he died, she desires passionately to discover. How he lived, she would rather not know.

On the Friday, my wife drives Bentley down for a visit, explaining to me in great detail how to take care of him, the way estranged spouses do. She pecks me on the lips and pats me on the back. She oohs and aahs over little Mary, gives my sister an unwanted hug, then heads back to Elm Harbor until Sunday, perhaps to do something with Lionel, perhaps because she just needs a break. I am careful to walk away from the door, leaning heavily on my cane, before she streaks down the drive. I am relieved to have my son back in my arms at last. But he seems skittish around me, preferring to spend his time with Mariah's brood. So, instead of hugging him for hours, which is what I would like, I watch him from a distance, in the yard, in the pool, in the basement playroom, and my heart sobs.

On the Monday, with Bentley back in Elm Harbor and Mariah off at some charity event, I borrow my brother-in-law's Mercedes and drive to Borders in Stamford, where I buy enough books to keep me occupied for a while. Reading is easier than feeling. But I am planning, too. Planning my approach to Angela's boyfriend. I not only know where he is; I also see the need for extraordinary caution. Even with Colin Scott dead and Foreman dead and Maxine and her employer fooled, there is another enemy out there, the one who hired the men who beat me up.

I ask my sister to try to find out who made the offer to buy the Shepard Street house, but she meets a blank wall. Some corporation, is all the broker will say.

Over breakfast on my ninth day in Darien, Mariah tells me that she will have a second houseguest next week, a divorced woman she knows from Stanford and her sorority, a fellow journalist, a mother of two, who will be leaving her children behind in Philadelphia to make this trip: "And Sherry is a wonderful person," Mariah enthuses, "intelligent, successful, and really, really gorgeous." When my sister adds shyly that Sherry will be taking the second bedroom in the guest house, I realize that her old friend's visit is for my benefit, not Mariah's, that even though I have been separated from my wife for perhaps a month—depending on whether one counts from Kimmer's ultimatum or my release from the hospital—my sister is already trying to fix me up with somebody else. I do not know whether to be furious or charmed; I do know that it is time to go.

I tell her so.

Mariah begs me to stay longer, no doubt because I am the living proof, bullet holes and all, of her conspiracy theories. When I insist that I have to get back to work, my sister insists on helping. So she spends three days driving me all over Elm Harbor and its suburbs, looking at rentals, and giggling ostentatiously every time some silly real estate agent sees the baby in her stroller, makes the obvious assumption, and calls her "Mrs. Garland." The agents giggle right back, even though they do not get the joke. None of the condos we see strikes my fancy. One is too small, another has no view. A big one on the harbor is too expensive, and Mariah, who has been unreasonably generous already, is too wise to offer me a subsidy. One of the agents says he has something in Tyler's Landing he thinks I would like, but Tyler's Landing is Eldridge territory, and the look on my face is enough to tell him to suggest another suburb.

Lemaster Carlyle finally resolves my dilemma. He strolls into my office on the third afternoon of my fruitless search, wearing one of his perfect suits, this one a lightweight navy worsted, handmade, featuring the faintest breath of chalk stripes, along with a monogrammed blue shirt, a tie of bright marigold and cobalt blue, and matching braces—an outfit any Wall Street lawyer would be delighted to own. His confirmation hearings are next week. I am in the building for only an hour or so, checking my mail, before Mariah comes to pick me up, so he must have been looking for me. I smile and we shake hands. Lem makes no mention of the events in the cemetery. He comes right to the point. He has heard about my problem, and we can help each other out. He and Julia, it seems, own a condo on the water—in a development just down Harbor Road from Shirley Branch's, as a matter of fact. Two bedrooms, three baths, a finished basement, fine views, even if not as fine as Shirley's. It was their first home in Elm Harbor, back when Lem was a promising young professor rather than a middle-aged academic superstar, and when they moved out to Canner's Point, the market was so dead that nobody made a serious offer to buy the place; they began to rent it out, and have never dropped the habit. Their most recent tenant, a visiting professor of Christian ethics from New Zealand, left early and unexpectedly, with six months' rent unpaid. They need a tenant, I need a place to live.

"I don't know how you feel about having a colleague as a landlord," says Lem, with the good grace not to look embarrassed. "But I suppose we won't be colleagues very much longer, anyway. Besides, we can offer you a nice deal on the rent."

I am beyond shame. Losing your wife to a student does that to you. "How nice?" He names a figure, which I recognize as a substantial discount from the going rate. I do not want charity, but I do not have much money. The mortgage payment on the Hobby Hill house is deducted monthly from *my* paycheck, not Kimmer's, despite her substantially higher income, because the university's Own-in-the-City program saved us two and a half points on the interest.

"So, what do you think?" he asks.

I make a lower counteroffer, just for form, and Lem has the further good grace not to display the annoyance he surely feels.

We split the difference, and Lem hands me the key. We are lawyers, of course, one of us on the verge of judicial office and therefore ethically painstaking, so he also hands me a lease to sign. As I scribble, he continues to chatter. He and Julia, he says, want to have me over for dinner as soon as the hearings end. As it is, Julia is already planning to deliver enough casseroles to keep me eating well into the summer.

I thank him.

So now I have a place to live. My sister dutifully exclaims over it, especially the rather distant view of the water, even though she is plainly disappointed that I am leaving her guest house and missing the gorgeous and desperate Sherry. But Mariah is a good sport. We drive over to Hobby Hill to pick up more of my things, mainly books and clothes, but only during the day, when Kimmer is not around.

Don Felsenfeld and Rob Saltpeter help me load the car.

"So now you have your bachelor pad," says Don, twinkling. But I am thinking of the need to wait, impatiently but necessarily, for the right moment to visit Angela's boyfriend.

I see Bentley as much as I can, which means as much as Kimmer will let me—which turns out to be quite a lot. She talks about how much she loves our son, how much he needs her with him, but her billable hours matter too. Kimmer has no au pair, and needs none: she has me. When she is running late, she calls me to pretty please pick him up, never asking whether it is convenient. When she has to go out of town unexpectedly, she calls on no more than an hour's notice to ask if I can take him for a few nights. After all, I have nothing to do all day but recuperate from three bullet wounds, a bruised kidney, two bent ribs, and a broken jaw. Dana Worth murmurs one afternoon over lunch at Cadaver's—her treat nowadays—that I should fight Kimmer for custody. I am tempted, but the truth remains what it has been all along: custody battles are ruinous to children's lives, and I love my son too much to tear him in half.

"That's what she's counting on," Dana points out.

"Then I guess she wins this round," I snap, although my dilemma is hardly Dana's fault. Yesterday marked Bentley's birthday, which meant presents from Daddy in the afternoon, more presents from Mommy in the evening. He seemed calm, although confused; weakened by my injuries, I went home and wept.

Dana is consoling, in her way: "See, Misha? That's what the same-sex-marriage folks have wrong. Why should I *want* to go through that nonsense?" For Dear Dana is no fan of what she calls the heterosexist lifestyle.

I refuse to let Dana discourage me. My four-year-old son and I stroll on the beach, or what passes for a beach in Elm Harbor, and I cannot believe the change in him. He does seem taller. He walks with an unexpected straightness. His gaze is more direct. And Kimmer is right: he cannot stop talking. Well, he never could, but now, suddenly, he is making sense.

"Do oh Daddy look the seagull, see the seagull Daddy?"

I nod, afraid to speak. My heart seems massive, a hot, painful weight in my chest. A few months ago this was a toddler whose favorite words were *Dare you*, and we worried about whether he was a little slow, and now he is absorbing language almost faster than the world can teach it.

I spend more time at the soup kitchen. Dee Dee and I compare canes: she can tell from the sound mine makes that it is second-rate. I grow fond of the women I serve. I know that few of them will see another decade, but I begin to admire their feistiness in the face of life's many disasters, their cleverness in foraging around the edges of the welfare state for the benefit of their children, and, in many, their surprisingly strong faith. Most of the women, I finally see, truly want to love their children but do not know how. I visit Dr. Young to talk about getting some of the women into his Faith Life Skills program. He sighs. The program is nearly out of money and has no more slots available, but he tells me to send a few of them over anyway, and he will see what he can do.

"God will provide," I remind him, smiling.

"In his own good time, not ours," he corrects me.

I begin to attend Temple Baptist, and listen with a hidden smile as pudgy Morris Young, who loves ribs and fried fish, preaches on self-restraint. I go to the YMCA with Rob Saltpeter. I can no longer run the floor, and, thanks to several pulled muscles around my ribs, I can shoot only a little, but I can coach and root. Alone in my condo at night, I get in the habit of building a fire and sitting in front of it, reading.

One afternoon, limping back to Oldie from the campus bookstore, I turn in my tracks, feeling somebody's eyes on me, but I see nothing. The next day, I give Romeo from the soup kitchen twenty dollars to walk through downtown Elm Harbor a couple of blocks behind me, trying to spot a tail. Maybe, he reports when we rejoin. Maybe not.

Nothing to do but go on.

March slips into history. I return to the classroom, hobbled a bit, not able to bounce up and down as I once did, but the students seem to like me better this way. Though I am nervous, there turns out to be no cause. My fifty-seven ad law kids, who have spent the past month being lectured by Arnie Rosen, offer a standing ovation when I walk back in the door. Arnie may be brilliant, but I have been shot, which seems to lend me a special authority. So impressed are they at the sight of a professor with three bullet holes in him that they do not bother to raise any of their usual clever challenges. When I ask questions, I am rewarded by blankly adoring stares, as though they are far too awed to concentrate on the subject matter.

So I set out to cure them of the adoration, by being as strict and demanding as I used to. Eventually, they realize that getting shot rarely turns men into saints, and then we are back to our usual arrangement, in which they do not particularly like me, but work their tails off in my class. Yet I have lost a little of my force, and they seem to sense it. It is like a playlet: *You know we know you're not what you used to be*, they are telling me, smiling behind their irritation.

My faculty colleagues are more restrained. They tell me how great it is to see me, in the loud, gentle voices we use to communicate with the hard of hearing, assuring ourselves, through our volume, of our physical superiority. At meetings of the Officers, my colleagues listen to me indulgently, compliment me on my perspicacity, then rush onward to their verdict as though I have not spoken.

I stop attending.

Once or twice I see the great Lionel Eldridge slouching around the halls of Oldie, but always from a distance. He never looks in my direction. I never call his name. Nothing in my years of teaching has prepared me to deal with the situation. What becomes of the paper he owes me? Is there a special rule that applies when you are required to grade a student who has stolen your wife? I consult Dana and Rob, each of whom advises me to hand Lionel off to somebody else.

One evening, just to be on the safe side, I ask Romeo to watch my back again, and this time, having fun, he does it for free. But still nothing to report.

April plods on. Kimmer announces that she is off to visit relatives in Jamaica for a week. I protest about safety, as usual, but she does not share my fear of flying. She does not say whether Lionel is going, and I do not ask. I do not even know if he has actually left his wife: I seem to be out of the loop on the rumors, and I am afraid to ask Dana, who could surely tell me the truth. Either way, I have Bentley for seven days straight. I am excited, but Bentley is uneasy; his new circumstance, living in two houses, his family sundered, is wearing him out. He displays a short temper that has never before been a part of his personality. When I burn the chicken on the third night, he throws his plate to the floor. When I punish him, sending him to his room for a time-out, the tantrum gets worse. He says he hates me. He says he hates Mommy. He says he hates himself. I hug him hard and tell him how much I love him, how much Mommy loves him, but he fights his way free and runs, wailing, to his bed. I am confused and frightened and furious at my wife. This is the moment when good parents call their own parents for help, but I have none to call, and I would no more ask my sister for child-rearing advice than I would swim to Antarctica. In the morning I contact Sara Jacobstein, Rob Saltpeter's wife, who is a child psychiatrist affiliated with the medical school. Presuming on our friendship, I catch her at home before she leaves for work. She is very patient. She tells me that Bentley's anxiety is normal, that I have to be firm with him but also loving and supportive, and that I should under no circumstances criticize his mother in front of him. Then she warns me that, sooner rather than later, Kimmer and I must settle on one of our two residences as his home, the other as a place he regularly visits. He will need that structure in the months and years to come, she explains gently. I experience Sara's words as a physical pain in the vicinity of my heart, and I make no comment: I know what the outcome of any negotiation with Kimmer will be. Sara is above all things a kind woman. Reading my silence correctly, she offers to see Bentley this afternoon, as a courtesy to me, if I think it important.

I decide to wait.

The following morning, Meadows calls to tell me that Sharik Deveaux, street name Conan, confessed killer of Freeman Bishop, was murdered in a jailhouse brawl while awaiting sentencing. The key witness against him, the posse member turned state's evidence, has disappeared. I hang up the phone and cover my face, wishing I had done more to get Conan released, but there was no time, and my energies were directed elsewhere. I pray for his soul, although, in truth, I have little sympathy to spare just now, especially for a drug dealer with a history of violence. Still, he did not commit the particular crime to which he pled guilty, and he died in that brawl, I am certain, so that nobody would find out the truth. I even know who somehow arranged this final murder.

Colin Scott, reaching out from the grave.

(1 1 1)

MAY. June. Final exams, caps and gowns. The graduating class rewards me for my bullet holes, or maybe for losing my wife to our most famous student, by electing me the commencement speaker. I march through the ceremony with the help of a new cane, heavy and dark and quite ornately carved, a gift from Shirley Branch, who brought it back from a March vacation in South Africa with Kwame Kennerly. It looks very smart with my drab academic gown. A few weeks ago, Kwame quit working for the mayor over some matter of high principle—I forget just what—and now Shirley tells me that he has decided to run against his former boss next year.

I am too busy missing Bentley to care.

In my remarks, I tell the students to use their skills for good, not evil, and they grow restless, because it is the same speech they hear every year. So I throw away my text and lean over the lectern and warn them that when lawyers place client service ahead of virtue, people die. They applaud wildly. I tell them that if they decide that their only role is to do what their clients tell them to do, they will be part of the destruction of a great nation, dying already from our stubborn refusal to look at life as more than an opportunity to get what we want. They applaud cautiously. I talk about the proliferation of handguns and the lack of political will to do anything about it. They applaud dutifully. I talk about the proliferation of abortions and the lack of political will to do anything about it. They do not applaud, but many of their parents do. I propose that both are signs of a self-indulgence that is replacing both capitalism and democracy as the nation's true ideology. Nobody applauds, because nobody thinks I am making any sense. I tell them that they need to find a vision of a greater nation and then to work toward it, not only in their professional lives but in their personal lives. I tell them that the contemporary dichotomy between the public and the private quite overlooks the fact that it is our so-called private lives that teach our children what it means to live rightly—and that living rightly, not using law to force others to live rightly, is the definition of the life well lived. I hear polite coughing. I am boring them. I imagine myself addressing Kimmer, stating my side of our unfinished argument. I paraphrase Emerson: the world is everything that is not *me*—including not only that which is outside of me, but much that is within me. So much of life today, I point out, seems to involve counseling people to be more of what they already are. But Emerson, I warn them, had it right. Sometimes even the body, its needs and desires at war with the will, is other.

They do not know what I am talking about. They do not want to know. They want to be congratulated on their achievements and sent out into the world to self-indulge. A titter runs along the rows of gowned students and suddenly uneasy parents. The members of the graduating class see now that they made a mistake inviting me to speak, that being shot and nearly killed in the Burial Ground has made me only angrier, not wiser; I am refusing to offer them the comfort that is expected on graduation day.

I try one last time. I select a story from Exodus. I tell them how, when God fed his people in the wilderness, Moses warned them to take only what they needed. It was easy to tell who had taken too much, I remind them, because those who had extra kept it overnight, in defiance of God's instruction, and the surplus rotted and filled with maggots. I look out over the sea of fresh young faces, excellently educated, ready to file off to staff the mighty law factories of the great cities. A good chunk of them, I remind myself, have never read Exodus, and probably remember Moses as the star of an animated movie. Still, I have to try. Take only what you need, I tell them. Not simply in terms of money—they know that part of God's law already, although ninety percent of them will ignore it once they enter upon the project of remuneration, as most of us do. Also in terms of what you take from others: emotional energy, for example. Take only what you truly need in love. In family life. In your relations with your colleagues.

They are silent.

And in what you demand of yourself, I add. Take only what you need from yourself. Law is a killing profession. I cite statistics: our absurd rates of suicide, of alcoholism, of clinical depression, of divorce. Because we do not listen to the wisdom of Exodus. Because we demand, even of ourselves, more than what we really need. We look at our bodies, our energies, and we think we own them: we do not recognize, with Emerson, that they are a part of the world to be husbanded with care, to be respected, not to be misused; we think they are ours to do with what we will. And so, thinking we have been liberated, we joyfully pave the paths to our own destruction.

They do not realize that I am finished. Neither do I, until I walk back to my seat. The students applaud, but only because they are expected to. Marching off the platform, I console myself with the thought that they probably would have booed Aristotle, from whom I cribbed my central idea.

Rob Saltpeter tells me later that I was brilliant. Dear Dana Worth kisses my cheek and says it made her sad. Stuart Land barks that it was certainly different. Lem Carlyle, attending his final commencement as a member of the faculty, informs me that it was gutsy, which could mean anything. Arnie Rosen pronounces it a little bit mystical for his taste. Betsy Gucciardini murmurs that it was fascinating, campus-speak for *I hated it*. Dean Lynda, shaking my hand, says it was just fine—another negative euphemism—but asks if I couldn't have tried to be a teensy-weensy bit more upbeat. Ben Montoya warns solemnly that Biblical analogies are exclusionary and very often offensive in our increasingly diverse society. Tish Kirschbaum confides that she knows what I meant about abortion, but the way I put it is likely to give comfort to the far right. Shirley Branch suggests that I should have talked explicitly about my subtext, which, she says, is racial subordination. Ethan Brinkley smiles that it reminded him of a chat he once had with the Dalai Lama.

Marc Hadley advises me that I got the quote from Emerson wrong.

CHAPTER 55

THE ELM HARBOR
CONNECTION

"You weren't at graduation," I say to Theo Mountain the next day. We are, once more, in his office, and I am standing in the huge bay window.

"No."

"Everybody noticed. You haven't missed one in—what? Twenty years?"

"I couldn't make it," he mumbles, but this is a new, shiftier Theo. All the triumphal condescension has been drained from his manner. He sits listlessly at his desk, waiting for the ax to fall. I know perfectly well why he was not present, and he knows I know. He has been able to read the fury in my face every time I have seen him over the past two weeks. The last thing he wanted to do yesterday was sit among the faculty on the stage and worry about whose fault it was that I got shot.

"You know, Theo, you have a great view from up here."

"So I've been told."

"You can see down the alley to the Original Quad. You have a straight line almost to the edge of the campus." I turn back to face him. He is a hunched, beaten shadow. I know now why he took so long to offer his condolences on my father's passing. He was ashamed of his own actions, as well he should have been. But trying to hate him does no good. I lean heavily on my cane. The pain is bad today. Dr. Serra says I will suffer from internal aches on and off for the rest of my life.

Which, if I miscalculate over the next few weeks, may not be very long.

"Why did you do it, Theo?"

"Do what?" he asks, in an unpersuasive stab at an innocent tone.

"Why did you send me the pawns?"

Still he will not look at me. Nor will he speak. He is gazing at the photographs on his desk: one of his late wife; one of his only child, a daughter, now in her early fifties and a very senior partner at a Wall Street firm, but in the photograph a shy undergraduate; and one depicting the three Mountain brothers climbing rocks somewhere, looking tough and strong, back in the days when, together, they ruled the world of legal academia. He just shakes his head.

"Come on, Theo, talk to me. I know most of it. I want the rest of it." When he says nothing, I move around to the front of the desk. "You saw me leave Oldie that day, because you can see everything from your window. You made a pretty good guess from my route that I was headed to the soup kitchen. It was lunchtime. I was rushing. And you're the one who hooked me up with Dee Dee in the first place. And so you called whoever you called and told her to drop off the first envelope. Who was it, by the way? That you called?"

"My granddaughter," he says at last, still hunched over. "I couldn't very well trust anybody else." So simple. His granddaughter, a student at the college. Had my wits been about me, I might have figured it out. "I told her not to go inside, and to make sure to leave before you came outside," he adds, stroking his beard thoughtfully. "I told her to give it to Romeo, and to tell him she was paid. No point in having you identify her."

Or you, I am thinking.

I hobble to a chair, shove aside the papers stacked on it, and manage to sit. Anger seems to make my lingering pains that much worse. "And the other pawn? The black one?"

"That was easier. I saw you and Dana go to lunch." His gaze bounces around the room, settling briefly on my glowering face before landing on the file cabinet where, for twenty clever years, Theo hid the evidence of Marc's plagiarism. Perhaps it should have stayed there. "It didn't matter whether you got them inside the law school or outside, so I did one of each. They were supposed to arrive close together, but . . . well, for a while, I chickened out."

"Instructions from my father," I propose. Who wanted to remind me that the Double Excelsior was a chess problem, revolving around two pawns, and wanted to signal me that white moved first . . . and wanted me sufficiently intrigued to keep hunting.

"Yes," he says grudgingly. "He asked me to do this for him . . . you know, if anything ever happened to him. We were on a television show together, oh, two years ago." He focuses on me again. "He asked me while we were in the greenroom."

"But he didn't give you the pawns at that time."

"No. No, he said they would arrive when they were needed. And they did, a week or so after . . . you know, after he died." He sighs. "And, before you ask, Talcott, I'm afraid the envelope didn't have a return address."

"Was it, by any chance, postmarked Philadelphia?"

Theo Mountain's sad eyes brighten briefly. "I think it might have been Delaware."

My turn to sigh. Good old Alma, in such a hurry to get away the morning after the funeral, the pawns probably hidden in her handbag, stopping on her way home to mail them to Theo. No wonder she went off to the islands. I wonder just how many people the Judge drew into his lunatic conspiracy.

"So, when you told me you weren't close to my father at the end, when you told me he was close to Stuart, you were lying. Trying to point me in the wrong direction."

"I was trying to point you in the wrong direction, yes, but I wasn't lying." Spoken like an elected official charged with perjury. "Your father and I weren't close any more. That was true. He and Stuart *were* close. That was true, too. When your father came to me, I asked him why he didn't want Stuart to do it. He got irritated and said he didn't really trust Stuart." Theo shakes his shaggy head, regaining, for that tiny instant, his old bonhomie. "Who could blame him? Stuart would sell his granddaughter for a nice fat consulting fee."

But I see that Theophilus Mountain has not penetrated to the truth. Stuart, whatever his politics, is a better man than Theo. More direct, less underhanded. Either Stuart turned the request down flat, or the Judge guessed that he would and never bothered to ask. He came to Theo precisely because of his old teacher's byzantine love of conspiracy.

"And what about Marc Hadley?" I ask.

"What about him?" Theo echoes faintly, exhausted from pretending to be strong.

"You told me you didn't tell the White House about his plagiarism. . . ."

"I didn't, Talcott! That was true!"

"I know it was. But somebody was feeding the White House transcripts of Marc's after-dinner talks, where he floated all those crazy ideas. That was you, Theo. Okay, so you didn't have the right political views to have any influence with the current administration. But Ruthie Silverman was your student, too, just like she was Marc's. She would have listened to you."

He shrugs.

My rage boils over. "And did you ever think, Theo, did you ever think for a moment that it would boomerang on my wife? That you would wreck her chances while you were in the act of sabotaging Marc Hadley's? That you would wreck what was left of my marriage, too?"

Theo says nothing. He looks genuinely shocked. By the cost? By his discovery? I find that I no longer care. I cannot bear his presence any more, this man I so admired. I stab the Oriental carpet with my cane, push myself to my feet.

"Goodbye, Theo," I mutter, making for the door.

"I would never have done it," Theo insists, his voice climbing a couple of registers into true shrillness in his urgent effort to persuade me, "if I had known how it would turn out."

From the door, I give him a look. "Yes, you would."

CHAPTER 56

A SUMMER STROLL

(1)

THREE DAYS LATER, Sally finally agrees to see me. She has been in her rehab facility past the requisite two months and can receive visitors. The old brick house perches on a bluff overlooking the Delaware River: if you happen to be crossing the bridge from New Jersey, you can probably see it, looking like the tumbledown mansion that it is. A high brick wall surrounds the property on three sides. The fourth is the river.

Sally and I walk the lavish grounds trailed at a dozen yards or so by a male orderly and the center's chaplain, the Reverend Doris Kwan, who is present because Sally wanted her to be. The orderly is present because of some rule. Before I was allowed to see Sally, I had a talk with Reverend Kwan in her sunny office. She is a compact, muscular, imperious woman of perhaps fifty, dark hair tied back heedlessly. The air around her crackles; if she turns out to run marathons in her spare time, I will not be surprised. She has a doctorate in social work to go with her divinity degree. The diplomas hang on her walls, along with a bad reproduction of *The Last Supper*. During our brief conversation, her skeptical glare never strayed from my face. *I was against this meeting*, she told me, *but Sarah insisted*. She explained the program: two group meetings a day, four one-on-one counseling sessions a week, mandatory chapel every morning, an hour in the gym every afternoon. *We are trying to heal her mind, body, and spirit. We take faith very seriously here. Sarah is coming around, but she has a long way to go.*

I assured Reverend Kwan that I am not going to upset the program. She allowed her patent disbelief to show on her face. I wondered what Sally had disclosed in therapy.

Now, walking with Sally, I marvel at the changes in her after her months of sobriety. She is a little slimmer and a good deal more graceful. She is wearing a track suit and sandals. She says she has seen her mother a few times but misses her kids, who are not old enough to visit. Her voice is quieter, her interjections are more contemplative. She has lost a bit of her spark, which grieves me, even if there was no other choice. The dark circles under her eyes tell me how hard it has been.

"I was so worried about you when I heard," Sally murmurs. She sounds tired but calm. "I would have come to see you, you know, in the hospital, but"—a small flick of the wrist, indicating the center, the grounds, the wall.

"I'm okay."

"You're limping. You didn't use to limp."

I shrug, my heavy cane plunging ahead like an extra leg. "I'm blessed to be alive," I assure her. Then it is my turn to ask how she is doing, and we go through the same routine the other way around.

Sally tells me she has learned a lot about herself over the past few months, and likes little of what she sees. I murmur something meant to be reassuring, but Sally does not want reassurance: she wants to discover the brutal truth of what she has done to herself, to help her avoid doing it again. And she wants, she adds, to fix what she can of the damage she has caused. "I'm sorry for the things I've said to you over the years, Tal. Especially about your wife. Your ex-wife."

I make a face. "Not ex just yet."

"Give it up, Tal. You're single now. Get used to it."

"I don't want to get used to it."

"You won't have to." Sally giggles and punches my shoulder gently. The laughter sounds tinny and determined, a faint echo of the way she used to effervesce. "The sisters will *all* be coming after you, just wait and see."

"I doubt it."

"Are you kidding me? A single black man, doesn't do drugs, doesn't drink, really into kids? Sweet, goes to church, doesn't have a temper? You'll be fighting them off with a stick."

I shake my head, genuinely less interested in these possibilities than Sally and my few friends seem to think. But I play along.

"You forgot good-looking."

"I didn't *forget*. I just don't want it to go to your head." Another soft punch.

We walk on in silence through the corridor of wise old maples, Doris Kwan hovering protectively like one of Jack Ziegler's bodyguards.

Sally's smile is starting to look pasted on, and I know my visit is a strain. Whatever other demons might have been driving her, the family, my father's side, certainly helped carry her over the edge. Right now, the less she sees of us the better. We emerge into a clearing overlooking the river. We sit side by side on a wooden glider, all painted white, gazing together at the Jersey shore. A chain-link fence spoils the view, but the hospital, obviously, cannot take chances.

"You didn't come here just to see how I'm doing," Sally finally says. She sounds less censorious than regretful. She misses being loved. I wonder if she knows about Addison.

"That was the main reason."

"It's maybe one of the reasons, but it's not the main reason."

I cannot meet her eyes. Down near the fence, an older woman is holding a younger, who is sobbing. They could be mother and daughter, but I do not know which is the patient. As they embrace, a pair of attendants keep anxious watch.

"I do have another reason," I say at last.

"Okay." Now I chance a look at her, but she is keeping a close eye on the grass, her slippered toe scraping the dirt.

"I need to ask you something."

"Okay."

"Why did you take the scrapbook?"

Sally slowly raises her head, the carefully crafted half-smile still in place. Her eyes are bright but wary. They glisten with a hint of tears, or perhaps pain. "What scrapbook?" she asks, unconvincingly.

"From Shepard Street. The day after the funeral. The scrapbook with all the hit-and-run accidents in it. You took it with you when you left." I can see the image again, Sally prancing down the front walk while I spoke to the fake FBI men, her tote bag hanging gaily from her shoulder. "Why did you take it, Sally?"

At first I think my cousin is going to persist in her denial. After a moment, she whispers a single word, a tender curse: "Addison."

"Addison? What about Addison?"

"He asked me to take it."

"But why? If he wanted it, why didn't he take it himself?"

"He couldn't take it. He had that stupid poet with him." She laughs unhappily. "He . . . he called me the day after your father died. At the house. You remember? He told me to go into the study and get the book, but I went in and you were there and . . . well . . . I guess I chickened out. But after the funeral, he asked me if I had the book yet, and I said no, so he said to please get it out of the house, it was important. So I did, the next day."

I think for a moment. "There must have been something in it he didn't want anybody to see."

She nods, toe still scuffing the lawn. "That's what I thought, too."

The million-dollar question: "So, what was in it?"

Sally draws in a sharp breath. The worried Reverend Kwan, who argued against this encounter, floats at the edge of my vision. "Addison said . . . he said Mariah was going to be looking into . . . into the Judge's past. He wanted me to take the scrapbook so she wouldn't find it. Then he asked me to work with Mariah, to . . . to keep an eye on her. To let him know whatever she found."

I can easily picture my brother manipulating poor Sally this way; her crush on him, as everybody in the family knows, never quite vanished. Watching my cousin as she sits here remembering and aching, I wonder whether the sexual side of their relationship really ended as long ago as everybody thinks, but I push the unworthy thought away, because it would be too easy to start hating him. Addison probably knows more about what is going on than the rest of us put together, but he has taken his knowledge with him to South America.

I must tread carefully now, asking my questions in the right order. "So he never told you what was in the scrapbook?"

"Never even mentioned it again. Had me on a *string*." The smile is gone.

Gently, gently: "And he also asked you to take Mariah's ledger, I guess. The one where she wrote down her notes when the two of you were in the attic? So he could read it?"

"I took that on my own. I wanted to impress him, if you can believe it. I was afraid Mariah would guess where it went, but she never did."

"And did it impress him?"

She shakes her head. "I called him up and told him, I was all excited, but he didn't even want it. All he ever cared about was the scrapbook."

"But why did Addison care so much, Sally? Did he say what he was worried about?"

The answer is a long time coming, as though even now she is working out how much to tell me. Worried that Doris Kwan might cut off the interview at any instant, I fight the urge to beg Sally to rush. "He told me . . . he said your father had done something terrible, a long time ago. And he said . . . he said if people found out he could get into trouble."

"Who could get into trouble? The Judge?"

"Addison."

"*Addison* could get into trouble?"

"Who do you *think?*" Somehow her voice has grown screechy.

"I just meant—"

"Who else would he ever worry about?" A strangled sob. "What a bastard! He made me lie for him, he made me steal for him, he turned me into a little spy! And he treated me like a whore! He *always* did! That bastard! I hate him!"

"Sally—"

She shoves at me. "You're *all* bastards! All you Garlands! You didn't love *me!* You loved each other and you loved yourselves, but you never loved my father and you never loved *me!*"

Reverend Kwan is beside us. "I think we're through here," she says firmly, drawing an unresisting Sally to her feet, and away from me.

"Wait," I protest, wanting to repair all her misconceptions, to assure her that I am one of the good guys.

"You have to go, Professor. Your cousin has been through enough."

"But I need to tell her—"

She shakes her head, putting her trim body between us. She has already handed Sally off to a female attendant who materialized from somewhere. The male orderly stands next to the good Reverend, the two of them an impenetrable barrier. Mariah and Howard have paid for the best. "I understand that you are in pain, Professor, that you, too, are suffering. But you cannot make your cousin the instrument of your deliverance. Sarah is a human being, not a tool. She has already been used by far too many people. She has been used up."

(I I)

THE REST OF WHAT I HAVE TO DO makes me feel grubby, but at least I am doing something. From a pay phone, I call Mariah in Darien, and ask her for Thera Garland's address and phone number, which, in the fashion of the men of the family, I do not seem to have written down anywhere. My sister is inquisitive, but she meets the brick wall I learned from the Judge how to build, and finally subsides and tells me what I want to know, exacting in return a promise to share "all the juicy details" later on. My sister still believes in the conspiracy and will be happy to fit into her model whatever I happen to be looking for.

Thera lives in Olney, Maryland, about fifteen miles north of Washington, and the drive from the hospital is less then two hours. Because of my bad leg, I ache all the way down. I stop twice, but I do not call until I am in the area, because I do not want to give her the chance to say no. Sally was Thera's only child, and her mother is fiercely protective of her—too protective, probably, because she has often shielded her daughter from the consequences of her own bad habits. Family legend says Thera has even lied to the police a time or two, and once committed insurance fraud to cover for the true driver in a car wreck.

Thera's unenthusiasm deadens her voice. I tell her I want to see the kids, which is true but incomplete. Although openly reluctant, she eventually yields to the inevitable and tells me to come over. She gives me directions to her condo, near the center of town.

I thank her and rush back to my car.

I am pursuing Thera on a simple theory: I have to get into Sally's apartment. Sally said Addison asked her to take the scrapbook. She also said he never mentioned it to her again, because he had her on a string. That he had her on a string can only mean he knew she would do what he asked. So, when she said he never mentioned it, she meant he never even asked if she had taken the book.

Which means she never gave it to him.

When I reach the sprawling development where Thera lives, I pause at the head of the driveway, letting the traffic pass me, for I have felt again that cool, alarming sense of being watched. But none of the cars behind me even slows down to see where I am going, so it is probably my imagination.

I ring the doorbell, and there is Thera, massive and dark, looking much like the barricade she always tried to build around Sally. She has Sally's fire, but uses the energy it generates to intimidate rather than to charm. She does not seem happy to see me, and I can hardly blame her: the Garlands, at least the men, have not been kind to her daughter. She is wearing loose jeans and a white blouse, and Sally's two shy children, ages seven and eight, are peering anxiously from behind their grandmother's strong legs.

"Hello, Thera."

She nods unpleasantly, then steps aside and sweeps me grandly into the small foyer. I stand on the blue ceramic tiles, which match the pale walls. In the front hall hang pictures: a black Jesus, a white Jesus. On the opposite wall are photographs: Derek, Malcolm X, Martin Luther King. Derek's is the largest. I lean over to shake hands with Sally's children, who goggle hopefully. When they ascertain that I have not brought them anything—an egregious omission in a relative they rarely see—they run off into the house to play.

"What's it been, Talcott? Four years? Five?"

"Something like that. I'm sorry, Thera."

Thera grunts what might be forgiveness. She leads me to the kitchen, where we sit on opposite sides of the counter drinking tea. A Bible is open on the Formica. Beside it is a book by Oswald Chambers. Next to the window hangs needlepoint: AS FOR ME AND MY HOUSE, WE WILL SERVE THE LORD. Thera sits there, seventyish and somber and strong, surrounded by her faith, worried sick about her daughter, wondering, maybe, why Sally seems to have more of her father than of her mother in her. Except, to hear Just Alma tell it, Thera, too, was a bit wild in her day.

"What do you want, Talcott?" This part of Thera's personality, this emotional honesty, she has indeed passed on to her daughter. Neither one of them is any good at pretending to feel what she does not, or at hiding what she is thinking. "You didn't come all this way just to see Rachel and Josh, so don't tell me that lie."

"I went to see Sally this afternoon."

Something moves in her face, and her voice grows less gruff. "How was she?"

"She's still having a hard time."

"I *know* that. What I mean is, how did she treat you?"

The question surprises me, both perspicacious and mean. I choose a diplomatic tone. "We apologized to each other."

Thera has no patience with euphemisms. "Oh, yeah? How come? Were you screwing her, too?"

An instant's silly panic. "No, no, please don't think that. No, of course not."

"Your family hasn't been good to her, Talcott." *Your* family. Thera herself was only married into it. And bore Sally before joining up.

"I know."

"You shouldn't have gone." A beat. Perhaps she decides to forgive me. "So, okay, why did you go?"

I have had time to think about how to answer this. "Thera, I can't tell you everything. I wish I could, but I can't. But Sally was . . . She and my sister have been looking into what happened to my father. I didn't want to disturb her, but there was a question I realized only she could answer. I went there to ask her."

Thera seems amused. She takes a sip of tea. Her massive hand swallows the cup. I cannot tell whether she believes me. "And did you get the answer?"

"Yes. Yes, I did." She waits. I hear the children whooping in the next room. Time to bite the bullet. "Thera, I have to get into Sally's apartment."

"What, you think I'm just gonna give you the key?"

"It's important. I wouldn't have driven all the way down here otherwise."

"What's important? What are you looking for, Talcott?"

"There's something . . . something I think Sally has hidden in the apartment. Something that came from my father's house. I need to find it."

"You're saying she stole something?"

I shake my head emphatically. "I think she was trying to help. I think she . . . thought she was doing the right thing by hiding it."

Thera's eyes narrow. "Help who? Your brother, right?"

"Why do you say that?" I fence.

"Because when she was crying for days before she . . . before she tried to do herself in? She kept talking about your brother and what he had done to her." A moment while we think that one over. Her next question takes me by surprise, but it is a mother's question: "Is the thing you want the reason she had her breakdown?"

"I don't know. I think it might be . . . a part of the reason."

"If you find it, will you take it away with you?"

"Yes, I think so."

"And that's why you want the key? So you can find it and take it away?"

"Yes."

"Wait here."

Thera trudges off down the hall. I hear her asking the children to quiet down. She is back a moment later with a shopping bag. "I think this is what you want, Talcott."

She hands it to me. I look inside. I see my old raincoat, the one I loaned Sally the morning she snuck out of the Hilton. I turn toward Thera, on the verge of explaining that this is not what I am worried about at all, that I still need that key, when I realize that the bag is heavier than it should be. I delve once more and discover, at the bottom of the sack, Mariah's missing ledger. I am about to protest that this still is not what I need. Then I unfold the coat and find, wrapped inside, the blue scrapbook.

"Get that devilish thing out of here," Thera orders me. "I knew it was from Satan the moment Sally brought it in. Can't you feel it?" She shudders, wrapping her arms around her chest. "I should have burned it. It's ruined too many lives already."

(I I I)

I HAVE NOT COME THIS FAR to grow impatient. Like my brother, I do not really care about the ledger, for it holds no secrets any longer. Only the blue scrapbook draws me. But I do not look at it, not at first. Instead, I head north again, quickly reaching I-95. I zip along for another hour, watching the rearview mirror, wishing Maxine were here to advise me. But maybe she is. I finally stop at a standard-issue motel in Elkton, just inside the Maryland border, to spend the night. Dinner is a chicken sandwich from McDonald's, after which I settle down at the not-quite-wooden table in the spartan room, fighting to concentrate through the reek of disinfectant. From the shopping bag I pull my ancient green coat, so badly wrinkled that the dry cleaner may not be able to rescue it.

Then I remove the blue leather scrapbook and center it on the table. A thing of the devil.

I remember the day I discovered it, the Friday after my father died, and my panic when I thought poor Sally might see it. Even then, instinct told me it was better that it not see the light of day.

Well, now it is night, and I can open it and try to figure out what frightened Sally so thoroughly that, added to the other, obscene pressures from my side of the family, she tried to take her life. So, once again, I flip through the nasty pages, the catalogue of deaths of others than my baby sister, every one a hit-and-run, every one a tragedy for some family somewhere: all of these people, I am sure, were loved.

Ugly, yes. But what were Sally's words?

I don't know why he had to get them both. That's what Sally said just before she took the pills. Paula, her Alcoholics Anonymous sponsor, assumed Sally was talking about me, because she also kept saying, *Poor Misha.* But maybe she didn't mean me. Maybe somebody else *had to get them both.*

I have made it all the way through the album again. The last pages are blank, because the Judge stopped collecting the clippings after he got well. But how did he get well? What led to the sudden change in attitude that my siblings and I remember so keenly?

I flip back to the last clipping, the final item my father pasted into the book before he stopped. Like all the others, this one is a story of a

THE EMPEROR OF OCEAN PARK

hit-and-run accident. Phil McMichael, I record, Dana's old boyfriend and the son of the Judge's old friend Senator Oz McMichael, run over in his Camaro by a tractor-trailer rig.

So? An interesting coincidence, but so what?

One of my father's crabbed annotations is in the margin. It takes me a moment to decipher it. Then I have it: *Excelsior.*

Excelsior?

Not a chess problem, but a page in a scrapbook? Or both?

Wait a minute. *Had to get them both.*

I begin to read the article, trying to figure this out. The first line of the third paragraph is underlined. *Ironically, Mr. McMichael's fiancée, Michelle Hoffer, was killed in a similar accident three months ago. . . .*

My fingers are sweating as I fumble my way to an earlier page where, sure enough, I find a picture of Michelle Hoffer, daughter of some other wealthy family, dead in a hit-and-run accident. And, right in the margin, the same word: *Excelsior.*

The Double Excelsior.

The folks in the car.

The folks. A driver and a passenger.

I can see Sally, sitting up in her apartment night after night, study-ing the scrapbook, trying to figure out why Addison wanted her to take it, waiting for Addison to call, which he never did. One day she hits upon the translation of the Judge's cryptic handwriting and she soon understands the whole mess. And wishes she didn't. So what does she do? She gives the book to her mother, trying to get it out of her life, trying to get the Garlands out of her life for once and all, but it isn't enough. She knows what my brother is hiding, and what the Judge did, and, in her fragile emotional state, she tumbles right over the edge.

No wonder the police did nothing about Abby's death. Back in those days, nobody was about to go after the son of the most powerful Sena-tor on the Hill. Certainly not for running over a black girl who had been smoking pot and was driving without a license in the middle of a rainstorm in a car that wasn't even hers. Nobody would touch this case.

Nobody except Oliver Garland.

Nobody except Colin Scott.

And it wasn't just vengeance, an eye for an eye. There were two people in the car that killed Abby, and the Judge decided in his madness that he had to get them both.

CHAPTER 57

SOME PIECES ARE
TRADED OFF

(1)

WITH THE ACADEMIC YEAR OVER, our small city of Elm Harbor is empty once more. Or seems to be. In the summer, not only do the students and faculty disappear, but even the year-round residents seem to withdraw to some hidden refuge, as though they do not have jobs to attend to, buses to ride, checkout counter lines to fill. I stay away from the law school. I am puttering again, arranging my condo, trying to make it livable. I play a little chess online, listen to a little music, write a little scholarship. Swallowing my terror of flying, I visit John and Janice Brown in Ohio for a couple of days, but their family is too happy for me to bear for very long. I still talk to Mariah two or three times a week, but we have little left to talk about. I do believe she is in touch with Addison, but she will never tell me if I am right.

I am waiting. I have set out criteria for action, and the criteria have not yet been met, so I am forcing upon myself a patience unfamiliar to my nature. I begin to keep a close watch on the weather reports, hoping for a hurricane, because only a hurricane will allow me to act.

I continue to gather information. One morning I wander over to the law school library to look up a name in Martindale-Hubbell, the national legal directory. That same day I lunch with Arnie Rosen, to ask him a tricky question about legal ethics. The next evening I attend a dinner party at the home of Lem and Julia Carlyle—shortly to be Judge and Mrs.—out in the suburbs, but when I realize that the only other single person there is a smart, pretty black woman a decade younger than I am, the noon anchor on the local news, and that my well-meaning hosts have seated us together, I make my excuses and depart early. She is probably wonderful, but I am far from ready.

Two days later, a group of conservative activists launches a public campaign for an investigation into "unresolved questions" surrounding the "tragic and suspicious" death of Judge Oliver Garland. Cringing, I watch the press conference on CNN, but only long enough to ascertain that no member of the family is involved; it pains me greatly, however, to see, in the midst of the crowd of conspiracy-hunters, the somber face of Eddie Dozier, Dana's former husband. As a onetime law clerk to the Judge, and a member of the darker nation into the bargain, he is a shining trophy for the group, and they display him right in the front row. I steel myself for a barrage of press inquiries, in response to which I intend to make no comment, but few reporters bother to call. My father, dead eight months, is very old news, and not even my old friend Eddie, who worshipped him, can bring him back to life.

At the end of June, I drive up to Woods Hole and ferry over to the Vineyard, my first visit since January. I take a few days to open up the house for the season—no vandalism this time—then return to Elm Harbor, by arrangement with Kimmer, to get my son. Back to Oak Bluffs again for three glorious weeks with Bentley, during which I treat him to absolutely everything I can. We spend hours riding the Flying Horses in the mornings, and hours playing on the beach in the afternoons. We eat every kind of fudge. We go to the playground every day. We walk the cliffs of Gay Head and the marshes of Chappaquiddick. We go to story time at the public library. We build a huge sand castle at the Inkwell. We wait in line at Linda Jean's. We rent bikes and I begin teaching my son to ride a two-wheeler, but he is only four and, in the end, the training wheels stay on. We consume enough ice cream to fatten an army. I buy him sweatshirts and hats and toys. I buy him his first pair of deck shoes, and he wears them everywhere. This does not represent the usual spoiling of the child of estranged parents of means; I am not, at this moment, in competition with Kimmer for our strange, marvelous son's affections; it is just that my unfinished business remains unfinished, and sooner or later I will have to finish it, and it may finish me first.

In short, I am afraid I am never going to see him again.

Kimmer calls to see how our son is doing, and also to tell me how happy she is. She seems to think I will be glad for these tidings. Mariah calls with the news that Howard is moving to another investment bank, where he will be vice-chairman and heir apparent. Just for moving, she confides, he will receive a bonus in the middling eight figures, although he will be required to plow much of it back into the firm's capital. Not sure what response is expected, I tell Mariah I am happy for them. Listening to my sister's joy, I wonder what *middling* means. I recall the line from *Arthur:* "How does it feel to have all that money?" "It feels great." Something like that. Certainly Mariah *sounds* great, and she does not mention autopsy photographs once.

Morris Young calls with a list of Bible reading assignments.

I make a point of perusing no newspapers from the mainland. I never watch the news and rarely listen to it. I want to live in a tiny, impossible world that includes just my son and myself, and also my wife, if she would only return.

Pathetic.

Lynda Wyatt phones, effusive. "I don't know what you said to Cameron Knowland, Tal, but he's not giving us three million for the library any more! He's giving us six! He doubled his gift! And you know what else Cameron said? He said that his son is a spoiled brat and it's about time one of his teachers straightened him out! He asked me to pass along his thanks. So, thanks, Tal, from Cameron, and also from me. As always, I am so grateful for everything you do for the school, and congratulations. You have the makings of a dean, Tal!"

Great. My academic standing is obviously on the ascendancy again, not because I have developed a stunning new theory in my field, but because I seem to be helping the Dean raise money, and lots of it. I do not mention to Lynda the flaw in her hearty analysis: I never got around to trying again to reach Cameron Knowland. The knowledge would only upset her. I will never be sure, but I will always suspect, that behind the doubled gift, possibly even supplying the cash, is the fine, mischievous hand of Jack Ziegler, who even now protects the family. I hope this doesn't mean I owe him a favor.

Dear Dana Worth calls with the news that Theo Mountain, her Oldie neighbor, has decided to retire. She is not reluctant to say it is high time. I share this sentiment, even though I do not tell her how glad I am, or why. I suggest that it will give him more time to spend with his granddaughter. But Dana has more to tell. She knows, it seems, how the plagiarism story got out. She has teased patiently out of Theo the fact that one more professor at the law school knew about what Marc had done. I see it coming before she is done.

"Stuart?"

"Bingo."

Of course. Stuart Land was the dean when Marc published his book.

Maybe Marc went to Stuart after Theo came to him; maybe Theo brought Stuart in. Either way, it would have been Stuart who brokered the deal to keep Theo quiet, for the good of the school. It might even have been Stuart who extracted, in return for Theo's silence, Marc's promise never to write another interesting word. No wonder Stuart tried to get me to persuade Kimmer to drop out! He wanted Marc to have that judgeship because he could no longer stand having Marc around to remind him of what he had done. And no wonder Marc was involved in the cabal that threw him over! Oh, what a tangled web . . .

"You can't trust anybody around this place," Dana chortles.

"Except you."

"Maybe me. Maybe not. This place is a regular den of iniquity." Another snicker. "You sure you want to come back?"

"No," I tell her honestly, although the other half of the truth is that I have nowhere else to go.

Walking along the Inkwell with Bentley half an hour later, watching the financially advantaged of the darker nation at play, I fill in the rest of the story for myself. Theo told me that the Judge would have known Lynda Wyatt from his service on various alumni committees. But that service took place mostly under Stuart's deanship, before my father's fall. Stuart, not Lynda, was the Judge's friend. Stuart might at some point have shared with him the story of Marc's plagiarism; might even have consulted him from the beginning. For all I know, the final deal between Theo and Marc could have been my father's idea. Either way, the Judge could have turned around and mentioned it to Jack Ziegler, maybe in passing, perhaps forgetting that Uncle Jack would catalogue every misdeed of every person of prominence on whom he could get his hands. Which would explain how Uncle Jack knew.

Bentley is chasing seagulls, his arms outstretched as though he, too, can fly. I keep turning the facts over in my mind, seeking another fit. Jack Ziegler, I remind myself, is a man of his word. He said he would not interfere with my wife's nomination, so I have to believe—*have* to believe—that Stuart, not Jack, tipped off the White House about Marc's plagiarism. Because the alternative is too horrible to contemplate. I do not want to think of what might have happened had Kimmer reached her goal, of how Jack Ziegler, or some surrogate, would one day have marched into her chambers and told her who got her the job, as well as who protected her family in a dangerous time, and what her new responsibilities were, and what would be revealed to the world if she tried to shirk. Turning her into the Judge's successor.

I tremble for the wife I still adore, and am suddenly thankful that Kimmer failed.

(I I)

I DO NOT KNOW why the telephone will not leave me in peace. I field two calls from the law firm where I have been consulting, and one from Cassie Meadows, with the news that the Bureau has no leads on the second gunman, but I do not need the Bureau to tell me who it was. Then Cassie whispers that Mr. Corcoran is worried sick about me.

"Good," I tell her.

"Try to see it from his point of view. . . ."

"No, thanks."

"But, Misha . . ."

"I know he's your boss, Cassie, and you look up to him. But I think he's a liar and a sneak." Surprised, she asks what I mean, but I am too worked up to explain.

Calls from the Registrar, reminding me to grade the rest of my ad law exams, and calls from two literary agents, asking if I want to do a book.

Shirley Branch phones, but she does not have any news. Mainly, she says, she just wants to see how I am doing. And to tell me how much she still misses Cinque, her vanished terrier. I ask after Kwame. She sings his praises for a few minutes, exults about how no other mayoral candidate can save the city, although she does not specify what it needs saving from. Then she sighs heavily and confesses that Kwame is so busy campaigning for the role of municipal savior that they really do not see much of each other any more. Oddly cloying, the significance, when you are lonely, of hints so faint and tiny they may not be hints at all.

But most of my attention is still lavished on Bentley. I teach him to fly a kite, badly, and how to swim, reasonably well. We check out a stack of beginner's books from the public library at the top of Circuit Avenue; we might as well get started on reading, too. As we walk back toward Ocean Park, Bentley carrying most of the books like the big boy he is all at once becoming, I wheel in my tracks, sensing unwanted attention, but the sleepy side street lined with tumbledown Victorians seems no different on this sunny July afternoon than on any other, and if people are watching me, I will never pick them out.

Bentley, eyes wide, asks if I am okay.

I ruffle his hair.

In the middle of our second week on the Vineyard, a nor'easter batters the island, and we lose electricity for nearly two days. Bentley is chipper, not at all bothered by the darkness of early evening as we eat supper by candlelight. For my son it is all an adventure. Now that he has some command of the language, he is storing up memories fast, and even talking about events that apparently occurred before he could speak. I allow him to sleep in my bed—no, I *require* him to—and, watching my son's peacefully slumbering brown face before I blow out the ancient hurricane lamp I found in the attic, I marvel at how a few short months can change everything. For, if this were January instead of July, I would have fled from the Island rather than risk a night without electric lights—and without an alarm system to warn me if the dangers lurking in the shadows draw too close to the house. But those fears died down in the Old Town Burial Ground with Mr. Scott, even if the mysteries that generated them did not. I lie awake, thinking of Freeman Bishop and Agent Foreman— really an agent, even if not really a Foreman—and marvel at God's providence. *Your sons will take the place of your fathers*, says Psalm 45. The thought of Bentley as my successor on earth fills me with awe and hope.

Protect the family, Jack Ziegler instructed me. Well, I'm doing my best. Only there is more left to do.

On Bentley's last day with me, we picnic boldly at Menemsha Beach, watching the sun drop beneath the most beautiful horizon on the East Coast. The same beach where Mr. Scott drowned another poor soul so we would think he was dead. I dare any of the ghosts of the past nine months to show themselves. Sitting on the blanket, I hold my boy so close that he begins to squirm. I cannot seem to let go. My eyes fill. I recall the night he was born, how both he and Kimmer almost died. My terror after the doctors forced me from the delivery room. The joy we felt when it was over, both of us, mother and father, on our knees praying for our son, making all the promises to God that people hardly ever keep after they get what they want. I catch myself wondering how it all slipped away, and that is when I know it is time to go home.

The next morning, I pack up the car, and Bentley and I sit in the short standby line for the early ferry. It is time to return Bentley to his mother; to his home. And time, finally, for me to confront my demons.

CHAPTER 58

A PLAUSIBLE ACCOUNT

MALLORY CORCORAN'S SUMMER PLACE is a wrecked farm sprawling over two hundred acres near Middlebury, Vermont: a restored
eighteenth-century clapboard house, half a dozen outbuildings, plenty
of meadows rented to locals to graze cattle, and tangled woods where
Uncle Mal likes to hunt. The farm is not difficult to find—it almost
jumps at you, spreading across the road, as you head down Route 30
toward Cornwall. I have not been here since I was a second-year law
student, when he invited me for Memorial Day weekend, while also
entertaining the Secretary of State and a couple of Senators. I suppose
he was trying to recruit me—*Someday this all could be yours!*—and it
might even have worked, except that his friendship with my father
already scared me, even if I did not, yet, know all its dimensions.

We sit on aging bentwood rockers on the front porch, lawyer and
client, sipping lemonade, while Edie plays with a couple of grandchildren and a horde of dogs and cats out in what real New Englanders call
the dooryard. Uncle Mal is wearing dirty jeans, work boots, and a
checked shirt: very much the gentleman farmer, or what a Washington
lawyer trying to be one looks like. I am in my usual summer attire of
khakis and windbreaker. My cane lies on the floor next to me, guarded
by another of the many huge dogs they keep, but I want Mallory Corcoran keenly aware of its existence.

"How much have you figured out?" he asks when we have exhausted
the small talk.

"I know you left the note at Vinerd Howse."

"Not me. Meadows." He smiles without apology.

"That's why you had her sit in that first time. She was already
involved."

"She was already involved," he agrees. "But we had to do it the way we did it. We were carrying out the last wishes of our client. Your father. He left us one of those, 'In-case-anything-happens-to-me-open-this' letters."

I remember the morning I left Aspen. "And he gave you the code to turn off the alarm at Vinerd Howse. So nobody would be the wiser." Uncle Mal nods. But I am confused. "So why didn't he just have you tell me what he wanted me to know? Why all this crazy rigamarole?"

Mallory Corcoran sips his lemonade, strokes another large dog between the ears as it rumbles at his side. He is not intimidated by me. He was not reluctant to see me. By his own lights, he acted honorably and has nothing to hide. "I think your father wanted you to know some things, but I am not sure he wanted to put them into ordinary language. I think he was . . . he was afraid that somebody else would come across it. So he made his arrangements and then hid them where only you could find them."

"A year ago," I murmur.

"I would say, almost two years."

I nod. "It'll be two years this October since he gave you the letter."

Uncle Mal is too savvy a lawyer to ask me immediately how I figured this out. But he does not know the story I heard from Miles Madison, my father-in-law.

"That sounds right," says Mallory Corcoran, still playing with the dog.

I nod. Earlier this summer, I consulted with my colleague Arnie Rosen, an expert in professional responsibility, who explained over lunch that an attorney's obligation survives the death of a client. The lawyer may no longer act in the name of the client, of course, but should generally carry out any deathbed instructions, as long as they propose nothing illegal or outside the scope of the lawyer's duties, and as long as the client is in his right mind. If what is asked seems wrong, the lawyer might try to dissuade the client or might even refuse to do it; but, if the lawyer accepts the task, the obligation exists. In other words, what Mallory Corcoran did in delivering the Judge's letter to Oak Bluffs was within his ethical responsibility to my father—whatever its twisted morality.

Why was it necessary to trash the first floor of Vinerd Howse? I ask. Or to break the glass?

He shrugs. "To make sure that you would be the only one to venture upstairs and find the note. Your father's idea."

"Meadows did that, too?"

"I didn't ask for the details."

"What if I had just waited for the police before going upstairs?"

"I don't know. I suppose they would have found the note and given it to you. The same if the caretaker—can't remember his name—had been the first one to find it. I must confess, however, I'm not sure your father considered the possibility that Kimberly might see it before you did. I suppose it all could have gone wrong. Or maybe he just figured you were too much a gentleman to send your wife to check upstairs after a break-in."

I cannot tell whether I am being complimented or mocked, so I drop the subject and, instead, ask the first of the two questions that brought me to Mallory Corcoran's dooryard. "Did you know what my father was doing? Why he left you the note?"

"Let me anticipate. You are asking me whether I know what his arrangements were, or exactly why he wanted you to know whatever he wanted you to know. The answer, Talcott, is no. I'm afraid I didn't know. I still don't."

"Do you know why he chose me and not Addison?"

This time the answer is longer in coming. "It was my impression that your brother was . . . oh, out of favor."

"Out of favor?"

"Your father seemed to think your brother had betrayed him."

This one puzzles me. But one look at Mallory Corcoran's super-lawyer face tells me I will get no more. So I ask the second question: "Did you know what was really going on? Between my father and Jack Ziegler?"

He has his answer ready. He has probably had it ready since the day the housekeeper called the firm to say the Judge was dead: "Your father was my partner and my friend, Talcott, but he was also a client. You know it is impossible for me to divulge what he told me in confidence."

"I take that as a yes."

"You should not construe it either way. You should not assume anything."

"Well, I'm your client, too. That means you have to keep my secrets."

"True."

"All right. Let me speculate for a moment." Uncle Mal is a statue. "I don't know exactly what my father and Uncle Jack were up to, but I know they were up to something. I don't know how much of it you guessed, but I don't think he would have told you very much, because . . . well, because he craved your respect." *And didn't quite trust you,* I think but do not say, for I am pouring on the butter here. *The Judge didn't fully trust you, which is the real reason he gave you only that one cryptic note and hid his arrangements someplace else.* "But I'd like to tell you what I think happened."

"I'd be very interested in hearing that, Talcott."

And so I tell him. I tell him I think at first it was reasonably innocent. Probably the Judge went to Jack Ziegler to find a private investigator, and Jack Ziegler recommended Colin Scott because Scott had been a colleague at the Agency and needed work. I doubt that my father was, at first, looking for a hired killer. Perhaps Jack Ziegler meant to put temptation in his path. Perhaps it just came together at the right moment. Either way, when my father received Scott's report, he decided not to share it with the police.

"Why not?"

"Because of who it named." But there is nothing in Uncle Mal's experienced face to tell him whether the Judge shared that particular truth. For my part, I have not shared it with Dear Dana—and never will.

Instead of going back to the police, I continue, the Judge asked Scott to kill the driver of the car. Scott refused. That was the argument overheard by Sally and Addison: *No rules where a daughter is concerned,* my father argued, or begged.

"And so my father went back to Jack Ziegler," I continue. He went to see Uncle Jack and asked him to use his influence with Scott, or to find somebody else to do it. Maybe Jack Ziegler was surprised. Maybe he was not. From what I have read, he has always possessed a remarkable capacity to seduce others into wrong. I suspect he would have started by tossing out objections, warning my father that he had no earthly idea what he was getting into, because he knew his old friend well enough to understand that, having started down the road into the other world, he would hardly turn back just because that other world turned out to have all the deadly features he expected. On the contrary, objections of that nature would draw him further in. My father would have pressed on, insisting that he wanted the driver of the car dead. He likely said he would pay any price, he did not care what obligations he undertook, he wanted justice done. Perhaps that was the moment when he asked Jack Ziegler to make a single promise to him: that, if anything happened to him, to my father, as a result of this mess, he, Jack, would see to it that his family never came to any harm. And he trusted Uncle Jack's word, because, as Agent Nunzio told me, his word was what Jack Ziegler lived by.

"You're guessing," says Mallory Corcoran, his unease growing, for I am speculating aloud now on the wrongs of two of his former clients, not one.

"I know. But it hangs together." He offers no disagreement, so I resume. Somehow, sooner or later, Jack Ziegler agreed to intercede, and went for permission to whoever makes such decisions in his world. A deal was consummated. Scott would do the killing. There would be no charge, just as there had been no charge for his investigative services. Instead, from time to time, the Judge would be asked for little favors. Nothing obvious: no votes to overturn the conviction of a Mafia don or a drug lord. Instead, he would be called upon to help out the companies in which illegal monies were invested. Throwing out a burdensome or expensive regulation. Overturning an antitrust verdict.

"That's why my father's voting record got more conservative after Abby died," I explain, with real pain. "Why he struck down so many regulatory schemes. He was covering his favors with a show of ideological purity."

"You're still guessing, Talcott."

"Yes, I am. But I can hardly go interview Jack Ziegler to check my facts." I hope he will offer to intercede, for Uncle Jack has returned neither of my calls since the cemetery, but the great Mallory Corcoran continues to sit, waiting to be impressed. Nothing has provoked a response. I know he can see my frustration, but it fails to move him.

I ponder. From what Wainwright told me, it is plain that the Judge felt burdened by his perfidy. He had ascended to the bench to do justice, not to remain in thrall forever to criminals. No doubt the special favors went on and on and on. Perhaps, as illegal money found its way into legal businesses, the pace increased. Who knows what stocks are in the Mob's portfolio? When the Supreme Court nomination suddenly came his way, Jack Ziegler's partners were surely ecstatic. My father was surely worried. Maybe the truth would come out, and he would be ruined. And then perhaps he had another idea. Maybe the truth *should* come out, and he could escape the hell into which he had sold himself.

"Which is where Greg Haramoto comes in," I say, but the words prompt no reaction. "I tried to talk to Greg, but he wouldn't."

Uncle Mal, a ghostly smile of reminiscence on his lips, finally makes an independent contribution: "I'm not surprised, the way your sister talked about him on television back during those very sad hearings. What was it she accused him of?"

"Of having a crush on the Judge."

"That's right. You know, people don't forget things like that, Talcott."

"I'm not criticizing Greg. I just want you to understand that I'm still just guessing."

"I never doubted it." He is on his feet, and I know the interview is over. "Everything you have said is guesswork. You can't know for sure if any of it is true."

"I realize that." We are walking toward my car. I had thought he would invite me to stay for lunch, but Uncle Mal has his ways, and his vacation time is sacrosanct. I suppose I should be grateful he has spared me this precious half-hour from whatever it is that big lawyers do when they own farms in the country. I cannot quite envision him milking a cow, although I seem to recall that he has a dairy herd hidden somewhere.

Uncle Mal is holding the door for me. "You know, Talcott, guessing is not always a terrible thing. Sometimes I do a little guessing of my own."

I stand very still, not daring to look at him. Around the side of the house, Edie and the kids are singing a song. The cats and dogs, most of them hideously fat, are now somnolent in the summer sun.

"I would guess that some of what you say could be true." His voice is soft, and a little sad. "Could be, Talcott, could be. And I would also guess that, when your father came to me and left me his letter and told me about the arrangements, he told me he was thinking of quitting the firm. If I were a guessing man, I would speculate that he was scared, that something out of his past had caught up with him. He wasn't scared of death, I don't think. If I had to guess, I would say he was scared of exposure. Something was going to come out."

I turn around finally. "The arrangements . . . all this . . . wasn't this about exposure?"

"On his own terms."

"What are you telling me?"

The weatherproof smile. "I'm not telling you anything, Talcott. You know I would never disclose a confidence. I'm only speculating."

"Okay . . . so what are you speculating?"

"I am speculating that your father was planning to hide the information he wanted you to have, and then commit suicide."

CHAPTER 59

ON THE OTHER HAND . . .

"THAT'S THE MOST RIDICULOUS THING I've ever heard," says Dear Dana Worth.

"What is?"

"That your father would commit suicide."

I shrug. "That's what he said."

Dana steams, not quite ready to accept my speculations about the man she once so adored, to say nothing of Mallory Corcoran's. We are strolling together along the bluestone walks of the Original Quad, which, nearly empty of students in the summer, can actually be quite pleasant. We have been seeing more of each other these days, although not, of course, romantically. We are both having what my parents used to call "trouble at home." My wife, proclaiming her love for me, has thrown me out, and Alison is angry at Dana these days for worrying so much about whether what they are doing is right. Alison wants Dana to stop hanging out at her little Methodist church with what she calls the right-wing homophobes, and Dana refuses, saying they are good Christian people and she wants to listen to their point of view. Alison asks if black people are obliged to worship with white supremacists, to get their point of view. Dana says it isn't the same at all. I am not about to get in the middle. Dana is stoic enough to qualify as an honorary Garland, but, when our various pains leak through our façades, we friends do our best to comfort each other.

"Suicide," Dana sneers again.

"It does happen, Dana. People do stupid things." One of our shared pains is that Theo Mountain suffered a massive stroke two days ago and is not expected to live. I want to blame the Judge, I want to blame Theo, but I cannot help blaming myself: was I too hard on the old man?

"So, the story is supposed to be that your father was going to kill himself because he was scared of being exposed? And then you were supposed to track down his arrangements and he would get his revenge?"

"Something like that."

"Sorry, Misha, that doesn't make any sense at all. No matter what kind of man your father really was. If some reporter or somebody was going to expose him, why would the fact that he was dead make them stop? A dead man can't even sue for defamation."

"I'm not sure it was that kind of exposure. Not public."

"What's the other kind?"

"Maybe somebody was threatening to tell his family what he had been doing."

"But why? What would that somebody want from him? And why would that somebody stop just because he was dead?"

I shake my head in frustration, still chewing on cotton, still sure of the existence, out there somewhere, of an interested party who has not been fooled. The only thing I can think of that somebody might want badly enough to threaten my father is the one thing I have not yet found: the arrangements. "I don't know," I confess.

Dana sighs, exasperated, maybe toward me. We continue through the empty Quad, where, in my student days, I used to walk with the Judge, who would reminisce for a while, then drag me along to drop in on those of his old professors who were still living, and those of his classmates who were now on the faculty. He would introduce me airily to my own teachers as though they had never seen me before, never embarrassed me in class, never commanded me to redo fifty-page papers in three days, and they fussed over me because they fawned over him; even then, my father had the magic that enraptured, the presence that demanded respect, and, besides, with Reagan in the White House, every one of them knew that the Honorable Oliver Garland would sit on the Supreme Court of the United States the instant that a vacancy occurred. When the visiting was done, I would drive the Judge to the lilliputian Elm Harbor airport in my shabby but earnest Dodge Dart, and we would sit in the coffee shop and eat stale Danish while waiting out the inevitable delay of the small commuter plane that would carry him back to Washington, and, to pass the time, he would bombard me once more with newer versions of the same old questions, as though hoping for a different set of answers—how were my grades, when would I hear about law review, whom was I dating these days—and, invariably, I was

THE EMPEROR OF OCEAN PARK

tempted to lie about the first two and tell the truth about the third, if only to see the look on his face, and to make him leave me alone.

By then, of course, he was already Jack Ziegler's judicial drone, so his desperate hopes for me, which I resented, take on a pathetic yet lovingly ambitious quality: he wanted his son the lawyer to wind up in a different place.

"Misha?" Dana has another question. "Misha, why would Jack Ziegler do it?"

"Do what? Let him out of the deal? Let him retire?"

"No, no. Why would he go to the courthouse? Wouldn't he know that somebody was bound to recognize him, that your father's judicial career would be wrecked?"

"Probably," I say, for I have considered this question. "But maybe the ruin of my father's judicial career was Jack Ziegler's final gift to him."

Dana nods. "And when your father finally got out, he would have warned them that he'd written it all down. That, if anything untoward happened to him, the whole story would make its way into the light." She is excited. "That must be what's in the papers, Misha! All the favors he did, the companies, who owned them—everything!"

"That would be my guess, too." I remember again how the Judge always demanded the names of the principals behind the shell companies litigating before him, and how few dared resist the demand. Justice Wainwright described my father's orders for disclosure as a mark of his obsession with detail. But there was another reason: he was protecting himself, squirreling away information.

Which would also explain who hired Colin Scott to follow me. The possibility that he might be implicated in the papers could have provided an additional incentive, but the notion that Scott reacted out of some personal fear remains the weak link in the FBI's chain of reasoning about what happened. I have no idea whether the Bureau suspected that Scott was the killer of Phil McMichael, the Senator's son, but, plainly, they thought he returned because he was worried about something in *the arrangements*. And that makes no sense. If he was safely overseas, living under another name, why would he come back to the United States and risk arrest for murder? No, he followed me for the benefit of somebody else, somebody who paid him well to follow the trail of his former employer, and I suspect I will never know who his clients were unless I find *the arrangements*, for they had to be those who profited from my father's corruption.

"You know, Misha, I really admired your father. I really did." Pain in her deep, black eyes. I wonder how much more pain there would be if Dana knew the secret I have kept from her, the identity of the driver of the red car, slaughtered by Colin Scott. "But this . . . What am I supposed to do now? Forgive him? Hate him? What?"

I have to smile. Dear Dana Worth, self-centered to the last. It does not seem to have occurred to her that I am struggling with precisely the same questions. I expect little from life other than mystery and ambiguity, so perhaps it is too much to demand of my feelings about my father that they come suddenly into crystalline focus. Dana, like Mariah, needs answers that are sharply defined. Searching for something to say, I hit upon another of my father's platitudes: "You have to draw a line, Dana. You have to put the past in the past."

"I feel like I never knew him. Like he was really . . . some kind of monster." She shudders. "He had all these sides. All these levels."

I remember Jack Ziegler's soliloquy. "He was trying to protect his family. He just . . . he kind of got in over his head."

"That's a pretty easy excuse."

"I don't mean it that way. I'm not trying to justify what he did. I just think . . . I don't think he set out to do it. I think he probably got caught up."

Dana shakes her head. She is never afraid of passing judgment, most mercilessly on herself. "I'm sorry, Misha, but that won't wash. Your father wasn't some kind of blundering innocent. He was an intelligent man. He knew who Jack Ziegler was. He knew *what* Jack Ziegler was. If it's really true that your father went to him and asked him to permit a murder, do you really believe he didn't realize he would be in Jack Ziegler's thrall for the rest of his life? He wasn't that naïve, Misha. Don't kid yourself." She allows herself a rare shudder, then touches her elbow, still sore where bullet chipped bone. "I don't know what to say about him, Misha. I don't want to say he was evil . . . but he wasn't just deluded, either. He made a *decision* to kill the driver of that car. He made a *decision* to become a corrupt judge." Another shake of the head. "I can't believe I knew so little about what was really going on in that head of his. It's scary, Misha. And it hurts."

"You should try being his son."

"Oh, Misha, I didn't mean it like that." She squeezes my hand. "I'm sorry."

"I know you didn't, Dana. But it isn't easy for me, either." I sigh. "Anyway, it isn't your problem any more."

Dana looks at me sharply, mouth wide, having heard something in my tone she does not like. She gives me my hand back. Perhaps she has realized, as I have been thinking ever since we both got shot, that our friendship will never be the same. She points a finger at me. "You don't think it's over," she says, wonder in her tone. "There's something you're not telling me, Misha."

"Let it go, Dana. Please."

"Is that what you're going to do? Let it go? Somehow I doubt it." Standing in the middle of the Original Quad, fists folded on her narrow hips. Her voice softens. "Do you really think the box fooled them, Misha?"

"I hope it did. I hope . . . I hope they'll think the Judge was just bluffing."

"What if there's some kind of test to show how long the box was in the ground?"

"I'm sure there is, but they can't possibly know when the Judge buried it. For all they know, he did it the day before he died. You buried it half a year later. Can a test really discriminate within a few months?"

"I hope not." A weak grin. "Otherwise, we're in big trouble."

We both think that one over. This is at our final moment together before Dana decamps for the rest of the summer—maybe with Alison, maybe not—to Cayuga Lake in upstate New York, where, a little north of Ithaca, Dana maintains what she calls her "little writing cottage," an old and naturally cool stone house on the water. I thought we would be hugging, sentimental. Wrong again.

"If we knew where the papers were," Dana says thoughtfully, "we might be able to use them to protect ourselves."

"Except we don't know where they are."

Worried, she studies my face. "Do me a favor, won't you, Misha, darling? When they come for you because the box was empty, and you decide to lie to protect me, please do a better job of lying than you just did."

"Nobody's coming for anybody," I soothe. "We fooled them, Dana."

But the expression on my best friend's pale face tells me she is not really sure. To tell the truth, neither am I.

CHAPTER 60

ENDGAME

(1)

So I KEEP WATCHING, waiting for them to come, while trying to live my life. Like most professors, I generally use my summers to write. But this year I am spending all the time I can with Bentley. Kimmer does not seem to mind, and, now and then, we do things as a threesome. Sara Jacobstein reminds me that Bentley needs to see his parents treat each other with respect. Morris Young tells me that God requires the same thing. We are not getting back together, my soon-to-be-ex-wife has made that clear, but these occasions—a walk in the park, a trip to a Broadway show—are somehow not too onerous, as though Kimmer and I are both growing up a little, even as we grow apart. Once, feeling particularly gay as we stand in the foyer of the house on Hobby Road after returning from a dinner for three, Kimmer even asks me if I would like to stay the night, and I am giddy until I realize that this is no promise of a resumption of our marriage, but only an impulse born of Lionel's temporary absence from town. When my polite refusal meets with a shrug, I know I am right.

When I am not with Bentley, I spend a lot of time driving through the countryside in my sturdy Camry, watching my rearview mirror with some care, because I have started to catch a whiff, just the faintest distant breath, of new shadows. Somebody, I am confident, is back there. Maybe Nunzio's people, maybe Jack Ziegler's, maybe his partners'. But I have a feeling that the breath on my neck belongs to somebody else; somebody who has not been around for a while. Somebody, however, I knew would return.

I am running out of time, but only I know it.

At the law school one midsummer's day, Shirley Branch cannot control her ebullience, running up and down the halls like a schoolgirl, embracing everyone she meets. "He's back!" she cries, literally cries, for she is sobbing through her joy. When it is my turn to be hugged, she all but knocks me over, cane and all, and I barely have time to ask who, exactly, is back before she shouts, "Cinque! He's back!" She came home from Oldie last night and he was there, sitting on the front step, wagging his tail in delight. I am astonished, and relieved, and more certain than ever of a small theory. The odd thing, Shirley adds, is that he was wearing a brand-new collar, with no name on it. But she is smart enough to have an explanation ready: "He must have lost his tag when he ran away, and somebody found him and didn't know where he lived and put a new collar on him, and then he missed me and he ran away from them and found his way home!"

A good story, even if it is not a true one. I remember, instead, a certain animal-lover on the Vineyard, who grew up with five dogs and ten cats, who could shoot me in the Burial Ground and call it just a job, but could not bring herself to harm Shirley's black terrier. I wonder where Maxine obtained the blood that she smeared on the tag when she followed me to Aspen. And why she didn't drop by to say hello when she slipped into Elm Harbor to deliver Cinque to Shirley's door.

That night, I telephone Thera to check on Sally's progress, but I reach her answering machine and she does not return the call. A few days later, Kimmer rings at 2 a.m., weeping and whispering my name for no reason I can discern. I ask her if she wants me to come over, and she hesitates and then says no. When I call to check on her later that day, she apologizes for troubling me and will say no more. Perhaps every disintegrated marriage has such moments.

The following day, the elegant Peter Van Dyke invites me to join him and Tish Kirschbaum for lunch, to talk about the many court cases involving the Boy Scouts; Peter says he cannot think of a better referee. The three of us banter and argue as though I am, almost, a respected member of the faculty again. And perhaps a respected member of the community as well, for my trio of bullet holes has brought me a certain local prominence: a couple of Elm Harbor pastors ask me to speak at their churches, and the Rotary and the local branch of the NAACP both inform me that their members would love to hear what I have to say. Most significant of all, Kwame Kennerly takes me out for coffee, trying to secure my support for his swiftly evolving mayoral campaign. He has traded in his kente hat and navy blazer for a beige vested suit, and he assures me that big changes are on the way in our town.

I tell him I have no interest in politics.

In the middle of the first week of August, my landlord, Lemaster Carlyle, is sworn in as a judge of the United States Court of Appeals. His beaming wife Julia holds the Bible. Half of the law school faculty is crowded into the city's brand-new federal courthouse, the half that is not on vacation. All the leaders of the local bar are in attendance. Judge Carlyle makes some brief remarks, solemnly promising to do his best to live up to the traditions of the bench—the better traditions, one assumes. He is applauded vigorously, for everybody has decided to love him. More friends thump him on the back than Lemaster probably knew he had. Standing at some distance from the hero of the day, I find myself still irritated that he never told us he was in the running. Despite everything that has occurred, I continue to feel, although I recognize its masochistic character, a degree of loyalty to my wayward wife, whose judicial ambitions Lem managed to trump. I remind myself that Lemaster Carlyle, he of the endless Washington connections, went behind *both* our backs—successfully, to be sure, but behind our backs nevertheless.

Still, I shake his hand and say the right things. Kimmer, too, attends, and is among the many back-slappers. Dahlia Hadley was right, and my wife knows it: there will be other chances for her, if she only continues to work hard and please those she must please. And if she can only settle this unpleasantness with her husband, and act sensible about Lionel. I even catch myself wondering whether a part of her calculation, when she decided to leave, was that her chances for the bench are better without me than with me. But that is an unworthy thought, and, with due credit to the Judge, I push it away. We make small talk, Kimmer and I, which is about all the talk we have left. I decide not to burden my wife with what I have figured out: that because she assumed the task of complaining to the alarm company after the break-in on the Vineyard, she must have learned immediately that the vandals possessed the correct code to turn the alarm on and off again. She never shared this vital clue with me, preserving the secret through the agonizing months of my search, because she did not want to jeopardize her chances at the nomination by supplying the evidence that I was right all along. I look at her tense face and forgive her. As it happens, the ceremony takes place on my forty-second birthday. Kimmer does not mention the coincidence, and I am not about to beg her to remember. So my only celebration is a late-night call from Mariah, who effuses on the subject of Mary, now six months old, but also confides that she plans to head back to Shepard Street soon: there are, after all, papers yet uncatalogued.

I wish her well.

Theo Mountain dies two days after Lem's swearing-in. His daughter, Jo, the New York lawyer, mistakenly believing that Theo was still my mentor, asks me to deliver one of the eulogies at his huge Roman Catholic funeral. I cannot think of a way to refuse that will not add to her grief. I write a few lines, trying to recall the way I once felt about Theo, but I cannot get through my text because I am weeping too hard. As everybody stares at everybody else in embarrassment, it is Lynda Wyatt who emerges from the congregation, puts a gentle arm around my waist, and leads me back to my pew.

I suppose people think I was crying over Theo. Maybe I was, a little. But, mainly, I was crying over all the good things that will never be again, and the way the Lord, when you least expect it, forces you to grow up.

(11)

Mr. Henderson shows up at the door of my condo on the second morning after the funeral. He was in the area, he says brightly for the benefit of any neighbors who might be listening, so he thought he would stop in and say hello. He is wearing a sports jacket to hide his gun, and he shows no obvious damage, so I suppose the fifth person in the cemetery the night I was shot must have been his alter ego Harrison. Dana and I were there, Colin Scott was there, and Maxine was there and stole the unburied box. That makes four. But I know there was a fifth, not only because the police think so, but also because I heard a man—not a woman—cry out in pain when the dying Colin Scott's desperate bullet struck him. The police found no sign of him, so it was someone close enough to the action to get shot, and tough enough to escape anyway.

I let Mr. Henderson in because I have no choice. Waiting for the guillotine's blade to fall, I lead him to the small kitchen table, an oft-painted wooden relic of my childhood salvaged from the basement of the house on Hobby Road. I offer water or juice. Henderson declines. Like gamblers who distrust each other, we both keep our hands in sight. We are very civil, although Henderson takes the precaution of setting up a small electronic device that will, he assures me, make it difficult for us to be overheard. All I know is that it gives me a sharp, sudden headache, even though it does not seem to be making a sound.

"Your friend understands why you did what you did," Henderson tells me in his smooth, sparkling voice. "He does not blame you for the fact that the contents of the box were . . . disappointing. On the contrary. He is pleased."

This surprises me. "He is?"

"Your friend is of the view that all involved parties are satisfied with this outcome."

Rubbing an aching ear, I think this one over. What Dana and I feared appears to be true: Jack Ziegler is too old a hand to be fooled so easily. I suppose the other *involved parties* are old hands too. Yet they are satisfied. And Henderson is here. Which means that . . .

"Somebody else ended up with the box," I murmur. The good guys, I am thinking. Not the great guys, the good guys. "My . . . friend doesn't have it. Am I right?"

Henderson declines to enlighten me. His strong face is smoothly impassive. "Your friend is of the view that if nothing was found, then perhaps there was nothing to be found. Some threats are bluffs."

"I see."

"Perhaps you agree."

I realize, finally, where I am being led: what I am being forgiven for, and what words I must recite to earn forgiveness. "I agree. Some threats are bluffs."

"Perhaps there were never any real arrangements."

"That is certainly possible."

"Even likely."

"Even likely," I echo, closing the deal.

Henderson is on his feet, wide shoulders flexing, catlike, under the loose jacket. I wonder how many seconds it would take him to kill me with his bare hands should the need arise. "Thank you for your hospitality, Professor."

"Thank you for stopping by."

Before folding up his electronic baffler, Henderson adds a final point: "Your friend also wants you to know that if you should, in the future, discover contents that are . . . less disappointing . . . he will expect to hear from you. In the meanwhile, he assures you that you will not be troubled further over this matter."

I think this one over, too. *Some threats are bluffs.* He is implying a little bit more than he is saying. "And my family and I . . ."

"Will be perfectly safe. Naturally." But no smile. "You have your friend's promise."

As long as I keep my end of the bargain, he means. Before, Uncle

Jack's ability to protect me was driven by his assurance to *involved parties* that I would track down the arrangements. Now that things have changed, his ability to protect me rests on his assurance that I will not. They cannot know whether I have found the real contents someplace else; whether, like my father, I have hidden them away, and made arrangements of my own, to be launched in the event of my unexpected demise. The *involved parties* and I shall live henceforth in a balance of terror.

"All right," I say.

We do not shake hands.

(I I I)

EVERY NIGHT I WATCH THE WEATHER CHANNEL. Near the end of the third week of the month, while Bentley is with me for a few days, I turn on the television and note with approval a terrible hurricane on its way up the coast. If it keeps on its present course, it will hit the Vineyard four days from now. Perfect.

The next morning, Saturday, I take Bentley back to his mother. My son and I stand together out on the front lawn, and Don Felsenfeld, tending his flowers, raises a trowel in greeting. I decide not to wonder whether Don, who notices everything, knew about Lionel before I did.

"When Bemley see you 'gain?"

"Next weekend, sweetheart."

"Promise?"

"God willing, Bentley. God willing."

His keen eyes search my face. "Dare Daddy?" he inquires, lapsing into the secret language we hardly ever hear any more.

"Yes, sweetheart. Dare Daddy. Absolutely."

I lead my son up the crooked brick path to Number 41 Hobby Road. Crooked because Kimmer and I, shortly after moving in, laid the bricks ourselves. A two-day job that took us, busy, love-struck rookies that we were, about a month.

My hand trembles on the cane.

The house is empty. The thought comes to me unbidden but with all the moral force of absolute truth. It is an empty house . . . no, an empty *home*. Kimmer is certainly inside somewhere, waiting for her son. Her BMW is parked in the turnaround, as usual, in defiance of my counsel. And if my wife has been careless and broken her solemn word—nothing new there!—Lionel Eldridge might be lurking around the place, his powder-blue Porsche safely hidden away in the garage. Yet the Victorian sits empty, for a home that once housed a family and now holds only its shards is like a beach whose sand has eroded to rock—retaining only the name, and none of the reason for the name.

At the door, I tell Kimmer I am returning to the Vineyard for a few days. She nods indifferently, then stops and peers at me. The resolution in my voice frightens her.

"What are you going to do, Misha?"

"I'm going to finish it, Kimmer. I have to."

"No, you don't. There's nothing to finish. It's over, it's all over." Hugging our son to her thigh now, wishing the truth away.

"Take care of him, Kimmer. I mean, if anything happens to me."

"Don't say that! Don't ever say that!"

"I have to go." I peel her hand from my sleeve. Then I spot the real panic in her face and I realize she has it all wrong. She thinks I'm going off to Oak Bluffs to kill myself. Over her! I love her, yes, I am in pain, sure, but suicide! So I smile and take her hand and lead her down the steps onto the lawn. She is savvy enough to shoo Bentley into the house.

"Please don't talk that way," Kimmer mumbles, shuddering. She does not object when I put my arm around her.

"Kimmer, listen to me. Listen, please. I'm not going to do anything foolish. There's a piece of the mystery that hasn't been solved yet. Everybody's forgotten about it. But I haven't. And I have to go and see."

"Go and see what?"

I think about the shadows I have sensed, ponder how to put it. I think about the still-unexplained attack on me in the middle of the campus. I think about my bullet holes. I think about my chat with Mr. Henderson. From my memory I draw the Judge's line: "The way it was before, darling. I have to see the way it was before."

She licks her lips. She is wearing jeans and a polo shirt and is as fetching as ever. Her hair is awry, and I wonder, with distress, if she was too busy in bed last night to braid it. She shoves her glasses up on her forehead and asks only one question: "Is it going to be dangerous, Misha? For you, I mean."

"Yes."

CHAPTER 6I

ANGELA'S BOYFRIEND

(I)

THE HURRICANE HITS on my second day in Oak Bluffs, and it is a triumph of a storm, one of the greats, a storm to be talked about for years to come, just as I hoped it would be. All morning the police go up and down the roads with megaphones, warning everyone living near the water to take shelter. The radio stations, both on the Island and from the Cape, predict horrific property damage. I stay in the house or on the porch, watching the storm arrive. By early afternoon, the wind has knocked down tree branches and power lines all over the Island, and my electricity is gone. I hear creaking up in the attic, as though the chimney is deciding whether to jump. A couple of decades ago, in a storm less severe than this one, the chimney fell over flat on the roof of the house. I open the front door. Rain forms a wet, shimmery shield just beyond the steps, as though to walk through the curtain would be to enter a magical world where leaves fly and lawn furniture tumbles aimlessly through the streets and trees crack sharply in two.

Still I wait.

No more cars on Ocean Avenue or Seaview, nobody playing in the park. As always, a few foolish souls are out walking along the seawall, perhaps waiting to see whether the storm surge will be high enough to wash them away. But they are no more foolish than Talcott Garland, Misha to his friends, sitting in the unboarded front window of his house in defiance of official orders to evacuate. Of course I cannot leave. I have planned for, searched for, hoped for this moment since the day I left the hospital and saw Kimmer standing militantly in the front hall of Number 41 Hobby Road and solved the mystery. I dared not let on, not to anybody, and only Dana even guessed that I might know. I cannot evacuate. I am waiting, waiting for the worst of the storm, waiting for the only instant since encountering Jack Ziegler in the cemetery when I can know, absolutely know, that I am alone. Nobody, I am betting, can maintain surveillance through a hurricane like this one.

At three-twenty, the storm surge strikes. Water careens over the seawall, carrying sand and seaweed and even fish onto Seaview Avenue. Another tree falls. I see a lone little car struggling along the road, but the wind turns it completely around, and the driver jumps out and flees. I watch to make sure he is not doubling back. I hear a terrible crack as a tree branch goes through a window of the house next door.

Still I wait.

Vinerd Howse is shadowy and shuddering. No power anywhere in the area. Nobody moving on the street. Not a car or a truck or an SUV. Not a bicycle. I see, literally, zero people, and when I step out into the storm, stabbing the endless gray with the powerful light I bought on the mainland, I can see the boarded fronts of every house on Ocean Park. I play the light over windows and porches, over trees and the bandstand, looking for any sign of a lurking human.

Nothing.

I repeat the process on both sides of the house and in the back. My rain slicker does little to protect me as I cross our narrow yard, shining my light into neighbors' windows.

I am alone. Everyone else in the world is sensible. The present moment belongs to the insane.

My moment.

Back inside, I leave my portable searchlight and pick up an ordinary flashlight. Passing the dining room, I see that silly *Newsweek* cover again: THE CONSERVATIVE HOUR. But not so silly after all. Perhaps the Judge kept it as a reminder. Of someone to whom he owed an apology of sorts. I remember the very different pictures on the wall in Thera's foyer. *The way it was before.* Over and over again, my father used that line, drumming it into me. Hoping I would never forget.

I hurry to the second floor of the house, then pull down the ladder into the attic.

(11)

THE LOW-CEILINGED ATTIC of Vinerd Howse is not a place to spend more than twenty or thirty seconds in the middle of the summer. Through some trick of physics—hot air rising, perhaps, or bad ventilation—the attic is stifling, the air all but unbreatheable, even when the rest of the house has cooled for the evening. In the hurricane, the air is even worse. Outside it is cold, but, in here, every step leaves me soaking with sweat. And I almost lose my nerve besides, because I can actually see the ceiling tremble. But the scholar in me takes over, fascinated by its chaotic movements. I have never seen a roof heaving and rippling, the very rafters shaking, the way I suppose they do in an earthquake.

I feel remarkably safe.

I begin to hunt around the cramped space. I know it is up here someplace. Hidden over the years by an accumulation of junk, but it is here. It has to be.

Uncle Derek, I am thinking. How could I have forgotten Uncle Derek? As Sally said, he gave me my name.

I stumble over trunks and aged crockery and lanterns, I sort through old clothes and older books, and I cannot seem to find it. Rain and wind crash against the lone window as though demanding entry. I hear a trickle or two and know the roof has sprung a leak. The room is not that cluttered, it is quite unlike the attic Mariah frequents down on Shepard Street: finding what I am looking for should not be this hard. I bark my shin on a wilted sofa, and marvel at the energy, and foolishness, required to get it up here. Under a coat, I find my old baseball mitt, which I had thought lost forever. I find a child's notebook filled with scrawling pictures of lighthouses. Mine, too? Abby's? I cannot recall. The chimney creaks. I find a beach umbrella that has not been opened in a decade or two, and a couple of beach towels that have gone about that long since being washed. I am ready to give up. Maybe my theory is wrong, maybe I am so far off base . . .

But I know I am right.

The way it was before.

B4. The first move of the Double Excelsior when the white side loses. Signifying, however, not a square on an imaginary chessboard in a cemetery, but a word. B4. *Before.*

The way it was before.

Meaning, before it all went bad.

But it didn't go bad when my father left the bench. It went bad long before that. It went bad—so he kept saying, according to Alma—it went bad when he split with his brother for the sake of ambition. Uncle Derek, his younger brother, who gave me my nickname. Uncle Derek, the lifelong Communist who, late in his life, got big into nationalism.

Not for him the peaceful protest—*praying while the cops beat your head in*, he used to call it—but fighting back. The armed struggle. When the Judge was not around, we all used to sit at Derek's feet, enthralled, especially Abigail. Uncle Derek would preach activism, activism, activism. But only with the right ideology. He liked the Panthers, even if he thought their ideology was a little bit thin. He liked SNCC. But most of all, Derek admired the black Communists who were active in the struggle.

And who was the most prominent black Communist?

Angela Davis. *Angela* Davis.

I move a rolled-up carpet, and, suddenly, there it is.

I straighten up.

I am looking down at the stuffed animal that Abby won at the fair so many years ago: the deteriorating panda my late sister named after George Jackson, who was shot dead trying to escape from San Quentin Prison. At the time, every black woman in America of a certain age seemed to be in love with him, as well as some who, like Abby, were way too young. George Jackson, the handsome, dynamic revolutionary. George Jackson, Angela Davis's supposed lover.

Angela's boyfriend.

(111)

I AM DOWNSTAIRS IN THE KITCHEN, thinking. The storm continues to shake the house. A few minutes ago, I took my portable searchlight outside again, braving wind and rain and lightning, all nature's summer fury, to be sure I am not being watched. For an eerie instant, shining the beam toward the bandstand, now clouded with rain, I almost caught that whiff of a shadow once more, so I raced across Ocean Avenue and hunted around to be sure.

Nothing. Nobody. But now I am sopping and my searchlight is showing definite signs of exhaustion. Too late to shop for fresh batteries.

I have a portable indoor lamp, which I now use to illuminate George.

The bear is on the butcher-block island, lying inert as though awaiting dissection. I am touching it lightly with my fingers, not missing an inch, carefully parting the fur, looking for evidence of a tear or cut that has been sewn up by hand. I find nothing. I lift the animal and shake it, waiting for a secret message to spill out, but none does. I scrape the plastic eyes with my fingernails, but nothing comes off. I pull the panda's little blue tee shirt (it once fit Abby) inside out, but I find no hidden missive. So I turn my attention to where, in truth, it has been from the moment that I moved the rug and discovered it: the seam where the right leg meets the torso, and from which some sort of hideous pink stuffing has been dribbling for thirty years. I insert a finger, then two, into the tear, but all I encounter is more stuffing. Slowly, carefully, not wanting to disturb whatever I am going to discover, I pull the filler out and spread it on the counter.

And, without going very much deeper, my fingers catch hold of something. It feels flat and hard, three or four inches wide.

Pulling, pulling, gently, don't break it . . .

. . . it feels almost like . . . like . . .

. . . like a diskette for a computer.

Which is exactly what it is.

(I V)

I LIFT THE DISK UP, using two fingers, holding it close to the light, checking for damage. I am furious at the Judge. All this searching, all the clues, all the death and mayhem, for this! A disk! In the heat of that attic for almost two years! What could he have been thinking? Maybe it never occurred to him that high temperatures could cause a problem. He was never technically inclined, my father; the digital revolution was, in his oft-repeated judgment, a gigantic mistake. Trying to calm down, I set the disk on the counter. It has warped a little, and I do not dare try to force it into the slot on the right-hand side of my laptop.

Unbelievable. What a waste.

But maybe there is something left. Who do I know who might have some expertise at retrieving data from a damaged diskette? Only one name comes to mind: my old college friend John Brown, professor of electrical engineering at Ohio State. The last time I was with John, he spotted Lionel Eldridge in the woods behind my house—not that either of us knew it was Lionel at the time. That same innocent afternoon, Mariah told me the private detective's report was missing, and my father's arrangements seemed infinitely distant. Now, at last, I hold the arrangements in my hand, and I need John again to help me unpack them.

Why wait? I can call him right now, unless the storm has knocked out the phones along with the power.

I first take the precaution of sliding the disk back into my little sister's bear. With the storm blasting the windows, that might be the safest place. I have just turned around to look for my address book in the family room when the kitchen door smashes open.

I spin around, expecting to discover that it is the wind.

It isn't.

Standing just over the threshold as rain sheets into the house, a small gun glittering in his hand, is Associate Justice of the Supreme Court Wallace Warrenton Wainwright.

CHAPTER 62

THE BATTLE FOR GEORGE

(1)

"HELLO, MR. JUSTICE," I say as calmly as I can.

"You don't seem terribly surprised."

"I'm not." Although I am, really. I watch his gun hand. I am tired of watching gun hands, but there is little else to do.

He closes the door firmly behind him, purses his thin lips. "Is that it?" He points with the gun. I was holding the bear when he broke in, and I am still clutching it in both hands. When I say nothing, Wainwright sighs. "Don't play games, Misha. It's too late for that. Your father obviously hid something inside the teddy bear. What is it?"

"A computer disk."

He rubs his neck with his free hand. His dark blue rain slicker, which would be hard to see in the middle of the storm, is dribbling water all over the floor. "He told me there was something. He didn't tell me what. He didn't tell me where." His voice is vague, distant, dreamy. I realize that the Justice is as exhausted, both physically and emotionally, as I am. "Everybody knew there was . . . something. But nobody was looking for a bear. And nobody thought there might be a disk. Not from your low-tech father. People were looking for *papers*. That was very clever. A disk." A long exhalation as he pulls himself together again. "So, how long have you been on to me?"

"Ever since I realized the obvious. That my father couldn't swing all those cases by himself. The federal court of appeals sits in three-judge panels. So, if he was fixing cases, he needed two votes, not one."

Wainwright moves farther into the room, winding up near the arched entryway into the hall. It occurs to me that his line of fire now covers both me and the back door, as though he is expecting a surprise. He seems to know what he is doing with the gun, so I am determined to make no sudden moves. My plan has succeeded, but it has also failed. I was sure nobody would be out in this storm, and I therefore have no serious hope of rescue.

"So what? It could have been any of a dozen judges. It didn't have to be me." He sounds worried, and it occurs to me that he is wondering whether he has done enough to cover his tracks. If I was on to him, who else might be?

"True. But you practically told me yourself. When I came to see you. You said my father was no more likely to fix cases than you were."

He offers me his famous twisted smile, which I now see is more sardonic than amused. Were all of us so badly fooled for all those years? Did we really mistake his moral arrogance for compassion? He probably enjoyed telling me the literal truth while also lying. Wallace Wainwright, like the Judge, has always known he is smarter than most people. He is not accustomed to having anybody keep up. "I suppose I was being too clever," he says.

"I suppose." No reason not to tell him the rest. After all, as long as we are talking, he is not shooting, and I have come to like not being shot. "I also suppose that Cassie Meadows kept you up to date on what was happening."

Perhaps it is my imagination. The gun seems to waver, just slightly. "What makes you think that?"

"I should have realized it from the start. Mallory Corcoran handed me off to Cassie because he didn't have time for my problems. He tried to impress me by telling me she was a former Supreme Court law clerk. It was clear to me that everything Cassie learned, somebody else was learning, too. I assumed it was Mallory Corcoran. But then it occurred to me she could just be keeping in touch with her former employer. The Justice whose law clerk she was. So I looked up Cassie in Martindale-Hubbell, and, sure enough, she clerked for Justice Wallace Wainwright. Probably just a coincidence that she was the associate assigned to the matter, but you still reaped the advantage." He has not told me to put up my hands. I am still holding George Jackson. I want to keep the conversation going. "So was she just a blabbermouth, gossiping with you, or was she part of it, too?"

"I have no intention of answering your questions." The wind is still whipping outside, and we hear a sharp snap as a tree loses a branch somewhere near the house. Rain continues its steady assault on the windows. In the hallway, Justice Wainwright frowns, stepping slightly to the side, as though unable to stand still. He considers what I have just said, still worried about whether he has somehow exposed himself. Then he shakes his head. "No. No, that wouldn't have been enough. You wouldn't jump to that conclusion just because Cassie clerked for me." The gun centers on my chest. I back toward the sink. He follows, just out of range of any kick or punch I might throw, even if I knew how. As for the bear, Wainwright has not asked for it and I have not offered it. "Why were you not surprised to see me? How did you even know that there was anybody else? You clearly thought your Uncle Jack was keeping tabs on you. Maybe his partners were, too. But why did there have to be a third party?"

"You're right. The fact that Meadows clerked for you wasn't enough." My palms and the small of my back are moist with perspiration. I still have a faint hope of escape. The storm that was supposed to keep me safe can still rescue me, if only I can keep Wainwright talking a little longer. "But I knew there had to be . . . like you said, a third party . . . because I knew that there was somebody out there who was unaware of Jack Ziegler's edict."

Genuine puzzlement. "What edict?"

"That I wasn't to be touched. The other people who were after me, they all knew the rules. I couldn't be hurt, and nobody in my family could be hurt. Jack Ziegler had made a deal with . . . well, whoever one makes such deals with. The word went out. I would not be harmed, and I would find what my father hid. So everybody just watched me and waited. Then, once I started to get hurt, it was clear that either the rules had changed or a third party was involved. I was . . . reassured that the rules were not any different. So it had to be an outsider. Someone without contacts in Jack Ziegler's circles."

"You'd be surprised where I have contacts, Misha."

I know what he means, but I shake my head. "It isn't enough that Jack Ziegler can reach you. You would have to be able to reach him."

Wainwright doesn't like this at all; I can see it in his face, which has morphed from sardonic to furious. Maybe he does not like remembering that he was never as close to Jack Ziegler as my father was. A new variation on the Stockholm Syndrome: the bribee wants to be the favorite of the briber. I remind myself not to try scoring points off an armed man.

"So Jack Ziegler put out an edict," he says finally, letting out a long breath. "He said nobody could harm you."

"Yes. And you didn't know about that, so you sent a couple of thugs after me. And there was one other thing." I have backed completely around the butcher-block table. Now Wainwright is in front of the sink. George Jackson, his leg just about ripped off, is still a shield between us.

"What thing?"

"Meadows. She started calling me Misha. Who could she have heard it from? Not Uncle Mal, he calls me Talcott. She could have heard Kimmer say it, but I doubt she would have been forward enough to pick a nickname only my wife used. I could only think of one person Meadows would know in D.C. who also called me Misha. You."

Justice Wainwright nods, smiling distantly. "That's very good. Yes. I will have to be more careful in the future." He sighs. "So, it's over, Misha. Give me the disk, and I'll be on my way." I glance at the kitchen door behind him. He sees me do it. "There's nobody else, I'm afraid. Nobody is coming to rescue you. It's just the two of us. So give me the disk. Please don't make me ask again."

Still I play for time. "What's so important about the disk? What's on it?"

"What's on it? I'll tell you what's on it. Protection."

"What kind of protection?"

"Oh, come, Misha, you have surely figured it out by now. You're not the dunce you pretend to be. Names. Names of the people with interests in all those corporations, all those years. Cabinet secretaries. Yes. Senators. A governor or two. Some CEOs and prominent lawyers. A man who has such a disk in his possession can buy a good deal of protection."

And then I see it. "Oh. Oh, no. You mean protection from Jack Ziegler. He still has his hooks in you, doesn't he? Or his partners do? And they won't let you stop, will they?"

"They won't even let me retire from the Court. They're so very demanding." I say nothing. Even though I had nearly figured it out, the implicit confession has rocked me. "But your father was no better. When I asked him to share his hidden information, he just looked at me and told me I was a part of his arrangements. And if I didn't stay away from him, everybody would know."

"A year before he died," I murmur, finally getting the point.

"What was that?"

"I, uh, was wondering what your cover story is for being on the Island." A lie, but I suspect that any call upon his vanity will lead to a disquisition. He has to show me how smart he is. Before he kills me, that is.

"Really, Misha. Everybody wants me as a houseguest. Yes. Well. You made a few mistakes of your own. You were too deliberate, Misha; it was clear you were preparing to do something. I heard about the hurricane, and that you were coming up here anyway. Well. I realized what you were up to. I accepted a long-standing invitation. This afternoon, when the storm came, I went for a walk." That crooked smile again. "I told my hosts I like storms. I am out walking at this very moment." The wind blows the back door open, then snaps it closed again. And Wainwright no longer wants to reminisce. "All right, Misha, enough talk. Now, give me the disk."

"No."

"Don't be silly, Misha."

I find a surprising stubbornness. "My father didn't leave it for you. He left it for me. I want to see what's on it, and then I'll decide what to do with it."

Justice Wainwright fires a shot. There is no warning and his hand barely flickers. The bullet zips past my head as I duck, too late of course, and buries itself in the kitchen wall.

"I was a Marine, Misha. I know how to use this gun. Now, give me the disk."

"It won't do you any good. It's useless. It's been up in the heat too long. It's all warped."

"All the more reason for you to give it to me." I shake my head. The Justice sighs. "Misha, look at it from my point of view. I can't do this any more. I have been in bed with these people too long. I need to get out. I need that disk." His eyes harden. "Your father refused to tell me where it was, but I can certainly get it from you."

"My father refused," I repeat. "Two years ago this October, right? That's when you asked him to tell you where it was hidden?"

"Possibly. So? Have I made another mistake?"

"No, but . . ." But that's what spooked the Judge, I am thinking. It was Wallace Wainwright—not Jack Ziegler, as I have assumed—who scared him so badly that he went to the Colonel to borrow a gun. And joined a shooting club to learn how to use it. Wainwright, tired and wanting to retire from the Court, went to see him, a year before he died, and tried to make him share the information he had hidden to protect himself from Jack Ziegler and his partners. The Judge refused, and Wainwright threatened him with exposure, which sent my father scurrying hat in hand to Miles Madison. A few months passed, nothing further happened, and my father put the gun away. Then, last September, a desperate Wainwright reappeared, and my desperate father went back to his gun club. I try to imagine these two judicial icons, one on the right and one on the left, jousting over the materials that now rest in this bear; battling because each wanted frantically to escape payment for a lifetime of corruption on the bench. "The gun," I whisper. "Now I see."

"What gun?"

"The Judge . . . obtained a gun. He was . . ." I thought the surprises were finished, and this one seems scarcely plausible. But it is the only explanation. Uncle Mal had it completely upside down. What my father told the Colonel was the literal truth: he wanted protection. But not, as Mariah imagines, from a would-be killer. He wanted protection from a blackmailer. On the screen of my mind, the last month of the Judge's life unscrolls. When Wainwright reappeared, my father called Jack Ziegler, and the two of them had their secret dinner. It is so easy, now, to see what favor the Judge must have asked that led his old friend and chief tempter finally to refuse him. Seeing the humor in our string of errors, I manage a laugh.

"What's funny, Misha?"

"I know you'll find this hard to believe, Mr. Justice, but I think my father planned to kill you. Seriously. If you didn't leave him alone, if you kept threatening to expose him. He bought a gun, and I think he planned to shoot you with it."

(11)

Wainwright's eyes darken. For a grim moment, he seems to be contemplating another way the story could have ended. Then his face twists in a snarl. "So now you know what kind of man your father really was. The great Judge Oliver Garland. You say he was prepared to murder me. Well, I can't say I'm surprised. He was a monster, Misha, a soulless, selfish, arrogant monster." Outside, another tree splits in two, the crunch loud and sudden. The gun quivers as Wainwright glances around. Then his wrathful eyes are on me again. I see now why he hasn't killed me yet. He wants the son to suffer first for the sins of the father. And it seems to be working. "Your father is the one who got me into this mess in the first place, Misha. He's the one who got me started. So what do you think of that?"

I say nothing. I am no longer capable of surprise where the Judge is concerned. But it is easy to see how the Judge might have enticed him. The poor boy from Tennessee trailer trash makes good. A rich wife?

Perhaps the fruits of two rich decades of taking bribes, laundered through his wife's family. Something. Too sophisticated, I am sure, for me to figure out, but the result is the same: Wallace Wainwright, the great liberal, the man of the people, got rich from fixing cases.

At least, if motive matters, my father did it for love.

"He was like a devil, your father. You have no idea how persuasive he could be! And quite thoroughly corrupt. Is that cold enough for you? Taking his orders from Jack Ziegler. Voting the way he was told. Think about that, Misha. But he was so clever that nobody knew. And when he approached me, he was very cagey, he talked his way around to it slowly. . . . Never mind. A love of money is the root of all evil, isn't it? I wanted to do good and do well, and your father . . . exploited that."

I am about to protest that my father never took money; and then I hold my tongue, for I see it as part of his evil genius that he kept this fact from Wallace Wainwright. I will never know just how the Judge seduced the future Justice, but I notice how Wainwright's self-pitying diatribe has caught the cadence of Washington: he took the bribe, but it was all the fault of the briber.

Wallace Wainwright seems to realize how he sounds, for he calls a halt. "We have spent too much time on memory lane, Misha. Now, the disk, if you please. Just put it on the table."

"No."

"No?"

"I'm not afraid of you. You don't dare hurt me." Desperation. "You saw what Jack Ziegler did to your drones."

"Ah, yes, my drones. Good word. Drones. Yes." A tone of pride. If I can just keep appealing to his vanity, I can keep him talking. "It's not that easy, you know. To find drones, I mean." That crooked smile. "I am, after all, a Justice of the Supreme Court of the United States. You have no idea what risks I took. I had to go back to my contacts from the old days, in the Marines. . . . Never mind. It was a risk, but that chain is broken. Yes. The drones never knew who hired them, and nobody can trace it back to me."

That chain is broken. Perhaps Wainwright himself has removed the key link. With, say, the very gun he is holding on me.

"I see." Just something to say. The casual admission that he, in his position, has recently murdered somebody has left me in little doubt about my own fate.

"No, you don't see." Reaching across the table with the gun, then drawing it back before I can figure out whether to try to grab his hand. He is unaccountably angry. The wind blows something against the porch. "You don't agree. You think if you were in my position you would have made a different choice."

"I just know the choice you made."

Without warning, Wainwright explodes. "You're judging me! I don't believe this. *You're* judging *me!* How dare you! You're even worse than your father!" He gestures wildly with his gun hand, which gets my adrenaline pumping harder. "You probably think I should have done something noble, like turning myself in. You don't know what you're talking about. Do you have any idea who I am? For the last decade, I've been the only hope, do you realize that? The Constitution is dying, in case you didn't notice. No. It's being murdered. It's fine for you to cast stones, you sit in your office and write articles that nobody reads. I'm the one who's been up there fighting for freedom and equality in this reactionary age! I've been leading a whole wing of the Supreme Court!" His voice softens. "And they needed me, Misha. They did. The work we've done up there for justice is too important to let it be derailed by . . . by something like this. I couldn't quit, Misha. Even if Jack Ziegler would have let me go, I didn't have the right. The Court needed me. The nation needed me. Yes, all right, I'm not a saint, I made some compromises a long time ago, I know that. But the issues matter, too! If I had left the Court, if my wing had lost its leader, the law would be inestimably worse. Don't you see that?"

Yes, I see it. I am dizzied by his hypocrisy, but I see it. Temptation, temptation: Satan never changes.

"So you . . . couldn't resign."

"No, I couldn't. This was bigger than me. My fate didn't matter, only the issues. It was a calling, Misha, the fight for justice, and I had no choice but to heed it. The Court needed me. To preserve some vestige, however small, of decency and goodness up there. People believe in the Court. If I had allowed scandal to damage the image of the Court, real people would have been hurt." He is back to the beginning and seems exhausted by his own argument. "Real people," he says again.

"I see."

"Do you, Misha?" Waving the gun again. "I wish I could fight on, I really do. But I'm tired, Misha. I'm so tired." A sigh. "Now, please, Misha, give me what I came for."

Still reeling from his diatribe, I muster a final bit of pluck: "And then what?" When he says nothing, I say what I am thinking: "You didn't just come here for the disk. You came here to kill me."

"True. I did. I won't lie about that. I wish there were another way. But, Misha, you still have a choice to make. I don't want you to suffer unnecessarily. Your death can be swift and painless, a bullet in the back of the head, or it can take time—if I shoot, say, your knees first, then your elbows, then maybe your groin. Hurts like hell but won't kill you for a while." He gestures with the gun. "Now, give me the disk."

"No."

"I killed people in Vietnam. I know how to use a gun, and I am not afraid to do it." I remember the photo in his office, a much younger Wainwright in Marine dress uniform. I have no doubts.

"You might be willing to shoot me," I try, "but you won't do it in the house, because there's too much chance of leaving some forensic evidence."

Outside, crunches and crashes as everything is dumped against everything else. The hurricane is, incredibly, getting worse. But maybe the eye has passed over us and we are getting the back part of the wind.

"I am perfectly willing to shoot you in the house," Wainwright says calmly.

"Then why haven't you?"

"Because that little bear might be another bluff. I am not about to underestimate you. You bluffed an expert in the cemetery. But we have talked enough. In thirty seconds, I am going to shoot off your kneecap, unless you give me the—"

A tremendous crash rattles the house, stunning us both. Pictures fall from the walls, crockery shatters in the cupboards. Justice Wainwright, no New Englander, is startled. He does not know what I know: that the bone-jarring impact was the sound of the chimney, blown loose by the hurricane, falling over flat against the sloping roof. Wainwright automatically looks up, alarm on his face, perhaps wondering whether the whole house is coming down.

The moment he is distracted, I dive, still clutching George Jackson, through the kitchen door and out into the storm.

CHAPTER 63

THE WATER BABY

THE KITCHEN DOOR opens onto a wooden stoop leading down into the tiny, pitted strip of browning grass that passes for a back yard. I leap down the steps and land with both feet in the marsh that the yard has become. I splash around the corner into the narrow alley that runs along the side of the house toward Ocean Avenue. I know Wainwright will follow me, because he has no choice, and I also know that my plan to use the hurricane has backfired in the worst way: I can run and shout as much as I want, but, even if I could be heard above the storm, there is nobody, not even a police officer, around to help.

For a moment, I am startled, almost overwhelmed, by the sheer majestic size of the angry clouds swirling low in the sky. Then I hear a gunshot smash into the side of the house next door, and I get my feet moving. Wallace Wainwright may be firing wildly, but that is bound to change, and I know too little about guns to figure out how many bullets he has.

Move!

My Camry, with its sparkling new rear bumper, sits parked on the verge, useless to me, because my keys are inside the house, in the pocket of my jacket. As I dart across the street, I hear Wainwright shouting and cursing somewhere behind me, but I dare not look back. He has nearly all the advantages. He has a rain slicker and a hat, while I am wearing sweats that are already sticking to my skin. He is wearing boots, and I am wearing sneakers that are already sloshing with water. He has a gun. I have a bear.

Emphasizing the point, a bullet thwangs off the pavement behind me. He is finding the range.

I have two advantages of my own, I remind myself as I slosh my way across the park, where the ground is saturated and water is simply collecting, nearly an inch deep, on the grass. One is that, ever since I was small, I have loved being outdoors in the weather when a storm strikes, at least on the Vineyard; my mother used to call me her water baby. My second advantage is that I am three decades Wainwright's junior. On the other hand, I have been shot a good deal more recently than he has, and I do not have my cane.

In the middle of Ocean Park, a gust of wind knocks me flat against the white bandshell, and, pressing away from the wall, I turn to look. Wainwright is a shadow in the storm, still negotiating the wooden rail fence lining the road, but he will soon gain on me, because I have few places to which to flee. I feel sutures separating, muscles freshly pulled. I am exhausted, my legs aching from the effort of this short run. Even as out of shape as I am, I should be able to keep well ahead of the aging Justice. Unfortunately, my leg has not yet recovered from Colin Scott's bullet, and I am hobbling, slowing inexorably as the trembling ache spreads outward from my wounded thigh.

Another gunshot, faintly heard beneath the roaring thunder. The storm is still my friend: the wind is ruining his aim.

I ran the wrong way, I realize. I should not have headed across Ocean Park, where I will be a sitting duck if he ever finds the range. I should have headed down the block, toward the stores—one might be open!—or the police station—a lone officer might be on duty! But Wainwright, the Vietnam combat veteran, has anticipated the tactic, circling in that direction, cutting off any hope I might have of running anywhere except toward the beach.

I will have to make my legs move if I want to see my son again.

And so I begin a sort of loping half-run, half-walk, beginning to hobble now because of a fresh searing pain in my abdomen, rushing toward the ocean, praying that the wind that keeps knocking me off stride and the drenching, buffeting rain that has already saturated my clothes will continue to keep him from aiming properly.

I cross Seaview Avenue, and a gunshot hits the metal railing separating the sidewalk from the beach. Wallace Wainwright is seventy-one years old and gaining on me.

For a moment I stand atop the rickety wooden stair running down to the Inkwell. Below me, savage waves lash the sand, stealing some of it forever. The jetty that usually marks the division between the lifeguarded and unlifeguarded parts of the beach is invisible. Most of the waves are spilling nearly all the way to the seawall before falling back.

I do not want to go down there.

Wainwright is behind me, and I have no choice.

I struggle awkwardly down the steps, longing for my cane to help with balance, and with the pain.

I hear Wainwright shouting.

Hurrying, but wary of the raging sea, I reach the bottom step.

Which, old to begin with and now weakened by the storm, immediately splits in two under my weight. I go sprawling into the waves covering the sand, and George Jackson goes flying, landing in the water a dozen feet away, where he bobs tantalizingly.

My entire body is singing with pain. I want to stay down here in the cold water, let it carry me away.

Wainwright is descending the steps, but carefully.

I climb awkwardly to my feet and splash toward Abby's bear, but the next wave knocks my legs out from under me again.

I struggle up again, lean into the water, stretch out my hand as something else tears, and then I have George Jackson in my arms again. But the chilly, whirling water is almost up to my waist, the waves are knocking me this way and that, and my energy reserves are nearly gone. The horizon is lost in angry gray-black clouds.

"All right, Misha, you did well." Wainwright, a couple of yards away, in shallower water. His voice sounds ragged. "Now, let's have it."

I look at him, in his blue rain slicker and boots, so practical, so well prepared, never fooled by me for a minute, never tripped up by the box in the cemetery. He knew I returned to the Vineyard, knew why I waited for a hurricane. He knew everything. I am dizzy now, from the cold and the pain, and my will is simply too weak. His brilliance, his patience, his planning have beaten me. Still clutching Abby's bear, I look at the small glittery gun, I look at Wainwright's coolly confident white face, and suddenly I simply cannot do this any more. I have given what I can. I am worn out. Emotionally as well as physically. Maybe he will shoot me. I am too tired, too cold, too miserable to care. Sorry, Judge.

The saga of the arrangements is finally over. I know I am going to give him the bear.

I take a stumbling step toward the beach, holding George Jackson out in front of me, and I see Wainwright's eyes go wide, and he backs away as though somebody is creeping up behind me, rising from the ocean to intervene at the last minute, Maxine or Henderson or Nunzio or some other armed avenger, but when I turn, what I see instead is a six-foot-high wall of black water, curling swiftly toward us.

Wainwright is already running for the ladder. I try to go after him, and then the wave crashes into my back and knocks me down. For a couple of seconds, my face is buried in the sand and there is water above me. I have lost track of the bear, of Wainwright, of everything, and if I do not move, pain or no pain, I am going to drown.

With what little energy I have left, I burst to the surface, only to tumble backward into the riptide, the giant wave drawing me helplessly along with it, and I have nothing left to fight with, so I ride the water, waiting to go under, until another wave replaces it and carries me to the beach once more.

I hear Wallace Wainwright, shouting something.

I sit up, shaking the water and sand out of my hair and eyes.

Wainwright is in the waves. He is trying to reach Abby's bear, which is riding out and out and out on the undertow. I watch. There is nothing I can do to help or hinder, for I have just about enough strength to sit here on the sand, soaked through, waiting for the next wave to arrive and drown me. Wainwright is nimble for his years, and strong, a jogger, but I can see even from this distance that he has no chance. Every time he reaches for the panda, another wave carries both of them further out. He does not seem to be holding the gun any longer; he is stretching for George Jackson with both hands. I find a momentary amusement in the vision of the great white liberal hero desperately trying to recover the great dead black martyr of the militant age. Then I frown, because it seems I was wrong. Wainwright has captured the bear. Cradling George against his chest, he is turning to struggle back to shore. And he is holding the gun. It must have been in his pocket. He is working toward me with grim determination, his face set in hard lines as he fights the undertow and, inch by inch, gets closer to the beach.

I even believe, briefly, that he is going to make it.

Then another six-foot swell washes over him and he is sucked under. His hand flails, his head comes up for air, once, twice, and then he is gone, carried out into the angry heart of the storm.

My head falls back onto the sand and, for a while, I die too.

CHAPTER 64

DOUBLE EXCELSIOR

(1)

Among the victims of the hurricane, says the pointedly solemn announcer, *was Justice Wallace Warrenton Wainwright of the United States Supreme Court, who drowned off the Island of Martha's Vineyard after apparently falling into the ocean while walking along the water to get a better look at the storm. Although the hurricane broke up three days ago, his body washed up on the beach just this morning. Wainwright, who was seventy-one, was on the Island to visit friends. Considered the last of the great judicial liberals, Wainwright was probably best known for his stirring defense of . . .*

Kimmer picks up the remote control and shuts off the fifty-three-inch television set that has become, absurdly, an issue between us. She turns to me and smiles. "Do you have any idea how lucky you are, Misha? That could have been you."

"I suppose."

"What were you doing out on that beach, anyway?" Maybe she is still thinking I might have tried to kill myself.

"Running away from Justice Wainwright. He was shooting at me."

"Oh, Misha, don't be morbid. That's not the least bit funny." She hops up to clear away the paper plates off which we have just finished eating carry-out pizza. Kimmer, although shoeless, is still dressed for work, in a cream-colored power suit and pale blue ruffled blouse. She has lost a little weight, maybe intentionally, maybe from stress. She looks more splendid than ever, and more splendidly unattainable. Over in the corner of the family room, Bentley is playing with his computer.

When I arrived to pick him up for the weekend an hour ago, he and Kimmer were just sitting down to a double-cheese pizza, and my estranged wife invited me to stay for a while.

"Bemmy zap, Bemmy zap!" our son cries happily. "Tree and six make nine! Nine! Bemmy zap!"

"Bemmy zap," I agree, still not opening my eyes. On the screen of my imagination, the final scene is played out so many different ways. Maybe I could have put together the energy to plunge into the waves and rescue Wallace Wainwright. Maybe my reserves were too thin or he was too far out. Sometimes I see myself pulling him out of the ocean. Sometimes I see myself dying in the attempt. Sometimes I remember to pray for his soul. Sometimes I am glad he is dead.

"Isn't our boy gorgeous?" murmurs Kimmer in a stage whisper.

"That he is."

"Your eyes are closed, silly."

"You know what? He's just as gorgeous with my eyes closed."

But I open them anyway and, for a golden moment, Kimmer and I are together, joined in love and admiration for the one thing in the world about which we both care. Then I recall the expensive leather jacket with the words DUKE UNIVERSITY stitched in blue that I found when I hung my windbreaker in the hall closet, and the gold turns to dross.

"Oh, Misha, by the way. Guess who called here looking for you?"

"Who?"

"John Brown. He said he was returning your call. I guess you forgot to give him your new number, huh?" Standing in the doorway, arms folded across her breasts. She has taken off her jacket. Still smiling. She has plenty to smile about. "Or are you trying to make some kind of statement?"

"I called him from the Vineyard." I am leaning back on the leather sofa, eyes closed, legs up on the ottoman, the way I used to when I lived here. "I guess I must have given him that number."

"You should get your new number listed."

"I like my privacy."

"I don't understand why you're so insistent," says Kimmer, who could not live five minutes without a telephone. A sudden thought strikes her, and she covers her mouth and giggles. "I mean, unless . . . unless you need so much privacy because . . . Hey, you're not hiding some woman in your condo, are you? Shirley Branch? Somebody like that?"

"No woman, Kimmer." Except you.

"Or maybe Pony Eldridge? You know, the two wronged spouses getting together?"

"Sorry to disappoint you. I'm still a married man."

Kimmer wisely ignores this dig. "It isn't Dana, is it? I hear she's having trouble with Alison. Or vice versa. Anyway, are the two of you gonna do anything after all these years?"

I recycle the old joke: "She's not into men, and I'm not into white women."

Kimmer waves this away. She leans in close, her proximity dazzling, then reaches around me, picks up her wineglass, takes a small sip. "Oh, everybody's into everybody these days," she assures me with an expert's authority before padding back into the kitchen. "Ice cream coming," she calls. "Butter pecan. Want some?"

"Sounds great."

"Chocolate syrup?"

"Yes, thanks."

Yes, I could have rescued him. No, I had no energy. Yes, I should have tried. No, I would have failed.

Another shout from the kitchen: "By the way, did you find what you were looking for? On the Vineyard, I mean?"

Good question.

"Misha? Honey?" I remind myself to attach no importance to *honey:* force of habit, nothing more. Kimmer is probably unaware that she said it.

"Not really," I call back. "No."

"I'm sorry."

"Me, too." A pause. It feels awkward, but I might as well do the polite thing and ask. "Mind if I use the phone?"

"Help yourself." Her grinning face appears around the doorjamb. "Your name's still on the bill." Disappearing again.

I walk into my old study. Kimmer has not converted it to any purpose. A couple of shelves are still in place; the others, along with the desk and the credenza and the chairs, are cluttering the basement of my condo. A few magazines lie here and there, a book or two, but, basically, the cozy room where I spent so many agonizing hours watching Hobby Road for surveillance is empty. The portable phone sits on the floor.

The room feels dead this way. I wonder how Kimmer can stand it. Maybe she just keeps the door closed.

I pick up the phone, push the buttons from memory, and wait patiently for John Brown to answer.

(I I)

THE OAK BLUFFS POLICE found me unconscious on the beach. They were sweeping the waterfront periodically, even in the storm. All I had to do was wait. I could even have fled to the police station in the first place. Only panic caused me to imagine they would close it.

By the time the ambulance arrived, I was already wide awake and sitting up, which is a very good thing, because, while the paramedics were lifting me onto the wheeled stretcher and preparing to insert a tube into my arm, one of the officers wandered over and said to his partner, *Some kid lost a bear.* I turned my head and saw a water-logged George Jackson nestled under his arm. The storm, passing on toward the Cape, had left George behind like an unwanted complication. I assured the startled cop that the bear was mine. They asked, more out of curiosity than duty, what I was doing out on the beach with a stuffed panda in the middle of a hurricane. *Good question*, I said, which did not exactly reassure them.

But they let it slide.

So here I am, finally, back in my condo, preparing for the opening of classes in two weeks, when I will once again teach torts to fifty-odd fresh young faces, trying my best not to bully any of them. Bentley races around my relatively cramped space, playing hide-and-seek with Miguel Hadley, whose father dropped him off two hours ago for a play date. Marc lingered for a few minutes, exuding great clouds of his raspberry tobacco, and we agreed it was a shame about Justice Wainwright, and played the old academic game of pretending we had the foggiest idea who the President will pick to replace him. I am grateful to Marc for trying, as the sad summer hurries to its close, to patch things up between us, but sundered friendships, like broken marriages, are often irreparable.

Although August still has a couple of days to run, the afternoon is chilly, for a storm front has moved in, and there are thundershowers. I have no real study in my condo, so I tend to work on my laptop in the kitchen, going back and forth to my bookshelves in the basement as needed. I am sitting at the laptop now, trying to get serious about an article taking a fresh look at the data on the effect of wealth on the outcome in tort cases—my own apology to Avery Knowland, taking the time to see if he might be right.

I stand up and walk to the kitchen window, looking down into my postage-stamp yard, the paved common area beyond it, and then the boardwalk and the beach. I strolled there in the brilliant afternoon sun yesterday, before driving over to Hobby Road to pick up Bentley, because I was trying to figure out what to do with the disk that remains nestled safely inside George Jackson. I am dithering still.

John Brown told me that even with the heat, even with the warping, even with the salt water in which the disk has now been soaked, there is probably still a fair bit of recoverable data. There is a need to act swiftly, because heat can "melt" bits of information off the disk, but the ocean water is the real problem: as the salt oxidizes, it could do further damage. He instructed me to rinse the surface with distilled water, which I did. But magnetic media, he assured me, are tougher than most people think. The only way to be sure of getting rid of stored information is to write over it completely, such as by reformatting the disk. And just to be sure, he said, you might want to go over the disk with a powerful magnet, then reformat it again. *After all that*, he laughed, *if you're really smart, you'll destroy the disk completely.* By cooking it in a microwave oven, say. Or tossing it in the incinerator. Short of steps so extreme, he said, yes, the likelihood is that some data have survived. There are experts who, for a fee, will retrieve whatever is there.

I know what is there. Wainwright said the disk was full of names: names of people now prominent whose cases he and my father fixed.

I could cause a lot of trouble.

I could read the Judge's tortured ravings and learn the details of his many crimes, I could blackmail corrupt Senators or bring them to justice, I could turn the disk over to the press and allow the media to have their frenzy. The allegations might turn some significant piece of the history of the seventies and eighties upside down. They are unproven, of course, possibly the last, desperate ravings of the Judge's tortured brain—but none of that has ever stopped journalists from doing as much damage as possible, with the smallest number of apologies, because the people's right to know equals, down to the last decimal place, the media's ability to profit from scandal.

I imagine my father on the front pages again, only this time with lots of friends along for the ride. I tremble. Senators, said Wainwright. Governors. Cabinet officers. Yes, I could do a lot of damage.

And perhaps a lot of damage is what my father craved—a final revenge on the world that so rudely spurned him. Perhaps that was the reason for his note and his pawns and the rest of the perilous, puzzling trail that finally led me back to the attic of Vinerd Howse. My father's cleverness suddenly terrifies me. The world destroyed my father, and I seem to be his chosen instrument to destroy it right back.

I experience a brief, delicious shiver of power, followed at once by a trembling of revulsion. No point in asking, *Why me?* No point in railing against fate. Or against God. Or against my father. Garland men do none of those things. Garland men bear troubles with a stoicism bordering on self-loathing, driving the women in our lives half crazy with our distance. Garland men make decisions with care, and then we stick to them, as the term implies, *de-cision*, cutting away, the elimination of other possibilities, even when the decisions we make are terrible. But the Judge may not have wanted me to decide at all; perhaps he died believing that the decision was made, that I would do what Addison, who had legal problems of his own, could not. Perhaps the Judge believed that I would read the names and set out to destroy, that I would do it not out of anger or a yearning for revenge, or even for the cold intellectual pleasure of seeing the guilty punished, but because my father asked me to.

The guilty *should* be punished—no question there.

But guilt comes in more than one variety. And so does punishment.

Addison. Now, there is a question nobody has raised, although Nunzio hinted around the edges. Alma said Addison could not be the head of the family. Sally said Addison told her to get the scrapbook. Mallory Corcoran said my father thought Addison had betrayed him. And my father's arrangements involved the younger son, not the older, whom he also loved best among his children. Could the reason be that Addison already knew it all? My brother said the Judge came to him in Chicago a year before he died, trying to get him to read Villard's report. This, surely, was in reaction to Wainwright's visit. My father's immediate idea was to tell his firstborn everything, so that Addison would be his insurance policy if anything went wrong.

Only Addison wouldn't play. I know he read the report, he knew the car that killed Abby had two people in it, not one. Maybe the Judge told my brother what happened next. Maybe Addison worked it out for himself. Either way, it upset him enough that he refused to listen to any more of the story. He did not want to know what the Judge did for Jack Ziegler in return for the murders of Phil McMichael and Michelle

Hoffer. And my father, as he told Uncle Mal, and as Just Alma knew or guessed, took this for a betrayal.

So he went on to his second son. Only, this time, he was more cautious. Worried, perhaps, that I would be as rejecting as Addison, he decided to leave me no choice, to design his arrangements the way he would design one of his chess problems, so that, once he died, events would be set into motion, and I would be able to follow only one path. The path that would lead me to Vinerd Howse, and to the attic, and to George Jackson.

Probably he hoped I would figure it out the first time I saw the note.

Or maybe Addison's involvement was not limited to telling the Judge he wanted no involvement. After all, somebody had to put the Judge's files on the disk. My father would not have known how to do it himself; but Addison loves computers. Maybe Addison gave him instructions, maybe Addison did it for him. Either way, my brother would have had at least a rough idea of what the Judge had hidden, and why, even if he did not know where. So, why did he refuse to help Mariah and me in our separate searches? Why, when I finally reached him, did he try to talk me out of going forward?

The same reason he arranged for Sally to remove the scrapbook. Because he was there in the kitchen at Shepard Street the night the Judge first tried to make his deal with the devil. Because he had buried that secret for more than twenty years. And because he was not ready to have it exhumed.

No wonder he never found time to come to the hearings.

I miss Addison. Not the way he is now, but the way he used to be. The way it was before, as the Judge would have said. I seem to miss the same thing in every corner of my life: the way it was before. I experience my family life as an unbroken chain of losses. My brother, my sister, my wife, my mother, my father, all of them gone but Mariah. Morris Young, like the Judge when he was at his best, preaches that we should always be looking forward, not back, and I try. Oh, how I try.

I have lost my wife. My father, for all his insanity, never lost his Claire, not until the day she died. In the last few years, I have been so obsessed with my father—first with living up to his standards, and, recently, with solving the terrifying mystery he thrust upon me—that I have scarcely given my mother a thought. It is time to correct the imbalance. It is time to get to know Claire Garland again, to study her life as painstakingly as I have studied Oliver's. I have been trying to find a place for my father in the way I remember the past. I must do the same for my wife. And I must spend enough time remembering my mother that she, too, can finally take a proper place in the rooms of my memory. If memory is our contribution to history, then history is the sum of our memories. Like all families, mine has a history. I would like to remember it.

(I I I)

BENTLEY AND MIGUEL are down in the basement now, whispering together, the way best friends do at that age. I check on the little fire I have going this cold afternoon, then climb the stairs to the second floor, go into my small bedroom, and close the door. I sit on my cheap mattress-and-box-spring bed and stare at the dresser, the only other piece of furniture in the room. From his perch atop the dresser, George Jackson seems to wink at me with dark plastic eyes. The disk, undisturbed, its information leaching away, remains inside him. The diabolical scrapbook is tucked away in a drawer, hidden beneath my underused exercise togs.

I close my eyes and remember Wainwright's flailing hand. I open them and remember his despairing words, how he wanted to retire and Jack Ziegler and his partners refused to let him step down. Probably Wainwright was the unnamed buyer who tried to purchase the house on Shepard Street, so that he would be able to search it top to bottom. Eventually he would have offered to purchase Vinerd Howse, too. With contents, no doubt.

Contents like Abby's bear.

A flash of lightning outside reflects in George Jackson's plastic eyes, making him wink again. He is magical, this ancient toy shedding his stuffing. I am astonished that he survived the storm, but storms are funny that way: sometimes what the riptide draws out bobs to the surface and floats back in on the next crashing wave, other times it is sucked under and disappears. The jetties extending from the sands of the Inkwell probably made his return more likely, turning some of the waves back in; but, the truth is, I got lucky.

Or maybe not. Had George never returned to shore, had the police officer never found him, had I remained unconscious, had a dozen small things been different, I would not now be facing this dilemma. Had the waves carried the bear away, I would not have to worry about what to do. There would be nothing to do, because there would be no disk to do it with.

No *arrangements*.

Jack Ziegler and his friends or enemies or whoever they are decided after the cemetery that I probably had already found the information my father hid, and I implicitly promised Henderson that I would keep secret what I knew. Now the belief is a fact: the arrangements are mine at last, and I feel the surging stir of temptation that power always brings.

I pick up the bear, slide the disk free, and put George back where he was. Holding the disk by its edges, I walk back down to my living-dining room. Outside the windows, the storm has yet to abate. True, it cannot hold a candle to the one that roared across the Vineyard while I was there, but a storm is a storm, and, despite the fire, the condo is growing colder.

Or maybe I am.

I remember my father's dream, to gain a measure of fame by creating the first Double Excelsior with the knight, the task that crazy old Karl called impossible. The Double Excelsior, but with black victorious in the end: two lonely pawns, one white and one black, pathetic in their powerlessness, beginning on their home squares and matching each other, move for move, until, on the fifth turn, each reaches the far end of the board and becomes a knight, the final move checkmating the white king. And the problem is not sound if there is any other option: a single line of play is all that is allowed. If the black king can be check-mated more quickly, or if either pawn can at any time make any other move and yet achieve the same result, the problem is cooked, which is to say, worthless.

My father left his Double Excelsior behind him, not on the board but in life, setting in motion his two pawns, one black, one white, matching moves, each stalking the other, one agonizing square at a time, until they reached the far side of their board on a storm-darkened beach in Oak Bluffs, where they faced each other for the final time.

One knight died. The other is left to give mate. Just as my vengeful father wanted. I hold in my hand the tool. I need only pick up the telephone and call Agent Nunzio or the *Times* or the *Post*, and the Judge's Double Excelsior is complete.

Except that the problem is cooked, as the jargon has it, if there is any other possibility. And the difficulty with knights is that they often move . . . eccentrically.

Impossible, said Karl.

The boys are running around the house again. In a few minutes, I will have to give them a snack, warming one of the countless casseroles that Nina Felsenfeld and Julia Carlyle have delivered. Then the three of us will squeeze into the Camry for the short drive up to the Hadleys' lovely home on Harbor Peak. I believe I have mentioned that Marc comes from money. Years ago, his Uncle Edmund was one of the founders of a little leveraged-buyout firm called Elm Harbor Partners. Kimmer had no conflict of interest, the Hadley money has long moved on, but I know from Dana, who should never have told me, that Marc once made a telephone call to the old family retainer who was then general counsel of EHP, urging him, as a favor, to ask for Kimberly Madison by name the moment she arrived in town. The request was part of the effort by Stuart Land, then the dean, to keep me from leaving, for I was as dreadfully unhappy during my first year in Elm Harbor as I had been during my final year in Washington. Had Marc not made the call, Kimmer might not have stayed; had she not stayed, she and I would never have married; which helps explain why I have never been able to dislike Marc as much as my wife does.

Marc has been man enough never to mention this favor to me. I do not think Kimmer knows. And I am not about to tell her. Besides, EHP might have asked for Kimmer as a favor to Marc, but it was through her exemplary skills as a lawyer that she earned her way into their—and Jerry Nathanson's—lasting confidence.

I check my watch and go into the cramped kitchen to warm the boys' snack. So much to do, so much to do. I want to be a better Christian, to spend time with Morris Young and learn the meaning of the faith I profess. I want to take more walks with Sally, apologize for the family, and help her, if I can, to heal. I want to visit Just Alma, to sit at her feet and listen to stories of the old days, when the family was happy—the way it was before. Then I want to visit Thera, and compare the stories. I want to help my sister out of her ennui. I want to believe in the law school the way Stuart Land does. I want to believe in the law itself the way I used to, before the Judge and his pal Wainwright shattered my faith.

And there is something else. I want to know what happened to Maxine. I want to know why she shot me, whether it was an accident, and, if not, on whose orders she did it. I want her to look me in the eye and tell me she was not working for either Jack Ziegler or the unknown partners with whom he conspired to murder Phil McMichael and his girlfriend and to corrupt the federal court of appeals. Maybe she can even make me believe it. In which case Maxine was working, just as she said, for the good guys—not the great guys, just the good guys, who vowed to destroy whatever my father left, rather than use it. Another faction? Another mob? Another federal agency?

I want to know why, despite my fervent prayers as I lay dying, so I thought, on the beach last week, I never saw her again.

Uncle Jack said some questions have no answers. Perhaps one day soon I will fly out to Aspen again and knock on his door and ask him a few anyway. And, if I do, I suppose I will owe him thanks of some kind for keeping me and my family safe all these months, when we could have been kidnaped, tortured, and murdered. Except that, had he not been who he was and done the things he did, we would never have needed protection in the first place.

The telephone rings, distracting me from my reverie, and I pick it up, reasoning that there is no more bad news to be had. As I should have guessed, it is my sister, calling to tell me about the new evidence she has found down at Shepard Street or on the Internet or floating in a glass bottle someplace: my stubborn mind refuses to focus on her words, which become a stream of noise, unrelated to any part of my reality. I surprise us both by interrupting her.

"I love you, kiddo."

A pause while Mariah waits for the punch line. Then her cautious yet happy rejoinder: "Well, that's a good thing, because I love you, too."

Another pause, as each of us silently dares the other to get mushy. But we are Garlands still, we are at our emotional limit, so conversation turns swiftly to her family. She promises not to try any matchmaking if I will come for her annual Labor Day barbecue. I agree. Five minutes later my sister is gone—but I know she will go on searching. Which is fine with me. Let Mariah continue to try to prove the Judge was murdered; that is her way of coping, and, with her journalistic tenacity, she may yet uncover a further unhappy truth. I admire her search but will not join it. I have long been comfortable living without perfect knowledge. Semiotics has taught me to live with ambiguity in my work; Kimmer has taught me to live with ambiguity in my home; and Morris Young is teaching me to live with ambiguity in my faith. That truth, even moral truth, exists I have no doubt, for I am no relativist; but we weak, fallen humans will never perceive it except imperfectly, a faintly glowing presence toward which we creep through the mists of reason, tradition, and faith.

So much to know, so little time. Wandering back into the living room, I stare at the cracked, warped disk in my hand, wishing I could unlock its secrets by sheer force of will, because knowing precisely what my father included, whether fact or fiction, could help me decide what to do. But I lack the time, or the trust, to do as John Brown recommends and hire somebody to decipher it. I will have to make my decision—my *de-cision*—based on the little I already know. *To be a man is to act.*

I notice that the fire is sputtering. Well, I can't have that on so chilly an afternoon. Back when Kimmer and I were more or less happy, snuggling in front of the fire was one of our favorite pastimes. If it is as brisk up on Hobby Road as it is down here by the beach, she is surely snuggling away. Just not with me.

I miss what I had. The way it was before.

But I can love a fire anyway.

I throw on another log and watch a few sparks fly. Not enough: the fire needs to be freshened. Seeing no kindling anywhere, I take the disk my father hid in Abigail's bear and, drawing a line and putting the past behind me, I feed it to the flames.

AUTHOR'S NOTE

THIS IS A WORK OF FICTION. It stems from my imagination. It is not a *roman à clef* on law teaching, or the bizarre process by which we confirm (or fail to confirm) Supreme Court Justices, or the tribulations of middle-class black America, or anything else. It certainly is not the tale of my own family, nuclear or extended. The story is just a story, and the characters are my own inventions, with the exception of a handful of genuine lawyers, legislators, and journalists who play peripheral but wholly fictitious roles.

My imaginary law school is not modeled on Yale, where I have taught for two happy decades, and my imaginary city of Elm Harbor is not a thinly disguised New Haven, although the careful reader will notice that the two communities share a few of the same ghosts. None of Misha Garland's rumbling complaints about his colleagues or students should be taken as representing my opinions of my own colleagues or students, whom I treasure and respect.

My character Oliver Garland, Misha's father and a former judge of the United States Court of Appeals for the District of Columbia Circuit, bears no connection whatever with the Honorable Merrick Garland, an actual judge of that very court, who was appointed long after my fictitious Garland family was invented. By that time it was too late to change the family name: they were already alive for me.

I have taken certain liberties with the geography of Martha's Vineyard, especially the wonderful village of Menemsha, where the shoreline behind the restaurants and shops is not lined with the fishing shacks that Misha investigates, and where I have never met anybody as selfish and unpleasant as the fisherman with whom Misha argues. The view of Oak Bluffs Harbor from the park where Misha and Maxine have their heart-to-heart is actually obscured nowadays by a hideous public bathhouse, but I prefer to remember the beauty of the vista before the monstrosity was built, so it does not exist in this novel. The Edgartown Road, as it nears the airport, is far flatter in reality than it is in my story. My only excuse is that the narrative works better if there are steep hills. The ancient wooden staircase from Seaview Avenue down to the Inkwell would not really be straight across the grass from a house on the south side of Ocean Park, but I needed it there, so I moved it a few hundred yards west of its actual location.

In 1997, the town of Gay Head was officially renamed Aquinnah, but, like Misha Garland and many who love the Island, I find the usage of three decades difficult to overcome. I am sure I will learn to do better with time. In Oak Bluffs, neither Murdick's Fudge nor the Corner Store would likely be open the week after Thanksgiving, when Misha and Bentley visit them, but I have taken a bit of poetic license to make late autumn on Circuit Avenue a little cheerier in my story than in real life. It is unlikely that Misha could have taken his car back and forth to the Island as often as he does in the story, because reservations for the auto ferry are scarce and the standby possibilities greatly reduced from what they once were. But one is permitted to dream.

Washington, D.C., is also not precisely the same in my novel as it is on the map. In particular, the downtown branch of Brooks Brothers moved a few years ago from its quiet location on L Street to a somewhat fancier and busier corner on Connecticut Avenue. But the new establishment is too close to Dupont Circle for the story to work, so I have kept the store where it sat for so long.

I have altered the history of America's past two decades in minor but noticeable respects, and I hope that none of the true-life figures whose lives I have rudely shoved around to fit the story will be offended. On the other hand, some things the reader may suspect are inventions are not. The Pro-Life Alliance of Gays and Lesbians, to take one example, is a real organization, and one of its national officers did indeed say to me, more or less in so many words, "Everybody hates us."

I am grateful to David Brown, a columnist for *Chess Life* magazine, for teaching me some of the intricacies of the chess problem that forms a part of the book's motif. I am also grateful to George Jones, Esq., a partner in the law firm of Sidley Austin Brown & Wood, L.L.P., a former member of the American Bar Association's standing committee on ethics, and president of the District of Columbia bar (2002–3), for guiding me through some thorny questions about the rules governing the lawyer-client relationship, and to Natalie Roche, M.D., F.A.C.O.G., at the time on the staff of Beth Israel Medical Center in New York City, for helpful conversations about medical problems that can occur during childbirth. Any errors that occur in the story, whether in these areas or any others, are mine, or perhaps my characters'.

And, indeed, some of the characters do make embarrassing mistakes. Misha Garland incorrectly states the law regarding cooperation with federal investigators in his argument with Agents Foreman and McDermott, but the reader should remember that criminal law is not his area of expertise. Marc Hadley, in his enthusiasm for his own ideas, misstates both the facts and the holding of the Supreme Court's decision in *Griswold v. Connecticut*, which had nothing to do with physicians or unmarried women. (He may be thinking of *Eisenstadt v. Baird*, or he may, as so often, be making it up as he goes along.) Lionel "Sweet Nellie" Eldridge always inflates his career scoring average from the National Basketball Association, rounding his points per game upward, from 18.6 to 19. Still, as Pony Eldridge, his wife and statistician, likes to say, this is permissible license, because his career scoring average would have been 19.5, had he not come back bravely after his injury for that last disastrous season—this is Pony talking—trying to reach ten thousand career points before retiring.

Most chess writers attribute the quotation used as the epigraph to this book to Siegbert Tarrasch, but it is sometimes said to have originated with the former world champion Alexander Alekhine. Different sources provide various renderings of the line from Felix Frankfurter quoted by Wallace Wainwright. I have chosen what seems to me the most authoritative, the late Bernard Schwartz's influential 1996 book *Decision: How the Supreme Court Decides Cases.* Professor Schwartz confirmed the quotation with a law clerk who was present when the statement was made.

Finally, I must confess that not every line in this book is my own creation. The precise wording of Bentley's announcement that he is riding on a boat was actually devised not by Misha Garland's son but by my own. Rob Saltpeter's *bon mot* about the United States as a Christian nation I first heard from the thoughtful David Bleich, who is both a rabbi and a law professor. The rules to the courtroom polka are not my own invention, nor are they Misha Garland's; they draw on a dim memory from my childhood, a joke about President Lyndon Johnson dancing the "press-conference polka." (I would be grateful to any reader who might direct me to the original source.) And Dana Worth's zinger about Bonnie Ziffren was actually coined, in a similar context, by my late Yale colleague Leon Lipson, whose subtlety, wit, and sheer joy in knowledge will always inspire but can never be replaced.

I must acknowledge my gratitude to my literary agent, Lynn Nesbit, who waited many patient years for me to finish the manuscript I kept promising next month. Lynn encouraged me through my frequent blocks and never tried to make me rush. The novel has benefitted immeasurably from the graceful and sympathetic editing of Robin Desser at Knopf, and from the thoughtful comments of the small circle of intimates who read the manuscript prior to publication.

Finally, as always, I have no adequate words to express my gratitude to my family: my children, Leah and Andrew, with whom I missed many a Saturday afternoon of fun because "Daddy has to write"; their great-aunt Maria Reid, who put up with my ignoring her for hours as I sat, chained to my computer, in my study; and, most of all, to my wife, Enola Aird, without whose steadfast love, clear-eyed readings, gentle cajoling, and spiritual guidance this novel could never have been completed. May God bless you all.

May 2001

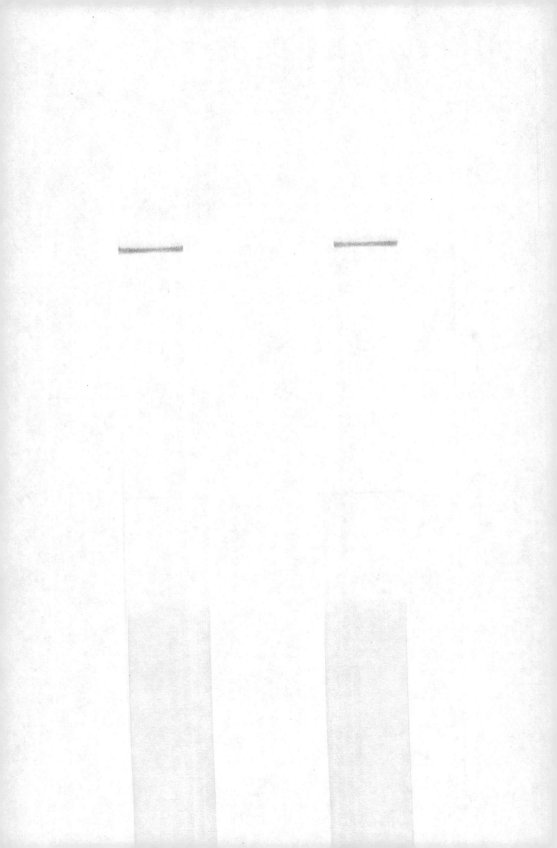